I AM CHARLOTTE SIMMONS

TOM WOLFE

I am

Charlotte Simmons

JONATHAN CAPE · LONDON

Published by Jonathan Cape 2004

2 4 6 8 10 9 7 5 3 1

Portions of this book originally appeared, in slightly different form,
in *Rolling Stone*, *The New York Times* and *Men's Journal*

First published in Great Britain in 2004 by
Jonathan Cape
Random House, 20 Vauxhall Bridge Road, London SW1V 2SA

Random House Australia (Pty) Limited
20 Alfred Street, Milsons Point, Sydney,
New South Wales 2061, Australia

Random House New Zealand Limited
18 Poland Road, Glenfield,
Auckland 10, New Zealand

Random House South Africa (Pty) Limited
Endulini, 5A Jubilee Road, Parktown 2193, South Africa

The Random House Group Limited Reg. No. 954009
www.randomhouse.co.uk

A CIP catalogue record for this book is available from the British Library

ISBN 0-224-07486-5

Papers used by Random House are natural,
recyclable products made from wood grown in sustainable forests;
the manufacturing processes conform to the environmental
regulations of the country of origin

Book design by Abby Kagan

Printed and bound in Great Britain by
Clays Ltd, St Ives PLC

This novel is not based on any real college, not even partly. Certain real
governmental and institutional offices are mentioned, but the characters
occupying them are wholly imaginary.

TO MY TWO COLLEGIANS

You have been a joy, a surprise, a source of wonderment for me at every stage of your young lives. So I suppose I shouldn't be astonished by what you have done for me and this book; but I am, and dedicating it to you is a mere whisper of my gratitude. I gave you the manuscript hoping you might vet it for undergraduate vocabulary. That you did. I learned that using the oath *Jesus Christ* establishes the speaker as, among other things, middle-aged or older. So does the word *fabulous*, as in "That's fabulous!" Today the word is *awesome*. So does *jerk*, as in "Whatta jerk!" It has been totally replaced by a quaint anatomical metaphor. Students who load up conversations with *likes* and *totallys*, as in "like totally awesome," are almost always females. The *totallys* now give off such whiffs of parody, they are fading away, even as I write. All that was quite in addition to the many times you rescued me when I got in over my head trying to use current slang. What I never imagined you could do—I couldn't have done it at your age—was to step back in the most detached way and point out the workings of human nature in general and the esoteric workings of social status in particular. I say "esoteric," because in many cases these were areas of life one would not ordinarily think of as social at all. Given your powers of abstraction, your father had only to reassemble the material he had accumulated visiting campuses across the country. What I feel about you both I can say best with a long embrace.

VOS SALUTO

Many generous people helped me gather information for this book:
college students, athletes, coaches, faculty, alumni, outriders,
and citizens of an Eden in North Carolina's Blue Ridge Mountains,
Alleghany County. If it were possible, I would thank each and every one
personally in these lines. I must certainly acknowledge a few who
went far out of their way on my behalf:

In Alleghany County: MACK and CATHY NICHOLS,
whose understanding and eye for details were superb; LEWIS and
PATSY GASKINS, who showed me the county's extraordinary
Christmas-tree farms, one of which was raising 500,000 trees; and the
gracious staffs of ALLEGHANY HIGH SCHOOL and the
ALLEGHANY CHAMBER OF COMMERCE.

At Stanford University:
media studies chieftain TED GLASSER; JIM STEYER, author
of *The Other Parent*; comparative literature savant
GERALD GILLESPIE; Mallarmé scholar ROBERT COHN;
young academic stars ARI SOLOMON and
ROBERT ROYALTY and their student entourages.

At the University of Michigan:
communication studies maestro M I K E   T R A U G O T T;
and P E A C H E S   T H O M A S, who enabled a fool to rush into
undergraduate nightlife where wise men never went.

At Chapel Hill:
C O N N I E   E B L E, lexicologist of college slang and
author of *Slang and Sociability*;
D O R O T H Y   H O L L A N D, whose *Educated in Romance*
blazed a trail in the anthropology of American college students;
J A N E   D.   B R O W N of *Media, Sex and the Adolescent* fame; and
two especially insightful students, alumni
F R A N C E S   F E N N E B R E S Q U E and D A V I D   F L E M I N G.

In Huntsville, Alabama:
M A R K   N O B L E, the sports consultant
famous for assessing, training, and healing Division I and professional
athletes; G R E G and J A Y   S T O L T, and G R E G   J R.,
University of Florida basketball star now playing professionally in Japan;
and Huntsville's colorful counselor D O U G   M A R T I N S O N.

At Florida, in Gainesville:
B I L L   M C K E E N, journalism chairman, author of *Highway 61*,
and a man with entrée to hot spots of undergraduate life,
including "the Swamp," a football stadium
with a city throbbing beneath the grandstands.

In New York:
J A N N   W E N N E R, who once again
walked me through the valley of the shadow of weary writing; and
C O U N S E L O R   E D D I E ("Get me Hayes!") H A Y E S,
who read much of the manuscript.

In dōmo:
My dear S H E I L A,
"scribere iussit amor," as Ovid put it. Scripsi.

—*Tom Wolfe*

CONTENTS

I AM CHARLOTTE SIMMONS

Victor Ransome Starling (U.S.), Laureate, Biological Sciences, 1997. A twenty-eight-year-old assistant professor of psychology at Dupont University, Starling conducted an experiment in 1983 in which he and an assistant surgically removed the amygdala, an almond-shaped mass of gray matter deep within the brain that controls emotions in the higher mammals, from thirty cats. It was well known that the procedure caused animals to veer helplessly from one inappropriate affect to another, boredom where there should be fear, cringing where there should be preening, sexual arousal where there was nothing that would stimulate an intact animal. But Starling's amygdalectomized cats had gone into a state of sexual arousal hypermanic in the extreme. Cats attempted copulation with such frenzy, a cat mounted on another cat would be in turn mounted by a third cat, and that one by yet another, and so on, creating tandems (colloq., "daisy chains") as long as ten feet.

Starling called in a colleague to observe. The thirty amygdalectomized cats and thirty normal cats used as controls were housed in cages in the same room, one cat per cage. Starling set about opening cages so that the amygdalectomized cats might congregate on the floor. The first cat thus released sprang from its cage onto the visitor, embracing his ankle with its forelegs and convulsively thrusting its pelvis upon his shoe. Starling conjectured that the cat had smelled the leather of the shoe and in its excitement had mistaken it for a compatible animal. Whereupon his assistant said, "But Professor Starling, that's one of the controls."

In that moment originated a discovery that has since radically altered the understanding of animal and human behaviour: the existence—indeed, pervasiveness—of "cultural para-stimuli." The control cats had been able to watch the amygdalectomized cats from their cages. Over a period of weeks they had become so thoroughly steeped in an environment of hypermanic sexual obsession that behaviour induced surgically in the amygdalectomized cats had been induced in the controls without any intervention whatsoever. Starling had discovered that a strong social or "cultural" atmosphere, even as abnormal as this one, could in time overwhelm the genetically determined responses of perfectly normal, healthy animals. Fourteen years later, Starling became the twentieth member of the Dupont faculty awarded the Nobel Prize.

—*Simon McGough and Sebastian J. R. Sloane, eds.,* The Dictionary of Nobel Laureates, *3rd ed. (Oxford and New York: Oxford University Press, 2001), p. 512.*

PROLOGUE: THE DUPONT MAN

Every time the men's-room door opened, the amped-up onslaught of Swarm, the band banging out the concert in the theater overhead, came crashing in, ricocheting off all the mirrors and ceramic surfaces until it seemed twice as loud. But then an air hinge would close the door, and Swarm would vanish, and you could once again hear students drunk on youth and beer being funny or at least loud as they stood before the urinals.

Two of them were finding it amusing to move their hands back and forth in front of the electric eyes to make the urinals keep flushing. One exclaimed to the other, "Whattaya mean, a slut? She told me she's been re-virginated!" They both broke up over that.

"She actually said that? Re-virginated?"

"Yeah! Re-virginated or born-again virgin, something like that!"

"Maybe she thinks that's what morning-after pills do!" They both broke up again. They had reached that stage in a college boy's evening at which all comments seem more devastatingly funny if shouted.

Urinals kept flushing, boys kept disintegrating over one another's wit, and somewhere in the long row of toilet cubicles somebody was vomiting. Then the door would open and Swarm would come crashing in again.

None of this distracted the only student who at this moment stood before the row of basins. His attention was riveted on what he saw in the mirror, which was his own fair white face. A gale was blowing in his head. He liked it. He bared his teeth. He had never seen them quite this way before. So even! So white! They vibrated from perfection. And his square jaw . . . that chin with the perfect cleft in it . . . his thick, thatchy light brown hair . . . those brilliant hazel eyes . . . *his*! Right there in the mirror—*him*! All at once he felt like he was *a second person* looking over his own shoulder. The first him was mesmerized by his own good looks. Seriously. But the second him studied the face in the mirror with detachment and objectivity before coming to the same conclusion, which was that he looked awesome. Then the two of him inspected his upper arms where they emerged from the sleeves of his polo shirt. He turned sideways and straightened one arm to make the triceps stand out. *Jacked*, both hims agreed. He had never felt happier in his life.

Not only that, he was on the verge of a profound discovery. It had to do with one person looking at the world through two pairs of eyes. If only he could freeze this moment in his mind and remember it tomorrow and write it down. Tonight he couldn't, not with the ruckus that was going on inside his skull.

"Yo, Hoyt! 'Sup?"

He looked away from the mirror, and there was Vance with his head of blond hair tousled as usual. They were in the same fraternity; in fact, Vance was the president. Hoyt had an overwhelming desire to tell him what he had just discovered. He opened his mouth but couldn't find the words, and nothing came out. So he turned his palms upward and smiled and shrugged.

"Lookin' good, Hoyt!" said Vance as he approached the urinals. "Lookin' good!"

Hoyt knew it really meant he looked very drunk. But in his current sublime state, what difference did it make?

"Hey, Hoyt," said Vance, who now stood before a urinal, "I saw you upstairs there hittin' on that little tigbiddy! Tell the truth! You really, honestly, think she's hot?"

"Coo Uh gitta bigga boner?" said Hoyt, who was trying to say, "Could I get a bigger boner?" and vaguely realized how far off he was.

"*Soundin'* good, too!" said Vance. He turned away in order to pay attention to the urinal, but then he looked at Hoyt once more and said with a serious tone in his voice, "You know what I think? I think you're demolished, Hoyt. I think it's time to head back while your lights are still on."

Hoyt put up an incoherent argument, but not much of one, and pretty soon they left the building.

It was a mild May night, with a pleasant breeze and a full moon whose light created just enough of a gloaming to reveal the singular, wavelike roof of the theater, known officially here at the university as the Phipps Opera House, one of the architect Eero Saarinen's famous 1950s modern creations. The theater's entrance, ablaze with light, cast a path of fire across a plaza and out upon a row of sycamore trees at the threshold of another of the campus's renowned ornaments, the Grove. From the moment he founded Dupont University 115 years ago, Charles Dupont, the artificial dye king and art collector, no kin to the du Ponts of Delaware, had envisioned an actual grove of academe through which scholars young and old might take contemplative strolls. He had commissioned the legendary landscape artist Charles Gillette. Swaths of Gillette's genius abounded across the campus. There was the Great Yard at its heart, the quadrangles of the older residential colleges, a botanical garden, two floral lawns with gazebos, tree-studded parking lots, but, above all, this arboreal masterpiece, the Grove, so artfully contrived you would never know Dupont was practically surrounded by the black slums of a city as big as Chester, Pennsylvania. Gillette had had every tree, every ground cover, every bush and vine, every grassy clearing, every perennial planted just so, and they had been maintained just so for the better part of a century. He had sent sinuous paths winding through it for the contemplative strolls. But although the practice was discouraged, students often walked straight through this triumph of American landscape art, the way Hoyt and Vance walked now beneath the brightness of a big round moon.

The fresh air and the peace and quiet of the huge stands of trees began to clear Hoyt's head, or somewhat. He felt as if he were back at that blissful intersection on the graph of drunkenness at which the high has gone as high as it can go without causing the powers of reasoning and coherence to sink off the chart and get trashed . . . the exquisite point of perfect toxic poise. He was convinced he could once again utter a coherent sentence and make himself understood, and the blissful gale inside his head blew on.

At first he didn't say much, because he was trying to fix *that moment* before the mirror in his memory as he and Vance walked through the woods toward Ladding Walk and the heart of the campus. But *that moment* kept slipping away . . . slipping away . . . slipping away . . . and before he knew it, an entirely different notion had bubbled up into his brain. It was the Grove . . . the Grove . . . the *famous* Grove . . . which said *Dupont* . . . and made him feel *Dupont* in his bones, which in turn made his bones infinitely superior to the bones of everybody in America who had never gone to Dupont. I'm a Dupont man, he said to himself. Where was the writer who would immortalize that feeling—the exaltation that lit up his very central nervous system when he met someone and quickly worked into the conversation some seemingly offhand indication that he was in college, and the person would (inevitably) ask, "What college do you go to?" and he would say as evenly and tonelessly as possible, "Dupont," and then observe the reaction. Some, especially women, would be openly impressed. They'd smile, their faces would brighten, they'd say, "Oh! Dupont!" while others, especially men, would tense up and fight to keep their faces from revealing how impressed they were, and they'd say "I see" or "uhmm" or nothing at all. He wasn't sure which he enjoyed more. Everyone, male or female, who was right now, as he was, in the undergraduate division, Dupont College, or had ever graduated from Dupont College knew that feeling, *treasured* that feeling, sought one way or another to *enjoy that feeling daily* if at all possible, now and for the rest of his life—yet nobody had ever captured that feeling in words, and God knows no Dupont man, or Dupont woman, for that matter, had ever tried to describe it out loud to a living soul, not even to others within this charming aristocracy. They weren't fools, after all.

He looked about the Grove. The trees were enchanted silhouettes under a golden full moon. Merrily, merrily the gale blew on and—a flash of inspiration—*he* would be the one to put it all into words! *He* would be the bard! He knew he had it in him to be a writer. He had never had the time to *do* any writing other than papers for classes, but he now *knew* he had it in him. He could hardly wait for tomorrow when he would wake up and capture that feeling on the screen of his Mac. Or maybe he would tell Vance about it right now. Vance was just a few feet ahead of him as they walked through the enchanted Grove. Vance he could talk to about such a thing . . .

Suddenly Vance looked at Hoyt and held one hand up in the gesture that says "Stop" and put a forefinger up to his lips and pressed himself up against the trunk of a tree. Hoyt did likewise. Then Vance indicated they should peek around the tree. There in the moonlight, barely twenty-five feet away, they could make out two figures. One was a man with a great shock of white hair, sitting on the ground at the base of a tree trunk with his pants and his boxer shorts down around his ankles and his heavy white thighs spread apart. The other was a girl in shorts and a T-shirt who was on her knees between his knees, facing him. Her big head of hair looked very pale in the moonlight as it pumped up and down over his lap.

Vance pulled back behind the tree and whispered, "Holy shit, Hoyt, you know who that is? That's Governor Whatsisname, from California, the guy who's supposed to speak at commencement!" Commencement was Saturday. Tonight was Thursday.

"Then wuz he doing here now?" said Hoyt a little too loudly, causing Vance to put his forefinger to his lips again.

Vance chuckled deep in his throat and whispered, "That's pretty fucking obvious, if you ask me."

They peeked out from behind the tree again. The man and the girl must have heard them, because they were both looking their way.

"*I* know *her*," said Hoyt. "She was in my—"

"Fuck, Hoyt! Shhhhh!"

Bango! Something grabbed Hoyt's right shoulder from behind in a terrific grip, and a tough-guy voice said, "What the fuck you punks think you're doing?"

Hoyt spun around and found himself confronting a short but massively muscled man in a dark suit and a collar and tie that could barely contain his neck, which was wider than his head. A little translucent coiled cord protruded from his left ear.

Adrenaline and alcohol surged up Hoyt's brain stem. He was a Dupont man staring at an impudent simian from the lower orders. "*Doing?*" he barked, inadvertently showering the man with spit. "Looking at a fucking ape-faced dickhead is what we're *doing!*"

The man seized him by both shoulders and slammed him back against the tree, knocking the breath out of him. Just as the little gorilla drew his fist back, Vance got down on all fours behind his legs. Hoyt ducked the punch, which smashed into the tree trunk, and drove his forearm into his assailant—who had just begun to yell "*Shiiiiiit*" from the pain—with all his might. The man toppled backward over Vance and hit the ground with a sickening thud. He started to get up but then sank back to the ground. He lay there on his side next to a big exposed maple root, his face contorted, holding one shoulder with a hand whose bloody knuckles were gashed clear down to the bone. The arm that should have been socketed into the stricken shoulder was extended at a grotesque angle.

Hoyt and Vance, who was still on all fours, stared speechless at this picture of agony. The man opened his eyes, saw that his adversaries were no longer on the attack, and groaned, "Fugguz . . . fugguz . . ." Then, overcome by God knows what, he folded his face into another blind grimace and lay there moaning, "Muhfugguh . . . muhfugguh . . ."

The two boys looked at each other and, possessed by a single thought, turned toward the man and the girl—who were gone.

Vance whispered, "Whatta we do?"

"Run like a bastard," said Hoyt.

Which they did. As they ran through the arboretum, the tree trunks and shrubs and flowers and foliage kept whipping by in the dark and Vance kept saying things like "Self-defense, self-defense . . . just . . . self-defense," until he was too winded to run and speak at the same time.

They neared the edge of the Grove, where it bordered the open campus, and Vance said, "Slow . . . down . . ." He was so out of breath he could utter no more than a syllable or two after each gulp of air. "Just . . . walk . . . Got'act . . . natch'rul . . ."

So they emerged from the Grove walking and acting natural, except that their breathing sounded like a pair of handsaws and they were soaked with sweat.

Vance said, "We don't"—gulp of air—"talk about this"—gulp of air— "to anybody"—gulp of air—"Right?"—gulp of air—"Right, Hoyt?"—gulp of air—*"Right,* Hoyt?"—gulp of air—"Fuck!"—gulp of air—*"Listen to me, Hoyt!"*

But Hoyt wasn't even looking at him, much less listening. His heart was pumping just as much adrenaline as Vance's. But in Hoyt's case the hormone merely fed the merry gale, which now blew stronger than ever. He had *deleted* that sonofabitch! The way he had flipped that muscle-bound motherfucker over Vance's back—ohmygod! He could hardly wait to get back to the Saint Ray house and tell everybody. Him! A legend in the making! He looked up and gazed at what lay just ahead of them, and he was swept by the male exhilaration—ecstasy!—of victory in battle.

"Look at it, Vance," he said. "There it is."

"There's *what,* for Chrissake?" said Vance, who obviously wanted to move on, and fast.

Hoyt just gestured at it all.

The Dupont campus . . . The moon had turned the university's buildings into a vast chiaroscuro of dark shapes brought out in all their sumptuousness by a wash of pale white gold. The towers, the turrets, the spires, the heavy slate roofs—all of it ineffably beautiful and ineffably grand. Walls thick as a castle's! It was a stronghold. He, Hoyt, was one of a charmed circle, that happy few who could enter the stronghold at will . . . and feel its invincibility in their bones. Not only that, he was in the innermost ring of that charmed circle, namely, Saint Ray, the fraternity of those who have been chosen to hold dominion over . . . well, over everybody.

He wanted to impart this profound truth to Vance . . . but shit, it was such a mouthful. So all he said was, "Vance, you know what Saint Ray is?"

The total irrelevancy of the question made Vance stare back at him with his mouth open. Finally, in hopes of getting his accomplice moving again, he said, "No, what?"

"It's a MasterCard . . . for doing whatever you want . . . *whatever you want.*" There wasn't a single note of irony in his voice. Only awe. He couldn't have been more sincere.

"Don't say that, Hoyt! Don't even think it! Whatever happened in the Grove, we don't know what anybody's talking about! Okay?"

"Stop worrying," said Hoyt, sweeping his hand grandly from here to there, as if to take in the entire tableau before him. "Innermost ring . . . charmed circle."

He was once more vaguely aware that he wasn't altogether coherent. He only idly noticed the look of panic that stole across Vance's moonlit face. What was Vance so squirrelly about? He was a Dupont man himself. Hoyt once more gazed lovingly upon the moon-washed kingdom before them. The great library tower . . . the famous gargoyles, plainly visible in silhouette on the corner of Lapham College . . . way over there, the dome of the basketball arena . . . the new glass-and-steel neuroscience center, or whatever it was—even that weird building looked great at this moment . . . Dupont! Science—Nobel winners! whole stacks of them! . . . although he couldn't exactly remember any names . . . Athletes—giants! national basketball champions! top five in football and lacrosse! . . . although he found it a bit dorky to go to games and cheer a lot . . . Scholars—legendary! . . . even though they were sort of spectral geeks who floated around the edges of collegiate life . . . Traditions—the greatest!—mischievous oddities passed from generation to generation of . . . *the best people!* A small cloud formed—the rising number of academic geeks, book humpers, homosexuals, flute prodigies, and other diversoids who were now being admitted . . . Nevertheless! There's *their* Dupont, which is just a diploma with "Dupont" written on it . . . and there's the *real* Dupont—which is *ours!*

His heart was so full he wanted to pour it out to Vance. But the coherence problem reasserted itself, and all he could utter was, "It's ours, Vance, ours."

Vance put a hand over his face and moaned almost as pitifully as the little thug on the ground in the Grove. "Hoyt, you are *so* fucked up."

1. THAT SINGLE PROMISE

lleghany County is perched so high up in the hills of western North Carolina that golfers intrepid enough to go up there to play golf call it mountain golf. The county's only big cash crop is Christmas trees, Fraser firs mostly, and the main manufacturing that goes on is building houses for summer people. In the entire county, there is only one town. It is called Sparta.

The summer people are attracted by the primeval beauty of the New River, which forms the county's western boundary. Primeval is precisely the word for it. Paleontologists reckon that the New River is one of the two or three oldest rivers in the world. According to local lore, it is called New because the first white man to lay eyes on it was Thomas Jefferson's cousin Peter, and to him its very existence was news. He was leading a team of surveyors up to the crest of the Blue Ridge Mountains, which form part of the Continental Divide. He reached the top, looked down the other side, and saw the same breathtaking sight that enchants outdoorsy outlanders today: a wide, absolutely clear mountain stream flanked by dense, deep green stands of virgin forest set against the immense ashy backdrop of the Blue Ridge, which from a distance really does look blue.

Not all that long ago the mountains were a wall that cut Alleghany County off from people in the rest of North Carolina so completely, they called it the Lost Province, when they thought of it at all. Modern highways have made the county accessible, but an air of remoteness, an atmosphere primeval, remains, and that is what the summer people, the campers, the canoers, the fishers, hunters, golfers, and mountain crafts shoppers love about it. There is no mall, no movie house, and not one stockbroker. To the people who lived in Sparta, the term ambition didn't conjure up a picture of hard-driving, hard-grabbing businessmen in dull suits and "interesting" neckties the way it did in Charlotte or Raleigh. Families with children who were juniors or seniors in the one high school, Alleghany High, didn't get caught up in college mania the way families in the urban areas did—college mania being the ferocious, all-consuming compulsion to get one's offspring into prestigious universities. What parents in Sparta would even aspire to having a son or daughter go to a university like Dupont? Probably none. In fact, when word got out that a senior at the high school, a girl named Charlotte Simmons, would be going to Dupont in the fall, it was front-page news in *The Alleghany News*, the weekly newspaper.

A month or so later, one Saturday morning at the end of May, with the high school's commencement exercises under way in the gymnasium, that particular girl, Charlotte Simmons, was very much a star. The principal, Mr. Thoms, was at the podium up on the stage at one end of the basketball court. He had already mentioned, in the course of announcing the various citations for excellence, that Charlotte Simmons had won the French prize, the English prize, and the creative writing prize. Now he was introducing her as the student who would deliver the valedictory address.

". . . a young woman who—well, ordinarily we never mention SAT scores here at the school, first, because that's confidential information, and second, because we don't like to put that much emphasis on SATs in the first place"—he paused and broke into a broad smile and beamed it across the entire audience—"but just this once, I have to make an exception. I can't help it. This is a young woman who scored a perfect sixteen hundred on the SAT and perfect fives on four different advanced-placement tests, a young woman who was chosen as one of North Carolina's two Presidential Scholars and went to Washington, to the White House—along with Martha Pennington of our English department, who was honored as her mentor—and met with the ninety-eight students and their mentors representing the other forty-nine states of our nation and had dinner with the President and shook hands with him, a young woman who, in addition, was one of the stars of our cross-country team, a young woman who—"

The subject of all this attention sat in a wooden folding chair in the first row of the ranks of the senior class, her heart beating fast as a bird's. It wasn't that she was worried about the speech she was about to give. She had gone over it so many times, she had memorized and internalized it just the way she had all those lines when she played Bella in the school play, *Gaslight*. She was worried about two other matters entirely: her looks and her classmates. All but her face and hair were concealed by the kelly-green gown with a white collar and the kelly-green mortarboard with a gold tassel the school issued for the occasion. Nevertheless, her face and hair—she had spent hours, *hours*, this morning washing her long straight brown hair, which came down below her shoulders, drying it in the sun, combing it, brushing it, fluffing it, worrying about it, since she thought it was her strongest asset. As for her face, she believed she was pretty but looked too adolescent, too innocent, vulnerable, virginal—*virginal*—the humiliating term itself flashed through her head . . . and the girl sitting next to her, Regina Cox, kept sighing after every *young woman who*. How much did Regina resent her? How many others sitting beside her and behind her in their green gowns resented her? Why did Mr. Thoms have to go on with so many *young woman whos*? In this moment of stardom, with practically everybody she knew looking on, she felt almost as much guilt as triumph. But triumph she did feel, and guilt has been defined as the fear of being envied.

". . . a young woman who this fall will become the first graduate of Alleghany High School to attend Dupont University, which has awarded her a full scholarship." The adults in the rows of folding chairs behind her murmured appreciatively. "Ladies and gentlemen . . . Charlotte Simmons, who will deliver the valedictory address."

Tremendous ovation. As Charlotte stood up to head for the stairs to the stage, she became terribly aware of her body and how it moved. She lowered her head to indicate modesty. With another twinge of fear of being envied, she found herself looking down at the gold of her academic sash, which went around her neck and down to her waist on either side, showing the world or at least the county that she was a member of Beta, Alleghany High's honor society. Then she realized she didn't look so much modest as hunched over. So she straightened up, a motion that was just enough to make her mortarboard, which was a fraction of an inch too big, shift slightly on top of her head. What if it fell off? Not only would she look like a hopeless fool but she would also have to bend way over and pick it up and put it back on her head—doing what to her hair? She steadied the board with one hand, but she was already at the stairs, and she had to use that hand to gather up her gown for fear of stepping on the hem as she ascended, since she held the text of her speech in the other hand. Now she was up on the stage, and the applause continued, but she was obsessed with the notion that the mortarboard might fall off, and she didn't realize until too late that she should be smiling at Mr. Thoms, who was stepping toward her with a big smile and an outstretched hand. She shook his hand, and he put his other hand on top of hers, leaned toward her, and said in a low voice, "We love you, Charlotte, and we're with you." Then he half closed his eyes and nodded his head several times, as if to say, "Don't worry, don't be nervous, you'll do fine," which was her first realization that she looked nervous.

Now she was at the podium, facing everybody sitting in folding chairs on the basketball court. They were still applauding. Right before her was the green rectangle formed by her classmates, the seniors in their caps and gowns. Regina was clapping, but slowly and mechanically and probably only because she was in the front row and didn't want to make her true feelings entirely obvious, and she wasn't smiling at all. Three rows back, Channing Reeves had his head cocked to one side and was smiling, but with one corner of his smile turned up, which made it look cool and sarcastic, and he wasn't clapping at all. Laurie McDowell, who had a gold Beta sash, too, was clapping enthusiastically and looking her right in the face with a genuine smile, but then Laurie was her friend, her only close friend in the class. Brian Crouse, with his reddish blond bangs—oh dear, Brian!—Brian was applauding in a way that seemed genuine, but he was staring at her with his mouth slightly open, as if she weren't a classmate, much less anything more than that, but some sort of . . . phenomenon. More applause, because all the adults were smiling and beaming at her and clapping for all they were worth. Over there was Mrs. Bryant who ran the Blue Ridge Crafts shop, Miss Moody who worked in Baer's Variety Store, Clarence Dean the young postmaster, Mr. Robertson the richest man in Sparta, owner of the Robertson Christmas-tree farm, beaming and clapping wildly and she didn't even know him, and over on that side in the second row Momma and Daddy and Buddy and Sam, Daddy in his old sport jacket it looked like somebody had wrestled him into, with the collar of his sport shirt pulled way out over the collar of the jacket, Momma in her short-sleeved navy dress with the white bows, both of them suddenly looking so young instead of like two people in their forties, clapping sedately so as not to seem possessed by the sin of pride, but smiling and barely holding back their overflowing pride and joy, and, next to them, Buddy and Sam, wearing shirts with collars and staring at their sister like two little boys in a state of sheer wonder. In the same row, two seats beyond the boys, sat Miss Pennington, wearing a dress with a big print that was absolutely the wrong choice for a sixty-some-year-old woman of her ungainly bulk, but that was Miss Pennington, true to form—dear Miss Pennington!—and in that moment Charlotte could *see* and *feel* that day when Miss Pennington detained her after a freshman English class and told her, in her deep, gruff voice, that she had to start looking beyond Alleghany County and beyond North Carolina, toward the great universities and a world without limits *because you are destined to do great things, Charlotte.* Miss Pennington was applauding so hard that the flesh of her prodigious bosom was shaking, and then, realizing that Charlotte was looking at her, she made a fist, a curiously tiny fist, brought it almost up to her chin, and pumped it ever so slightly in a covert gesture of triumph, but Charlotte didn't dare respond with even so much as a smile—

—for fear that cool Channing Reeves and the others might think she was enjoying all the applause and might resent her even more.

Now the applause receded, and the moment had come.

"Mr. Thoms, members of the faculty, alumni and friends of the school"—her voice was okay, it was steady—"parents, fellow students, fellow classmates . . ."

She hesitated. *Her first sentence was going to sound awful!* She had been determined to make her speech different, not merely a string of the usual farewell sentiments. *But what she was about to say*—only *now* did she realize how it would sound—and now it was too late!

"John, Viscount Morley of Blackburn"—*why had she started off with such a snobby name!*—"once said, 'Success depends on three things: who says it, what she says, and how she says it. And of these three things, *what* she says is the least important.'"

She paused, just the way she had planned it, to let the audience respond to what was supposed to be the witty introduction to the speech, paused with a sinking heart, because her words had all but shrieked that she was an intellectual snob—

—but to her amazement they picked up the cue, they laughed appropriately, even enthusiastically—

"So I can't guarantee this is going to be a success."

She paused again. More laughter, right on cue. And then she realized it was the adults. They were the ones. In the green rectangle of her classmates, a few were laughing, a few were smiling. Many—including Brian—looked bemused, and Channing Reeves turned to Matt Woodson, sitting next to him, and they exchanged cool, cynical smirks that as much as said, "Vie count wha'? Oh gimme a *break*."

So she averted her eyes from her classmates and looked beyond to the adults and soldiered on:

"Nevertheless, I will try to examine some of the lessons we seniors have learned over the past four years, lessons that lie beyond the boundaries of the academic curriculum—"

Why had she said *lie beyond the boundaries of the academic curriculum*, which she had thought was so grand when she wrote it down—and now sounded so stilted and pompous as it fell clanking from her lips—

—but the look on the faces of the adults was rapt and adoring! They looked up in awe, thirsty for whatever she cared to give them! It began to dawn on her . . . they saw her as a wonder child, a prodigy miraculously arisen from the rocky soil of Sparta. They were in a mood to be impressed by whatever she cared to say.

A bit more confident now, she continued. "We have learned to appreciate many things that we once took for granted. We have learned to look at the special environment in which we live, as if it were the first time we had ever seen it. There is an old Apache chant that goes, 'Big Blue Mountain Spirit, the home made of blue clouds, I am grateful for that mode of goodness there.' We seniors, centuries later, are grateful, too, grateful for the way . . ."

She knew it all so completely by heart, the words began to roll out as if on tape, and her mind began to double-track . . . Try as she might to avoid it, her eyes kept drifting back to her classmates . . . to Channing Reeves . . . Why should she even care what Channing and his circle of friends and admirers thought of her? Channing had come on to her twice, and only twice—and why should she care? Channing wasn't going to *any* college in the fall. He'd probably spend the rest of his days chewing and spitting Red Man while he pumped gasoline at the Mobil station or, when he lost that job from shiftlessness, working out in the Christmas-tree groves with the Mexicans, who did all the irksome toil in the county these days, a chain saw in his right hand and the nozzle of a fertilizer spreader in his left, bent from the weight of the five-gallon tank of liquid fertilizer strapped on his back.

And he'd spend his nights rutting around after Regina and girls like her who would be working in the mail room at Robertson's . . .

"We have learned that achievement cannot be measured in the cold calculations of income and purchasing power . . ."

. . . Regina . . . she's pathetic, and yet she's part of the "cool" crowd, the "fast" crowd, which shuts Charlotte Simmons out because she's such a grind, such a suck-up to the faculty, because she not only gets perfect grades but *cares* about it, because she won't drink or smoke pot or go along for drag races at night on Route 21, because she doesn't say *fucking* this and *fucking* that, because she won't *give it up* . . . above all, because she won't cross that sheerly dividing line and *give it up* . . .

"We have learned that cooperation, pulling together as one, achieves so much more than going it alone, and . . ."

But why should that *wound* her? There's no *reason*. It just *does*! . . . If all those adults who were now looking up at her with such admiration only knew what her classmates thought of her—her fellow seniors, for whom she presumed to speak—if they only knew how much the sight of all those inert, uncaring faces in the green rectangle demoralized her . . . Why should she be an outcast for not doing stupid, aimless, self-destructive things?

". . . than twenty acting strictly in their own self-interest . . ."

. . . and now Channing is *yawning*—yawning right in her face! A wave of anger. Let them think whatever they want! The simple truth is that Charlotte Simmons exists on a plane far above them. She is not like them in any way other than that she, too, happened to grow up in Sparta. She will never *see* them again . . . At Dupont she will find people like herself, people who actually have a life of the mind, people whose concept of the future is actually something beyond Saturday night . . .

". . . for as the great naturalist John Muir wrote in *John of the Mountains*, 'The mountains are fountains of men as well as of rivers, of glaciers, of fertile soil. The great poets, philosophers, prophets, able men whose thoughts and deeds have moved the world, have come down from the mountains—mountain-dwellers who have grown strong there with the forest trees in Nature's workshops.' Thank you."

It was over. Great applause . . . and still greater applause. Charlotte remained at the podium for a moment. Her gaze swept over the audience and came to rest on her classmates. She pursed her lips and stared at them. And if any of them was bright enough to read her face—Channing, Regina,

Brian . . . Brian, from whom she had hoped for so much!—he would know that her expression said, "Only one of us is coming down from the mountain destined to do great things. The rest of you can, and will, stay up here and *get trashed* and watch the Christmas trees grow."

She gathered up her text, which she hadn't looked at once, and left the stage, and for the first time she let herself bathe in the boundless admiration, the endless applause, of the adults.

The Simmonses had never before had a party out at their place on County Road 1709, and even now Charlotte's mother wasn't about to call this a party. Being a staunch member of an up-country denomination, the Church of Christ's Evangel, she regarded parties as slothful events contrived by self-indulgent people with more money than character. So today they were just "having some folks over" after commencement, even though the preparations had been under way for three weeks.

It was a beautiful day, and thank God for that, Charlotte said to herself, thinking mainly about the picnic table, which was over next to the satellite dish. The folks were all out back here in the yard in the sunshine, although it wasn't exactly a yard, more like a little clearing of stomped dirt with patches of wire grass that blended into the underbrush on the edge of the woods. The curiously sweet smell of hot dogs cooking was in the air, as her father manned a poor old spindly portable grill. The folks could help themselves to hot dogs from the grill and potato salad, deviled eggs, ham biscuits, rhubarb pie, fruit punch, and lemonade from off the picnic table. Ordinarily the picnic table was inside the house. If it had rained and all these people—Miss Pennington, Sheriff Pike, Mr. Dean the postmaster, Miss Moody, Mrs. Bryant, Mrs. Cousins who had painted the Grandma Moses–style mural in Mrs. Bryant's shop—if they had had to cram themselves inside the house with all her kinfolk and her father's and mother's friends and had discovered that the only table the Simmons family had in their house to eat on was a picnic table, and not only that, the kind that has a bench—a plain plank, built in on either side in place of chairs—Charlotte would have died. It was bad enough that Daddy was wearing a short-sleeved shirt. Everybody could get a good look at the tattoo of a mermaid that covered the meaty part of his right forearm, product of a night on the town when he was in the army. Why a mermaid? He couldn't recall. It wasn't even drawn well.

The house was a tiny one-story wooden box with a door and two windows facing the road. The only halfway ornamental touch was the immovable awnings over the windows, made of wooden slats nailed in place. The door opened directly into the front room, which, although only twelve by fifteen feet, had to serve as living room, workroom, TV room, playroom, and dining room. That was where the picnic table stood ordinarily. The ceilings were right down on top of your head, and the whole place was soaked with a countrified odor that came from using coal stoves and kerosene space heaters. Until Charlotte was six, they had lived belowground in what was now the foundation. Charlotte had thought nothing of it at the time, since they were far from being the only ones. A lot of families started out that way if they wanted their own place. Folks would buy themselves a little scrap of earth, maybe no more than one-fifth of an acre, dig a foundation, put a tar-paper roof over it, stick the pipe from the potbellied stove—used for heating as well as cooking—up through the tar-paper roof, and live down in the pit until they could scrape together enough money to build aboveground. When they finally did, the result was always pretty much what you saw right here: the little box of a house, the rusting septic tank off to the side, and the stomped dirt and wire grass out back.

Laurie McDowell had just left the picnic table carrying a paper plate of food and a white plastic fork and seemed to be going over to talk to Mrs. Bryant. Laurie was a tall, slim girl with quite a head of curly blond hair and a face that absolutely glowed with goodwill—and goodness—even though her nose was curiously wide and blunt atop the graceful and lissome rest of her. Her father was an engineer with the state, and her house was a palace compared to Charlotte's. But Charlotte didn't worry about Laurie. She had been here many times and knew how things were. Nobody else from the class had been invited. There were only kinfolk and genuine friends here, and they were having themselves a real picnic, or seemed to be, and making a fuss over the star of the moment, Miss Charlotte Simmons, who stood in their midst in the sleeveless print dress she had worn under the commencement gown.

"Well, I'll be switched, little lady!" exclaimed her father's former foreman at the Thom McAn shoe factory in Sparta—since removed to Mexico— or China—a big, paunchy man named Otha Hutt. "Everybody told me"—*everbuddy tole me*—"you was smart, but I never knowed you could get up and give a *speech* like that!" *Like'at.*

Sheriff Pike, who was even bigger, chimed in. "The way you did up there"—*up'ere*—"I'm claiming you as a kissin' cousin, gal, and best not be nobody trying to tell me any different, neither!"

"I can remember you when you was no more'n thhhhhis high," spluttered one of her real cousins, Doogie Wade, "and shoot, you could talk circles around everybody way back thhhhhen!" Cousin Doogie was a tall, rawboned rail of a man, about thirty, who had lost two front teeth one Saturday night, although he couldn't remember exactly where or how, and spluttered whenever he had to use words with *th* in them.

Her aunt Betty said she didn't want Charlotte to go and forget everybody once she got to Dupont, and Charlotte said, "Oh, you needn't worry about that, Aunt Betty! Right here's *home!*"

Mrs. Childers, who did dress alterations, called her "honey" and told her how pretty she looked and bet she wouldn't have any trouble finding beaux at Dupont, no matter how grand a place it was.

"Oh, I don't know about that!" said Charlotte, smiling and blushing appropriately but also genuinely, since it made Channing and Brian flash into her mind. Thank God nobody else from the class was here, just Laurie.

For Charlotte's benefit, Joe Mebane, who had a little diner out on Route 21 that offered liver-and-kidney hash for breakfast and had a lineup of chewing tobaccos and snuffs in the front window, yelled over to her father, who was busy at the grill, "Hey, Billy! Where'd all this girl's *brains* come from? Must be Lizbeth's side a the family!"

Her father looked at Joe, forced a smile, then returned to his hot dogs. Daddy was only forty-two, handsome in the ruddy, rugged fashion of a man who worked outside with his hands. After the Thom McAn shoe factory closed and then Lowe's laid off some of its loading-dock crew over at North Wilkesboro, the only job Daddy had was fill-in caretaker of a place on the other side of the ridge in Roaring Gap for some summer people from Hobe Sound, Florida. Momma's pay working half days at the sheriff's office was what they actually lived on. Daddy was depressed, but even when he was happy, he was at a loss when it came to conversational banter. No doubt he was tending the grill with such diligence in order to minimize talking to all these people. It wasn't that he was bashful or inarticulate—not in the ordinary sense. Charlotte was just old enough—just detached enough for the first time—to realize that Daddy was a product of Carolina mountain country, with the strengths and shortcomings of his forebears. He had been raised never to show emotion and, as a result, was far less likely than ordinary men to give way to emotion in a crisis. But also, as a result, he was instinctively reluctant to put a feeling into words, and the stronger the feeling, the more he fought spelling it out. When Charlotte was a little girl, he was able to express his love for her by holding her in his arms and being tender and cooing to her with baby talk. But by now he couldn't bring himself to utter the words necessary to tell a big girl that he loved her. The long stares he sometimes gave her—she couldn't tell whether it was love or wonder at what an inexplicable prodigy his daughter had become.

Mr. Dean, the postmaster, was saying, "I sure do hope you like basketball, Charlotte! What they tell me is, at Dupont everybody's just plain-long *wild* about basketball!"

Charlotte only halfway heard what he was saying. Her gaze had strayed over to her little brothers—Buddy, who was ten, and Sam, who was eight—as they chased each other, dodging and weaving between the adults, laughing and carrying on, excited by this extraordinary thing, a party, that was taking place at their house. Buddy ran between Miss Pennington and Momma, who tried, but not very hard, to get him to slow down. What a contrast they made, Miss Pennington and Momma, Miss Pennington with her thinning gray hair and her fleshy bulk—Charlotte would never entertain a word like obese where Miss Pennington was concerned—and Momma with her lovely lean figure, so youthful looking, and her thick dark brown hair done up in a complicated plaited bun. When Charlotte was a little girl, she used to love to watch her put it up that way.

At this moment the two women were deep in conversation, and Charlotte experienced a surge of anxiety, two kinds of it. What did Miss Pennington make of all this? Over the past four years Charlotte had spent many hours talking to her at school and at Miss Pennington's house in Sparta, but never out here. What did she think of Cousin Doogie and Otha Hutt with his *I'll be switched* and, for that matter, Momma and her *Cain't git'm do a thang* and her *Arland* for Ireland and her *cement* for cement and her *Detroit* for Detroit? Miss Pennington probably didn't make all that much more money than Momma and Daddy. Miss Pennington's house, which her parents had left to her, wasn't much bigger than theirs, either. But Miss Pennington had taste—a relatively new concept to Charlotte—and cultivation. Her house was *decorated*, and everything was kept just so. Her property out back was even smaller than theirs, but she had a real *yard*, planted all over with real lawn grass and bordered with boxwood and flower beds, all of which Miss Pennington took care of herself, even though any real exertion left her out of breath. Charlotte used to talk to Momma about Miss Pennington a lot, but she didn't anymore. She was beginning to have the guilty feeling that Momma was jealous. In her own roundabout way Momma would ask Charlotte if Miss Pennington was sophisticated, worldly-wise, and erudite, and instinct told Charlotte to tell a little white lie along the lines of "Oh, I don't know."

While Mr. Dean talked on about Dupont and national championships, in the peculiarly male compulsion to display knowledge, Charlotte cut another quick glance at her mother. Momma's face had strong, regular features, and she should have been beautiful, but her expression had narrowed and hardened within the tight limits represented by this tiny little place out on County Road 1709. Moreover, she was intelligent and shrewd enough to know most of that. She had found two means of release from her bind. One was her fervent religious faith; the other was her daughter, whose phenomenal intelligence she had recognized by the time Charlotte was two. Throughout her elementary and junior high school days, she and Momma were about as close as a mother and daughter could get. Charlotte kept nothing from her, *nothing*. Her mother led her by the hand through every crisis of growing up. But Charlotte reached puberty shortly after entering Alleghany High, and a curtain closed between them. Perhaps in any age, but certainly in an age like this, there was nothing more critical in a girl's life than her sexuality and the complicated question of what boys expected from it. From the very first time she brought it up to the very last, her mother's religious convictions, her absolute moral certainty, ended discussions as soon as they began. In Elizabeth Simmons's judgment, there were no dilemmas and ambiguities in this area, and she had no patience for sentences that began *But, Momma, these days* or *But, Momma, everybody else*. Charlotte could talk to Momma about menstruation, hygiene, deodorants, breasts, bras, and shaving her legs or armpits, but that was the limit. When it came to matters such as whether or not she should hook up in even a minimal way with a Channing or a Brian and whether or not girls who *kept it* until they got married were becoming rare, Momma closed any such line of inquiry as soon as Charlotte tried to open it up, no matter how indirectly, since there was nothing to discuss. Momma's will was stronger than hers, and she wasn't about to experiment in this area in willful repudiation of Momma's dictates. Instead, she worked it out in her mind that she was going her own way and wasn't about to sink to the level of Channing Reeves and Regina Cox; and if they called her uncool, then she was going to wear Uncool as a badge of honor and be as different from them morally as she was in intelligence. The terrible moment had come, how-ever, when even someone as nice as Brian gave up on her.

The less Charlotte talked to Momma, the more she talked to Miss Pennington, and Momma was aware of that, too, which gave Charlotte something else to feel guilty about. She talked to Miss Pennington about schoolwork, writing, and literature, and Miss Pennington assigned her books to read, including books in history, philosophy, and French, that she would never encounter in the regular curriculum at Alleghany High. Miss Pennington persuaded the biology teacher, Mrs. Buttrick, and the mathematics teacher, Mr. Laurans, to recommend advanced textbooks in their fields and to go over her answers to the questions and solutions to the problems that appeared at the end of each section. But most of all, Miss Pennington talked to her about her future and why she should aim for Harvard, Dupont, Yale, or Princeton—and for the limitless triumphs that waited beyond such universities. But Miss Pennington was a spinster and, despite her unlovely appearance, a dignified woman with perfect manners, and her interests were in things higher than the question of how far a girl should or shouldn't go with Brian Crouse if they happened to be alone in a car or someplace after dark. The only person Charlotte could talk to about all that was Laurie, and Laurie was as confused and innocent as she was.

She was still gazing at Miss Pennington when she heard, or thought she heard—above the general burble of voices and Mr. Dean's discourse on Dupont's current basketball stars—the throaty revving roars of a car somewhere out front of the house, the kind of car that boys used for drag racing. Then the noise stopped, and she once again set about keeping track of what Mr. Dean was saying, in case she had to respond.

It wasn't long, however, before she heard a boy's loud mocking voice. "Hey, Charlotte, you never *told* me you were having a *party*!"

Coming around the side of the house, by the septic tank, were four boys, Channing Reeves, Matt Woodson, and two of their buddies, Randall Hoggart and Dave Cosgrove, both of them great big football players. A couple of hours ago all four had been wearing the kelly-green robes and mortarboards, but now Channing and Matt had on T-shirts, ripped jeans, sneakers, and baseball caps on backward, and Randall Hoggart and Dave Cosgrove wore shorts, flip-flops, and "beaters," which were white strap-style undershirts—an ensemble calculated to display their huge calves, arms, and chests to maximum effect. Channing, Matt, and Randall had big lumps of chewing tobacco in their cheeks and were expertly spurting great brown streams of tobacco juice on the ground as they came swaggering toward Charlotte.

"Yeah, Charlotte, but we know you'd a invited us if you'd a thought of it!" said Matt Woodson in the same sort of loud, arch voice as Channing's, whereupon he looked to Channing for approval.

All four of them began flicking glances at one another and laughing in tribute to their mutual fearlessness and the finesse of their sarcasm. Dave Cosgrove had a twenty-ounce "tall boy" can of beer in his hand, but the voices, the smirks, the laughs, and the swaggers were quite enough to make it obvious that they had been drinking ever since commencement and perhaps before.

Charlotte was stunned, and in the next instant—before she could possibly explain to herself why—she was humiliated and shamed. The party grew silent. You could hear the sound of a hot dog sizzling on the grill. And then she felt fear. Smirking, the drunken band of intruders headed straight toward her with huge strides, as if oblivious to the adults and any respect that might conceivably be due them. She felt rooted, as in a dream, to the spot where she stood. In the next moment, Channing was right in front of her. She was frightened by the insolent way the flesh of his forehead showed through the sizing gap in the back of the baseball cap even more than by the noxious lump in his cheek.

Leering, he said, "I just come for a little graduation *hug*." With that, he reached out and tried to take hold of her upper arm. She jerked it away, he reached out to try again, and she screamed, "STOP IT, CHANNING!"

Suddenly a huge arm was between Charlotte and the boy. Sheriff Pike—and now the entire mass of his body separated them.

"Boys," said the Sheriff, "you're gonna turn right around and go home. You don't git two chances, you git one."

Channing was clearly startled to see the sheriff, whose arms were so big they stretched the sleeves of his polo shirt. He hesitated and then evidently decided he dare not lose face in front of his comrades.

"Aw, come on, Sheriff," he said, mustering a big grin, "we been working hard for four years to graduate. You know that! What's wrong with a little celebrating and coming by to see Charlotte? She was our *valedictorian*, Sheriff!"

"You're drunk, is what's wrong," said the Sheriff. "You're either going home right now or you're going *in* right now. What's it gonna be?"

Still looking at Channing, Sheriff Pike reached over and took hold of the can of beer in Dave Cosgrove's hand. Dave took such a deep breath he seemed to swell up. He stared at the Sheriff, then stared at someone behind the Sheriff, and surrendered the big can without a peep. It was only then that Charlotte realized that three men had come up beside her, just a step back from Sheriff Pike—Daddy, big Otha Hutt, and Cousin Doogie. Daddy still had the big long fork from the grill in his hand. Doogie was about half the size of Sheriff Pike, and Randy and Dave, for that matter, but the way he narrowed his eyes and curled his lips back in a hideous smile, revealing the big gap in his front teeth, made the teeth that remained look like fangs. Everybody in the county knew how much Doogie Wade loved to go brawling. Slugging, kicking, biting, elbows to the Adam's apple, or plain-long old-fashioned Saturday-night rock fights, it was all the same to Doogie Wade.

The Sheriff raised the beer can up to his nose, sniffed it, and said, "If one a you's not drunk, you git to drive the whole bunch a you outta here. Otherwise, you're gonna walk."

"Well now, hey, Sheriff," said Channing, but his proudest weapon, insolence, had disappeared. He spat, but without the gusto of a moment ago.

"Filthy," said the Sheriff, eyeing the arc of the brown spittle. "And 'at's another thang. This ain't your property to spit on."

"Aw, Sheriff," said Channing, "how can anybody"—*innybuddy*—"keep from—"

Before he could utter another word, Daddy, standing right beside Charlotte, said in a strange, low, even, toneless voice, "Channing, if you ever set foot on this property again, you gon' git crawled. If you ever try to touch my daughter again, that'll be the last time you got anythang left to want a woman with."

"You threatening me? You heard what he said, Sheriff?"

"That's not a threat, Channing," said Daddy in the same eerie monotone. "That's a promise."

For an instant—stone silence. Charlotte could see Buddy and Sam staring at their father. This was a moment they would never forget. Maybe this was the moment the mountain code would take hold in their hearts, even now, in the twenty-first century, the same way it had in Daddy's and his daddy's and his granddaddy's and his great-granddaddy's in the centuries before. Her little brothers would probably glory in this moment, which would define for them without a word of explanation what it meant to be a man. But Charlotte saw something more, and that was what she would never forget. Daddy's expression was almost blank, utterly cold, unblinking, no longer attached to the variables of reason. His eyes were locked on Channing's. It was the face of someone out on an edge where there could be only one answer to any argument: physical assault. Did Buddy and Sam see that? If they did, they would no doubt come to admire their father all the more for it. But for Charlotte, those words—"the last time you got anythang left to want a woman with"—completed the humiliation of the dreadful event that was occurring.

Sheriff Pike was saying to Daddy, "Ne'mind all that, Billy." Then he looked straight at Channing while seeming to still be talking to Daddy. "Channing's not stupid. Like he said his ownself, he's a high school graduate now. He knows from now on, won't nobody have any truck with it if he acts like some damn-fool little boy. Right, Channing?"

Trying to salvage one last shred of impudent honor, Channing didn't say yes and he didn't say no, and he didn't nod this way and he didn't nod that way, and he gave the Sheriff one last look that didn't signal respect and didn't signal disrespect. He kept his eyes away from Charlotte's father altogether. He turned tail and said to his comrades in a voice that didn't say surrender and didn't say hold fast, either, "Let's go. I've had enough of this bullsh—" He said the word and didn't say the word, and they retreated, managing to summon up their old swagger until they got beyond the septic tank and around to the front of the house. None of them spat, not even once.

Charlotte stood there with her fingers pressing into her cheeks. The moment the intruders disappeared, she bent over and surrendered herself to hopeless sobs that seemed to well up from out of her lungs. Daddy lifted his hands and tried to think of what to do with them and what to say to her, while the Sheriff, Otha Hutt, and Cousin Doogie looked on, paralyzed, in the age-old way, by a woman's tears. Momma took charge and put her arm around Charlotte's shoulders and squeezed until Charlotte's head rested against her own, just the way she had always done when Charlotte was younger, and said to her, ever so lovingly, "You're my good girl, darling. You're my dear, sweet good girl, and you know that. It don't do for you to waste one drop a tears on trash like those boys. You hear me, darling? They're trash. I've known Henrietta Reeves all my life. As ye sow, so shall ye reap, and I can tell you one thang. *They* won't be bothering you any more." How eagerly her mother was seizing this chance to treat her once again as a child, a genius-in-embryo in the womb of Momma's devotion. "You see the look on that boy's face when your daddy looked him in the eye? Your daddy looked him deep down inside. That boy's never gonna get fresh with you again, my little darling."

Get fresh. How completely Momma misunderstood! Channing's behavior once he and his sidekicks got here—it was irrelevant. That they *wanted* to hurt her in this way—that was what mattered. Looks, boys, popularity—and what good were looks if you had failed so miserably at the other two? And Daddy's solution to the problem—his mountain man's *promise*—to castrate Channing if he ever dared approach his little girl again—ohmygod! How grotesque! How shaming! It would be all over the county by nightfall. Charlotte Simmons's great day of triumph. She couldn't stop crying.

Laurie came over, and Momma let her take over the consoling for a moment. Laurie embraced Charlotte and whispered that underneath Channing Reeves's supposed good looks and cool personality was a cruel bastard, and everybody in the class knew that when they were honest with themselves. Oh, Laurie, Laurie, Laurie, not even you understand about Channing, do you? She could still see his face. Why *not* me—Channing—

Miss Pennington was a few yards away, looking on, not sure it was her place to step in and do something or say something that might be construed as maternal. When Charlotte finally pulled herself together, the guests tried to continue the party, to let her know they weren't going to let four drunken louts spoil things. It was no use, of course. There was no breathing life back into this particular corpse. One by one the guests began saying their goodbyes and slipping away, until it became a general exodus. Momma and Daddy were heading around the house to where the cars were parked along the road. Dutifully, Charlotte was following them, when Miss Pennington came up from behind and stopped her. She had a sort of live-and-learn smile on her broad face.

"Charlotte," she said in her deep contralto, "I hope you realize what that was all about."

Crestfallen: "Oh, I think I do."

"Do you? Then what *was* it about? Why did those boys come here?"

"Because—oh, I don't know, Miss Pennington, I don't want—it doesn't really matter."

"Listen to me, Charlotte. They're resentful—and they're attracted, intensely attracted. If you don't see that, I'm disappointed in you. And they went out and got drunk enough to make a spectacle of it. All they got out of that commencement was that one of their classmates is exceptional, one of their classmates is about to fly out of Alleghany County to the other side of the Blue Ridge Mountains, far above *them*, and there's always the type of person who resents that. You remember we read about the German philosopher

Nietzsche? He called people like that tarantulas. Their sole satisfaction is bringing down people above them, seeing the mighty fall. You'll find them everywhere you go, and you'll have to be able to recognize them for what they are. And these boys"—she shook her head and gave her hand a little dismissive flip—"I've taught them, too, and I don't like saying this, but they're not even worth the trouble it takes to ignore them."

"I know," said Charlotte in a tone that made it obvious that she didn't.

"Charlotte!" said Miss Pennington. She raised her hands as if she were about to take her by the shoulders and shake her, although she was never demonstrative in that fashion. "Wake up! You really are leaving all that behind. Ten years from now those boys will be trying to sound important by telling people how well they knew you—and how lovely you were. It may be hard for them to swallow right now, but I'm willing to bet you even *they're* proud of you. *Everybody* looks to you for great things. I'm going to tell you something I probably shouldn't. I started to tell you when we were in Washington, but then I figured it would be a mistake, because I ought to wait until you graduated. Well . . . today you graduated." She paused and smiled her live-and-learn smile again. "I think I know about what most students think of somebody being a high school teacher, but it never has bothered me, and I've never tried to explain how mistaken they are. When you're a teacher and you see a child achieve something, when you see a child reach a new level of understanding about literature or history or . . . or . . . anything else, a level that child would have never reached without you, there's a satisfaction, a reward, that can't be expressed in words, leastways not by me. In some way, no matter how small, you've helped create a new person. And if you're so fortunate as to find a student, one student, a *single student*—like Charlotte Simmons—and you spend four years working with that student and seeing that student become what you are today—Charlotte, that justifies all the struggle and frustration of forty years of teaching. That makes an entire career a success. So I'm not going to *let* you look back. You've got to keep your eyes on the future. You've got to promise me that. That's all you owe me— that single promise."

Charlotte's eyes misted over. She wanted to throw her arms around this big, gruff woman's neck, but she didn't. What if Momma happened to come back around the corner and see her?

———————

Daddy, Momma, Charlotte, Buddy, and Sam, just the five of them, had supper at the picnic table, which Daddy and Doogie had managed to move back into the house. It weighed a ton. It was a pretty morose suppertime, since Daddy, Momma, and Charlotte couldn't forget what had happened earlier, and the boys sensed their mood.

As soon as they finished eating, while they were all still sitting on the picnic table's plank benches, Daddy turned on the TV. The evening news was on, and so Buddy and Sam ran off to play outside. Some correspondent or other wearing a safari jacket had a microphone in his hand out in front of a hut, talking about something that was going on in the Sudan. Charlotte was too depressed to care, and she got up and went back to her room, which was in fact nothing but a five-foot-wide enclosure that had been partitioned off from one of the house's two bedrooms when Buddy was born. She propped herself up on the bed and started reading about Florence Nightingale in a book called *Eminent Victorians* she had taken out from the library on Miss Pennington's recommendation, but she couldn't get interested in Florence Nightingale, either, and she began aimlessly studying the dust dancing in a shaft of light from the sun, which was so low in the sky it hurt her eyes to look out the window. Out there, about now, all over the county, people would be talking about what happened at Charlotte Simmons's this afternoon. She just knew it. A rush of panic. All they would have heard would be Channing Reeves's version. He and Matt and Randall and Dave went over to visit Charlotte after commencement, and it turned out the Simmonses were having a party and didn't want them there, and so they sicced the sheriff on them, and Charlotte's daddy threatened Channing with a big grill fork and said he'd castrate him if he ever tried to have anything to do with his precious genius daughter—

Just then Daddy called from the front room, "Hey, Charlotte, come here. You wanna see this?"

With a groan Charlotte got herself up off the bed and returned to the front room.

Daddy, still sitting at the picnic table, gestured toward the TV set. "Dupont," he said, smiling at her in a way that was obviously intended to dispel the gloom.

So Charlotte stood by the picnic table and looked at the TV. Yes, it was Dupont, a fact she noted with an empty feeling. A long shot of the Great Yard with the breathtaking library tower at one end and a mass of people in the center. Charlotte had been there only once, for the official tour during the application process, but it wasn't hard to recognize the famous Yard and the stupendous Gothic buildings around it.

"... in his appearance today at his alma mater amid the pomp and ceremony of the university's one hundred and fifteenth commencement," the voice on the TV was saying. A much closer shot of a vast audience. Up a broad center aisle a procession of mauve robes and mauve velvet academic hats was marching toward a stage erected in front of the Charles Dupont Memorial Library, a structure as grand as a cathedral, with a soaring tower and a three-story-high compound arch over its main entrance. At the head of the procession a figure in mauve carried a large golden mace. The pageantry of it made Charlotte blink with wonder, despite her conviction that all was surely ruined. A closer shot . . . the stage . . . mauve robes from one side to the other against a backdrop of gaudy medieval banners. In the center, a podium made of a rich-looking polished wood with an intricately carved cornice, bristling with microphones, and at the podium, also in mauve robes, a tall, powerful-looking man with square jaws, an intense gaze, and thick white hair. He's orating . . . You can see his lips moving and his arms gesturing and his voluminous mauve sleeves billowing, but you can hear only the voice-over of a broadcaster: "The California governor struck what is likely to be the keynote of his all but certain bid for the Republican presidential nomination next year—what he calls 're-valuation,' and what his harsher opponents call 'reactionary social conservatism.'" A closeup of the Governor as he says, "Over the next hundred years, new sets of values will inevitably replace the skeletons of the old, and it will be up to you to define them." The face of the broadcaster filled the screen: "He called upon the current generation of college students to create a new moral climate for themselves and for the nation. The governor arrived in Chester two days ago in order to spend time with students before speaking at today's commencement."

The evening news switched to the accidental beheading of two workers in a sheet metal factory in Akron, but Charlotte was still forty miles southeast of Philadelphia, in Chester, Pennsylvania, at Dupont . . . That wasn't the local news, that was the national network news, and that wasn't just any commencement speaker, it was a famous politician the whole country was talking about, and he was a Dupont alumnus speaking there, in the Great Yard!—robed in Dupont mauve!—calling for a new moral order to be created by *this* generation of college students—*her* generation! A surge of optimism revived her depleted spirits. Sparta, Alleghany High, cliques, hookups, drinking, resentments, tarantulas—Miss Pennington was right. All that was something happening up-hollow in the mountains at dusk as the shadows closed in, something already over and done with, whereas she . . .

"Just think, Charlotte," said Momma with a smile as earnestly encouraging as Daddy's, "Dupont University. Three months from now, that's where you'll be."

"I know, Momma. I was thinking the exact same thing. I can hardly believe it."

She was smiling, too. To everybody's relief, including her own, the face she had on was genuine.

2. THE WHOLE BLACK PLAYER THING

hree men in polo shirts and khakis were sitting high up in the cliffs of seats, so high that from down here on the court their faces looked like three white tennis balls. Below them sat thousands— *thousands*—of people who had somehow—but *how?*—heard about what was going on and were fast filling the first twenty or thirty rows— off-season in a vast half-lit basketball arena—on a sunny Wednesday afternoon in August.

Only a few were students. The fall semester didn't officially begin for another two weeks. Biggie-fried fatties wearing baseball caps and mustaches that drooped down below their lip lines at the corners and work shirts with their first names in script on the breast pockets were making themselves at home in seats that cost $30,000 apiece for Dupont's fifteen home games during the season. They could scarcely believe their good fortune . . . dream seats in the Buster Bowl . . . and you could come walking right on in.

On the court, lit up by the LumeNex floodlights right above it, all that was going on was nothing but ten young men, eight of them black and two white, playing a "Shirts and Skins" pickup basketball game. All five Shirts were wearing shorts and T-shirts, but no two shirts or shorts were identical. The only thing uniform about this bunch was their size. They were all well over six feet tall, and two, one black and one white, were seven feet tall or close to it. Anybody could see that. The upper arms and shoulders of all ten players were pumped up bodybuilder-style. The trapezius muscles running from their necks to their shoulders bulged like cantaloupes. They were sweating, these bodybuilt young men, and the mighty LumeNex lights brought out their traps, lats, delts, pecs, abs, and obliques in glossy high definition, especially when it came to the black players.

During an out of bounds in which the ball got away and had to be retrieved, one of the white players on the court, a Shirt, came over to the other white player, a Skin, and said: "Hey, Jojo, what's going on? Maybe I'm blind, but it looks like that kid's pounding the shit outta you."

He said it in a pretty loud voice, too, causing the one called Jojo to look this way and that, for fear the black players had heard it. Satisfied that they hadn't, he twisted his mouth to one side and nodded his head in sad assent. His head was practically shaved on the sides and in back and had a little mesa of a crew cut of blond hair on the dome. It sat atop a thick torso without an ounce of fat visible, supported by a pair of extremely long legs. He was six feet ten, 250 pounds.

Once he got through nodding, he said in a low voice, "If you really wanna know the truth, it's worse than that. The fucking guy's talking shit, Mike."

"Like what?"

"He's like, 'What the fuck are you, man, a fucking tree? You can't move for shit, yo.' Shit like that. And he's a fucking freshman."

"*What the fuck are you, man, a fucking tree?* He said that?" Mike began to chuckle. "You gotta admit, Jojo, that's pretty funny."

"Yeah, it's cracking me up. *And* he's hacking and shoving and whacking me with his fucking elbows. A fucking freshman! He just got here!"

Without even realizing what it was, Jojo spoke in this year's prevailing college creole: Fuck Patois. In Fuck Patois, the word *fuck* was used as an interjection ("What the fuck" or plain "Fuck," with or without an exclamation point) expressing unhappy surprise; as a participial adjective ("fucking guy," "fucking tree," "fucking elbows") expressing disparagement or discontent; as an adverb modifying and intensifying an adjective ("pretty fucking obvious") or a verb ("I'm gonna fucking kick his ass"); as a noun ("That stupid fuck," "don't give a good fuck"); as a verb meaning *Go away* ("Fuck off"), *beat*— physically, financially, or politically ("really fucked him over") or *beaten* ("I'm fucked"), *botch* ("really fucked that up"), *drunk* ("You are so fucked up"); as an imperative expressing contempt ("Fuck you," "Fuck that"). Rarely—the

TOM WOLFE

usage had become somewhat archaic—but every now and then it referred to sexual intercourse ("He fucked her on the carpet in front of the TV").

The fucking freshman in question was standing about twenty fucking feet away. He had a boyish face, but his hair was done in cornrows on top and hung down the back in dreadlocks, a style designed to make him look "bad-ass," after the fashion of bad-boy black professional stars such as Latrell Sprewell and Allen Iverson. He was almost as big and tall as Jojo and probably still growing, and his chocolate brown skin bulged with muscle on top of muscle. No one was likely to fail to notice those muscles. The kid had cut the sleeves off his T-shirt so aggressively that what was left looked like some mad snickersnacker's homemade wrestler's strap top.

The Shirt named Mike said to Jojo, "So whatta *you* say to *him?*"

Jojo hesitated. "Nothing." Pause . . . mind churning . . . "I'm just gonna fucking kick his ass all over the fucking court."

"Yeah? How?"

"I don't know yet. It's the first time I've ever been on the court with the fucking guy."

"So what? Seems to me you're the one who told me how you grew up taking no shit from—" Mike gestured in the general direction of the black players who were standing around. Mike had a swarthier complexion than Jojo and short, curly black hair. At six-four, he was the second shortest man on the court.

Jojo twisted his mouth again and nodded some more. "I'll think of something."

"When? Seems to me you're also the one who told me how you can't dick around. You gotta give'em an instant message."

Jojo managed half a smile. "Fuck. *I'm* bright. Why do I ever tell you these things?"

He looked away at approximately nothing. Jojo had big hands and long arms, which were considerably bulked up through the biceps and triceps. Proportionately, he wasn't all that big through the chest and shoulders, but he was certainly big enough to intimidate any ordinary male, especially in view of his height. At this moment, however, he looked whipped.

He turned back toward Mike and said, "*Every* year I gotta lock assholes with one a these sneaker-camp hot dogs?"

"I don't know. *This* year you gotta."

The two of them didn't have to dilate on the subject. They already knew the theme and the plot. Jojo was a power forward and the only white starter on the Dupont team. That was why he was a Skin in this game. The Skins were the starting five, and the five Shirts were backups who had only one thing on their minds: cracking the starting team themselves. The Shirt guarding Jojo—and punishing him physically—and talking shit—was a highly touted freshman named Vernon Congers, the usual case of the high school sensation who arrives at college brash, aggressive, and accustomed to VIP treatment, obsequious praise, and houri little cupcakes with open loins. Other grovelers were the most famous basketball coaches in America, including Dupont's legendary—on the sports pages he was always "the legendary"—Buster Roth. Typically, coaches discovered these young deities at AAU summer games or at summer basketball camps. Both the games and the camps were run expressly for college recruiters. Only hot high school prospects were invited to either. The big sneaker companies, Nike, And 1, Adidas, ran three of the major ones. Vernon Congers had been The Man at last summer's Camp And 1, where flashy play—"hotdogging"—was encouraged; also cornrows and dreads, if Congers was any example. Jojo understood the breed, since one Joseph J. Johanssen had been The Man himself a few summers ago at Camp Nike. In fact, being white, he had gotten even more "pub"—publicity, of which most youngsters invited to the sneaker camps had been keenly, greedily aware since junior high—than Vernon Congers last summer. Every coach, every agent, every pro scout was looking for the Great White Hope, another Larry Bird, another Jerry West, another Pistol Pete Maravich, who could play at the level of the black players who so completely dominated the game. After all, most of the fans were white. It was unbelievable, the wooing and the cooing and the donging, as it was called, lavished upon big Jojo Johanssen that summer; so much so that he just naturally assumed Dupont would be mainly a warm-up, a tune-up, a little stretch of minor-league ball on the way to the final triumph in the League, as players at Jojo's level referred to the National Basketball Association. After all, Jojo had set what was probably the all-time sneaker-camp record for donging. At the camps, the college coaches, who were there in droves, were forbidden by NCAA recruiting rules to talk to a player unless the player initiated the conversation. So how could a coach get close enough to a player to make him want to initiate a conversation? Buster Roth—and plenty of others—tagged along whenever Jojo went to the men's room during the camp's all-day sessions. Coach Roth was fast. Jojo couldn't even remember all the times Coach had wound up at the urinal next to his, with *his* dong out, too, waiting for Jojo to say something. One afternoon there had been seven nationally known coaches standing with dongs unsheathed and unfurled at the urinals flanking Jojo's, four to his left and three to his right, with Buster Roth at his usual post, at the urinal to Jojo's immediate right. It turned out Coach could hear better with his left ear. Had there been more urinals, there might have been still more NCAA Division I coach dongs rampant for Jojo Johanssen that afternoon. Jojo never said a word to Coach or any others. But he knew who Coach was—after all, this was the Legendary Buster Roth—and he was flattered and gratified, even moved, by how many times Coach had taken his aging dong out of his pants that summer in homage to The Man of Camp Nike, all nineteen years of him. Of course, once he wooed and won and had your signature on the scholarship contract, which was legally binding, Coach turned into a holy terror. It was the holy terror who was the Legend. It was the holy terror thanks to whom this 14,000-seat basketball hippodrome—officially named Faircloth Arena—was universally known as the Buster Bowl. Even the players called it the Buster Bowl. Ordinarily players called a basketball arena a "box." But this one had a circular façade and a steep funnel of stands inside. It looked just like an enormous bowl with a basketball court at the bottom.

Jojo and Mike were the only white players, or bona fide players who were white, on the team this season. The three swimmies were white, making the squad five whites and nine blacks on paper, but they didn't count. Mike's real name was Frank Riotto. Mike was short for "Microwave." One of the black players, Charles Bousquet, had come up with that nickname. By now it was hard to remember he had ever been called Frank.

The game was about to resume, and it was the Skins' ball. Jojo was down inside, along with the center, Treyshawn Diggs. On the Dupont basketball team, Treyshawn was The Man. Everything on offense revolved around Treyshawn Diggs. Jojo glanced over at him to make sure of his position. Treyshawn was seven feet tall, agile, well coordinated, and nothing *but* muscles, a chocolate brown giant with a shaved head. A white player could be just as jacked as Treyshawn, but his light skin would make it all look flat. Not only was Jojo white, but he had very fair skin, and to make things worse, he was blond. That was why he had his hair cut so close on the sides and in back, practically shaved, leaving just that little blond flattop. He wished he could shave his whole head, the way Treyshawn, Charles, and practically all the black players did—excluding Congers—in imitation of the great Michael Jordan. It was an awesome look, an intimidating look, the look of not only Jordan but also one of those wrestlers who has built himself up into a brute of sheer muscle and testosterone—the shaved head, the powerful neck, the bulging shrink-wrapped traps, delts, pecs, lats, and the rest of it. But according to the unspoken protocol of basketball, it was a black thing, the shaved head was, and if you tried to imitate the black players, they lost respect for you, fast. So he had to keep the mesa of unfortunately blond hair on top.

The ball was back in play. Despite the noise of the crowd, Jojo could hear every shrill screech of the boys' sneakers as they started, stopped, pivoted, changed direction. The point guard, Dashorn Tippet, fed the ball to the shooting guard, André Walker. The Shirts double-teamed André, so he bounced a pass inside to Jojo—and Congers was all over him again, practically lying on his back, pushing, elbowing, hacking, bumping him with his midsection, and going, "Now what the fuck you gon' do, Tree? Caint jump, caint shoot, caint move, caint do shit, Tree."

The sonofabitch wouldn't stop! A freshman! Just got here! Made Jojo *feel* like a tree, rooted to the spot . . .

Cantrell Gwathmey and Charles, the Shirts guarding Walker, were pulling back toward Jojo, and he knew he should feed the ball back to Walker, who was open for one of his patented three-pointers, or to Treyshawn, who had muscled his way around Alan Robinson, the Shirt guarding him, but he wasn't about to, not this time. At the Division I level, basketball players were like dogs. They could smell fear or nervousness, and Jojo knew that his young nemesis had picked up the scent. He steeled himself for what he had to do.

He glanced over his shoulder. He was looking for only one thing, Congers's chest level. Now he had it. He pump faked, as if he were about to try a jump shot. Instead he rammed his elbow straight back, throwing all 250 pounds of himself into the thrust.

"Ooooooooof," went Congers. Jojo pushed off, wheeled around him, drove straight to the basket and slam-dunked the ball as hard as he had ever slam-dunked a ball in his life—and held on to the rim of the basket with both hands and swung on it in a triumphant rimbo, as it was called. Bull's-eye! He had elbowed the bastard right in the solar plexus! He had . . . kicked . . . his . . . fucking . . . ass.

A roar rose up from the crowd. That coup de grâce they couldn't resist.

Play had stopped. Treyshawn and André were standing over Congers, who was bent double, both hands to his solar plexus, taking jerky little steps toward the sideline and going, "*Uh uh uh uh.*" Every time he went *uh,* the dreadlocks down the back of his neck lurched. He was only eighteen or nineteen, but he looked like an old man with a stroke, the disrespectful sonofabitch.

Jojo walked up and stood over him, too, and said, "Hey, man, you okay? Whyn'tchoo go over there and stretch out, man. Take a break."

Congers looked up and gave Jojo a stare of pure old-fashioned hate, but he was speechless. He was still struggling to get his breath and his locomotion back.

Dis me? Fuck you! thought Jojo. The roar of the crowd! The rush of euphoria!

Mike came over with an expression appropriate in the wake of a teammate's injury. Jojo put on a long face, too.

"Yo, blood," said Mike, who considered himself adept at imitating the black players' fraternal lingo. "I take it all back. You're one cool motherfucker, motherfucker. That was off the fucking chain."

Jojo felt so exultant he could barely keep his voice down. "That dickhead . . ." He nodded in the general direction of the black players who were standing around. "Any'm say anything?"

"Nah. Coupl'm gave you a funny look when you slammed it in his fucking face, but whatta they gonna say? The kid was asking for it, and you did it coo-oo-ool, dude." That was another piece of protocol. The slam with the swing on the rim was the black players' thing, too. It was a way of saying, "I didn't just get the better of you, I *kicked your ass and shoved your fucking face up it.*"

The two white boys cut their eyes over toward the bench, where Congers was sitting with his head down between his knees. Treyshawn and André were still leaning over him.

"Don't turn around," said Mike, "but Coach's standing up and looking down here. I bet if it wouldn't look so fucking bad, he'd be running down the stairs to see what's happened to his baby."

Jojo was dying to look, but he didn't. The three tennis balls, Coach Buster Roth and two assistant coaches, had to stay up there in the cheap seats, far removed from the players, because it was a violation of NCAA regulations to start basketball practice before October 15, and this was only August. That was also why the boys were playing in shirts and skins. Uni-

forms, or even the gray practice T-shirts with nothing but DUPONT ATH-
LETICS on them, would be an indication that what was taking place was . . .
what in fact it *was*: basketball practice seven weeks before the permissible
starting date. Of course there was nothing to prohibit somebody from coming to the campus in August, before school started, and playing a little
pickup ball and working out in the weight room—and any player who didn't
make that completely voluntary decision was going to be in deep trouble
with Coach Buster Roth.

"Hey, look what they're doing," said Mike. "You'll like this. They're
bringing in one of the swimmies to take his place."

Jojo glanced over. Sure enough, one of the three lanky white boys was
up off the bench and hustling out onto the court to play for the Shirts.
Charles had dreamed up "swimmies," too, and now all the real players,
black and white alike, called them that. All three swimmies had been excellent prep school players, but they didn't measure up to Division I standards.
On the other hand, they were awesome in the classroom. Under Conference regulations, each team—not each player but the team as a whole—was
required to maintain a grade point average of 2.5, which was a C. The three
prep school boys' grade point averages were practically off the chart. They
were like those inflated orange flotation devices parents put on young children before they let them go in the water: Swimmies. They were lifesavers,
the three prep school boys were. They kept the whole team from drowning
academically.

Charles came walking over to Jojo and Mike and said, "Hey, Jojo, what
the fuck'd you do to my man Vernon?" But he was smiling.

Jojo kept a straight face. "Nothing. I guess he sorta lunged into my
elbow."

Charles let out a whoop, then turned his back to Congers and lowered
his voice. "Sorta lunged into my elbow. I like that, Jojo. Sorta lunged into
my elbow. Who says you white boys don't know how to kick butt? Not me!
You won't catch me lunging into your elbow, man."

He went away smiling, but Jojo kept his straight face on tight. He didn't
dare gloat. Inside, he was elated. Approval and perhaps admiration by a
black player who was as cool as they come!

Play resumed, and Jojo breathed easier. The Shirts had switched
Cantrell over to guard him, and Charles was sent over to guard the Skins'
other forward, Curtis Jones, who liked to slash through the big guys inside

and go to the hole. They let the swimmie guard André Walker. Cantrell gave Jojo a battle, but he was respectful about it, and so Jojo was content to stick to Coach's game plan, which was for him to set up picks, block shots, rebound, and feed the ball to Treyshawn and the other scoring machines.

As the game wore on, Jojo began to hear more bursts of cheering and applause. It was as if his TKO of Congers had turned the crowd on. He'd hear people singing out names: "Treyshawn!" . . . "André!" . . . "You the man, Curtis!" . . . Somebody yelled, "Go go, Jojo!"—a familiar cry here at the Buster Bowl when the season was on. During a break in the game, Jojo checked out the stands. Thousands! Part of the charade of the "pickup game" was to leave the doors to the arena open and let anybody wander in. But who *were* these people? University employees? People from town? Where did they come from? How did they know? They were like those gawkers who seem to—*bango!*—rise up from out of the concrete and asphalt wherever there's a car wreck or a street brawl. Now they had materialized by the thousands in the Buster Bowl to watch a game of Shirts and Skins in the middle of the afternoon. The young gods of basketball. Ranked first in the country last season, the fifth Buster Roth Dupont team to reach the Title Two in his fourteen years here . . . three national championships . . . *nine* teams in the Final Four. What an extraordinary elevation Jojo Johanssen dwelled upon! How far above the great mass of humanity his talent and fighting spirit had already taken him! Oh, he knew who some of the people in the stands were, the usual, inevitable, freelance groupies, for example. But sometimes scouts from . . . the League . . . would materialize, scouts and agents . . . looking for a piece of those who might reach the League and make millions . . . tens of millions . . . But then Vernon Congers popped into his head, and he lost heart. Congers hadn't vanished from his life, he was merely off the court . . .

During the breaks, Mike kept drifting over to the stands and chatting up this girl with a storm of blond hair sitting in the first row. You couldn't miss her. Her hair was very curly but very long. It gave her a wild look.

Jojo said, "Like what you see over there, Mike?"

"You know me. I'm always friendly with the fans."

"Who is she?"

"She's a senior. She's doing something with freshman orientation. All the freshmen come in tomorrow for orientation."

"You know her?"

"No."

"You know her name?"

"No. I know what she *looks* like."

Freshman orientation. Jojo had never gone through freshman orientation, because basketball recruits were exempt from things like that. They barely saw nonathlete students except in the form of groupies, fawning admirers or students who happened to be in the same classes they were. If you played basketball for Buster Roth, you got your freshman orientation on the court. Well . . . *one* freshman got his orientation just now. That was the last time Vernon Congers was going to *Yo! Tree!* Jojo Johanssen . . . He lost heart again. Maybe it was only going to get the kid more fired up.

Finally Coach signaled from way up there in the stands that practice was over, and the Shirts and Skins left the court. The fans descended from the stands in a pell-mell rush and thronged the players. So easy! No security guards to impede their worship! They could *touch* them! Jojo was surrounded. He was mainly aware of the crop of ballpoint pens and notebooks, notepads, cards, pieces of paper—one hoople held up the ripped-off corner of a cardboard NO SMOKING sign—thrust up toward him . . . by the little people way down there. Nearby, a fan kept yelling, "Great give-and-go, Cantrell! Great give-and-go, Cantrell!" As if Cantrell Gwathmey had the faintest interest in some hoople's learned analysis of his play. Jojo kept walking slowly toward the locker room as he signed autographs, carrying a great buzzing hive of fans with him. There were a couple of obvious groupies, their bosoms jacked up by trick bras, who kept smiling and saying "Jojo! Jojo!" and searching his eyes for a look *deeper* than the ones he gave to ordinary fans. Over there was Mike. Being a second-stringer, he didn't attract a real hive, but he sure had attracted the blonde with all the wild curly hair. She was giving him that same groupie grin, searching his eyes for a look loaded with meaning profound. As usual Treyshawn had the biggest hive of all. Jojo could hear him saying, "No problem, Sugar," his slacker-cool way of saying "You're welcome" to girls who thanked him for his autograph. To Treyshawn, all females, any age, any color, were named Sugar. Consciously, the players regarded this hiving as a tedious fate that befell them as part of their duty as public eminences. Unconsciously, however, it had become an addiction. If the day should come when the hives disappeared and they were just a group of boys walking off a basketball court, they would feel empty, deflated, thirsty, and threatened. By the same token, bored and irked by it all as they were, somehow they never failed to notice which player attracted the biggest hive. In fact, any of them could have ranked hive sizes, player by player, with startling accuracy.

"Vernon!"

"Yo! Vernon!"

"Vernon—over here!"

With a chilling realization Jojo looked . . . over there. They—fans—groupies—university groundskeepers—were all over Vernon Congers, and he had yet to play in a single game for Dupont or anyone else at the Division I level! Congers probably struck them as a good-looking guy, assuming they could stomach the cornrows and dreads. That was it, nothing more than looks. Of course, he *had* gotten a lot of pub due to speculation last spring that, as one of the hottest high school prospects in the country, he might skip college and go straight to the pros. That was it, nothing more than pub. That was it . . . and yet there it was. The young shit-talking hot dog already had one hell of a hive.

Finally the young gods reached the locker room.

> *"Know'm saying?*
> *Fucking gray boy say, 'Yo, you a beast.'*
> *I take my piece, yo, stick it up yo' face.*
> *Yo li'l dickie shaking, it won't cease*
> *Faking you got heart. You ain't got shit, yo.*
> *Know'm saying?"*

Rap music by Doctor Dis was kicking and screaming from one end of the room to the other. Rap of some sort was *always* kicking and screaming from one end of the room to the other. Thanks to a nonaphonic wraparound sound system, there was no getting away from it, not in this locker room, where black giants ruled. The team captain always got to choose the CDs on the loop. Charles, who was a senior, was the captain this year, even though he was no longer a starter. Nobody was cooler than Charles. No one commanded more respect. In Jojo's opinion, Charles was totally cynical about the music. If most of the boys wanted rap, he'd give them rap . . . the most rebellious, offensive, vile, obnoxious rap available on CDs. Curtis swore he had seen Charles coming out of Phipps one night after a Duke Ellington and George Gershwin concert by some white symphony orchestra from Cleveland. He said he knew for a fact that was the kind of shit Charles

really liked. Nevertheless, Doctor Dis was who Charles had chosen for the
locker room. Doctor Dis was so sociopathic and generally disgusting, Jojo
had the suspicion that Doctor Dis himself was a cynic who created this stuff
as a parody of the genre. He'd stick in words like "beast" and "cease," words
more than half the Dupont national basketball champions had never uttered in their lives. At this very moment, in fact, the Doctor was singing?—
saying?—

> "Know'm saying?
> Call yo'self a cop? Swap yo' dick and yo'ass,
> Ev'ry time you shit, yo' balls go plop plop.
> Wipe yo' dick, and it bleeds choc'late.
> You needs to fuck with yo' butt, cocksucking cop cop.
> Know'm saying?"

But the locker room itself was luxurious beyond anything the thousands
of hooples who had watched the "pickup game" could have imagined. The
lockers were made not of metal, but of polished oak in its natural light color
with a showy grain. Each one was nine feet high and three and a half feet
wide, with a pair of louvered doors and all manner of shelves, shoe racks,
beechwood hangers, lights that came on when the doors opened, and a fluorescent tube near the floor that was on twenty-four hours a day to keep things
dry. Above the door was a brass strip with the player's name engraved on it,
and above that, framed in oak, a foot-high photograph of the player in action
on the court. Jojo's was one from the publicity department. It showed him
soaring above a thicket of upstretched black arms and tapping in a rebound.
He loved that picture.

As Jojo entered the room, four black players, all with the shaved heads,
he noticed, Charles, André, Curtis, and Cantrell, were standing around in
front of Charles's locker. Jojo couldn't resist joining them. *Had* to . . . Their
conversation offered the possibility of recognizing the triumph of Jojo Johanssen, the white boy who took no shit.

As Jojo approached, Charles was saying, "Say what? What's that motherfucker know about *my grades*? What's he *care*? He's one dumb motherfucker, that motherfucker."

André, grinning at him: "I'm just telling you what the man said,
Charles. Man said you go over the library every night after study hall and
hump the books. Said he saw you."

"The fuck he saw me. That motherfucker's so dumb he don't know where the library's *at*." Charles was no longer his witty and ironic self. He had just been accused of not only getting good grades—it was rumored that his GPA was 3.5—but of *trying* to get them. "What's he talking about—*books*. He don't know what a book *looks* like. Motherfucker's so dumb he counts on his fingers and can't get past one." Whereupon Charles extended his middle finger.

"Ooo-ooo-weee!" said Cantrell. "Gil hear that, man, he gon' come gitchoo!"

"Shit, he ain' gon' come git nothing. He gon' put his finger up his ass's all he gon' do. Talking about *my grades* . . ."

"Hey, man," said Curtis, "what grades you be getting anyway, you don't mind me asking."

"*Heghhh heghhh heghhh* . . ." André began laughing from deep down in his belly. "Maybe we don't need no more swimmies. We got Charles."

Jojo sidled up to the group and said, "Take no shit from'm, Charles. You got grades!"

He glanced at the others to register their amusement at this witty turn on the expression "You got game." Instead, he got three blank faces.

"Whaz good, Jojo?" said Charles with an empty expression of his own. Charles always said "Whaz good?" instead of "Whuzzup."

"Not much," said Jojo. "Not much. I'm beat." He figured that would give them an opportunity to think about what had forced him to work so hard—and whom he had put in his place.

Nobody picked up on that, and so Jojo tried to amplify his point. "I mean, that kid Congers was all over my back out there. I felt like I was in a fucking sumo wrestling match for three hours."

They looked at him the way you might look at a not particularly interesting statue.

Nevertheless, he doggedly pursued his mission and risked the direct approach. "Anybody know what happened to Congers? He okay?"

Charles cut a quick glance at André and then said to Jojo, "I assume so. He isn't hurt, he just had the breath knocked out of him."

Assume so! Isn't hurt! Every time! Never failed! Every time the black players talked among themselves, they'd go into an exaggerated homey argot, with all sorts of *motherfuckers* and *he don'ts* and *I ain'ts* and *don't need no mores* and *you be gettings* for *you are gettings* and *where's it ats*. The moment

Jojo arrived, they'd drop it and start speaking conventional English. He didn't feel deferred to, he felt shut out. Charles's expression was unreadable. Charles, who had laughed about it in front of him and Mike after it happened! He wasn't even going to talk about it in front of André, Curtis, and Cantrell. The cool Charles Bousquet was treating him like some random fan he'd had the misfortune of running into.

A conversational vacuum ensued. It was too much for Jojo. "Well . . . I'm gonna take a shower." He headed off toward his locker.

"Hang in there," said Charles.

And what was *that* supposed to mean? Even after two seasons Jojo never knew where he stood with the black players. What had just happened? Why had they suddenly treated him like a hoople? Was it because he had just walked up and assumed he could join in a conversation among the four of them—or *wot*? Was it that none of them was going to talk to him about any friction he might have with a black player if another black player was present? Or was it because he had made a crack that was a play on "You got game," which was a black expression? It made your head hurt . . . He tried to tell himself it wasn't him, it was the whole racial divide. He was one white boy who had competed with black basketball players all his life, and he could play their game. He prided himself on that. He was so proud, in fact, that he had opened his big mouth to Mike about it, hadn't he? Nevertheless, it was true, starting back when he was growing up in Trenton, New Jersey. His dad, who was six-six, had been the center and captain of the basketball team the year Hamilton East reached the state finals; he had a couple of feelers from recruiters, but no college wanted him badly enough to offer him a scholarship, which he would have needed. So he became a burglar-alarm mechanic, like his father before him. Jojo's mom, who was plenty bright enough to have been a doctor or something, was a technician in the radiology lab at St. Francis Hospital. Jojo adored his mother, but she centered her attention—it seemed to him, anyway—on his brother, Eric, His Majesty the Brilliant Firstborn, who was three years older. Eric was a whiz in school, the best student in his class, and a lot of other things Jojo got tired of hearing about.

Jojo was an indifferent student who would show flashes of intelligence and ability one day and then inexplicably slump and drag his grades back down the next. Well, if he couldn't be the student Eric was, he would be Mr. Popularity, the cool dude Eric never had been. Jojo became the class clown and class rebel, a pretty mild rebel, in point of fact, and then he became something else: very tall.

By the time he entered junior high school, he was already six-four, and so naturally he was steered toward the basketball team. He turned out to be not only tall but also a real athlete. He had his father's coordination and drive. His mom worried about his size because people were going to expect him to be more mature than he actually was. But his dad was excited. His son was going to *make it*. Dad believed he knew why he himself never had, despite all his clippings and stats. He'd had the misfortune of playing in the 1970s, when the black players had begun to dominate the game at the college level and captivate the recruiters. Perennial basketball powers like Bradley and St. Bonaventure were daring to put all-black teams on the court. Jojo's dad was no genius perhaps, but he had figured out one thing: the advantage the black players had was *absolute determination to prevail in this game*. To them it was a disgrace to let yourself be pushed around by anybody and a terminal humiliation to let yourself be pushed around by a white player.

That summer, when Jojo was fourteen, his father started driving to work in the morning and dropping Jojo off at a basketball court on a public playground in Cadwalader Park, a mainly black area—Jojo and a brown paper bag with a sandwich in it. The court was asphalt with metal backboards and hoops with no nets. His father wouldn't pick him up until he got off work late in the afternoon. Jojo was on his own. He was going to learn to play black basketball or else, sink or swim.

This wasn't as drastic a form of education as it would have been in a big city. Trenton wasn't the sort of place where the presence of a white boy on a mainly black playground would create an automatic flash point. But it was drastic enough. The black kids played a physical game with *absolute determination*. If you were white and backed down from them, they wouldn't *do* anything or *say* anything. They would merely run right over you with a cool aloofness. Without so much as a word, they'd let you know that you deserved no respect. After one day of it, Jojo resolved never to back down from a black player again.

The playground game wasn't so much a team sport as a series of duels. If you had the ball and passed it to the open man under the basket, nobody considered that admirable. All you'd done was throw an opportunity away. The game was outdueling the man guarding you. Making a terrific jump shot from outside didn't get the job done, either. The idea was to fake your man out or intimidate him, outmuscle him, drive past him "into the hole," soar above him, score a layup or dunk the ball if you were that tall, and then give him the look that said—this was where Jojo first learned it—"I'm kicking your ass all over the court, bitch."

One day Jojo was defending against a tall, aggressive black player they called Licky. Licky feinted this way and that, then gave Jojo a shoulder in the chest, drove for the basket, and soared for a layup. But Jojo soared higher and blocked the shot. Licky yelled, "Foul!" They began arguing, and Licky decked Jojo with a single punch to the face. Jojo got up seeing red, literally. A red mist formed in front of his eyes, and he threw himself on Licky. They exchanged a few wild punches, then went crashing to the asphalt and rolled in the grime. The other players stood there rooting for Licky but mainly just enjoying the beano. After a while they broke it up because Licky and Jojo were running out of the energy required to make it interesting; they wanted to get back to the game. When it was over, Licky was on his feet, heaving for breath to the point where he was unable to enunciate the curses he intended to direct at Jojo, who was sitting on the asphalt with a bloody cut over one eye, a split lip, a fat nose, and blood running down from the nose and the lip and dripping off his chin. He struggled up, wiped the blood off his face with the tops of his forearms, walked to the center of the court, and made it obvious that he was ready to resume play. He heard one player say to another, sotto voce, "*That* white boy's got heart." He took it as the greatest compliment of his young life. He had it in him to command the respect of black players.

If so, why had Charles and them just frozen him out? Well, if that was the way it was going to be, he couldn't let it bother him, could he . . . All the same, it *did*! The black players ruled in basketball, but he couldn't believe they'd distance themselves from *him*. On the court there was no color line. All were close-knit and worked together as one—and joked together as comrades-in-arms—on a team that had won the national championship last season with him in the bruising position of power forward. He looked at the picture above his locker . . . Jojo Johanssen *soaring* above a lot of flailing black arms and *stuffing* the ball against Michigan State in the Final Four in March. He had broken through the glass ceiling in this game . . . or he thought he had.

Such speculations kept rolling around in his head while he took a shower and got dressed. He was so lost in his thoughts, he was surprised when he realized that he was the last player left in the locker room. Him and the polished oak lockers and the foul mouth of Doctor Dis were all that remained. As usual, the doctor was venting his vile spleen:

"Know'm saying?
What you saving yo' cunt for, bitch?
Some rich old sucker you be hunting for?
Motherfucker he be stuffing shit up his nose, too,
For a brain fuck, ain't having no truck with ho's, yo.
Know'm saying?"

Then Mike, already dressed in his T-shirt and jeans, came back in.

"You still here?" Mike said. He headed for his locker. "Forgot my fucking keys."

"Where you going?"

"See my girlfriend," said Mike.

"What girlfriend?"

"The girl I'm in love with"—he gestured in the general direction of the court.

"Oh, come on, not the one with—you *didn't* . . . I hope to hell you're shucking me."

"I wouldn't shuck you, Jojo. What are *you* gonna do?"

"You've gone fucking balls to the walls, Microwave." Jojo shook his head and gave Mike the twisted smile you give an incorrigible but amusing child. "Me? I don't know. I'm beat. Go get a beer, I guess. That fucking game went on forever. Coach just sits up there in the stands . . ."

"Ummm."

"You know we scrimmaged for three hours? Without one fucking break?"

"Well, it beats running," said Mike. "Last August, eighty-five degrees and you're out on a track running laps."

"Everybody has such a fucking edge on," said Jojo.

"Edge?"

Jojo looked about to make sure nobody else was in the room. "The first day of so-called practice, and I'd like to know who the hell was *practicing*. Everybody's out there playing as if their whole goddamn season depends on impressing Coach on August whatever this is. Everybody's out there trying to cut your legs off to get their minutes."

"You mean Congers?"

"Yeah, him, but it's not just him. I'm sick of the whole black player thing. Coach—now, he's white. Most of the coaches are white. But they just assume if two players have equal ability and one's black and the other's white—they just assume the black player's better. You understand what I'm saying?"

"I guess."

"When I was at the Nike camp that year, I practically had to dunk the ball with my fucking feet before they noticed me."

"They noticed you, or you wouldna been at the camp, and you wouldn't be here."

"But you know what I mean. And it's actually worse than that. They think—the coaches think, I know this for a fact—they think that in a clutch situation, like the last seconds of the game, you gotta give the ball to a black player to take that last shot. He's not gonna choke. The white player of equal ability will. The white player will choke. That's the way they think, and I'm talking about white coaches. It's gotten to the point where it's a fucking prejudice, if you ask me."

"You know that for a fact? *How* do you know that for a fact?"

"You don't believe me? Look at your own situation. You're the best three-point shooter on this team. There's no fucking question about that. I bet you not even André himself would dispute that. If Coach ever had one of those three-point contests like they have at the All-Star game, you'd annihilate André. But he's the starting shooting guard and you're not."

"Well . . . Coach thinks he's better on defense."

"Yeah, *thinks*. That's just the point. *You* know that's bullshit, and so do I. You're just as fast as he is, maybe faster. The fact is, he *assumes* André is faster, and he assumes he's gonna be more aggressive and less intimidated if he's gotta defend against some hot black player."

"Oh, I don't know about that—"

"Why do you think they call you Microwave?"

"I don't even remember," said Mike with a shrug. He began smiling at the recollection, however.

"You think it's a compliment, don't you? Well, it is, up to a point. They know Coach can pop you into a game and you'll score a whole batch of three-pointers right away, just the way you can pop a piece a meat into the microwave and get yourself an instant meal. But they don't think you're a finisher, and Coach dud'n, either. Coach'll take you off the bench and put you into the game to close a big gap in the third quarter, but he won't put you in to make the big shots at the end of the game—and you're the best shot on the team, maybe the best shot in college basketball!"

"Jojo, you're so—"

"My situation is the same! Okay, I'm starting, but Coach dud'n think of me as a real player. Treyshawn, André, Dashorn, Curtis, the black players, they're the real players. He comes right out and tells me. He dud'n want me taking shots. I'm not out there to score points. If I try anything other than a dunk or a little bank from two feet out or a tap-in or something, he holds it against me, even if I make it! A jumper from fifteen feet away? Dud'n wanna know about it. He comes right out and *tells* me! I'm out there to set picks, set screens, block shots, rebound, and feed the ball to Treyshawn, André, and Curtis, the *real* players."

"What's so unreal about that?" said Mike. "You think you're the only one? What about that guy Fox at Michigan State or Janisovich at Duke? You don't think they're real players? I sure as hell do."

"They're real players, but coaches don't think of them as real players. The only real players are black players. You and me, we just play a role. You're the team microwave. Why? Because Coach can't believe the best shooting guard in college basketball isn't black."

"Jojo," said Mike, "stop thinking so hard."

"You don't have to think. You only have to use your eyes."

"You're straining your brain, Jojo. I don't know why the fuck you're feeling so neglected. *I* heard them in there. Go go, Jojo. It id'n as if nobody knows you're on the fucking court."

Now it was Jojo's turn to feel good despite himself. That was true. *Go go, Jojo.* Mike hadn't been able to hide his pleasure over "Microwave." Jojo, all six feet ten inches, 250 pounds of him, was just as transparent. *Go go, Jojo.*

Mike was eager to go meet this afternoon's love of his life and soon departed the Buster Bowl. Jojo finished dressing. He was putting on his khaki pants when he noticed an unusual weight in the right-hand pocket. *Odd*—but in the next moment it didn't seem odd at all. He knew what it would be, but he didn't know exactly what kind it would be. He didn't want to exaggerate the possibilities . . . On the other hand, he *had* been power forward for the national champions last season . . . That gave him a *Christmas* sort of excitement. He didn't want to spoil the surprise by looking right away. He stepped inside his locker to fetch his T-shirt, which had sleeves not likely to deny the public a look at the density of his upper arms. Inside the locker, the oak walls had not been stained or polyurethaned but, rather, left natural and polished and oiled. At this moment they gave off a rich smell, those walls, and Jojo treated himself to a huge lungful. He was as excited as a child, and everything seemed especially wonderful, even the inside of his locker.

He walked all the way down the hall to the players' entrance to the arena . . . and still managed to fight off the impulse to look at what precisely was in that pocket, which now seemed to create heat and vibration along with the drag of its weight. He swung open one of the double doors—and there—right in front of him—there it was!—poised against a backdrop of chestnut trees and maples, which in turn looked luxuriant against the ultimate backdrop, a flawless summer afternoon sky—*oh shit*, it was too good to be true, but there in a no-parking zone of the arena drive: a brand-new Chrysler Annihilator SUV pickup . . . white, gleaming in the sun, massive, perfect for a six-foot-ten, 250-pound national champion power forward, a four-door SUV with a five-foot pickup truck-bed extension covered by a sleek white lid. And *oh shit oh shit*, there were chromed Sprewell spinners on the wheels! It was the most magnificent object Jojo had ever laid eyes on, a monster, but a luxurious monster, with 425 horsepower and every extra known to American automobile manufacturing. Jojo stood still on the sidewalk about fifteen feet away from this awesome manifestation of beauty and power and slowly withdrew from his right-hand pocket . . . sure enough, a set of keys on a ring that also bore a little black remote-controlled transmitter and an inch-long, lozenge-shaped tab with a piece of white enameled metal—just like the car's—on one side and a license plate number on the other.

Jojo pushed the unlock button and heard the *rat-tat-tat* of the four SUV doors unlocking. He pushed the pickup button, and the sleek white lid of the truck bed rose silently. He closed it, then opened the driver's door, stepped way up—the roof of this monster was almost as high as his head—and slid behind the wheel. Tan leather seats . . . *the smell!* It was even richer than the smell of the lockers, just this side of intoxicating. On the passenger seat was what looked like a small white leather album, no bigger than a wallet. And inside . . . but he really already knew: the vehicle's registration and insurance cards in the name of his father, David Johanssen. It was no doubt the same arrangement they—the booster club, known as Charlie's Round-table—had made for the Dodge Durango he had, in fact, driven over to the Buster Bowl this afternoon. The monthly leasing bills came to his father, but the boosters paid them in an under-the-Roundtable way Jojo didn't particularly want to know about. Jojo liked the Durango. It was a great SUV. But *this*! The Annihilator, pure white, gleamed before his very eyes and gleamed and gleamed some more. It was bigger and more powerful than an Escalade or a Navigator.

He loved it. It was like a dream. He felt as if he were in a control tower overlooking . . . the world. The instrument panel looked like what he imagined an F-18 fighter plane's looked like. He turned the ignition key, and the monster came to life with a deep, highly muffled roar. Jojo thought of an underground nuclear test. *The ultimate power.* He loved it. On top of the dashboard was a four-inch-square card embedded in plastic. In the middle of it were two bold capital letters, AD, for Athletic Department, in the center of a corn-yellow circle, around which was a ring of black against a mauve background. That was all it said, AD . . . aside from a small black ID number in one corner. It was the most coveted parking permit on campus. It allowed you to park practically anywhere, anytime.

Basketball players seldom walked through the campus. They drove, as Jojo did now. All the boys preferred SUVs. Subconsciously, they maintained the height advantage and muscular advantage they enjoyed in life on the ground. Whether by design or not, it was one more thing that isolated them from ordinary students and ordinary mortals generally.

But sometimes you developed a craving for all those earthlings to get a load of your astonishing physical presence up close. And so it was to be with Jojo on this lovely, in fact enchanting, late summer afternoon.

He tooled around on the campus drives a bit, so that people could envy him for his great 32-valve behemoth; but shit, there was almost nobody around, and too few of those who were seemed sufficiently staggered by the sight, not even with the chrome Sprewell spinners playing tricks on their eyes. He didn't even spot any of the other guys' SUVs. They had had to walk over to the parking lot to get them. Come to think of it, he'd have to go back to the lot himself to retrieve the Durango and return it to the Chrysler/Dodge dealership.

Yet the sense of added magnificence the Annihilator provided him remained strong. He was heading back to his suite in Crowninshield, and cruising along past the Great Yard on Gillette Way, looking down upon the world, when on an impulse he pulled over to the side and parked—in a no-parking zone, but what did that matter? He got out, stretched his big frame, and began strolling along a path that cut across the Great Yard on a diagonal. *Go go, Jojo.* He was feeling triumphant and in a mood to be noticed, although he told himself he just needed some fresh air and sun. *Go go, Jojo.* There were no students to be seen, only some old people, tourists or whatever they were, walking around and looking at the buildings.

Surely *someone* would show up. Here he was, at the heart of a great university, one of the five best-known people on the campus . . . Nobody, not the president of the university or anybody else, was nearly so recognizable or awesome as the starting five of the national champions. *Go go, Jojo.* Of course, Dupont was just a stop on the way to the final triumph, which was playing in *the League.* In the meantime, being at Dupont was cool. Everybody was impressed that you were playing ball for Buster Roth. For that matter, everybody was impressed that you were even *attending Dupont.* The sweet irony was that he had wound up at a better university than Eric. If the unthinkable happened and you didn't make it to the League, it was pretty good credentials just to be able to say you graduated from Dupont—assuming you managed to keep your grades above water and *did* graduate. Well, that was what tutors were for, wasn't it?

Doubts began to form. What if something *did* happen? In high school, teachers would tell him that he had a perfectly good mind, but it wasn't going to do him any good if he didn't apply himself and develop it; and if he didn't, someday he'd regret it. He took it as an inside-out compliment. He didn't have to apply himself and develop his mind and all that stuff. He was of a higher order of student. He was a basketball star. The high school would make sure he had the grades he needed to stay eligible. Which they did. Several times he got really interested in courses and did pretty well, but he was careful not to let on. One time he wrote a paper for history that the teacher liked so much he read part of it to the class. He could still feel how exciting and at the same time embarrassing that had been. Luckily, word of it never got beyond the classroom.

His brother, Eric, had made all these good grades and gone to Northwestern and then to the University of Chicago Law School—and big deal. For the past four years, two at Dupont and his last two in high school, Jojo had completely overshadowed His Majesty the Brilliant Firstborn. In the general sense, nobody knew who the hell Eric Johanssen was, and tens of thousands, hundreds of thousands maybe, knew who Jojo Johanssen was.

But . . . *what if something did happen and nobody in the NBA drafted him?*
The problem with Vernon Congers was not so much that he might take his
starting position away from him, but that Coach might bring Congers in off
the bench more and more and cut into his, Jojo's, minutes, which would
mean that he would fade in the stats and in every other way. If that happened, he could forget the NBA. Suddenly he'd be that pathetic animal, a
college has-been with a piece of paper from Dupont and nowhere to go.
He'd be nothing. Maybe he could get a job coaching basketball at Trenton
Central—and Eric would be what he was right now, a lawyer in Chicago on
the threshold of a limitless future . . . The hell of it was, Congers was so goddamned good! Big, strong, quick, aggressive, and *absolutely determined to
prevail in this game!* Far faster than it would take to recite it, all this rushed
together in Jojo's midsection. Now there was no mistaking the feeling,
which was fear.

Had to stop thinking about it. He looked around the Great Yard. The afternoon sun, the summer light, brought out the warm undertones in the
gray stone of the Gothic buildings. Glints of yellow, ocher, brown, and purple made it all look richer and somehow even more massive and imposing.
The library tower . . . it was like a cathedral . . . He'd seldom been inside it,
except with a tutor. Actually, there were a couple of times after midnight he
had gone in there to hook up with this girl he knew studied in there late at
night . . .

A man was walking toward him. He recognized the guy, but who the
hell was he? In his early forties, probably, wearing a polo shirt, a pair of khaki
cargo shorts, and sneakers . . . terrible posture . . . completely undeveloped
muscles . . . a little paunch bulging out over his belt . . . scrawny legs. Jojo
knew he was a body snob, but he couldn't help it. How could a man let himself go like that? The man was carrying one of these hoople attaché cases.
He was coming closer . . . Who the hell was he? The guy started smiling.
Jojo gave him a befuddled smile in return. Just before they passed each
other, the guy looked him right in the face and said, "Hello, Mr. Johanssen."
Jojo gave him an embarrassingly unconvincing, "Hey—how are you?" Each
walked on. *Mr. Johanssen?* That wasn't a fan talking. Now, too late, it dawned
on him: that was his sociology professor from first semester last year. Like a
lot of athletes, Jojo was majoring in sociology, which was known as an athlete-
friendly department. But what was the guy's name? . . . Pearlstein, that was
it . . . Mr. Pearlstein. Nice guy, Mr. Pearlstein . . . He had given him a break
on a paper he *knew* he couldn't have written. More doubts . . . Had he

detected a note of irony in the man's voice? Hello, Mr. Johanssen, you dumb jock?

Jojo walked around some more, putting a slight roll into his shoulders, hoping to be noticed. The T-shirt he had on certainly wasn't meant to hide the fact that he was not only very tall but very buff. Damn! . . . Nobody! . . . Maybe they were looking at him out of windows. He scanned the buildings . . . Nobody . . . but wait a minute. A pair of casement windows were open on the ground floor of Payson College—and what was that he saw on the wall? He walked closer. He was *right*! It was *himself*! A huge poster, at least four feet high, of Jojo Johanssen, triumphant, springing above a whole cluster of black players—and kicking their asses. He walked still closer, as close as he could without seeming to take an abnormal interest in some student's room. He was transfixed . . . couldn't take his eyes off it . . . Whoever it was . . . *worshiped* Jojo Johanssen. He just stood there staring, as long as he possibly could without seeming weird. Finally he turned away, suffused with an exhilaration indescribable, but as real, as corporeal, in fact, as any of the five senses . . .

He scanned the Great Yard again . . . nobody. Bereft of an audience, he now felt very tired. He must have really pushed himself in that endless scrimmage. He began to think of the big TV screen and the easy chairs that awaited him in the suite he and Mike shared. Suddenly it seemed like the most delightful prospect in the world, and absolutely *necessary*, to be sinking into one of those chairs and turning on the TV and emptying his mind of . . . all the stuff that had gone on this afternoon and all the stuff he'd been brooding about . . .

So he walked back to Gillette Way, got back in the Annihilator, and headed on to Crowninshield College. Under NCAA regulations, you could no longer have special dorms for athletes. They had to be housed with the general student population. So the basketball players were all put at one end of a big hallway on the fifth floor of Crowninshield. For the basketball players, they had knocked down the walls between the two bedrooms on either side of the suite's common room, so that each player had one large bedroom, with a private bath and an outsize bed. To make up for the space lost by doubling the size of the athletes' rooms, they had converted some storerooms and unused kitchens into a bunch of pretty wretched singles for the leftover ordinary students. On top of all that, the basketball players' suites, and theirs alone, were centrally air-conditioned.

As Jojo walked along the hall to the suite, his very hide anticipated the luxury of that ever so nicely conditioned air, of his big, tired body sinking back into an easy chair, of the TV irrigating the interior of his parched skull. He opened the door—

—two young white people were lying stark-naked on the floor of the common room amid a litter of T-shirts, jeans, underpants, and sneakers, their arms and legs intertwined, right there on the carpet in front of the TV— fucking. In and out, in and out, and the girl was going, "*Unhh unhh unhh.*" Their legs were toward him. They were lying on their sides. The view was mainly the fleshy, meaty swells of buttocks and thighs and the storm of curly blond hair that concealed Mike's face. Idly, Jojo wondered if this girl had shaved her crotch. Last spring and so far this year he had been seeing more and more of them completely shaved—although this girl he had hooked up with a couple of days ago said she'd had a "Brazilian wax job." But what he really wondered about was how the fashion spread from one girl to another. As a basketball player, you could easily keep tabs on girls' grooming down there, but how did the *girls* themselves stay au courant? Did they actually discuss such things—or what?

"That you, Jojo?" Mike didn't so much as lift his head.

"Yeah."

"Whew. I was afraid it might be the maid." Mike didn't stop what he was doing for an instant or change the rhythm. "Say hello to Jojo."

But the girl, evidently preferring to remain in the passionate mode, kept her face turned to Mike's and continued to go "*Unhh unhh unhh.*"

"Jojo, say hello to—what's your name?"

"*Unhh unhh unhh* Ashley *unhh unhh unhh.*"

"Say hello to Ashley, Jojo."

"I need the remote," said Jojo. "Skooz."

So saying, he stepped over the couple, looking down to make sure he didn't step *on* them. The girl had her eyes squeezed shut. Mike cut an annoyed glance up at Jojo.

Fuck, thought Jojo. He had begun *thinking* in the Fuck Patois, too. He picked up the remote from the TV table and—"Skooz"—stepped back over the couple. In two strides he reached one of the big easy chairs, started to sink back into it—and froze before his bottom hit the cushion. It was too fucking gross. Mike and what's her name, Ashley, remained on the floor in front of the TV, making noises and doing the in-and-out.

And Mike had given *him* an annoyed look. Ordinarily Mike used good judgment, but sometimes . . . What was so special about this particular piece of ass that he couldn't make it ten more feet to his bedroom? Anybody on the basketball team could point at any girl on campus and have her in his room in ten minutes or close to it—so what was the big deal? One time when there had been *four* of them at once . . . all four completely shaved . . . The memory of it aroused him a bit . . . but annoyance quickly overcame the stirring in his loins. Mike could be so goddamned thoughtless. He, Jojo, had had a rough afternoon. For the past ten minutes he had been thinking about only one thing in the world: coming back to this suite, sitting in this easy chair, and zoning out on a little TV. And now, on the floor right in front of the TV, was a two-backed beast slogging away and going *unhh unhh unhh.*

With an accusing sigh, Jojo tossed the remote onto the seat of the easy chair and went into his room and shut the door. He could see them in his mind's eye, and for a moment, despite himself, he felt the old tingle again. He focused on his resentment and fought it off.

3. THE MERMAID BLUSHED

Daddy, at the wheel of the pickup truck, Momma, over by the passenger-side door, and Charlotte, sandwiched in between, were driving down Dupont University's showiest approach, Astor Way, an avenue flanked by sycamores whose branches arched over from either side in the summer months until they met to form a lush, cool green tunnel with a thousand little places where the sun peeked through. The sycamore trees were so evenly spaced they made Charlotte think of the columns she had seen in Washington when she was there with Miss Pennington.

"Well, I'll be switched," said Momma. "I never in my life—"

Instead of finishing the sentence, she lifted her hands and made a tunnel shape like the arch of trees and looked at Charlotte with a wide-eyed smile. It was about two p.m. Ever since four-thirty this morning, when they left Sparta in the dark, Momma had been primed to be impressed by Dupont.

Daddy turned into a tree-shaded parking lot marked LITTLE YARD, and their old pickup became part of a busy swarm of cars, vans, SUVs, and at least one yellow Ryder rental truck, disgorging freshmen, parents, duffel bags, wheelie suitcases, lamps, chairs, TV sets, stereos, boxes . . . and boxes . . . box after box . . . boxes of every conceivable size, or every size Charlotte could think of. What on earth were her new classmates bringing in all those boxes—and what did *she* lack? But that was a fleeting concern.

Young men wearing khaki shorts and mauve T-shirts with DUPONT in yellow letters across the chest were helping people unload their cargo, piling it on heavy-duty dollies, and pushing the immense loads out of the lot and toward the building. Charlotte had been assigned to Edgerton House, "house" being the term Dupont used instead of such unclassy, bureaucratic State U. terminology as "Section E, freshman dormitory." It wasn't part of any "dorm," either. It was a house on Little Yard. Little Yard would be home to all sixteen hundred incoming freshmen. It was the first dormitory ever built at Dupont. A hundred years ago it had housed every student in the university.

The parking lot was so busy and the trees had such dense foliage, Charlotte barely saw the building itself at first. In fact, it was gigantic and seemed even more so thanks to its heavy, brownish rusticated stone walls. The wall she was looking at extended the entire length of the long block it was built on. No fortress ever looked more formidable, but only intangible matters concerning that huge structure were on Charlotte Simmons's mind. They had obsessed her thoughts throughout the ten-hour drive from Sparta: namely, what her roommate would be like and just what the ominous term "coed dorm" actually meant.

All spring and all summer Dupont had been a wondrous abstraction, the prize of a lifetime, the trophy of all trophies for a little girl from the mountains; in short, a castle in the air. Now it was right in front of her at ground level, and this was where she would be living for the next nine months, and dealing with—what? Her roommate was a girl named Beverly Amory, from a town in Massachusetts called Sherborn, whose population was 1,440, and that was really all she knew about Beverly Amory. Well, at least she was a small-town girl, too. They had that much in common . . . As to what coed dorm life really was, she knew even less. Whatever it was, the concept, now that the time had come, was alarming.

Charlotte, Momma, and Daddy had gotten out of the pickup, and Daddy was heading toward the rear to open the fiberglass camper top and the tailgate, when one of the young men approached, pushing a dolly, and said, "Welcome! Moving in?"

"Yeah," said Daddy in a wary tone.

"Can I give you folks a hand?"

He was smiling, but Daddy wasn't. "No thanks."

"You sure?"

"Yep."

"Okay. If you change your mind, let one of us know." Whereupon he went off, pushing the dolly toward another vehicle.

Daddy turned to Momma and said, "He'd want a tip."

Momma nodded sagely over this insight into the wiles of life here on the other side of the Blue Ridge.

"I don't think so, Daddy," said Charlotte. "They look like students to me."

"That don't matter," said Daddy. "You'll see. When we git in'ere, you're gonna see those 'students' standin'ere waiting and folks digging into their pockets. 'Sides, what we got, h'it won't take much to tote it."

So Daddy opened the fiberglass camper top and lowered the tailgate. Charlotte really hadn't brought a whole lot, just a big duffel bag, two suitcases, and a box of books. Daddy had gone to the trouble of putting the camper top over the bed of the pickup, not so much to protect her things from the weather, which the TV said would be fine all over the East, as to provide some privacy in case he and Momma had to spend the night here for some reason. They had their sleeping bags rolled up on the truck bed and an Igloo cooler with enough sandwiches and water to get by.

True to his word, Daddy toted the two heaviest things himself. He put the duffel bag up on his shoulder and somehow carried that whole box of books under his other arm. Goodness knows how he did it, except that he was strong as a bull from all the hard work he'd done in his life. The literature from Dupont had said to come dressed ready for "moving in," and so Daddy had on an old short-sleeved plaid sport shirt that hung out over a pair of the thorn-proof gray twill pants he wore when he went hunting. Charlotte immediately monitored the parking lot and was relieved to see that most of the other fathers were dressed more or less the same as Daddy: casual shirts and pants and, in some cases, shorts . . . although there was something different about theirs. Naturally, she checked out the other female freshmen with that same swift sweep of the eyes, and that was a relief, too. She was afraid they might be all dressed up, although she didn't really think they would be. Practically all of them were wearing shorts, just the way she was. Hers were high-waisted denims with her sleeveless cotton print blouse tucked in—"blouse" was the word Momma used—an ensemble designed to show off not only her trim athletic legs but also her small waist. She saw immediately that most of the other girls were wearing flip-flops or running shoes, but she figured her white Keds fit in fine with the running shoes. She didn't see any other mothers dressed quite like Momma, who had on a T-shirt and a denim jumper that came down below her knees. A pair of athletic socks rose up from out of her striped sneakers as if to meet the hem of the jumper. Never in her life had Charlotte possessed the strength to entertain . . . Doubts . . . about Momma's taste, any more than her authority. Momma was Momma, which was all there was to say about Momma.

Momma carried the bigger suitcase and Charlotte the other one, and they were heavy enough, but Daddy's feat was really something. People were staring at him, probably because they wondered how one man could carry such a load, which made Charlotte proud, or marginally proud; but then she noticed that the way Daddy had his arm around the box made his forearm look huge, which in turn made the tattoo of the mermaid look huge . . . and reddish from the strain . . . which in turn made the mermaid look as if she were blushing. Was that what they were all actually staring at? Despite herself, Charlotte felt shamed, for she did entertain doubts about Daddy's taste and the tattoo in particular.

Amid a rumbling caravan of dollies, they went through the Little Yard's great arched entryway and its fifteen-foot-high stone corridor and out into a courtyard . . . the Little Yard, which turned out to be a quadrangle the length of a football field, with ancient trees on a lush green lawn bordered by boxwood hedges and big red-orange poppies blazing amid beds of lavenderish blue nepeta and crisscrossed by worn walkways that looked as if they had been there forever. The entire yard was enclosed by the rows of houses, which, by the looks of them, had been built in different stages and in slightly different styles. The place conjured up a picture of a fortress whose interior drill ground has been magically transformed into an idealized, arboreal, floribunda landscape. The rumbling, the rattling, the aluminum clanking, the creaking, the squeaking, the jerking, the jouncing of the dollies ricocheted off the walls. What colossal heaps of *things* the young men in the mauve T-shirts were pushing and pulling and humping to the houses! At Edgerton, they, the boys in mauve, were carting everybody else's belongings onto the elevator, but Daddy was having none of that. He marched right on with his prodigious load. He was sweating, and the mermaid was really blushing now.

Charlotte caught two of the boys in the mauve shirts sneaking glances at it. One said to the other in a low voice: "Nice ink." The other tried to suppress a snigger. Charlotte was mortified.

Charlotte's room, 516, was up on the fifth of the building's six floors. When she got off the elevator, she found herself looking down a long, gloomy old corridor in which frowning adults were popping in and out of doorways, pointing this way and that, yammering about God knows what, amid a tumbled clutter, extending as far as the eye could see, of empty boxes, some gigantic, lying every which way from one end of the corridor to the other, with so much in the way of lurid lettering and illustrations and so many closure flaps thrust out it looked like an explosion. Boys and girls stood by phlegmatically, secretly appalled in varying degrees that their parents insisted on walking the face of the earth in plain view of their new classmates.

The young men in the mauve T-shirts were pushing their heavy dollies through this cardboard chaos like icebreakers. On the landing of a stairwell near the elevator, there was a huge garbage can the color of drained veal with boxes, bubble paper, lacerated shrink-wrapping, Styrofoam peanuts, and other detritus gushing out of it. On the floor of the hallway, what you could see of it, were . . . dust balls . . . more dust balls than Charlotte had ever seen in her life . . . everywhere, dust balls. Toward the far end of the corridor Charlotte spied two barefoot boys. One was clad in only a polo shirt and the towel he had wrapped about his waist. The other wore a long-sleeved shirt with the tail hanging out over a pair of boxer shorts, and he had a towel slung across his shoulders. Boxer shorts? Both boys were scampering across the corridor into the men's bathroom, judging by the towels and the toilet kits they were carrying. But no pants? Charlotte was shocked. She glanced at Momma—and was relieved to see that she hadn't noticed. Momma would have been more than shocked. Knowing Momma . . . she would have brought God's lightning down on somebody's head. Charlotte hurried her into the room, 516, which was fortunately just ahead of them.

Given the grandeur that was Dupont, the room seemed terribly bare and, like the hallway, worn and exhausted. A pair of tall double-hung windows, side by side, equipped with yellowish shades but no curtains, looked out onto the courtyard. The courtyard appeared rather grand from up here, and the windows let in plenty of light. That much you could say for the room. But the rest of it was gloomy and tired: a pair of single beds with cheap metal frames and mattresses rather the worse for wear, a pair of plain wooden bureaus that had seen better days, a pair of small wooden tables that couldn't properly be called desks, a pair of straight-backed wooden chairs, yellow ocher walls that could have stood a coat of paint, small dark wood baseboards and ceiling cornices that might have been handsome once, a wooden floor gone gray with use . . . and crawling with dust balls.

Daddy unzipped the big duffel bag and allowed as how they might as well take out the bedclothes and get started making up the bed, but Charlotte thought she ought to wait for her roommate and not just arbitrarily decide which side of the room would be hers, and Momma agreed. Then Momma went to the windows and said you could see the top of the library tower from here and a couple of smokestacks. Daddy was of the opinion that the smokestacks meant that Dupont had its own power plant, it was so big. And they waited.

They could hear the dollies rolling out in the hallway and the young men in the mauve DUPONT T-shirts grunting and occasionally swearing under their breath as they bulled their loads through the sprawling dump of boxes. At one point, there was the unmistakable shriek of two girls thrilled by the fact that they had run into each other. That gave Charlotte a hollow feeling. It hadn't occurred to her that there might be entering freshmen who already . . . had friends. From somewhere down near the elevator a boy exclaimed, "Gotcha! Who's your daddy?" Came the reply: "Oh, man, 'Who's your daddy.' How completely douche-baggy is that?" Then a woman's mannered voice: "Kindly spare us your . . . 'colorful' terminology, Aaron." Charlotte could tell by the boys' stressed voices that they were trying to assert themselves as manly and cool purely out of a nervous fear that the other males in this dorm might think they weren't.

By and by, she heard a girl talking out in the hall near the door, apparently to herself: "Edgerton. We just got here. Eeeeeeyew, there's like trash all over the place, and they've got this like big plastic garbage can—are they all like this? This one's beat up and busted, if you ask me . . ." The voice was coming closer. "Ummmm, we *did* . . . He's cute . . . Ken, I think, but it could've been Kim. Would they name a boy Kim? . . . I can't just walk up and say, 'So, what's your name?' . . . Ummmm, I don't really think so . . ." Now the voice was just outside the door. "Fresh *meat?*"

In the doorway appeared a tall girl with a cell phone to her ear, a canvas sling over her shoulder . . . a girl so tall and thin that Charlotte thought she must be a model from a magazine! . . . long, full, straight brown hair with blond streaks . . . big blue eyes set in a perfectly suntanned face . . . but a terribly thin face, now that Charlotte got a better look, so thin it made her nose and her chin look too big, giving her a slightly horsey look. A long, terribly thin neck rose up out of a pale, chalky blue T-shirt . . . even Charlotte could tell it was one of those fine cottons, like lisle . . . hanging outside a pair of khaki shorts . . . perfectly tanned, long, long, oh-so-slender legs . . . so slender they made her knees seem too big . . . just as her elbows seemed too big for her awfully skinny arms. Still on the cell phone, she kept her eyes cast down at some nonexistent point in midair without so much as a glance inside the room . . . a mock grimace, and she said, "Eeeeeyew, that's gross, Amanda! *Fresh meat.*"

Then she looked up, saw Charlotte, Momma, and Daddy, and—the cell phone still at her ear—opened her eyes wide as if in surprise, gave them a big smile, and made a little fluttering gesture with her other hand. Then she cast her eyes down again, as if drawing a curtain, and said into the cell phone:

"Amanda— Amanda—Amanda—I'm sorry, I have to go now. I'm at my room . . . Uh*hunh*, exactly. Call me later. Bye."

With that, she pushed a button on the cell phone, slipped it into the canvas bag, and beamed another big smile toward Momma, Daddy, and Charlotte.

"Hi! *I'm* sorry! I *hate* these phones! I'm Beverly. Charlotte?"

Charlotte said hello and managed a smile, but she was already intimidated. This girl was so confident and poised. Somehow she immediately took over the room. *And* she already had a friend at Dupont, apparently. They shook hands, and Charlotte said in a timid voice, "These are my folks."

The girl directed her smile toward Daddy, looked him right in the eye, extended her hand, and said, "Hi, Mr. Simmons."

Daddy opened his mouth, but nothing came out. He just nodded deferentially and shook her hand . . . limply, Charlotte could tell, and she could feel shame weighing down her confidence. *Oh God, the mermaid!* Charlotte thought she saw the girl flick a glance at Daddy's forearm . . . When he took her hand, it disappeared inside his. *What does that big callused hand feel like to her?*

The girl turned to Momma. "Hi, Mrs. Simmons."

Momma wasn't at all intimidated. She shook the girl's hand and sang out, "Well, hi there, Beverly! It's *real* nice to meet you! We been looking *forward* to it!"

A woman's voice: "That says five sixteen, doesn't it?" Everyone turned toward the doorway.

In came a middle-aged woman with a lot of pineapple blond hair teased and fluffed and brushed back in a certain way, followed by a tall, balding man, also middle-aged. The woman wore a simple sleeveless dress that came down to just above her knees. The man had on a white open-necked polo shirt, revealing the puffy onset of jowls, and a pair of khakis and some sort of leather moccasins—and no socks. Behind them, in came one of the young men in the mauve T-shirts . . . rather handsome . . . carefully pushing a dolly over the threshold. There must have been a *ton* of stuff on it, piled six or seven feet high.

"Mummy," said the girl, "come meet the Simmonses. Dad . . ."

With a big, friendly smile the man came over to Daddy and shook hands—Charlotte could have sworn that he, too, took a quick look at the mermaid—and said, "Hey! How are you? Jeff Amory!"

"Billy," said Daddy. That was all he said: "Billy." Charlotte was mortified. The man shot a glance at Daddy's gray work pants. Charlotte shot a glance at Mr. Amory's khakis and at Mrs. Amory's dress. To a girl from Mars, or Sparta, North Carolina, they were dressed essentially the same as her parents. So what was it about them—

Mr. Amory was greeting Momma, saying, "How are you? Jeff Amory!" Then he turned to Charlotte, pulled his head back, beamed a big smile, opened his arms as if coming across a long-lost friend, and said, "Well—you must be Charlotte!"

Charlotte couldn't think of what on earth to say, and so she just said, "Yes, sir," and felt like a child.

"This is quite a day," said Mr. Amory. "Are you ready for all this?" He swept his hand toward the windows, as if to take in the whole campus.

"I think so," said Charlotte. "I hope so." Why couldn't she come up with anything more than this juvenile politeness?

"When I was starting out as a freshman here—"

"In the Dark Ages," said his daughter.

"Oh, thank you, dear. See what a respectful roommate you have, Charlotte? Anyway, as I recall"—he aimed a wry smile at his daughter—"through the fog of my Alzheimer's onset"— he beamed once more at Charlotte—"is that it's big, or it seemed big to me at the time, but you really get used to the place very quickly."

Beverly's mother was saying to Daddy, "How do you do? Valerie Amory. It's *so* nice to meet you. When did you arrive?"

Before Daddy could say anything, Mr. Amory said, "Oh, brother. Let's see where we're gonna put all these things."

He had turned around and was talking to the young man who was tending the dolly . . . tall, slender, athletic looking . . . sun-bleached brown hair brushed down just slightly over his forehead. Charlotte took in every detail. The dolly bore an enormous heap of . . . stuff.

Mrs. Amory was greeting Momma. She took her hand and said, "Mrs. *Simmons* . . ." with a smile, a deep look into the eyes, and an inflection that bespoke a sympathetic if inexplicable confidentiality. "Valerie Amory. This is such a pleasure."

"Why, thank you, Valerie," said Momma, "it's just real nice to git the chance to meet you all! And you can call me Lizbeth. Most everbuddy does."

Out the corner of her eye, Charlotte caught, or thought she caught, Beverly staring at her waist-high denim shorts.

"*Beverly*," Mr. Amory said, "you sure you didn't for*get* anything?" He stared at the mound of things on the dolly and shook his head and then smiled at Momma and Daddy. He surveyed the room and said to his daughter, "Where do you think you're gonna put all this?"

From the graphics on the cartons, Charlotte could make out a kitchenette refrigerator—that was the really big box—a microwave, a laptop computer, a fax machine, a digital camera, an electric toothbrush, a television set . . .

Mrs. Amory had turned to Charlotte and, clasping her hand with both of hers, was saying, "Well . . . *Charlotte*." She brought her face closer to Charlotte's and peered profoundly into her eyes. "We've been *so* anxious to meet you. I can remember this very day so well myself. It wasn't here, it was at Wellesley, and I'm not going to tell you *when*! But four years from now"— she snapped her fingers—"you'll wonder where on earth—"

"Oh, *Dad*," Beverly was saying, "you have to *worry* about everything. Just put it anywhere. I'll take care of it."

Mrs. Amory turned abruptly to Beverly and said, "Hah hah hah, darling." Then she said to Momma, "I hope Charlotte's better organized than—"

A thump on the floor—"Oh, shit!" said Beverly.

Everyone turned toward her. She was already stooping over to pick up her cell phone. She stood up again and, surprised by the silence, looked about quizzically. Charlotte saw Mrs. Amory glancing sideways at Momma, who looked like she had turned to stone. If anyone had said *Oh, shit* in her presence in her house—anyone—Momma would have let her know she had no mind to tolerate it.

Mrs. Amory forced a laugh and, smiling and shaking her head, said, "*Beverly* . . . did I just hear you say, 'Oh, darn'?"

Beverly obviously didn't know what she was talking about. Then it dawned on her, and she opened her eyes wide and put her fingertips over her lips in the classic attitude of mock penitence.

"Oops," she said, looking about and misting the air with more effusions of irony. "Sorry." Without skipping a beat, she turned toward the handsome young man in the mauve T-shirt who was beginning to unload the dolly. "Just anywhere . . . Ken." She gave him a coquettish smile. "I'm terrible with names. It *is* Ken, isn't it?"

"*Just anywhere?*" said Mr. Amory. "You'll need a loft for *just anywhere.*"

"Kim," the young man said.

"*Anhh* . . . I *thought* I heard Kim, but I just didn't—I'm Beverly." It seemed to Charlotte that she looked at him a couple of beats longer than necessary before continuing in a small but somehow flirtatious voice, "What year are you?"

"I'm a senior. All of us"—he gestured toward the trolley—"are seniors."

Mrs. Amory had turned back to Daddy, eager to change the subject to . . . any subject, and Boring be damned. "I'm sorry, *when* did you say you arrived?"

"Oh, 'bout half hour ago, I reckon."

"You live in the western part of North Carolina." She smiled. Charlotte thought she noticed her eyes dart ever so quickly to the tattoo.

"Yep. 'Bout as far west as you kin git and still be in the state of North Carolina. Well—not quite, but it took us purt' near ten hours to drive here."

"My goodness." She smiled.

Daddy said, "How did you folks git here from Massachusetts?"

"We flew." She smiled.

Charlotte could see Mr. Amory's eyes run up and down Daddy . . . his ruddy face with its reddish brown field hand's sunburn . . . the mermaid . . . the sport shirt out over the gray twill work pants, the old sneakers . . .

"Whirred you fly *into*?" said Daddy.

"An airport five or six miles out of town—Jeff, what's the name of the field we flew into?"

"Boothwyn." He smiled at Momma, who wasn't smiling.

"Well, I'll be switched," said Daddy. "I didn't even know they had an airport here."

Charlotte could see Beverly Amory running her eyes up and down Momma . . . down to where the denim jumper descended below the knees and the athletic socks rose up . . .

"Oh, it's very small," said Mrs. Amory. She smiled. "It's not really an airport, I guess. That's probably not the right term." She smiled some more.

The smiles seemed not so much cheery as patient.

"Anything else I can help you folks with?" said the porter, Kim, who had now removed everything from the dolly. The way he had pushed them together, the boxes created a massive little edifice.

"I think that's just about it," said Mr. Amory. "Thank you very much, Kim."

"No problem," said the young man, who was already heading out the door with the dolly. Without stopping, he said, "You all have a good time." Then he looked at Beverly and Charlotte. "And a good year."

"We'll try," said Beverly, smiling in a certain way.

She'd practically struck up an acquaintance with him! Charlotte felt even more inadequate. She couldn't think of anything to say—to anybody, much less to some good-looking senior.

Momma cocked her head and stared at Daddy. Daddy compressed his lips and shrugged his eyebrows. All right—the boy *hadn't* stood around waiting for a tip.

A muffled ring, oddly like a harp being strummed. Mr. Amory reached into the pocket of his khakis and withdrew a small cell phone. "Hello? . . . Oh, come on . . ." His sunny demeanor was gone. He scowled into the little mouthpiece. "How could that possibly . . . I know . . . Look, Larry, I can't go into all this now. We're in Beverly's room with her roommate and her parents. I'll call you back. In the meantime, *ask around*, for God's sake. Boothwyn isn't so small that they don't have *mechanics*."

He closed up the cell phone and said to his wife, "That was Larry. He says there's some sort of hydraulic leak in the rudder controls. That's all we need."

Silence. Then Mr. Amory smiled again, patiently, and said, "Well . . . Billy . . . where are you and . . . Lizbeth . . . staying?"

Daddy said, oh, they wouldn't be staying, they were going to turn around and drive back to Sparta, and Momma and Mrs. Amory had a little discussion about the rigors of such a long round-trip in one day. Mrs. Amory said they would be flying back as soon as they could to get out of Beverly's hair and let her and Charlotte arrange things for themselves, and besides, wasn't there a meeting of all the freshmen in this section in a couple of hours? Hadn't she seen that on the schedule? That was true, said Beverly, but would they mind terribly not getting out of her hair until they had something to eat—*hello-oh?*—since she, for one, was starving? Both Mr. and Mrs. Amory gave their daughter a cross look, and then Mr. Amory smiled at Momma and Daddy like Patience on a monument smiling at Grief and said that, well, it looked like they were going to go have a quick bite to eat, and if Momma, Daddy, and Charlotte would care to come along, they were welcome. As he remembered, there was a little restaurant in town called Le Chef. "Not fabulous," he said, "but good; and quick." Daddy gave Momma an anxious glance, and Charlotte knew what that was about. Any unknown restaurant named Le Chef or Le anything sounded like more money than he was going to want to spend. But Momma gave Daddy a little nod that as much as said that they probably should sit down and have one meal with Charlotte's roommate's parents, since they had suggested it.

Daddy said to Mr. Amory, "There's a Sizzlin' Skillet just before you git to the campus? Bet it's not more'n half a mile from here. I ate at a Sizzlin' Skillet near Fayetteville once"—*wunst*—"and it was real nice; real good and real quick."

More silence. All three Amorys looked at each other in a perplexed fashion, and then Mr. Amory turned on the most patient smile yet and said, "All right . . . let's by all means go to the Sizzlin' Skillet."

Charlotte stared at Mr. and Mrs. Amory. They both had deep suntans and absolutely smooth, buttery skin. Compared to Momma and Daddy, they were so soft—and sleek as beavers.

Daddy excused himself and left the room. A few minutes later he returned with a bemused look on his face. "Strangest darn thing," he said to the room. "I was looking for the men's bathroom? And some folks down 'eh, they told me iddn' any men's bathroom. Told me this is a coed dorm, and there's one bathroom, and it's a coed bathroom. I looked in 'eh, and I seen boys *and* girls."

Momma compressed her lips severely.

"Oh, I wouldn't worry about that," said Mrs. Amory. "Apparently they get used to it very quickly. Isn't that what Erica said, Beverly? Beverly has a good friend from school, Erica, who was a freshman here last year."

"Certainly didn't bother Erica," said Beverly in an airy, nothing-to-it manner.

"I gather the boys are very considerate," said Mrs. Amory. Charlotte could tell she was making an effort to calm the country folks' fears.

Momma and Daddy looked at each other. Momma was doing her best to hold herself back.

The six of them went down to the parking lot, and Daddy pointed out their pickup truck with the camper top and said, "Whyn't we all go in our pickup? Me'n' the girls can sit in the back." He looked optimistically at Beverly. "We got some sleeping bags back 'eh we can sit on."

"That's nice of you, Billy," said Mr. Amory with his patient smile, "but we might as well take ours. We've got six seats." He pointed at a huge white Lincoln Navigator SUV.

"Well, as I live and breathe!" said Momma in spite of herself. "Whirred you folks git that? I don't mean to pry."

"We rented it," said Mr. Amory. Anticipating the next question, he said, "You call ahead, and they'll bring it right out to the pla— to the airport for you."

So they drove to the Sizzlin' Skillet in the Lincoln Navigator. It was all leather inside, with windows as dark as sunglasses and strips of exotic wood, polyurethaned, here and there. Charlotte was glad they hadn't seen what was under the old pickup's camper top, or inside the cab, for that matter.

The Sizzlin' Skillet had quite a sign on its roof: an enormous black skillet, eight or nine feet in diameter, with THE SIZZLIN' SKILLET written in huge curvy letters on the pan. Around the skillet were rings of red and yellow lights.

From the moment one walked in, an astounding array of hot, slick colors screamed for attention from every direction. Everything was . . . *big* . . . including, straight ahead, up on the wall, some alarmingly detailed color photographs of the house specials: huge plates with slabs of red meat and gigantic patties of ground meat fairly glistening with . . . ooze . . . great molten slices of cheese, veritable lava flows of gravy, every manner of hash brown and french-fried potato, fried onion, and fried chicken, including a dish called Sam's Sweet Chickassee, which seemed to consist of an immense patty of skillet-fried ground chicken beneath a thick mantle of bubbling cream sauce, all of it blown up so large in the photographs that slices of tomato—the only vegetable depicted, other than lettuce and the fried potatoes and onions—created an impression of overwhelming weight.

There seemed to be a lot of people peering into the dining area but not going in, and Mr. Amory said rather hopefully, "Looks pretty crowded, doesn't it. I guess we ought to try someplace else."

Charlotte swung her head about to see what Beverly thought—and there she was, her back turned, holding on to her mother's arm and leaning her skin and bones against her shoulder, pointing at the photographs of the deluges of gravy and cream, and, no doubt thinking the Simmonses were looking the other way, made an *eeeeyuk* face, as if she wanted to throw up.

Suddenly talkative, or talkative for him, Daddy assured Mr. Amory that they'd get a table sooner than it looked like. See there?—you go up to that podium there and let them know you're here, and you'll be surprised how fast things move. So Mr. Amory set his jaw and led their procession up to the podium, which turned out to be a gigantic wooden thing, like a podium on a stage but much wider and made of massive slabs of wood. Everything at the Sizzlin' Skillet was . . . *big*. There was a short line just to get to the podium, but it did move along.

Behind the podium stood a bouncy-looking young woman dressed in a red-and-yellow—evidently the Sizzlin' Skillet colors—shirt-and-pants outfit. The shirt was adorned with some kind of brooch—in fact, a three-inch-long miniature of the Sizzlin' Skillet sign outside.

She gave Mr. Amory a perky smile. "How many?"

"Six. The name is Amory. A, m, o, r, y."

She wrote nothing down. Instead she handed him something the size and shape of a television remote. It had a lot of little lenses in a circle on one end and a number—226—on the other. "We'll signal you when your table's ready. Have a sizzlin' good meal!"

Mr. Amory looked at the object as if it had just crawled up his leg. On its shaft was an advertisement: "Try our Sizzlin' Swiss Steak. You'll yodel!"

"It'll go off when our table's ready," said Daddy, pointing to the device. "That way we don't have to git in a line. We kin go over't the gift shop or something."

Daddy led them to the gift shop, where there seemed to be a lot of souvenirs, dolls, and candy bars, all of them abnormally big, even the candy bars. Mr. Amory held the . . . device up in front of his wife without comment. "Hmmm," she said, cocking her head and smiling in a way that made Charlotte uneasy.

The Amorys kept looking at the people milling about. Many, like Mr. Amory, were holding the device. Immediatcly in front of Daddy and Mr. and Mrs. Amory was an obese man, probably forty-five or so, wearing a cutoff football jersey with the number 87 on the back. Between the bottom of the jersey and the top of his basketball shorts a roll of bare flesh protruded. Next to him was a young woman in black pants who was so wide her elbows were cushioned on the tube of fat around her waist, and her forearms stuck out to the side like little wings.

"Do you and your parents go to Sizzlin' Skillets often?" Beverly said to Charlotte.

Charlotte caught a whiff of condescension. "We don't have anything like this in Sparta," she said.

Near the see-through, where you could look in and see the cooks working in the kitchen, a single sharp piping whistle sounded, and red and yellow lights began whirling around. It was the thing in the hand of a big woman wearing what looked like a mechanic's jumpsuit. She beckoned impatiently to two little girls and headed for the dining area.

"See?" said Daddy. "Now she's gonna go over't the podium and show the woman the lights going around and the number, and somebody'll show 'em straight to their table." Over *there* . . . another piping whistle. "What'd I tell you?" said Daddy. "It don't take long. And I pledge you my word, you won't be leaving hungry." He was smiling at all three Amorys, going from one face to the other.

Mrs. Amory smiled briefly, but her eyes had gone dead.

Even though he was prepared for it, when the high-pitched whistle burst out of *the thing* and the red and yellow lights started whirling, Mr. Amory jumped. Daddy couldn't help laughing. Mr. Amory gave him a 33° Fahrenheit smile and a single chuckle: "Huh." He carried the thing to the podium with his thumb and forefinger, the way you might transport a dead bird by the tip of one wing.

Their table had a slick bright yellow vinyl-laminate top. The room was packed. The surf of what seemed like a thousand enthusiastic conversations rolled over them. Cackles, chirps, and belly laughs erupted above the waves. The waitress, wearing one of the little skillet pins, arrived not with an order pad but with a black plastic instrument that looked like a pocket calculator with an aerial. The menus, coated in clear plastic, must have been fifteen inches tall and were full of color photographs similar to the outsize ones on the wall. After considerable study, Mrs. Amory ordered a fried-chicken dish and asked the waitress to please leave off the skillet-fried hash browns and the deep-fried onion rings. The waitress said she was sorry but she couldn't, because—she held up the black instrument—all she could do was enter the number of the dish, which was instantly transmitted to the kitchen. Mr. and

Mrs. Amory looked at each other and accepted this setback patiently, and everybody ordered, and the waitress pushed a lot of buttons.

The dishes arrived with astonishing speed—prompting Daddy to give Mr. Amory a cheery, comradely smile, as if to say us fellas are in this thing together, aren't we.

The dishes were . . . *big*.

"Jes what I told you, iddn' it, Jeff!" Daddy was now *beaming* at "Jeff," as if good times among comrades didn't come much better than this.

Each plate was covered, *heaped*, with skillet-fried food. Daddy launched into his cream-lava-ladled Sam's Sweet Chickassee with gusto. Mrs. Amory inspected her fried chicken as if it were a sleeping animal. No more smiles, no conversation.

So Momma, apparently recovered from the *Oh, shit* incident, said to Mr. Amory, by way of filling the conversational vacuum, "Now, Jeff, you have to tell us what Sherborn's like. I been real curious about that."

A smile of tried patience: "It's a . . . just a little village, Mrs. Simmons. The population is . . . oh . . . perhaps a thousand? . . . perhaps a little more?"

"Go 'head and call me Lizbeth, Jeff. That's whirr you work?"

A frown of tried patience: "No, I work in Boston."

"Whirr at?"

Patience at the breaking point: "An insurance company. Cotton Mather."

"Cotton Mather! Oh, *I've* heard a them!" *They-em.* "Tell us what you do at Cotton Mather, Jeff. I'd be real interested."

Mr. Amory hesitated. "My title is chief executive officer." As if to cut off all queries regarding this revelation, he quickly turned to Daddy. "And Billy, tell us what *you* do."

"Me? Well, mainly I take care"—*keer*—"of a house some summer people got over't Roaring Gap? Used to be I operated a last-cutting machine over't the Thom McAn factory in Sparta, but Thom McAn, they relocated to Mexico. Maybe you know about these things, Jeff. I keep hearing on TV that this 'globalization' is good for Americans. I don't know why they think they *know* that, because nobody ever tried it before, but that's what they keep telling us. All I know is, it ain't particularly good for you if you live in Alleghany County, North Carolina. We lost three factories to Mexico. Martin Marietta came in and built a plant in 2002. They only employ forty people, but thank God for'm anyway. That's Mexico, three, Alleghany County, one."

Momma said, *"Billy."*

Daddy smiled sheepishly. "You're right, Lizbeth, you're right as rainwater. Don't let me git started on 'at stuff." He looked at Mrs. Amory. "You know, Valerie, one thing my daddy told me. He told me, 'Sonny'—he never called me Billy, he called me Sonny—'Sonny, never talk about politics or religion at the dinner table. You either gon' rile 'em up or else clean bore'm to death.'"

Mrs. Amory said, "Sounds like a wise man, your father."

Daddy said, "Oh, 'deed he was, when he had a notion."

Part of Charlotte was proud of Daddy for not caring to put the slightest gloss on the way he made a living. He was perfectly comfortable with who he was. Part of her cringed. She had a general idea what a chief executive officer was, and Cotton Mather was so big, *everybody* had heard of it.

Mr. Amory had no response to Daddy's remarks except to nod four or five times in a ruminating mode.

To rescue a drowning moment, Mrs. Amory said, "Charlotte, I feel like we know hardly anything about *you*. How'd you happen to come to—to choose Dupont? Where'd you go to secondary school?"

"Secondary school?"

"High school."

"In Sparta. Alleghany High School it's called. I had an English teacher who told me to apply to Dupont."

"And they gave her a full scholarship," said Momma. "We're real proud of her." Charlotte could feel her cheeks turning red, and not because of modesty. Momma said, "Whirred *you* go to high school, Beverly? How many high schools they got in Sherborn?"

Beverly glanced at her mother. Then she said to Momma, "Actually, I went to school in another town, called Groton."

"How far away was 'at?"

"About sixty miles. I was a boarder."

Charlotte didn't know exactly what Beverly was saying to Momma, but somehow the way she had put it to her was patronizing.

"Jeff," said Daddy, chowing down the last forkful of his gigantic plate of Sam's Sweet Chickassee, french fries, and tomato slabs, "this was a great idea of yours! You need sump'm that'll stick to your ribs if you're gon' do what we're fixing to do, drive all the way back to Sparta, North Carolina, tonight. One thang they know at these Sizzlin' Skillets, they know how to give folks *enough to eat*."

From Mrs. Amory's plate only one thing had disappeared—a morsel of chicken breast, less than an inch square, from where she had peeled back the fried skin. The vast plate remained a mountain of food. Warily, gingerly, Beverly put a piece of hamburger about the size of a nickel into her mouth and chewed it slowly for a very long time. Without a word, she got up and left the room. In a few minutes, she came back, her face absolutely ashen. Her mother gave her a look of concern—or censure.

Charlotte barely noticed. A single phrase, *drive all the way back to Sparta, North Carolina, tonight* had hit her with a force she would never have dreamed possible—not her, not Sparta's prodigy whose future would be filled with great things on the other side of the mountains.

A little later on, once the Amorys and Simmonses had gone their separate ways, Charlotte stood in the parking lot of the Little Yard next to the pickup truck as Momma and Daddy said their good-byes.

Momma was smiling and saying, "Now, you remember what I said, honey, don't you forgit to write. Everbuddy's gonna want to know 'bout—"

Without a word Charlotte threw her arms around Momma and nestled her head next to Momma's, and her tears began rolling down Momma's cheek.

Momma said, "There, there, there, my good, good girl." Charlotte clung to Momma for dear life. Momma said, "Don't you worry, little darling, I'll be thinking of you every minute of the day. I'm real proud of you, and you're gonna do real well here. But you know what I'm the proudest of? I'm the proudest of who you are, no matter whirr you're at. I 'spec' there's ways Dupont iddn' gon' be good enough for *you*."

Charlotte lifted her head and looked at Momma.

"There's gon' be folks here wanting you to do thangs you don't hold with," said Momma. "So you jes' remember you come from mountain folks, on your daddy's side and my side, the Simmonses and the Pettigrews, and mountain folks got their faults, but letting theirselves git pushed into doing thangs iddn' one *uv*'m. We know how to be real stubborn. Can't nobody make us do a thang once we git hard set against it. And if anybody don't like that, you don't have to explain a thang to'm. All you got to say is, 'I'm Charlotte Simmons, and I don't hold with thangs like 'at.' And they'll respect you for that." *They-at.* "I love you, little darling, and your daddy loves you, and no matter whirr you're at in the whole wide world, you'll always be our good, good girl."

Charlotte laid her head back on Momma's shoulder and sobbed softly.

She could see Daddy standing right there, and she took her tears to him and threw her arms around his neck, which clearly startled him. Daddy didn't hold with public displays of affection. Between sobs she whispered into his ear, "I love you, Daddy. You don't know how *much* I love you!"

"We love you, too," said Daddy.

He also didn't know how much it would have meant to her if he could have only brought himself to say *I*.

Charlotte kept waving, and Momma stuck her head out the window and looked back and kept waving, until the poor, sad, brave pickup truck with the fiberglass camper top disappeared beyond the shade trees. Finally Charlotte turned around and headed back toward the stone fortress alone.

As she walked through the great arched entrance, a boy and a girl, presumably freshmen, too, passed her, chatting away. The arch was so deep, their words echoed off the stone. Did they already know each other, or had they become friends this very day? . . . *I'm Charlotte Simmons . . . You are unique. You . . . are Charlotte Simmons* . . . Momma's and Miss Pennington's words gave her a spurt of confidence. She had faced envy and resentment and social isolation at Alleghany High, hadn't she . . . and been imperiously uncool . . . and gone her own way . . . and never let any of it hold her back in her destined ascension to one of the finest universities in the world. And nothing was going to hold her back now . . . *nothing*. If she had to do everything by herself, then she would do everything by herself.

But God . . . she felt so alone.

Beverly was already there when Charlotte reached room 516. They decided on who was going to have which side of the room—the two sides were identical, identically bare and spare—and they set about making up their beds and unpacking. What a lot of . . . *things* . . . Beverly had! She left her computer, fax machine, television, refrigerator, microwave, and the rest of her electrical devices in their cartons, but she unpacked more pairs of shoes than Charlotte could even imagine one girl owning—at least a dozen—a dozen or more sweaters, most of them cashmere, skirts, skirts, skirts, shirts, shirts, shirts, camisoles, camisoles, camisoles, jeans, jeans, jeans . . . Charlotte possessed not even the smallest of Beverly's various types of machines. For a computer, a necessity at Dupont, Charlotte was going to have to depend entirely on the so-called computer clusters in Dupont's main library. Rather than a dozen or more pairs of shoes, she had three: a pair of loafers, some sturdy leather sandals—"Jesus sandals," Regina Cox used to call them—and the pair of Keds she had on.

Beverly chatted with Charlotte in a dutiful fashion. Nothing she had to say bore even a hint of the excitement of a girl heading out with another girl, her new roommate, from another part of the country, on a four-year adventure at a great university. She spoke to Charlotte from an amicable distance. She spoke with the inflections of someone who was *showing an interest*. When Charlotte mentioned how fascinating the French courses listed in the Dupont catalog sounded, Beverly's comment was that the French are *so* resentful of Americans these days you can like *feel* it in the air when you're around them. They were majorly boring, the French.

Beverly had only halfway squeezed her clothes into the closet and the bureau when it was time to go downstairs for the house meeting. The two hundred or so boys and girls in Edgerton House convened in what was known in Dupont (and British) parlance as the Common Room. It was a little bit run-down, but its proportions and decor bespoke grand origins. The ceiling must have been fifteen or sixteen feet high, with all sorts of dark wooden arches Charlotte didn't know the name for converging in the center. Huge luggage-brown leather sofas and easy chairs, an incredible number of them, had been arranged in a vast semicircle upon the room's acres of Oriental rugs. More leather easy chairs remained in ornate reading bays with parchment-shaded wrought-iron floor lamps. The freshmen of Edgerton House, most of them in shorts, either crammed themselves into the leather seats or stood behind this great upholstered crescent in several rows. Others sat behind them on the edges of long oaken monk's tables that had been brought in for the meeting. As soon as she and Charlotte entered the room, Beverly drifted away to the side, where she stood with two girls she obviously already knew. Well, so what . . . Charlotte already felt entirely separate from her roommate, and trotting along after her at this meeting wouldn't change that. Actually, standing in the center amid so many other girls and boys made her feel almost . . . whole again. They certainly did not look intimidating. In fact, with all their shorts, flip-flops, and T-shirts, they looked like large children. Surely this room must be filled with people just like herself, bright young people anxious because they knew so little of what was to come and exhilarated by the very fact that they had come this far. They were Dupont men and women—starting with this moment.

Facing the assembly was a young woman in jeans and a man's-style button-down shirt. Charlotte was fascinated by her. She stood there in front of two hundred strangers with such an easy confidence. She was beautiful but casual, with an athletic figure—and such amazing blond hair! It was very curly but very long, wild, yet combed just so. She seemed the very essence of collegiate glamour. She identified herself as a senior and the R.A., the resident assistant, of Edgerton House. She was there to help them with any problems that came up. They should feel free to ring her up, e-mail her, or knock on her door at any time. Her name was Ashley Downes.

"The university no longer plays the role of parent," she was saying, "and certainly I don't. You're on your own. But there *are* some rules—not a lot, but some, and I'd be doing you a disservice if I wasn't frank about that. First of all, alcohol is prohibited in Edgerton and every other house on Little Yard. That doesn't just mean no drinking in public, but no alcohol in the building, period. It may not surprise you to learn that there *is* alcohol on the Dupont campus." She smiled, and many of the freshmen laughed knowingly. "But it's not gonna be here. Okay?" She smiled again. "In case you're worried, you're gonna discover this won't put an end to your social life."

Charlotte came close to letting her breath out audibly. What a relief! In Sparta she had been able to avoid the sodden, drunken milieu of the Channing Reeveses and the Regina Coxes simply by going home in the evenings and studying and ignoring the upside-down contempt she felt from them and their crowd. But here? It was well known that there was a lot of drinking in colleges, probably even at Dupont. At least she wouldn't have to deal with it in this building where she lived, thank God. If the R.A. could just reassure her about one other thing—

But in no time, it seemed, the meeting was over, and the freshmen departed the Common Room far more animated and vocal than when they arrived. They were already getting to know one another. Charlotte started to hang back, in hopes of having a word with Ashley Downes privately. But eight or ten freshmen were clustered about her, and Charlotte didn't want to ask her question in front of other people. She dawdled . . . and dawdled . . . for five minutes, ten minutes, before she finally gave up.

When she returned to the room, Beverly was there, standing in front of her bureau looking into a prop-up vanity mirror with tiny bulbs ablaze along the edges. She turned around. She was wearing black pants and a lavender silk shirt, sleeveless and open three or four buttonholes' worth in front. It showed off her suntan—but also her arms, which looked almost emaciated. She made Charlotte think of an all-dressed-up stork. Her makeup did nothing for her nose and chin. They seemed even bigger somehow. She had put a peach-colored polish on her nails; it looked great on the tips of her perfectly tanned fingers.

"I'm meeting some friends at a restaurant," she explained, "and I'm late. I'll put away all that stuff when I come back." She gestured toward a mountain of bags and boxes piled this way and that.

Charlotte was astonished. The very first day wasn't even over, and Beverly was *going out to a restaurant.* Charlotte couldn't imagine such a thing. For a start, she didn't know a soul. And what if she did? She had a grand total of five hundred dollars to cover all outside expenses to the end of the first semester, four and a half months from now. She was going to have to eat every meal, seven days a week, in the university dining hall. That was provided for by her scholarship. Unless somebody took her to one, the Sizzlin' Skillet was the last restaurant she was going to eat in for a long time.

Beverly left. Charlotte sat on the edge of her bed, hunched over, hands clasped, thinking and thinking, glancing at Beverly's edifice of cartons, looking out the window at the dusk. She could hear people talking and occasionally laughing in the hall outside. Finally she worked up her nerve. Ashley, the R.A., had said they could knock on her door anytime. This would be pushing it perhaps, approaching her barely an hour after the meeting, but . . . She stood up. Now was the time to do it, if she was going to do it at all.

The R.A.'s room was on the second floor. As Charlotte walked down the hall, she was startled to see a boy in cargo shorts, no shirt, emerge from a doorway and come dashing toward her. He was holding a small spiral notebook in one hand and glancing back over his shoulder and laughing in breathless bursts. As he hurtled past Charlotte, he said, "Sorry!"—scarcely even looking at her. Now running toward Charlotte was a girl in a T-shirt and shorts, yelling, "Gimme that back, you little shit!" She wasn't laughing. Charlotte noticed that she was barefoot. She didn't say a thing as she ran by.

Charlotte hesitated in front of the R.A.'s door. Then she knocked. After a few seconds the door opened, and there was Ashley Downes, with her amazing mane of curly blond hair. She had changed into pants and a rather low-cut tank top. "Hi," she said in a puzzled fashion.

"Hi," said Charlotte. "I'm really sorry, Miz Downes—"

"Oh, come on, *please.* Ashley."

"I'm really sorry. I was just at the meeting, and I tried to get to talk to you afterward, but there were so many people." Blushing and lowering her chin: "You said come by anytime, but I know you didn't think *this* soon. I'm really sorry."

"Well—come on in," said the R.A. She smiled at Charlotte the way you might smile at a lost child. "What's your name?"

Charlotte told her and, once inside the room, stood there and began expounding, in an embarrassed way, upon how valuable the meeting had been and how much she thought she had gotten out of it, all the while noticing that this was a single room and a surprisingly messy one . . . bed unmade, clothes strewn on the floor, including a pair of dirty thong underpants. "But there was one thing . . ." Now that she had come to the point, she didn't know how to put it.

"Why don't you sit down," said the R.A. So Charlotte sat in a plain wooden chair, and Ashley Downes sat on the edge of her messy bed.

Charlotte struggled some more with her phrasing, finally saying, "But you didn't really talk about the coed dorm part. I mean you *did*, you certainly did talk about it, but there's one thing . . ." Words failed her again.

The R.A. now looked at her as if she were about six. She leaned forward and said quietly, "You mean . . . sex?"

Charlotte could feel herself nodding like a six-year-old. "Yes."

Ashley Downes leaned forward still further, resting her forearms on her knees and intertwining her fingers. "Where are you from?"

"Sparta, North Carolina."

"Sparta, North Carolina. How big is Sparta?"

"About nine hundred people," said Charlotte. "It's up in the mountains." Just why she had added this bit of geographical intelligence, she couldn't have explained, not even to herself.

Ashley Downes averted her eyes and thought for a moment, then said, "Let me put your mind at ease. Yes, this is a coed dorm, and yes, there is sexual activity in coed dorms here at Dupont. What floor are you on?"

"Five."

"Okay. This is a coed dorm, but that doesn't mean boys are going to be running back and forth across the hall and jumping into bed with girls. Or for that matter, boys from any other part of Edgerton. In fact, if anything, it means they *won't*. There's no actual rule against it, but it's looked down upon. It's considered pathetic and dorky to be reduced to hooking up with someone from your own house. It's called dormcest."

"Dormcest?"

"Dormcest. You know, like incest. As a matter of fact, Edgerton always has a T-shirt for everybody at the end of the year listing all sorts of funny or stupid things that have happened in the house. Last year's had a line that said DORMCEST: THREE. That's three cases out of two hundred students. That's how dorky it is."

Now Charlotte could feel herself smiling like a six-year-old who has just stopped crying. She kept smiling and nodding and expressing profound thanks, and she really hadn't meant to take up her time on the very first night.

Charlotte stood up, and Ashley stood up and put her arm around her shoulders as she walked her to the door. "I'm sorry, tell me your name again?"

"Charlotte Simmons."

"Well, Charlotte, I'll tell you something. This isn't Sparta, North Carolina, but I think you're gonna find it isn't Sodom and Gomorrah, either."

By eight-thirty, back in room 516 once more, Charlotte felt as tired as she had ever been in her life. She had been up since three o'clock this morning and on edge the entire time. Watching "Jeff" and "Valerie" of Sherborn, Boston, and Mather Insurance and "Billy" and "Lizbeth" of County Road 1709, Sparta, and the next thing to unemployed, fend with the problem of breathing the same air—had been draining, excruciating. She decided to take a shower, get in bed, read for a bit, and then go to sleep.

Her heart sank. My God . . . take a shower? In a coed bathroom? The thought was mortifying, yet she had no choice. She changed into her pajamas, her slippers, and her Scottish plaid polyester flannel bathrobe, picked up her toilet kit and her towel, screwed up her courage, and headed down the corridor. Things were quiet, thank God. On the way she nodded tentatively at a girl and then a boy, each alone and looking as lonesome as she felt.

She entered the bathroom slowly and softly, as if stealth was of the essence. It was a large, windowless, feebly lit room with rows of weary old yellowing white basins and urinals, gray sheet-metal toilet cubicles, narrow shower stalls with old mauve-gone-russet curtains for privacy . . . One of the showers was running . . . Other than that, the place seemed to be miraculously empty. Perhaps if she hurried—into a toilet cubicle. She had been sitting down no more than fifteen seconds when she thought she heard a faint grunting sound. Then—a prodigious pig-bladdery splattering sphincter-spasmed bowel explosion, followed by, in rapid succession, *plop plop plop* and a deep male voice—"Oh fuck! Splashed right up my fucking asshole!"

Filthy! The crudeness, the grossness, the vulgarity—above all the fact that there was a *boy* or a *man* in here . . . *egesting* . . . no more than three or four cubicles down the row from her!

"Shit—a—brick!" said a deep male voice in a cubicle only slightly farther away. "What the fuck you been eating, Winnie—month-old sushi?" He made a mocking vomiting sound. "You're fucking . . . morbid, dude. I need a gas mask."

Sure enough, a nauseous, putrid, gaseous odor was in the air.

Charlotte lifted her legs and pressed her feet against the door, lest these *brutes* see her slippers in the space beneath the door or the walls and become aware of her presence.

"Don't be so fucking heartless," said the first voice. "My asshole's cold. That was a fucking bull's-eye."

The second one laughed. "You're a human disaster area, Winnie, is what you fucking are."

"Yeah?"

"Yeah. That was a *terrible* performance, dude! *Terrible!* You want to see a perfect, noiseless turd? I mean *perfect*? Just swing on by here before you leave. I won't flush it."

"And you know what *you* are, Hilton? You're a pervert."

"Don't try to talk your way out of it. You got to come by here and learn how to take a shit."

Charlotte didn't know whether to sit here with her feet up—or run for it. But oh God, she couldn't sit here with her feet up forever. So in a frenzy she stood up, hoisted her pajama bottom and put her bathrobe back on, picked her toilet kit up off the floor, departed the cubicle, rushed to the row of basins. She had to wash her hands! She heard a toilet flush and then the clack of somebody sliding a cubicle side-bolt lock open. Then another.

"Hey! Yo! You didn't come by to see, dude."

"You're weird. Why don't you hang it up on the wall over your bed?"

Same deepened manly voices . . . Charlotte lifted her eyes, and in the mirror she could see two boys—mere boys! Neither looked more than fifteen or sixteen! Babies dropping their voices a couple of octaves in a desperate desire to sound like men! Each had a can of beer in his hand. *But that was not allowed!* Both were bare from the waist up. One wore a towel around his waist, only that and flip-flops. He had such a tender coating of baby fat over his cheeks, neck, and torso, it made Charlotte think of diapers and talcum powder. The other wore khaki shorts and boots. He was the leaner of the two but still at that mooncalf stage in which the nose looks enormous because the chin hasn't caught up with it yet. He threw his head back, lifted the can to his mouth, tilted it almost straight up, drank for what seemed like forever with his Adam's apple pumping up and down like a piston, then jackknifed his body and shook all over, as if in ecstasy, and cried out, "IT TASTES SO GOOD WHEN IT HITS YOUR LIPS!"

The baby face in the towel laughed and laughed.

They were walking straight toward Charlotte—and wound up at basins not far from hers. They clanked their cans of beer down on the narrow shelf of glass. Charlotte began drying her hands on her towel. With peripheral vision she could tell the baby-fat, baby-faced boy was looking at her.

"Hi," he said. "Nice bathrobe."

She ignored him.

"Seriously," said the other, the thin one with the teenager nose. "Awesome plaid. What's your clan?"

The baby face laughed and laughed and said, "Kmart."

Then the outsize nose laughed and laughed.

Charlotte ignored them both and picked up her toilet kit. Her face was burning. She knew it must be scarlet.

The boy with the nose said behind his hand in a mock whisper, "No capeesh. Must be a foreign student. The Scotch count as foreign students, don't they?"

Laughter, laughter, laughter.

Just before she turned to leave, Charlotte saw in the mirror a girl coming toward the basins. She was clad in a towel, too, but had somehow wrapped it around her body from just beneath her arms to just above her knees. There was no longer the sound of a shower running. The girl had a chubby, freckled face and wet, reddish hair plastered against her head and hanging down her back.

When she reached the basins, the baby-fat boy said, "Hi, there. We're looking for some friendly conversation and a little sympathy."

The girl barely even glanced at them. She turned to the mirror and brought her forefingers to one eye and spread the lids apart as if looking for something lodged in it. Still looking straight ahead, she said, "I hope you find it."

As of the moment Charlotte left the bathroom, the boys hadn't thought of a comeback, and the girl was ignoring them.

On the way back to the room, Charlotte realized her heart was banging away. She was appalled . . . Coed Bathroom had seemed like a plausible, if uninviting concept, the way the Amorys had talked about it. But *this* was what it was! The vulgarity, the *rudeness*, the *impudence*, the virtual nudity — people parading around in towels — and *drinking* — barely two hours after the resident assistant Ashley's assurances there would be no alcohol in this building, much less public drunkenness . . . Now Charlotte was more than appalled. She was frightened. How was she supposed to live like this? — stripped of all privacy, all modesty . . . Her heart kept banging away . . . How could this be real? This was *Dupont* . . . Channing, Matt, Randy Hoggart, and Dave Cosgrove at their drunkest would never be so vulgar.

Once inside her room, Charlotte quickly changed back into her denim shorts and her blouse, picked up her toilet kit and her towel, and went down to the Common Room. She remembered a powder room near the entrance. In the Common Room . . . quite a jolly burble of laughs and voices . . . the furniture massed in the center of the room had been moved, back to its original places, presumably. Plenty of boys and girls, her classmates, were sprawled on the leather couches and easy chairs or standing around them, having a merry time . . . making friends . . . Charlotte was too distraught to even imagine joining in . . . Suppose people saw her going into the powder room with a toilet kit and a towel? What would they think — or assume?

It was about as cramped as a powder room could be. She carefully locked the door and took a seat on the toilet, only to find that her excretory and egestive systems had shut down, totally. She got up. She would bathe as best she could manage. She took off her blouse and her bra. There she was in the mirror . . . a wretched, panicked little half-naked creature . . . She had forgotten to bring a washcloth. She wet one end of the towel in the tiny basin, tried to use the squirt-by-squirt soap dispenser on the wall to lather it, creating a mess mainly, and washed her armpits —

Someone was trying to open the door — only to find it locked —

Charlotte tried to speed up her primitive toilette. She needed to lower her shorts and panties, but the room was so small that if she bent over, her bottom pressed into the wall. So she stood up straight and tried to wriggle her clothes off straight down —

The doorknob began turning again, this time several times, in . . . an accusatory way? An ostentatious groan of a sigh came from the other side of the door.

From just outside the door a girl's voice said, "Anybody in there?" Not very nicely, either.

Thoroughly frazzled, Charlotte said, "Not yet!"

The voice said, "Not *yet?*"

"I mean I'm not through yet!"

Long pause. Then the voice said, "How obvious is that?"

But she had to brush her teeth! *Had* to! . . . Finally she managed to squeeze some toothpaste onto her toothbrush. She began furiously brushing her teeth.

The voice from the other side said, "Are you really *brushing your teeth* in there?"

That did it. Charlotte snapped. "Shut up!" she cried. "Leave me alone! Stop sniffing at the door!"

Silence . . . prolonged silence . . . It was hard to believe, but the voice had shut up. Nevertheless, Charlotte hurried. The whole thing was too much. How long could she use a powder room as her bathroom? Maybe if she got up really early every day and brought a washcloth . . .

She emerged from the powder room carrying a toilet kit and a wet towel. Standing back four or five feet was a small angry girl, arms crossed over her chest. She stared sullenly at the towel and the toilet kit. She had a wide face, olive skin, a grim visage, and a mane of very long, very thick dark hair parted down the middle. As Charlotte rushed past her, the girl muttered, "Why don't you, like, *move in?*"

At long last, Charlotte sat propped up against the pillow on her bed, at peace, reading a paperback of a novel Miss Pennington had recommended, *Ethan Frome* by Edith Wharton. As the pages went by, Ethan and Mattie's unrequited passion became more and more poignant. Involuntarily, Charlotte found herself pulling her knees up closer to her chest and wanting to close her bathrobe more protectively about her pajamas. Poor Ethan! Poor Mattie! You just wanted to *help* them, *tell* them what they could do. It's *all right* for you to embrace—to declare your love—to leave that frigid little New England town where you're trapped!

So absorbed was she that she was only faintly aware of how the noise level was rising out in the hall. Even though the door was closed, every now and then she could hear a girl shriek, and sometimes two or more girls shriek, and these were not the shrieks of girls happy to see each other after a long time, but girls expressing their hilarity, genuine or otherwise, over something stupid and juvenile some boy was doing. But these were considerations merely drifting along the margins of *Ethan Frome.*

Soon she felt terribly tired, however, overwhelmingly tired. She got up, pulled the shades down, turned the lights off, took off her bathrobe, and slipped under the covers. She thought she would go to sleep immediately, but the noise—the activity—in the hallway kept intensifying. Well . . . everybody was no doubt as wound up and excited as she was, and not everybody bottled it up the way she did. She thought she heard a boy cry out, "Not her—you'll get awfuck's disease!" But it couldn't have been that, because it wasn't followed by any shrieks or juvenile laughs. Then things quieted down a bit. She heard a little scampering, some sort of scraping on a wall somewhere, but by and by, as she lay there with her eyes shut, the sounds began to float beyond the reach of analysis. For a moment she could see Beverly's peach fingernails framed by the tan of her fingers, but it meant . . . nothing. It dissolved into an eyelid movie, and she fell asleep.

She woke up with a start. A shaft of light shot across the counterpane on her bed. Heavy, syncopated thumps on a bass drum, a grunting voice—*rap?* What time was it? She propped herself up on one elbow and looked toward the door. As soon as she did—

"Whaaazzup, dude?"

Silhouetted in the doorway was the gangling frame of a boy in a floppy T-shirt and baggy pants. He had a long neck and a mass of curly hair that popped out above his ears. In his hand, up near his head, was the unmistakable silhouette of a bottle of beer.

"Wake you up?"

"Yes—" She was so shocked and disoriented that it came out like a dying sigh.

"Courtesy call, dude. Time to chill." He tilted the bottle up and took a long swallow. "Ah, ah, ah."

Groggily, "I'm—trying to sleep."

"'S all right," said the boy. "Needn'pologize. Zits happen." He smiled goofily and said, "Oohoooo, oohoooo."

Charlotte remained on one elbow, staring. *What's he doing!* The heavy bass thuds—it *was* rap. Someone down the hall was playing a CD, very loudly. She could barely find her voice. Imploringly, "What—*time* is it?"

The boy lifted his other wrist up near his face. It was all so eerie, because he was in silhouette, with just a highlight here and there. "It says here . . . lemme see . . . it says . . . time to chill."

Down the hall, a tremendous crash, followed by a boy yelling, "Well, you sure fucked *that*, dawg!" Raucous laughs. The rap music pounded on.

The boy's curly head turned to look, then turned back. "Barbarians," he said. "Exterminate the brutes. Look—uhhhh, needn't stand on ceremony—"

With a burst of anger Charlotte pushed herself upward in bed with both arms. "I *told* you! I'm trying to *sleep!*"

"Okay!" said the boy, pulling his head back and holding his palms out in front of his chest in a gesture of mock defensiveness. "Whoa! Skooz!" He walked backward with a mock stagger. "I wasn't even here! That wasn't me!" He disappeared down the hall, going, "Oohoooo . . . oohoooo . . ."

Charlotte got up and shut the door. Her heart was pounding away inside her rib cage. Could she lock the door some way? But even if she could, Beverly hadn't come in yet. She turned on the light. It was ten minutes after one. She got back into bed and lay on her back with her heart still pounding, listening to the noise. *No alcohol in Little Yard.* That boy was absolutely drunk! The third drunk boy she had seen with her own eyes since the R.A.'s solemn pronouncement, and it sounded like there were many more. She had the terrible fear that she wasn't going to be able to get to sleep at all.

An hour or more must have gone by. The ruckus finally began to subside. Where on earth was Beverly? Charlotte stared at the ceiling, she stared at the windows, she lay on this side, she lay on that side. *Dupont.* She thought of Miss Pennington. She thought of Channing and Regina . . . Channing and his strong, even features. Regina was Channing's girlfriend. Laurie said they had gone all the way. Oh, Channing, Channing, Channing. How much more time passed, she didn't know, because she fell asleep at last, thinking of Channing Reeves's strong, even features.

4. THE DUMMY

Most of them hadn't seen each other all summer, and classes had just begun this morning, but by evening the boys at the Saint Ray house had already sunk into a state of aimless lassitude. First day or not, it was still that nadir in the weekly cycle of Dupont social life, Monday night.

From the front parlor came the sound of "quarters," a drinking game in which the boys gathered around a table in a circle, more or less, each with a jumbo translucent plastic cup of beer before him. They bounced quarters on their edges and tried to make them hop into the other players' cups. If you were successful, your opponent had to tilt his head back and the container up and chugalug all twenty ounces. There was also a cup out in the middle. If you bounced a quarter into that one, all your opponents had to drink up. Much manly whooping when a quarter bounced home or just missed. Needless to say, the tables, magnificent old pieces that had been here ever since this huge Palladian mansion was built before the First World War, were by now riddled with dents. It was hard to believe there were once Saint Rays rich enough and religious enough about the great fraternal chain of being to build such a place and buy such furniture, not merely for themselves—after all, their own Dupont days would be few—but for generations of Saint Rays to come.

From the terrace room came the music of a Swarm CD banging out of a pair of speakers that were fixed in place for parties. Everybody was beginning to get tired of Swarm's so-called bang beat; nevertheless, Swarm was banging away tonight in the terrace room. Terrace room, front parlor, back parlor, dining room, entry gallery (cavernous), billiard room (ancient pool table, felt chewed up and stained because one evil night a bunch of blitzed brothers used it to play quarters), card bay, bar—the variety of rooms for entertaining on this one floor would probably never be built in a house again.

Here in the library a dozen or so of the boys were sprawled back on couches, easy chairs, armchairs, side chairs, window seats—most of them wearing khaki shorts and flip-flops, watching ESPN SportsCenter on a forty-inch flat-screen television set, drinking beer, needling each other, making wisecracks, and occasionally directing sentiments of awe or admiration toward the screen. About ten years ago a flood from a bathroom up above had ruined the library's aged and random accumulation of books, and the once-elegant walnut shelves, which had the remains of fine Victorian moldings along all the edges, now held dead beer cans and empty pizza delivery boxes funky with the odor of cheese. The library's one trove of mankind's accumulated knowledge at this moment in history was the TV set.

"Ungghh!" went two or three boys simultaneously. Up on the screen a huge football linebacker named Bobo Bolker had just sacked a quarterback so hard that his body crumpled on the ground beneath Bobo like a football uniform full of bones. Bobo got up and pumped his enormous arms and shimmied his hips in a dance of domination.

"You know how much that fucking guy weighs?" said a boy with tousled blond hair, Vance by name, who was sitting back in an armchair on the base of his spine, holding a can of beer. "Three hundred and ten fucking pounds. And he can fucking *move*."

"Those guys are half human and half fucking creatine," said another boy, Julian, a real mesomorph—his short, thick arms and long, ponderous gut made him look like a wrestler—who had sunk so far back into a couch, he was able to balance a can of beer on his upper abdomen.

"Creatine?" said Vance. "They don't take creatine anymore. Creatine's a boutique drug. Now they take like gorilla testosterone and shit like that. Don't give me that look, Julian. I'm not kidding. Fucking gorilla testosterone."

"The fuck, they take gorilla testosterone," said Julian. "How do they get it?"

"They buy it. It's out there for sale on the drug market." Vance had managed to make an entire statement without using the word *fuck* or any of its derivatives. The lull would be brief.

"Okay," said Julian, "then answer me this. I don't care if you're the greatest fucking drug lord in the history of the world. Who the fuck's gonna go out there in the jungle and harvest the fucking crop?"

Everybody broke up over that, and they immediately turned to a boy sitting in a big easy chair in the corner, as if to say, "But . . . do *you* think it's funny, Hoyt?"

Hoyt was genuinely amused by Julian, but mainly he was aglow with the realization that this happened all the time now. The boys would crack a joke or make what was meant to be an interesting observation, particularly in the area of what was or wasn't cool, and they'd all turn to him to see what *Hoyt* thought. It was an unconscious thing, which made it even greater proof that what he had hoped for, what he had predicted, had come to pass. Ever since word had spread about how he and Vance had demolished the big thug bodyguard on what boys in the Saint Ray house now referred to as the Night of the Skull Fuck, they had become legends in their own time.

So Hoyt laughed, by way of bestowing his blessing upon Julian, and knocked back another big gulp of beer.

"Holy shit," said Boo McGuire, a roly-poly boy who had one leg slung over the arm of a couch and one elbow crooked behind his head, "I don't care how big they are. If they're taking gorilla testosterone, then they've all got balls the size of fucking BBs."

And everybody broke up over that, since it was well known to habitués of SportsCenter that the downside to taking testosterone supplements to build muscle was that the body's own testosterone factory shut down and the testicles atrophied. The room glanced at Hoyt again, to ratify the fact that Boo McGuire had indeed gotten off a funny line.

Just then Ivy Peters, a boy notable for how fat his hips were—and the way his black eyebrows ran together over his nose—appeared in the doorway and said, "Anybody got porn?" Sticking up in front of his chin was the sort of microphone one wears in order to use a hands-free cell phone.

This was not an unusual request. Many boys spoke openly about how they masturbated at least once every day, as if this were some sort of prudent maintenance of the psychosexual system. On the other hand, among the cooler members, Ivy Peters was regarded as one of the fraternity's "mistakes." They had been carried away by the fact that his father, Horton Peters, was

CEO of Gordon Hanley, and a majority of Saint Rays with no particular aptitudes assumed they would become investment bankers, Hoyt among them. At first behind his back and now sometimes to his face, they had begun calling him Ivy Poison or Mr. Poison or I.P., which they made sure he knew didn't stand for Ivy Peters. Hoyt's own face went glum all of a sudden, as it often did when he saw I.P. these days . . . Gordon Hanley . . . to get hired by an i-bank like that these days you needed a transcript that shined like fucking gold . . . and his grades . . . He refused to think about them. That's next June's problem, and this was only September.

Vance was making an insouciant upward gesture for I.P.'s benefit. Barely even looking at him, he said, "Try the third floor. They got some one-hand magazines up there."

"I've built up a tolerance to magazines," said the mistake. "I need videos."

Boo McGuire said, "What's the microphone for, I.P.? So you can call your sister while you jack off?"

I.P ignored that. Julian got up off the couch and left the room.

Hoyt lazily knocked back some more beer and said, "Oh, f'r Chrissake, I.P., it's ten o'clock at night. In another hour the cum dumpsters will start coming over here to spend the night. Right, Vance-man?" He gave Vance a mock leer of a look, then turned back to I.P. "And you're looking for porn videos and a knuckle fuck."

The mistake shrugged and turned his palms up as if to say, "I want porn. What's the big deal?" He didn't seem to realize that Julian was sneaking up behind him . . . *Bango!* Julian wrapped his arms around I.P.'s chest, pinning the mistake's arms to his sides, and began thrusting his wrestler's gut and pelvis against the mistake's big rear end like a dog in the park.

Everybody broke up again.

"Leggo a me, you grotesque faggot!" screamed I.P., his face contorted with anger as he thrashed his pinioned body about.

Convulsive laughter, waves and waves of it.

"What makes you so fucking *grotesque*, Julian?" said Boo McGuire, coming up briefly for air. The repetition of the fancy word threw everybody into a new round of paroxysms.

I.P. broke loose and stood there for a moment glowering at Julian, who put on a sad face and said, "Don't I get one little hump?"

The mistake then turned and glowered at everybody in the room and started shaking his head. Without another word he stormed out into the entry gallery, toward the stairs.

A big, rugged varsity lacrosse player named Harrison Vorheese yelled after him, "Happy hand job, I.P.!"—and everybody cracked up, convulsed, and dissolved all over again.

Julian's rutboar embrace was a form of fraternal gibe known as humping, generally inflicted upon brothers caught doing dorky things such as covertly working on a homework assignment in the library while Sports-Center was on or coming into the library at ten o'clock at night looking for porn videos, especially if you were a mistake in the first place.

"What *is* all this walking around the house with a fucking microphone in his face?" said Boo. "I.P.'s become some kind of wireless nut. You should see the shit he has up in his room."

Once they finally got control of themselves, Harrison, invigorated by the success of his "hand job" crack, said to Hoyt, "Speaking of cum dumpsters, did you know—"

Boo broke in. "What the fuck's this cum dumpster shit, Hoyt? Didn't I see a little cutie-pie in disco clothes coming out of your room at seven-thirty this morning?"

Everybody went "Woooooooooooo!" in mock dismay.

Harrison said, "Like I was saying—"

"I was speaking generically, not specifically," said Hoyt. "Specifically, I only allow discriminating visitors in my room."

Horselaughs and groans. "Oh, brother" . . . "Discriminate *this*, Hoyt" . . . "Where'd *she* come from?" . . . "What's her name?"

"Whattaya think I am," said Hoyt, "a fucking playa? I wouldn't tell you her name even if I knew it."

Harrison said, "Like I was saying—" Laughs and groans directed at Hoyt drowned him out.

"What the fuck *were* you saying, Harrison?" said Vance.

"Thank you," said Harrison. "It's nice to run into a gentleman in this fucking place once in a while. What I was saying was"—he looked at Vance and then at Hoyt—"did you know Crawdon McLeod's started hooking up with you guys' favorite ice-cream eater?"

"Craw?" said Hoyt. "You're kidding."

"I'm not kidding."

"Does he know who she fucking *is*?"

"I don't know. Maybe he can't fucking resist. After all, she's a fucking documented genius at skull work."

They all convulsed and disintegrated yet once again. Harrison's beefy square face was beaming. He was on a roll.

Julian said, "Does she know you guys know she was the one going down on the fucking governor?"

"I don't know," said Hoyt, who now tilted the beer can up almost vertically to get one last swallow. Idly he wondered how many of these things he had drunk tonight. "Probably not. I don't think she ever got a real look at us. We were behind a tree." He indicated with his arms how big around the tree was.

Then he noticed that Vance was grilling him with a certain stern look he was very familiar with by now. Vance didn't want to be a legend in his own time. He continually beseeched Hoyt to bury the whole incident. They'd been lucky. So far nobody had come looking for them. Or maybe they had. Politicians had their own ways of getting even, and so forth and so on. Hoyt looked at Vance's pained expression for a couple of seconds. A pleasant breeze was beginning to blow inside his head. Nevertheless, he decided to drop the subject.

But Julian said, "You think they're ever gonna come looking for you guys?"

Vance got up and walked to the doorway in exasperation, pausing only long enough to say to Hoyt, without even a suggestion of a smile, "Hey, why don't we talk about it some more?" He pointed toward the TV screen. "Why don't you get SportsCenter to broadcast a replay for you? That way you can let the whole fucking country in on it." He turned his back and left.

Hoyt hesitated, then said to Julian, but more for Vance's benefit than Julian's, "They ain't coming looking for *no*body. All they're looking to do is *over*look the whole fucking thing. Nothing they could do to anybody at Dupont would be worth the risk. The guy got himself fucking gobbled in the bushes by a little girl. Syrie's nineteen, twenty years old, and he's the fifty-whatever-year-old governor of California. She's a little blond college girl, and he's a big old cottontop—two and a half, maybe three times her age. Talk about grotesque."

The others were watching Hoyt with big eyes. Hoyt and Vance weren't boys any longer. They were real men who had been in an elemental physical fight with a bona fide professional tough guy. They had been in a real-life rumble with no rules, and they had won.

Hoyt looked up at the TV screen with a steady gaze and a somewhat cross expression, to indicate that this particular topic of discussion was now terminated. Not that he really cared; in fact, he did it mainly for effect. The happy wind was rising. Nobody said a word. Everybody became conscious all over again of the quarters bouncing in the front parlor and the boys whooping ironically and Swarm's bang beat banging away in the terrace room.

Up on the screen, the SportsCenter anchorman was interviewing some former coach from the pros, an old guy whose bull neck creased every time he turned his head. The guy was explaining Alabama's new "tilt" formation. A play diagram comes on the screen, and white lines start squiggling out to show how this guy blocks that guy and this guy blocks *that* guy and the running back goes through this hole *here* . . . At first Hoyt tried to concentrate on it. Of course, what they don't fucking tell you is that *this* guy who blocks *that* guy better be the size of Bobo Bolker, because *that* guy's gonna be three hundred pounds of gorilla-engineered cybermuscle. Otherwise that running back's gonna be another sack of bones . . . After perhaps thirty seconds of it, Hoyt was still gazing at the screen, but his brain was no longer processing any of it. A thought had come to him, an intriguing and possibly very important thought.

A replay of what happened in the Grove up on the screen . . . Too bad that was impossible . . . Every Saint Ray *should* see something like that. They ought to all think about what that little adventure really meant. It was about more than him and Vance. It was about more than being a legend in your own time. It was about something serious. It was about the essence of a fraternity like Saint Ray, not a fraternity merely in the sense of him and Vance fighting shoulder to shoulder and all that . . . A concept was taking shape . . . Fraternities were all about one thing, and that one thing was the creation of real men. He would like nothing better than to call a meeting of the entire house and give them a talk about this very subject. But of course he couldn't. They'd laugh him off the premises. Besides, he wasn't sure he could *give* an inspirational speech. He had never tried. His strong suit was humor, irony, insouciance, and being coolly gross, *Animal House*–style. In the American lit classes, they were always talking about *The Catcher in the Rye,* but Holden Caulfield was a whining, neurotic wuss. For his, Hoyt's, generation it was *Animal House.* He must have watched it ten times himself . . . The part where Belushi smacks his cheeks and says, "I'm a zit" . . . awesome . . . and *Dumb and Dumber* and *Swingers* and *Tommy Boy* and *The Usual Suspects, Old School* . . . He'd loved those movies. He'd laughed his head off . . . gross, coolly gross . . . but did anybody else in this house get the serious point that made all that so awesome? Probably not. It was actually all about being a man in the Age of the Wuss. A fraternity like Saint Ray, if you truly understood it, forged you into a man who stood apart from the ordinary run of passive, compliant American college boys. Saint Ray was a MasterCard that gave you carte blanche to assert yourself—he loved that metaphor. Of course, you couldn't go through life like a frat boy, breaking rules just for the fun of it. The frat-boy stuff was sort of like basic training. One of the things you learned as a Saint Ray—if you were a real brother and not some mistake like I.P.—was how rattled and baffled people were when confronted by *those who take no shit*. His thoughts kept drifting back, almost every day, to one particular moment that night in the Grove . . . He cherished it . . . The pumped-up thug (he could see his huge neck), the bodyguard guy, grabs him from behind, totally surprises him, and says, "What the fuck you punks think you're doing?" Ninety-nine out of a hundred college boys would have (a) been frightened by the brute's tough-guy pose and bulked-up body and (b) tried to mollify him by taking the question at face value and saying, "Uh, nothing, we were just—" Instead, he, Hoyt Thorpe, had said, "*Doing?* Looking at a fucking ape-faced dickhead is what we're *doing!*" That was the last thing in the world that motherfucker had expected to hear. It rattled his tiny brain, ruined his tough-guy intimidator act, and provoked him into launching the wild roundhouse punch that led to his downfall. The phrase *fucking ape-faced dickhead* and the insolent way he had thrown the dickhead's own word, *doing,* back in his face—that wasn't some strategy he had *thought up.* No, it was a *conditioned reflex.* He had shot that line quickdraw, like a bullet from the hip, in a moment of crisis. He had triumphed, thanks to a *habit of mind,* a take-no-shit *instinct* . . . He began to see something even bigger . . . Everywhere you looked at this university there were people knocking "the frats" and the frat boys—the administration, which blamed them for the evils of alcohol, pot, cocaine, ecstasy . . . the dorks, GPA geeks, Goths, lesbos, homobos, bi-bos, S and Mbos, blackbos, Latinos, Indians—from India and the reservation—and other whining diversoids, who blamed them for racism, sexism, classism, whatever the fuck that was, chauvinism, anti-Semitism, fringe-rightism, homophobia . . . The only value ingrained at this institution was a weepy tolerance for losers . . . The old gale began blowing, and the concept enlarged . . . If America ever had to go to war again, fight with the country's fate on the line, not just in some "police action," there would be only one source of officers other than

T
O
M

W
O
L
F
E

the military academies: frat boys. They were the only educated males left who were conditioned to think and react . . . like *men*. They were the only—

The concept would have grown still larger had not a boy named Hadlock Mills—known as Heady, which was short for Headlock—come in from out of the entry gallery and said with a slight smirk, "Hoyt, there's a young lady here to see you."

Hoyt rose from the easy chair, put his dead beer can up on a walnut shelf, and said, "Sorry, guys, hospitality calls," whereupon he left the room. He soon reappeared at the doorway with a pretty little brunette—clad in halter top, shorts, and flip-flops—behind him.

He looked back at her and said, "Come say hello to some of my friends, uhhh—come say hello."

As she stepped forward, he put his arm lightly on her shoulders, and she said, "Hi!" and gave a little wave. She had a charming smile, which made her look even prettier.

The boys responded with smiles of their own, in a pleasant and gentlemanly fashion, plus a few *Hi*'s and polite waves and even a "Welcome!" from big Julian. Whereupon Hoyt said, "Well, see you guys," and, his arm still resting lightly on her shoulders, steered the girl toward the stairway.

The boys sat in silence, merely exchanging glances. Then Boo said in a low voice, barely audible above the SportsCenter anchorman's, "That's the same girl, the one from last night. And couldn't you tell? He *still* doesn't know her fucking name."

Charlotte looked from the professor, Dr. Lewin, to the windows to the ceiling and from the ceiling to the windows to Dr. Lewin. She was well into her second week of classes, and the puzzles and contradictions of Dupont kept mounting, unabated. She reckoned it was inevitable. She could now see that she had led a sheltered life up there behind the wall of the Blue Ridge Mountains—but even allowing for that, *this* . . . was odd.

The classroom was a spacious one on a corner, with two great English Gothic leaded-glass casement windows comprised of multitudes of small panes. Here and there, seemingly placed at random, were panes exquisitely etched with pictures of saints, knights, and what looked like characters from old books. If Charlotte had to guess, she would say that a couple of them came from *The Canterbury Tales*. And that knight . . . over there . . . certainly did look like Don Quixote on Rosinante . . . If anything, the ceiling was even grander. It was higher than any classroom ceiling she had ever imagined and was transversed by five or six shallow arches of a dark but warm wood. Where the arches met the walls, they rested atop carved wooden heads with comic faces that appeared to be looking down at open books, also carved of wood, just below their chins.

All that elegance was what made the personage of Dr. Lewin seem so curious. Last week, when the class first met, he had worn a plaid cotton shirt and pants—nothing remarkable about that. The shirt had had long sleeves, and the pants had been long pants. But this morning he had on a short-sleeved shirt that showed too much of his skinny, hairy arms, and denim shorts that showed too much of his gnarly, hairy legs. He looked for all the world like a seven-year-old who at the touch of a wand had become old, tall, bald on top, and hairy everywhere else, an ossified seven-year-old, a pair of eyeglasses with lenses thick as ice pushed up to the summit of his fore-head—unaccountably addressing thirty college students, at Dupont, no less.

The title of the course was the Modern French Novel: From Flaubert to Houellebecq. At last week's class Dr. Lewin had assigned Flaubert's *Madame Bovary* for today. And today, as the transmogrified seven-year-old addressed the class, things, to Charlotte's way of thinking, grew stranger and stranger.

Dr. Lewin had his nose in a paperback book he held open just below his chin, rather like the wooden heads that served as finials to the arches. Then he lowered the book, let the glasses flop down onto the bridge of his nose, looked up, and said, "For a moment let's consider the very first pages of *Madame Bovary*. We're in a school for boys . . . The very first sentence says"—he pushed the glasses back up on his forehead and brought the book back up under his chin, close to his myopic eyes—"'We were at preparation, when the headmaster came in, followed by a new boy dressed in "civvies" and a school servant carrying a big desk.' And so forth and so on . . . uh-mmm, uhmmm"—he kept his face down in the book—"and then it says, 'In the corner behind the door, only just visible, stood a country lad of about fif-teen, taller than any of us—'"

He lowered the book, flopped the glasses down onto his nose again, looked up, and said, "Now, you'll notice Flaubert begins the book with 'We were at preparation' and 'taller than *us*,' referring to Charles Bovary's school-mates collectively, presumably, but he never tells the story in the first person plural again, and after a few pages we never see any of these boys again. Now, can anybody tell me why Flaubert uses this device?"

Dr. Lewin surveyed the students through his binocular lenses. Silence.

Evidently, everybody else was stymied by the question, even though it didn't seem difficult to Charlotte. Charlotte was puzzled by something else entirely. Dr. Lewin was reading this French classic to them in *English*—and this was an upper-level course in French literature. Thanks to her high advanced placement scores, Charlotte had been able to skip the entry-level French course, but just about everybody else must be an upperclassman—and he's reading to them in *English*.

She was in the second row. She started to raise her hand to answer the question, but being new, only a freshman, she felt diffident. Finally a girl to her right, also in the second row, raised her hand.

"So the reader will feel like part of Charles's class? It says here"—she looked down at her book and put her forefinger on the page—"it says here, 'We began going over the lesson.'" She looked up hopefully.

"Well, that's it up to a point," said Dr. Lewin, "but not exactly."

Charlotte was astonished. The girl was reading one of the greatest of all French novels in an *English* translation—and Dr. Lewin hadn't so much as made note of the fact. Charlotte quickly glanced at the girl on her left and the boy on her right. They were both reading the book . . . in *English translation*. It was baffling. She had read it in translation way back in the ninth grade under Miss Pennington's tutelage, and she had spent the better part of the past three days reading it in the original, in French. Flaubert was a very clear and direct writer, but there were many subtle constructions, many colloquialisms, many names of specific objects she'd had to look up, since Flaubert put a big emphasis on precise, concrete detail. She had analyzed every line of it, practically disassembled it and put it back together—and nobody else was reading it in French, *including the professor*. How could that be?

Meantime, three other girls had taken a stab at the question, and each answer was a bit more *off* than the one before. As she craned about to see the girls, Charlotte noticed that the boys in the class seemed extraordinarily . . . big . . . reared back, as they were, in their desk–arm chairs. They had big necks and big hands, and their thighs swelled out tightly against the fabric of their otherwise baggy pants legs. And none of them lifted a hand or uttered a peep.

Although she couldn't have said why, Charlotte somehow felt a compulsion to rescue the reputation of the entire class. So she raised her hand.

"Yes?" said Dr. Lewin.

Charlotte said, "Well, I think he does it that way because what the first chapter really is, is Charles Bovary's background up to the time he meets Emma, which is when the real story begins. The last two-thirds of the chapter are written like a plain-long biography, but Flaubert didn't want to start the book that way"—she could feel her face reddening—"because he believed you should get your point across by writing a real vivid scene with just the right details. The point of the first chapter is to show that Charles is a country bumpkin and always has been and always will be, even though he becomes a doctor and everything." She looked down at her text. "*Une de ces pauvres choses, enfin, dont la laideur muette a des profondeurs d'expression*'"—she looked up at Dr. Lewin again—"*comme le visage d'un imbécile.*' So you start the book seeing Charles the way *we*—the other boys—saw him, and the way *we* saw him is so vivid that all the way through the book, you never forget that what Charles is, is a hopeless fool, an idiot."

Dr. Lewin looked at her and said nothing for what seemed to Charlotte ten or fifteen seconds, although of course it wasn't nearly that long.

"Thank you," he said. Then he turned to the rest of the class. "That's *precisely* why. Flaubert never simply *explained* a key point if he could *show* it instead, and to show it he needed a *point of view*, and as"—he turned toward Charlotte, but since he had no idea what her name was, he simply gestured in her direction—"has just said . . ."

Dr. Lewin continued in this vein, implicitly verifying the superiority of her intellect, but Charlotte kept her head lowered and didn't dare look at him. Her cheeks were burning. She was overcome by a familiar feeling: guilt. The rest of the class would resent her, this freshman girl who had turned up in their midst and made them look bad.

She kept her eyes turned down toward *Madame Bovary* and made out like she was busy taking notes in her spiral notebook. The class discussion continued with the same fits, stops, silences, and starts as before. Gradually it deteriorated into Dr. Lewin asking students about nothing more than how the plot was developed. The girls—there weren't many—supplied most of the answers.

By and by Dr. Lewin was saying, "In chapter eleven, Charles, who's not even a surgeon, attempts a radical operation that's supposed to correct the clubfoot of a stable hand named Hippolyte. He botches it and ruins his reputation, which becomes a turning point in the book. Now, can someone tell me what drives Charles, who is not exactly a cutting-edge medical pioneer—if you'll pardon the unintentional pun—to attempt something so risky?"

The usual silence . . . Then, in a suddenly lively voice, Dr. Lewin said, "Yes! Mr. Johanssen?"

Charlotte looked up, and the professor was pointing toward the rear of the class. His sallow face had brightened. It was the first time he had called a student by name. Charlotte craned about to see who this Mr. Johanssen might be. In the back of the room, a big boy, a giant of a boy, was just lowering his hand. His neck was a thick white column rising up out of a muscular torso only barely obscured by his T-shirt. His head was practically shaved on the sides and had just a little crew cut crop of blond hair on top.

"He did it," said the giant, "because his wife had all these ambitions, and the thing is—"

"Hey! Jojo read the book!" It was a gigantic black youth in the row in front of the white giant; he was so twisted about that Charlotte could see only the back of his completely shaved head. "The man *read the book!*"

"Aw-*right!*" said another huge black youth with a shaved head who was sitting next to the white giant, whereupon the two black giants bumped each other's fists together in a celebratory gesture called "pounding." "Outta *sight!*"

A third black giant, next to the second one, joined in. "Go go, Jojo! You the man!" Now all three were exchanging fist pounds. "Where's *Charles* at? We got us another *scholar!*" . . . "Awwww yeah!"

All three had turned toward the white giant, Jojo, and were holding out their fists so he could join in this merry mockery of scholasticism.

The white giant started to raise his fist, then withdrew it. He started to smile, but the smile turned into lips parted in bewilderment. He crossed his arms in front of his chest as if to rescue his hands from their ribaldry, but then he summoned up a smile, as if to say he was amused, too.

"All right, gentlemen," said Dr. Lewin in a placating tone, "let's see if we can't settle down. Thank you . . . Mr. Johanssen? As you were saying."

"Lemme see," said Mr. Johanssen, "lemme see . . ." He adopted a faint smirk as he reflected. "Oh yeah. He did the operation because . . . his wife wanted some money to buy some stuff?" He now smiled, as if sounding ignorant was funny.

Dr. Lewin spoke coldly this time. "I don't think so, Mr. Johanssen. It's made quite clear that he charged no fee for the operation." He turned his gaze away from Mr. Johanssen and looked for other hands.

Charlotte was aghast. It was obvious that the boy had been serious when he raised his hand and started to answer the question. Moreover, he was right on target. Emma Bovary's social ambitions *were* at the bottom of it. And then he'd decided to play the fool.

Her eyes scanned the leaded-glass windows . . . the arches, the carvings, the ceiling murals . . . the treasures of Dupont University. Whatever was taking place in this grand old room, she couldn't comprehend.

After class she tarried, hoping to have a word with Dr. Lewin. That wasn't difficult. Nobody else stuck around. He was stuffing his papers into a nylon backpack. Yet another subteen touch. His childish ensemble made him look not more youthful but more decrepit. Somehow it underscored the scoliotic slump of his shoulders, the concavity of his chest, the hirsute tabescence of his limbs.

"Dr. Lewin? Excuse me—"

"Yes?"

"My name's Charlotte Simmons. I'm in your class."

A dry smile. "I'm well aware. By the way, here at Dupont we don't use 'Professor' or 'Doctor.' Everybody is 'Mister'—or 'Miz' or 'Mrs.' Unless you're referring to a medical doctor."

"I'm sorry . . . Mr. Lewin . . . I didn't know that."

"Oh, it's just a harmless bit of reverse snobbery, actually. The idea is, if you're teaching at Dupont, *of course* you have a doctorate. Anyway, that's the custom. But I cut you off."

"Sir, I'm—well, I guess I'm sort of confused." Her voice sounded so mousy and hoarse, from nervousness. "I thought we were reading *Madame Bovary* in French, but everybody else is reading it in English, and I read it in French."

Mr. Lewin flipped his glasses down from the crest of his forehead and studied her for a moment. "What year are you, Ms. Simmons?"

"I'm a freshman."

"Ah. Advanced Placement."

"Yes, sir."

Big sigh. Then his entire demeanor changed, and he looked at her with a world-weary but confidential smile. "My dear . . . We're not supposed to call you that—I gather it's considered demeaning to the female student— but anyway—I don't think this is the course for you."

Charlotte was taken aback. "*Why?*"

Mr. Lewin pursed his lips and slid them back and forth across his teeth. "To be perfectly honest with you, you're overqualified."

"Overqualified?"

"This course is designed for upperclassmen who are . . . uhmmm . . . linguafrankly challenged but nevertheless have to fulfill their language requirements some way. You're obviously a very bright young woman. I'm sure you can figure out who most of these students are."

Charlotte's mouth fell open slightly. "I liked the title so much. It sounded wonderful."

"Well—I'm sorry. I completely understand. I wish someone had red-flagged it for you. I'm not particularly enthusiastic about teaching this course myself, but it seems to be a necessary thing. One tries to think of it as community service."

Jojo didn't hurry anywhere after he left the class. His next class wasn't for another hour, and breaks between classes gave him just about his only opportunities to stroll about the campus and . . . be noticed. It wasn't something he thought about consciously. It was more like a mild addiction. What was best—and it happened a lot—was when some student he had never laid eyes on before would hail him with a "Go go, Jojo!" and a big grin and a little wave, which was in fact a salute.

It was one of those September days when the air is nice and dry and the sunshine is warm, toasty, and gentle, even to fair skin like his. He had a warm feeling inside, too. Treyshawn, André, and Curtis had treated him like . . . *one of them.* They'd even wanted to pound him. Mr. Lewin had gotten a little frosted off . . . but *they had treated him like one of them.*

Fiske Hall, the building he had just departed, was right on the Great Yard. Everywhere you looked were the old-fashioned stone buildings that said "Dupont" even to people who had seen them only in photographs. The famous library tower was right over there . . . All over the Yard's lush green lawn, students were hustling along the walkways to their next classes. Jojo stood on a walkway pondering the matter of which direction would satisfy his urge quickest . . . He could already see, or thought he could see, some students nudging each other and discreetly pointing out his famous towering figure. Yes, it was a good feeling . . . His eminence at this particular crossroads of American college life, the Great Yard at Dupont, was incalculable . . . What an awesome day it was. He filled his lungs with the perfect air . . . He opened his very pores to the perfect sunshine . . . It wasn't a question of whether, but when, some student would salute and sing out *Go go, Jojo!*

A girl from behind him walked past, heading in the direction of the library, a trim girl with nice legs, good calves, and long brown hair, who evidently hadn't recognized him at all as she approached him from the rear. He liked what he could make out of the nice, firm bottom inside those denim shorts . . . *Hey, wait a minute* . . . It was the girl from the class, the brainy one. He recognized that hair. He had taken a long look at it from where he sat . . . It didn't matter what a brain she was. In fact, there was something nice and feminine about that. It went with a *look* she had. She wasn't just some hot number. She wasn't beautiful in any way you usually thought about at this place. He couldn't have given it a name, but whatever she had was *above* all that. She looked like an illustration from one of those fairy-tale books where the young woman is under a spell or something and can't come to until she gets a kiss from the young man who loves her, the kind of girl who looks pure—yet that very thing about her gives you even *more* of the old tingle. And she had come walking by him obviously not even knowing what an eminence she had just been so close to.

He strode after her with his big long legs. "Hey! Hi! . . . *Hi!* . . . Wait a second!"

She stopped and turned, and he walked up to her, beaming a certain winning smile and waiting for the usual. But she didn't even yield up a girlish grin, much less say, "You're—Jojo Johanssen!" In fact, she didn't make any positive response at all or exhibit even the slightest sign of vulnerability. She looked at him—well, like some guy she didn't know, who had just accosted her. Her apprehensive expression seemed to be asking, "Why are you delaying me?" Aloud she said nothing at all.

Broadening his smile, he said, "I'm Jojo Johanssen" . . . and waited.

The girl merely stared.

"I'm in the class." He gestured toward the building they had just left . . . and waited. Nothing. "I just wanted to say—you were really terrific. You really know this stuff!" She didn't even smile, much less say thanks. If anything, she looked more apprehensive. "I'm not kidding! Honest! I was genuinely impressed." Nothing; her lips didn't move in any way, shape, or form. He vaguely realized that saying "I'm not kidding," "Honest!" and "genuinely" one after the other was like erecting a billboard that said PHONY. Her eyes looked frightened. There was nothing left to say but what he was leading up to in the first place: "Wanna grab some lunch?"

To anybody on the basketball team, that—or something like it—was just clearing your throat before saying, "Would you like to see my suite?" which in turn was a polite formality before putting your hand on her shoulder and getting it on. In his mind he could see Mike going at it with that wild-haired blonde . . . gross, but a turn-on . . .

She stared at him but didn't say a word.

"Well . . . how about it?"

For the first time her lips moved. "I can't." She turned her back and headed off at a good clip.

"Hey! Come on! Please! Whoa!"

She stopped but didn't turn completely toward him. He tried on a look of as much warmth, friendliness, tenderness, and understanding as he was capable of and said softly, "You can't—or you won't?"

She turned away again, then spun about and confronted him. Her little voice was trembling. "You knew the answer to that question Mr. Lewin asked, didn't you?"

He was speechless.

"But then you decided to say something foolish."

"Well—you could maybe say—"

A hoarse little whisper: "Why?"

"Well, I mean, shit, I didn't . . ." He was still ransacking his brain for an answer when she turned away once more and hurried in the direction of the library.

He called after her. "Hey! Listen! I'll see you next week!"

She slowed down only enough to say over her shoulder, "I won't be there. I'm switching out."

He shouted after her, "What for?"

He thought he heard her say, something something "for dummies," something something "cruise-ship French."

Jojo stared after her retreating little figure. He was stunned. She had not only completely rejected him, she'd as much as called him a fool or a dummy or a dumb fool!

Godalmighty . . . the old tingle stirred and stirred and stirred his loins.

5. YOU THE MAN

The next night, before dinner, Vance, an ultra-solemn look on his face, beckoned Hoyt into the otherwise empty billiard room, crossed his arms over his chest, and said, "Hoyt, we've got to have a serious talk about this shit."

"What shit is that, Vance?"

"You know 'what shit.' This governor of California shit. You think the fucking thing's funny. I don't. And you want to know why?"

I already know why, Vancerman, thought Hoyt. You're scared shitless, that's all. As he stood there waiting for Vance's lips to stop moving, his mind wandered . . .

. . . those who cower and those who command . . . Europe in the Early Middle Ages, taught by a wizened old Jew named Crone, as Hoyt thought of him, whose droning voice would put you right under but who was a notoriously, or gloriously, easy grader. To Hoyt's own surprise, the course had captured his imagination. He had experienced the sort of moment that real scholars, as opposed to Saint Rays, lived for: the *Aha!* phenomenon. In the early Middle Ages, according to old Crone, there were only three classes of men in the world: warriors, clergy, and slaves. That was it—China, Arabia, Morocco, England, everywhere. Ninety-nine times out of a hundred, a leader of the people was, or had been, a warrior, baptized in battle. In the hundredth case, the man was the high priest of the local religion. Mohammed had been both warrior and high priest. Likewise Joan of Arc. Everybody else on earth was some sort of slave: serf, indentured servant, or outright chattel, including artists, poets, and musicians, who were merely entertainers existing at the sufferance of warrior-leaders. In the Bible, according to Crone, King David had started out as a boy of the slave class who had volunteered to fight the Philistines' champion of "single combat"— Goliath. When, against all odds, David defeated the giant, he became Israel's warrior of all warriors. He ascended to King Saul's royal household and became king when Saul died, leapfrogging over Saul's own son, Jonathan.

Hoyt loved that story, the Nobody who was King. His own ambitions were analogous. His father, George Thorpe, was—

"—hire a bunch of goombahs to intimidate witnesses—"

Goombahs. Every now and then some phrase from Vance's earnest, frightened lips would snag in Hoyt's mind.

"What's a goombah?" he said, not because he wanted to know, but just to make Vance think he was paying attention.

"An Italian thug," said Vance. "And these guys . . ."

Goombahs. Oh, give me one fucking break, Vancerman, thought Hoyt. My dad would have eaten your goombahs for breakfast. As Hoyt remembered him, his dad, George Thorpe, was handsome and a half, with a thick stand of dark hair, a strong, square jaw, and a cleft chin. His old man loved it when people said he looked "just like Cary Grant." He spoke through his nose with a New York Honk accent that intimated a boarding school background. He made oblique references, stuck inside relative clauses, to his days at Princeton, and *his* dad's before him, too, not to mention his stint with the Special Forces in Vietnam, where he had seen, literally *seen*, swarms of AK-47 bullets coming straight at him at five times the speed of sound. They looked like green bees. But since he had been a member of the elite of the elite, Delta Force, he couldn't really go into details. Strictly speaking, he shouldn't even have told his family he was *in* Delta Force. It was that elite. On the strength of these New York Honked-out credentials, he managed to gain membership in the Brook Club. There was no more socially solid club in New York. With the Brook escutcheon on his shield, he gained entry to four more swell clubs of the Old New York sort. Thus established, he recruited club brethren into three esoteric hedge funds he had set up based on a strategy of selling corporate bonds short. This was during the Wall Street bond boom of the 1980s. In the late eighties, he changed his legal name from George B. Thorpe to Armistead G. Thorpe. Even at age eight Hoyt found that strange, but both his dad and his mother explained that Armistead was his dad's mother's—his grandmother's—maiden name and he had loved her profoundly, and Hoyt swallowed it.

Hoyt's mother, the former Peggy Springs, a pretty, brunette, washed-out, submissive lab rabbit of a woman, was a certified public accountant with a master's degree in economics from her alma mater, the University of Southern Illinois. She cooked George B. Thorpe's books for him and Armistead G. Thorpe's, too, backed up his stories even when they became so tall they collapsed of their own lack of foundation, and was willing to keep her timid Peggy Rabbit self at home, at his suggestion, when he went trolling for investors over lunches and dinners at his clubs.

Hoyt always hung on to the assumption that his father's intentions had been on the up and up. But not even a son could fail to see that toward the end his father had been setting up the new hedge funds for no purpose other than to get cash with which to assuage the investors in the old ones who were getting cranky and threatening to sue. He had even convinced a bank teller—a twenty-four-year-old Estonian girl who had grown up on an island in Maine called Vinalhaven, a lissome little blonde he liked to flirt with when he was at the bank—to invest all her savings, a $20,000 Treasury bond her parents, a night watchman and a nurse's aide, had given her on her twenty-first birthday, in a hedge fund based on selling *futures* on bond sales short. It was complicated stuff but absolute dynamite . . . She should think of it as a "hedge against a hedge with a multiplier or 'whip' effect" . . . *Bango!* He told Peggy to print up the necessary letterhead stationery, contract, and prospectus using computer fonts, *tout de suite*, and open a commercial bank account to receive her check. This was one of but many last desperate contortions before all of his funds crashed in a pile.

Hoyt and his parents were living at the time in a house built originally by the old cowboy movie star Bill Hart in the Belle Haven section of Greenwich, Connecticut, close to Long Island Sound. George Thorpe now found it advisable to disappear for "a while," until things smoothed over. Ever mindful of the potential wrath of his creditors and investors, he had long since put the house in passive Peggy's name. Now he wanted the title back— fast. For the first time Hoyt's mother allowed her brain to take over from her faint heart. She stalled and stalled and stalled. She knew her husband's "things" inside out, and there was no way they were going to smooth over this time. One Thursday morning, he mentioned, in the Oh-I-didn't-tell-you? mode, a weekend real estate conference he was going to on Sea Island, Georgia. That afternoon he packed two garment bags and headed off to La Guardia Airport. They never saw him again. The bankers, insurance companies, and investors descended on Peggy. She gave them nothing but an innocent, clueless face and managed to hang on to the house. She got a job in the accounting department at Stanley Tool in nearby Stamford and was able to bring home just enough honest dollars to pay the mortgage installments. But Hoyt's days at the pricey Greenwich Country Day School were over.

In the course of settling George's affairs, Peggy called the Princeton alumni office for some amplification of his record there, but they couldn't find his name, or that of his father, Linus Thorpe. Similarly, the army drew a blank on Captain George Thorpe. Peggy found a cache of aging, intimate letters from women—addressed to George Thornton, George Thurlow, and George Thorsten.

In short, she never found a single documented record of her husband's background—or of his existence on this earth, come to think of it. Hoyt, being only sixteen, explained all doubts away. To him the old man remained— he had to remain—a tough, aggressive military hero. It all had to do with Delta Force being a secret unit of the Special Forces. They probably had to destroy records.

When Hoyt had moved from the lower school to the middle school at Greenwich Country Day, he was a short, slight boy, and two outsize bullies in the class above him picked him out for special torment. Their favorite torture was to lock him up in a janitor's broom closet in a seldom-used hallway and leave it up to him to shout and bang on the door until he got somebody's attention. He had missed entire classes that way, to the detriment of his academic standing. Naturally, there was no way he could explain to the teachers what had happened, because there was nothing—*nothing*—worse than a boy being a snitch. After three weeks of the ordeal, he finally told his mother about it, first making her swear not to tell his father, which of course was the first thing Peggy did. His father gave Hoyt his grimmest Vietnam search-and-destroy look and said he was going to the school tomorrow and lift the headmaster up by his shirtfront, if necessary, and tell him that this bullshit *will* cease. "Bullshit" was the word, since George regarded sharing vulgarities, father and son, as a part of helping the son grow up as a man's man.

Oh God, no! Tell the headmaster? There *was* something worse than being a snitch; it was having Mommy or Daddy being a snitch *for* you.

In that case, said the old man, you've got to make a choice. Hoyt could either give one or both of the bullies a good pop on the nose—Dad demonstrated by administering an imaginary clout, not with his fist but his forearm (which Hoyt assumed must be the Delta commando way)—or he, the old man, would head straight for the headmaster. But such a pop on the nose was impossible! They were bigger than he was! They'd destroy him! Not so, said his father. One good pop on the nose, especially if it drew blood, and they would never bother him again; and neither would anybody else at that school. Not only that, but from then on, ninety-nine times out of a hundred, you'll be able to dominate every confrontation with nothing more than an intimidating stare and a couple of give-a-shit words. "Give-a-shit" he shared, too.

But—but—there was no way it could work out like that!

His father shrugged and said okay then, you've got a big problem. You're gonna have one totally pissed-off—"pissed-off"—parent storming into that school and raising holy hell.

That did it. The next morning, one of the bullies approached Hoyt and began taunting him. Hoyt croaked out his usual nervous response—and then, with no preamble whatsoever, lunged at the astonished kid and gave him a good whack on the beak with his forearm. Blood gushed out all over the place. Everything his father predicted had ensued. This was one sixth-grader nobody was going to mess with. Furthermore, never again did he run into a situation he couldn't handle with an unblinking stare and a few superior give-a-shit comments.

But that was sweet little Greenwich Country Day. Now he had to go to a public school, Greenwich High. Greenwich High had a not-bad academic reputation, as public schools went, but it drew a certain element . . . The third day Hoyt was there, a group of four Hispanic-looking guys blocked his way in the hall between classes. The group's spokesman had a week's worth of stubble on his face and a tight T-shirt with sleeves so negligible you could see the tubelike pumping-iron veins on his biceps as well as his forearms. He wanted to know Hoyt's name.

"Hoyt, hunh? That suppose a be a *name*—or wot? A fart?"

The thought of going through all the preliminaries, all the stupid words, all the moronic sneers, all the ritual challenges, depressed Hoyt tremendously. So without a word or the slightest change in expression, he smashed the guy in the nose with his forearm. Something cracked, and blood poured out of his nose like Niagara Falls. The bigmouth, the group wit, fell back with half a whimper and half a cry and brought both hands tenderly to his hemorrhaging nose as if it were his child. Blood poured through the crevices between his fingers and down his arms. The other three piled on Hoyt and would have probably given him a pretty good drubbing except that a couple of teachers happened along and broke up the melee. The four tough guys vowed several types of crippling foggin' revenge upon the white mottafogga, but in fact that was the end of it, and Hoyt spent four years at Greenwich High as one white mottafogga you didn't mess with.

After that, he was regarded as cool by all factions. As he began to fill out and his cleft chin took on manly contours, he was regarded as hot by all the girls. He was fourteen when he first scored, as the expression went. It was one night on the couch in the den in the girl's own house, while her parents were directly overhead in their bedroom. The girl didn't go to Greenwich High, however, but to Greenwich Country Day. Without consciously planning it, Hoyt kept himself insinuated into the student social circles of Greenwich Country Day. He dressed in the marginally preppier, neater Greenwich Country Day boys' clothes, and he wore his thatchy hair in their longish, but not truly rebellious, style. That only made him hotter in the eyes of girls at Greenwich High — "hot" being the comparative degree of "cool" in teenage grammar. Hoyt didn't altogether neglect the Greenwich High girls by any means. In fact, it was they who, in short order, got him through the usual teenage male sexual trials, such as premature ejaculation and "how to do it."

Thanks to his comparatively rigorous preparation at Greenwich Country Day, Hoyt was a good year ahead of most of his classmates at Greenwich High. He was diligent about maintaining that advantage, not because of any true interest in academic excellence, but rather because good grades were a sign that you were part of the better element. At the beginning of his junior year at Greenwich High, his Greenwich Country Day friends began to talk about how good grades alone weren't enough to get you into the top colleges. You needed a "hook," sometimes called a "spike," some area of remarkable achievement outside the academic curriculum, whether it be athletics, the oboe, summer internships at a biotech lab — *something*. Hoyt had nothing. He thought and thought. One night on television he saw a brief segment about a charity in New York City called City Harvest, which sent trucks with refrigeration units around to restaurant kitchens at night and collected unused food that would have otherwise been discarded and brought it to soup kitchens for the homeless. A lightbulb went on over Hoyt's head. He talked a nerdy classmate who had access to his parents' Chrysler Pacifica minivan into joining him in a venture called the Greenwich Protein Patrol. Thus read the professional-looking posters taped to the front doors of the minivan. Hoyt had prevailed upon the new blond twenty-three-year-old art teacher, who was a real number—she obviously had a thing for Hoyt but restrained herself—to do the graphics, which included two white sweatshirts with THE GREENWICH PROTEIN PATROL appliquéd in dark green. In fact, the Protein Patrol gathered no protein—only carbohydrates in the form of leftover bread at two bakeries—since they had no refrigeration for meat, leafy greens, or other protein-heavy food. This the two eleemosynary youths dropped off at the First Presbyterian Church, which had a soup line for the homeless. Hoyt laid eyes on the ultimate recipients of his generosity only once. That was when an idea-starved feature writer for the *Greenwich Times* named Clara Klein heard about the Patrol from the church's Reverend Mr. Burrus and wrote a story about it, accompanied by a three-column photo of Hoyt in his white sweatshirt with his arm around a little old soup-line regular who provided a striking contrast. There was Hoyt, the knight in white; and there was the poor little man, all in dark tones of brown and gray: dirty gray hair, sickly grayish brown skin, the turd-brown thirty-nine-gallon vinyl garbage bag he had converted into a poncho, the blue jeans that by now had turned soot gray, as had his Lugz sneakers, lurid stripes and all.

Attached to Hoyt's Dupont application, the photo was dynamite as far as the admissions office was concerned. Here was a good-looking young man who was not only sympathetic to the downtrodden but also imaginative and enterprising. He had created and organized a mobile food-collecting service, complete with uniforms, to provide the needy with nutritious food from the best restaurants in a wealthy town, an implication that Hoyt let stand. It didn't hurt that he himself was from a broken home and his mother had been reduced to drudgery at a place called Stanley Tool. These days such things were a definite plus at college admissions offices.

Hoyt had to emphasize his "deserving poor" credentials in order to get a partial scholarship, which was essential. Putting himself in this light galled him, however, and he had never revealed it to a soul at Dupont. If anybody asked, he said he had gone to a "day school" in Greenwich. Anybody who knew anything about Greenwich took this to be an unpretentious way of referring to Greenwich Country Day—even people who didn't assumed that "day school" referred to a private school. He said that his parents were divorced and his dad was an investment banker who operated internationally (the fleeced little Estonian morsel at the bank). Stanley Tool and its accounting department he took care not to mention.

It never occurred to Hoyt that here was another tendency he shared with his father: blithely covering up his past and manufacturing a pedigree. In short, he was a second-generation snob. He looked so great, had such confidence, projected such an aura, had cultivated such a New York Honk, it never occurred to anyone to question his autobiography. He had no trouble getting into what everybody knew was the most socially upscale fraternity at Dupont, Saint Ray—far from it. Four fraternities had vied for him. None was quite what Saint Ray was, however. Saint Ray was the natural home of the ideal-typical socially superior student, who would be someone like Vance, whose father, Sterling Phipps, a golf nut, had retired at fifty after running a wildly successful hedge fund called Short Iron and had villas in Cap Ferrat and Carmel, California (on the beach), Southampton, New York (with memberships at both the Shinnecock and National Links golf clubs), as well as a twenty-room apartment at 820 Fifth Avenue in New York, which Vance called home. One of Vance's uncles had put up most of the money for the Phipps Opera House. That the Vance Phippses of Dupont looked up to him and were in awe of his aristocratic daring meant the world to Hoyt. As he looked at Vance's anxious face here in the billiard room, Hoyt's blood alcohol level was not far from perfection. He became more convinced than ever that his role in life was to be a knight riding through throngs of students trapped by their own slave mentality—but that made him think of next June. The Knight was going to need a job at an i-bank . . . It was the only way . . . but his fucking *grades*! *Stop thinking about it!* Don't get a long face in front of Vance—

"—here looking for us!" Vance was saying, his voice rising an uncool octave or so.

"Vance," said Hoyt, "we're not gonna wait and see if the governor comes here looking for us. We're gonna *invite* him here."

"Gonna what?" said Vance. "What the hell are you talking about?"

Hoyt loved the fear on Vance's face. He, Hoyt, didn't really know what he was talking about, either. But the general idea *felt* right.

He couldn't resist shaking Vance up a little more. "If we can get him here, we can make that fucker fucking sit up on his hindquarters and beg."

For a moment Vance said nothing. Then he said, "Hoyt, if you—has anybody ever been honest with you and told you you're insane?"

Hoyt couldn't hold back a laugh and a big grin. He loved it . . . an even bigger legend in his own time . . . It only remained to figure out how to get the governor of California to the campus on Chevalier Hoyt's terms . . . He knew of one thing that turned the governor of California to a quivering gob of jelly . . .

Vance was saying, "You think that's cool, don't you, somebody saying you're crazy. You think it's a compliment." He couldn't believe the dreamy look that had stolen across Hoyt's face. "Well, it's not. You're not crazy cool, Hoyt, you're just crazy."

Hoyt couldn't suppress another laugh. "Hey, this is your chance, dude! Stick with me and you'll be a *real* legend in your own time."

"Me? I don't think so. I've had enough legend. Legend gives me mud-butt, if you want to know the truth."

"Aw, come on. You're money, baby, and you don't even know it. Let me grab a beer, and I'll tell you how we do it."

As Jojo entered the study hall, Charles Bousquet and Vernon Congers were just in front of him, and he could hear Charles dogging the big freshman, as he often did, because Congers was (a) a rookie and (b) such an easy mark.

"Aw, mannn," Charles was saying, "I can't believe you just said that, Vernon. What's the matter witchoo? You want people going around thinking you got room to rent upstairs?"

Congers just stared darkly. He always had trouble processing Charles's gibes and was apparently puzzling over "room to rent upstairs."

"Okay, here's an easy one," said Charles. "What state are we in?"

"What state?"

"Yeah, what state. The United States of America is made up of fifty states, and we're in one of them right now. Which one, Vernon?"

Congers paused, perhaps wondering if this might be a trick question. Frowning: "Pennsylvania."

"Right," said his tormentor. "Okay, what's the capital of Pennsylvania?"

Now Congers was obviously stumped, and at the same time, he didn't have the wit to deflect this entire demeaning quiz. Testy hesitation. Then: "Philadelphia."

"Godalmighty, Vernon! *Philadel*phia? The capital of Pennsylvania's a town called Harrisburg. H, a, r, r, i, s, b, u, r, g. It's about 150 miles west of here. *Harris*-burg."

By now Curtis, Alan, and Treyshawn had started listening in, and Curtis let out a low chuckle.

Congers said, "Who gives a good fuck."

"Come on, Vernon," said the inquisitor, "you gotta know these things. You're a high-profile guy now. Think about the fucking press. What if the press starts asking you questions? This ain't no And 1 camp, baby, this is the big-time hoops!"

Muffled, reined in, but clearly audible laughs this time. Congers's eyes were narrowing with anger.

Charles wouldn't let up. "You gotta know some geography, man! Go get a map or look at a globe or watch the History Channel or something. Whatta you tell yo' mama when she ax you where you at?"

Open laughter. Congers was now plainly furious. He glowered at Charles and then at the whole bunch of them.

"Fuck you," he said, and stormed off into the room, a small classroom in Fiske used for the basketball team's compulsory two hours of study every night after dinner.

Unrestrained eruptions of laughter. Jojo drew in his breath. He was glad he had been behind Congers's line of vision. The schadenfreude side of him enjoyed seeing his young rival ridiculed, but Charles had gone too far. He had started dogging the kid in a ghetto accent, which even Congers could tell was sheer mockery. Worst of all, Charles had brought in the subject of Congers's mother. It was only a joke, and he hadn't said anything bad about her, although come to think of it, he *had* sort of insinuated that she couldn't figure out where her own son was. Jojo was close enough to the black players to know that the subject of their mothers was touchy stuff, especially in the case of somebody like Congers. He didn't know a whole lot about Congers, but he did know that he was a fairly typical case of a boy whose mother had raised him entirely on her own, ghetto-style, in a town outside of New York City called Hempstead, if he remembered correctly. Charles, on the other hand, had grown up in a reasonably affluent suburb of Washington, D.C., and had a father who was chief of some sort of security operation at the State Department and a mother who taught English in the local school system.

Congers took a seat in a desk chair near the back, and—*whap*—slapped a loose-leaf binder on the surface of the chair's desk arm, as if terminating a fly. Boyish face and all, he was a lot bigger and stronger than Charles. He was six-nine, maybe 240 pounds, jacked, ripped, and *thick*. Charles was six-six and well built, thanks to Mad Dog the strength coach, but he was slender, with a fine-boned face, and was close to forty pounds lighter than

Congers. Jojo took note of the dimensions because Congers was so furious, he wondered if it *just might come to that* . . .

The study hall started off as usual—which is to say, unless you were deaf or had the concentration powers of a Charles Bousquet, you might as well forget about studying. The usual suspects were making fart noises, cracking jokes in stage whispers, frogging each other, launching sneak attacks using Blue Shark candy drops as missiles, or otherwise horsing around. An assistant coach, Brian Glaziano, sat in a chair near the podium, facing these student athletes, supposedly to make sure they kept their noses in the books, but he was young, white, and a hoops nonentity compared to the elite players he was assigned to preside over.

Jojo had a loose-leaf binder and a couple of textbooks with him. He sat at his desk riffling through an auto accessories catalog, daydreaming about cool ways in which he might tart up his Chrysler Annihilator. He happened to be sitting one row behind Congers and ten or twelve feet off to the side. Hearing Congers unsnap the rings on his loose-leaf binder, Jojo glanced over idly. He found himself witnessing a strange thing. Congers took a sheet of paper out of the binder—ordinary lined school paper—and stuffed it into his mouth. Then he started chewing. Must have tasted like hell, all that acid or whatever it was they put in cheap paper. Then he took out another one and started chewing that one, too . . . and then a third one . . . chewing and chewing but not swallowing. By now his cheeks were ballooned out like one of those frogs or whatever they were on those learning videos they used to make you watch in elementary school. His eyes were angry slits. The next thing Jojo knew, Congers was forcing a prodigious wad of gray mush out of his mouth and into his cupped hands. He began shaping it into a sphere, the way you'd make a snowball. Saliva and a mushy gook began oozing out between his fingers and dripping onto his lap. Then he stood up, all six feet nine of him, holding the huge mushball aloft, and he hurled it with all his might—*splat*—against the back of a shaved brown head three rows ahead of him. Charles, of course. Until that moment, since the back of one shaved brown head looked much like another, Jojo hadn't even noticed that Charles was sitting there.

Charles did nothing at first except raise his nose from his books and look straight ahead. Then, deliberately, coolly, in the Charles Bousquet fashion, still without turning around, he reached back and scraped the mush off the base of his skull with his hand and inspected it. Then he felt the neck of his

TOM WOLFE

T-shirt where the slimy pulp had soaked it. Only then did he twist about and look back.

The first person he saw was Jojo, who, transfixed, was looking him right in the face. Charles eyed him for an instant and then, apparently concluding that Jojo was a highly unlikely suspect, lasered in on Congers, who now had his head way down, practically buried in his loose-leaf binder, scribbling away with a ballpoint as if he were taking notes.

In a deep voice Charles yelled out, "Yo!"

Naturally, everybody in the room craned about to see what was going on, everybody except Congers, who still had his head down and his ballpoint squiggling like mad.

"Yo!" Charles yelled again. "Yeah, I mean *you*, ni—you moronic motherfuckin' shitfa brains!"

Charles had started to say "nigger," but he checked himself because Jojo and Mike were right there. The black players never uttered the *n*-word, not even in jest, if he, Mike, Coach, a swimmie, or any other white person was within earshot.

Congers had no choice now. There was no way he could pretend he hadn't noticed. He stood up, shoving his chair over backward with a *thwack*, and took a deep breath. His tight T-shirt was more like a film than a fabric, and his mighty pecs, delts, traps, lats seemed to pump up before your very eyes. Seething, he stared at Charles and said in a strained, constricted, strangely high-pitched voice, "Who the fuck you think—" He broke off the sentence and then said, "Motherfucker."

Whereupon he stepped out into the aisle and began walking slowly toward Charles. No professional wrestler ever looked bigger or meaner. Charles stood up and stepped out into the aisle, too. He faced Congers, took a spread-legged stance, folded his arms across his chest, cocked his head, and put his tongue in his cheek. Congers was now barely four feet from Charles. For a moment that seemed interminable to Jojo, the two of them confronted each other stock-still in a stare-down.

Then Congers pointed his forefinger at Charles, one, two, three times, not uttering a sound, before saying in the same strained, constricted voice, "Open your mouth one more time, motherfucker, and—" Once more, he didn't finish the sentence.

"And *what*, Shitfa Brains?" said Charles. He sounded gloriously bored. He didn't move a muscle. He just stood there with his arms folded across his chest and his head cocked skeptically to one side.

Congers glowered for a moment and said portentously, "*You* heard me." With which, he turned, muttering, "Motherfucker," and returned to his desk.

Not a sound in the room, not a laugh, not a chuckle, not even an *unhh unhh unhh* under the breath. Everybody, even Jojo, was too embarrassed for the big freshman, pitied him too much, to call any more attention whatsoever to the way he had tried to start something with Charles the Coolest and then backed down like a pussy.

Jojo and Mike remained aroused by the incident after they returned to their suite. The suite's common-room casement windows were open, but it was so dark outside, you couldn't even make out the library tower or the smokestacks of the power plant. Jojo sat down in an easy chair and got comfortable, but Mike began pacing back and forth. A lungful of the mere atmosphere of male physical combat can start a young man's adrenaline pumping that hard.

Mike was saying, "It was the 'moronic' and 'shitfa brains' that got him. He couldna gotten any madder over 'nigga' than he did over that. When he got up from that desk and started heading for Charles, I thought he was gonna—"

Jojo interrupted. "You know something, Mike? That fucking study hall is a farce. Studying in there is a fucking impossibility. Somebody's always horsing around or cracking jokes or making fart noises . . . and we sit there for two fucking hours doing nothing."

"Seriously," said Mike.

"And what the fuck's Charles doing in there in the first place? Coach dud'n make the swimmies go to study hall, and everybody knows Charles's grades are as good as theirs. Why make him sit there for two hours while a buncha guys throw mushballs and do fuck-all?"

"Oh ho ho." Mike chuckled ironically. "Don't you get it, Jojo? Coach don't care what the swimmies do at night, because they're not gonna be playing. They're not really part of the program. But us? Us—he wants to fill up the day so we're totally into the program and nothing else. He dud'n want Charles or anybody else just rattling around the campus at night . . . *thinking* . . . or anything counterproductive like that."

Jojo nodded pensively. Maybe Mike had a point. They got up in the dark, had breakfast in their own dining room, went over to the weight room and pumped some iron, or else went running. The only time they saw anybody else was when they went to class, and even then, who did they actually talk to? Maybe some hoochie groupie who would come over later and provide you some ass.

Into his head blipped the girl with the long brown hair, the one in the French class . . . But she was no hoochie, not that girl, and certainly no groupie. She had frozen him out from word one. *Pure!* The *purity*—that was what made her beauty unique, that and the fact that she was unobtainable. His loins stirred so, he could feel the tumescence against the fly of his jeans. Oh *God* . . . he wanted some of that . . . He had never laid eyes on her since then. True to her word, she had never turned up in Whatsisname's French class again.

". . . practice for three and a half fucking hours, and then where do we go? Back to the dining room where we see the same fucking faces—"

Jojo had become so absorbed in his sublime vision he had lost track of what Mike was talking about.

"—or maybe spending time in the fucking library writing his own papers, getting all interested in something besides basketball—"

"Oh shit!" said Jojo, thrusting his hands up, fingers spread, as if he were holding a big physioball over his head. "I totally fucking forgot. I got a paper due tomorrow."

"What in?"

"American history, that fucking guy Quat. I don't know where they ever got the idea he's an athlete-friendly professor. If he's athlete friendly, then I'm . . . I'm . . . I don't know what. What time is it?"

"About twelve."

"Shit . . . he's really gonna be pissed if I beep him now."

"Who is?"

"My history tutor, kid named Adam. But I don't see that I got any choice. Shit, I hate to do this to him. He's a nice kid . . . Thank God he's a nerdy little guy. He'll take it without breaking my fucking balls."

So he got on the telephone and beeped the nerdy little guy, and in due course the guy called back, and Jojo said he needed to see him right away.

Meantime, Mike had turned on the TV set, some sitcom, but he was already bored with it, so he prevailed upon Jojo to play a video game while he was waiting for the tutor. Jojo didn't take much persuading. Mike had a new PlayStation 3 set, and it was awesome. The images had depth and fluid motion; the sounds rose and fell just the way they should, and they had a wraparound effect, and you felt like you really were competing—football, baseball, basketball, boxing, judo, whatever—before cheering fans in some huge stadium. It was all eerily realistic. How the hell did they come up with these things? So Jojo and Mike sat down and picked up the handsets for their current favorite, which was called Stunt Biker. You were on a bicycle on a huge half-pipe, doing double, triple flips in the air and full gainers and everything else, while thousands cheered. What they both liked best about Stunt Biker were the wipeouts. If you miscalculated on your flips and crashed, you usually landed on your neck. In real life, although not on PlayStation 3, you'd be dead. Gales of laughter when your opponent broke his neck on the concrete surface of the half-pipe . . .

They became so absorbed in Stunt Biker and the cheering multitudes that God knows how much time had gone by before they realized that somebody, no doubt the tutor, was repeatedly knocking on the common-room door. Jojo got up and opened it.

"Hey, Adam!" said Jojo. He opened his arms in a gesture of welcome. The tone of his voice and the smile on his face were the sort one would ordinarily save for some dear but long-absent friend. "Come on in!"

By the looks of him, Adam the history tutor wasn't feeling nearly so cheerful about this house call.

"Adam," said Jojo, "you know my roommate, don't you, the old Microwave here?"

"Hey, how's it going?" said Mike, smiling broadly and putting out his hand.

The tutor took it with a noticeable lack of enthusiasm, said nothing, and put a look on his face that said, "Okay . . . I'm waiting."

Stunt Biker was still on the TV screen, and you could hear the yammer of the crowd waiting for more action.

The tutor seemed half as tall as Jojo and about a third as heavy, although if he stood next to ordinary students at Dupont, he would have looked neither very tall nor very short. His face had fine, almost pretty features, and he wore a pair of glasses with pin-thin titanium rims, but it was his hair that people were likely to notice. His hair was longish, with a profusion of soft dark brown curls that came down in bangs in front and a bohemian ruff in back. And he *parted* his hair—unbelievable! His baggy khakis and his black sweater, with just a T-shirt beneath it, seemed to hang rather than lie upon his frame. He seemed as delicate as Jojo was massive, and even though they were both seniors, he appeared to be much younger.

An awkward pause. Jojo realized that he had to plunge into the void.

TOM WOLFE

"Adam . . . you're gonna kill me." He averted his eyes, lowered his head, and shook it, all the while smiling as if to say, "Wouldn't you just know it?" Finally he removed the smile, looked at his tutor, and blurted out his problem.

"All right," the boy said in a measured voice, "what's this paper supposed to be about?"

"It's about . . . ummm . . . something about the Revolutionary War."

"*Something* about the Revolutionary War?"

"Yeah. Wait a second. I got it printed out." Jojo hurried into his bedroom.

By now Mike had returned to PlayStation 3 and was playing Stunt Biker solo. From time to time he said, "Oh fuck!" as he broke his neck. The crowd cheered and groaned.

Jojo returned with a printout of an e-mail, which he now scrutinized. "It says here . . . it says here . . . it says it's supposed to be about . . . Here it is: 'The personal psychology of George the Third as a catalyst of the American Revolution.' Eight to ten pages the guy wants. What's a catalyst, anyway? I've heard of the damned things but I don't really know what they are."

"Oh fuck!" said Mike, intent on the TV screen, which flared with stadium lights and hot colors.

The boy, Adam, said, "When is this due, Jojo?"

"Uhh . . . tomorrow. The class is at ten." Ingratiating smile. "I *told* you you'd kill me."

"Ten o'clock *tomorrow*? . . . Jojo!"

The way he said it allowed Jojo to relax. What did Adam the tutor amount to? He amounted to a male low in the masculine pecking order who is angry, deserves to be angry, is dying to show anger, but doesn't dare do so in the face of two alpha males, both of them physically intimidating as well as famous on the Dupont campus. Jojo had enjoyed this form of unspoken domination ever since he was twelve. It was a source of inexpressible satisfaction. Literally inexpressible. Only a complete fool would ever own up to such a feeling out loud—to anybody.

Out loud: "Yeah, I know." He feigned the sort of grimace that indicates you're disappointed in yourself. "I just like totally forgot, man. I been in study hall for two hours studying for a French test I got coming up, and I just like, you know, drew a blank on the fucking history paper."

Adam said, "Well . . . have you got any *notes*? Any *texts*?"

"Nawww . . . I think the guy said he wanted this to be a research paper or something."

"Oh—fuck—all!" said Mike. The crowd groaned louder than ever, and the screen flared with a change of background color.

A rising whine from Adam: "Jojo, do you have any idea what this is gonna involve? Researching the life of George the Third and the history of the Stamp Act and all that stuff and putting them together and writing eight or ten pages"—he looked at his wristwatch—"in the next ten hours?"

Shrugging: "I'm really sorry, man, but I got to get that paper in. The fucking guy's already on my case. Mr. Quat. He's just *waiting* for some excuse to flunk my ass."

The atmosphere was heavy with the realization that failing a course could make an athlete ineligible to play during the following semester.

The roar of the crowd swelled, and then—"Fuck! Fuck! Fuck!"—turned into a bottomless groan.

Adam stood there looking glum, and whipped. "Okay . . . give me the sheet of paper."

Jojo threw a big arm around the boy's back and shoulders and squeezed so hard he practically lifted him off his feet. "You the *man*, Adam, you the *man*! I *knew* you wouldn't let me down!"

The little tutor squirmed helplessly in Jojo's powerful grip. When Jojo relented and released him, the boy stood there for a moment with a desolate look on his face. He shook his head slowly and headed for the door. Just before he went out, he turned around and said, "By the way, a catalyst is something that precipitates—something that helps set off something else that's not directly related to it, like the way the assassination of a Serbian archduke nobody ever heard of was the catalyst for World War One. You might want to know what the word means, just in case you ever have to make somebody think you know what you've written."

Jojo didn't know what the hell he was talking about, but he did know it was supposed to be some kind of sarcastic reprimand, as close as a nerd could get to saying how totally pissed off he actually was. The alpha male smiled and said, "Hey listen, man, I'm really sorry. I appreciate the hell outta this. I owe you one."

The boy was not even all the way out the door when Jojo turned toward Mike and said, "What are all these *oh fucks*, man? You may be the microwave of treys, but you can't stunt-bike for shit."

No sooner had Adam closed the door and taken a few steps down the hall than he heard the muffled sound of Jojo and his roommate at the controls of PlayStation 3, crying out in triumph or pain and laughing . . . laughing at *him,* no doubt. The two morons would sit there playing their stupid video game, like they were twelve-year-olds, and yelling *Oh fuck* and laughing at Adam Gellin . . . while he had to hustle to the library and ransack some source material, cobble together some notes, and stay up all night turning out 2,500 or 3,000 words that would read like something a cretin such as Jojo Johanssen might conceivably have written. Actually, Jojo wasn't all that stupid. He just refused to use his head, as a matter of principle. It was sad. It was worse than sad. It was pathetic. Jojo was a brute, but he was also a weakling who didn't dare violate the student-athlete code, which decreed that it was uncool to act in any way like a student. For that reason, he, Adam, was doomed to an all-nighter, while Jojo put in a few more vacuous hours in front of the TV screen and slept the sleep of the child who knows everything he needs will be there when he wakes up in the morning.

Adam's face began to burn with anger and humiliation. Goddamn it! The smug, heavy-handed way the big lout had acted happy to see him . . . the utterly transparent simulation of contrition, when he had undoubtedly known for a long time that this paper would be due tomorrow . . . the way he had put his arm around him in a sickeningly fake show of camaraderie . . . *You the man!* . . . Goddamn that muscle-bound sonofabitch! He had grabbed him and lifted him off the floor as if he owned his very hide! "You the man"—and what he was really saying was, "You're not a *man* at all! You're my servant! You're my little slavey boy! I *own* your ass!"

A great muffled yawp of manly laughter from behind. Jojo and his roommate were laughing at him! Couldn't contain themselves! Adam scurried back on tiptoe and stood outside the door to their suite. They were laughing again!—but it turned out they were laughing about Vernon Congers and how Charles kept teasing him, and Congers hadn't a clue about how to deal with it. All right, so they weren't laughing at slavey boy . . . at that moment . . . Nevertheless, Adam trudged along the hallway, head down, thinking of all the devastating remarks he should have obliterated the giant with. He had long ago come to terms, at least on a rational level, with the master-servant aspect of the job. For that matter, not every athlete he tutored acted superior. A few were grateful the way any needy child might be or should be, in which case a traditional teacher-pupil relationship existed, and the psychic rewards were his. In any event, the three hundred dollars a month he was paid for this service was crucial to his existence at Dupont, as was the approximately one hundred a month—all of it in tips, none in wages—he made delivering pizza, mainly to students' rooms, for a franchise operation called PowerPizza. Of course, delivering pizza for tips created a master-servant relationship, too, but these days, students and young people generally shrank from being anything but egalitarian in their dealings with the working poor.

No matter which job he was working at, he had to make a trade-off. The downside of delivering pizza was that it was mindlessly repetitive, and your time wasn't flexible. Whenever you worked the job, you were committed to a six-hour stretch. In tutoring athletes, you had to submit to the egos of large, stupid people who could summon you by beeper anytime they felt like it, and you had to accept the fact that you were abetting an institutional farce known as "the student-athlete." On the other hand, the work was varied and occasionally interesting, you could do much of it on your own time . . . and your dim-witted charges were in some way dependent upon you, regardless of how they behaved.

A little farther down the hall, he could hear, coming from behind the door he was just passing, an old Tupac Shakur CD going full blast—the classic track, the song about his mother . . . That would be the freshman hotshot Vernon Congers, whose room looked like a Tupac Shakur shrine—two entire walls papered with photographs of that legendary martyr of the rap music wars. Adam had substituted for one of Congers's regular tutors once. He passed another door, which was open a few inches . . . Fireball movie sounds and a male voice saying, "Treyshawn, just between you and me, I don't play 'at shit. You know what I'm saying?" Ah, yes, Treyshawn "the Tower" Diggs . . . Inside the suite opposite it, two males were laughing, and a female was squealing in mock denigration, "Curtis, you a *girl's* what *you* are!" Louder squeal: "Keep yo' hands offa me, you old nancy!" . . . Curtis Jones. Adam kept on walking . . . From behind that door, this door, this door, that door, came the unmistakable cracking sound of opposing forces colliding in video games. Ah, the hallway symphony of the basketball greats, the living legends at their midnight ease. Adam smiled. But fuck! "The personal psychology of George the Third as a catalyst of the American Revolution" . . . for a brick skull that didn't contain a clue as to what "catalyst" meant . . .

T
O
M

W
O
L
F
E

Far from being quiet at midnight, the historic Charles Dupont Memorial Library was humming. The rustle of many people in motion—plus the occasional sharp, piping chirp of sneakers on the great stone floor—echoed off the vaulted arches of the main hall. So grand and so gloomy, the cavernous space swallowed up the light from the chandeliers and rendered it feeble. Nevertheless, the hall and the huge computer cluster off to this side and the vast reading room off to that side and the circulation and reference desks up there were alive with students. Many undergraduates never began doing homework until midnight, and there were always plenty of them still at it when the sun rose. Dupont Memorial never closed. Staying up until two, three, or four a.m., weekdays included, was part of the conventional, if eccentric, cycle of student life at Dupont.

Two girls, chattering away in hushed voices while glancing this way and that, walked right across Adam's path. Whatever they were looking for, it wasn't him. Both had on eye makeup, lip gloss, and earrings. One wore a low-cut, lacy peignoir-sort-of top, the other wore a tight T-shirt, and both were deeply cloven behind by tight jeans. None of this was remarkable except that these girls were *totally* slutted up. Many girls got dressed up to go over to the library at midnight for the simple reason that boys would be there.

The sight roused within Adam a familiar, smug feeling of superiority. So many students treated Dupont as an elite playground where they played for four years with bright and, for the most part, wellborn people like themselves . . . while he and a small Gideon's army, most of whom he knew personally, were here at Dupont as "Millennial Mutants"—his friend Greg Fiore's term—who would . . .

Another surge of anger. Long after Jojo Johanssen and his ilk had been reduced to pissing away the remainder of their lives sitting on the curb somewhere drinking malt liquor out of brown paper bags, Adam Gellin and his confreres would—

—would *what? Poof.* All his superiority vanished in an instant, *just like that,* as if it had never been anything but air in the first place. Jojo could get laid anytime he felt like it. He had only to step outside onto the campus and point. Jojo had expressed it to him just that way once—"and point"—and Adam believed him. Whatever else he was, Jojo wasn't boastful. He had described actual examples. He thought it was funny. One had stuck in Adam's mind. Jojo had finished a class and was walking across the Yard, not even thinking about any such thing, when he saw an athletic-looking blonde in a tennis outfit, a tall, slender girl with "these long legs and buff shoulders and tits like *this*"—he had cupped his hands to indicate the size and where on the torso they were placed—hustling toward the tennis courts where she and a friend had booked a court, and he just stepped in her way and came on to her, and ten minutes later they were in his room slogging away at it. It was simple as that if you were a basketball star. And that girl's voice in Curtis's room—she wasn't in there to ask him for a basketball ticket. Adam wheeled about and took a second look at the girls in the tight jeans. Both these little midnight scholars would get themselves laid within the hour. He could be sure about that. Sex! Sex! It was in the air along with the nitrogen and the oxygen! The whole campus was humid with it! tumid with it! lubricated with it! gorged with it! tingling with it! in a state of around-the-clock arousal with it! *Rutrutrutrutrutrutrutrutrut*—

He tried to visualize how many of Dupont's 6,200 students were rutting away at it at this very moment, visualize in the sense of being able to see through walls and spot the two-backed beasts herkyjerky humping bang-bangbang . . . up *there*, in that bedroom in Lapham—*there*, in that room in Carruthers—up *there*, on the floor of that empty seminar room in Giles—over *there*, in the euonymus shrubbery because, bursting with lust, they couldn't make it all the way back to a bedroom—and *there*, up against a locked rear door on the other side of the tower, because doing it where they might get caught gave it a fetishistic kick they couldn't resist—and here was himself, Adam Gellin, so superior in so many excellent ways . . . and a virgin. A senior at Dupont and still a virgin. Even in his own thoughts he said it softly. It was a failing he was desperate that the world not know of. The whole campus was rutting away like dogs in the park, and he remained a virgin. As soon as he could, at the end of his sophomore year, he had moved out of Carruthers College, away from roommates for good, and into a squalid little apartment off campus—nothing more than a slot for humans created when two ordinary bedrooms in a rotting nineteenth-century town house were converted to four "apartments," all using one bathroom out in the hall—rather than have others gradually come to realize . . . there was something wrong with him—namely, a bad case of virginity—and now it was getting terribly late, because he knew nothing about it . . . and he would be perfectly inept—he *felt* it—and whatever he could do wrong, he would do wrong—nervous impotence, premature ejaculation—and how did they

T
O
M

W
O
L
F
E

manage to stop just *before* . . . and put on the condom in some suave way—did it require a joke?—would just unsheathing the damned thing and touching the tip of his dong with it cause him to ejaculate?—

Damn. The library catalog computer cluster was mobbed. There were some twenty computers arranged in a horseshoe behind a low retaining wall of oak carved with High Gothic tracery, and he had to locate some volumes of British and American history, and all those computer screens glowing with twenty-first-century electronic jaundice behind grand fourteenth-century flourishes of conspicuous wood-sculptural waste were occupied. But wait a minute—in the very back corner, hard to spot, a screen with nobody sitting in front of it. He began speed-walking toward the cluster. If it wouldn't have looked so totally dorky, he would have made a run for it. Barely fifteen feet away when—*Shit!*—a girl with long brown hair, looked like a kid, came in from the side and went straight to that one last screen.

His mind spun. He couldn't afford to be his passive, play-by-the-rules self, not this time. Besides, the girl looked so young. Unless his judgment was seriously off, she would be the sweet, pliant type who gives way to avoid friction. He entered the bull pen. It was packed with the hunched-over backs of students clattering away on the keyboards. The glow of the screens gave their faces a sickly dry-ice pallor. Resolute, he marched up to the girl, who was already seated, and said:

"Excuse me, but I was getting ready to use that one"—he gestured toward the screen—"when you cut in front of me, and I mean, I've *got* to use it." He spoke as sternly as he could. "I've got a paper due in the morning. How about letting me use it for just a minute? Okay? Do you mind? How about it?"

He stood right over the girl. Stern insistence; no smile. She looked up at him warily, a touch of fear in her eyes, studied his face, deliberated, and finally managed to say in a frightened little voice, "Yes."

"Grrrrreat! Thanks! Hey, I really appreciate it." He let his face soften for the first time.

The girl hesitated again and then said in the same small voice, "I meant yes I *do* mind."

She didn't move, she didn't change her expression, and he couldn't stare her down. Her big blue eyes were fixed on his face. She wouldn't budge.

It was he who wilted, as a flood of impressions swept over him all at once. The way she pronounced the *i* in *I* and *mind—Iiii meant yes Iiii do miiind—*a flat, drawn-out way that made him think of one of those Southern racial-conflict-turned-racial-amity movies where everybody sings "Amazing

Grace" at the end. She wasn't pliant, wouldn't yield in the slightest, and she was beautiful in a way he wasn't used to seeing, not in the slutty atmosphere of Turning Boys On at Dupont. She had an absolutely clear, open, guileless beauty. A graceful neck, big wondering eyes, no earrings, no eye makeup, no lip gloss—and such perfectly formed, untouched lips they were! Virginal . . . that was the only word for this sort of face. And she wouldn't give an inch.

It was he who became pliant. "Well . . ." He lapsed into a weak, ingratiating smile. "Okay if I just stand here and wait till you're through?"

The girl said, "All right." Came out *allriot.*

"Thanks. I promise I won't *hover* or anything." Bigger ingratiating smile. "By the way, I'm Adam."

6. THE MOST ORDINARY PROTOCOL

About eleven o'clock the next night, Charlotte happened to be standing by the window in her pajamas and bathrobe, taking a break from medieval history, when a round of shrieks and manly laughs erupted in the courtyard below. Not that there was anything unusual about that; various adolescent cries were part of the ambient sound of Little Yard. But this time she peered down and searched the darkness. There had been a shower earlier, and the ground gave off a damp, ionized smell. Was it just girls *and* boys or girls *with* boys? She wanted to see them, but the lamps on the perimeter of the courtyard and the light from the windows across the way were hopeless against the gloom.

Now the cries were echoing in the big tunnel-like corridor that led from the courtyard out to the street. It definitely sounded like girls *with* boys. Moreover, they were *leaving*, going out, and it was eleven p.m. on a Thursday. What easy, sly, glib, coquettish charm did you have to have? She thought of the blond giant, who she had since learned was some sort of celebrated basketball player. She could still see the way the veins wrapped around his huge forearms. He was so sure of himself, and he had wanted her to go with him somewhere . . . The boy last night in the library, the one who was so rude and hostile one minute and suddenly came on to her the next—

there was nothing frightening about him, and he wasn't bad-looking, but he seemed so devious. He was totally manipulative and opportunistic.

She remained standing by the window, imagining she could still hear the songs of other students' happiness heading off into the unimaginable world of "going out." Her pity for herself knew no bounds . . . no longer had any home whatsoever . . . just a tiny room poisonous with the scorn of a tall, skinny, sarcastic, snobbish Groton girl who wouldn't be caught dead having a normal conversation with some nobody of a country girl from the Blue Ridge Mountains . . . a bathroom where she could find only the opposite of privacy . . . the intrusion . . . the vulgar affront! . . . of bands of adolescent boys who gloried in the noxious noises and smells of bowel movements— *gloried* in them!—groaned, strained audibly, sighed ostentatiously with satisfaction, laughed at basso pig-bladdery blasts from the rectum and things that went *plop* or *poot*, and shouted running commentaries glorifying their own adolescent grossness.

She turned away from the window and became aware of the happy, noisy—drunken?—traffic of boys and girls in the hallway outside her door. She could hear the simpleminded chords and percussion of a CD somebody was playing too loud . . . Well, they could all go on living from impulse to impulse. Self-discipline was one of the things that had always made Charlotte Simmons . . . Charlotte Simmons . . . that, and her power of concentration. She had a medieval history test in the morning, and it was time to return to her desk for a final thirty minutes over the pages of *Blue-eyed Bondage: Caucasian Chattel Slavery in Northern Europe in the Early Middle Ages*.

Could have been lively, this book . . . the part about how Welshmen were sold as slaves on the Dublin slave market, so many, in fact, that the Old English word for slave was *walsea*—Welshman—just as the word *slave* came from the *Slavs* the Germans routinely kidnapped and pressed into forced labor . . . but it was so pedantic . . . lying there on the desk under her nose reflecting light, thanks to the cheap, slick paper university publishers printed pedantic books on . . . on . . . on the other hand they had singled her out on their own . . . No matter what they were like, the blond giant and the darkhaired conniver, they *had* been attracted, hadn't they, they *had* noticed something about her . . . and they liked it . . . But why kid herself? Two wholly accidental encounters lasting a few blinks of the eye . . . What on earth could they do for a girl who was *so lonely*!

"Ohmygod, ohmygod . . . Seriously . . . *Me?* . . . Me, I wouldn't give him the satisfaction . . ." A girl's voice just outside the door—Beverly.

The door opened, and in she came. As usual, she had her head cocked, the cell phone at her ear, and her eyes cast down and to the side toward some point in midair that didn't exist. Walking in behind her was another girl, a blonde. Quite striking she was, thanks to her fine square jaws. Without really looking at Charlotte, Beverly flashed a smile and gave a distracted wave by way of acknowledging her roommate's presence by the window. She removed her lips from the cell phone just long enough to gesture behind her at the blonde and say, "Charlotte . . . Erica," whereupon she sat her skin and bones down on the edge of her bed and poured herself back into the little black device.

"Hi," Charlotte said to the girl, Erica. Vaguely she recalled the Amorys talking about an Erica who had been a year ahead of Beverly at Groton.

"Hello," said the girl in a clipped, perfunctory fashion. She gave Charlotte a wide, flat, dead smile, then ran her eyes over Charlotte's plaid bathrobe, pajamas, and slippers . . . slippers, pajamas, and bathrobe. That done, she turned her attention to Beverly and never looked at Charlotte again.

Beverly was saying into the device, "I mean, I was sitting at this table at the I.M. with Harrison and this other lacrosse player who's a Phi Gam and some girl named Ellen, and I had on my low-cut Diesels? And I happened to look down, and *eeeyew*, my ass—it was like I just gave birth! It was like my waist had this tube the size of a garter snake around it—and you're the one who's always telling me, 'Oh, go ahead! One slice of chocolate cake won't kill you.' I had this little . . . *tube*—and *my ass!*"

Erica emitted a short burst of laughter and said, "Ohmygod, Beverly, the day you get a big ass—"

Beverly said into the cell phone, "That was Erica. She thinks I'm joking . . . Come on, I'd be honest with *you* . . . What? Him? I know you're only trying to change the subject, but did I tell you he wanted to hook up in this little sports car he has? It's got two seats with all this manual shift shit sticking up in between—"

The square-jawed blonde chuckled, sighed, covered her eyes with her hands, said, "Ohmygod," and pulled faces.

"I'm glad it was dark in the I.M., anyway," Beverly was saying. "I mean, whatta I do about my fucking waist? . . . Hahhh! You always say that. I wish I *was* skinny."

The friend, Erica, laughed and laughed. She never looked at Charlotte to get her reaction to all this, not even once.

"I'll *be* there!" Beverly was saying. "But can I borrow the prick-tease shirt? . . . The one that's open down the front. It'd make me look like I've got boobs."

Charlotte was plunged into consternation, four or five kinds of it. Beverly's language shocked her. She had heard her use the occasional expletive, usually *Oh shit,* once or twice an *Oh fuck,* but she had never heard her go on and on in this completely smutty fashion like . . . like . . . like *Regina Cox,* only worse. The sheer sexual bluntness shocked her. The fact that she would blithely say such things in front of other people shocked her. The fact that her friend Erica, far from being shocked, thought it was hilarious shocked her. And the fact that neither of them deigned to bestow so much as a flick of the eye upon her throughout this extraordinarily vulgar cell phone performance—somehow that made it worse. For a moment she felt that the whole awkward situation must be her own fault. The very fact that she existed in this room had become an unfathomable embarrassment. How could she remain standing here by the window, watching and listening to two girls who ignored her?

Neither gave her so much as a glance as she went to her desk and sat down. She resumed reading *Blue-eyed Bondage.* Or rather, staring at it; she couldn't very well keep her mind off the two girls, who were barely three feet behind her, talking and laughing.

Beverly had at last snapped her cell phone shut and was declaring, "I have nothing to wear."

Out of the corner of her eye Charlotte could see that she had her fists on her hips. Then she opened a bureau drawer and slammed it shut.

"I have . . . *nothing to wear!*"

"I think I'm gonna have to cry, Bev," said Erica.

Beverly began sighing and going through more drawers and then her closet. Erica seemed to find all this immensely amusing.

"Well, I guess it's not the end of the world," said Beverly.

"Oh, no, Bev, it totally *is* the end of the world."

They chattered away. Charlotte tried to tune out, but she heard Erica saying, "That's not Sarc Three, Bev, that's only Sarc Two. I mean, it's almost as obvious as Sarc One. I can't believe they let you out of Groton without passing Sarc. Sarc One is when I look at you, and I say, 'Ohmygod, a *cerise* *shirt. Cerise is such an *in color* this year.'* That's just ordinary intentionally obvious sarcasm. Okay?"

"You really don't like this shirt, do you?" said Beverly.

"Oh, please give me a fucking break, Bev! I'm just giving you an example. I'm trying to enlighten you, and you—touchy, touchy, touchy. Now . . . in Sarc Two you say the same thing, only in a sympathetic voice that sounds like totally sincere. 'Oh, wow, Bev, I love that color. *Cerise*. That's like so-o-o-o cool. *Unnhhh* . . . no wonder it's so like . . . *in* this year.' By the time you get to the 'so *in* this year,' your voice is dripping with so much syrup and like . . . sincerity, it finally dawns on the other person that she's getting fucked over. What you've really been saying is that you *don't* love the color, you *don't* think it's cool, and it's *not* 'in' this year. It's the delay in it dawning on her that makes it hurt. Okay?"

"And you're sure you're just being nice and giving me an example?" said Beverly.

"I'm sure you're going bitchcakes on me, be-atch. That's what I'm sure of. If you don't cool it, I'm not going to explain Sarc Three to you."

Silence.

"Okay. In Sarc Three you make the delay even longer, so it *really* hurts when she finally gets it. We've got the same situation. The girl's getting ready to go out, and she has on this cerise shirt. She thinks it's really sexy, a real turn-on, and she's gonna score big-time. You start off sounding straight—you know, flattering, but like not laying it on too thick. You're like, 'Wow, Bev, I love that *shirt*. Where'd you get it? How perfect is *that*? It's so *versatile*. It'll be perfect for job interviews, and it'll be perfect for community service.'" The very thought made Erica laugh.

Beverly said, "Hah hah. You sure that's not Sarc Four—and you're just fucking with me??"

Erica laughed and laughed. "Bev, I love you—you're totally paranoid!"

"I'm taking this shirt off," said Beverly.

"If you take that shirt off, I'm gonna—Bev, that's an awesome shirt, and you know it."

Charlotte flushed with anger. Ignorant snobs! Beverly's square-faced Erica had said a single word to her—a single, curt hello—and then treated her as if she were invisible. *Just like that,* she knew why. Beverly had told her friend ahead of time that her roommate was a person of no significance. Hence the bare-minimal hello and the dead smile. And who did they think *they* were? Charlotte had an idea of who they *thought* they were. By now she knew what Beverly had actually meant when she said, the day they met, that she had gone to "high school in Groton, Massachusetts." Groton was the name of a high school, but it was no high school in the sense that a Charlotte Simmons thought of a high school. It was a private school, so fancy, so prestigious it needed no descriptive appendage after its name. It was enough to say "Groton," and students didn't just "go" there, they boarded there, away from home.

Beverly Amory of Groton didn't "room" with Charlotte Simmons of Alleghany High School, either. She put up with her. She was never unpleasant. In fact, she was always cheerful, in her distant fashion. She conversed with her only about impersonal subjects, such as the cost of cell phone service. Even then she was vague about it; obviously somebody else took care of the bill. Charlotte wasn't about to humiliate herself by asking or coaxing or trying to steer Beverly into sharing this year at Dupont with her on a more comradely level. She had thrived alone in Sparta, and she could thrive alone here. The invincible truth was, *she possessed a brilliance unparalleled here or anywhere else.* The day would come, in due course, when Beverly and the cold fish with her would look up to Charlotte Simmons in awe and berate themselves for not having made friends with her *when they had the chance.* And when that day came, she would — cut — them — dead.

While Charlotte stared at *Blue-eyed Bondage* and seethed, Beverly changed clothes rapidly. Charlotte could hear her groaning and saying *Oh shit* and breathing hard. The room became brighter. Beverly must have turned on her vanity mirror. There was a waft of perfume.

Presently Charlotte was aware that Beverly was standing just behind her.

"Well, Charlotte, bye-bye."

Charlotte looked up. Beverly had done something amazing with her face. Mauve-purple shading and pencil liner and mascara or something made her eyes stand out like two big jewels. At the same time, she had somehow whitened the creases below the lower lids. Her lips were their natural color, but they glistened. Charlotte couldn't imagine how she had done it, but she looked *sexy* and, more than that, *provocative.* Erica was finally deigning to gaze upon Charlotte . . . benevolently, the way you might bestow a moment's attention upon some deserving urchin.

"Have a good time," said Charlotte. *Tiiiime.* She said it without a trace of a smile or a note of goodwill. No doubt the resentment showed on her face.

She should have been cool about it, of course, and acted breezily congenial, but she couldn't begin to summon up the artful hypocrisy required to do it.

As the pair went through the door, Charlotte could see Erica leaning in toward Beverly's ear and moving her square jaws. No doubt she was whispering, "What's *her* problem?"

After they had gone, Charlotte got up from the desk and headed back toward the window to catch them laughing at her expense as they went out into the courtyard. But why lacerate herself like that? She stopped and stood there in the middle of the room instead, staring at Beverly's vanity mirror, which was still on. Where were they going at this hour? Who would they see? Boys . . . and what would Beverly talk to boys about? Her *ass*? Would she talk that same way to boys? And to think that one of the bonuses, supposedly, of being so brilliant as to be admitted to Dupont was that I, Charlotte Simmons, will now ascend forever above the cheap, sordid, vulgar milieu and aimless vices of the Regina Coxes and the Channing Reeveses. What exactly did Beverly expect to achieve with a cerise silk shirt open down to *there*?

Charlotte went over to Beverly's vanity mirror and studied her face under its hot little lights. Then she went to Beverly's closet and opened the door and studied herself in Beverly's full-length mirror. She wasn't merely smarter than Beverly, she was prettier. There was something emaciated about Beverly . . . There was something . . . sick . . . about all of Beverly.

Charlotte returned to the desk and took another look at *Blue-eyed Bondage*. It was either that or contend with the juvenile noxiousness and pseudo-macho foul mouths of the privileged late-teenage American males in the courtyard below and the hallway outside . . . and the bathroom down the hall.

Upside down she was, way down here, a band of light across the ceiling, and something had her by the shoulder, shaking it, shaking it—

"Charlotte! Charlotte! Charlotte!" Barely above a whisper, but it wouldn't stop.

Charlotte turned her head toward it and tried to prop herself up on one elbow. A wall of light streamed through a crack in the doorway and backlit the thin, bony silhouette leaning over her.

"Charlotte! Wake up! Wake up! You gotta do me a favor!" The low, urgent voice of a close confidante. Beverly.

Charlotte managed to raise herself on both elbows. She groaned and tried to adjust her eyes to the light and make sense of things. "What time is it?"

Same low, intimate voice, as if they were the very closest of roommates: "Two, two-thirty, I don't know. It's not late. I need a big, big favor from you." Billows of alcohol.

"I was sleeping," said Charlotte. It was a complaint, but she realized it came out sounding like merely a foggy statement of the obvious.

"I know, and I'm really sorry, but you gotta help me just this one time, Charlotte." Now Beverly was massaging her shoulder, the one she had just been shaking. "Just this *one time*," she said. "I promise I'll never ask you again, I promise." Her voice was so *urgent*.

Charlotte remained propped up on her elbow, stupefied, hypnopompic. "One time . . . what?"

The same hushed, urgent tone: "There's this guy—Harrison—*please* don't let me down. I really, really like him. Ever since we got here—*you* know what I mean, Charlotte!"

Beverly had sunk to her knees by the bed, so that her head was almost even with Charlotte's. Billows and billows of alcohol. Her eyes seemed enormous . . . ablaze in the sockets of a skull. Charlotte turned away.

"Charlotte!"

Charlotte looked at her roommate again. The shaft of light from the hallway made her dizzy. It came from directly behind Beverly and created brilliant highlights on the shoulders of her silk shirt. The shirt was scarcely buttoned at all.

"I need to bring him up here. I really do. You've gotta, gotta, *gotta* help me out! How about sleeping somewhere else? Just this one time? I *promise* I'll never ask you to do this again. *Charlotte!*" Beverly closed her eyes, thrust her chin upward, stretching out her neck, brought her fists up beside her cheeks, and shook them in the vibrating gesture that is supposed to convey desperate supplication among chums.

Bewildered: "I have a *test* tomorrow!"

"You can sleep next door, in Joanne and Hillary's room! They have a futon."

"How? I hardly even know them!"

"*I* know them. They'll understand. People do it all the time."

"I have a test! I need to sleep!"

Beverly turned her head aside and went *Unnhhhh!* in a way that made clear her astonishment that anyone on this earth could be so dense and un-

T
O
M

W
O
L
F
E

cooperative, so ignorant of the most ordinary protocol. Then she looked Charlotte in the eye and, in a voice that indicated she was doing her very best to keep her temper in check, said to her, "Charlotte, listen to me. You're not gonna lose any sleep. You'll lie down on that futon, and you won't be awake three seconds. *Please*. Do I have to *beg* you? It's not a big thing. I gotta have the room. Come . . . *on*, Charlotte! Can't you do this one little thing for me? I'd do it for *you*."

Charlotte could feel her willpower weakening. She was so groggy. Beverly was drunk, but she had somehow established the notion, by the *way* she put it rather than what she said, that to refuse such a request was to expose yourself as ignorant of the most elementary etiquette—or else stubborn or even spiteful, a willful violator of the unwritten rules of life among college women.

Charlotte pushed herself up to a sitting position. She knew she should say no, she knew there was no reason why she should give up a night's sleep on the eve of a test in a difficult course, give up her very bed—yet she heard herself saying, "Whose futon is it? I don't know either one of them." With that, of course, she had already given in.

"Hillary's, I think," said Beverly, rushing to reinforce her advantage. "Ask Hillary, but it won't matter. Hillary—Joanne—but ask Hillary. They'll like totally understand, either one."

Slowly, dizzily, and with the sinking feeling that she had just suffered a great defeat through sheer inability to stand her ground, Charlotte slid her legs off the bed, fished about for her slippers with her feet, and wriggled into her bathrobe.

"All you have to do is knock on the door," said Beverly. "Hillary's like totally awesome, she's so great about everything. She'll do anything for anybody, she's so great—" The hushed words gushed out in a flood aimed at sweeping her wavering roommate right out the door.

Which they did. Without knowing how it happened, Charlotte found herself out in the hall, petrified at the thought of knocking on the door of somebody she barely knew at two-thirty or whatever it was in the morning. This Hillary had never struck Charlotte as the charitable type. She had a shrill voice and such an affected accent that Charlotte had thought she must be from England or something. In fact, she was from New York City, and about every time Charlotte had ever heard her say anything, she had worked the phrase "at St. Paul's" into the conversation. St. Paul's, Charlotte had deduced, was a boarding school much like Groton.

Charlotte stood there for a moment, trying to work up some courage and despising herself for being weak. Somewhere down the hall a monotonous, drawling rap CD—"Yo', you take my testi-culls . . . Suck 'em like a popsi-cull"—not terribly loud but loud enough to hear out here in the hall. She looked this way and that, halfway expecting to see the boy, the one Beverly was so eager for. Instead, here came two boys and three girls, laughing as if fun couldn't get any more intense. One of the boys kept saying in a put-on deep voice, "Your ego's writing checks your body can't cash, your ego's writing checks your body can't cash." Laughter, laughter, laughter. When they saw Charlotte standing there, they grew quiet. As they came by, they looked her up and down. Bathrobe, full set of pajamas, snuggy slippers . . . After they passed, one of the boys said, "Oh-kaaaayyyy," and they all started laughing again.

The laughter, the mockery of that *Oh-kaaaayyyy*, struck Charlotte in her very solar plexus and invaded her body, her very neural pathways. She had just suffered a *catastrophic defeat* without fighting back. She had let herself be thrown out of her own bed, her own room, and that was all she had at the eminent Dupont, a bed in one half of a miserable room. All she had left now were the pajamas, slippers, and bathrobe she had on to cover her naked body—and somehow they made her an object of ridicule by total strangers. Charlotte Simmons! Her own name cried out inside her skull. *Nothing!* All that was . . . *Charlotte Simmons* . . . had been scoured out, and all that was left was this . . . this . . . this husk . . . dead but too helpless to fall down the way it should . . . it stands here to be mocked! *Utter defeat* . . . a feeling that immediately gave way to a desperate loneliness . . . not mere emotion but a condition, an affliction . . . Lethe! Oblivion! Not one soul to turn to—

—which left Hillary, next door, whom she didn't even know. She took a deep breath and approached the door of 514. She took another breath, hesitated, and then knocked. Nothing. She knocked harder. From within, a boy's voice said, apparently to somebody else in there, "Who the fuck is *that?*"

Dismay—but she didn't know what else to do. She put her mouth close to the door. Softly: "Hillary, Hillary." Nothing. Whispery but much louder: "Hillary! Hillary!" Nothing. "It's Charlotte! From next door! Beverly's roommate! I need—"

"Go away!"

That was Hillary. There was no mistaking that voice. She didn't sound like the awesome person Beverly had described, the one who would do anything for anybody, but what alternative was there? "Hillary—please, can I—"

"I said GO AWAY!"

The boy was saying, "Who the fuck *is* that?"

Charlotte couldn't believe it. She was stranded out in the hall, and she had a medieval history test in the morning. Crone was a very exacting professor. She had to get some *sleep*, but where?

"Yo, take my johnson . . . Knock it on some fox's box, my cock, sucker, I'm the fucker you forgot . . ." The CD rapper droned on.

She abandoned 514 and stood in front of 512. Wait a minute. Two guys lived in 512. She moved on to 510. Two girls lived in there. She didn't even know their names. But what else was there to do? She knocked on the door. Nothing. Please, God! She knocked louder. She knocked still louder. Nothing. She turned the doorknob and pushed gently. The door wasn't locked. She pushed it open far enough to stick her head in. A slice of light entered the room. A girl groaned and turned over. There was a girl asleep on each bed, and there was one on a futon on the floor. Charlotte recognized her. It was Joanne, Hillary's roommate. Obviously Hillary had forced Joanne out the same way Beverly had forced *her* out. Charlotte was conscious of her heart rattling away in her rib cage. She was beside herself. She had a *test* in the morning—and no place to go, no place to sleep. She was stranded out in a hallway in her nightclothes at two-thirty a.m., all because somehow another girl's desire to bring a boy up to the room in the middle of the night took precedence over everything else.

Where could she go to even get off her feet? The R.A., Ashley . . . It was two-thirty, but that was what R.A.'s existed for, wasn't it—to help?

In the elevator on the way down, she tried to think of how she might put it, and the truth of the matter hit her. She could see Ashley's wild hair and the thong panties lying on the floor. What a naïve little child Ashley must have thought her to be! With the straightest of faces Ashley had led her to believe that there would be no alcohol in Edgerton, because that was the regulation. Sex? No problem, since "dormcest" was looked down upon. She had sent her on her way relieved and even more clueless than when she arrived. She could see Ashley holding forth with such aplomb that first day in the Common Room on the ground floor . . . smiling so reassuringly at all her anxious young charges. She could see all the freshmen of Edgerton House, eager for the lowdown on life at Dupont, huddled together on the leather couches and chairs that had been shoved together in a great semicircle. Barely three weeks ago it was, and already that little show seemed so cynical. To ask Ashley about anything at this point would be a humiliation.

Well, Charlotte thought as the elevator reached the ground floor, at least there's the Common Room. She would have someplace to lie down while she despised herself for her innocence and her weakness in giving in to Beverly's sudden, besotted, utterly phony posture of friendship and intimacy.

In the Common Room, the couches and easy chairs were back at their appointed posts beneath the glum light of three big medieval-type wooden chandeliers, along with an array of dark wooden tables and straight-backed chairs.

Charlotte scanned the room. In the middle, amid this sea of furniture, a pair of enormous old couches upholstered in chestnut-brown leather were backed up, one on this side, one on the other, against a long, heavy old dark wooden library table, lit by a pair of tall but dim old Arts and Crafts lamps. In this gloomy, elephantine cluster of furniture sat the only three souls Charlotte could spy. At the far end of one couch sat a girl with her chunky legs crossed, reading a paperback book. On the other couch, a slender girl, her back to Charlotte, sat on the edge of a seat cushion, leaning forward, talking in a low voice to a slender boy who was leaning toward her from the edge of the armchair. Both wore T-shirts and blue jeans.

The girl reading the book—what on earth was *she* wearing? Apparently nothing but a floppy T-shirt and a pair of plaid boxer shorts, the kind boys wore. Not only that, the fly was popped open from the way her legs were crossed. Charlotte couldn't imagine a girl just sitting like that in a public place, not even at two-thirty in the morning. It was bad enough having to be here in pajamas and a bathrobe.

She decided to sit far from all three, somewhere deep in the Middle Gothic recesses of the Common Room. She started walking that way—but her body wouldn't obey. It was as if something independent of rational motor control was taking command. The new commander had had enough of isolation, enough scouring loneliness, and refused to venture beyond the settlement before her, with its plush leather, its ancient hand-carved wood, the snug light of its olden lamps, and its human beings.

But not even the commander could make her actually approach a human and strike up a conversation, and so she sat in a chair at the other end of the couch from the chunky girl with the open fly. True, this put her opposite the couple in the blue jeans, but there was the depth of both huge couches plus the width of the table plus the fact that both were leaning forward from the edges of their seats seemingly engrossed in each other . . . to make her feel properly distanced from them.

T
O
M

W
O
L
F
E

The chunky girl with the open fly glanced up at her from the depths of the couch as Charlotte sat down in the chair, but she immediately returned to her book. Her book . . . reading her book—Charlotte felt an overwhelming need to not appear to be some hopeless refugee adrift in the dead of the night, not even to these three young strangers. Now it was essential to be busy at something, which is to say, anything.

She looked about . . . At the end of the table, near her, was a magazine. Blushing—actually feeling the rush of blood to her face—for fear one of them would notice that she was so desperate as to start reading anything she could lay hands on, she got up, put one knee on the seat of the couch, reached way over and picked up the magazine, and hurried back to her chair.

Only then did she notice the title: *Cosmopolitan*. Charlotte had heard of the magazine, and had the impression it had been around a long time, but she had never read it. It wasn't in the Alleghany High library, and she had certainly never bought it. The price on the cover was $3.99, and that wasn't for a year's subscription. That was for this *one issue*. She had never seen *any* slick magazine in their house at home. Who was going to go out and pay *four dollars* for a magazine? On the cover a blond girl with big eyes was smiling at her in a friendly way. There were headlines all over the cover. The biggest one said, "99 SEXY WAYS TO TOUCH HIM. These Fresh, Frisky Tips Will Thrill Every Inch of Your Guy (Our Favorite Requires a Glazed Doughnut)." Couldn't possibly mean what it suggested. She riffled through the magazine, which was very thick, until she found it . . . "You want to be his best *ever*. And that's a goal we can definitely get behind. So get ready to step up and assume your rightful title of sex deity. After consulting some eager experts (gorgeous guys with loose lips and tons of sex-rated secrets to spill), we have 99 of the most erotic and ingenious ways for a girl to tantalize, tease, and thrill every inch of him." The first one said, "Help me button my shirt or adjust my tie in the mirror. When you dress me, I just want to get undressed again." The second one said, "Tugging on my earlobe just a bit with your teeth makes me lose all sense of the English language" . . . Sort of naughty overtones, Charlotte reckoned, but otherwise— then she hit "When we're having sex and you're on top, cup my balls and tug on them lightly. It's an unexpected, awesome feeling." And "Put the condom on me. It's such a turn-on to see you prep me that way" and "Swirl your tongue around the tip of my penis, and then, without warning, take all of me in your mouth" and "Take your panties off, throw them in the freezer, then caress my bod with them. Don't laugh. It's actually awesome" and "My girl-friend gets a glazed doughnut and sticks my penis through the hole. She nib-bles around it, stopping to suck me once in a while. The sugar beads from her mouth tingle on my tip"—

Charlotte closed the magazine and studied the cover again. Was this some sort of pornographic parody of *Cosmopolitan*? She opened it to the contents pages . . . a list a mile long of directors, managers, assistant man-agers, associate publishers, and then: "Published by Hearst Communica-tions, Inc., President and Chief Executive Officer: Victor F. Ganzi." It was all quite unbelievable. She put the magazine in her lap and looked straight ahead at nothing. The chunky girl glanced up at her but, as before, imme-diately returned to her book.

Charlotte's face was blazing red. Suppose somebody—anybody—even one of these three strangers—*saw* her reading this . . . blatant pornography! It would be mortifying—terminally!

As nonchalantly as she could, which is to say, with her hands shaking only a little, she got up, knelt on the couch again, reached over, and put the magazine back on the table, then turned it over so that the cover would be face-down. *Oh my God!* She didn't try to get back to her chair. Instead, she sank as deeply as she could into the couch, there being no available crack in the earth into which she could disappear.

She kept very still. Her heart was drumming away. Now she was directly across the table from the couple, the boy and girl in blue jeans. She had no interest in eavesdropping, but all at once the boy's voice rose just enough for her to overhear.

"What? I don't get it. You want *me* . . . to do . . . *that* for you?"

The girl's whisper reached an audible level, too. "*Please*, Stuart . . . don't you see? I'm a freshman. I don't know any of these guys—and for you it wouldn't be such a big thing. You're a senior. And I trust you."

"Yeah, but what's in it for *me*?" said the boy.

"Don't you think I'm attractive?"

"You're gorgeous, in case you don't already know it, which I'm sure you do, but what's that got to do with it?"

"I'd think it would have a little . . . *something* to do with it."

"No it wouldn't. You'd just be using me."

"Well, I'll bet there've been plenty of times—"

"Brittany! I've known you since you were nine and I was thirteen. I al-ways felt like your uncle. My God, it would be like *incest* or something."

"I'll bet you've—"

"I'm not sure I could even . . . you know, *do* it."

"Unnhh. Then what am I gonna do?"

At that point their voices fell again, and Charlotte could no longer hear what they were saying, other than that the girl, Brittany, was using a lot of *unnhs* and *ohhhhs* and other sighs.

Charlotte's chin sank down to her collarbone as what she had just heard began to register.

"Sexiled?"

Charlotte's head jerked about. It was the girl in the boxer shorts at the other end of the couch. She was looking straight at Charlotte and smiling in a perfectly friendly manner. Charlotte must have looked dumbstruck, because the girl said it again.

"Sexiled?"

By now Charlotte had taken the term apart and put it back together again, and she said, "Yeah . . . I guess I am."

"Me, too."

"You *are*? That's what it's called, sexiled?"

"Unh hunh." The girl shrugged, as if resigned to her fate. "This is the third time in two weeks. What about you?"

Charlotte was appalled to realize that any such abomination was so common, it had a name. "It never happened to me before. I just can't—my roommate promised she'd never do it again."

"Hah hah," said the girl. She seemed rather jolly about it. "That's what mine said. I can tell you, all she means is, she won't do it again tonight. Maybe. If you're lucky."

Charlotte pursed her lips grimly. The whole thing was overwhelming. "Well—I'm not gonna put up with it."

Dismissively: "Ahhhch . . . It's like totally—it's the way it works. You've just done her a favor, so she can't very well say no when it's your turn. Who's your roommate?"

"Her name's Beverly." She said it in a distracted fashion. What was on her mind was, Good Lord! When it's *my turn*?

"Mmmm, don't know her. You have a boyfriend yet?"

Stunned. "No."

"Me, neither. Oh, well. Guys come up to me, and I think they're interested, and then they ask me to introduce them to some girlfriend of mine, or whatever." She smiled and lifted her eyebrows in a self-deprecatory fashion.

The girl had a pretty face, in a rubicund country girl sort of way—Charlotte had seen that face plenty of times around Sparta—but she was buttery, stubby, and chubby. The chances of her ever achieving the twenty-first-century female ideal of a lean, hard, slim-hipped, well-defined body were remote, if not nil. She just wasn't made for it. Yet here she was, sitting in her boxer shorts in a public lounge in the middle of the night, looking forward to boyfriends and having her turn at sexiling her roommate. A nice, cheery normal-looking girl—who assumed all this was the natural order of things!

"I'm Bettina," said the girl.

"Charlotte."

They were members of the first generation to go through life with no last names.

The girl looked at Charlotte with a slightly amused expression and said, "Where are you from?"

"Sparta, North Carolina."

"Don't know Sparta. I *thought* I detected a little bit of the South, though. Where'd you go to school?"

Charlotte stiffened. She had regarded herself as the cosmopolitan of the Alleghany High student body, and she fancied her speech was nearly accent-free. But all she said was, "In Sparta, at Alleghany High School." Then, to shift the subject away from Sparta, Alleghany High, and Southern accents, "What about you?"

"I'm from Cincinnati. I went to Seven Hills School," said Bettina. "You always wear pajamas?"

The very same once-over Beverly's snobbish friend had given her! And the boys and girls in the hallway! What was wrong with pajamas, for God's sake? They were certainly better than a pair of plaid boxer shorts with an open fly! But before she could work up a good head of resentment—

—a shriek. A girl came running from the entry hall into the Common Room. She shrieked again. She was slim and blond and wore shorts that showed off her perfect legs, and the shrieks were ones that any girl on earth could have interpreted. They were the cries of the female of the species feigning physical fright at the antics, probably physical, of the male. Sure enough, running in after her came a tall, lean boy with short brown hair and little bangs. Moving like an athlete, he cornered her against the back of a couch and threw his arms around her as if to drag her back into the hall. As she squirmed, she cried, "No! No! Put me down, Chris! You can't make me! I'm not going to!"

TOM WOLFE

The boy said, "You have to! That was the deal, dude!"

He dragged her out of the room. It was almost . . . choreographic, this gorgeous, lissome girl and this gorgeous, tall, lean, athletic boy and their charade of a struggle. The two departed Edgerton House in melodious combat.

Charlotte and Bettina sat there without saying a word, but Charlotte knew they were both thinking the same thing. The perfect *her* intertwined with the perfect *him*—while they sat marooned in this lugubrious desert of dried-out leather upholstery, the two sexiles.

Part of Charlotte wanted to get out of the place immediately, even if it meant walking around aimlessly until dawn. She refused to be lumped with this . . . well . . . homely girl.

Then she faced up to it: leaving was the last thing in the world she was about to do. She could live with the business about the accent. She could forgive the implied insult regarding pajamas. She could roll with those punches and a dozen more like them. She was dislodged, rooted out of her own bed, thrown out of her own room, discarded, adrift, helpless, deracinated practically, but at least she was not *alone*. At least, for however brief an interval, she had a sunny, friendly face to look into. She was eye to eye with a human being whose fate she shared—and never mind how demeaning or miserable the fate—someone she could talk to . . . even open up to, assuming she could find the courage—

If only she could call Miss Pennington . . . or Momma . . . Hello, Miss Pennington? Momma? You know Dupont, on the other side of the mountains? The Garden of Athena, Goddess of Wisdom, where great things are to be done? Well, Miss Pennington, Momma, I plumb forgot to ask: did anybody ever tell you about being sexiled? About being marooned in a public lounge in the middle of the night so that your roommate, so-called, can rut like a pig with some guy she just picked up?

It seemed terribly important to keep the conversation with Bettina going. She ransacked her brain and finally came up with "Who were they?"—nodding toward the corner where the perfect guy had swooped up the perfect girl.

"I don't know who *he* is," said Bettina, "but she's a freshman. I saw her the other two times I was sexiled, too. She's always up late and got some guy chasing her. She's *hot*, I guess, but she's terribly, *you* know, all *Oooo Oooo Oooo Oooo Oo*." Bettina cocked her head and opened her eyes wide and fluttered them in the baby coquette fashion. "If she wanted to swap legs, I wouldn't say no, though."

"Yeah, I know what you mean," said Charlotte. But she said it in a dull, flat manner, because she was merely being agreeable. Deep down inside she wanted to say, "Then wait'll you see mine. I used to run cross-country in the mountains."

That revived her a bit. So gutted, disemboweled, scoured out had she been, by loneliness, she had all but forgotten the Force: *I am Charlotte Simmons.*

LOST PROVINCE ENTR'ACTE

"Dear Momma and Daddy,

"I'll admit my eyes blurred with mist when I saw you drive off in the old pickup."

The old pickup? . . . my eyes blurred with mist? . . . She sighed, she groaned, deflated. What on earth did she think she was writing? She lifted her ballpoint from the top sheet of a pad of lined schoolroom paper and slumped back, or as far back as you could slump in an exhausted wooden chair with no arms. She looked out the window at the library tower. It was lit up ever so majestically in the dark. She saw it, and she didn't see it. Beverly's cast-off clothes mashed on the floor, Beverly's web of extension cords plugged into surge-protector strips and knuckle sockets in midair, her rat's nest of a percale-sloshed unmade bed, her littered CD cases, uncapped skin-care tubes, and spilled contact lens packets, her techie alphabet toys, the PC, the TV, the CD, DVD, DSL, VCR, MP4, all of them currently dormant in the absence of their owner, each asleep rattlesnake-style with a single tiny diode-green eye open—her roommate's slothful and indulgent habits were all over the place . . . Charlotte was sort of aware of it and sort of wasn't really.

She rocked forward with another trill of low-grade guilt to confront her letter home . . . *the old pickup.* Daddy is totally dependent on that poor, miserable old truck, and I'm treating it like it's something quaint. *Eyes blurred with mist* . . . Yuk! She could just imagine Momma and Daddy reading *that.* The "pretty writing" . . .

She riiiiiiippped the sheet off the pad—then saved it. She could use it for scratch paper. She hunched over the desk and started again:

"Dear Momma and Daddy,

"I hope I didn't seem too sad when you left that day. Watching you all drive off made me realize"—she starts to write, *what a long journey I have set out upon,* but the pretty-writing alarm sounds again, and she damps it down to "how much I was going to miss you. But since then I have been so busy studying, meeting new people, and"—she grandly thinks of *figuring out Dupont's tribal idiosyncrasies,* already knowing she's going to settle for "getting used to new ways of doing things, I haven't had time to be homesick, although I guess I am.

"The classes haven't been as hard as I was afraid they would be. In fact, my French professor told me I was 'overqualified' for his class! Since he had a peculiar way of teaching French literature, in my opinion, I wasn't unhappy about switching to one a little more advanced. I have a feeling that it is harder to get into a university like this than it is to stay in it. I suppose I shouldn't even think like that, however"—she starts to write *lest I have a rude awakening*—and how is *lest* supposed to sound in Alleghany County?—then downscales it to "because it might be bad luck."

"The library here is really wonderful. You remember it, I'm sure, the tower, the tallest building on campus? It has nine million books, on every subject you can imagine, sometimes so many you hardly know where to start. It is really busy, too. There are as many students using the library at midnight as there are in the middle of the day. The other night I went there"—changes it to "I had to go there"—"kind of late, to use a computer, and there was only one computer not in use in a cluster of about 25 of them. I made a new acquaintance when we"—starts to write *got into an argument,* instead writes—"couldn't figure out which of us was next in line." So much for that—no name, no gender.

"My best friend so far is a girl from Cincinnati, Ohio, named Bettina, who lives on my floor. We met one night when each of us was having a hard time sleeping and decided to go down to the Common Room on the first floor and read for a while. Bettina is a very cheery and energetic person and not shy at all. If she wants to meet somebody, she just pipes right up and says hello.

"Generally I sleep very well. The only problem is that Beverly goes to bed really late"—starts to write *3, 4, even 5 a.m.*, instead writes—"2 a.m. sometimes, and it wakes me up when she comes in."

She slumped back in the chair once more and stared out the window a few light-years into the darkness. This, she figured, was it. Right here was the point where she either cried out or she didn't cry out. Momma, only you can help me! Who else do I have! Listen to me! Let me tell you the truth! Beverly doesn't just return in the dead of the night and "go to bed really late"! She brings boys into bed—and they rut-rut-rut *do it*—barely four feet from *my* bed! She leads a wanton sex life! The whole place does! Girls *sexile* each other! Rich girls with fifteen hundred SATs cry out, "I need some ass!" "I'm gonna go out and get laid!" The girls, Momma, the girls, Dupont girls, right in front of you! Momma—what am I to do . . .

But she stiffened and swallowed it all. Just one little mention of . . . sex . . . and Momma the Wrath of God would head east in the pickup, and haul her back to Sparta, and the whole county would hum like a hive: "Charlotte Simmons has dropped out of Dupont. Poor thing thinks it's immoral there."

So she writes, "By the same token, when I get up in the morning at my usual time, it wakes Beverly up. We are getting used to each other, however, even though we don't have many opportunities to spend time together. There seem to be a lot of her prep school friends here, and she also spends a lot of time with"—starts to write *her boyfriend(s)*, instead crosses out the *also* and writes—"a lot of time with them. I'm not sure she has ever heard a Southern accent before." She strikes out the previous sentence. Despite what a couple of people have said, she essentially has no regional accent. "Beverly and I get along fine, however.

"You wouldn't believe how important sports are here! The big football and basketball stars are celebrities. Everybody on campus knows them by sight. There were four basketball players in the French course I started out in, and they were so tall they made everybody else feel like a midget. I met one of them. He was very friendly and complimented me on my performance in the class. The athletes like to pretend they don't care about academic work, but I think this one really is interested, even though he acts as if he isn't." Dying to write *He immediately invited me to grab some lunch, which is the prelude to grab some ass*—but doesn't take even one step down that road.

"Living in a coed dorm was strange at first. Pretty soon, though, the boys just seem like neighbors 'across the way.'" Dying to write, *By now I hardly notice them except when Beverly brings her hookups up to the room to give them some fresh meat.* Actually writes, "That doesn't mean I don't have a lot to learn about Dupont, but every freshman is in the same boat. The freshmen girls go around in little 'herds'"—puts quotation marks around *herds*, doesn't want to characterize them to Momma and Daddy as dumb animals, especially since that is what they are, dumb, frightened, rich rabbits, chronically, desperately, in heat—"so that they won't feel both confused and lonely. Confused is bad enough!

"So everything is going along pretty much the way I hoped it would. I have to pinch myself to make sure this isn't just a dream and I really am a student at one of the best universities in the country." Thinks: where one and all make Channing and Regina look like harmless four-year-olds. "Dupont isn't Sparta, but I've already come to believe that growing up in Sparta has advantages that people I've met from places like Boston and New York have never had." Would love to write, *They don't realize that not everything you say has to be ironic or sarcastic and cynical and sophisticated and sick, virulent, covered in pustules, and oozing with popped-pustular sex.* If only there were a way to slip that sentiment into a letter to Momma—without her exploding! Settles for "Some things money can't buy."

"I didn't mean to make this letter so long. I should have written you before now to bring you up to date. Give my love to Buddy and Sam; also to Aunt Betty and Cousin Doogie. Tell them I miss them and that everything is going fine.

I love you,
Charlotte."

She slumped back again . . . There it was—one long, well-intentioned lie.

For a long time she just sat in the chair and looked out the window in something close to a trance. The floodlights down below sent shadows up the sides of the library tower as if they weren't shadows at all but great washes of watercolor. The undersides of the compound arches and decorative outcroppings caught the light here and there. What if she called Miss Penning-ton? She would be a lot more objective than Momma. She was wise as well as intelligent . . . Miss Pennington . . . She tried to imagine it—but what did Miss Pennington know about sex on the other side of the mountain? Noth-ing. How *could* she know? She was an old, homely spinster who had lived all her life in Sparta. Charlotte immediately chided herself for thinking that way about someone who had been so good to her. Yet it was true. "Spin-ster"—would anybody at Dupont even be *aware* of the word? No, the sex-obsessed know-it-alls of Dupont would sneak through Miss Pennington's blood/brain barrier and swim through her arteries and veins like liver flukes until they found evidence, no matter how far-fetched, of lesbianism or tran-sexuality or something else disgusting. They would roll her in their muck, all the while piously "defending" her right to her "orientation." What hyp-ocrites they were! Still, what did—how could—Miss Pennington know about it all? And she already *knew* what Miss Pennington would say: "Get busy, start a project, ignore them." Be yourself, be independent, march to a different drummer, swim against the current—they'll admire your courage, the way they do here—Oh, Miss Pennington! You don't understand. In Sparta that was so easy. It was easy maintaining my pose, looking down my nose at the Channings and the Reginas all day with a Little Scholar's sneer as they called me an "uptight cherry" and a lot of other things, and asked me—Regina once said it to my face—when I was going to "give it up." It was easy, because at nightfall the skirmish was over, and I went home to Momma and Daddy and Buddy and Sam. Oh, I was superior to *them*, too, even to Momma. How backward I knew my family to be by the time I was thirteen! But that poor old shack out County Road 1709 was always there; it was mine. It reeked of kerosene and a coal grate, but no one could touch me, no one would try, no one could look Daddy in the face when his eyes went cold, no one dared provoke Cousin Doogie to the point where he bared his fangs. Once he threw rocks—"thhhhhhoo rrrocks," as he spluttered it out later—at big Dave Cosgrove when Dave winked a sarcastic wink and said, "Reckon you ain't fixing to give me no cherry on ice, hunh, Charlotte?" . . . rocks might'near big enough to kill him. Then Cousin Doogie stood there with another rock in his hand and said, "Try talking that way again, fat boy. I ain't rammed a spit up a pig's ass in a long time." Dave, who must have weighed eighty pounds more than Cousin Doogie, just slunk away. That was why he went limp when he crashed the party after commencement. There was Cousin Doogie.

Here, now, at Dupont, when she came "home," she wasn't getting away from it all—right here was where she had to wallow in it all. Right here, in her "own" room, which was supposed to be a place of peace, sleep, and refuge—right here was where she got her nose shoved in the filth. It wasn't so much a thought as an instinct: what she needed was somebody wise who also *knew* and who would assure her that yes, her situation was unjust, and yes, it was her duty to hold firm and remain independent, a rock amid the decadence all around her. That person, in the Dupont catalog, would be the R.A. Ha ha, a joke. Her R.A., Ashley, had immediately taken her for a hopelessly innocent little country girl and told her a sentimental lie about "dormcest." She could just *see* Ashley's "sincere" face and her flyaway tangles of blond hair—

Bango!

—the blond hair, the blond hair and the freckles: Laurie. Only a freshman herself, at North Carolina State, but Laurie was levelheaded and mature, at least compared to other girls at Alleghany High, and she was religious—New River Baptist Church, the Better Sort of Baptists, the in-town Baptists, as opposed to the foot-washing Baptists out in the countryside, even though the Better Sort also baptized people with full immersion in the New River at Easter when the water was still ice-cold. Laurie had convictions!

Charlotte got up from the chair and picked up the "room" telephone, a white portable. The instrument itself belonged to Beverly, but Charlotte could use it, entering her own code when she made a call. It was hardly ever used. Beverly lived on her cell phone, and Charlotte, like her folks, would do almost anything to avoid "calling long distance." She felt reckless and oddly exhilarated. She punched in Information in Raleigh, North Carolina, for North Carolina State, hung up, and then punched in General Information at State. All this was going to cost money, but with giddy abandon she refused to think about that now. A recorded voice answered and instructed her to press *this* if she wanted this, or this for this, or this for this or . . . It was bewildering. She had to hang up and dial again . . . *flinging* money out the window. This time she concentrated on the disembodied instructions and pressed *this* for *this* . . . and *this* referred her to this or this or this, and *this* instructed her to punch in the first four letters of the last name, which she did, MCDO, which led her to a series of automated voices that went through the McDodds, McDolans, McDonoughs, and McDoovers before finally reaching the McDowells, whereupon another voice took over and ran A. J., Arthur, Edith, F., George, H. H., and Ian McDowell by her before reaching

L. McDowell. Charlotte was frantic. She had never been in phone-mail jail before. She took a wild stab and responded yes to L. A squad of patched-together digital voices gave her L. McDowell's number.

God knows what the Information calls alone cost. But now she's drunk on her own heedlessness. She punches in the number, stretches the coiled cord, and sits back down in her chair. Seven rings, eight rings—not there, even if L. is Laurie—

"Hello?" Loud rap music in the background.

Terribly embarrassed: "May I speak to Laurie McDowell?"

Hesitation . . . "This is Laurie . . ."

Charlotte is elated! Laurie! Why hadn't she called her in the first place? Laurie will *know*! Laurie will understand! Shivers of delight. She wants to laugh, she's so happy. Almost a shriek: "Laurie! You know who this is?"

"No-o-o-o . . ."

Carried away by joy, she giggled, "Regina Cox."

"Regina?—*Charlotte!*"

Shrieks, laughter, interjections, I-can't-believe-its, more shrieks and laughs. The rap music is banging away. "Knock it on some fox's box, my cock"—blip: Doctor Dis. Since when was Laurie interested in rap?

"Regina . . . Charlotte, you are like totally—Ohmygod, I mean the day Regina—where are you?"

"In my room in the dorm."

"At Dupont?"

"Yeah . . . at Dupont . . ."

"I can't say you sound very excited. What's it like? I can't believe this! Like a hundred times I've been on the verge of calling *you*! I totally *have*!"

"Me, too—same thing."

"The Dupont girl!" said Laurie. "Tell me everything! I've been like totally dying to know. Wait a minute, let me turn down this music. I can hardly hear you."

Laurie and . . . all these *totallys*? The rap band banging in the background began to digit down, and the last thing Charlotte heard distinctly was Doctor Dis making one of those crude rap half rhymes, ". . . take my testi-culls, suck 'em like a popsi-cull . . ." For a moment she worried that the distraction would make Laurie forget what they were about to discuss, namely, Dupont. At the same time she didn't want to pounce right back onto the subject herself, for fear of revealing how eager she was to talk about it.

Laurie returned to the telephone. "Sorry, I didn't know I had it on so loud. You know who that was, the singer?"

"Doctor Dis," said Charlotte. She left it at that. She didn't want things to go off on a tangent about some stupid illiterate singer, if you could call rap singing. At the same time, she had a terrible itch of curiosity. "I didn't know you liked rap."

A bit defensive: "I like *some* of it."

Dead air. Silence. It was as if the conversation had leaked out a hole. Charlotte ransacked her brain. Finally, "Is it like *here*? All *anybody* plays at Dupont is rap and reggae, except for the ones who like classical music and all that. There are a lot of musicians in my class."

"Rap and reggae are really popular here, too," said Laurie, "but there are a lot of kids, guys especially, who listen to country and bluegrass? I got enough of that in Sparta. But other'n'at, N.C. State's like totally cool. It's big! The first two weeks it liked to drive me crazy, it's so big." *Liiiiked*—sounded almost like *locked*. It was a relief to Charlotte to know that somebody else was in college with the Sparta accent, the Sparta diction, the Sparta "other'n'at," the Sparta "liked to" for "almost," the Sparta declarative sentence that modestly questions itself at the very end. Laurie would *understand*, if she could ever get her back on the subject. "At Dupont," Laurie was saying, "do you have to do everything online?"

"Well, a lot of—"

Laurie talked right over the top of her. "Here you register for classes online, you turn in assignments online, if you need to ask a T.A. something about homework, you do it online—but I don't mind." With great enthusiasm she proceeded to tell Charlotte about the endless number of things that made N.C. State cool. "Everybody's always talking about how State is an aggie college and all that? Well, there are a lot of really cool kids here. I've made so many friends?" *Free-uns.* "I'm glad I came here."

Charlotte didn't know what to say. Laurie *liked* it there. Since misery loves company, that was a disappointment.

Laurie said, "Well—what's up with you? You've got to tell me all about Dupont!"

"Oh, it's great, or I guess it's great," said Charlotte. "They sure *tell* you enough it's great."

"What do you mean?"

Charlotte told her about the speech by the dean of Dupont College at the "frosh" convocation, the medieval banners, the flags of forty-three nations, the name-dropping, the Nobel-dropping—

"That's what *they* say, and what do *you* say?"

"Oh, I don't know," said Charlotte. "It probably *is* that great, but I don't know what difference it makes."

"Oh wow," said Laurie. "You're sure jumping for joy."

Charlotte said, "Do you live in a coed dorm?"

"Do I live in a coed dorm? Yeah. Practically everybody does. Do you?"

"Yeah," said Charlotte. "What do you think of it?"

"Oh, I don't know," said Laurie. "It was weird at first. The guys were totally *loud* all the time. But now it's like calmed down. I don't think about it much anymore."

"Have you ever heard of sexiling?"

"Yeah . . ."

"Has it ever happened to you?"

"*To* me? No, but it happens."

"Well—it happened to me," said Charlotte. "My roommate comes in about three o'clock in the morning and—" She proceeded to tell the story. "But the worst thing was the way *she* made *me* feel guilty. I was supposed to *know* that if she gets drunk and picks up some guy somewhere and brings him up to the room, that's more important than me being able to stay in *my* room and get some sleep before a test in the morning."

A pause. "I guess it's the same way here."

"At Dupont," said Charlotte, "everybody thinks you're some kind of—of—some kind of twisted . . . uptight . . . pathetic little goody-goody if you haven't had sex. Girls will come right out and ask you—girls you hardly even know. They'll come right out and ask you—in front of other girls—if you're a V.C., a member of the Virgins Club, and if you're stupid enough to say yes, it's an *admission*, like you have some terrible character defect. They practically sneer. If you don't have a boyfriend, you're a loser, and if you want a boyfriend, you have to have sex. There's something perverted about that. Don't you agree with me? This is supposed to be this great university, but it's like if you haven't 'given it up,' as Regina used to say, then you just don't belong here. *I'd* say that's perverted. Am I right—or do I just not get it or something? Is it like that there?"

Pause. "More or less."

"So what do *you* do when it comes up? What do you *say*?"

Long pause. "I guess I like . . . don't say anything."

"Then what do you *do*?" said Charlotte.

Longer pause. "I guess I try to look at it in a different way. I've never lived anywhere but Sparta before. College—I don't know, I guess I think of college as this opportunity to . . . to experiment. I needed to like get away from Sparta for a while."

"Well—me, too," said Charlotte. She couldn't imagine why Laurie was saying anything so obvious.

Still longer pause. "You think maybe it's possible you got away, but you brought a lot of Sparta with you to Dupont?" said Laurie. "Without knowing it?"

"What do you mean?"

"I'm just asking . . . like suppose it's something to consider. I guess what I really mean is college is like this four-year period you have when you can try anything—and *everything*—and if it goes wrong, there's no consequences? You know what I mean? Nobody's keeping score? You can do things that if you tried them before you got to college, your family would be crying and pulling their hair out and giving you these now-see-what-you've-gone-and-done looks?—and everybody in Sparta would be clucking and fuming and having a ball talking behind your back about it?—and if you tried these things after you left college and you're working, everybody's gonna fucking blow a fuse, and your boss or whoever will call you in for a—"

—the *fucking* just slipped out and hit Charlotte in the solar plexus— *Laurie!*

"—little talk, he'll call it, or if you have a boyfriend or a husband, he's gonna totally freak out or crawl off like a dog, which would be just as bad, because it'd make you feel guilty? I mean, look at it that way, Charlotte. College is the only time in your life, or your adult life anyway, when you can really *experiment*, and at a certain point, when you leave, when you graduate or whatever, everybody's memory like evaporates. You tried this and this and this and this, and you learned a lot about how things are, but nobody's gonna remember it? It's like amnesia, totally, and there's no record, and you leave college exactly the way you came in, pure as rainwater."

"Tried *what* things?" said Charlotte. "What's an example?"

"Well—" Laurie hesitated. "You were talking about boyfriends and what boyfriends expect and everything . . ."

"Yeah . . ."

Laurie's voice rose. "Charlotte! That's not the end of the world! This is the time to cut loose! To really learn about everything! To learn about guys, to really get to know them! Really find out what goes on in the world! You just have to let yourself fly for once, without constantly thinking about what you left behind on the ground! You're a genius. Everybody knows that. I'm being sincere, Charlotte. Totally. Now there's other things to learn, and this is the perfect time to do it. Take a chance! That's one reason people go to college! It's not the only reason, but it's a big reason."

Silence. Then Charlotte said, "So you're talking about . . . going all the way . . ."

Silence. Then, "Not *just* that, but, well—yes."

Embarrassed pause. "Have *you* done that, Laurie?"

Bravely, nothing to be ashamed of: "Yes, I have." Silence. "I know what you're thinking, but it's not all that big a deal." Silence. "And it's a relief. I mean—well, you know." Silence. "If you decide you want to, all you have to do is call me up, and I can tell you—I can tell you some things."

Laurie went on for a while, in the abstract, about how little the deal was. Charlotte kept the receiver at her ear. She let her eyes wander . . . the pale gray wash up the side of the tower . . . the curious ragged diagonal the lit-up windows on the other side of the courtyard made . . . the bra that had somehow gotten tangled around the high heel of a shoe underneath Beverly's bed. Laurie was going on about how every girl was on the pill, and it didn't cause you to gain weight, the way she'd always heard . . .

Charlotte had a picture in her head of thousands of girls getting up out of bed in the morning and shuffling to the bathroom with sleepers in their eyes and standing in front of a small, discolored cream-gray enameled basin with an old-fashioned zinc-gray chain attached to a black rubber stopper and a medicine cabinet with a mirror on the door, and they're all reaching up, in a fog, thousands of college girls—she can see thousands of arms and hands reaching up, in this building, that building, the one across the way, the one behind that—incalculable numbers of buildings—they're all reaching up and opening the cabinets and taking The Pill, which she imagined must be the size of the pills they give mules on the Christmas-tree farms for heartworm.

That was the picture, but she didn't actually hear anything after "Yes, I have."

7. HIS MAJESTY THE BABY

It was very nearly dark, and along the footpath on the edge of the Grove, blinking yellow lights came bobbing and bouncing by, one after the other, weak yellow lights, bunched together here, spread out there, but a whole train of them, all going in the same direction, bouncing and bobbing and blinking along the footpath by the arboretum. Adam squeezed the brake levers on his bicycle and stopped, even though he was already late for his meeting at *The Daily Wave*.

It took a moment or two to figure out this spectral locomotion: joggers. The yellow lights, which blinked in order to alert motorists at night, were built into the CD players they wore Velcro'd around their upper arms. But their arms—they were hardly even there! These joggers were girls, every one of them, so far as Adam could make out, and half of them were terribly thin, breastless, bottomless, nothing but bones, hair, T-shirts, shorts, big sneakers, and blinking lights. They were determined to burn up every last calorie they could squeeze out of their juiceless hides—or die, literally die, trying.

Adam saw a story in it immediately—THE ANOREXIC MARATHON— and nobody at the *Wave* was going to grouse about his being late if he arrived with a good idea like this one—on top of the real bombshell he was delivering this evening concerning—he could already envision this story's headline, too—THE GOVERNOR, THE BLOW JOB AND THE BRAWL.

He hurried on, pedaling past Crowninshield, past the Little Yard, all the while wondering if it was hard to get anorexics to agree to pictures. THE LIV-ING DEAD WHO WON'T LIE DOWN . . . The interviews? No problem for an enterprising reporter like him. None of these wimp-out caveats—"the names have been changed"—either. He could see it in print. He could *feel* it in print. There was something almost chemical about new story ideas. They gave him a visceral rush. THE GOVERNOR, THE BLOW JOB AND THE BRAWL—although little Greg Fiore would never have the guts to put BLOW JOB in a headline. He pedaled faster.

Out in the real world, as opposed to Dupont's cocoon, the typical news-room of a daily newspaper wasn't much different from the home office of an insurance company: the same somber, invincible synthetic carpeting, the same rows of workstations with young backs humped over in front of low-grade-fever-blue computer screens. Only college newspaper offices such as the *Wave*'s preserved the lumpen-bohemian clutter of newsrooms in the fa-bled *Front Page* era of the twentieth century, not that anybody at the *Wave* other than Adam himself or possibly Greg, the editor in chief, had ever heard of *Front Page* or its era, more than seventy years ago, back in the last century, which to college students today was prehistory.

As Adam walked in, Greg was rocked back on the rear legs of the old wooden library chair he used, holding forth to five other staff mem-bers, two boys and three girls, who had perched themselves wherever they could, against a backdrop of discarded pizza take-out boxes glistening with their greasy cheese residue, cardboard baskets that buffalo wings and chicken fingers had come in, cracked translucent tops from containers of coffee and jumbo Slurpees and smoothies, mealy-feeling molded gray composite-cardboard trays, various crumpled bags, and sheets of news-paper and computer printouts strewn upon an exhausted carpet splotched with raspberry Crazy Horse caffeine-jolt spills or worse. The bombness of it all! The pizza boxes . . . after this meeting he would have to hustle over to PowerPizza and put in four frantic hours of pizza deliveries.

A skinny Chinese girl named Camille Deng—that skank, thought Adam—was saying, "I think we've still got some unresolved homophobia is-sues here. I don't buy the administration's cop-out that the maintenance staff 'thought they were *combating* homophobia.'"

"Why not?" said Greg, leaning back even farther on the chair's hind legs and eyeing Camille down his nose. Greg and his gotta-be-tough-newspaperman pose, thought Adam. Greg and his scrawny neck and receding chin.

"Well," said Camille, "do you think it's just a coincidence that Parents Weekend is coming up, and the administration, which is always telling us how they're a hundred percent behind diversity and everything, you think they might just possibly not want the parents to see descriptions of how Dupont guys make love written in chalk all over the sidewalks? 'We're Queer and We're Here'—you think Dupont Hall wants to let that big cat out of the bag? Because they *are* here."

"How come you're saying *they*?" said a boy with shaggy red hair. Randy Grossman. "You sure you don't have an issue yourself? Like maybe a little covert pariah-ism? Like maybe a little self-loathing lesbianism?"

Camille went *Unnngghh* in a groan of utmost contempt.

I've got an issue of covert pariah-ism, too, when it comes to Randy, thought Adam. Randy had turned into an aggressive pain in the ass ever since he came out. Like everybody else on the *Wave*, Adam had admired him for his courage. Now he wished to hell he'd go back in the closet.

Greg ignored Randy and said, "Look, Camille, some night-shift security guy spots all this writing on the sidewalks describing 'cock-and-ass jobs' and sticking fingers up the ass and stroking the prostate—I saw the remains of that one myself—and it's two or three in the morning, and Security tells Maintenance, and Maintenance decides—remember, we're talking about the night shift here—"

Camille broke in. "What difference is that supposed to make? Night-shift maintenance personnel are automatically retarded?"

"Let me finish. Maintenance figures this is antigay vandalism. 'We better get rid of it before daylight.' What's so hard to believe about that? These guys—it's the middle of the night, and how are they supposed to know this is the Lesbian and Gay Fist striking a blow for gay freedom? So they spend the rest of the night scrubbing it all off, and in the morning there's nothing left but chalk smears, and they think they've done the right thing. I can get down with that, but the Fist goes postal. Whattaya think happened—a buncha guys got together at three a.m. and had a public relations meeting about Parents Weekend?"

Greg's right, thought Adam, and Camille's a skank, but Greg's right from the wrong motive. Greg, like every *Daily Wave* editor in chief, was supposed to be a fiercely independent journalist who pulled no punches. Greg was not alone in *Wave* history in his inclination to pull lots of punches, since the administration, and fellow undergraduates, had an infinite number of ways—moral, social, and substantive—to make life miserable for any editor who took his charter of independence at face value. Nevertheless, it was important, not only for Greg's public face but also for his private soul, for him to believe that he was one tough journalist who would rake the muck whenever it needed raking. In fact, the chances of Fearless Greg Fiore denouncing the administration for not proudly upholding the right of the Fist to write anal sex exotica all over the sidewalks for Parents Weekend never existed in the first place.

Of course, Adam, as he himself realized, was not altogether objective when it came to Greg Fiore. It went without saying that he, Adam, was the senior who should at this moment be sitting in that rickety chair looking down his nose at staffers from his eminence as editor in chief. He couldn't blame Greg for the situation, but he found it in his heart to resent him all the same. No, at bottom it was his parents who were to blame, most specifically his father, who had left him and his mother in the shabby circumstances that made it necessary for him to work two jobs in order to get through college. Editing a daily like the *Wave* was a full-time commitment that left no time for things like delivering pizza and filling in for Jojo Johanssen's brain. Adam couldn't have accepted the job of editor if they had come on their knees begging him. Jews without money. Adam's father was the grandson of some Jews without money—*Jews Without Money* was a 1930s "proletarian" novel that Adam had read just because of the title—who had immigrated from Poland to the United States in the 1920s and wound up in Boston, where they remained Jews without money. His father, Nat Gellin, had been the first Gellin, or Gellininsky—Adam's great-grandfather had given the name a little trim—to go to college. Strapped for money, he had been forced to drop out of Boston University after two years, at which point he considered himself lucky when he got a job as a waiter at Egan's, a big, popular, glossy downtown restaurant that attracted the sort of businessmen who liked to dine breathing the same air as bigger businessmen, flashy politicians, TV anchors, journalists from the *Globe* and the *Herald*, and the odd visiting show-business celebrity. In sum, Egan's was irresistible to that creature of the big city, he who must be "where things are happening." Nat Gellin had the three qualities essential for success in such an establishment: punctiliousness, tact, and charm; and in just under ten years he had worked his way up from waiter to captain to maître d' to manager. Adam barely remembered him, but his father must have had the gift of glib bonhomie, too, because Egan's, historically, was Irish through and through. The joint had a bar trade that by six o'clock in the evening fairly roared with the boisterous conversations of people who knew they were drinking in the right place. The bar featured massive swaths of oak with polished brass accoutrements, inch-thick glass shelves bearing ranks of liquor bottles lit from below as if they were onstage—and Nat Gellin in a gray unfinished-worsted suit, a freshly starched shirt, and a navy tie with white pin dots, a look he had picked up from the team of official greeters at "21" in New York City. He greeted one and all at Egan's with a smile set between a pair of rubicund round cheeks. He had the knack of never forgetting a name, not even if the fellow came in only once in a blue moon. It was while he was a mere waiter and college dropout that he met pretty, cute, bouncy little Frances "Frankie" Horowitz, a high school graduate who had a job routing customer accident and theft calls for Allstate Insurance.

Adam's mother idolized the incomparable restaurateur Nat Gellin. Even years later, in the midst of monologues of pure old-fashioned hate, she would come out with something like "There isn't another Jew in Boston who coulda done what your father did with that Irish restaurant." What Adam took away from all that was the idea that a successful Jew was one who was a hit with the goyim.

Nat Gellin of Egan's was a hit with the goyim, all right. Two years before Adam was born, Nat charmed an old-line Brahmin bank, First City National, into a prodigious loan and bought a half interest in Egan's from the original Michael F. X. Egan's five children, who were happy to get some cash out of the place in the here and now. Then he bought a house in Brookline to go with it, even though it meant he was now leveraged over the moon. Adam spent the first five years of his life in what he would recognize years later was a big, elegant Georgian house in Brookline, built about 1910 on a small lot, after the urban fashion of the day, in what was no doubt the right section back then and wasn't bad now. Nat's hubris was leveraged up to the ultimate, too. His ascension from salaried manager to profit-sharing full partner made him feel that he had risen to a higher social and, one might say, romantic level. One night, while wafting bonhomie in his restaurant, he met a blond twenty-three-year-old recently graduated from Wellesley, a WASP with all sorts of Ivy League and Beacon Hill connections, and in due course he began having to stay later and later at night to wrap up all the loose ends in his establishment, the operation of which was a matter of infinite complexity, after which, nevertheless, came the inevitable drive back to Brookline and to Frankie.

Frankie. He had grown, and she hadn't grown with him. She *had* grown older, however, and no longer looked pretty, cute, and bouncy as much as she did chunky, prematurely middle-aged, and not much different from any other uneducated American mom putting on weight and growing more and more remote from where things were happening, as she cooed and cooed in Brookline over her baby, Adam.

It was one Sunday, while Nat was in just such a gloomy yet hubristic mood, and she was in the sunroom watering some Lollipop Stamen lilies, that he decided he had to tell her straight out. He actually used those words: "I know it's not your fault, Frankie, but I've grown, and you haven't grown with me."

He couldn't have worded it in a worse way. He was not only telling her he was leaving her, he was also informing her that it was because she was an unsophisticated dimwit, an embarrassing *zhlub*. Adam was so young when it all happened that his memory contained nothing more than a single snapshot of his father—specifically, of his porky belly and his genitals emerging naked from the bathroom. He also had a snapshot of the moment his mother informed him Daddy was moving out, although he couldn't remember how she put it. He was old enough a couple of years later to be quite aware that they were moving from the grand house in Brookline to the second floor of a not-so-great house in the West Roxbury section of Boston, although he was still too young to have any more than a vague idea of the status implications. His own personal status was fabulous. He was His Majesty the Only Child. His mother put him on that throne, sang his praises, worshiped him, strewed petals of adulation upon his every path. Inasmuch as his teachers also made a fuss over him, it never occurred to him that the elementary school he attended, along with a lot of unruly Irish, black, Italian, Chinese, Canuck, and Ukrainian children, might be somewhere toward the soggy bottom of the Boston public school system. He was royalty in the school building, too; His Majesty the Prodigy. It was only after he was thirteen and had a scholarship to Roxbury Latin, a famous and prestigious old private school, that he realized what a free fall it had been from Brookline to West Roxbury—and learned how it happened.

Nat Gellin's divorce papers had roused all the bouncy spunk Frances Horowitz Gellin had possessed the day she met him, except that now it came out not as "cute," but as revenge. There had been a time when Nat used to love regaling Frankie with war stories of the restaurant business, and she knew that restaurateurs treasured customers who paid cash. At that time, the only record of cash receipts was the tape that came out of the register—and the tape was thrown into the trash the moment the joint closed at night. The cash itself was a pie, up to the owners to divide as they thought best. For three months, Frankie and her lawyer went out in the middle of the night and retrieved those tapes from the trash outside Egan's. The lawyer thought she was going to use the evidence as a threat to squeeze a better settlement out of her prosperous entrepreneur husband, but Frankie went straight to the federal government. Nat got off with a fine, but the fine was so enormous that he had to sell his half interest in Egan's and the house in Brookline, and even after that he remained nailed to the ground by the bankers. The settlement, the alimony, the child support—those became nothing but words on a document. There was no longer any more than a pittance to be extracted from that well-known host and boulevardier Nat Gellin. And boy, did Frankie leave one dumbfounded, flummoxed, outstanding-billoxed lawyer staring at the remains of her case.

At the time, Frankie didn't care, because she had had her revenge, and yes, it was sweet. She cared later on, when things got so bad that she had to take a job making cold telephone calls for the retail sales department of a cable television company, the sort of calls that interrupt people at home and make them wonder what kind of loathsome creep was so hard up as to take a job doing that. But not even free-floating scorn daunted her, since she was serving a higher cause: turning Adam into a star who would light up her life.

Until Adam started going to Roxbury Latin, no two people were more devoted to each other. Adam was an academic star throughout his school days, and the constant praise of others and the glitter of success in the boy's own eyes did, indeed, light up Frankie's life. As her part of the deal, Frankie kept Adam's confidence—and ego—pumped up to astonishing proportions. There was nothing that could hold him back from going forth from West Roxbury and conquering the world. Frankie had never gone to synagogue again after her social downfall, and Adam grew up without any religion—or any but the most cursory knowledge of Judaism. But she did tell him about the Jewish people. Again he couldn't remember exactly how she put it, but it was clear that the Jews were the greatest people on earth and Israel was the greatest nation on earth, and the United States, although a wonderful country in other ways, was riddled with anti-Semitism. Such was the foundation upon which Adam Gellin's Weltanschauung, like many another's, was built.

At Roxbury Latin, Adam learned a little too much about status distinctions for Frankie's good. Roxbury Latin was anything but a snobbish school. In fact, it had an atmosphere of old-fashioned Protestant scrubbed-wood asceticism about it. Nevertheless, there were quite a few socially well-placed boys who went there and lots of sophisticated parents active in school projects. It was at Roxbury Latin that it first dawned on Adam that his mother, Frankie Gellin, the former Frances Horowitz, the woman who had not only nurtured him but fed his ego, fed his ego, fed it, fed it, fed it, fed it until he was a giant amid Boston's swarms of ordinary people—this woman who had done all that was in fact a very ordinary person, an aging, tiny, round-shouldered woman with no education, no sophistication, no knowledge of the world and no curiosity about it, a poorly read person who couldn't possibly converse with him about Shakespeare, much less Virgil, and still less Emily Dickinson or J. D. Salinger. It was pretty hard to understand irony or allusion or metaphor if you didn't have the faintest notion of what it was playing off of. His mother didn't get it and never had. Adam went into his later teens believing himself to be a brilliant and infinitely promising young star who had been born to the wrong parents.

From worshiping his mother, he veered overnight into resenting her. Why? He had no idea. He didn't even know it was resentment. He thought it was a matter of cultivation, her lack of it and his Roxbury Latinized depth of it. He was unable to face the truth, which was that he didn't want to believe that it was an intellectual and social nullity like this, his mom, his embarrassing, ill-spoken cipher of a mom, who had created Destiny's Adam Gellin. That would have made his grand ego seem like a fraud. (Nor was his the first case of Shrunken Mommy complex among those who regard themselves as intellectuals.)

"—or was that before you got here?"

With a start, Adam realized Greg was looking straight at him and asking him a question, probably containing a barb about his being late for the meeting, but he hadn't a clue as to what the question actually was. His mind churned for a moment, and then he said, "Sorry about being late"—he made a point of looking at the others when he said it, to avoid the appearance of apologizing to Greg—"but I've just come across something like totally incredible but totally true."

Greg sighed in an impatient I-don't-have-time-for-this manner. "Okay, like what?"

Adam now realized this was the wrong moment to pitch his story, but the drive known as information compulsion overrode common sense. "Well, the speaker at commencement last spring is the leading contender for the Republican nomination for president, right?"

Greg nodded even more impatiently.

"Well, one night two days before commencement last spring, the guy's already on campus, and two frat boys—two Saint Rays, in fact—catch him getting a blow job out in the Grove from this girl, a junior—and I know her name, although I guess we can't run it—and there's a brawl with the guy's bodyguard—"

Greg broke in. "This is something that's supposed to have happened two days before *commencement?*"

"Exactly," said Adam.

"That was what—one, two . . . *four* months ago? That's really awesome, Adam, but we've got to go to press three hours from now, okay? And the story I got to deal with right now happened this morning, okay?"

"I know that," said Adam, "but I'm talking about one of the most important politicians in America here, and—"

Greg broke in again, sarcastically. "That's bangin', Adam, but—"

Camille broke in on Greg: "Did it ever occur to you, Adam, that all your story ideas are like designed to make women look pathetic? Or is the problem that it *does* occur to you?"

Oh you pathetic skank. But what he said was, "Whattaya mean, all my story ideas?"

"I mean like this Predatory Professor thing you want to do. You want to make women look like—"

"Whattaya talking about, Camille? That's not a story about women; it's a story about male faculty members."

Greg said, "Can we please get back to—"

"What am *I* talking about?" said Camille. "The question is, what are *you* talking about? You know very well that the subtext is, Oh, wow, nothing has changed, has it. Female students are still little sexual lambs who need protecting against all-powerful males who want to seduce them. We can't just let them go around having affairs with whoever they feel like, can we. Your narrative is the same old story, the same as"—she paused, her mouth slightly open, obviously searching for some historical or possibly literary analogy—"the same story it's always been," she concluded lamely. "The subtext makes sure female undergraduates remain the stereotypical Little Red Riding Hoods."

"Oh, *fuck*, Camille, subtext me no subtexts. Let's *talk* about the text. The text is—"

"THE TEXT IS WE GOTTA COME TO A CONCLUSION ABOUT THE FIST AND THE 'WE'RE QUEER' SHIT! IT'S ONLY TWO HOURS TO DEADLINE!" Greg's voice had become shrill.

"Why is 'We're Queer' shit?" said Randy.

Greg sighed, rolled his eyes, looked away, and tamped the side of his head with the heel of his hand. Softly, his gaze panning from Randy to Camille to Adam, he said, "We—haven't—got—time—for—semantics. We haven't got time for deconstructing texts, we haven't got time for four-month-old blow jobs, we haven't got time for horny professors. We only have time for—"

Adam tuned out. He knew exactly what poor Greg would do, as did everybody in the room who stopped and thought about it. Not only would Greg be afraid to touch THE GOVERNOR, THE BLOW JOB AND THE BRAWL, he would run a completely straight-faced account of today's WE'RE QUEER fiasco, even though the whole thing was comical, and he would write one of his nevertheless editorials, assuming he had the nerve to run any editorial at all. In his nevertheless editorials, Greg always said something like, "While the administration is probably not being evasive in referring to the erasure as an honest mistake, nevertheless the Gay and Lesbian Fist has every right to hold the administration to the strictest standards of yackety yackety yak . . ." And Greg would see to it that he never had time for THE BLOW JOB. The very mention of it had scared poor Greg to death.

Greg was arguing with Camille and Randy and looking at his watch, as if the sheer logic of the deadline would make them willing to acquiesce. Greg didn't have the balls to just assert his authority and say—as he, Adam, would have—"Look, it's getting late, and here's what we're going to do . . ."

Adam looked at his own watch and realized, resentfully, that he wouldn't have the luxury of hanging around long enough to see his prediction come to pass. He had fifteen minutes to get over to his night job. Destiny's Adam Gellin would spend the next four hours in a little Bitsosushi hatchback delivering slices of anchovy-and-olive, pastrami-mozzarella-and-tomato, prosciutto-Parmesan-red-pepper-and-egg, sausage-artichoke-and-mushroom, smoked-salmon-stracchino-and-dill, and eggplant-bresaola-arugula-pesto-pignoli-fontina-Gorgonzola-bollito-misto-capers-basil-crème-fraîche-and-garlic cheese pizza to every indolent belly-stuffing time-squandering oaf on or off the Dupont campus who picked up the phone and called PowerPizza.

Adam couldn't stand pizza, but tonight, as he stood at the stainless-steel take-out counter inside the alley entrance to PowerPizza, the sound of the Mexicans dicing all the onions and red peppers and the smell of sausages cooking in their cheese lava cut right into his stomach and made him painfully hungry. He hadn't eaten since noon and wouldn't be able to eat for four more hours, and here he was staring into a hot maw, the PowerPizza kitchen, where a motley hive of people were furiously shoveling food in gross quantities. The counter girls up front were yelling at the cooks, the cooks were yelling at the Mexicans, the Mexicans were yelling at each other, in Spanish, and Denny, the owner, was yelling at the whole lot of them in what passed for English.

"'Eyyyyy, whattayou do standin'eh?" He had spotted Adam. He threw both hands up in the gesture that said "Useless!"

"I've only got seven orders!" said Adam, indicating the stack of pizza flats beside him on the counter. "I'm supposed to have eight!"

"Okay. You get a you eight, you get a you ess moving."

Denny, whose actual first name was Demetrio, was like a caricature of a pizza parlor proprietor, an immigrant from Naples, too fat, bald, hot-headed, and harried, and he couldn't even yell at you without using his hands. In the evenings his entire business depended on speed—speed at the front counter, in the kitchen, and above all in the take-out deliveries, which were supposed to go out fast and arrive hot. To ensure that, Denny had devised a shrewd form of bottom-dog capitalist motivation. Delivery boys like Adam got no wages, only tips. Adam's take each night depended solely on how fast he could get the orders to their destination. Volume was what counted, because students were not the greatest tippers in the world. He wished he could arrive at every door with a sign around his neck that said I DON'T GET PAID TO DO THIS, I ONLY GET YOUR TIPS.

One of the Mexicans slid another pizza box down the counter, and Adam had barely touched it before the all-seeing Neapolitan yelled, "You got a you eight! You get a you ess on da road! You stan' aroun' when you t'ru!"

Adam staggered away from the counter holding a stack of pizza flats that rose up higher than his head. Delivery boys used a battered, underpowered eight-year-old Bitsosushi hatchback. PowerPizza was part of a gaudy strip of student-oriented shops, and Adam's first stop would be six or eight blocks behind it in an apartment building he was only vaguely aware of, since he had never heard of any student living there. On the other hand, he couldn't imagine anybody other than students with rude animal appetites craving five full-size flats of pizza. The order came to more than fifty dollars, in any event. It would take somebody mean or clueless to tip him less than five dollars. Off the job, he was cautious at the wheel of a car. On this job you had to be a stock-car driver if you wanted to make any money. He sped through the seedy, feebly lit old residential area behind PowerPizza, barely even one-pumping the stop signs.

The apartment building was a dingy brick affair, four or five stories high, with a small entry vestibule containing a deck of about twenty mailboxes, a panel of apartment buzzers, and a glass interior door through which Adam could see a lobby that wasn't much but had an elevator, thank God. The five flats of pizza were so unwieldy, Adam had to put them down in order to study the buzzer panel. Jones 3A . . . Jones 3A . . . Found it, pushed the button, waited for the clicking sound, pushed the door open, and did the usual acrobatics, holding the door open with the heel of his sneaker while he bent over and lifted the five flats up off the floor. Christ! Did something to his back, which put him in an even worse mood. What was Destiny's child doing in a situation like this? How could it be that he, Adam Gellin, was a delivery boy backing his way into a third-rate apartment building in a shady part of a dreary little city in Pennsylvania, carrying five boxed slabs of idiot food while a lock-mad security-hinged plate-glass door pressed against his butt, trying to deny him entry? And his back hurt like hell.

When he reached the third floor, he found himself in a hallway with seven or eight identical flush doors, but he didn't have to guess which one was waiting for five orders of pizza. Belly laughs, whoops, the rumble of a lot of people talking at once, and the languid synthesizer sounds of a piece of so-called Sample Rap called "Elliptical Rider" by C. C. Good Jookin' were audible behind the door of what was undoubtedly Jones 3A. They sound black, Adam said to himself. Consciously, that made no difference. Inside his rib cage his heart had other ideas, however, and sped up. He took a deep breath and pressed the button. Nothing but the sound of people partying inside. He had to push it four times before the door opened. Adam found himself looking up at a towering young black man with a shaved head, clad in cargo pants and a T-shirt that showed off his muscles. His shoulders, biceps, and forearms were so thick and highly defined they made Adam blink. Behind the brute, a hazy, smoky dimness was punctuated by flares of electric color, apparently from a television set. Black faces were chundering conversation, through which pulsed the slow, eccentric beat of "Elliptical Rider." An oddly sweet odor hung in the air.

In the next instant Adam realized who Jones 3A was: Curtis Jones, the basketball team's shooting guard. On the court he looked small, since he was only—only, by Division I standards—six-five. Standing there in an ordinary apartment doorway, he looked gigantic. Adam felt relieved. The man might be a brute in a foul mood, but at least Adam knew who he was. Like the other players, Jones lived in Crowninshield, and Adam had been around him from time to time while tending Jojo. He started to say, Hi, Curtis, but thought better of it and settled for, "Hi—PowerPizza."

If the big man recognized him, if he was at all happy that his five flats had arrived, or if he was in any other way pleased by Adam's presence, he successfully contained his enthusiasm. He motioned toward a table just inside the door and said, "Over there." *Over there*—not even *put it* over there, much less *please*.

Adam did as he was told and glanced about the room, which was big but practically unfurnished except for an outsize DVD television screen tuned to ESPN SportsCenter, which nobody seemed to be watching, and a set of quadraphonic speakers currently devoted to the drones and percussions of "Elliptical Rider." Jones was not the only tall, powerfully built young man in the room with a shaved head. Treyshawn Diggs over there—hard to miss him. André Walker, Dashorn Tippet . . . but also some young black men who didn't look like athletes or students, either. Smoky in here. The sweet odor—marijuana. The black athletes, Adam had noticed, liked weed—that was invariably the term—while the white athletes preferred alcohol, and nobody even paid lip service any longer to the rule that athletes shouldn't get high during the season. The TV screen flared and lit up a huge white head. Jojo! That was him, Jojo. He was in the back of the room talking to Charles Bousquet. That huge white head happened to turn his way.

"Hey, Jojo." Somehow it seemed very important that the morose and intimidating Curtis Jones realized that he, Adam, knew someone here. Jojo gave him nothing but a blank stare. Couldn't he see who it was? Adam raised his voice this time—"Hey, Jojo!"—and waved.

Jojo nodded once, without a smile, then turned and resumed his conversation with Charles Bousquet. Adam couldn't believe it—but then he knew it was true. Jojo was avoiding him. He didn't want to acknowledge his tutor's existence in the same room as his cohort of fellow giants. Just two days ago he had stayed up all night researching and writing a paper for him on a complicated subject—saved him from a catastrophic F—and now the big, ungrateful dummy cuts him half dead with a single stone-faced nod!

Curtis Jones was glowering. "Okay. How much I owe you?"

Adam fished the PowerPizza check out of the pocket of his Windbreaker, looked at it, and said, "Fifty dollars and seventy-four cents."

Jones snatched the check from between his thumb and forefinger. "Lemme see that." He stared at it until his eyebrows came together. "Shit." He looked at Adam as if he were trying to perpetrate some outrageous scam. Belligerently he jammed his hand down into a pocket of his jeans, withdrew a thick fold of money clamped with a broad gold clip, riffled through it with his thumb, extracted two bills, handed them to Adam, and turned away without so much as another word.

The man's wide back was toward him before Adam comprehended what was in his hand. A fifty and a one. A fifty and a one? *Twenty-six cents?* Surely Curtis Jones was going to turn back and give him his real tip.

But he didn't. Adam was stunned. This was a fifty-dollar order! It didn't matter who the man was. He couldn't let himself get stiffed like this. He screwed up his courage. "Hey, wait a minute." He'd started to say, "Wait a minute, Curtis," but he wasn't brave enough to act that familiar, and he was too angry to grovel and say Mr. Jones. Not that it would have made any difference; Jones hadn't even heard him above the noise of the conversations and C. C. Good Jookin's Sample Rap.

Adam stared at the two bills again. *Twenty-six cents.* Anger wrestled with fear. Fear was winning. Okay, he'd—he'd—he knew what he'd do. He'd take twenty-six cents in change out of his pocket and say *Hey, you forgot your change* and then throw it at him. Well, not exactly throw—more like toss. He searched his pockets. He didn't have any change, not even a single coin. He ransacked his mind.

"Hey! Curtis!" It just came blurting out.

Jones, who had begun walking toward Treyshawn Diggs, stopped, turned his shoulders slightly, and looked back.

"What about my tip!" The trigger had been pulled now, and there was no holding back.

The big black man merely tilted his head, raised one eyebrow, narrowed his eyes, and gave Adam a certain look of male challenge that as much as said, "Okay, what *about* it?" Adam was speechless. Jones turned his back and started toward the center of the room.

"THEY DON'T *PAY* ME TO DELIVER THIS STUFF! ALL I GET IS THE TIPS!"

The room grew quiet except for C. C. Good Jookin's synthesizer beat, which in the sudden silence seemed swollen with amplification. The odor of weed seemed somehow stronger. The lurid flashes of ESPN SportsCenter hurt Adam's eyes. He knew his face was a burning red.

Without even looking at him, Curtis Jones said, "Hey, the man says he wants a tip." He sounded gloriously bored. Sniggers, chuckles, and the deep rumble—*hegghhh hegghhh heggghhhh*—of somebody's belly laugh. "One a you guys wanna give the man a tip?"

A few more low, restrained *hegghhh hegghhh heggghhhhs*, but nobody said a word, and nobody reached into his pocket, either. Adam was acutely conscious of a roomful of black faces, all turned toward him.

And one white face: Jojo's. Adam opened his eyes wide, imploringly, and fixed them upon Jojo. Jojo! You know these guys—don't let them do this to me!

Jojo stood there like a building. Finally he screwed his lips up to one side, shrugged his shoulders, and rolled his head in the direction of Curtis Jones, as if to say, "Hey, it's his party."

The others were already tired of the spectacle of the whining delivery boy. Conversation resumed, and C. C. Good Jookin's "Elliptical Rider" sank into the general hubbub. Jojo turned back to Charles Bousquet as if his tutor had never existed. Out in the middle of the room, silhouetted against the garish rectangle of the big television screen, some black guy was nudging the great hulk of Treyshawn Diggs. Adam couldn't see their faces very well, but he was sure they were having themselves a good laugh at his expense: the little white boy, his face contorted into a wretched plea, standing there atremble, begging a room full of black males for his tip . . .

Aghast at his own abasement, Adam slunk out through the door. Why even bother slamming it? It would only make his humiliation complete, if by any remote chance it wasn't already. They—and Jojo—had treated him like the lowest form of servant and, worse, as the lowest form of male, a bitch who didn't dare do anything more than bleat for his tip.

As he shitkicked his way along the hallway's steel-wool–colored carpet toward the elevator, his chin hooked down over his clavicle, Adam tried to console himself. After all, what could he have possibly done about it? He had been on alien terrain in a room full of young males of a different race, half of them giant pumped-up trained athletes. Was he supposed to loathe himself for not confronting the alpha-male challenge in Curtis Jones's eyes and fighting him? But that hadn't been his only choice, had it. He could have told him off. He could have told them all off. He could have informed them of what vulgar, illiterate, childish, ego-inflated, brain-stunted, reverse-racist bastards they actually were. Except for Jojo, of course—and you're *worse*, you towering buzz-cut blockhead! You're so terrified of looking un-cool in front of the other players, you're afraid to show even the most minimal common courtesy to someone who just rescued you from disaster, you nine-hundred-SAT, ninety-IQ, PlayStation 3 cretin! You didn't even want to be caught *knowing* me, you craven snob!

But he hadn't uttered a word of all that, had he. He had been the craven one. He had just stood there pleading for a tip, too much of a coward to do anything else. He could rationalize it all he wanted, but there was no getting around the simple fact of the matter. He had caved in at the first sign of male challenge.

He had almost reached the elevator when the belly laughs began in earnest. They came rolling out from behind the door of Jones 3A. The bastards had given him a few moments' grace, and now they were letting it all out. *Hegghhh heggghhh hegggggghhhhh!* . . . His public unmanning was now complete.

Adam left the building and looked this way and that in the morbid darkness without actually taking in anything he saw. He got back into the Bitso-sushi and just sat there, even though he had seven more orders to deliver, seven more orders that would soon grow cold.

All at once something stirred within him. It was Frankie Horowitz's His Majesty the Child coming out of his coma.

The Child blinked, stretched, and gulped some fresh air. As Adam sat there in an exhausted eight-year-old small-size hatchback, Frankie's prince's crown popped up magically on his curly head.

Destiny's Adam Gellin. In that very moment, he made himself a promise, the sweetest promise the human beast can make to himself: vengeance is mine, and I shall be repaid.

8. THE VIEW UP MOUNT PARNASSUS

The next morning, shortly after ten o'clock, Charlotte had just come down from Mr. Crone's classroom on the third floor of Fiske, where she had spent the past hour in the blessed company of about ninety others taking the medieval history test. Two students she recognized from the class, a guy and a girl, juniors or seniors it looked like to her, were standing by the magnificent spiral finial of a brass balustrade that ornamented the wide swath of steps that swept from the Great Yard up to the Fiske entryway.

The girl was saying to the guy, "How'd *you* feel about the test?"

"How'd I *feel*?" He put his head back, rolled his eyes up until the irises almost disappeared, and expelled a noisy jet of air between his teeth. "I felt like I was getting ass-raped by a very large animal."

The girl laughed and laughed, as if that were the wittiest thing she had ever heard in her life. Then she said, "What was that second *essay* question all about? 'Compare the Dublin and Baghdad slave markets of the eleventh century and'—what was it?—'the differing nature of the chattel trade in northern Europe and the Middle East'?"

"I had to wing it with that fucker," said the guy. "Do you think he'll give me a few points for truly *inspired* bullshit?"

The girl laughed and laughed, as before. Nevertheless—blessed company!

Charlotte only wished she were *still* in the middle of the test! At least for that hour she was part of a group of human beings all doing the same thing. At least she had been completely engrossed in a task that made it impossible to think of . . . *how lonesome she was.*

Loneliness wasn't just a state of mind, was it? It was *tactile*. She could *feel* it. It was a sixth sense, not in some fanciful play of words, but physically. It *hurt* . . . it hurt like phagocytes devouring the white matter of her brain. It wasn't merely that she had no friends. She didn't even have a sanctuary in which she could be *simply* alone. She had a roommate who froze her out in order to remind her daily what an invisible nonentity Charlotte Simmons, the erstwhile mountain prodigy, really was—and to underscore it by throwing her out when she felt like it in the dead of the night. Out to where? To a public lounge . . . which also burned with lust and sexual fear . . . in the dead of the night.

Charlotte scanned the Great Yard and all the scurrying bodies, all the happy heads atilt as they *bonded* with their *friends* over their cell phones, on the odd chance that somehow she might spot Bettina. Bettina might *become* a friend. *Sexiled?* Bettina seemed to regard sexiling as a perfectly normal part of college life. Charlotte was willing to make allowances—if only she could have a friend! Oh, how steadily the phagocytes devoured devoured devoured devoured . . .

In this mood, she *knew* there would be no Bettina to be found upon the sunny, shaded, majestic, massive, oh so delicately glinting tableau of the Great Yard, and there wasn't. So she finally pulled herself together and headed up the walkway that led to the library tower. In the library she could study . . . and sit alone in a setting where that didn't seem pathetic.

She was halfway there, walking through a stretch of deep, ancient leafy shadows, when she became aware of the scritching sound of someone in sneakers running up behind her. She didn't turn around; but then: "Yo! Hey! Excuse me!"

She looked back over her shoulder—and was so startled she stopped, paralyzed with dread. It was the huge guy from the French class, the wantonly stupid one who had tried to pick her up. *How about lunch?* She wheeled about and stiffened. He was almost upon her—the same hulk, the same tight T-shirt displaying the same grotesque muscles, the same odd little plateau of buzz-cut blond hair. He came to a stop barely two feet from her. The urge to run clashed with her desire not to look childish. The yearning for mature status prevailed. Motionless, paralyzed, aghast, she managed, but barely managed, to say in a strangled voice, "What do you want?"

His mouth fell open, and he slowly raised his hands, palms upward, as if lifting a huge plastic exercise ball. He was the very picture of a good soul misunderstood.

"I just wanted to apologize, that's all. Honest."

Still afraid: "For what?"

"For the other day," said the giant, "for the way I acted, the way I just walked up . . ." He blushed, which to Charlotte was an indication he just might be sincere and hadn't simply devised a new way to "hit on" her, as the terminology here at Dupont seemed to be. But it was no more than that, an indication, and she said nothing.

He rushed in to fill the conversational vacuum. "I was sort of hoping I would run into you again. I was thinking about what it must have looked like to you, and I'm really sorry."

Charlotte didn't say a word. She just glowered. He was so big, he was abnormal. His neck was so wide, his arms were so long, so packed with slabs of muscle . . .

"Come on, let me make it up to you. Let's go have lunch at Mr. Rayon—only this time, *lunch*. That's all. I swear."

Charlotte continued to grill him with a malevolent stare. On the other hand, there was a certain . . . supplication in his voice.

"You don't know who I am, do you," he said. Somehow the way he said it didn't reek of self-importance.

Charlotte oscillated her head as slowly as an electric fan, as if to say, "I don't know, and you're not even capable of conceiving how little I care about finding out," even though she did know he was some sort of basketball player, and now a little flame had lit up her curiosity.

"My name is Joseph Johanssen, and I'm on the basketball team. Everybody calls me Jojo."

Charlotte debated with herself.

"Come on," said Jojo. "We'll just go in and grab a little something."

All she had to do was say she was late for class or . . . In fact, she didn't owe him any explanation at all. All she had to do was say no and leave.

But she couldn't budge. It was as if her autonomic nervous system had taken over. The other her, the autonomic her, the one aching so with lone-liness, ruled.

So, without knowing why—the other her kept mum—she found herself saying, "All right." She said it in a faintly disgusted way, as if she were doing him a reluctant and essentially pointless favor.

Charlotte had never set foot in Mr. Rayon before. It was on the ground floor of a huge and rather overbearing Gothic classroom building, Halsey Hall, whose exterior offered not the vaguest hint of the visual explosion that hit Charlotte as she and Jojo entered the restaurant. Slick white walls seemed to scream from all the winking electrographics and industrial light-ing they reflected. Medievalish banners hung in martial ranks high above the floor. On the floor, a flotilla of black tables bordering on the cafeteria "sectors" were so slick they *smacked* with reflected light like the white walls. *Sectors*—six—different cafeterias, in effect, but not separated by walls, each with the same gleaming parallel U-shaped rows of chromed stainless-steel tubing for trays to slide on, stretched from one side of the hall to the other, presenting six different cuisines: Thai, Chinese, BurgAmerican, Vegan, Ital-ian, and Middle Eastern. The sound system was playing an old number called "I'm Too Sexy," whose mindlessly repeated disco sounds made the place seem far more crowded than it was. The real lunch traffic wouldn't build up for another hour.

The giant, Jojo, got a hamburger in the BurgAmerican sector and a can of Sprite. Charlotte refused to get anything, partly because she couldn't af-ford it and partly so that the giant wouldn't think she was deigning to "dine" with him or in any other fashion allowing this to be turned into some sort of "social" situation.

As they headed for one of the slick black tables, one of a group of four guys a couple of tables away halfway rose up from his seat, waved, and yelled, "Go go, Jojo!" The giant gave him a somewhat begrudging smile and nod and kept on going. A terrible thought crossed Charlotte's mind: If he *was* a basketball player, he might be very well known on campus, and sup-pose *she* were seen with him? . . . She wished she could put up a sign saying, THIS IS NOT A *DATE*. I DON'T KNOW HIM. I DON'T LIKE HIM. I'M NOT IMPRESSED BY HIM. I'M UNIMPRESSED. On the other hand, seen by whom? There was no one at Dupont University who could possibly care, ex-cept maybe Bettina. And what would *she* care?

They sat down, and this Jojo leaned forward over his plastic plate with the hamburger on it, as if to make sure nobody else heard him. "Remember what you said to me that day? After Mr. Lewin's French class?"

Charlotte shook her head no. She remembered very well.

"You asked me why I 'decided to say something foolish'—to Lewin when we were discussing *Madame Bovary*."

Charlotte couldn't hold back any longer. "Well, why did you?"

"That's the question I've been asking myself ever since!" His voice was barely above a whisper. "I *liked* that book. It really made me think. And you remember what else you said?"

This time Charlotte didn't shake her head no. She looked at him for a moment and then ever so slowly nodded yes.

"You said, 'You knew the answer to that question, didn't you?' And I *did*. And you wanna know why I acted as if I didn't?"

He paused, obviously eager for a response. So Charlotte obliged: "Why?"

"Three other players, my teammates, are in the class. It's okay to do the work, because you have to pass the courses, and you might even get away with good grades—although there's this one really bright guy on the team, and he always tries to keep anybody from knowing his grades. But you can't let anybody know you're actually *interested* in a course—you know, like you actually enjoyed the book?—then you're really fucked."

"Don't talk that way," snapped Charlotte, genuinely offended.

Jojo stared at her, motionless, as if he had been stunned. "Hey, I'm sorry! It just slipped out!" Awkward pause . . . Finally he said, "Where are you from?"

Charlotte fired back rat-tat-tat: "Sparta, North Carolina—it's up in the mountains—you never heard of it—nobody ever heard of it. Far's that goes, you don't even know my name, do you?"

Jojo was speechless.

Afraid she had gone too far, Charlotte said with a small, forgiving smile, "It's Charlotte. All right, you were saying how you're terrified of peer pressure."

Jojo compressed his lips into a slit. "It's not like—it's not peer *pressure* exactly—" He broke it off. Charlotte had him pinned with a cold and dubious stare. "I mean, this thing starts in high school. In *junior* high school. Coaches, everybody, start telling you you've *got* it. You know what I'm saying? You're very big for your age, you're something special, you're on the way to being a great athlete. Three different high schools, I'm talking about public high schools, three of'm tried to recruit me out of junior high school! My

TOM WOLFE

dad told me to go to the one that had the best record for getting players into the Division One basketball programs, and I ended up going to the one the furthest from where I lived, Trenton Central."

"Where'd you live?" *Whirred*, she realized.

"Trenton, New Jersey. But everybody on the team, Treyshawn Diggs, André Walker, went through the same thing. You're a freshman in high school, and everybody's treating you like you're way up here, and down there's all the other students. The other students, they're worrying about books and tests and homework, but you're 'special.' I mean like I'd sit in the last row of the class and kinda, you know, sprawl back in the chair and hold the book upside down. All the kids thought that was really cool. Then in high school I started getting all this ink in the local newspapers—for playing basketball—and that was a great feeling."

Still timidly: "Well . . . isn't that what you wanted?"

"I guess. But now I'm getting interested in some things, like literature, even if it's only Frère Jocko."

"Frère Jocko?"

"That's what everybody calls that course. That's French for Jocks. There's a German class they call Jock Sprache. There's a geology class they call Rocks for Jocks. There's a course in the Communications Department they call Vox for Jocks. I never got the Vox part."

"*Vox* is voice in Latin," said Charlotte. "You know, 'vox populi'?"

Jojo drew a blank.

"The voice of the people?" said Charlotte.

Jojo nodded yes in a distracted fashion that as much as declared he didn't get that, either. "Oh yeah, and I take a course in econ they call Stocks for Jocks," he said. "At first you think, wow, this is cool. But one day somebody says something to you, the way you did, and it sort of like . . . *zaps* you."

"Why would you care what *I* think? I'm just a freshman."

Jojo cast his eyes down and massaged his huge forehead with his thumb and two fingers. Then he looked up at Charlotte with wide-open eyes. "I don't *have* anybody to talk to about things like this. I don't fucking *dare*! 'Scuse me. I just get—"

Without finishing his sentence, he leaned farther over the table. "You're *not* just a freshman. What you said to me—it was like . . . like you had just arrived from Mars. You know what I mean? You didn't come here already affected by a lot of—a lot of the usual sh—*stuff*. It's like you came here with clear eyes, and you see things exactly like they are."

"Sparta, North Carolina, is a long way away from here, but it isn't on Mars." She was conscious of smiling at him for the very first time.

Charlotte immediately detected that something other than his concern for academic achievement was now seeping into that sincere expression of his. She knew this was the moment to put a stop to it. The thought of his starting to "hit on" her again was unpleasant and even frightening . . . and yet she didn't *want* to put a stop to it. The present moment was much too early in her experience for her to have expressed it in a sentence, but she was enjoying the first stirrings, the first in her entire life, of the power that woman can hold over that creature who is as monomaniacally hormono-centric as the beasts of the field, Man.

"Charlotte . . . I love that name," said Jojo.

Charlotte rheostatted her expression down to a completely blank look.

Jojo apparently took that as the rebuke Charlotte meant it to be. He mopped up the hormonal seepage of his expression and said, "My problem is, I don't know any a this . . . cultural stuff. You know what I mean?"

"No."

"I mean like where did this idea come from and where did that idea come from. People mention these *names*, like everybody knows who *that* is, but I never know. I never paid attention before! It's embarrassing. I mean like I got this teacher in American history, Mr. Quat, and he's saying the first settlers in America were Puritans—" He stopped short. "That's not right. What he said was not Puritans but Protestants, although there *was* something about Puritans, okay? Then he's saying in England, the Protestant revolution—wait a minute, or did he say reformation?—yeah, that was it, reformation—he's saying the Protestant Reformation—this is what he said almost exactly: 'The Protestant Reformation fed on rationalism, but rationalism didn't cause it.' Okay? So I'm looking around, waiting for somebody to raise their hand and say, 'What's rationalism?' But nobody does! All these kids have like ridiculous GPAs, and they know what he's talking about. And here's me, and I'm afraid to raise my hand, because they'll all look at me and say, 'You dumb jock.'"

"They'll say, 'You dumb jock'?"

"They'll *think*, 'You dumb jock.' Do *you* know what rationalism means?"

Charlotte found herself feeling sorry for him. "Well, yeah, but I had a teacher who took a special interest in me? And she had me read all about Martin Luther, and John Calvin and John Wycliffe and Henry the Eighth and Thomas More and Descartes? I was sort of lucky."

"All the same, you know what it means, just like all those kids in the class. I never read about Day Cart and—those other people. What did you say—Wycliff? I never even heard a any those names."

"You never had to take philosophy?"

Self-pitying: "Jocks don't take philosophy."

Charlotte looked at him in a teacherly fashion. "You know what 'liberal arts' *means*?"

Pause. Rumination. ". . . No."

"It's from Latin?" Charlotte was the very picture of kind patience. "In Latin, *liber* means free? It also means book, but that's just a coincidence, I think. Anyway, the Romans had slaves from all over the world, and some of the slaves were very bright, like the Greeks. The Romans would let the slaves get educated in all sorts of practical subjects, like math, like engineering so they could build things, like music so they could be entertainers? But only Roman citizens, the *free* people?—*liber?*—could take things like rhetoric and literature and history and theology and philosophy? Because they were the arts of persuasion—and they didn't want the slaves to learn how to pre-sent arguments that might inspire them to unite and rise up or something? So the 'liberal' arts are the arts of persuasion, and they didn't want anybody but free citizens knowing how to persuade people."

Jojo looked at her with arched eyebrows and a compressed smile, a smile of resignation, and began nodding nodding nodding nodding. Dawn was breaking inside that big head of his. "So that's what we are . . . athletes—we're like slaves. They don't even want us to think. All that thinking might distract us from what we were hired for." He was still nodding. "That's kind of cool, Charlotte." It was the first time he had called her by name. Now he gave her an entirely different kind of smile. "*You're* kind of cool."

The look on his face as he said that frightened Charlotte all over again. She stuck rigidly to her role as schoolteacher: "Take some philosophy. I bet you'd like it."

Jojo seemed to get the message, because he pulled his elbows back from where they supported his yearning hulk on the table and sat up straight. "I wouldn't know where to begin."

"That's easy," said Charlotte. "You begin with Socrates and Plato and Aristotle. That's where all philosophy begins, with Socrates, Plato, and Aris-totle."

"How do you *know* all this stuff?" said Jojo.

What crossed Charlotte's mind was, "Everybody knows *that*." What she said was—shrugging, "I guess I just pay attention."

Jojo remained seated upright. But the smile became even warmer, and he couldn't take his eyes off her, and what had been mere seepage now flowed and flowed and flowed and flowed.

She couldn't very well let that continue. Nevertheless, her very loins were astir with the power.

9. SOCRATES

his wasn't the first time Jojo had had an appointment with Coach Roth in the Rotheneum, but it was the first time he had made an appointment on his own initiative . . . and oh, man, had he had to do some double-talking to avoid having to tell Coach's secretary among secretaries, Celeste, what he wanted to see the great man for . . . Jojo's going-on-seven-foot self now entered the Rotheneum lobby feeling small and devious.

The Rotheneum was a section of the Buster Bowl building, created specially as an office facility for Buster Roth and his minions. Some young cynic on the school newspaper had come up with "Rotheneum," and now everybody called it that, although not within Coach's earshot. "Rotheneum" was a play on the word "atheneum." Jojo didn't know what an atheneum was, but he knew the word had to do with the higher things, things intellectual in nature. *The Wave* obviously thought of Buster Roth as a lower thing, a big-time college coach who made more than a million in salary plus at least twice that in endorsements, public appearances, life-is-like-a-basketball-game motivational speeches for businessmen, and swoosh deals, as they were known because of the swoosh symbol of the Nike company, still the biggest swoosh dealer of them all. In a swoosh deal, the coach dresses the entire team, from top to bottom—jerseys, shorts, basketball shoes, and socks—in the company's products, with each item identified by a logo—in return for . . . nobody ever seemed to know exactly how much. But it was known that Nike all by itself had a $200 billion advertising budget and that swooshing, also known as "branding," was their most important form of advertising. As coach of last year's national champions, Buster Roth had just signed a new swoosh deal, this time with the up-and-coming And 1. The numbers being bruited about were phenomenal. Whatever the sum, every cent of it went to Coach.

And there you had the mental atmosphere of the Rotheneum. It was the palace of the sports empire bearing a benign relationship with one of its most important colonies, Dupont University. The Rotheneum lobby had stark-white walls featuring glassed-in niches lined with mauve velvet to display Coach's many trophies. Last year's NCAA national championship trophy was in a niche directly opposite the main entrance. Everywhere you looked, star gleams were exploding off the trophies, thanks to high-intensity pinhole spotlights within the niches.

Coach's domain took up the entire third floor. There was a screening room with a sloping theater floor and forty seats—posh upholstered theater seats that popped up when you stood up—solely for the analysis of Dupont basketball games and practice sessions and the play of upcoming opponents. "Now, keep your eye on Number 8, Jamal Perkins . . . See that! . . . I'm gonna rewind . . . Okay . . . You see the way he sticks his fucking knee out when he executes a pick? Fucking refs never call it!" Jojo could hear Coach's exasperated voice in his head.

The elevator opened into a waiting room with a high ceiling, twelve feet at least . . . Downlighters cast dazzling beams upon epic-scale photographs framed in the most minimal (1.5 mm) brushed aluminum strips and hung upon more smacking white walls. There was a horseshoe-shaped banquette upholstered in a smart tan leather, on which sat three fortyish white business types with neckties. Opposite the banquette was a glass fence etched with diagonal lines of Dupont D's leaning in cutting-edge italic. Behind the fence, at workstations, as they were called, was Coach's harem of secretaries and assistants, all of them young women with short skirts and glistening shanks. Queen of Coach's harem was Celeste, a tall, willowy brunette with alabaster-white skin. More than one was the basketball player who entertained the desire to hit on Celeste, and Jojo was among them, but she was said to be the

T
O
M

W
O
L
F
E

"office girl" of Coach himself. As Jojo walked in, she stood up and said, "Ahhh, the man of mystery arrives! Have a seat, Jojo." She gestured toward the banquette.

Jojo said, "Yo, Celeste," and let it go at that. He didn't take a seat immediately. He eased his shoulders back to emphasize the swell of his pectorals beneath his T-shirt and gave the business types a few seconds in which to fully admire his overpowering height and muscles and to register the fact that *here*, even if they didn't happen to recognize him, was a Dupont athlete.

And if they didn't know it then, they certainly got it just a few minutes later when Celeste summoned him into Coach's office ahead of them.

And there he was: Coach—reared back grandly in a modernistic leather-upholstered swivel chair before a gigantic slab of mahogany—his desk—in the bay created by the great curved wall of glass at his corner of the building. He had his fingers interlaced behind his head and his elbows winged out on either side. Still vain about his once-athletic body, he had tensed his biceps, which in this posture protruded from the short sleeves of his polo shirt, and inflated his chest to create a mighty shelf above his gathering paunch. The room was not big in square feet, but with the sweeping curve of glass, the high ceiling a-dazzle with downlighters, the mahogany, the startlingly white walls, and stainless-steel furniture upholstered in tobacco-brown leather, it was dramatic.

"Come in, Jojo," he said—quietly, for him.

Then he gave Jojo a look every player on the team was familiar with. He lowered his head slightly, looked upward into Jojo's eyes with his teeth touching and his lips parted in a slight smile. It made Jojo feel as if Coach had just MRI'd his innards and found all his secrets, including the ones he didn't even know about.

"So—to what do I owe this pleasant surprise, Jojo?" said Coach. "Celeste calls you the man of mystery."

Jojo just stood there, beginning to feel extremely awkward. He realized he had never thought out, in so many words, what he wanted to say. "Well, I guess I should—I mean, I really appreciate you taking the time—"

Coach interrupted: "Go ahead, have a seat, Jojo." He motioned toward a semicircular chair of stuffed brown leather in a stainless-steel frame. So Jojo sat down—and couldn't get comfortable in the damned thing. The back was at a right angle to the seat, and the seat was too low. He felt like his head was a foot lower than Coach's.

Buster Roth gave Jojo a kindly smile. "You don't look one hundred percent yourself, Jojo. What's up? Anything wrong?"

"Well . . ." Jojo began rubbing the backs of his hands with his palms. "I wouldn't say 'wrong,' exactly."

"Okay, then . . . what, Jojo?"

"It's about academics, Coach."

Coach's voice turned a bit stern. "What *about* academics, Jojo? What class? I've told you guys a hundred times, you don't let things *develop*. The first sign of some issue, you come to one of us. You don't let these damned things just drift along."

"It's nothing like that, Coach." Jojo was rubbing his hands so hard, Coach glanced at them. "It's—I guess—what I want to say is—I guess I just don't feel I'm getting enough out of it, that's all."

"Out of *what*, Jojo?" Coach had pulled his eyebrows together over his nose. Obviously he hadn't a clue as to what Jojo was trying to say.

"Out of the academics, Coach, out of my classes."

"*What* classes? You're not having any trouble passing, are you? You had a two-point-two grade point average last time I heard anything about it. So what's the problem, Jojo?"

"Well . . ." said Jojo, struggling—he now had the fingers of both hands intertwined and thrust deep down between his thighs, which caused his whole upper torso to hunch over—"like . . . like I'm taking this upper level French course for my language requirements?"

"Yeah . . ."

"And we read the books in English instead of French, that kind of thing."

"Mr. Lewin, right?"

Jojo nodded yes.

"He's terrific. He's a real friend of the program, Jojo. He understands the importance of athletics in higher education. Most professors at Dupont are fine people. But every now and then, as you know, you run into some prick who's got a hard-on for athletes. Lewin's not like that. He's a stand-up guy."

"But we do all our reading in English, Coach. I'm not really learning any French."

"So what? Whattaya wanna be, a language scholar? Jesus Christ. Besides, that's not true. You learn plenty of French in that class, plenty of French literature. Plenty of our guys have taken that course. They all tell me he's a great lecturer. They learn all about the great French writers—you know, like Proust . . ." Coach was obviously rummaging through his memory bank for more names and coming up short. "And you actually learn *more* . . . about more great writers, because Lewin don't make you do all this translating. I had to take a foreign language when I was in college, too, you know. All that translating does for you is eat up time and break your balls. Don't forget, this is Dupont, Jojo. You couldn't be taking a better French course anywhere in this country. Jesus Christ, count your blessings. Lewin is great."

So Jojo gave up on From Flaubert to Houellebecq. "Well . . . that's not the only thing, Coach. The other day I'm talking to this student, and she says something about Socrates. I don't mean something like . . . complicated or anything. She wasn't trying to show off. She just assumed everybody would understand that much about Socrates. I mean, I knew the *name*, Coach, but that was all, and like Socrates is the foundation of philosophy."

"The foundation of philosophy, hunh? Who told you that, Jojo?"

"This girl."

"This girl," said Coach. "Well, I can tell you about Socrates, Jojo. He committed suicide. He drank a glass of hemlock. You know what hemlock is?"

"Like a tree?"

"Very good," said Coach, although Jojo wasn't sure about the look on his face. Was he making fun of him? "In this case," said Coach, "it's a poison made from the leaves. Socrates was a man of great principle, Jojo. He committed suicide rather than . . . Well, anyway, it all had to do with his principles. And you know what, Jojo? That's all you're gonna need to know about Socrates for the rest of your life. That's all *anybody* needs to know. You're still too young to understand this, but you'll get by fine as long as you have some vague idea of who these characters are when their names come up. Nobody you meet's gonna know any more than that, either, except for a few learned nerds, and they can't do anything about anything anyway."

"I know, Coach, but shouldn't I learn some of this stuff, all the same? I mean, here I am, and like you say, this is Dupont, and maybe while I'm here, shouldn't I—I mean, as long as I'm here and there are all these courses you can take instead of—like this econ course I'm taking?"

A weary note slipped into Coach's voice. "*What* econ course, Jojo?"

"It's called Fundamentals of Market Fluctuation. Mr. Baggers."

"I know him well. Great guy. Great teacher, too."

"I guess so, Coach, but it's also sort of econ for dummies."

Tersely: "Yeah? Which means *what?*"

"The other students call it Stocks for Jocks."

"Oh? Maybe you got a better idea."

"There's this philosophy course, Coach. Somebody told me about it."

"'This girl,' I suppose."

"Well . . . yeah. But it sounds like a great course. It's called the Age of Socrates."

Coach stared at Jojo for what seemed an eternity with the kind of astounded, malevolent look a father might give a teenager who has just walked in and told him he totaled the old man's Lamborghini in a drag race. Then he pressed an intercom button. "Celeste, get me the course catalog . . . Right. For Dupont College . . ."

Then he resumed the stare, saying nothing. Jojo felt as if he were being shriveled and shrunk by some sort of ray.

In no time, Celeste popped in and gave Jojo a flirtatious, almost leering smile—*hunhhh?*—and handed the course catalog to Coach. Coach swiveled in his chair so that his back was to Jojo as he opened the catalog to a certain place and began running down the pages with his forefinger; then he swiveled back to face Jojo.

Tonelessly: "Could this be the one, Jojo?" He read from the catalog: "'Philosophy 308. The Age of Socrates: Rationalism, Irrationality, and Animistic Magic in Early Greek Thought. Mr. Margolies.'"

"Yeah, that's it," said Jojo, brightening. "I remember there was this part about animalistic magic!"

Coach rolled his eyes but made no comment. Pause . . . Then: "Philosophy 308. You know what the 308 means, Jojo?"

Jojo shook his head no.

"It means it's the highest level. The three hundreds are the hardest courses they got. You ever had a three hundred course before?"

Jojo shook his head no.

Coach looked at the catalog again. "You know what Rationalism, Irrationality, and Animistic Magic mean?"

"Sort of," said Jojo, "more or less."

"Sort of more or less. That's great."

Jojo could feel emotion rising in his throat. "Okay, Coach, you're right, I'm kidding myself if I say I know, but I want to *learn* something, Coach! If

I'm gonna be sitting in classes anyway, I'm tired of—you know, skimming and scamming by the way I've been doing. I'm not just a stupid jock, and I'm tired of treating myself like one!"

Coach ignored all of that and said, "You know who Mr. Margolies is, by any chance?"

"No, but I hear he's really good."

"Yeah, really good," said Coach in a thoughtful, contemplative tone. Then—*bango!* "REALLY GOOD AT BEING ONE OF THOSE *PRICKS* I TOLD YOU ABOUT! THAT FUCKER'D LOVE TO GET HIS HANDS ON SOMEBODY LIKE YOU! HE'D CHEW YOUR ASS UP AND SPIT IT OUT THE CORNER OF HIS FUCKING MOUTH! The Age of Socrates . . . You simpleminded shit, I got news for you. As far as you're concerned, THIS IS THE FUCKING AGE OF JOJO! You got it? You got any fucking idea what I mean? YOU GOTTA MAKE IT RIGHT OVER THERE!" He thrust his right forefinger in the general direction of the basketball arena so hard, his whole shoulder and upper torso jerked. "AND YOU GOTTA MAKE IT *THIS* YEAR!—OR YOUR ASS IS FUCKED! The Age of Socrates . . . YOU'RE HERE TO DO THINGS WITH A ROUND ORANGE BALL!" He made a basketball shape with his hands—"THAT'S THE ONLY FUCKING AGE *YOU* GOT TO THINK ABOUT!"

Jojo had never shown his anger to Buster Roth, but the "simpleminded shit" crack had breached the Coach/coached barrier. "You're just like everybody else! You think I'm stupid, don't you! You—"

"That isn't what I was saying—"

"You think I'm good for one thing in this world! You think I'm this animal you put out there to take your goddamned round orange ball off the boards and set up picks so other—"

"That isn't what—"

"—other animals can shove your round orange ball through your—"

"Jojo! Listen to me! That ain't—"

"—fucking basket and whack the shit outta the big motherfuckers the other team's got inside—" It occurred to Jojo that he had just mentioned three things instead of one. That caused just enough of a hiccup in the gusher of anger for Coach to break in successfully:

"Jojo"—he had his palms up in the *whoa whoa* stance—"come on! You know me better than that! We been close for a long time. Ever since that night—remember that night?—one second, one *split* second after midnight,

July first—I had your whole telephone number already punched in except for the last digit—and as soon as my watch said twelve-oh-oh, I punched that last digit—it was a *seven*—right?—I even remember the fucking number— am I right or not!—and I said, 'Jojo, this is Coach Roth. I want you here at Dupont as much as any player I've ever tried to recruit in my entire career.' That was God's own truth then, Jojo, and it's—"

"Yeah, but you just called me a simpleminded shit!"

"—and it's true now! Christ, I don't wanna sound sappy, Jojo, but I've always though of you as a son. Like my firstborn. If I didn't, I wouldna used a term like—like what I said. But you and me, we're so close we can exaggerate to each other to make a point, and I wasn't even talking about *you*, in the sense of you, Jojo Johanssen"—he spread his arms out wide, as if Jojo Johanssen were about as grand as things got in this world—"I was talking about this one decision you wanted to make, a course with a prick like Margolies. That's all. I just thought it wasn't savvy, and you're as savvy as any player I've ever coached. Why do I depend on you to set picks? I'll tell you why. You *know* this game, Jojo. Other players just *play* the game. But you *know* the game while you *play* the game. You see what I mean?"

Part of Jojo didn't believe a word of it for one moment. And yet . . . another part of Jojo purred, however reluctantly, under the stroking.

"Yeah, but you shouldna called me that, Coach."

Coach. Even Jojo realized that his anger had just gotten flattered back down below the Coach/coached barrier.

"Of course I shouldna. But I get emotional when the subject's a great player like you. I guess that's a personal defect I got, Jojo, but having somebody like you to coach is what this game is all about, if you're a coach. Someday, someday *way* down the line, *years* from now, when you decide to call it a career on the hardwood, you might wanna be a coach yourself. Oh, you'll have plenty a other options. Sometime remind me to tell you all the different great things our players have gone on to do. When you play the game the way you do, a lot of doors open, Jojo. You'll have a *lotta* options. But if you wanna coach, you'll be a *great* coach, Jojo, a *great* coach, and you'll understand how much it means"—he tapped his fist against the center of his chest—"to have a player as talented and smart as you are right now."

Jojo averted his eyes, set his lips into an angry twist, heaved his great chest, and sighed . . . and nodded his head several times, ever so slightly, in assent, as if to say, "Don't think for one minute I'm not still angry at you . . . but I *am* willing to be justly praised."

Coach said in as calm a voice as you please, "You know, this is big-time basketball we play here at Dupont, Jojo. It's as big-time as it gets. But it's also college, and I think of myself as a teacher, and I *am* a teacher. I know some players hear me say that, and they think it's just something I say because it sounds good, but I mean it. I mean it as much as anything I've ever meant in my life. We were just talking about Socrates, right? Well, Socrates was a Greek, and in the age of Socrates the Greeks had a saying: *Mens sana in corpore sano*, a sound mind in a sound body."

Jojo didn't know the first thing about Greek, but for some reason that didn't sound Greek. It sounded more like—that was the problem, he didn't even know what it sounded more like. He was dying to interrupt Coach and demonstrate the wattage of the Johanssen brain, yet he couldn't very well interrupt and say something told him Coach was wrong, but he didn't have the remotest idea what it was.

"See?"—Coach went on—"The Greeks knew something we've lost sight of. A good mind don't mean much unless it's one and the same thing"—he held up his hands and interlaced his fingers—"with a good body. *Mens sana in corpore sano*. That's Greek for 'If you want a great university, you damn well better have a great athletic program.' Whether you know it or not, you're an educational leader here at Dupont. Yeah! A leader. You're a role model for the whole campus." He lifted his right hand to eye level and made an almost 180-degree sweep of the hand to indicate the whole campus. "They see a guy like you, and they see what they gotta shoot for. Now, none a those kids are gonna get a body like yours"—he gestured toward the Johanssen body. "A body like yours is a gift from God plus a lot of hard work. But that's what they oughta shoot for. The reason our program has to put a slightly greater emphasis on the *corpore* is because it's our program that teaches the entire student body what protects and fortifies and energizes the *mens* and enables it to make a difference in the world. We're all educators—me, you, the whole program. Like I say, you're a role model. You're helping teach all of this great university the Greek ideal: *Mens sana in corpore sano*. Every time they see you out on that hardwood—hell, every time they see you on the campus—they all know you by sight—they all say *Go go Jojo*—you're teaching, teaching, teaching, teaching them the Greek ideal: *Mens sana in corpore sano*, Jojo, *mens sana in corpore sano*."

With that, Coach sank back comfortably into the swivel chair and beamed Jojo a Solomonic look.

Shit. Jojo felt like he was treading water in a vat of mineral oil. The goo made him feel like anything he tried to do would be half speed. Was this how his big decision, his big academic turnaround, was winding up—with him floating like a dead bug in a vat of slippery Buster-brand bullshit? With his last ounce of moral courage he said oh so slowly and oh so hoarsely, "I never thought about it that way before, Coach—"

"Of course you didn't. There was no reason for you to. You're a great guy and totally committed to the program. Now you step back a few feet and take a look at the big picture and realize what a big part you're playing."

"—and I'd like to take the Socrates course, too."

Coach put his hand over his eyes, massaged his temples with his wide-spread thumb and middle finger, swiveled about twenty degrees away from Jojo, and let out the kind of sigh that sounds like an eighteen-wheeler's air brakes. Without turning back toward Jojo or lifting his head or removing his manual eyeshade from his brow, Coach said calmly, softly, albeit wearily, "Jojo, do me a favor. Take a nice long walk before practice tomorrow. Think about what I've just told you. Think about your role on this campus and your obligations and loyalties in life. Or if you don't wanna think about that, then think about a big, enormous, resentful prick. His name is Margolies. Anyway, think about something. Anything. Anything that'll make you use your head and not just your impulse of the moment."

He still didn't look at Jojo. He didn't budge from his posture of pain. And he didn't say any more.

So Jojo got up from his chair and stood there a moment. The whole thing was damned awkward.

"Coach—" But he decided not to continue. If he made one final pitch for the Age of Socrates—he wasn't even up to imagining what might happen.

So he just turned around and left.

10. HOT GUYS

Bettina, Charlotte, and their new friend, a freshman named Mimi, had just returned from PowerPizza to Bettina's room and the usual stew of unmade sheets and blankets, contorted pillows, strewn clothes and towels, abandoned catalogs, manuals, instruction sheets, CD cases, beauty-enhancement magazines, empty contact lens packets, stray rechargers, and dust balls dust balls dust balls.

"That place is a rip-off!" said Charlotte.

"Forget rip-off," said Bettina. "My jeans will never fit again."

"Yeah, I'm so-o-o-o full!" said Mimi. "But that was so good."

"Now what should we do?" said Charlotte.

Silence. That was, indeed, the question, for that question led straight to a larger one.

Bettina's roommate, Nora, was out . . . naturally. After dark she was always out . . . and Bettina, wearing a polo shirt and tight blue Diesel-brand jeans that made her legs look even chunkier than they were, had settled back into Nora's techie-looking desk chair. Mimi, wearing likewise fashionably exhausted Diesel jeans and a sweatshirt, sat on one bed with her back propped up against the wall and her knees pulled to her chest. Mimi was a big-boned blonde with a lot of hair, the type boys at Dupont called a Monet, meaning a girl who looks great twenty-five feet away and not that great up close. Up close you became aware that Mimi's nose was too long for her face. Charlotte sat on the edge of the other bed in a T-shirt, sweater, and shorts. Wearing shorts at night this late in October was pushing it, but she was determined to show off her legs, and besides, she now realized that her only jeans, the inky-blue ones Momma bought her just before she left Sparta, were not faded, were not low-cut at the waist, had tapered legs, and made you look about as un-Diesel as you could get. So here they were, the three of them, assessing their situation, which was that it was Friday night and they were sitting in a dorm room with nothing to do.

Finally Mimi said, "I need—I'm gonna go to the gym."

"It's ten-thirty on a Friday night!" said Bettina. "The gym's probably closed. Besides, that would be lame. We're not that pathetic."

"Well, what do you propose we do?" said Mimi.

Charlotte said, "Anyone have any cards or board games?"

"Oh—come—on!" said Bettina. "We're not in high school anymore!"

"Wanna play drinking games?" said Mimi.

"Drinking games?" said Charlotte. She tried not to reveal her alarm.

"Yeah, ever heard of them?"

"Yeah—" said Charlotte, who hadn't.

"Where are we going to find alcohol?" said Bettina.

"Good point," said Mimi.

More silence. Charlotte felt enormously relieved. She didn't want to look like a moralistic little mouse in front of her new—and only—friends. On the other hand, there was no way she was going to take a drink of alcohol. Momma's powerful embrace had her arms pinned to her sides when it came to something like that. Did Bettina drink? Charlotte rather desperately hoped not. Bettina was the motor, the energy, the gregarious force, the enterprise, that had brought the three of them together on a Friday night, so that, whatever their circumstances, at least they weren't alone. But Mimi was the one with . . . experience. Mimi had gone to a private day school in Los Angeles. She was the one who was up on subjects Charlotte had never heard of, everything from "morphing" with computers to "doing lines" of cocaine and "rolling" at "raves"—which seemed to be some sort of orgies people who used the drug ecstasy went to—and sexual matters such as "the seven-minute seduction," which Charlotte still didn't comprehend but didn't want to ask too many questions about, for fear of appearing hopelessly innocent. In short, Mimi was the sophisticate of the trio, the one with the sharp wit, the amusing cynicism, the world-weariness. She also seemed to have plenty of money to spend on things like going out for supper at a restaurant just because it might be fun. To Charlotte, even going out to PowerPizza was an extravagance. The real reason she had called the place a rip-off was to manufacture a reason why she had ordered so little.

Bettina got up and turned on her absent roommate's television set. An unseen commentator was yelling, "That did it! That did it! Look at that choke hold! Now she wants to twist her head off!"

"Eeeeyew," said Bettina, "mud wrestling." She turned to Mimi and Charlotte. "WWE, CNN, or 90210 reruns?"

"Um—90210, I guess," said Mimi.

"Reminds you of home, hunh?" said Bettina.

"Totally not," said Mimi. "It's so-o-o-o unrealistic, if you actually know anything about Beverly Hills. But I like it anyway."

Bettina looked at Charlotte.

"Oh yeah," said Charlotte, "90210, definitely."

"So 90210 it is." Bettina began clicking the remote.

Screams rose up from the courtyard, the unmistakable screams, once more, of girls singing their mock distress over the manly antics of boys. Very loud they were, too. The boys sang their choral response of manly laughs, bellows, and yahoos. To Charlotte, this bawling had become the anthem of the victors, namely, those girls who were attractive, experienced, and deft enough to achieve success at Dupont, which, as far as she could tell, was measured in boys.

"What are they doing screaming so loud?" she said.

"It's Friday," said Mimi. "Hello-oh?"

"Well, they don't have to be *that* loud."

Still more silence. Then Bettina stood up and put her fists on her hips. "This is ridiculous. We're not sitting here watching 90210 reruns on a Friday night. What happens when people ask us what we did all weekend? What are we gonna say? 'Watched TV'?"

Charlotte said, "We could go bowling?"

"Okaaay . . ." said Mimi, drawling the word out dubiously. "Do either of you two have a car?"

"No."

"No."

"Well, that kind of rules that idea out."

"Still, why don't we go out," said Bettina. "You know . . . like try a frat party or something. There's supposed to be a big party at the Saint Ray house."

"Are you invited?" said Charlotte. She looked at Mimi, too, including her in the question.

"Doesn't matter," said Bettina. "Sometimes they keep guys out, but they always let girls in."

"We won't know anybody," said Charlotte.

"That's the whole point," said Bettina. "We're supposed to meet people there. How are we supposed to meet anybody if we never go outside this dorm full of rejects?"

"How far is it?" said Charlotte. "How would we get there? How would we get back?"

"Hopefully we won't," said Mimi.

"What do you mean?" said Charlotte.

"Well, maybe we'll meet some hot guys and not have to come back."

"Nora certainly has that one down." Bettina motioned with her head toward her roommate's side of the room. "She used to sexile me. Now . . ." She rolled her eyes meaningfully.

"Oh, I've *seen* Nora," said Mimi. "I bet she hasn't slept in this room for like two weeks, has she?"

"Nora's okay," said Bettina, "but she's such a slut. Did you see what she was wearing tonight to go to dinner?"

"Yeah," said Mimi. "Could her skirt be any tighter?"

"Maybe she has a date," said Charlotte.

"Yeah," said Mimi, "a date with her pimp."

"Do we really have to stay over there?" said Charlotte.

"No, of course not," said Mimi. "Let's go. Seriously. It could be fun."

"But suppose it's real late? How do we get back?"

This provoked such a sigh from Mimi that Charlotte discarded the travel barrier and returned meekly to the first roadblock she had tried to erect. "And you're sure we can get in?"

"Yes! Come on!"

"They're not even gonna notice us," said Bettina. She turned to Mimi. "What do we wear?"

Charlotte broke in. "Have you ever been to one before?"

"Obviously! Yes, of course," said Mimi. "They're like totally cool. Up-perclassmen are way hotter than freshmen. They don't look like they just got off the school bus."

"Was everyone really drunk?" said Charlotte.

"Where are you from? What do you think? No, they drank apple juice the whole time."

That left Charlotte speechless. She knew she should act cool about it; in fact, she looked anxious.

"Come on!" said Mimi.

"Well, maybe," said Charlotte. "I mean if we're all gonna go."

"I'll lend you my makeup case," said Bettina. She was brimming with enthusiasm for the adventure ahead.

"Hey, can I borrow that red halter top of yours?" said Mimi.

"Yeah sure," said Bettina.

"Do you think it would be flattering?"

"Yeah, it looks good on anyone."

"What should *I* wear?" said Charlotte.

"Black pants," said Bettina. "And a bright-colored top. That way you'll stand out."

"I don't want to stand out. I'd rather look like I was supposed to be there."

"Then wear all black," said Mimi.

"I don't know . . ." said Charlotte. "I was looking at a magazine, and that's what they wear in New York. I'm not from New York."

"Help yourself to my closet," said Bettina.

"I don't think anything will fit me," said Charlotte. "I'm gonna have to run down the hall to my room."

"Well—don't take all night," said Bettina.

In 516, all the lights were on, but Beverly was not there, not that Charlotte had thought for a second she would be. Her heart was hammering so hard that when she opened her mouth, an odd chafing sound rose from her chest with each beat, as if her heart were rubbing against her sternum. Beverly's side of the room was as much of a mess as Bettina's room. A pair of Beverly's jeans were on the floor at the foot of her bed. It was as if they had dropped straight off her hips and telescoped at her feet. A round, crushed, prefaded denim pie on the floor was what they looked like. Diesels, needless to say. Charlotte's side of the room was a model of neatness by Little Yard standards. For a start, she didn't have enough clothes to be lazy or absent-minded enough to leave some of them lying around mashed up like that. For another thing, when you grew up in a five-by-eight-foot bedroom, most of which was taken up by the bed, leaving stuff on the floor and stepping through it was more trouble than keeping it neat—not that Momma had ever left her any choice. Charlotte's eyes remained fixed on the abandoned blue jeans, but they no longer registered. Crashing a fraternity party—and what did she *think* they drank, apple juice? She was breathing too fast, and her underarms and her face were abloom with heat. Somehow she had just committed herself to a dreadful test that wasn't worth taking in the first place. Well, that was crazy, wasn't it? One of the things that made Charlotte Simmons Charlotte Simmons was the fact that she had never let herself be bent by peer pressure. Nobody could *commit* her to doing anything. But Mimi was already fed up with her doubts and fears, and if she didn't go, then there would just be Mimi and Bettina, and maybe it would remain that way, and she would have no friends. She had had only one real friend at Al- leghany High, Laurie—four years at the same school, and one friend. What was it—this implacable remoteness, this inability to surrender herself to the warmth and comradely feelings of others? Could being an academic star, being applauded over and over again as a prodigy, take the place of all that? She shuddered with a feeling she couldn't have put a name to. It was the congenital human fear of isolation.

She was no star here at Dupont, not so far. Nothing had altered her in- expressible conviction that she would be the most brilliant student at this fa- mous university—but how was anyone supposed to know about it, even if she was? At Alleghany High, there was a steady flow of recognition in one form or another. If you skipped a grade in a certain subject, if you were re- ceiving special advanced instruction, if you were chosen to represent the school in some sort of academic competition, if you made nothing but A pluses, everybody knew about it. Here, if you were so brilliant, who would know and who would care, especially if you were a freshman? At this exalted institution, what was that compared to success as a girl? What should she wear? She didn't have any black pants, and she didn't have any black top, even if that was what she had been dying to put on. Her blue jeans—they weren't even a conceivable choice. She looked again at Beverly's, lying in a clump there on the floor, faded and worn out to near perfection . . . She'd never even miss them. But suppose somehow she *did*! Besides, they were bound to be too long. Desperately she scanned the room . . . Mimi and Bet- tina were probably already drumming their fingers. Unable to come up with anything better, she put on her print dress, the same one she had worn un- der the kelly-green gown at commencement. It wasn't the right thing, but at least it showed off her legs—although not enough . . . Ohgod. In a frenzy

TOM WOLFE

she took off the dress and raised the hem a good two and a half inches, using safety pins . . . By now they'd be ready to kill her . . . She looked at herself in Beverly's door mirror. A bit primitive, the hem job, but lots of leg . . . Anything else? . . . On top of Beverly's bureau there was Beverly's makeup case and her vanity mirror. Charlotte snapped on the mirror lights. The face she saw, lit up that way, looked like somebody else's, but somebody else not bad at all. She put her hand on the makeup case. She took her hand away. She'd rather die than have Beverly somehow figure out that she had used her makeup. Besides, she wasn't sure exactly how you were supposed to use the things in that forbidden container. She left the room frantic, a little soldier about to plunge, feebly equipped, into a dangerous battle for no other reason than to keep up with some girls she knew.

Sure enough, down the hall in Bettina's room Bettina and Mimi had severely tested patience written all over their faces. Mimi was wearing her jeans and Bettina's Chinese red halter top, and Bettina had on jeans and a tight T-shirt, the expensive, dressy kind. But above all, there was the makeup. Both girls' eyes were set in the shadows of the night, just the way Beverly's always were when she went out. Both girls were fair-haired, but their eyebrows and eyelashes were now black.

Mimi looked Charlotte up and down and said, "I'm glad you don't want to stand out."

"Is it terrible?" said Charlotte. How inadequate she was! "Is it all wrong?"

"It's fine," Mimi said. "You look great. Let's go."

"But you're both wearing jeans."

"Sooner or later you'll need to get some jeans. But not tonight. Tonight you look great."

"Yeah, you totally do," said Bettina. "You've got the body for it. I think we ought to get going."

"It looks awful, doesn't it?" said Charlotte. "Listen, I'm gonna—"

"Gonna what?" said Mimi. It was more of a challenge than a question.

"Oh—I'm just gonna go like this, I guess."

Soon they were walking in the dark along Ladding Walk, which was in the very oldest part of the campus. The Walk was an extravagantly wide promenade paved with stone and lined with huge ancient trees and late-nineteenth-century mansions, built close together, now used mainly for administrative offices, and, at some juncture, if Bettina had it right, the Saint Ray fraternity house. The light from the ornate old streetlamps overhead succeeded mainly in casting the trees and the buildings into monstrous, indecipherable shadows. Such a heavy stillness enveloped the place, it was hard to believe that they were going to come upon a big fraternity party in this vicinity.

That gave Charlotte a flicker of hope. Perhaps Bettina had it wrong, and the fraternity wasn't on Ladding Walk, or the party wasn't tonight but some other night, or it was already over or something. Up ahead in the dark, a *ping,* as if someone had thrown an empty beer can onto the pavement, followed by the *wooooooo!* that boys cut loose with to express mock astonishment—and Charlotte's last hope guttered out.

Soon they heard laughter and voices, although not very loud, and then music, which sounded like nothing more than a dull throbbing. Nevertheless, Charlotte's heart sped up all over again. As they came closer, a light at the entrance was sufficient to bring a grand Palladian villa out of the shadows. The portico close to the pavement had columns, like Monticello's. The windows were exceptionally tall but heavily curtained, so that only the faintest sort of light seeped out.

Fifteen or twenty boys and girls, mostly boys, were hanging around in clumps in the little yard out front, chatting and laughing in the subdued voices of people on edge about what might or might not happen. Just then a girl's voice piped up. "Oh, wow, you *think you're in love.* Like I totally care. You think all girls look the same upside down, is what you think."

This rated a chorus of *Woooooooo!* from the boys.

A tall, bony boy appeared in front of them. He had long light brown hair parted in the middle and flopping over his ears, and he was clad in khaki shorts, flip-flops, and a polo shirt with a Dupont golf team emblem. He had a drunken, I'm-very-amusing look on his face. "Where've *you*—I mean, *where've* you been?—I mean where've you *been?*" It seemed to be directed at Charlotte. His I'm-very-amusing voice degenerated into small-animal sounds: "*Enh enh enh enh enh enh enh.*"

Mimi murmured out the side of her mouth, "Just make out you're talking to somebody else."

They went up four or five low steps onto the portico and through a pair of dignified old double doors into—*bango!*—whines, thuds, shrieks, cries, and other agonies of electric guitars, electric basses, electric keyboards, amped-up drums, digital synthesizers, and young singers screaming their throats raw in defiance of God knew what—a regular storm, in short, raging through a swarm of boys and girls yammering, yawping, squirming this way and that, rooting about like weevils in a delirious twilight rank with a sour, rich, rotting sweet odor swelling up like a gas in the heat—the ungodly heat!—of so many bodies mashing in on one another and combusting with adrenaline—

Panicked, Charlotte turned toward Bettina and Mimi with the intention of saying "Let's leave!" but already the pressure of people who had come in behind them was forcing her toward the center of the swarm. Mimi had a vacant look, far from sophisticated. Bettina arched her eyebrows and pulled a face, as if to say, "I'm as bewildered as you are! Just press on!"

Blocking the way was a heavy wooden table commanded by two boys in blue button-down shirts, open at the throat, with great half-moons of sweat under their armpits. God it was hot in here! Behind them, arms crossed, face deadpan, stood a massive boy with a neck wider than his head and a tight green T-shirt that brought out the heft of his chest and the slabs of meat that were his upper arms, glistening with sweat. The boys in the blue shirts were shaking their heads no to three boys, two of them black, who were leaning over the table, supporting themselves on the heels of their hands. Immediately in front of Charlotte, a big girl with low-cut jeans and a bare midriff squeezed past the boys without so much as pausing at the table, and Charlotte could hear Bettina, just behind her: "Go ahead! Go ahead!" So Charlotte squeezed by, too, feeling reckless, guilty, frightened, baking with heat. She turned about. Bettina and Mimi had made it through, and the three of them huddled together.

Mimi leaned in close to Charlotte, to overcome the uproar of the revelry, and said, "See? Nothing to it!" Her face didn't look all that confident.

They stood still for a moment, trying to get their bearings. The storm bore down on them from . . . where? There were evidently two different bands at opposite ends of the house. In the darkness of the far side of the hall, strobe lights were flashing, illuminating a mob of white faces one moment and abandoning them to darkness the next, so that the faces themselves seemed to be flashing on and off amid laughter, shouts, and inexplicable ululations. Ostentatiously drunk boys weaved through the crowd carrying big twenty-ounce translucent cups, grinning with their mouths open, and bouncing off people. Two boys stood side by side, their faces, eyes, necks, and hands twitching spastically, while three others looked on, convulsed with laughter. The feverishness of it all dumbfounded Charlotte. Here were hundreds of boys and girls in a state of bawling rapture — over what? . . . Her eyes jumped from one girl to another out in that heaving disco gloaming.

So many wearing makeup — talking to boys . . . So many with glistening lips — talking to boys . . . So many eyes blazing like jewels in their dark occipital orbits — looking up, as if enchanted, at boys . . . So many leather skirts ending a foot or more above the knees, so many low-cut jeans and black pants, so many abbreviated halter tops, so many belly buttons winking in between — at boys. Their flesh, wherever it showed, seemed oiled. In fact, they were merely sweating, and the sweat reflected what little light there was. The sight of it made Charlotte feel the heat herself. Her armpits were humid. She wondered if the sweat would discolor her dress. She literally couldn't afford to ruin a dress, not even a pathetic one like this . . . hem hiked up by safety pins . . . She felt like a child . . . with her pale, unadorned face, her long little-girl hair, and her little print dress — hanging onto Bettina and Mimi for dear life. The very hair on her head was getting wet with sweat.

And the targets of the seductive artifices she saw all around her? The boys looked the same as they did every day, except that they were sweating. They still wore their shirts pulled out and flopping down over their jeans and khakis . . . They still wore T-shirts, polo shirts, khaki shorts, sneakers, and flip-flops. Exact same clothes as fifth-graders', Charlotte said to herself — fifth-graders with faces grizzled by seven- or eight-day growths of beard . . . They still wore their hair unparted and unruly, so that it tumbled down over their foreheads in half bangs . . . except for some who had combed in hair gel to give it shape . . .

A group of girls walked past, bunched together, blocking Charlotte's line of sight. They didn't look happy. She recognized two of them as freshmen. They all wore jeans, and they were practically stepping on one another's heels as they coursed through the crowd, glum and sweaty . . . a little herd of freshmen. The heat was becoming ferocious. Sweat was breaking out on Charlotte's forearms. She felt grungy and dirty, and she just got here. Over there . . . another bunch of freshman girls moving about like a single organism with many denim legs, blank looks on their faces — or, if not blank, anxious, as was she, and she didn't even have the saving grace of blue jeans. A little country girl's daytime print dress! How could she have let Mimi intimidate her from going back to her room and taking this thing off?

She turned back toward Bettina and Mimi, but Mimi was no longer there. She leaned close to Bettina's ear. "What happened to Mimi?"

Bettina shrugged and gestured vaguely into the midst of the crowd all around them.

"Bettina! Bettina!" Amid the heaving bodies, a girl was waving and grinning. She wore heavy scarlet lipstick, and her eyes beamed from out of a pair of deep purple dreamlike sockets. She seemed to be with three or four other girls. Charlotte recognized two of them as freshmen.

"Hadley!" Bettina shrieked the name, and Charlotte knew precisely why. She would have shrieked, too, had she been so blessed as to find a friend somewhere in this drunken rout and thereby be rescued from social oblivion on an alien planet to which she hadn't been invited in the first place.

Bettina headed toward her Hadley, looking back at Charlotte just long enough to smile and raise her forefinger, as if to indicate she'd be back in a moment. But Charlotte knew she wouldn't be, and sure enough, in no time Bettina and Hadley and those other girls had been swallowed up by the mob of revelers.

Barely five feet from Charlotte, a boy with big hips and heavy black eyebrows that ran together above his nose lurched through the crowd, drunk, proudly drunk, carrying a white plastic drink container and bawling, "I WANT SOME ASS! I NEED SOME ASS! ANYBODY KNOW WHERE'S SOME ASS?" and vastly enjoying the laughs he got from the boys and the mock shock on the faces of the girls. One of the boys yelled back, "Who you kidding, I.P.? You're ass negative! All you want is a knuckle fuck!" And everybody laughed again.

The rawness left Charlotte numb and frightened, and a fast-rising fear of some as yet nameless catastrophe made things worse. Charlotte Simmons was now a castaway in the hellish uproar—and everyone would see that! How she must look in their eyes! A little country girl dressed as inappropriately as a girl could be in an atmosphere like this, wearing no makeup—a waif alone in the storm.

She stood on tiptoes and searched the crowd for Bettina and Mimi. She would fight her way through the mob and attach herself to one of them, no matter how hopeless that would make her look.

Why not just leave, for God's sake!

But the walk back alone in the dark, back to the hollow place from which she had come—she could hear Bettina or Mimi or both asking her tomorrow, "What happened to you?" and not really caring in the slightest and not asking her to go anywhere again. She had no choice but to persevere and undertake the grim task of making this houseful of bawling boys and shrieking girls believe she was actually with someone and as deliriously happy as everybody else.

She tried smiling smugly and staring confidently at blank spots on the walls, as if she had just seen someone she knew only too well—and she was convinced they would all see that for what it was, namely, a look of curdled fear. The electric wails, whines, thuds, percussion, the bawling, the screaming, louder and louder—

Over near a wall—a line of girls. Some were talking into each other's ears, the only way to make yourself heard in the storm, but others were talking to no one. They were merely in line. Well—no matter how haplessly, she would be . . . with somebody. So she got in line, too. Soon enough it became apparent that this was a line to a bathroom. Pathetic . . . but an identifiable role, however temporary, however lowly—that was the main thing. She could catch stray overtones of girls chattering up ahead but couldn't make out what they were saying. The girl immediately ahead of her, a brunette with short, bobbed hair, had a worried, distracted look on her face and seemed to be alone. She should strike up a conversation with her—but how? What was there to say to a stranger in a line of girls waiting to get into the bathroom? Did she dare put her mouth up to the ear of someone she never laid eyes on before? That wouldn't hold back Bettina for a second. Bettina had just piped up and said, "Sexiled?" Charlotte couldn't imagine saying such a thing to a girl she didn't know.

The line inched forward, inched forward, while the party raged. That was all right with Charlotte. The slower the line, the longer she would have her protective cover. When she finally came close to the bathroom door, there was an amateurish but big sign on it: BOOTING ROOM. Booting? She could hear someone inside retching and vomiting. Or was it two people? Presently a tall, skinny girl came out, her face a ghastly white. Beverly! Charlotte thought at first. But that's not her. On the other side of the door the sound of retching went on, unabated. The only way Charlotte could kill more time before having to face social humiliation once again was by actually entering the bathroom. Finally her turn came. Two toilet stalls—one closed—the unmistakable sound of someone throwing up—and the overpowering odor of vomitus swept over her like something liquid and tangible in the air. She turned about and hurried back out into the storm.

Once more she threaded her way through the crowd, looking for Bettina and Mimi. She came upon a huddle of girls and was passing only inches from one of them, an exotic-looking girl with very long, straight black hair parted down the middle and streaming down either side of her face. The girl was saying, "Are you kidding? No way! We didn't do anything!"—when a big, laughing boy backed up and bumped Charlotte, and Charlotte's shoulder bumped the girl's. The girl turned her head and glowered from out of her hood of hair.

"Sorry!" said Charlotte.

The girl inspected Charlotte's face and her print dress without saying a thing, not even a word of reproof. She merely turned back to her friends. As if Charlotte had vanished into thin air, she said, "I get so bummed out by these freshmen. I'm a junior, and I don't have a boyfriend, and they prance around like, 'Hey, fuck *me!*' And the guys totally love it! They're like totally into fresh meat!"

More desperate than ever for cover, Charlotte wriggled and squirmed on through the crowd.

Another line, boys and girls—heading for what? It didn't matter. Charlotte tucked herself into the end of the queue and began another slow shuffle forward. This one was heading for a table, behind which two old black men in white jackets were serving drinks. Drinks . . . what would she say when she got there? What could she possibly ask for? As she drew closer, she could see big forty-ounce plastic bottles of Diet Coke, ginger ale, Sprite, seltzer, and a big pitcher of orange juice. By the time she reached the table, she realized that in fact the two black servitors weren't serving any alcoholic drinks at all. She walked away with a big plastic cup of ginger ale in her hand, relieved and vaguely puzzled. If they were only serving soft drinks— what about all the drunken boys? The storm raged on.

She stood at the edge of the crowd, slowly sipping her drink. A drink, a drink in her hand . . . not much, but as good as—perhaps even slightly better than—being in a line. Holding a drink was certification, however low-grade, that you were part of the party and not hopelessly adrift.

She sipped and sipped, slower and slower. She scanned the crowd, no longer really counting on finding Bettina and Mimi. The uproar, the lurching boys, the relentless music, the dank smell, the epileptic flashes of the strobe lights . . . how grueling it had become, how stultifying. Her shoulders slumped; her face went slack . . .

She felt the pressure of a hand on her upper arm. She turned and faced a guy who was bound to be in his twenties. He was startlingly good-looking, even though his face was flushed and his forehead was slick with sweat.

Everything about him struck her as imposing—the cleft chin and square jaws, the perfect thatch of light brown hair, the hazel eyes that were unquestionably mocking her, the smile that had just a hint of smirk, the white button-down shirt so freshly washed and ironed it still had a pair of folding lines down the front, a pair of khakis not worn dirty and shapeless, as other boys' were, but impeccably laundered and ironed with crisp creases. Everything about him said to her: authority. She had been caught. She dreaded the words he was about to utter, which would be *who invited you* and *then what are you doing here.*

"Hi!" he said, leaning his head close to hers so she could hear him. "Mind if I ask you something? I bet you get *really tired* of people telling you you look like Britney Spears."

What on earth was he talking about? He had a white plastic drink container in one hand—was he drunk? It took a moment for her to entertain the notion that he might, in fact, be flirting with her. Her face turned hot, and she smiled to try to keep from looking flustered. She finally managed to say, "I don't think so." But in such a little voice! With such a weak, stupid smile—and such clumsy ambiguity! Was he going to think she was saying she *didn't* get tired of being mistaken for Britney Spears? How awkward she was amid this swarm of sophisticates with naked belly buttons and little low-slung leather skirts!

The boy put his hand on her arm again, as if he were only trying to steady the two of them while he leaned in closer. "Well, I say you do, and Saint Rays don't joke around."

He *must* be drunk. He was so extraordinarily good-looking, it intimidated her. She ransacked her brain again for something light and deft, and came up speechless. She stood there smiling a smile she knew imparted nothing but the embarrassment of a little girl who had no experience in encounters like this.

He patted her on the arm and said, "Okay, I *am* kidding. You *do* look like Britney Spears, but if you wanna know the truth, I just wanted to say hi." He began staring deep into her eyes from no more than six inches away. He put his hand on her shoulder and grasped it, the way a mentor might if he were about to ask his young protégée a very important question. "You having fun?"

You having fun? She had been miserable from the moment she entered this house, but how could she be frank with someone so blasé? She couldn't even get the sickly smile off her face. "I guess so," she said. "Mostly."

He took his hand off her shoulder, turned it palm up, and stared at her with his mouth open. "You *guess* so! *Mostly!*" Then he put his hand back on her shoulder. "How can we change that?"

She kept smiling, gamely, which made her feel stupid. "I'm just looking for two friends of mine."

"Male or female?"

"Two girls who live in my house in Little Yard."

"Hey, that's a relief. In that case—wanna dance?"

The thought terrified her. She knew practically nothing about dancing, other than the square dancing she used to do out at the Grange Hall in Sparta. At the same time, the attentions of a good-looking boy like this would certainly validate her presence here.

She finally started nodding yes and said in a little voice, "Okay."

"Awesome!" He patted her on the arm again.

He took a sip of his drink. He placed his other hand on the small of her back and began steering her through the crowd. Well—he was only helping her, wasn't he? It wasn't easy getting through this mob. It was so hot, and she was sweating so much she could feel the pressure of his palm pasting the cotton dress to her skin. Wails! Thuds! The percussion shook her rib cage.

They were heading toward the back, where the strobe lights were flashing. In the roaring surf of polo shirts, T-shirts, camisoles, sleeveless jerseys, halter tops, and indefinable gossamer tops, they came upon a roly-poly boy in a blue button-down shirt and khakis, with a big plastic cup in his hand. He grinned in a cockeyed way and cried out, "Yo, Hoyto!"

Charlotte's escort said, "W'as happenin', Boo-man?"

There was an awkward pause as the roly-poly boy, who had a drunken, openmouthed grin on his face, gave Charlotte a frank appraisal.

"We're taking a house tour!" said Charlotte's escort, shouting to be heard, whereupon he slid his hand off her back and put it around her. "Boo, this is—uhhh—" He turned to Charlotte. "Have you met Boo?" He gave her a little squeeze.

The roly-poly boy chuckled and looked at his wristwatch and said at the top of his voice, "Okay, Hoyto, seven minutes, and the clock is running!"

Charlotte looked up and said, "What's he mean, seven minutes and the clock is running?"

Good. She didn't know. Her escort pretended to tip his plastic cup back three times in the semaphore that says, "He's drunk," and then added, aloud, "Beats me."

Every few yards, it seemed, some boy or other would cry out "Hoyt!" "Hoyto!" "Hoyt-man!" or some other variation of the name Hoyt. Charlotte found herself looking up at him and smiling, not from pleasure but from the need she felt to make people think she actually knew this obviously well-known boy who had his hand on her back.

A great strapping boy wearing a polo shirt that showed off his build came up and said, "Yo, Hoytster! Where'd you get that drink?"

"I'm not drinking," said Hoyt. "It's water." He lowered and tilted the cup, and sure enough, it was water. Charlotte was greatly relieved.

"Ve-ry int-ter-rest-ting," said the great strapping boy in some sort of mock foreign accent. "So to-night . . . the snowman cometh."

Hoyt shook his head. "Come on, Harrison." Harrison put his forefinger under his nose and made a profound *sniff sniff sniff* sound and grinned.

Now they were very close to all the white faces flashing in the strobe lights. Charlotte could see arms and hands flashing, too—a whole mob of people dancing on a big terrace enclosed by glass. At night the glass reflected like a mirror, so that it seemed as if there were strobe lights pulsing on and off from here to beyond Ladding Walk and on to infinity. The music was so loud it hurt her ears. Scores of white people, flashing in slices. Five black men, the musicians, flashing in slices, glossy with sweat. A cadaverously thin singer with dreadlocks. His head was thrown back, and he seemed to be swallowing a handheld microphone—in slices. He was screaming, "Mackin'n'jackin'—*ungggh*—mackin'n'jackin'." Next to a wall near the band— flashes of a boy and girl who were dancing on top of a table—in slices. Their faces bobbed, flashed on and off—light, dark, light, dark—in slices, their arms were flailing in slices, their legs were shimmying in slices, but they were joined at the pelvis. Their pelvic saddles bucked and reared in slices but never parted. Her jeans were so low-cut that when she torqued far enough, you got a flash of the top of the cleft of her slick, sweating buttocks. The mocking *wooooo wooooo wooooo*s of the boys massed about the table skimmed along the crest of the noise. Hoyt was now in slices. Charlotte's own arms were in slices. Gradually her eyes adjusted to the phenomenon, and she could see there were couples everywhere on the floor, dancing that way, locked mons pubis to mons pubis. She couldn't believe her eyes! They were simulating . . . *intercourse*! Right out in the open! It made her think of Regina's filthy phrase, "dry-humping." They were pressing their genitals to-gether! Some girls were bending over so that boys could thrust thrust thrust thrust simulate intercourse from behind, like dogs in a barnyard!

Hoyt put his arm around her again, tilted his head very close to hers, and said, "You wanna dance?"

Charlotte couldn't speak, she was so appalled. She shook her head no, almost ferociously. Hoyt said, "Hey, you can't do that to me!"

He said it in a jocular way—or did he? Charlotte opened her mouth—and managed only a sickly smile—after all, it wasn't *his* fault—as she shook her head again.

"Come *on*! You said you wanted to dance! I took you all the way through that mob so we could dance! Humor me! One song! That's it!" He had to shout to be heard.

Again she shook her head and mouthed the word no.

He cocked his head and stared at her for a moment, his tongue in his cheek, as if to say, "You really think I'll take that for an answer?"

"Let's go!" He seized her by the hand and tried to pull her toward the dance floor.

"*You*"—a rush of uncontrollable outrage. "Stop it! Let go of me! I changed my mind! I don't want to dance!"

He let go, startled by her outburst.

He held his hands up in a defensive posture. "Hey! Okay. Chill!" He smiled broadly. "Who said anything about dancing? I said house tour, and I meant house tour!"

That's better, she thought. He couldn't take her for granted anymore. This speck of encouragement expunged her angry stare. In fact, she found herself giving him a rueful little smile. But she still resented his attitude. All these people rubbing . . . their genitals together! . . . like dogs in heat . . . How dare he? She was better than the whole bunch of them! She was better than *him*! What did he have to be smug about?

When he put his hand on the small of her back again and began steering her out of the terrace room and into the grand hall, she knew she should jerk away from him—but *Bettina and Mimi*! There they were in the midst of the mob with Bettina's friend Hadley and some other girls—and Bettina was looking straight at her! They were too far apart to even shout to one another, but Bettina arched her eyebrows and pulled a face that as much as said, "Whoa! Look at you—with a hot guy like that!" Mimi's face fell. She stared at Charlotte with amazement and envy. She and Bettina were still stuck in a freshman herd.

Charlotte immediately looked up at Hoyt and smiled and tried desperately to think of a question to ask so he would have to turn his face toward hers and Bettina and Mimi and their herd would think they were having a great time. This Hoyt represented social triumph.

"Uh . . . what uh—" Why couldn't she come up with a question! "Uh . . . I—"

"Beat it up!" said Hoyt, smiling and revolving his hand, encouraging her to get the words out.

"What's uh—what's the name of the band?"

"The Odds!" he shouted.

"The odds?"

"The name of the band! The Odds! Fuck! I can't hear anything! Let's go downstairs."

Downstairs?

"The secret chamber!" Hoyt arched his eyebrows several times in an exaggerated way to indicate he was only being funny.

But what if he wasn't! Why had he put it that way? On the other hand, she was still floating on the awed face Bettina had made and Mimi's sullen wonder—Mimi, who had made her feel so timid, hicklike, and awkward, in short, unconnected with anything at this elite place. Charlotte craned about for another glimpse of the two of them, who she was sure were tracking her every step, but she could no longer see them.

Absentmindedly she said to Hoyt, "All right." Whatever his so-called secret chamber was, she now felt adventurous enough to take it. *The looks on their faces!*

Before she knew it, Hoyt had steered her down a dim, hazy corridor paneled with carved walnut. There were small, ribbed half columns of the same wood where the panels joined. The panels were so dark they soaked up what little light there was. The haze became a churning fog, and revelers wandered about yawping and cackling in a lunatic way.

Hoyt stopped behind two boys and two girls who were hovering over a table next to the wall. Seated at it was another brute—white, massive, young, but fast going bald, with a green T-shirt tight enough to show off great slabs of muscle, those and the dark triangle of wet sweat where the two bulging halves of his chest joined above the midsection. An argument was in progress.

"Well, how do you think we got in in the first place?" said a tall boy with a wide neck and a tough-guy face softened only by the thatch of brown curls coming down over his forehead.

The brute seated at the desk crossed his arms, which made them seem twice as big, and leaned back in his chair and shrugged his shoulders. "I don't know. I just know you gotta be a member or have a ticket to go downstairs."

The flat-faced boy, who had the dull stare of somebody drunk, launched into some heated remonstrances. Hoyt stepped forward and said to the sentinel behind the desk, "We got an issue here, Derek?"

The sentinel, Derek, said, "He says they had tickets, but they"—he motioned upward with his head, indicating the monitors on the floor above—"took them from them when they came in."

Hoyt slipped his arm away from Charlotte's waist, stepped forward, and said in a challenging tone, "Who invited you? Who gave you the tickets?"

A pause. Sensing, hoping for a rude confrontation, random onlookers began gathering around. Finally the guy said, "His name's Johnson."

"Eric Johnson?" said Hoyt.

"Unh hunh, Eric Johnson."

"Well, there's nobody in this fraternity named Johnson, and there's nobody named Eric," said Hoyt.

A couple of the gawkers laughed. Realizing he had been made to look like a fool in front of his friends and an audience, the guy felt compelled to begin the male battle. "And so who the hell are you?"

"God, as far as this conversation is concerned," said Hoyt. "I'm a Saint Ray." He had no expression except for an accusing stare and a slight thrust of his chin.

The guy set his jaw and lowered one eyebrow. Charlotte, like the others, quickly sized the two of them up in terms of male combat. The would-be crasher was taller, heavier, tougher looking, and more powerfully built. "That's very cute," he said to Hoyt, "but you wanna know what I think?"

"Not particularly," said Hoyt, "unless you'd like to explain why you shouldn't be a pal and fuck off."

The boy took a step closer, opened his mouth slightly, pressed the tip of his tongue against his lower lip, and narrowed his eyes to slits, as if trying to decide exactly which way to tear his adversary limb from limb. Hoyt maintained his insulting stare. The brute manning the desk was on his feet. He held an open hand up in front of the boy's chest. His bare forearm was the size of a cured ham.

"Time out, tiger," he said. "We can't let you go downstairs, and you don't want beef. Okay? Do like he said and take a walk."

Furious and powerless, the boy turned and walked away. His bewildered friends followed him, and the gawkers took it all in, disappointed that things hadn't progressed to bloodshed, cracked bone, and loosened teeth. After he had taken five or six steps, the guy wheeled about and pointed his forefinger at Hoyt.

"I'll remember you! And next time it'll be one on one!"

Hoyt raised his cupped hand to his mouth and pantomimed knocking back three gulps. You're just another drunk. The gawkers laughed some more.

Charlotte flashed back to Daddy and Sheriff Pike's confrontation with Channing Reeves and his buddies. Despite the language he had used, Hoyt's attitude of cool command impressed her.

The brute, Derek, smiled, shook his head, and said to Hoyt, "I always love these guys who are gonna come back and do something." Then he put the heel of his hand on the carved walnut panel on the wall behind him. It swung inward. It was like a secret door from out of a movie. The brute gestured, indicating that Charlotte and Hoyt should come on through, and then he scanned the remaining gawkers to make sure they didn't have any ambitions of their own.

Hoyt slipped his arm around her waist again, as if he was just steering her through the doorway. She stiffened for a moment but didn't disengage. It was just . . . his way of being a host.

"Where are we going?" she wanted to know.

"Downstairs," said Hoyt.

"What's downstairs?"

"You'll see."

"I'll see what?"

"You'll *see!*" said Hoyt. He assessed her wary expression and sighed. "Oh, okay, you're ruining the surprise, but I might as well—no—I can't do that—I can't tell you, but there'll be a lot of people there. We won't stay very long. You just ought to see it."

She was wary—no, plain-long scared.

Charlotte hesitated. Fear of the unknown and a chance at social triumph wrestled on the edge of a cliff above the abyss of doom . . . and . . . the social striver won. She followed Hoyt. The door closed behind them with a heavy *thunk.* The noise of the party was suddenly faint. Wherever they were, it was ten or twenty degrees cooler. They were on a landing, which was the threshold of a narrow, poorly lit stairway with black rubber treads that twisted downward around a curved wall. They headed down and around. The stairway, it turned out, led to a small cellar chamber consisting of a concrete

TOM WOLFE

floor painted furnace-room gray, tired-beige walls, and a wide metal door of the same color with a small square window in it. The ceiling was so low it seemed to Charlotte like some immense mass about to crush her. Hoyt pressed a button beside the door, and a scowling face appeared at the window. The face saw Hoyt and relaxed, and the door opened.

"Yo, Hoyto!"

The face belonged to a suddenly cheery big boy wearing the ever-present—fashionable?—khakis with the tail of a button-down shirt hanging outside it. The dank, sour, oddly rich odor Charlotte had detected upstairs—in here it was ten times stronger—and she realized what it was: a room the size of a living room saturated, re-saturated, eternally soaked in spilt beer. Downlighters recessed in a low ceiling cast light on a bare wooden floor, and cigarette smoke hung in the beams. The ceiling and the walls were painted a lumpy dark brown. Over the sound system came a squeaky, staccato jazz saxophone and a voice that talked the lyrics and kept saying, "Chocolate City." Some boisterous students were clustered about something or other on the wall opposite . . .

"Hey, Hunter," Hoyt said to the keeper of the gate. "Had any issues?"

"Not so far," the boy said. He embarked on a long discourse about how "the monitors" were supposedly everywhere tonight, about how you tell one from a genuine student, and why you had to be extremely careful all the same. Throughout this conversation, neither one, Hoyt or this Hunter, made the slightest acknowledgment of Charlotte's presence, even though Hoyt had his arm about her waist.

Her resentment was rising fast as he began steering her into the room, his arm still around her. Make him let go! On the other hand, this underground room, with its loud drinkers and smokers, made her claustrophobic, and he was her protector and her validation for being here at all. So she let him lead her that way toward the crowd. The students were hiving about an old-fashioned bar of dark wood, with a brass footrail. Happy—abnormally happy—to have made it into a special place where others couldn't go, they babbled, laughed, and shrieked. The bottom end of a bottle arced up above the head level of the swarm. It took a moment for Charlotte to realize that the bottle was in the grip of a boy who was pouring whatever was in it straight down his throat.

Cries of "Hoyt!" and "W'as up, Hoyto!" from the crowd. The party had reached the stage at which conversation disintegrates into inarticulate jubilation over being young, drunk, and immune to disapproval in the company of others who are likewise young and drunk and what of it. Off to the side, a boy and girl were lying together on a couch in a profound embrace, bodies pressed together. No one seemed to take any notice.

Behind the bar were two middle-aged black men in white shirts, their sleeves rolled up over their forearms, their black neckties pulled up tight at the throat. The shirts had great crescents of sweat beneath the armpits. Before them, on the bar, was a lineup of bottles of whiskey, rum, wine, vodka, and other things harder to figure out. Everything—big drinks, small drinks, beer, or vodka—they served in identical plastic cups.

Still holding Charlotte tightly, Hoyt said, "What would you like?"

"Nothing, thanks." She forced a smile.

"Oh come on. You wouldn't dance with me! So you gotta at least have a drink!"

He said it so loud! People at the table were turning around.

Barely above a whisper: "I don't drink."

Hoyt boomed out, "Not even *beer*?"

She croaked out, "Uh . . . no. *You're* not drinking."

The boomer: "I will if *you* will!"

More people were turning around. Charlotte could feel the color surging into her face. She tried to utter the word no, but could only say it by shaking her head. The smile on her face was meant to indicate to *them* that this was all in fun. In fact—and she was conscious of it—it was the sickly smile of someone who thinks she has just committed a terrible gaffe.

"Well then, how about some wine? Wine isn't even drinking! It doesn't even count!" *Everyone* could hear him.

"Don't listen to him! He's a lapsed recovering alcoholic!"

Out the corner of her eye Charlotte could tell that came from a big, strapping boy—khakis, blue button-down shirt, tail out—near the table. He had his arm around a lissome girl in a miniskirt. Her eyes were bleary and switched off. She looked as if she would fall to the floor if he took his arm away. But Charlotte didn't dare look at the guy, since she had no idea how she might possibly come up with an answer.

Once more looking at her, the boy said, "You know you're standing next to the poster boy for Mothers Against Binge Drinking?"

"Fun-nee," said Hoyt. "Why don't you sing us a song, Julian? They say drunks can sing songs even after they start bubbling at the mouth."

Hoyt still had his arm around Charlotte. He looked down at her, smiled, gave her a mighty squeeze, and began steering her toward the bar.

She had no idea what to say to this big guy who kept directing questions to her—or supposedly to her. Her face was aflame with embarrassment over the proprietary hugs Hoyt was giving her in front of everybody. She wanted to show everybody she didn't belong to him—but did she dare make a scene in this secret cellar or wherever she was? Worst of all, she could feel one of her greatest strengths, the fact that Charlotte Simmons was one of those rare young people who never caved in to peer pressure, ebbing away moment by moment. She couldn't have all these people, these sophisticated upper-classmen, staring at her as if she were some naïve freshman oddity. In the next moment, she heard herself saying to Hoyt, "Maybe some wine."

"Way to go!" said Hoyt. Arm still around her, he led her into the throng by the table.

The big guy, Julian, edged over toward them and said, "You are so bad, Hoyt." He said it as if she wasn't even there.

Hoyt leaned over toward him and said in a low voice, "You know what a cock block is, Julian?" To Charlotte: "Red wine or white?"

"I don't know. Red?"

He let go of her for a moment and started to muscle his way through the crowd to the table. He stopped and looked off to the side. Then he yelled out, "Yo! Get a room!"

The boy on the couch had thrust one denim leg between the girl's denim thighs, and she had wrapped one leg way up practically around his waist, and they were making little thrusting motions. People started laughing, and three or four others yelled, "Yeah, get a room!" The couple disentangled and propped themselves up on their elbows, staring stupidly at their audience. The girl Julian was supporting started making a sputtering sound, like air escaping from the tiny opening of a party balloon. Her lips were flapping. Her eyes were open but saw nothing. *Just like that* she collapsed. Julian barely managed to keep her from hitting the floor.

"Aw, shit," he said. He lifted up her inert form and flung it over his shoulder. "Fucking Roofies."

He turned to carry the girl out of the room—and a sludgy brown stream was running down the back of one leg. It was putrid. Feces.

Charlotte went, "Hoyt—Hoyt—" She was horrified.

"Ecch," said Hoyt. "Nothing to worry about. Girl's crazy. She takes muscle relaxants."

In due course, Hoyt came back from the bar with two cups, one for her and one for himself. He raised his, as if making a toast. Still terribly embarrassed and convinced that the entire room was waiting to see what she would do, she raised her container, and Hoyt tapped it with his. Not knowing what else to do, she put hers to her lips and took a sip. It wasn't all that horrible—but she felt a jolt of shame. The only reason she was holding this drink in her hand was to keep from looking uncool in front of a bunch of drunks she didn't even know. But she took another sip, a bigger one, and then another, bigger still. Only then did she notice Hoyt hadn't even brought his drink to his lips.

He kept sneaking glances down into her cup. Spreading the warmest and sincerest smile imaginable across his face, he looked deep into her eyes. Then he motioned toward the metal door. "I told you we wouldn't stay down here very long," said the man you could always trust. "Let me show you what's upstairs."

Charlotte nodded and took another gulp.

Charlotte hadn't felt this relaxed—or trustful—all evening. Instead of the chill of anxiety that had gripped her ever since she first stepped into this house, something warm and mellow now coursed through her veins. This good-looking boy, Hoyt, who had excited and frightened her at the same time, had proved to be a gentleman, albeit an extremely "hot" gentleman, to use Mimi's word. The look on her face!—and Bettina's! That was what she could see as she looked into Hoyt's eyes. She didn't mind at all when he took her by the hand as he led her back up the winding stairs.

At the top he turned the handle of the secret door, but it wouldn't open. No doubt the bouncer had locked it, he told Charlotte. The guy must have spotted a monitor, or somebody who might be a monitor. It seemed that the university sent snoopers around to report underage drinking—meaning serving alcohol where people under twenty-one were present—and it was hard to keep them out. That was why both the alcohol at the secret bar downstairs and the soft drinks at the bar on the main floor were served in identical white containers. That way the monitors couldn't tell a container of beer from a container of Sprite. The administration had begun enforcing the drinking rule with a vengeance. The vengeance was directed at the very system itself: fraternities. The administration was looking for any way possible to force them off the campus and eliminate them, and—

Charlotte didn't hear anything after underage drinking. She was at this very moment doing something illegal. It had never occurred to her! But the jolt of panic soon passed. She took another swallow of wine. While delivering his exegesis, Hoyt put his arm around her again. This time it wasn't at all disturbing. Somehow he had become her protector.

Hoyt tried the door again, and now it opened. They emerged into the full onslaught of the music. The bouncer turned around in his seat at the desk, smiled wryly, and said something to Hoyt. It sounded like, "All clear, Hoyto."

The crowd in the great hall had swollen. Boys and girls, practically all of them white, were crammed together from one end to the other. The heat was worse than ever. The girls grinned with their mouths open and laughed at anything and nothing at all. The music was a never-ending chain-reaction freeway pileup with slivers of human cries and shrieks.

She hadn't wanted anybody seeing him touch her in any way, least of all Mimi and Bettina, but now a thrill of sudden social ascension—she had a hot guy hovering over her!—was overriding everything else. And what if they did see her with his arm around her? What was actually wrong with that? Was there a better-looking boy in the whole place? Take a good look, Mimi! Mimi's condescending attitude would never survive seeing her with this boy in tow . . . Charlotte looked about, halfway expecting to see them. But there were so many bodies, so much noise, such a delirious humid haze . . . and the strobe lights kept throbbing . . .

Hoyt was steering her toward the grand staircase. It was just ahead, its banister sweeping upstairs in a luxurious curve. She stiffened with a twinge of the Doubts . . . Was it really wise to go "upstairs," whatever that might possibly mean? But there were already boys and girls going up the staircase and coming down the staircase, a regular stream of them. It wasn't as if she and this boy would be up there by themselves.

Getting through the crowd wasn't easy. Boys kept trying to get over to Hoyt. "Hey, Hoyt!" "Yo, Hoyto!" Charlotte Simmons—magically beamed up into the very center of things!

Boys and girls, pelvises locked together, were grinding away as before, except that now they were sweating so much their arms and faces looked luminous—and frenzied—when the strobe flashes hit them.

Up close, the staircase wasn't quite so grand. Coats of paint had dulled the great curved banister. The steps, which must have been four feet wide, had patches of practically bare wood in the center.

"Yo, Hoyt! Where you going?" *Whuh yuh gon'?* "Crawl the hall—or sump'm else?"

It was a fat boy yelling in a slurred voice from below. He was leering. An egregious pair of black eyebrows ran together over his nose. Wait a minute. Hadn't she seen him before? He held a white drink container at a perilous angle in one hand. His shirtfront was sopping wet.

Hoyt ignored him.

"Who's that?" said Charlotte. "What's he mean, crawl the hall?"

Hoyt shrugged in a *Who knows?* sort of way and said, "That's I.P. He's one of our mistakes."

At the top of the stairs was a landing three times the size of Charlotte's living room in Sparta. She never saw such a high ceiling upstairs in a house. In the center, where there had no doubt once been a chandelier, was a fluorcscent fixture that gave off a harsh, gaseous blue light. Down a wide hallway Charlotte could see students crowded in front of open doorways, convulsing with laughter, erupting with cheers, whoops, and applause of obviously mock approval, and groans and boos of mock disappointment, all the while drinking from their big cups.

"What are they doing?" said Charlotte.

Hoyt didn't even pause. He never let up on the pressure of his arm on her back as he steered her toward the staircase that went up. "I don't know," he sighed, shaking his head as if to say that whatever it was, it was something pointless, wearisome, and juvenile, not even worth investigating. "Come on, I'll show you the rooms. They'll blow your mind."

Leading off the third-floor landing was a hall as wide as the one below, but the doors seemed to be closed, and there was nobody hanging out in the corridor. Hoyt steered her along it, his arm ever more tight around her. From behind the doors came random muffled laughter, real and from TV laugh tracks, drunken male yawps, the burble of conversations, the deep *unghhs* of animated brutes getting pulverized in video games . . .

Hoyt stopped in front of a door, paused to see if he could hear anything, then opened it. It was a large bedroom packed with boys and girls sitting on the edges of the beds and on the floor in a cloud of funky, sweetish smoke, not saying a word. They stared at Hoyt and Charlotte with the wary, wide-eyed look of raccoons caught out back by the trash bin at night—except for a girl who held a wrinkled cigarette up to her lips between her thumb and forefinger and inhaled deeply with her eyes shut.

"Peace," said Hoyt as he closed the door and withdrew.

He opened another. It was dark except for the light from the hall, which was enough to reveal a double-decker bunk bed on either side. Hoyt clicked a wall switch on. A sandy-colored blanket with American Indian designs on it was tucked beneath the upper mattress, pulled straight down, and tucked beneath the lower mattress, creating a sort of tent. Charlotte heard a male voice whisper, "Who the fuck's that?"

Hoyt switched the light off and closed the door.

"Did you hear somebody say something?" Charlotte asked.

"Maybe in their sleep or something," said Hoyt. "I think there's somebody sleeping in there."

He hurried her down the hall. Another door. He opened it and stuck his head in. The lights were on. Two beds. One bed—what a rat's nest! Sheets, blanket, and a pillow all twisted together, and a lot of bare mattress showing. On the other bed the blanket was pulled all the way up over the pillow in a stab at neatness, but there were inexplicable lumps and humps under it. Hoyt beckoned Charlotte in and closed the door. Resting an arm lightly across her shoulders, he gestured toward the wall opposite.

"Look at those windows. Must be eight or nine feet tall."

They were big, all right, but their eminence in the world of windows was compromised by splotched and mottled old shades that sagged down full length, helplessly, never to roll up again, from bare wooden spindles whose spring mechanisms were done for.

". . . and look at the height of that ceiling," Hoyt was saying, "and those what do you call them? Cornices, cornice moldings. And this place was built as a *fraternity house*! Two alumni back in whatever it was put up the money for it. They'll never build anything like this again. Of that you can be sure."

"Is this your room?" said Charlotte.

"No," said Hoyt. "Mine's downstairs where all those people were. It's actually bigger than this one, but this one's pretty typical. You know what? I really love this house."

He compressed his lips and shook his head, as if to indicate that he was feeling an emotion too profound to express. Then he gave her the smile of a man who has seen an awful lot in his time on this earth. He looked deep into her eyes—deep, deep, and deeper—and gave her an almost bashful smile.

At that moment the door to the room opened and a virtual yodel of happy conversation filled the doorway. Without relaxing his grip on Charlotte, Hoyt swung about. Coming into the room was a tall, slim boy with tousled blond hair. He had his arm around a cute little brunette who was practically popping out of a short spaghetti-strap camisole and a pair of low-cut jeans, while her belly button winked in between.

Hoyt barked out, "Damn it, Vance, get outta here! We've got this room!"

The little brunette stood stock-still with a now irrelevant smile frozen on her face.

"*Sor-ree*," said Vance, his arm still around her. "Chill, chill, chill. Howard and Lamar told me—"

"Do you see Howard and Lamar in here?" said Hoyt. "*We're* here now. We got this one."

The boy looked at his watch and said, "I don't know, Hoyt, but it looks like a lot over seven minutes to me."

"Vance—"

Vance turned the palms of his hands up toward Hoyt and said, "Okay, that's cool. Just let me know when you're through? Okay? We'll be down on the second floor."

We got this room! Okay, let me know when you're through!

Charlotte's hands went cold. Her face was on fire. She wrenched herself free of Hoyt's grip and said, "For your information, you're wrong! *We* don't have this room—*you* have this room! And *we* won't ever be through— because *we* won't ever begin!"

Hoyt shot a quick glance at Vance and the brunette in the doorway, then canted his head back and off to one side, rolled his eyes upward, and opened his arms in a helpless, crucified way. "I know—"

"You *don't* know!" screamed Charlotte. "You're gross!"

"Hey! Keep it down!" said Hoyt. "I mean—shit!" The eternal male, eternally mortified by the female Making a Scene.

"I *won't* keep it down! I'm leaving!"

With that, she stormed past him, tears streaming down her face, past Vance and his little brunette—

Hoyt called out, lamely, "Hey—wait!"

Charlotte didn't look back. She tossed her long brown hair over her shoulder in anger and kept going. As she ran down the big curved stairway, the bacchanal below raged on. All was uproar. Downstairs in the big entry hall, she frantically, physically, bodily forced her way between the revelers, who bobbed and shrieked and ululated and exulted in bawling music drunken screaming stroboscopic girls in slices boys dry-humping in-heat bitches he's not cool got little dickie his cum dumpster is what she is oh fuck that sucks it's so ghetto scarfed a whole line with a green straw from the heel of her Manolo gotta get laid she scored Jojo—

—"she scored Jojo?" That little lick of conversation caught Charlotte's attention, but she was far beyond the gravitational pull of gossip in her headlong flight through the double doors and out onto Ladding Walk into God's own air!—not befouled by decadence and lust—

—except for five or six stricken boys and girls crawling, lolling stuporously, bending over on the little fringe of a lawn in front of the Saint Ray house vomiting and chanting into the void in Fuck Patois. Charlotte ran down the Walk into the darkness and the monstrous shadows until her throat ached and she could no longer hold back the tears. She slowed to a walk, let her head slump over, held her forehead with her hand, and convulsed with sobs. Get outta here! We've got this room! Okay, that's cool. Just let me know when you're through. Okay? Oh dear God, was there any way Bettina and Mimi could find out?—about her *cool guy* and her terminal humiliation and what a fool she was?

She felt so small here in the infinite terminal darkness of Ladding Walk, all alone, sobbing and sobbing and racking her thorax, slogging pointlessly toward Little Yard, a little mountain girl—she couldn't have pitied herself more—in an old cotton print dress hiked up two and a half inches with pins so she could show off more of her legs.

The dark hulks of the buildings along Ladding Walk, which were menacing, the stony silence—except for her own sobs, which she held back and then let out—held back, let out—there was a certain morbid, self-destructive *pleasure* in letting them out, wasn't there?—a sick, morose self-abnegation in surrendering to the swirl of deceit she had been subjected to by Hoyt Whoeverhewas—the walk back to Edgerton was a nightmare, part of whose pain was that it seemed like it would never end.

When she stepped out of the elevator on the fifth floor, into that dead-silent vestibule, it seemed like a sanctuary, or the only one Charlotte Simmons would have, and she indulged herself in a real wailing sob as she headed down the hallway—then she heard whispers . . . *Ohmygod!*—six? seven? eight? girls sitting in a row, bottoms on the floor, backs against the wall, legs, or most of them, sticking straight out in a lineup of distressed jeans, shorts, sneakers, flip-flops, bare feet, lumpy knees—eyes, every eye, pinned on her. They were all freshmen who lived on this floor. What were they *doing* here out in the hall in the middle of the night? What must she look like to them? Tears, puffy eyes—her nose felt twice as big as it was, it was so congested from crying—and they were *bound* to have heard her wail when she left the elevator. They were a *gauntlet.* They would have to lift their legs in order for her to get to her room. If she had to speak to them, ask them to let her by—she *couldn't!*—she would burst into tears again! She bit her lip and told herself to be strong, be strong, come on, don't let on, hold it in. The first pair of knees and ratty jeans jackknifed to let her by. The puniest pair imaginable they were, too, those of a skinny, chinless girl with the palest of faces and hair the color of chamomile tea and cut like a young boy's, a girl called Maddy—a wretched case despite the fact that she had won some big national science competition last spring, Westinghouse or something. Charlotte couldn't stand looking at her, but she couldn't escape those abnormally big eyes as they turned up toward her and runty Maddy said, "What happened?" Charlotte kept her head down and shook it, which was as close as she could come to a gesture signifying, "Nothing." That only sharpened Maddy's appetite. "We heard you crying." The knees ahead began pulling up to the chests one by one. Each time, the big eyes studied her face, which Charlotte knew very well was contorted like that of a girl who would convulse with tears if she so much as opened her mouth. From behind, little Maddy wouldn't give up. "Can we help?" A couple of other girls in this strange crew of now tiny, now skinny, now keg-legged, now obese, now plain ugly girls said, "Yeah, what happened?" She couldn't tell which ones, because she avoided looking at any of them—these . . . these . . . these *witches*, assembled on the floor solely to torment her! But then she made the mistake of peeking—and locked eyes with a big black girl named Helene. As Helene raised her knees, she said with a voice of deep sisterly concern, "Hey, where've you *been?*" implying "Who did this to you?" Charlotte couldn't think of any way to answer that one with a head motion—and besides, she had it in her mind, from social osmosis, that it was proto-racist to slough off what black students had to say—even a black girl like this one, whose father, as everybody on the floor seemed to know, was one of the biggest real estate developers in Atlanta—no doubt richer than all the Blue Ridge Mountain Simmonses in history put together—and so Charlotte fought to reinforce the dam holding back the flood and uttered just two words, "Frat party." That did it. That was more than enough. The dam broke, and she staggered the rest of the way sobbing and convulsing. The little witches fired away from the rear. "Which frat?" . . . "What'd they do?" . . . "Sure you don't want us to come help you?" . . . "Was it a guy?"

By the time she turned the doorknob, she could hear the whole misshapen gauntlet clucking, whispering, sniggering, mock-sympathizing . . .

"This really rounds it out," Charlotte said to herself amid the tears. The wreck of Charlotte Simmons was *their* Friday night.

11. ONSTAGE, A STAR

Well past ten o'clock the next morning, Charlotte was still in bed, lying flat on her back, eyes shut . . . eyes open . . . long enough to gaze idly at the brilliant lines of light where the shades didn't quite meet the windowsill . . . eyes shut . . . listening for sounds of Beverly, who occasionally sighed or moaned faintly in her sleep . . . eyes open, eyes shut, running the night before through her mind over and over to determine just how much of a fool she had made of herself. She was at her most vulnerable, her most anxious, during this interlude between waking and getting up and facing the world . . . which she knew, but that didn't make the feeling any less real . . . How could she have let him keep *touching* her that way? Right in front of everybody! Right in front of Bettina and Mimi! She had fled the Saint Ray house without even trying to look for them . . . walked back to Little Yard alone through monstrous shadows in the dead of the night. How could she ever look them in the eye? How could she have talked herself into believing that a predator the likes of Hoyt was just a friendly, hospitable protector who was rescuing her from social oblivion and validating her presence . . . at what? . . . a drunken fraternity wallow . . . when he was just a plain out and out . . . out and out . . . out and out . . . *cad*? . . . That was the word . . . even though she had never heard anyone say it out loud, including herself . . . She had even let him pressure her into drinking alcohol . . . and strutting around with the drink in her hand and his arm around her—in front of everybody . . . Momma would die! Barely a month, and already she had gone to a fraternity party and started drinking and letting herself be pawed, publicly, by some totally deceitful . . . cad . . . who only wanted to get her into a bedroom . . .

Well, she couldn't lie here like this forever . . . but she dreaded waking Beverly up . . . Even on weekdays, when Charlotte got out of bed and got dressed, no matter how quiet she tried to be, Beverly would thrash about under her covers and huff great groans, as if she were still asleep but just barely, because Charlotte's hayseed habit of getting up early was about to destroy all chance of rest and, for that matter, her entire day. One way or another, Beverly always made her feel like some rural throwback. When Beverly came in, much more noisily, in the middle of the night, Charlotte felt like giving *her* the thrash-and-groan treatment, but she didn't have the nerve. Somehow, perhaps through sheer aloofness, Beverly had established the notion that she was the eminence in this room. She was a rich boarding school girl. Who would be so foolish as to deprive her of even thirty seconds of her heedless Saturday morning sleep?

Without a creak, without a rustle, holding her breath, Charlotte slipped out from under the covers, eyes pinned on the inert form of the eminence. In the same fashion, she slipped her slippers on and her bathrobe inch by inch, fetched her towel, soap, and toilet kit, and tiptoed toward the door . . . lost her grip on the bar of soap and it hit the floor with an impact that, under the circumstances, might as well have been an explosion. Paralyzed with dread, she stared at Beverly, the sleeping lion. Miracle of miracles! The lion didn't so much as moan or move a muscle. Charlotte stooped down, retrieved the soap, and tiptoed out of the room, meticulously restraining the handle so that the door wouldn't make even the slightest click as it closed.

Thank God there was hardly anybody in the bathroom. A pale girl with practically no waist, emerging—naked!—from a shower stall in a fog of steam . . . some guy in a cubicle making the usual rude bowel noises . . . *So gross* . . . She studied her face in the mirror to see what the night had done to it. Slightly ashen, wasn't it, its vitality leached away by guilt and shame . . . Hurriedly she washed her face and brushed her teeth, returned to the room, and opened the door as carefully as could be . . .

Sunshine! The shades were up. Beverly was looking out of one of the windows, leaning forward, arms propped on the sill, wearing the panties and short T-shirt she slept in. From behind like this—the *bones* of her pelvis sad-dle stood out. She was a pale version of one of those starving Ethiopians you see on TV with bugs flying around their eyes. Beverly straightened up and turned about. With no makeup to help, her eyes seemed abnormally big and bulging, like an anorexic's. She stared at Charlotte with a crooked little smile on her face. Charlotte braced for a reprimand, oozing with sarcasm, for waking her up "this early" on a Saturday morning.

"Well!" said Beverly. An arch and ironic *Well*. She paused and looked Charlotte up and down, still smiling with one corner of her mouth up higher than the other. "Did you have a good time last night?"

Startled, Charlotte paused, too, then managed to say timidly, "I guess so—it was all right." *Last night!*

"I see you made a new friend."

Charlotte's heart palpitated for several seconds before snapping back into a normal—albeit speeding—rhythm. *It had already spread every-where! Ten-thirty in the morning, and everybody already knew!* In a wavering voice:

"What do you mean?"

"Hoyt Thorpe," said Beverly.

Her smile was the smug one that says, "I know more than you think I do." Charlotte felt as if the lining of her skull were on fire. She was speech-less. She wondered if her expression looked frightened or merely wary.

Beverly said, "So? What do you think? You think he's hot?"

Charlotte was swept by an overwhelming need to dissociate herself ut-terly from Hoyt and everything that had happened.

"I don't know *what* he was," said Charlotte, "except drunk and . . . and . . . and . . . rude." The word she had started to use was "deceitful," but she didn't want to give Beverly that strong a word to pry with. "How did you know I met him?"

"I *saw* you. I was there, too."

"You were? At the Saint Ray house, at that party? You know, I thought I saw you"—she started to mention the BOOTING ROOM but thought better of it—"for a fraction of a second, but then you weren't there."

"Same with me. It was a mob scene, totally. Besides, you seemed like . . . otherwise occupied."

A bit too emphatically: "I wasn't occupied with *him*!"

"You weren't?"

Unconvincingly: "No."

"Maybe a little bit?"

"How did you know his name?" said Charlotte. "I never even heard his last name until you just said it, and now I can't even remember what you said. Hoyt what?"

"Thorpe. You really had no idea who he was?"

"No."

"Nobody said anything about how he caught some girl, some junior, giving head to this governor—from California?—what's his name?—out in the Grove last spring?"

"No."

Beverly proceeded to tell her the story, which had swollen in the five months since the incident. Hers had Hoyt knocking two of the governor's bodyguards unconscious with his bare fists.

Charlotte got hung up on the phrase "giving head." It took her a moment to figure out what it meant, and when she did, she found it trashy that Beverly had used such an expression. She didn't absorb anything after that until Beverly said, "Do you want to see him again?"

"No."

"Oh, come on, Charlotte. It didn't look like that last night."

It occurred to Charlotte that this was only the second time since the day they met that Beverly had addressed her by name.

Charlotte didn't want to be at a campus crossroads like Mr. Rayon on this particular morning, but Abbotsford Hall (the Abbey), the great, gloomy Gothic dining hall she had to use in order to take advantage of the food allotment of her scholarship, stopped serving breakfast at nine a.m. That left Mr. Rayon, which was already a swarming, buzzing hive by the time Charlotte walked in carrying a text for her Introduction to Neuroscience course called *Descartes, Darwin, and the Mind-Brain Problem*, which she intended to read over breakfast. There were long lines at all six cafeteria counters. Elsewhere, students were weaving among one another in droves, raggedy to near perfection, wearing children's clothes of every sort (so long as they weren't wool or silk), especially ersatz sports and military gear: baseball caps on backward, hooded jerseys, Streptolon warm-up pants with bold stripes down the sides, tennis shorts, starter jackets, leather cockpit jackets, olive green wife-beaters, camouflage pants . . . The restless motion of such heroic, motley faux-warrior rags amid this smooth digital backdrop made Charlotte dizzy. She kept her head down. All she wanted was enough food to stave off hunger for a few hours and a cranny in a wall to consume it in.

By and by, she maneuvered her way through the crowds, head still down, carrying a tray on which rested her breakfast—four slices of health-nut bread (at the deli counter they scratched their heads and let her have them for 40 cents), a metallically wrapped little square of butter and a vacuum-sealed miniature jar of jelly (both free), and a 50-cent cup of orange juice (cheaper than the only water available, which came in bottles at 75 cents each). She found a small table against a wall. There were two chairs. She put *Descartes, Darwin, and the Mind-Brain Problem* across from her by way of discouraging anyone who might consider occupying the other seat. The health-nut bread, which seemed to be made of dried husks, was tough going, as were Descartes, Darwin, and the mind-brain problem. "Whereas the doctrine that cultural changes represent nothing more than the organism's constant probing in the process of natural selection begs the question of whether or not the 'mind' is in any way autonomous, the argument that 'minds' are capable, through a process of organized 'wills,' of creating cultural changes wholly independent of that process revives, ultimately, the discredited notion of the ghost in the machine." Charlotte understood the gist of it, but the effort of dealing with such stultifying rhetoric at breakfast made her . . . "mind" . . . "brain" . . . "will"—all those quotation marks were like dermatitis!—feel unbearably heavy. Besides, she had to use one hand to keep the book open, which created an annoying problem when she tried to put butter and jelly on the health-nut bread. So she closed it and looked up to give the room a quick survey—

Dear God. There were Bettina and Mimi, not thirty feet away, threading their way between tables. At Mr. Rayon, finding the right place to sit seemed to strike everybody as a vital, crucial, all-consuming matter. Charlotte ducked her head back down over the book, but it was already too late. Even though it was for only an instant, her eyes had locked with Bettina's in a way that made it impossible to pretend she hadn't seen her. So she lifted her head just as Bettina, in the heartiest Bettina fashion, sang out, "Charlotte!"

Charlotte put on a flat smile and waved, at the same time tilting her book up with the other hand, as if to say, "I'm acknowledging your presence in a friendly way, but you can see I'm busy reading, so you'll just keep on walking, won't you?"

If that got across to Bettina and Mimi, they didn't show it for a second. They immediately changed direction and headed straight for Charlotte.

Both had big smiles. She did her best to look enthusiastic as Bettina made herself at home at the little table's other chair and Mimi pulled over a chair from a table nearby. Charlotte braced herself for . . . last night.

"Where'd you go last night?" said Bettina. "We looked all over for you before we left." Bettina and Mimi were both leaning forward in their chairs.

"I walked back," said Charlotte. "I couldn't find you all, either, so I figured I'd get on back by myself. It was sort of scary walking all that way in the dark."

"I thought maybe you didn't *have* to get back," said Mimi with a suggestive smile.

"Yeah," said Bettina. "Who *was* that guy? He was *hot*." Her smile and her gleaming eyes said she wanted to hear it all, every tasty detail of it.

"What guy?" said Charlotte.

"Oh—come—on!" said Mimi. "What guy. Were there ten guys or something?" But it wasn't the irritated tone of last night. She was looking at her with the glittering eye of someone pumped up for an exciting story and waiting to be impressed.

"I guess you mean . . ."

"I guess I mean the guy who was all over Charlotte Simmons at the Saint Ray party, that guy. Who is he?" Big eyes, hungry smile.

Charlotte was overwhelmed by the urge to make it clear that whatever they had seen, the patting, the pawing, the squeezing, meant nothing. "His first name's Hoyt. Or that's what everybody called him. He never told me himself. He's in that fraternity. That's all I know about him, except that you can't trust him."

"What do you mean?" said Bettina. "What did he do?" Her eyes said, "Come on, every detail."

"Oh, he pretended he was just being a good host. He was going to give me a tour of the house and this stupid secret room he was so proud of and everything. Then he kept *touching* me. All he really wanted to do was get me alone in a bedroom. It was so . . . so . . . He was really gross."

"Hold on a second," said Mimi. "How did you meet him in the first place?"

"I was just standing there, and he came up behind me and tapped me on the shoulder and said—oh, it was so corny . . . I'm too embarrassed to tell you. I can't believe I fell for it."

"What'd he *say*?" Mimi and Bettina said, practically in unison.

"I'm too embarrassed," said Charlotte. She hesitated, but then the pleasure of being at the center of a drama outweighed everything else. "He said, 'I bet you get tired of being mistaken for Britney Spears.' It was *so corny*!"

"And then he started touching you?" said Mimi.

"Yes."

"But not *really*, not touching you . . . ummm—"

"Well, not like *that*!"

"And then he asked you if you wanted to dance, and you went out there and started grinding, right?" Mimi leaned back in the chair and rotated her hips.

"He tried to—how did you know?"

Mimi shrugged and cocked her head and rolled her eyes in an arch mime show of ignorance. "Just a wild guess. And then I guess he said, 'Why don't we go somewhere?'"

"I wouldn't dance with him," said Charlotte. "I saw the way they were all dancing out there. It was *so gross*. I just wouldn't do it."

"And how did he take that?" said Mimi.

"He kept on insisting that I had to dance with him. He begged, and then he practically got mad. He finally gave up and took me to see this stupid secret room they've got down in the basement."

High on stardom, Charlotte gave a full account of the secret door in the wood paneling upstairs and getting past the bouncer sort of guy—she tucked her chin down into her clavicle to pantomime his bulked-up body—and the scene in "the stupid secret room" . . . it was all "so immature" . . . omitting, however, the big cup of wine she had accepted. She treated them to the trip upstairs and, indignantly, the incriminating lines *We've got this room* and *Let me know when you're through*, and the way she stormed out. Mimi and Bettina were hanging on every word.

"You're sure you left?" said Mimi.

Charlotte looked at her quizzically for a moment. "Of *course* I'm sure!"

"Okay, okay, just *asking*. You know, these frat guys like to brag to each other the next day about how fast they scored with some girl, some total stranger. They time it! They actually time it with a watch!"

Charlotte hated Mimi for that. She was trying to ridicule the very idea that Hoyt had found her genuinely attractive, that he actually *felt* something toward her, even if he did want to . . . *score*, as she put it.

But then the roly-poly guy Hoyt called Boo-man popped into Charlotte's head—*You got seven minutes, Hoyto, and the clock is running.* That was the *last* thing she was going to reveal.

"They love to run that game on freshmen," said Mimi. "You've probably heard the expression 'fresh meat.' I *hope* you didn't do anything. You can count on them telling all their buddies about it—*everything*, from the size of your tits to—well . . . everything."

Charlotte raised her head and looked past Mimi in an ostentatious pantomime of boredom. Mimi wanted her to feel small, didn't she—yet another clueless victim of a heartless sexual prank, another piece of fresh meat, anything but a beautiful girl who had attracted a hot guy. Mimi . . . one of the tarantulas Miss Pennington had talked about, only this was not Alleghany High but Dupont—

—*wait a second.* Charlotte had to clinch her teeth to suppress a smile. When you thought about it, all three of them, Beverly, Mimi, and Bettina, had paid her an involuntary compliment, which was of course the only reliable kind among girls. In the six weeks she had roomed with Beverly, she had treated her as a person—as opposed to a rural alien who had somehow been billeted to her space—exactly twice. The first time was the night Beverly had come in drunk and had begged, cajoled, wheedled, pressured her into sexile with many utterly insincere cooings of "Charlotte" this and "Charlotte" that. From that night to this morning, Beverly hadn't even so much as addressed her by name. But this morning she had become "Charlotte" again, and not because Beverly wanted anything—except personal information about this suddenly interesting roommate of hers, Charlotte Simmons. Mimi was no longer the California sophisticate rolling her eyes and sighing over the naïveté of this clueless mountain girl. Mimi was suddenly . . . jealous—*jealous*! It was so obvious now! As for Bettina, the most forthright and good-hearted of the three, she was openly impressed.

Charlotte turned back to Mimi. She found herself smiling with an unaccustomed aplomb. "Wow. How do you know all this, Mimi?"

Glumly: "*Everybody* knows it."

"Oh, one thing I didn't tell you," said Charlotte, feeling a surge of confidence. "When I got back, there were all these girls sitting in the hall on our floor? Right on the floor they were sitting, backs against the wall and their legs sticking out, and you couldn't get by unless they moved their legs? They *did*, but they all stared at me and wanted to know where I'd been. They were like . . . so *weird*."

"Oh, they're the Trolls," said Bettina. "That's what I call them. They sit there every weekend, and all they do is watch other people go out and come in and then gossip about them. Talk about losers . . ." She laughed to herself. "*We're* far superior. We're the Lounge Committee."

The three of them, the whole Lounge Committee, laughed and laughed.

Charlotte gazed off again, grinning as if still amused by the "Trolls" and "the Lounge Committee." What she was actually grinning about was the rankings. She wasn't at the bottom like the Trolls. But neither was she stuck in the ever-hopeful middle class, the Lounge Committee.

And she had been mortified by the thought that she had disgraced herself in front of people she knew! Instead, she had become a new person in their eyes, an interesting person, a person to be reckoned with—and jealous of—a pretty girl very much *on the scene* . . . all because some *hot guy* had gone to the trouble of chasing her, no matter how perfidious his motives.

She rocked back in her chair and tilted her chin up and invited the whole world—all those boys and girls in their ludicrous Active Life outfits milling about in the big, slick supergraphic box that was Mr. Rayon—to get an eyeful of Charlotte Simmons. Idly she thought of the cleft chin, the ironic grin, the exotic hazel eyes, the preppy thatch of brown hair . . . which didn't make him any less vile, of course.

"Hold it! Hold it! Jesus H. Christ, Socrates! You fucking—" He didn't complete the impending insult.

The players froze in their tracks. They froze every time they heard one of Coach's *fuckings*. Vernon Congers, who had just outdueled Treyshawn and Jojo for a rebound, stood frozen with the ball up near his right shoulder, his elbows sticking out at cockeyed angles, exactly the way they had been when Coach yelled *Hold it! Fucking* was Buster Roth's all-purpose, universal term of disapproval. Charles once told Jojo, "After practice it's two hours before I realize my name isn't U. Fucking Bousquet."

Here the man came, walking onto the court with a slow, menacing, rocking, straddling gait, as if his thighs were so dense with muscle he couldn't get them any closer together if he tried, and his face was compressed into the full, furrowed Buster Roth scowl. Jojo hated it when Coach was like this. Jojo saw . . . Doom. He felt trapped on Doom's domain, the court, its blond wood brilliantly lit by the LumeNex lights up above. The court was a little rectangle at the very bottom of Doom's hellishly black bowl. Cliffs of seats rose up all around in the darkness like walls of an infinite height.

When Coach was ten feet away, he scowled at Vernon Congers as if he had just done something terribly wrong and said in a seething, low voice, "Give me the fucking ball."

Zombielike, Congers tossed him the ball in a gentle arc. Buster Roth caught it and rested it on his right palm. Then he began tossing it up three or four inches and catching it, three or four inches and catching it, three or four inches and catching it, while he glowered at Jojo. Without another word he pivoted, reared back, and threw the ball about twelve rows up into the Buster Bowl's seats, where it glanced off the top of a backrest and ricocheted crazily among the seats and the concrete tiers higher up.

He turned back toward Jojo, looking more furious than ever. "Well, well, old Socrates," he said in a normal, if sarcastic, tone of voice. "You're a famous thinker. So whyn't you tell me what you think you're doing here, Socrates . . . ONE A YOUR FUCKING PERIPATETIC DIALOGUES? YOU FUCKING GREEK PHILOSOPHERS TOO DIGNIFIED TO JUMP UP IN THE AIR FOR A BALL? WHY CAN'T YOU PRE-TEND YOU'RE STILL ALIVE INSTEAD OF A FUCKING GREEK STATUE? WHO THE FUCK YOU THINK'S YOUR COACH NOW, PROFESSOR NATHAN MARGOLIES? YOU'RE SUPPOSED TO BE COVERING THE FUCKING BOARDS, NOT STANDING THERE LIKE A SEVENTY-ONE-YEAR-OLD GEEZER CHUGALUGGING HEMLOCK! IF YOU WANNA ACT LIKE A FUCKING DEAD MAN, WHYN'TCHOO GET A PART IN A GREEK PLAY! I HEAR FUCKING SOPHOCLES IS AUDITIONING! FUCKING GUY'S NINETY YEARS OLD, AND HE DON'T LIKE JUMPING UP AND DOWN, EITHER! YOU TWO FUCKING GUYS'LL HIT IT OFF FAMOUSLY, YOU AND SOPHOCLES! HE'S FUCKING NINETY AND YOU'RE FUCKING SEVENTY-ONE AND O-DEEING ON HEMLOCK! WHYN'TCHOO—"

Jojo knew you had to just stand here and let him finish his rant. Every-body had been through it at one time or another, so there was no need to feel humiliated . . . Still—there was something *about* . . . *this* rant. It was like Coach had been planning it or something. He'd been reading up on a lot of

stuff like peripatetic dialogues and Socrates dying at seventy-one and Sophocles writing plays when he was ninety. Reading up! Coach resented the fact
that one of his players had ignored his instructions and gone ahead and en-
rolled in a 300-level course in philosophy. He truly *resented* it. There was
something weird, something poisonous about this particular tirade.

Now Coach was turning toward the rest of the players. He was speaking
in his "normal" voice, which in this case meant his most insidious and sarcastic voice. "Oh, I forgot. Maybe some a you ain't been reintroduced yet to
the hoopster formerly known as Jojo. So please give a big hello to a real
philosopher's philosopher, a real thinker, Professor *Socrates* Johanssen—"

Out of the corner of his eyes Jojo could see three student managers at
courtside drinking this all in, feasting their eyes, gobbling it up. The student
managers were students who willingly served as the team's slaves, doing all
the dirty work you couldn't get a starving Mexican to do, cleaning up after
the players, picking up their jockstraps and sweaty practice jerseys and putting them in the laundry, mopping up the vomit when they got drunk on the
road. One of them was a fat-hipped, sullen little girl named Delores. She
had long dark hair parted down the middle, which made her look like an Indian, and she wore heavy mealy-gray sweatpants, which made her look like
an Indian in the shape of a bowling pin. She was the one who disturbed Jojo.
Maybe he was being paranoid, but in practice, every time he did something
wrong, he would catch her snickering into the ear of one of the other managers. She never smiled *at* him, only at his expense. One time after he
passed by, he distinctly heard her say "the big stoop"; and another time, "not
the sharpest knife in the drawer." If she was such a genius, what was she doing working for free as a glorified men's-room attendant?

Now Coach was looking straight at Jojo. "So okay," Buster Roth was saying, "you bulked up over the summer. Fine. But if all it is, is fucking dead
weight, then we might as well give the job to the fucking Safe. He can stand
still bigger than you can."

Jojo detected sniggers and stifled chuckles on the sidelines and among
a couple of players on the court. The Safe was a 345-pound offensive tackle
on the football team named Reuben Sayford. Jojo's breathing accelerated.
Coach was Coach, but this was pushing the outside of the envelope.

Buster Roth stopped talking but continued to stare at Jojo in a certain
way. Then he crooked a forefinger and wiggled it and said, "Come here."

Jojo was sweating terribly as he walked toward him. Sweat had soaked
through the upper part of his sleeveless mauve basketball shirt to the point

where it seemed to have a dark bib. Coach turned toward Vernon Congers, who had been in on the battle for the rebound and was no more than four feet from Jojo.

"Congers," he said with another beckoning crook of the finger, "you come here, too."

The two of them now stood before Coach. Congers was sweating also, and the sweat gave his brown skin a glossy sheen. His strength-coached muscles stood out in high relief, especially his deltoids, which popped out from his shoulders like two big apples.

In a perfectly ordinary voice Coach said, "You two trade shirts."

All the ramifications of those four words hit Jojo at once. He was stunned, dumbstruck, paralyzed. Demoted to the second team. Six days before the opening game—which was here at Dupont! Against a pushover, Cincinnati—but the first game of the season! Students, alumni, the Charlies' Club donors! The press!—scouts from the League!—they'll all see Jojo Johanssen sitting on the bench! What team in the League was even going to consider a demoted has-been power forward! The very people who had looked at him as if they were looking at a god—the students, ordinary fans, sports junkies in front of the TV sets, all those hooples who wanted a little piece of Go go Jojo, an autograph, a smile, a wave, or just the chance of being in the same place he was, breathing the same air he breathed—even they would avert their eyes! Jojo Johanssen, object of pity!—assuming anybody bothered thinking of him at all . . . Congers was already taking off his yellow shirt, revealing his abdominals, which stood out like cobblestones, and his obliques, which surmounted his pelvic saddle like plates of armor.

Jojo just stood there staring at Coach, as if any second he was going to say, "Just kidding. Only wanted to get your attention." But Coach was not the just-kidding type. His eyes were not dancing with merriment. The moment stretched out . . . stretched out . . . stretched out . . . stretched out . . . until finally Jojo had no choice but to start taking off his mauve shirt. A dishonored knight surrendering his sword and suit of mail. Every eye was pinned on him as the LumeNex lights beamed down on the blond wood stage . . . It might as well have been the whole world, because the whole world would soon know, anyway. Dead silence . . . not a sound . . . but what was there to say when you were watching a man being broken? The final indignity was putting on the yellow shirt and feeling the sweat left over from Congers's magnificent, exhilarated, triumphant black body chill his own deflated pale white, bled-white, dead-white carcass.

The scrimmage resumed, and in a sheerly intellectual sense, Jojo knew that this was the time to show what he was made of, to dog Congers on defense in a way no power forward had ever been dogged before, to outrun him, outjump him, outmuscle him, fake him out, shoot him out of the water, *crush* the sonofabitch. Oh, yes; that he knew intellectually. But his spirit was in ruins, and that was all his body knew. It was Congers who did the outdogging, outrunning, -jumping, -muscling, -faking, -shooting—and the crushing. Within fifteen minutes it couldn't have been more obvious that once more, Buster Roth, lord and wizard of the Buster Bowl, had shown himself to be an unerring judge of horseflesh. Jojo left the floor feeling as humiliated as any athlete on earth had ever felt.

Sure enough, the rest of them were diligently not looking at him, not even Mike. Mike was making a big point of keeping himself wrapped up in conversation with Charles. On the edge of Jojo's peripheral vision, however, one big pair of eyes was fixed right on him. He turned his head. It was Delores, the student manager with the Indian face and the big bottom. She was the only person still sitting on the bench.

"Hang in there, Jojo," she said.

If she had said it out of sincere concern, it would have been bad enough. All he needed at this point was some pity poured on him by a "student manager." As it was, a smile seemed to be playing at the corners of her mouth.

A red mist formed in front of Jojo's eyes. He squared his stance toward her and said, "What the hell's that supposed to mean?"

Abashed, she shrugged her shoulders and her eyebrows. She never took her eyes off him, however, and kept on giving him a what—ironic?—stare. "I was just trying—" She didn't finish the sentence.

"You were just trying bullshit, is what you were just trying," said Jojo.

"Well, you don't have to take it out on *me*." The calmness of her voice somehow made it worse.

"Take *what* out?" He didn't wait for her to answer. He thrust his chin forward and gestured toward her. "Why do you do this? Tell me that."

"Do what?"

"This 'job' you got, this student manager"—he started to say *shit* but thought better of it—"thing?"

"Well—"

"Nobody respects you for it. You know that, don't you?"

The girl shrugged nonchalantly, which made Jojo furious.

He stepped closer. "Everybody laughs at you, if you wanna know the truth! Everybody wonders how you can get yourself down low enough to take this shit! Student manager . . . Student manager, my ass! Student slave is more like it! Student urinal puck supplier!" He stepped still closer. "The whole team spits on you people!"

Jojo was now the very picture of looking down at somebody. The six-foot-ten hulk of him towered over the little ball of Indian hair and nappy gray cotton rag down below him on the bench.

She looked frightened, but she didn't budge. In a tiny voice she said, "That's not true, and I'm sorry about what happened out there—but I didn't do it."

Of course she was right—which made it that much worse.

"You think it's not true! How about a little experiment? If I spit on the floor, you're the one who's got to get down on all fours and wipe it up!"

She looked up at his huge white blond-tipped head, which was now florid with anger. She was afraid to attempt any reply at all. The giant was at the point of detonation.

Jojo swelled up his chest, lifted his head upward as high as it would go, and snuffled, scouring his sinuses, nasal pathways, and lungs so furiously it was as if he wanted to suck the bench, the girl, the entire Buster Bowl and half of southeastern Pennsylvania up into his nostrils. He grimaced until his neck widened, striated by muscles, tendons, and veins, swelled up his chest to the last milliliter of its capacity—and spat. The girl stared at the edge of the court where it landed: a prodigious, runny, yellowy pus-laced gob of phlegm.

"Clean it up," said Jojo, halfway between a hiss and a snarl, whereupon he started walking away.

The girl, Delores, didn't move or make a sound. At that moment, Buster Roth, heading off the court and back to his suite of offices, walked past, did a double take, stopped, and stared at the virulent mess on the floor.

He turned toward Delores. "Jesus Christ, what the hell is that? Clean it up!"

Delores pointed at the retreating Jojo and said, "Get *him* to do it."

Roth was so astounded that anybody at Dupont, especially a creature so insignificant as this one, would dare talk back, he was speechless.

"*He* put it there," said Delores.

The analog chemical computations within Buster Roth's brain were almost visible. It was obvious that she was right. No doubt his flattop blond giant was the slob who had put it there. So he had a choice: order this little girl to do what he said—or make Jojo do it. But the girl was smart as a whip, a tireless worker who did most things before he had to ask her, the best student manager he had had working for him since God knew when. On the other hand, did he really want to make Jojo's humiliation total and complete by ordering him to get his 250-pound hulk down on all fours in the Buster Bowl and clean up an oyster like that one? Jesus Christ . . . it was an insoluble dilemma. So without a word and without so much as looking at either of them, Buster Roth went behind the bench, picked a crumpled towel up off the floor, walked over and dropped it on top of the noxious mess, and began rubbing it around with his foot. It wouldn't be a perfect job, but he was damned if *he* was going to get down on all fours, either. He figured he'd just smush it around like this until it was no longer identifiable.

When he finished, the floor at that spot had become a glaze of mucus about two feet in diameter. The mighty LumeNex lights of the Buster Bowl highlighted it in a viscous relief, or was he just seeing things? In any case, he'd get some other manager to clean up the remains later on.

Jojo, heading down the ramp to the dressing room, had heard the exchange. His humiliation took a further nosedive . . . into guilt. How could he have done what he just did? How could he have called the girl a slave and all that other stuff? And she had stood up to him, and to Buster Roth, too! He envisioned her twenty pounds lighter, slim in the hips, and naked.

The moment Hoyt got a glimpse of the guy coming toward them, he pegged him as a dork.

"Yo," he said to Vance, who was seated across from him in the booth at Mr. Rayon, "who is that guy?" He made a slight motion with his head.

Vance turned his head in that direction as inconspicuously as he could. "No clue."

Hoyt took another glance. The guy was wearing a red Windbreaker with BOSTON RED SOX on the front. It was unzipped, revealing a "lively" sport shirt, which was tucked into his pants, which were black flannel. And what was it about his hair? It was dark, curly, too long—and had a part in it. A *part*! By now long hair was very Goth. Now you wore your hair short with no part. The guy wore his hair *parted*! On top of that, he was skinny without looking in any way wiry, much less buff. He might as well have had a sign around his neck saying DORK.

The guy came right over to their table. He looked down at Hoyt with these big, wide-open, timorous eyes and said, "Hi! You're Hoyt?" Then he managed a grin that was probably supposed to look affable. In fact, the small muscles in his lower lip were twitching.

"That's right," said Hoyt, looking him in the eye in a challenging manner.

The dork turned toward Vance and tried another smile and said, "And you're . . . Vance?"

Vance didn't say a word. He just nodded yes . . . in a cool fashion that as much as said, "And therefore . . . ?"

The dork looked from Vance to Hoyt and from Hoyt to Vance and said, "I'm Adam. I don't mean to . . . uh . . ." He couldn't think up the word for what he didn't mean to do, and he smiled, averting his eyes.

"Then why the fuck are you doing it?" Hoyt said under his breath.

"What?" said the dork.

Hoyt made a small dismissive motion with his hand.

The dork soldiered on. "You guys mind if I ask you something for just a second?"

Vance looked at Hoyt. Hoyt eyed the guy for a couple of beats and said, "Go ahead."

"Thanks," said the dork. Almost without looking, he leaned backward, grabbed a chair from the next table and pulled it up and sat down, hunching forward with his forearms resting on his thighs and his hands clasped between his knees. "I'm from the *Daily Wave*." His eyes darted this way and that at Hoyt and Vance. "Several people have told my editor that you guys" — now he smiled as if he were about to bring up that merriest subject imaginable — "pulled a helluva prank on the governor of California last spring when he was here for commencement."

His eyes darted even faster, and he held on to the smile for dear life. Evidently the smile was supposed to cover up a case of rapid ataxic eyeblink and the fact that his Adam's apple went way up and then way down in an involuntary swallow.

Hoyt could see Vance staring at him in alarm. He said to the dork in a bored manner, "Who told you *that*?"

The dork said, "I guess — well, nobody told *me* exactly. They told my editor, was the way it happened. And he asked me to check it out. So I'm just here to —" He couldn't find the word to complete that sentence, either, and resorted to a few shrugs. His shoulders shrugged, his eyebrows shrugged, and his lips smiled innocently.

Hoyt looked at Vance. "You know what he's talking about, Vance?"

Vance shook his head no; *too* emphatically, if the truth be known.

Hoyt looked at the dork. "The governor of California . . . What's supposed to have happened to the governor of California?"

The dork said, "Well, just before commencement—a day or two before—I'm trying to remember when the Swarm concert was—I need to check all this out—that's why I'm asking you guys"—he lifted his eyebrows in a way that suggested a helpless plea—"to get it all straight. Anyway, what these people told my editor was—it wasn't just one person—I mean, we probably wouldn't even care if it was just one person—but this is one of those things that's all over the place—"

"*What* is?" said Hoyt. He began rolling his forefinger toward himself in the semaphore that says, "Hurry up, get it out."

"Well—this is what these people, these students I'm talking about—they're all students—or at least I don't know for a *fact* that they're all students, but that's what my editor told me—he didn't go out *looking* for this story, *nobody* did—they came to us—" The dork broke off. He could no longer recall the syntax of what he was supposed to be saying. "Anyway, they told us that it was after the Swarm concert at the Opera House, and it's after midnight or something, and you guys were walking back to campus through the Grove and you see the governor right out there in the Grove and this girl is giving him a blow job—" He stopped to look at Hoyt and Vance, as if to give them a chance to answer. "Am I right so far?"

"Wow," said Hoyt in a bored, Sarc 1 fashion. "So what happens next?"

"Well . . . then—this is what we were told—I'm not saying it's necessarily true one way or the other—I'm here to ask you guys"—a look filled with fathoms and fathoms of sincerity—"because the way we hear it is, the governor has these two bodyguards who are out there in the Grove, but they're not, you know, right there *watching* or anything, but they spot you two guys and they come running up, and you guys jumped them and beat 'em up."

"*Two* guys," Vance blurted out, "and *we* jumped *them* . . ."

Vance, thought Hoyt, you are *sooooo* uncool.

"That's why I wanted to ask you guys personally," said the dork. "That's not the way it happened? I'm just interested in . . . *you* know . . . how it *did* happen."

The dork now knew he was onto something. He'd have to be retarded not to.

"Vance," said Hoyt with another Sarc 1 smile, "you're a vicious mother-fucker, man." To the dork: "And that's the 'prank'?"

"I guess 'prank' isn't exactly the right word," said the dork, "but you know, 'prank' in the sense of you guys didn't go out there to jump anybody and you didn't go out there to see the governor of California get some head—the people who were telling us about it, they called it the Night of the Skull Fuck. It was like it was a really unusual, funny thing that happened, that's all. So is that the way it happened? Is it close to the way it happened?"

Hoyt could practically feel Vance's eyes boring into his head, beseeching him . . . Hoyt said to the dork, "I tell you what. Whyn't you call the governor of—what state was it?—California? See what *he* has to say."

"I already have," said the dork.

Vance couldn't hold it back: "You did? What'd he say!"

"They never put me through to him personally," said the dork. "I talked to some kind of . . . spokesperson. She said it was beneath comment. That was her expression, 'beneath comment.' But if you ask me, that's not the same as saying it never happened."

Vance, alarm still in his voice: "So now the guy knows you plan to write something about it?"

"Well . . . sure," said the dork. "I *told* them."

Vance, you are *so-o-o-o-o-o-o-o* uncool. To the dork: "Who's the girl supposed to be in this story, the one giving the governor of California a blow job?"

"I don't know her name," said the dork, "but one of these people—we got the first name of her current boyfriend."

"Which is what?" said Hoyt.

"Something like Crawford. You guys know who that might be?"

Crawdon McLeod, thought Hoyt. Now that was weird. Who the fuck could've or would've told these dorks about Crawdon and Syrie? "Crawford . . . Don't know any Crawford," he said.

"Wait a minute," said Vance. "Back up a second. You came in here—how'd you know who we were? How'd you know *where* we were?"

Vance, Vance, Vance-man Vance . . .

"Well, I—I called the Saint Ray house and asked to speak to you," said the dork. "They told me you were over here."

"How'd you know what we looked like?"

"I asked some people." He motioned vaguely in the direction of the entrance. "You guys are pretty well known!"

Big grin from the dork, big flattering grin. The flattery left Hoyt with conflicting impulses. On the one hand, it was time to let the dork know that dorks existed on a plane . . . way down *there*. On the other hand, was it really so bad . . . to be well known? Was it really such a frightening prospect . . . the possibility of becoming *better* known? "Looking at a fucking ape-faced dickhead is what we're *doing*!" What would be so bad if that line, that *great* line, were recorded in print?

"I never read the *Daily Wave*," he told the dork. "You read the *Daily Wave*, Vance?" He addressed Vance with a Sarc 3 inflection.

"No, I don't," said Vance. Hit the *don't* just a little too hard. It made him sound petulant. "So you write for the school newspaper?" he said to the dork.

"Yeah . . ."

"What do you guys do if you want to run some story and it's a great fucking story and *you ain't got one fucking fact to go on?*"

The dork was jolted by the suddenly aggressive tone. His lips did some funny things, as if he could no longer control the little muscles that enabled them to go this way and that.

Timorous again, the dork said, "We just hope we can . . . *get* the facts. Look"—the big eyes again, pleading, pleading—"that's why I wanted to talk to you guys directly! A story like this, we try to double-check the facts with the principals. We can always go with what other witnesses said, and I guess we will if we have to."

"*What* other witnesses?" said Vance. Still in the alarm mode.

"Well, like you guys and the governor and the girl weren't the only people there."

"Like who else was?" said Vance.

"The bodyguards," said the dork.

"The body*guards*?" said Vance.

"Well, they were there."

"Body*guards* . . . plural?" said Vance.

"Are you denying there were bodyguards there?" Then to Hoyt: "Can *you* deny or confirm it?"

Hoyt could hardly believe it. The little fuck had ratcheted his courage up again. Vance was staring at him, dumbstruck.

"'Do you deny it or can you confirm it,'" said Hoyt, contempt dripping from the legalistic phrases. "Deny and confirm my ass . . . 'Do you deny it or can you confirm it' . . ." He shook his head and twisted his lips in the way that says, "You . . . pussy."

Pleading, pleading: "I have to ask you that! It's not up to me, it's up to you guys. My editor's going with the story either way! We'd rather go with your version of the whole thing, but it's like up to you guys."

"What's *it*?" said Vance. "I don't even know what you're talking about." Petulant again.

"See those two guys over there?" said Hoyt, pointing to two students, a couple of real porkers sitting about three tables away, laughing and carrying on. "Go ask *them*. Maybe they did it."

The dork's big eyes began bouncing from Hoyt to Vance to Hoyt again. Silence. Both were giving the dork okay-and-now-what stares.

The dork stood up and said, "Well, thanks for talking to me, guys . . . and here . . ." He twisted and slipped his backpack off his shoulders and fished around in it and came up with a *Daily Wave* calling card and a ballpoint pen. "If you want to get hold of me, here's the number at the *Wave*, and I'm going to give you my cell number," which he did, using the pen. He gave the card to Hoyt. "Thanks," he said again.

Hoyt said nothing and didn't stow the card anywhere. He just held it insouciantly between his first two fingers. He gave the dork a small Sarc 1 smile as the guy turned and headed off. The guy's backpack was mauve with a yellow Dupont D on the flap. It was very dorky to go around with Dupont backpacks and jackets and things, as if you thought that the mere fact of being a student at Dupont was a big deal in and of itself. The fact that it *was* a big deal in and of itself was part of the inverse spin of the snobbery.

Vance sighed a high-blood-pressure sigh and fixed Hoyt with accusing eyes. "Goddamn it, Hoyt, how many times did I tell you to stop talking about it! Now we got this shit-bird at the *Daily Wave*—"

Hoyt said, "Relax. What's the worst thing that can happen?"

"We get fucked, is what happens. This fucking tool has us assaulting two bodyguards, like *we* started it. *Two* bodyguards—I mean the fuck, the fucking guy's talking about *two* bodyguards, and who the fuck needs to get caught in the middle of some goddamned story about the governor of California getting himself sucked off by Syrie Fucking Stieffbein?"

"Ea-ea-ea-ea-sy, Vance-man. Chill. Chill *out*! We didn't make the guy's gorilla go insane!"

"Yeah, but this guy's gonna get it all fucked up. He's already got it all fucked up. And now they're gonna run the bodyguard's version! You can imagine what that's gonna be! Why didn't you just deny the whole thing, the way I did? You strung it out. You strung it out so far, now the guy's telling himself it's obvious we were there."

Hoyt broke into a grin. "*Me?* I don't believe what I'm hearing! The little shit says 'two bodyguards,' and you say, 'Whattaya mean, two? There weren't two! I only saw one!'"

"I didn't say that!"

"Well, you might as well have," said Hoyt.

Vance eyed Hoyt for a few beats. "You know what I think? I think you'd *like* for somebody to write about it. That's what I think."

Hoyt turned his palms upward. "Who sent the guy packing? Who told him to kiss my ass?"

He stared Vance down, but *hmmmm* . . . the Vance-man had just painted him a little picture . . .

"Let me see the fucking guy's card," said Vance.

As he handed it to him, Hoyt flicked a glance at it himself. Adam Gellin.

"Never heard of him," said Vance, handing it back.

Hoyt shrugged in as bored a fashion as he could. But he wasn't bored. He jotted the name down in his mind. Adam Gellin was the little shit's name.

Fuck! Why the fuck did that make him think of his fucking grades? He could be a legend in his own time—one of the very greatest. But what the fuck was he going to do next June?

12. THE H WORD

Where is the poet who has sung of that most lacerating of all human emotions, the cut that never heals—male humiliation? Oh, the bards, the balladeers have stirred us with epics of the humiliated male's obsession with revenge . . . but that is letting the poor devil off easy. After all, the very urge, *Vengeance is mine,* gives him back a portion of his manhood, retaliation being manly stuff. But the feeling itself, *male humiliation,* is unspeakable. No man can bring himself to describe it. The same man who will confess with relish and in lavish ghostwritten detail to every sort of debauchery and atrocity will not utter one peep about the humiliations that, in Orwell's phrase, "make up seventy-five percent of life." For confessing to humiliation means confessing that he has cringed, caved in, surrendered his honor without a fight to another man who has intimidated him—that he has been unsexed and has plunged into a misery worse than the prospect of imminent death. Eternally, the sheer fear of physical confrontation—even now—in the twenty-first century!— when life's major victories are won not by knights in armor on the field of battle but by sedentary men in central-heating-weight worsted suits inside glass-walled electronic chambers. Nor will a man ever free himself from that sickening moment of capitulation. A word, an image, a smell, a face will bring it flashing back, and he will experience the very *feeling,* every neural sensation of that moment, and he will drown all over again in the shame of lying still for his own unsexing.

Fortunately, Adam Gellin was not flashing back to *that moment* as he walked across the Great Yard at sunset, even though his destination, the new Farquhar Fitness Center, had everything to do with it. Indian summer was fading, the days had become noticeably shorter and chillier, and Adam had put on his quilted forest-green Patagonia jacket, the kind that extends all the way down to the hips and has a drawstring enabling one to tighten it at the waist for greater snugness. Random souls went in and out of the great arch-ways of the library, but there was hardly a soul in the Yard itself. As the sun sank, bands of soft purples and pinks rimmed the horizon, and the low light did something wondrous to the Gothic buildings. Adam no longer saw them as individual structures, each with its distinctive details, but rather as a single, vast gray Gothic abstraction of stone tinged with pink, purple, and the sun's last faint gold. The elms that rose to towering heights here were gray, but backlit by a soft golden mauve. He had never seen Dupont in quite this light before . . . solid, deep-rooted, unassailable, aglow . . . Fortunes fluctuated, but not Dupont . . .

Adam Gellin was high on the rush of optimism a young man enjoys when he first decides to transform his body by pumping iron.

He had begun working out on the Cybex machines at Farquhar. Not that he thought he would ever bulk up enough to overcome giants such as Curtis Jones and Jojo with his bare hands. He wasn't crazy. All he wanted was a certain look that said, "Don't even *think* about fucking with *me*. Don't even *try* to make me your patsy. Save your patronizing cracks—You the man, Adam!—for wusses. You can't play *me* like that."

Adam ruminated upon some of the terminology of his new quest—pecs, abs, delts, traps, lats, tri's, bi's, obliques—as he approached the crossing of the Great Yard's two big interior walkways. In the center of the intersection was the Saint Christopher fountain, featuring a huge, heroic granite sculpture of the saint himself in a toga, carrying the infant Jesus across a turbulent stream created by the rushing water of the fountain. The late-nineteenth-century French sculptor Jules Dalou had done the figures, which were now cast into the deep shadows of the verging twilight. What pecs Dalou had given Saint Christopher! What bulging delts! As he walked, Adam straightened his left arm and raised it to shoulder level, then felt the deltoid muscle with his right hand. Not much there yet, but—

Down in the locker room, Adam changed into an extra-large T-shirt and extra-long shorts, then headed up to the weight-training floor. Powerful over-head lights gave a slick look to the floor's black-trimmed beige expanse and its regiment after regiment, rank after rank, of Cybex machines with white frames, black iron arms, and stainless-steel weight axles, all doubled in number by the mirrored walls. On his first day up here Adam had taken a look at the other weight lifters and decided that he needed a shirt with sleeves that came down to the elbows, so serious were his shortcomings in the upper arm, chest, and thigh departments. And these young brutes weren't even athletes! Real athletes, the recruits who played on the football and basketball teams, never went near Farquhar. They had their own gyms, weight rooms, and training rooms. The muscular students here at Farquhar were merely subscribing to the new male body fashion—the jacked, ripped, buff look. They were all over the place here on the weight-lifting floor! Ordinary guys with such big arms, big shoulders, big necks, big chests, they could wear sleeveless T-shirts and strap-style I'm-Buff shirts to show off in! What were they going to do with all these amazing muscles? . . . *Nothing*, that's what. They weren't going to be athletes, and they weren't going to fight anybody. It was a fashion, these muscles, just like anything else you put on your body . . . cargo shorts, jeans, the preppies' pink button-down shirts and lime-green shorts, Oakley sunglasses, black rubber L. L. Bean boots with the leather tops . . . whatever. Pure fashion! Nevertheless, Adam wanted in.

Look at these fucking guys checking themselves out in the mirror . . . Practically every wall is a vast sheet of mirror. The cover story, you understand, is that the mirrors are here so you can see if you're doing your exercises correctly. Pure bullshit, of course . . . They're here so you can drink in and drool over the beauty of your fashionable body! Between exercises, our dense fashion plates *sneak* looks at themselves. They can't even *wait* for the next exercise. Look at that one over there . . . casually straightening his arm down by his side . . . so he can sneak a look at the way his triceps pop out . . . and *that* one . . . he's pretending he's just stretching . . . so he can make his latissimi dorsi fan out like a giant stingray . . . and *that* one, over there . . . pretending to rub his hands together at waist level . . . when he's really pressing them together with all his might so he can watch the mighty pectoral muscles pop out . . . Behold! The fashionable brutes! The diesels, they called them! Every thirty seconds—you could count on it—some brute-in-embryo would straighten an arm and sneak a look in the ubiquitous mirrors at his burgeoning triceps. Muscles were very much in fashion.

Adam stood there in his droopy clothes, panning his head this way and

T
O
M

W
O
L
F
E

that, searching for—*there!* Up on the balcony he spotted it: a shoulder-shrug machine, designed expressly for bulking up the trapezius. Once he laid eyes on it, he *yearned* for it. Nobody had ever yearned more for a drug. *Nothing* could make you look tougher faster than a big neck merging with a trapezius bulging, *swollen* from shoulder to shoulder . . . But there was an unspoken piece of protocol that said only heavy lifters used the apparatus on the balcony. Adam agonized; the very thought of the diesels he would find up there made his arms and legs feel like noodles . . . but he couldn't help that, could he? He all but ran up the treaded metal stairs, fearful that somebody else, some bona fide brute, would get to the shoulder-shrug machine before he did.

Sure enough, once he reached the balcony, he was in the realm of *the thick, the dense, the swell, the diesels.* From throughout the balcony came the strangled basso profundo of gonnabe buff boys pumping iron, lying on their backs on padded benches within the bench-press frames, bent legs atremble in the squat frames, bellying into strange, padded inclined planes for biceps curls and vertical lifts for the latissimi dorsi.

"Hey, dude, spot me, wouldja!"

"That's it! That's it! One more! Don't be a pussy! One more!"—accompanied by ostentatious groans.

" . . . did five hundred."

Groaning out of a strangled throat, "Bullshit—you—did—five—hundred—you—couldn't—fucking—*budge*—five hundred," followed by a desperate interjection halfway between a groan and a cry—"Oonaggh!"—and a dense young mesomorph emerges from the squat frame wearing a wrestler's low-cut strap-style shirt (in order to display the pecs as well as the bi's, tri's, delts, and traps), inflating and deflating with deep breaths, holding his arms slightly curved and away from his body, as if the muscles through his chest, back, bi's, and tri's are too big for his arms ever to hang down straight again, and walking about with a curious, apelike straddle gait.

Adam involuntarily tugged on the arms of his T-shirt to bring them down below his elbows to make sure none of the brutes got a look at those sad little pipes of his. He imagined that every eye on the balcony was pinned on him . . . the featherweight weakling who had dared ascend to the balcony of the jacked . . . not realizing that *every* bodybuilder thinks the entire gym is watching him . . . to check out how much weight he's lifting, how many reps he's doing . . . and whether or not he's going to try to sneak a look in the mirror afterward to see how much bigger his traps, delts, pecs, bi's, tri's, lats, quads, and obliques look, now that the exercise has gorged them with blood . . .

Adam loaded up the shoulder-shrug machine with weights—had to make it look respectably heavy—tried it . . . couldn't budge it . . . had to take a lot of weights off . . . mortified at the thought of the brutes' no doubt mounting scorn . . . finally reduced the weight enough to do three sets . . . ten, eight, and a final puny five repetitions. Between sets he took deep breaths, looked down at the floor with his face set in a terribly manly grimace, rolled his shoulders, and walked with a straddle in the accepted apelike fashion.

After an hour of lifting, Adam felt gratifyingly pumped up, and he headed downstairs, stealing glimpses of his traps where they were visible at the extra-big neck of his T-shirt as he passed mirrors, and wondering if they really did look a bit bigger or if it was just his imagination. No . . . they *did* look bigger.

He was enjoying that temporary high the male feels when his muscles, no matter what size they may be, are gorged with blood. He feels . . . *more of a man.*

The Farquhar Fitness Center had elevators, but it also had a wide, well-lit stairway, and Adam, high on muscle building, chose the scenic route. On each floor's stairway landing you could look through a pair of big plate-glass doors and see what was going on within. One floor down, the sign above the double doors said CARDIOVASCULAR, which struck Adam as a pathetically medical term connoting the sickly, not the manly . . . but the sight of students, many of them girls, running in an odd fashion on a machine caught his eye, and he went inside . . . The machine, called a StairMaster, allowed you to run—if you could really call it running—without taking your feet off a pair of huge pedals. It was a bit like standing up and "pumping" on a bicycle. There were many girls . . . Some wore plain, sexless gym clothes, T-shirts, sweatshirts, roomy shorts, and sneakers. More, however, came dressed as . . . girls. Super-low-cut sweatpants they had! And short T-shirts! And lots of nubile young flesh and belly buttons in between! From the back . . . was he seeing a little buttocks décolletage, a little cleavage . . . Right in front of Adam, a girl with long blond hair pumped away on the StairMaster in low-waisted lavender nylon running shorts and an abbreviated royal blue basketball jersey. She didn't have large breasts, but with each rotation her nipples pressed out against the thin nylon of the halter, and her belly button winked this way and that in the long expanse of bare flesh. Four machines down the row, a girl wore black tights, which gripped every curve and crevice of her loins like a second skin, and a flesh-colored athletic bra. The tops of her breasts bobbed up and down like flan. You had to look twice to make sure she had on any bra at all. The sight aroused Adam. His own loins were on the qui vive, as if something were about to . . . *happen* in this so-called fitness center . . . The push of a button, the flick of a switch . . . and they would stop pretending anymore and plunge into a full-blown rout, an out-and-out orgy, and rutrutrutrutrut . . .

Just beyond the StairMasters were rows and rows of treadmills, an extraordinary number of treadmills . . . wide black keyboards . . . green and orange diode lights. The noise was almost deafening. Row after row of boys and girls were running on the treadmills, some of them at quite a clip, adding the thuds of a hundred, perhaps two hundred feet pounding the treadmill belts, whose motors ground away in a bass register. Adam could see scores of breathless young buttocks . . .

He started to turn back to the StairMasters when a mane of long brown hair caught his eye. The girl was running, really running, on a treadmill next to a mirrored wall. He could see her from behind at a three-quarter angle. She was wearing ordinary sweatpants, not low-cut, but they fit tight on her buttocks—and that *line*! That *line*! A dark line of sweat had formed in the crevice between the two buttocks. It clove the declivity and reached down under into the very mystery of her loamy loins. He couldn't keep his eyes off it—the dark, wet rivulet that led to . . . Oh, loamy, loamy loins! He caught sight of her profile in the mirror. He stared—he stared—and he was sure of it! It was that girl, that freshman, the one he had run into that night in the library when he had to do an all-nighter writing a paper for Jojo. All he had gotten out of her was her name, Charlotte. Other than that, she had frozen him out. She had cut him to shreds with her eyes. He had longed to run into her again—and, oh God, that *line*!

How to approach her, though. She was flying on that treadmill—looked as if she were running a four-minute mile . . . eyes fixed straight ahead. The treadmill next to hers was vacant. No more than eight inches between machines. He drew closer, walking slowly down an aisle between rows of treadmills. What a racket! It was her, all right. Such untouched, innocent beauty—with a temper! Well—if he worked up his nerve and got on the vacant treadmill, what would he do then? How could he even operate the damned keyboard? And could he run? Not the way she was running . . . maybe not at all . . . When was the last time he had done *any* kind of running? And how could he make himself heard if he got up on the thing? But—this was his chance.

Adam got up on the treadmill and looked at the girl, hoping she would notice him before he had to do any running at all. But her eyes remained pinned on some abstract vanishing point straight ahead. It took him a full minute—seemed like ten—to figure out how to start the thing. There were buttons for every damned thing in the world, including his own weight—*weight?*—the incline of the treadmill—*incline?* The racket was so loud he felt as if he were in the innards of a machine, a printing press. He finally punched the speed button until the treadmill belt beneath his feet reached 2 miles an hour, now 2.5, now 3 . . . There was nothing to it, he could keep up with it by walking . . . then 3.5 . . . By the time he got to 4 miles per hour, however, he had to walk so fast it became an effort . . . Maybe it would be easier to jog it, and she might show an interest in a runner rather than a walker . . . He started jogging, but the machine was actually going too slow for jogging, so he punched it up to 4.5. He kept jogging, but still she took no notice of him. Barely thirty seconds had gone by when he realized that his lungs weren't up to this. So he leaned forward with his forearms resting on the big keyboard console, frantically trying to make his feet keep up with the belt while he reached beneath his chest to slow the machine down—*damn!*—hit the speedup button instead, and—*whoa!*—his legs went out from under him. He pushed against the console to try to straighten himself up . . . and in a helpless slow motion . . . he knew precisely what was happening but couldn't do anything about it . . . he did a belly flop on the treadmill belt, which transported him and his whole body and dumped them on the floor. He was still lying there, thoroughly dazed, when the girl leaped acrobatically onto the frame of her own treadmill—which was really speeding—leaned over, hit a button that stopped his belt, then stopped her own, leapt like a goat, and—*just like that*—was on one knee by his side.

"Are you all right? What happened?"

Her face, framed by the flowing brown hair, was not only young and angelic but also, somehow, maternal. He was torn between the ignominy of a hopeless fool and the impulse to rise up on one elbow and press his cheek against hers and embrace her and say, "Thank you!" He settled for just propping himself up, smiling, shaking his head self-deprecatingly, and saying, "Wow . . . thank you."

"What happened?"

In a daze: "I don't know . . . My feet went out from under me . . ."

He started to get up, and a pain shot through his hip, and he winced—"Oooo!"—and settled back down.

"What's wrong?" She had to shout to be heard over the ruckus of the machines.

"I did something to my hip!" He shook his head again to indicate that this wasn't serious, merely stupid.

He started to get up again, and the girl extended her hand and said, "Here!"

He took her hand, and she pulled, and he finally got his feet beneath him. Adam tested his hip; and the pain, while not terrible, made him limp.

"Why don't you sit down," said the girl. She was pointing toward an exercise bench just beyond the regiment of treadmills.

So he limped over and sat down on the bench. The girl stood in front of him with her hands on her hips. It wasn't quite so noisy over here. He looked up into her eyes and smiled and said, "Thanks." The smile was supposed to carry more meaning than the word. He hoped she wouldn't remember that night in the library.

She frowned. "Wait a minute, aren't you the—"

"Yeah . . . I am . . ." said Adam. He lowered his head sheepishly and had to roll his eyes upward to keep looking at her. "I was hoping you wouldn't notice . . . Charlotte, right?"

She nodded.

"I'm Adam. I guess I owe you an apology, but I was desperate that night."

"Oh?"

"Yeah . . . I had to write a ten-page paper for some athlete by ten o'clock in the morning."

"You *had* to?"

Adam shrugged. "I have a job tutoring athletes. Otherwise I couldn't even afford to be here."

"You have to write their *papers* for them? Isn't that illegal?"

"*Oh* yeah—or a serious academic violation anyway. But around here the athletes are the athletes, I guess. Far as I can tell, the faculty just sort of looks the other way."

"I never heard of such a thing," said Charlotte. "The athletes—what do they do? Do they just say, 'Hey, write me a paper'?"

"That's about it, I guess. Ordinarily, I wear a beeper."

"Do they all do it? Aren't some of them ashamed?"

"Maybe, but I've never met one. Some of them are just your ordinary dummies, eight-forty combined SATs, that sort of thing. The rest of them find it socially unacceptable to work hard. They're *above* all that. Besides, their teammates would resent it and make fun of them, but it wouldn't be fun fun, if you know what I mean. It's sort of a point of honor not to make the others look bad. The one or two of them who actually make good grades, like this guy Bousquet on the basketball team, they try to hide it."

"Who were you writing a paper for that night?"

"Another basketball player. Jojo Johanssen. He's practically seven feet tall, and he must weigh three hundred pounds, all muscle, and *white*. He's the only white player on the starting five. He's got a big white head and a little blond buzz cut on top." Adam made a level motion over the top of his head from back to front.

Charlotte gave her lips a rueful twist. "Oh, *I* know that guy."

She proceeded to tell him about Jojo's performance in a ridiculous French class known as Frère Jocko. After class he started hitting on her, and she told him what a fool he was and walked away, leaving him blathering like an idiot.

Adam chuckled and said, "I wish I'd seen *that*! These guys think they can come walking up to any girl on campus and she'll fall down on her back in awe. The pathetic thing is, they're usually right. I could tell you some stories . . ." He let his eyes drift off, and then he turned back. "The whole campus gets all excited—over *what*? What does it *matter* what Dupont does in basketball against Indiana or Duke or Stanford or Florida or Seton Hall? What does it *mean*? Our freaks beat their freaks, that's all."

The frown had disappeared from Charlotte's face. She looked prettier than ever. Her face glowed with color from all the running. "I used to wonder the same thing when I was in high school," she said, "'xact same thing. What was everybody all excited about?" *Exact* was *'xact*, and *about* was *abay-ut*.

"Where'd you go?" said Adam.

"It was a little town"—*tayun*—"called Sparta? In North Carolina? Nobody here's ever heard of it." *Uv* it.

"I *thought* I detected a little Southern accent there," said Adam.

He gave her a warm smile, but she seemed to stiffen a bit. "I'm a real pushover for Southern accents," he added quickly. "How'd you happen to come to Dupont?"

"I had this English teacher? Miss Pennington? She wouldn't even *let* me apply anywhere but Dupont, Harvard, Yale, and Princeton. My safety school was Penn."

Adam started chuckling. "Your *safety* school, hunh? So you got into Dupont."

"I got into all five *uv*'em." Charlotte blushed bright red, then tried to cover it up with a modest-looking smile. "Dupont gave me the best scholarship? And I really liked the French department. I was going to major in French."

"And now you're not?"

"Well, I'm kind of confused about it now. I'm taking this—" She broke off the sentence and gave him the tenderest of looks. "Are you feeling better?"

"I'm fine. I'll be okay." Adam slid himself over a bit on the bench. "Here . . . have a seat. You don't have to stand like that."

So she sat down . . .

The treadmills were still grinding and rumbling like a factory, but Adam was afraid that if they moved, it would . . . break the spell.

That *look*. Here was this girl from someplace called Sparta, North Carolina, and so young, and she had just given him a look so tender, it was maternal and at the same time it was opening, opening, opening like the tender virginal bud of the most gorgeous flower revealing its virginal petals to the world with a sublime innocence and at the same time a sublime invitation. Inside Adam's head all this horticulture was no mere figure of speech, no mere extended metaphor, no mere conceit. He could *see* the pinkness of the petals opening, *her* petals, in the flesh. He wanted to lean forward and embrace her and press his lips upon the tender buds of hers. But if he did that, should he take his glasses off first? Or would that be like too much of an announcement of what he intended to do, thereby destroying the ineffable magic of the moment? Or should he leave the glasses on and risk poking her in the eye with the frame when he bent his neck at a forty-five-degree angle to make his lips fit hers right? *Pop.* What the hell, it was only an *urge*, in the first place, and so all he said was, "Anyhow, you were saying you're taking this—this what?"

"Oh. This class in neuroscience? It's the most exciting subject in the world. It's like in the future it's going to be the key to just about everything. And the teacher is *so* good. Mr. Starling."

"He's the one who won the Nobel Prize, right?"

"That's right." *Riot.* "But I didn't even know that when I signed up for the course."

A lightbulb went on over Adam's head. "You know what? You ought to come by and meet this sort of group we have. We call ourselves the Millennial Mutants. I bet you'd really enjoy it."

"The Millennial Mutants?"

"Yeah. This girl Camille Deng thought up the name. She writes these like long political pieces for the newspaper, the *Daily Wave.* I write for it, too. A lot of us do. In fact, one of the group, Greg Fiore, is the editor of the *Wave.*" Adam figured that might impress the girl. For once that arrogant little sonofabitch Greg might be of some use. The same went for Camille. "Anyway, Camille thought up the name. The idea is—well, here's the thing. This school is full of smart kids. They've hosed the SATs and the APs and the GPAs like it's their job. Then they come here and party and 'network' and like make a 'transition from adolescence to adulthood' and all of that ridiculous bullshit, which really means a transition from adolescence to preadolescence. You know? I mean, why not! I mean, here we are in one of the greatest universities in the world, and all these kids act like—like they're taking four years of classes for . . . I don't know . . . for—well, like they're paying dues so they can enjoy Club Dupont for four years. Then there's a whole bunch of kids who work very hard so they'll end up with a transcript from Dupont that'll be like a ticket to a lot of money. Investment banking for example—I mean, you could go to the Great Yard at noon and close your eyes and throw a rock, and you'd hit somebody who assumes they're going to work for Gordon Hanley or some place like that. As a matter of fact, the son of the CEO of Gordon Hanley—" Adam decided to drop that subject. "I mean, the whole thing is *pathetic,* if you want to know what I think. We want to leave here and *do* things, and I don't mean like working for some fu—god-damn"—somehow you just didn't say *fucking* to a girl like this—"investment bank and crunching numbers fourteen hours a day to make money off evaporated property, which is what Schumpeter called it."

"Doing what things?" said Charlotte.

"What things? The best thing is being a Bad-Ass Rhodie, capital B, capital A, capital R."

Charlotte said, "What's a—what's that?"

"The Bad-Ass Rhodie . . . that's an idea that just sort of developed after the end of the cold war, or right after the Gulf War, the first one, in 1991, I guess you could say. Up to then students like us—you know, students interested in ideas and concepts—which are what *really* move the world, not politics or plain military power, okay?—I mean, like Marxism—I mean, here's this guy, this alien, this guy from Austria nobody ever heard of, sitting by himself in the British Museum in the 1880s writing a like really abstruse book on economics called *Das Kapital*, and that book, that idea, is what creates the history of the entire twentieth century!"

His eye strayed to another girl who had that sweat stain . . . that lubricious line . . . down the crack in the back of her sweatpants . . .

He grinned sheepishly. "Now I can't even remember what I was saying."

"You were talking about 'students like us'? After the Gulf War in 1991?" *Nine-teen niney wuh-un?*

"Oh, yeah. Up 'til then, students like us used to just go to graduate school and become college teachers. But after that, a new type of intellectual comes on the scene: the bad-ass. The bad-ass is sort of a rogue intellectual. A bad-ass doesn't want to do anything so boring and low-paid and like . . . codified . . . as teaching. The bad-ass types, they're the types who don't want to spend their twenties, they don't want to spend the prime of life as a graduate student cooped up in some cubicle up in the stacks of the library. You're an intellectual, but you want to operate on a higher level. This is a new millennium, and you want to be a member of the millennial aristocracy, which is a meritocracy, but an aristo-meritocracy. You're a mutant. You're an evolutionary advance. You've gone way beyond the ordinary 'intellectual' of the twentieth century. You're not just some dealer in ideas who's content to sell the ideas of a Marx or a Freud or a Darwin or a . . . a . . . a Chomsky . . . to the unenlightened." He didn't seem all that sure about Chomsky. "Those guys weren't transmitters for other people's ideas. Each one of them created a *matrix*, a mother of all ideas. That's what a Millennial Mutant aims for. This is a new millennium, the twenty-first century is, and you're going to create the new matrixes yourself, or *matrices* I guess it is, if you see what I'm saying?"

No, said the blank look the girl gave him.

"All right. You're not going to be a graduate student, which to most people means some kind of geek or creep, and you're not going to teach, which means some poor old guy who ends up with humped-over shoulders—you know the kind of professor I mean? Who wants to end up as this like . . . pathetic object of pity? So in college you don't sign up for a conventional major. If you're at Dupont, you do what I did. You go into the Hodges

Fellows Program and you create your own major, along with a faculty adviser. I'm not bragging, because it's not all that hard to do. But I have to tell you, I came up with the perfect title for my Hodges: 'The Intellectual Foundations of Globalization.' 'Global' is a key concept. It's a big plus if you show an altruistic interest in the Third World. Tanzania is very hot right now. East Timor is not bad. Haiti will do, but you haven't like . . . you haven't like gone deep enough into the Third World. You know what I mean? It's too easy to get to Haiti. I mean, you can take a plane from Philadelphia and be there in an hour and a half, that sort of thing."

"What do you mean, 'get there'?" said Charlotte.

"You actually *go* there. You go to Tanzania or some other country that's hot for your junior year abroad. You never pick Florence or Paris or London, least of all London. It has to be the Third World, and you have to show what they call 'service opportunity leadership.' I went to Kenya, but it turns out everybody has this idea Kenya's too civilized. I taught English in a village out in the *re*-mote, out in the bush about four hours west of Nairobi by pickup truck, and I mean there wasn't a ballpoint pen within a fifty-mile radius, much less a word processor, and I got malaria like everybody else in my village. They gave me the best house they had, this little brick hut with two windows, since I was the teacher come all the way from America, but it didn't have any screens—so I got malaria like everybody else—and I come back and other Mutants are telling me I made a bad choice. Kenya is too civilized. If I had it to do over, I'd do a project like a documentary photo study of Tanzania, with text, something like that."

Adam detected a touch of reproof in the look Charlotte was giving him. Sure enough, she then said, "You went—people go all the way to Africa just to look good?"

"No, no, that's not what I'm saying," said Adam. It was time to back out of this particular dead end—and it had seemed so light and captivating and sophisticated while he was saying it. "Not at all. I mean if you don't have a genuine interest, you don't even think about anything like this. You don't live in a brick hut with no screens and let toxic insects have their run of your hide. But it's like anything else you want to do. There are strategies . . . and there are *strategies*." He shook his head several times. "No, no, no, don't get me wrong. But if you're a bad-ass, you have a specific goal. You want to get a Rhodes scholarship. That's the goal, and there are only thirty-two of them awarded in the whole country. If you get one, you go to Oxford and get a D.Phil. degree, and then it's like magic. Every door opens. You can go into politics like Bill Clinton or Bill Bradley. Remember Bill Bradley? You can be a policy wonk like this guy Murray Gutman, who advises the president on demographics and cultural shifts. He's only twenty-six, *but*—he's your classic Bad-Ass Rhodie. You can write, like this guy Philip Gourevitch who does all these long pieces for *The New Yorker* on Africa and Asia or this guy Timmond who did the big coffee-table book on African leaders. I mean, Africa's perfect, especially when you think about Cecil Rhodes's idea when he set up the Rhodes scholarships. The idea was to bring bright young American barbarians over to England and make them citizens of the world. He wanted to lift them up to a higher plane and extend the reach of the British Empire with its American cousins in tow. The British Empire is gone, but a Rhodes still lifts you to a higher plane. You're not doomed to being some obscure college teacher. You become a public intellectual. Everybody talks about your ideas."

Charlotte said, "There are only thirty-two Rhodes scholarships?" Adam nodded yes. "Well, golly, that's not very many. What if you're a bad—what if that's what you're counting on and you don't get one?"

"In that case," said Adam, "you go after a Fulbright. That's a pretty long way down from a Rhodes, but it's okay. There's also the Marshall Fellowships, but they're the last resort. I mean that's bottom-fishing. During the cold war a bad-ass couldn't've accepted a Fulbright or a Marshall, because they're government programs, and that would've made you look like a tool of imperialism. A Rhodes was okay because there was no British Empire left, and you couldn't be accused of being a tool of something that wasn't there anymore. Today the only empire is the American empire, and it's omnipotent, and so if you don't get a Rhodes you have to make use of it, the new empire. It's okay as long as you're using it for the sake of your own goals and not theirs."

"Theirs?" said Charlotte. "What do you mean, theirs?"

Oh-oh; let's back out of this alley, too. "I don't mean 'theirs' like 'ours' and 'theirs' in the ordinary sense." He realized this wasn't very expert doubletalking, but he hurried on, hoping to sweep her along with his momentum. "I just mean there's no conventional role, no existing codified role for a badass. There's no existing slot for the new aristo-meritocrat. 'Theirs' in that sense, in that circumscribed sense. You know?" Let's get outta here! "Or that's why some bad-asses go into consulting for like . . . McKinsey. That's the one they shoot for, McKinsey. I mean, consulting is better than i-banking, because let's say you're starting out as an i-banker—"

"What's an i-banker?" said the girl.

"An investment banker," said Adam. Thank God. At least he'd faked and kept her from digging her heels in for some kind of anti-anti-Americanism number. "If you start out in investment banking, you're going to be putting in hundred-hour weeks. You make a lot of money, but they use you like a slave. Some of these banks have dormitories, so if you're still working at two or three in the morning, you can sleep over and be back at your desk at eight, in time to work another sixteen or eighteen hours straight. If you're a consultant, you don't make quite as much money, but you make plenty, and you travel out of town three or four times a week and you rack up incredible frequent-flier miles."

The expression on the girl's face as much as said, "You're not making any sense."

Adam rushed on: "The thing about all those frequent-flier miles is, you can fly all over the world for nothing. Let's say you want to go to this new super-resort they've got in New Zealand—awesome golf course, the whole deal— you can fly there first-class for a vacation, and it doesn't cost you anything."

"I don't understand," said Charlotte. "What does that have to do with concepts and ideas and being an intellectual and having influence and everything?"

"Well, nothing directly," said Adam. "It's just an example of how you use the empire to live like an aristocrat without having to have a family pedigree or any of that stuff."

"I don't see why you call it the empire," said Charlotte.

Damn. He'd blundered back onto that terrain again. "It's sort of a . . . figure of speech," he said. "I'm not even interested in consulting, myself, although if you're invited for a McKinsey recruiting weekend, that shows you're on the right track."

"Have they invited you on one?"

"Yeah, and it's coming up in about three and a half weeks."

"Are you going?"

"Uh . . . yes. I mean I might as well."

"Even though you're not interested?"

"Well—I'm curious about it, I guess. And it won't hurt to be seen there. *You* know—the word gets around that you're out there on the right track. Actually, the track starts early, in high school, although I didn't know that when I was at Roxbury Latin. If you're interested in being a scientist, the big thing is being invited to the Research Science Institute at MIT or the Telluride Institute at Cornell. Princeton has one in the humanities, and it's also a big thing to be invited to the Renaissance Weekend as one of the student attendees. You know about the Renaissance Weekends?"

"No."

"They have them every year at Christmastime at Hilton Head, in South Carolina. All these politicians and celebrities and scientists and businessmen go there and talk about ideas and issues and things. They have student attendees so they can find out what's on the minds of 'the young' and all that. That anoints you as somebody who's already on the Millennial track, and you're only seventeen or eighteen."

"But I still don't understand consulting," said Charlotte. "What do you consult *about*?" *Abay-ut.*

"You get sent to these corporations, and you tell them how to improve their . . . oh, I don't know, management techniques, I guess. But the important thing—"

"How could they know how to do that?"—*they-ut*—"if they've just graduated from college?"

"Well, I suppose they . . . uh . . . have some kind of—to tell you the truth, I don't know. I've wondered the same thing. But I know they do it, and they make a lot of money. The important thing is to be an aristo-meritocrat and live at that higher level I was talking about. If you want to have some influence, then you've got to have the freedom to ram your ideas home." Adam leaned back against the wall and gave her as warm, and at the same time as confident, a smile as he could. She seemed slightly bewildered, but that only made her open her eyes wider to look more lovely. Her eyes were so blue, blue like . . . he could see the flower . . . grew low to the ground, but he didn't know its name—

"But the *really* important thing," he heard himself saying, "is that you come meet the Millennial Mutants. You'll see what Dupont *ought* to be about. Every Monday we get together for dinner."

"Where?"

"Different places. I could let you know."

She just looked at him, although not in a way one could attach any particular emotion to. Finally she said, "Monday nights? I reckon I could do that. Thank you."

"Great," said Adam. And it *felt* great. He looked into her eyes with the intention of looking deeply, profoundly . . . and then pouring his whole self into her through her optic chiasmas.

But—*pop*—her eyes were on his sweatpants, at hip level. "How does your hip feel now?"

His hip? "Oh, it's okay," said Adam. "I'll be fine."

"Well, I've got four and a half more miles to go, I guess I'd better . . ."

"Oh sure," he said, "you go ahead. And hey, thanks!"

By the time he said "thanks," she was already on her way to the machine. But then she looked back over her shoulder and smiled and gave him a little wave.

Walking home in the dark, through the campus, through the streets of Chester, Adam kept visualizing that smile. Surely it wasn't mere politeness, for there was definitely a certain gleam, a kind of . . . promise . . . or maybe the word was confirmation or like . . . *sealing* . . . and the way she tossed her hair when she looked back . . . sort of like an . . . unfurling . . . He began whistling a tune, "You Are So Beautiful," even though it was a hard tune to whistle.

The next morning, a little past eleven-thirty, no sooner had the class begun than the professor, Mr. Quat, dissed Curtis Jones, fo'shizzle, as Curtis himself might say.

The course was called America in the Age of Revolution, referring to both the Revolution of 1776 and the industrial revolution. The class's twenty-eight students convened in a ground-floor room of Stallworth College that had four large, solemn leaded casement windows looking out on a courtyard landscaped in the Tuscan manner. The room was lined with six-foot-high intricately carved oak bookshelves, replete with books. What with the early Renaissance look of the windows and the Old World woodwork, the room all but spoke aloud of the wisdom of the ages and the sanctity of learning and scholarship.

Everybody sat around two great oak library tables set end to end, creating the impression of a conference room. Mr. Quat was probably in his mid- to late fifties. He was a passionate, even hotheaded, pursuer of knowledge, and not even the most buff-brained athlete was likely to nod off during Quat time. But his physique was enough to make an athlete's flesh crawl. He had a perfectly round head, thanks to his fat cheeks, his fat jowls, and the fact that his curly iron-gray hair had receded to the point where his forehead had the contours of a globe from the equator up to the North Pole. He had a mustache and a close-trimmed goatee. His torso was swollen with fat to the point where little breasts had formed on his chest, a detail all too apparent thanks to his penchant for too-tight V-neck sweaters with only a T-shirt underneath and no jacket on top. The T-shirt, ordinary white cotton, always showed in the V. But no athlete, least of all Jojo, was going to challenge him on any level. Mr. Quat always stood up at the table as he taught, while Jojo, André Walker, and Curtis Jones, along with the twenty-five authentic undergraduates, remained seated. Mr. Quat treated all students as antagonists, but he acted as if student-athletes—the sarcasm fairly dripped from his eyeteeth as he used the term—were cretins he would like to *kill*. This unpleasant situation was the result of a colossal blunder by a blond twinkie named Sonia in the Athletic Department. She had confused Quat with Tino Quattrone, a young associate professor who came to all the basketball games even though he could only get standing-room tickets, with this character, Jerome Quat, who would obviously like to blow up the entire Buster Bowl, given the chance, when she prepared the list of approved athlete-friendly teachers in the History Department. Speculation as to why Coach had ever hired this bimbo always ran in the same direction. On top of everything else, Mr. Jerome Quat lectured and hectored them in a highly scholarly, lofty manner pockmarked by unpleasant pronunciations, which were in fact a residue of his upbringing in Brooklyn, New York.

Mr. Quat, standing, was staring at a stack of papers on the table as if he hated them. Then he looked up and said, "All right—" *Awright*—he paused, as if he had just caught them in the act, some act, any act. "Last time we saw that by 1790 such social eccentricities had been exacerbated"— *We sawr that by seventeen ninedy such social eggzendrizzidies had been eggzazzerbated*—"by her further attempts—" *Huh fuhthuh attempts*—

He stopped abruptly and stared toward the far end, where Jojo, Curtis, and André were sitting.

"Mr. Jones," he said, "do you mind telling me what's that you have on your head?"

Curtis was in fact wearing an Anaheim Angels baseball cap with the bill sticking out sideways. He now touched it and said in a tone of mock bemusement, "You mean *this*?"

"Yes."

Curtis chose the cool and amused route. "Aw, hey, Prof, check it out! You looking at a—"

Quat cut him off. "Are you an orthodox Jew, Mr. Jones?"

"Me?" He looked around at his basketball buddies with bemusement and amusement. "Naw."

"Does that cap have any other religious significance, Mr. Jones?"

Still cool and amused: "*Aw* naw. Like I say—"

Cold and not amused: "Then kindly remove it."

"Aw, come on, Prof, the other—"

"*Now*, Mr. Jones. And by the way, starting now, you will not address me as Prof. You will say 'Mr. Quat' or, if three syllables is expecting too much, 'Sir'—'Mr. Quat' or 'Sir.' Do I make myself clear?"

Their eyes locked. Jojo could tell that Curtis's mind was scrolling scrolling scrolling scrolling, trying to figure out how much of his manhood was actually on the line here.

"I—"

"One of us will remove your headgear, Mr. Jones. Either you or me. *Right now.*"

Curtis was the one who broke. He removed the cap, looked away, and began shaking his head in a manner that was supposed to say, "I'm going to indulge you this time, but you're one sick puppy."

Mr. Quat's angry gaze panned over every student in the room. "Other teachers may not care what you wear to class. I can't speak for them. But you will not wear any form of headdress in *this* class, unless your particular religious faith requires it. Do I make myself clear?"

No one said a thing. Mr. Quat resumed his discourse on class, status, and power among the American colonials. Curtis lounged back in his library chair with his hands folded in his lap, craning his head this way and that, in any direction other than one that might make it seem as if he was paying any attention whatsoever to Mr. Quat. Smoke was coming out of his ears. Jojo could hear him muttering now and again. Had he been dissed? Obviously, he had come to the conclusion that he had been.

At the end of class Mr. Quat went around the table handing students back the ten-page papers they had turned in the week before. When he got to Curtis, Curtis took his with exaggerated nonchalance, as if Mr. Quat were nothing more than a stewardess handing out those slimy miniature "hot towels" they dispense on airplanes. Glancing sideways, Jojo noticed that both Curtis and André had received C's. Jojo looked up at Mr. Quat, but the professor skipped over him entirely and resumed handing them out farther down the line.

Like the rest of the class, Jojo got up to depart . . . but then hung back a bit just in case Mr. Quat discovered he had failed to give him his paper. Finally he started following André and Curtis. Curtis kept leaning close to André and nudging him, going *heghh heghh heghh*, presumably settling Quat's hash and explaining how he hadn't backed down, it was actually something else or other . . .

Jojo was almost out the door when a voice behind him said, "Mr. Johanssen."

Jojo stopped and turned around.

"May I see you for a moment?"

Sure enough, Mr. Quat had Jojo's paper in his hand. He could make out the capital letters typed on the otherwise blank first page: THE PERSONAL PSYCHOLOGY OF GEORGE III AS A CATALYST OF THE AMERICAN REVOLUTION.

Mr. Quat held the paper up in front of Jojo—there was no grade on it—and said, "Mr. Johanssen, this is your paper?"

"Yeah . . ."

"Did you write it yourself?"

Jojo could feel the blood draining from his face. It was all he could do to answer in a halfway normal voice, "*Yeah,*" and arrange his eyes and lips in a fashion that registered astonishment over the very question.

"Well then, perhaps you can tell me what this word means." The professor was pointing at CATALYST.

Jojo panicked. He couldn't *think*. His tutor had just *told* him the other night! He had even said, albeit a bit sarcastically, "You might want to know what the word means, just in case you ever have to make somebody think you know what you've written." But *what had he said*? Something about *precipitation? Assassination?* Damn! The rest of it had vanished from his memory.

"Well, I *know,*" Jojo sputtered, "but it's one of those words you *know* you know, but you don't know how to put it into words? You know what I mean?"

"It's one of those words you *know* you know, but you don't know how to put it into words," Mr. Quat said drily. Then he flipped to an interior page. "You say here, 'When George was a young boy, his mother is said to have exhorted him constantly, "You must become a great king." When he at last became king, he could never free himself of the memory of that metronomic maternal exhortation.' What does *exhortation* mean?"

Fear turned Jojo's very powers of logic to mush. He couldn't even come up with a rationale for not knowing. All he could think of was why the hell the little twerp, Adam, had ever thrown in words like that. Finally he said, "It means . . . what she said?"

"*Exhortation* means 'You must become a great king'?"

"No, but I mean, the meaning—I *know* the meaning and everything, but just *defining* the meaning by itself and that kinda thing—"

"Is meaning the meaning but not defining the meaning like knowing the word but not knowing how to put the word into words, Mr. Johanssen?"

Jojo knew the professor was purposely messing up his mind with all these *meanings* and *knowings* and *words*, but he couldn't figure out how to break up the game. "I didn't mean that," he said. "All I meant was—"

Quat broke in. "What does *maternal* mean, Mr. Johanssen?"

"Mother!" Jojo blurted out.

"Wrong part of speech," said Mr. Quat, "but I'll accept that. Now, how about *metronomic*?"

Panic and uproar reigned inside Jojo's head. He hadn't a clue—and Mr. Quat had closed the door to waffling around with *knowing* and *meaning*. He just stood there with his mouth half open.

"Oh, I'm sorry, Mr. Johanssen," said Mr. Quat, oozing with sarcasm, "that really wasn't fair of me, was it? That's a difficult word."

Jojo remained speechless.

Mr. Quat flipped to another page. "Let's try this one. You say here, 'George regarded himself as the cleverest of political infighters, but what he took to be subtle strategy often struck others as the most—'" He put his fingertip upon the next word, which was "maladroit," without pronouncing it. "'—sort of meddling.' How do you pronounce that word, Mr. Johanssen, and what does it mean?"

"I—" The first-person pronoun just hung in the air. Jojo felt that he had lost all power of articulation.

"Okay, *maladroit* is difficult, too—after all, its roots are French—so let's try meddling. What does *meddling* mean, Mr. Johanssen?"

Jojo could feel his armpits sweating. "Meddling"—he certainly knew that one, but the words!—the words! The very words had fled his brain! "Well—" he said, but that was as far as he got. *Well* now hung in midair with *I*.

"Okay, let's try *subtle*. What does *subtle* mean, Mr. Johanssen?"

With the most profound effort, Jojo managed to say, "I know what it means—" But that was it. *I know what it means* floated away and joined the others.

"Let's bring this rather dreary demonstration to a conclusion," said Mr. Quat.

"Honest, I *know* all these words, Mr. Quat! I *know* them! The only problem I have is saying the meaning the way you want me to!"

"Which means you know the words but you have just one little problem: you don't know what they mean."

"Honest—"

"Stop displaying your ignorance, sir! Here's your paper."

Still holding it up before Jojo, he flipped it to the first page once more. Jojo thought he was giving it back, and he reached for it. But Mr. Quat withdrew it and held it close to his chest. Then he reached inside his jacket and produced a big mechanical china marker. He set the paper down on the table and with a furious flourish printed a huge red F on the first page beneath the title. Then he handed it to Jojo, who, shocked, accepted it robotically.

"When this is averaged in with your other grades, Mr. Johanssen, you are in deep trouble in this course. But that's a secondary problem. I have the grounds here for filing a serious honors violation . . . and I intend to file it immediately. I have no idea how much you've enjoyed making a mockery of the academic life of this university, but your fun is over. Do I make myself clear? *Over* . . . And if you try to get anybody to intervene on your behalf— *any*body—can you possibly imagine who I mean by *any*body?—that will only make it worse. Do I make myself clear?"

Jojo was speechless.

The fat man gathered up his papers and, without so much as another glance at Jojo, walked out of the room. Jojo stood there, bewildered, holding the tainted paper as if his fingers were frozen to it.

Mr. Quat reappeared in the doorway. "By the way," he snapped, "in case you're wondering, that's a xeroxed copy." Then he was gone.

Jojo's mind whirled and whirled . . . Fuck! So he got help from a tutor. *That's what they were there for!* Besides, he *knew* those words! All right, he didn't know *maladroit* and *metro-whateveritwas*, but damn it, he knew *catalyst*, or he knew it last week. He just couldn't remember what his twerpy goddamn tutor had told him. He knew *meddling* and *subtle*, too, and he knew the gist of *exhortation*, more or less. He could use them in a sentence! No problem at all! Okay, he might have an issue with *exhortation*, but *meddling* and *subtle*—Goddamn it! It was just that he couldn't rattle off formal definitions. What was he supposed to be, a CD-ROM? And what the hell was that scrawny little fuck Adam doing, throwing in *maladroit* and *metro-*

whuzzywhuzzy and all that stuff. That kid was as bad as Mr. Quat! Had he sabotaged him intentionally? Why else would he stick in words nobody ever heard of? Except for those two words, hell, he knew the whole thing cold! And all these insults . . . Don't display your ignorance, sir . . . and threats! Nobody but *nobody* can help you . . . If worse came to worse, he'd just have Coach come over and twist the guy's head off for him and shit down his windpipe. Then he remembered: Jojo Johanssen was on Buster Roth's shitlist, too. He felt bolted to the floor of this, the scene of his second devastating . . . uh . . . uh . . . experience.

He was not the first man to throw the *h* word down the memory hole when it applied to himself.

13. THE WALK OF SHAME

In the lichen twilight, dusky, rusky as could be, around the corner of the house he swaggers, stops, puts his fists on his hips, paralyzes Charlotte with a stare. It's already too dark to see his face, but she knows it's him, and she knows he's staring straight into her eyes, and she can't move her legs at all, much less run. Desperately she looks toward the house, for Daddy, Momma, Cousin Doogie, the Sheriff, but there's no one, not even a light, and Channing swaggers straight up to her, smirking and saying, "Party time," even though she can't actually hear the words. He reaches around to the back side of his jeans and produces a chaw bag of Red Man, digs in with his fingers, and shoves a plug of it into his mouth until his left cheek lumps out the size of a walnut. Smirks—sneers?—at her, does Channing, with a tilted smile, vile brown juice dribbling out of the lower corner of his mouth. He twists his body halfway around so she can see him slide the chaw bag into the jeans' rear pocket, leaving two inches of it sticking out in the accepted fashion. He starts patting it, the chaw bag in his pocket, and leering at her and doing some heavy breathing, *Unggh hunh, unggh hunh, unggh—*

*—hunh, unggh hunh—*Charlotte woke up in the dark, and she could still hear it, *Unggh hunh, unggh hunh,* and her heart started pounding. It's

in here, in this room! Utter darkness! Lunged for the lamp on the little bed-side table—*crash*—knocked it off onto the floor beside the bed. With another lunge jackknifed herself over the side of the bed, and even before she could find the stem switch on the lamp's neck, *it* had started crying and whimpering, "Charlotte . . . Charlotte . . ." Charlotte turned the lamp on—

Not two feet away, on the floor, on all fours—Beverly. The crashed lamp cast a huge shadow of her onto the wall opposite. She was on—all fours!—slowly crawling forward on her hands and knees. The way her high heels stuck up in the air behind her made them seem ludicrously superfluous. Her black pants were stretched across her scrawny rear end. A mess of flattened streaked-blond hair hung this way and that.

Charlotte, still in the hypnoidal state: "What's the matter, Beverly . . ."

Beverly looked at her blearily, trying to stanch her tears, her gasps, her whimpers, her bleats of "Charlotte" long enough to say—

Before she uttered a word, even the hypnoidal mind knew that the big high-heeled creature on all fours was drunk, and not just a little bit.

"Charlotte . . . Charlotte . . . Where are the lacrosse players? Where are the *lacrosse* players?"

"What lacrosse players?"

"This guy—I've got to go back and talk to him . . . Charlotte, *Charlotte!*"

"How can you go anywhere? You're like—I think you've had too much to drink."

Beverly looked up into her face with the eyes of a bewildered patient. "Him, too, *Charlotte!* That's the only time they *talk*—when they're drunk! *Charlotte!* . . . This is my only chance . . . He was *talking* to me, Charlotte! . . . He says he doesn't want to get involved . . . But I don't care! I *have* to hook up with him tonight." More tears, whimpers, gasps. "Where are the lacrosse players!"

Charlotte said, "He says he doesn't want to get involved? Isn't that a kind of a hint?"

"But he was *talking* to me! I gotta go find him while he's still interested . . ."

"Then why did you leave him?"

"He said he had to talk to some guy and he'd call me on my cell in ten minutes. That was five minutes ago—my cell in ten minutes five minutes ago . . ." Beverly lowered her head and began sobbing . . . on all fours. "I'm gonna drive back. I *gotta* drive back! I have to hook up with him! *Charlotte!*"

"Back where?"

"The *I.M.!*" Exasperation, as if she were repeating something for about the tenth time: "The *I.M.!*"

The I.M. . . .

Charlotte said, "You can't drive a car to the I.M., Beverly. You can't drive a car, period."

"Then *you* gotta drive me. Here are the keys." Without getting up off her hands and knees, she tried to fish her keys out of her pants pocket. But the pants were so tight she had to twist her body and straighten one leg and dig into the pocket while supporting herself on one arm and canting her neck to one side, grimacing, eyes shut, all the while. She finally retrieved the keys and held them up toward Charlotte.

"I can't drive you anywhere," said Charlotte, "least of all the I.M. You've had enough to drink. Here, why don't I help you go to bed."

Charlotte was just about to swing her legs over the side of the bed when Beverly grabbed one sleeve of her pajama top and tried to drag her toward the door. She was strong, too.

"Hey, let go! You're going to rip my pajamas!"

"You gotta drive me! — drive me! — drive me!"

"Stop it, Beverly!"

Beverly let go and keeled over on her back, then struggled up into a sitting position. "Aw right, aw right, *don't* drive me. Next time, no thanks, I'll do the same for you. Don't do me any favors . . ." Baffled, she began feeling about on the floor for her keys, finally found them, and looked up angrily at Charlotte. "Thanks a lot. I'm gonna go, I don't care —"

She tried to get her feet beneath herself, but the high heels skidded and her bottom hit the floor hard. She began crying again. She rolled over toward her own bed, got up on all fours, and managed to pull herself upright by steadying herself on the metal bed frame. She glowered at Charlotte, then lurched off balance toward the door.

Charlotte sprang up and blocked her way. "You can't do that, Beverly. You can't drive! You can't even walk!" Big sigh. "Okay, I'll drive you there. I don't even know why you want to, but I'll drive you. You'll get yourself killed. Just let me put on some pants."

She stepped out of her pajama pants and into a pair of shorts without stopping to put on underwear, slid on her sandals and said, "Okay, now give me the keys."

Beverly handed them over with the smile of a little girl who has gotten her way.

Outside in the dark, in the dead of the night, Charlotte regretted her generosity. She was still groggy. The massive wall of Little Yard seemed to pitch forward at an ominous angle, about to collapse and bury them under tons of stone. Windows were lit up here and there, and somebody was playing a country music song whose hook went "I'm not slick's you, but I'm gon' fix you. I'm gon' eighty-six you hick sombitch." There appeared to be no one else about down here at ground level. Beverly had left her car almost three feet from the curb in a no-parking zone on the drive that ran between Little Yard and the parking lot. The vehicle was enormous. Charlotte knew that Beverly had a car, but she never dreamed she had a monster like this one. It was a black thing called a Denali, an SUV, but as big and heavy as the pickup truck Daddy drove. The driver's seat was so high Charlotte had to take two great pumping steps, one up to a running board, the second up to the seat itself. It was like sitting on a leather-upholstered throne. There was tan leather everywhere and superfluous panels of wood with a showy, highly polyurethaned grain. The windows were tinted black. The whole thing was disorienting. How could it be that she was way above the ground at the wheel of a leather-upholstered monster of a vehicle, getting ready to take a besotted girl back to a bar . . . in the dead of the night?

The I.M.—the bar's name came from the Internet function "Instant Message"—was near PowerPizza and other enterprises geared mainly to students, on a strip just off campus on the edge of a slum known among students as the City of God, after a cult movie of that name about packs of homicidal boys in Rio de Janeiro. Under other circumstances it would be an easy walk.

As she drove, Charlotte said to Beverly, "Why do you like lacrosse players so much?"

"Why?" said Beverly. She turned away and looked out the side window, as if the matter was too obvious to bear explaining.

After a bit Charlotte said, "What's his name?"

Beverly continued looking straight ahead. "His name?" A dark cloud formed, and she burst into tears again.

Charlotte said, "How about if I take you back and you go to bed? Come on."

"No!" Beverly abruptly stopped crying but still didn't bother to look at

Charlotte or wipe off the tear tracks where they coursed through the makeup on her cheekbones. "I know his *room number*. He lives in Lapham. They all live in Lapham! All the lacrosse players!" Now she looked at Charlotte. "And he's *drunk*." (Don't you understand?) "That's the only time they *talk* to me!" (*Please* understand!)

"I thought you said he was at the I.M."

"He *is*! Where'dya think I just fucking *came* from?"

Charlotte pulled up in front of the I.M. At this hour there was almost no traffic. Beverly opened the door, wriggled and lurched out of her soft leather bucket seat. The high heel of her right shoe slipped off the running board, and she nearly pitched face forward onto the pavement, finally staggering to a stop like an ice-skater who has lost control. She was listing perilously to port.

"I'll come in with you!" said Charlotte.

"No!" said Beverly, offended, like most drunks, by any insinuation that she needed someone to babysit her.

A row of downlighters illuminated the front entrance. Beverly's blond hair, cerise shirt, and the waifish bones of her backside beneath the black pants shimmered as she passed beneath the lights and opened the big plate-glass door. A rush of drumbeats, electrified wails, and the voice of an adolescent curdling his vocal cords in an attempt to sound like a hardened country-slacker, veteran of a thousand jook houses . . . and the door closed. Charlotte kept the engine running. *What am I doing here?* . . . Two-thirty a.m. . . .

By and by Beverly emerged, walking at a terrific pace even though weaving slightly, opened the door of the Denali, and began blubbering and sobbing again.

"He . . . wasn't . . . there . . ." She broke *there* into two long, plaintive, tear-sodden syllables.

"That's all right," Charlotte said almost maternally. "Let's get in, and let's go back and get some sleep."

"No! I gotta find him! He was *talking* to me before! I know where he lives. You gotta take me to Lapham. You *gotta*!"

Beverly said it with such monomaniacal belligerence, Charlotte was intimidated. She was afraid of what the inebriated girl would do if she said no. So she drove her over to Lapham College. Everybody knew Lapham, thanks to the huge baroque gargoyles along the edges of its parapets. Here in the middle of the night, the faint streetlights threw the gargoyles and the building's architraves, compound arches, and stone facing into deep relief.

This time Charlotte insisted on going inside with Beverly. She wasn't going to wait out here in the SUV for the rest of the night.

Obviously this wasn't Beverly's first visit. She headed immediately for a side entrance secured by heavy, ornate wrought-iron gates and an oak door studded with iron bolts in the medieval fashion. Without hesitation, she punched a numerical code into a lock panel to the right of the gates. A low hum sounded, and she opened the gates and the door. They entered a small Gothic vestibule; straight ahead, a narrow staircase; to the right, another stout wooden door; to the left, the door to the elevator. The elevator took forever to arrive. Beverly was swearing under her breath. At last, with much ancient rattling and clanking of the outer and inner doors, it appeared, and they ascended. When they reached the fourth floor, Beverly lurched out, still listing to port. As she staggered down a corridor, she managed to do a regular tattoo on the floor with her high heels. The noise reverberated between hard-plastered yellow-ochre walls. Halfway down, she stopped—then flung herself upon a door and began hammering it with her fists. The door was so thick, this produced nothing more than muffled thumps, whereupon she started crying again and screaming, "Harrison! I know you're in there! Harrison!" A couple of doors opened down the way; boys' heads poked out, saw it was only some drunk girl, and withdrew. From inside the room . . . nothing.

Charlotte pulled back a few steps to distance herself from her roommate. Beverly hung her head and cried some more. In a burst of fury, she took off her shoes and began hammering the door with the high heels. A terrific racket. The door opened, and a tall, lean youth appeared, clad in nothing but a pair of boxer shorts hanging on his hip bones, exposing the slabs of weight-room muscle on his shoulders, chest, arms, and abdomen. He had close-cropped curly brown hair and a lean face that at this moment looked fatigued and annoyed. He stared at Beverly and took a stance blocking the doorway.

Wearily, contemptuously: "What the fuck are you doing, Beverly?"

Beverly shrank into a little-girl voice. "You said you'd call me."

Exasperated sigh. "I said if I *could*."

"The fuck you said *if I could*!"

Male controlled rage: "Goddamn it, Beverly, I'm trying to sleep, and you're fucking blitzed outta your mind. Go *home*."

"Go . . . home," said Beverly, breaking into a mournful sob and sinking, obviously on purpose, to her knees and then to all fours. "Go . . . home . . ."

Charlotte stepped forward to try to put an end to the spectacle.

The all but naked lacrosse player noticed her for the first time. "You with her?" He said it rather crossly.

"Yes." Quickly adding, "I'm trying to get her to come back to the room."

Still stern: "Good." Then he took a second look at Charlotte, who at a glance appeared to be wearing nothing but a pajama top.

Beverly was on all fours, whimpering.

"You're her roommate?" He beckoned Charlotte closer and said in a very low voice, "Your roommate's got an issue. You think you can get her outta here?"

"I think so."

The athlete crossed his arms over his bare chest and tightened his abdominals, causing the boxer shorts to drop still lower. He gave Charlotte a second look. "You know, I could swear you and I've met someplace."

"Maybe," said Charlotte with a slight smile. "But I don't think so."

"Well, you and me, we got to figure it out—we got to get her some—you know—help in the long term."

Beverly was still on her hands and knees, her head lowered, beginning to hit the high notes of a sob.

"We?" said Charlotte.

Same low voice: "Yeah . . . you're her roommate. I'm her friend. I tell you what. You doing anything Saturday afternoon?"

"No . . ."

"You can come see me at the tailgate."

Charlotte stared at him for a moment. He had an ever so slight smile. He wasn't even looking at Beverly. "I don't think so," said Charlotte. She wondered what a tailgate was.

The athlete shrugged. "Aw . . . come on . . ." He gave her a blip of a wink, and grinned. "I couldn't stand it if *both* roommates mean-mugged me. That's where I'll be, anyhow." He gave her a certain smile, the smile of the coconspirator. Then he went back inside his room and shut the door.

Beverly remained on the floor on all fours. She had settled into the forlorn mode and didn't want to be moved. It took Charlotte a good five minutes to roust her up and onto her feet again and maneuver her back to the car.

When they returned to their room in Edgerton, Beverly was on another crying jag, with lyrics such as, "Why did he think he had to *lie* to me?"

Charlotte put an arm around her shoulders to steady her. With a wail,

Beverly broke free, teetered precariously on her high heels, and pitched face forward onto her bed. In no time her muffled sobs gave way to a low snore. She still had all her clothes on. Charlotte started to remove the high-heeled shoes, then decided not to do anything that might wake her up.

She turned off the lights, put her pajama pants back on, and slipped into bed. She lay there thinking about the lacrosse player, Harrison . . . He was very good-looking, very well built . . . What exactly was he saying to her? . . . But pretty soon she fell asleep.

She woke up in the dark in a stupefied haze. *Click click,* high heels. She was vaguely aware that Beverly had gotten up off the bed and was heading for the door, but she no longer cared. Even after she heard the jingle of car keys, she rationalized that Beverly was just going across the hall to the bath-room.

Well, she had tried, she had tried. She had done all she could . . .

When she next woke up, the first thing she noticed was the light com-ing in between the bottoms of the shades and the windowsills. It was alarm-ingly bright. *My French class!*

The little windup clock by the bed: 10:35! Forgot to set it! The class was already over! *Couldn't* happen! A scalding feeling at the base of her skull . . . The long night wasted babysitting Beverly . . . Beverly—not in her bed—hadn't touched it since she last staggered out. Must have finally sobbed, whined, wheedled her way back into the bed of her lacrosse player. Slut! Her crawling, drooling, sobbing, slobbering slut of a roommate had done this to her. And into the adrenal panic over heedlessly, pointlessly cutting a class came an ashy resentment.

Charlotte got out of bed and walked toward the windows. She was so groggy. She got down on her knees before she raised the shade about a foot. Brilliant sunlight. Gothic Dupont rose up almighty.

On a walkway out in the middle of the courtyard, near the statue of Charles Dupont, a girl was teetering along on high heels. From up here, five floors above, Charlotte was looking down at a disheveled rick of straight, flat streaked-blond hair on a head hung over toward the ground . . . the bony processes of her breastbone were showing from the way she had left her cerise shirt unbuttoned *way* down . . . a pair of tight black pants—then the sway and staccato of the gait, *click teeter click teeter click teeter.* Oh God . . . Her heart misfired—a premature ventricular contraction—Beverly. It couldn't have been more obvious that she was wearing clothes from last night and was just now returning home, still intoxicated.

From a window across the way a boy yelled out, "You're money, baby, and you don't even know it!"

Laughter from another window somewhere.

Beverly started walking faster—*clickteeterclickteeterclickteeterclickteeter-clickteeterclickteeter*—and broke into a run for the entryway to Edgerton, sprinting on the pointed toes of her shoes. She had gone no more than a few yards when one of her high heels struck the walkway. She pitched forward, fell, rolled over the walkway's border of green-and-white liriope and onto the lawn, where she wound up on her back. She put a forearm up in front of her face to shield her eyes from the sun. Not a sound from the windows now. She rolled over onto her abdomen and struggled up into a crawling position. Her pumps were still on. One high heel had almost completely torn away from the sole and hung at a crippled angle. On all fours now, she lifted one leg and tried to kick the pump off. No luck. A couple of students down in the courtyard just stood there, absorbed in the spectacle. After a clumsy struggle Beverly managed to stand upright. She looked about in an abstract, unseeing way and began limping the rest of the way to Edgerton, one heel high, one heel dragging lengthwise on the walkway.

Charlotte pulled the shade down and stood up. She was torn by competing emotions: sympathy for the weary and heavy-laden, revulsion at what was revolting, guilt over feeling more revolted than sympathetic at the sight of a drunken slut on her Walk of Shame. She had heard the term. Now she was witnessing it. A twinge of sympathy . . . a twinge of guilt . . . a surge of revulsion. She caught the wave and rode it for all it was worth. She got dressed even faster than she had before her mission of mercy in the middle of the night. She had babysat this . . . bitch . . . enough for one day. Her roommate was on her own now, the Sodom-bottom rotten Groton . . . whatever . . .

Charlotte gathered up some books and notes and hurried down the five flights of fire stairs to avoid having to deal with her. Halfway down, she began to relax. But the French class! She panicked all over again. Never before in her whole life had she ever just plain-long missed a class.

"*Why* is it your fault? I'll *show* you why the fuck *why*," said Jojo. He could feel the muscles in the front of his neck contracting tight as wires, he hit the *why* so hard. He was genuinely angry, but he wanted to look insanely angry, just to see Adam cower and squirm with fear, see him surrender his very ass in submission.

He stabbed the offending word on the offending page with his forefinger. "See that? *Mally-dro*-it. I mean *shit*, Adam, first he gets sarcastic because I can't pronounce it, and then he's straight-out making me because I don't know exactly what it means. I *know* what it means, but when some asshole's got a gun at your head saying '*define* the motherfucker'—whattaya trying to do to me? I'd never use a fucking word like that! *Mally-dro*-it . . . I can't even pronounce it. Shit! He made me *pronounce* the fucker. How do *I* know how to pronounce the fucking word!"

"Maladroit," said Adam. "It's not that unusual a word."

Jojo eyed him with loathing. The little nerd had a way of sounding mousy and know-it-all at the same time. "Okay, what's it mean? Lemme hear *you* define it. The bastard was always telling me to '*define* it.'"

"It means like 'clumsy' or 'awkward.' "

"Then why the fuck didn't you write 'clumsy'? I mean, *shit*, Adam."

The mouse said in its little voice, "I thought it went well with *meddling*. 'Maladroit meddling.'"

"Yeah, *you* think. But you know damned well that fancy shit's not *me*. I don't think that way." Sardonically: "Subtle strategy and mal—that's another thing. He'd take a word I *know*, a word I know how to use, like *subtle*, and then he'd like put a gun at my head and say, 'Define it!' I *know* the fucking word, but if somebody tells you like point-blank *define* it—what would *you* say? Lemme hear you just straight-out *define* it."

"It means like 'cunning' or 'crafty' or 'with a nice touch.'" A mousy voice and then an infuriating shrug, as if to say you have to be pretty stupid not to know that. Jojo could have strangled him.

"Well, I don't care. You fucked me over, Adam, you fucked me over big time. Did you get some sick satisfaction out of getting me in trouble? This guy's a prick! If I'm lucky, I just get an F and fail the course, and I can't play next semester, which means the whole season, and if I'm unlucky, the prick tries to get me thrown out of school. Great fucking options. You . . . totally screwed me, dipshit!"

Pleading—Jojo took a morbid, useless satisfaction in the plea in his little tutor's voice—Adam said, "Jojo, come on—you gotta back up. I mean, do you remember what time it was when you called me to write that paper? It was almost *midnight*! And you had a ten-page paper to hand in at ten o'clock! And that wasn't a paper where you could just go to a textbook or go online or get some Cliffs Notes!" He went on—pleading, pleading, to describe his grueling all-nighter in Jojo's behalf. "I was lucky to get the words down at all, Jojo! There was no way I could go back and—you know"—the little bastard was obviously ransacking his brain for a euphemism—"go back over it and translate it into like another . . . idiom."

For an instant Jojo wondered if "idiom" had anything to do with "idiot," but he had to admit, although he didn't feel like doing so out loud, that Adam had a point. That had been pretty bad . . . He'd been embarrassed to even call the poor sonofabitch so late. His anger began to diminish.

More pleading, whining: "You didn't even come over to the *library* with me, Jojo. You stayed here with Mike and played *video* games."

The anger spiked back up. "What the fuck did it matter *what* I did!"

"I don't know why you're so angry, Jojo. I mean, come on, didn't you at least read it over before you handed it in?"

"Who had the fucking time to do that?"

"Jojo, I slipped it under your door about *eight-thirty*. How could you not have time?"

Jojo felt his whole frame go slack. He clasped his hands in front of him and lowered his head. He looked away from Adam. "Aw, shit . . ." Then he turned back toward him. "Okay, I'm sorry, Adam. It wasn't your fault . . . But I'm still fucked. Quat is one of those pricks who's so anti-athlete—I don't know how the fuck I even got steered into that fucking course. Nothing would give him more pleasure than kicking my student-athlete ass out of the fucking school." Jojo looked away again and now, feeling a bit guilty about how he had been yelling at his tutor, suddenly realized something. "You know, this guy's vicious. He's the kind that would come looking for you, too."

Adam practically flinched with shock. The blood drained out of his face.

"Me?"

"He's the type, that's all I can tell you. He knows I didn't write it. So he's gonna say 'Who?' you know? Don't worry, I'm not admitting *any*body did. But if he decides to get really shitty and start asking around and all that shit . . ."

"Well, I didn't actually *write* it for you, Jojo . . ."

"Hah. In fact, that's what you actually did do." He smiled, but it was a smile of fellow feeling. "Don't worry, you didn't even help me, okay? I wrote it all myself, I got those words out of some book, all right?"

Adam was biting his lower lip. "If worse comes to worst—maybe I helped you smooth out some rough edges. What about that?"

"Awww, don't get worked up. If worse comes to worse, Coach'll take care of it." Everything had gotten turned around. Now he felt like he had to be Adam's therapist or camp counselor.

"You think he can?"

Or mommy. The poor little omega male was *looking* at him in the most frightened way.

"Well, sure he can. But I shouldn't have even mentioned it. It's not gonna come to that. I'm gonna hang tough. The guy can't prove a god-damned thing. At least it wasn't downloaded from the Internet. They can check that shit with computers now. Treyshawn got in trouble last year . . . or sort of . . ." He laughed. "Treyshawn can't *get* in trouble around here. If it comes to *that*, the fucking president goes first, not Treyshawn the Tower Fucking Diggs." Big grin.

Adam tried to smile, too, but he was too shaken up. "Okay. Okay." He looked away with his eyebrows contorted, obviously thinking, thinking, thinking. Then he turned back with an urgent expression. "Look. Here's what we have to do in the meantime. In fact, why don't we do it right now. We go over the paper together, word by word. The thing to do is, you get to know every word, every idea, every bit of history in the damned thing. Then, if anybody asks you anything—you were just rattled when Quat first brought it up. I say let's get started."

Adam's expression was so nerve-wracked, Jojo couldn't help saying, "I can't do that now."

"Why not?"

"I got to make a booty call."

"Jojo!"

"I'm just kidding, I'm just kidding." His eyes wandered. He was stricken with remorse. "There's no reason something like this shoulda ever happened. Shit . . . I can do better than this. I'm not a fucking moron . . ."

14. MILLENNIAL MUTANTS

Less than fifteen minutes left, and Charlotte was still leaning forward in her seat high up in the amphitheater, spellbound. The slender and surprisingly debonair figure down there on the stage, Mr. Starling, who must have been close to fifty, walked from one side to the other, not lecturing, but using the Socratic approach, asking his students questions and commenting on their answers, as if he were talking to twelve or thirteen souls gathered around a seminar table rather than the 110 who now sat before him in steep tiers, filling a small but grandiose amphitheater with a dome and a ceiling mural by Annigoni of Daedalus and the flight of Icarus from the labyrinth of Minos.

"All right," Mr. Starling was saying, "so Darwin describes evolution in terms of a 'tree of life,' starting with a single point from which rise limbs, branches"—with his arms he pantomimed a tree rising and widening—"offshoots of infinite variety, but what is that *point* where it all starts? What does Darwin say this tree has ascended *from*? Where does he say evolution begins?"

He surveyed his audience, and a dozen hands shot up. "Yes," he said, pointing to a plump blond girl in the topmost row, not all that far from one of the molten wings of Icarus.

"He said it began with a single cell, a single-cell organism," said the girl.

"Somebody asked him where the single cell was located, and he said, 'Oh, I don't know, probably in a warm pond somewhere.'"

An undercurrent of laughter ran through the amphitheater. Everybody looked to Mr. Starling to see how he would take it.

He smiled in a shrewd sort of way, paused, then said, "You happen to be exactly right. In fact, he suggested there might have been a whole *school* of single-cell organisms in that warm pond. But that leaves us with the question of where the single-cell organisms came from and, as far as that goes, the warm pond—but let's forget about the pond for the time being. Where did Darwin say the single cell or cells came from?"

He crossed his arms and cocked his head to one side, a challenging pose he often struck. "Okay, my little geniuses," the pose said, "what are you going to do with *that* one?"

One of the amphitheater's downlighters happened to hit him dramatically, theatrically . . . just so . . . and he held the pose during the silence that ensued. In Charlotte's estimation, the vision was . . . sublime. Victor Ransome Starling's thick brown hair, which he combed straight back, was definitely still brown despite a rising tide of gray. The current fashion among male professors at Dupont was scrupulously improper: cheap-looking shirts, open at the throat, needless to say, and cotton pants with no creases—jeans, khakis, corduroys—to distinguish themselves from the mob, which is to say, the middle class; but Victor Ransome Starling always bucked the tide with the sort of outfit he was wearing right now, a brown-and-white houndstooth suit that looked great on his slender frame, a light blue shirt, a black knit tie, and a pair of ginger-brown suede shoes. To Charlotte he was elegance itself amid a motley crew.

Yes, Mr. Starling was sublime, to look at and to listen to, and he had posed a question. Swept away, Charlotte raised her hand and was immediately frightened by her own audacity—a freshman in an advanced class taught by a Nobel Prize winner in a daunting amphitheater overflowing with upperclassmen.

The vision below looked up at her, gestured, and said, "Yes?"

Charlotte's heart began racing, and she became acutely conscious of the sound of her own voice. "Darwin said—he said he didn't know where the original cells came from, and he wasn't going to guess?" Even as the words left her lips, she was aware that she was reverting, in her nervousness, to the way she spoke before she arrived at Dupont. She had broken *guess* into two syllables and uttered it on a rising note, as if she were asking a question rather than making a statement. But she plowed on. "He said the origin of life itself was a hopeless *inquiry*?" *Inquiry* rose, too! And she had come down on the *in* like a farm boy driving in a stake with an ax head. "And it would be way, way in the future before somebody figured that out, if they ever did?"—which not only rose but also came out *dee-ud*. "And I think he said—in *The Origin of Species*?—I think he said that in the beginning it was the Creator?—with a capital C? It was the Creator, and he breathed life 'into a few or into one'—a *few* single-cell organisms or *one* single-cell organism, I guess." *Geh-ess*—in spite of herself.

"Right," said Mr. Starling, looking up at her from the stage. Then he turned away to address the class as a whole. "Now you'll notice—" He stopped abruptly and looked up again in Charlotte's direction: "Very good. Thank you." Then he turned away again and continued. "You'll notice that Darwin, who probably did more than any other single person to extinguish religious faith among educated people, doesn't present himself as an atheist. He bows to 'the Creator.' He always professed to be a religious person. There's one school of thought that says he was only throwing a sop to the conventional beliefs of his day, since he knew *The Origin of Species* might be attacked as blasphemous. But I suspect it was something else. He probably couldn't *conceive* of being an atheist. In his day, not even the most daring, most rationalistic and materialistic philosophers, not even David Hume, professed to be atheists. It's not until the end of the nineteenth century that we come upon the first atheist of any prominence: Nietzsche. I suspect Darwin figured that since nobody had the foggiest idea as to *what* created life in the first place, and might never know, why not just say it was created by the Creator and let it go at that?"

He looked up in Charlotte's direction again and gestured. "You've made a very fine and very important distinction." Then his eyes panned over the entire class. "The origin of the species, which is to say, evolution, and the origin of life itself, of the impulse to live, are two different things."

The student on Charlotte's right, a cheery brunette with pale but striking features whom she knew only as a junior named Jill, whispered, "Hey! Charlotte!" and opened her eyes wide and pulled a face of mock astonishment. Then she mouthed the words "Not bad!" and smiled.

A flood of joy, so intense it seemed tangible in her nerve endings, ran through Charlotte's entire body. She was giddy. She barely took in anything anybody said in the last few minutes of the class.

One thing she did remember was something Mr. Starling said about "the conscious little rock":

"If anyone should ask me why we're spending so much time on Darwin," he was saying at one point, "I would consider that a perfectly logical question. Darwin was not a neuroscientist. His knowledge of the human brain, if any, was primitive. He knew nothing about genes, even though they were discovered by a contemporary of his, an Austrian monk named Gregor Johann Mendel—whose work strengthens the case for evolution tremendously. But Darwin did something more fundamental. He obliterated the cardinal distinction between man and the beasts of the fields and the wilds. It had always been a truism that man is a rational being and animals live by 'instinct.' But what is instinct? It's what we now know to be the genetic code an animal is born with. In the second half of the last century, neuroscientists began to pursue the question, 'If man is an animal, to what extent does *his* genetic code, unbeknownst to him, control his life?' Enormously, according to Edward O. Wilson, a man some speak of as Darwin the Second. We will get to Wilson's work soon. But there is a big difference between 'enormously' and 'entirely.' 'Enormously' leaves some wiggle room for your free will to steer your genetically coded 'instincts' in any direction you want—if . . . there is such a thing as 'you.' I say 'if,' because the new generation of neuroscientists—and I enjoy staying in communication with them—believe Wilson is a very cautious man. They laugh at the notion of free will. They yawn at your belief—my belief—that each of us has a capital-letter I, as in 'I believe,' a 'self,' inside our head that makes 'you,' makes 'me,' distinct from every other member of the species Homo sapiens, no matter how many ways we might be like them. The new generation are absolutists. They—I'll just tell you what one very interesting young neuroscientist e-mailed me last week. She said, 'Let's say you pick up a rock and you throw it. And in midflight you give that rock consciousness and a rational mind. That little rock will think it has free will and will give you a highly rational account of why it has decided to take the route it's taking.' So later on we will get to 'the conscious little rock,' and you will be able to decide for yourself: 'Am I really . . . merely . . . a conscious little rock?' The answer, incidentally, has implications of incalculable importance for the Homo sapiens' conception of itself and for the history of the twenty-first century. We may have to change the name of our species to Homo Lapis Deiciecta Conscia—Man, the Conscious Thrown Stone—or, to make it simpler, as my correspondent did, 'Man, the Conscious Little Rock.'"

Once it ended, five or six students went up onstage and gathered about Mr. Starling. By the time Charlotte had made her way down from the upper rows of the amphitheater, he was just descending from the stage, and they came within two or three feet of each other. He excused himself from a tall young man who was hovering over him and turned toward her.

"Hello," he said. "It was you—I'm afraid I have a hard time distinguishing faces in the upper rows—you're the young . . . uh . . . the one who mentioned the Creator?"

"Yes, sir."

"Well, you made a very nice summary of a very subtle point. Can I assume you actually read *The Origin of Species*?"

"Yes, sir."

Professor Starling smiled. "I assign it every year, but I'm not sure how many actually go to the trouble, although it's well worth it. What's your background in biology?"

"I went as far as molecular biology. My high school didn't have that, so they sent me over to Appalachian State twice a week."

"Appalachian State University? You're from North Carolina?"

"Yes, sir."

"What year are you?"

"I'm a freshman."

He nodded several times, as if pondering that. "You took the A.P."

"Yes, sir."

He did some more nodding. "I try to get to know every student before Christmas, but we've got a very large class this year. I'm afraid I don't know your name."

"Charlotte Simmons."

Still more nodding. "Well, Ms. Simmons, keep going to the primary sources if you can, even when we get to neurobiology and some of the prose gets a little—a little steep."

With that, he gave her a businesslike smile and turned back to the students who had been clustering about him.

Charlotte left the building and began walking aimlessly across the Great Yard. He had singled her out! The midmorning sun cast immense shadows of the buildings on this side upon the Yard's lawn, which looked more lush and a richer green in shadow than in light. Beyond the shadows, the sun had transformed the Gothic buildings on the other side into gleaming monoliths. The bells of the Ridenour Carillon were tolling "The Processional," and not knowing the lyrics Kipling had written for it, Charlotte found it stirring. The verdant foreground, the brilliant backdrop, the stirring music—all somehow arranged expressly for her! Sailing! Sailing! Gloriously drunk on cosmological theories and approbation.

On this sparkling, sunny morning, with its perfect, cloudless blue sky, amid the century-old majesty of the Dupont campus, it came to her in a rush . . . Yes! She had found the life of the mind and was . . . *living it!*

She gazed about at all the other students who were walking across the Great Yard. She was among the elite of the youth of America! Back home in Sparta, she was known as the Girl Who Went to Dupont. Here at Dupont she would be known, in the fullness of time, as . . . she didn't know precisely what, but a radiant dawn had arisen . . . Before her, behind her, walking this way and that way across the Great Yard, enjoying the sun, enjoying the shade and the majesty of the ancient trees, chattering away into their cell phones, which their daddies could pay for as easily as drawing their next breath, suffused with the conspicuous lapidary consumption of all this royal Middle English Gothic architecture and the knowledge that they were among that elite minifraction of the youth of America—of the youth of the world!— who went to Dupont—all about her moved her 6,200 fellow students, or a great many of them, in midflight, blithely ignorant of the fact that they were merely conscious little rocks, every one of them, whereas . . . *I am Charlotte Simmons.*

The thought magnified the light of the sun itself. She was now beyond the Great Yard, but here, too, the lavish lawns, the way the sun lit up the tops of the leaves of the great trees and at the same time turned the undersides into vast filigrees of shadow—to Charlotte it became a magical tableau of green and gold. Just ahead, Briggs College . . . and even Briggs, generally regarded as a bit of an eyesore, had come alive as a pattern of brilliant stone surfaces incised by the shadows of arches and deep-set windows. Four or five guys and one girl were out on the steps of the main entrance. One of the guys, a string bean with a huge mass of dark curls, was on his feet. The others were sitting on the steps near him. Students hanging out on the front steps was a familiar sight at all the colleges, but Charlotte did a second take. If she wasn't mistaken, one of them was the guy she had run into the other night at the gym: Adam.

On the steps, it so happened, Greg Fiore, the one standing, was saying to Adam, "Why do you keep pitching this Skull Fuck story? How many times do I have to tell you, this is something that may or may not have happened . . . *last spring*. People have been talking about this . . . this rumor . . . ever since school started. But there's nothing concrete—*and* it's not news anymore."

Adam realized he was getting too worked up about it—this story required a *smooth* pitch—but he couldn't hold back. "You're not *listening* to me, Greg. I've got the whole thing on tape from a participant—*two* participants. This is strictly *entre nous*, okay? One is Hoyt Thorpe himself. *He* called *me*! He couldn't tell me enough. He *wants* everybody to know about it, as long as we don't say it came from him. That's one. Now, the other—do you remember I finally found out the name of the governor's bodyguard? They took him to a hospital in Philadelphia so his name wouldn't be in the books in Chester? Well, I found out who he is! I've talked to him! He was a California state trooper. He just got canned, and he's really pissed. He thinks it's because some newspaper called about the story, and they want him long gone and out of the way. And guess who 'some newspaper' was?"

"You?" said Greg.

"Me. Me and the *Wave*. He'll give us an affadavit if we want it."

Greg sighed. "You're a terrific reporter, Adam. I mean that. And you've done a lot of work. But I'm sorry—we can't dredge up some random blow job from last May and run a story about it."

Adam wanted to tell Greg the truth—namely, that he was one scared shitless fearless editor—but he knew that would only make him dig in for good. So he said, "Well . . . okay. I still think it's a great story. So how about the other story, the basketball thing?"

Greg sighed again and said, "You don't give up, do you? I don't know why you're taking the basketball thing so seriously. I don't see how you can call it *hypocrisy*—"

Adam watched Greg's lips move, and he tuned out . . . and fumed. Greg always positioned himself as the eminence of the Millennial Mutants, not merely in terms of authority but often physical stance. At the *Wave* office he sat in an outsize oak library armchair that overwhelmed any other stick of furniture in the dismal dump. And now out here on the steps, he ends up the only one standing, while the rest of the Mutants—Camille Deng, Roger Kuby, Edgar Tuttle, and himself—sit perched on the steps . . . at his feet, as it were.

All Adam could come up with was, "I don't believe what I'm hearing."

That was so lame, he looked away in an instinctive bid to disengage from combat. He blinked. Coming toward them on the walkway in front of Briggs was that girl, the Southern girl, the pretty freshman with the innocent look, Charlotte.

He stood up and waved. "Hey, Charlotte!"

So it *was* him. He couldn't have sought her attention at a more propitious moment. Charlotte didn't know quite what to make of this Adam, whom she had met only in awkward circumstances, but she could say one thing for him. He was the only student she had met who shared—or openly shared—her vision of what the university should be like intellectually. Millennial Mutants . . . She couldn't say she really *got* it, but all the same—and he really wasn't bad-looking.

"Come here!"

So she walked on over to the front steps of Briggs, and Adam introduced her to Greg, Camille, Roger, and Edgar Tuttle. Greg was the skinny one with a pencil of a neck supporting his head and the huge mop of curly hair she had noticed. Camille's Asian face was smooth and symmetrical, but she seemed irritable. Roger Kuby's pudginess covered up what were probably some fundamentally handsome features, but he was prone to stupid jokes. "Charlotte O'Hara?" he said when Adam introduced her as Charlotte. Edgar Tuttle was tall and good-looking but terribly reserved.

"I told Charlotte I'd introduce her to some real Millennial Mutants," Adam said to Greg, who appeared a bit put off by the remark.

"What makes you think we're real?" said Roger. "That's unreal."

Charlotte smiled out of courtesy and from nervousness, but none of the others reacted in any fashion.

"Charlotte," said Adam, "tell Greg what you told me about Jojo Johanssen in that French class. I think he doubts my assessment of our revered student-athletes. What was that course called?"

Charlotte hesitated before saying, "The Modern French Novel from Flaubert to Houellebecq?" She wasn't sure she wanted to tell the story in front of five upperclassmen she didn't even know.

"Well—who?" said Roger.

"Well-beck?" said Charlotte, to give him an approximation of the French pronunciation of Houellebecq.

"Oh—Well-*beck*," said Roger, as if there were something funny about that.

"He's a young novelist?" Charlotte said. "He's sort of nihilistic?"

"Anyway," said Adam, "Charlotte enrolls in this so-called advanced French course, and they're reading the books in . . . English translation! Advanced French!" He looked toward her for confirmation. "Right?"

She nodded yes.

"And tell'm why," said Adam.

The implication that she had some great exposé to relate made her uncomfortable. She wanted to say, "I'd rather not get into it," but she didn't have the nerve. She tried to get off by saying only, "The teacher said the course was for people having trouble completing their language requirement."

"Who is this teacher?" the Asian girl, Camille, wanted to know.

"What was that term?" said Adam. "Linguafrankly challenged?"

Charlotte didn't know what to say to either one of them. The girl hadn't asked her question like someone who just wanted to hear some gossip. She sounded more like an inspector. Charlotte suddenly had the feeling that if she identified Mr. Lewin, who in fact had been nice to her, this irritable girl would see to it that there were consequences.

Fortunately, Adam just couldn't wait to parade his new inside information. "Half of them were Greg's beloved basketball players, whose combination of ignorance and pseudo-ignorant malingering he's so eager to overlook."

"Oh, give me a fucking break," said Greg. "All I was saying was—"

Feeling that he now had Greg on the defensive, Adam seized the moment to ram his argument down Greg's cynical gullet. "One of them was my tutee—I guess that's who tutors tutor—tutees?"

Roger broke in: "SAT tutors tutor tutees for SAT twos. Try saying that fast—SATtutorstutortutees—"

Goddamned Roger! So he rammed Roger's interruption aside. "One of them was my boy Jojo Johanssen. Jojo—"

Greg said, "You totally miss—"

Adam rammed Greg aside, too. "Charlotte, tell our basketball groupie here about Jojo and that question he started to answer in that class. He doesn't even want to be *mistaken* for intelligent. Now, how did that go, that question he started to answer?"

"I don't remember the details," said Charlotte. "Besides, it was too complicated." She was depressingly aware that she had just pronounced *besides* with a very long, flat *i*—*besiiiiides*—whereas everybody else at Dupont gave it three syllables: *be-sy-ids*.

"Beautiful!" Greg said to Adam. "Your own star witness—"

Camille Deng spared Adam the trouble of ramming his way back in. "Tell me this," she asked Charlotte. "Did this guy hit on the women in the class?" What a grim set her lips had!

Charlotte could see Jojo's enormous hulk approaching her—as vividly as if he were right here on the steps.

"I don't know," she lied. "I wasn't in that class but one day. I transferred out of there as fast as I could."

"You're lucky," said Camille. It was hard to tell whether her bitter tone came from personal experience or from some profound moral repugnance or ideological belief. "They think this campus is Testosterone Valley and they've got all-American dicks, and if a woman comes here, it's only for one reason. They just *assume* . . ."

Edgar Tuttle spoke up for the first time. He had a sheepish voice. "That's what cheerleaders are all about."

"What is?" said Camille.

"Well, you know—they're a chorus line," said Edgar. "They kick their legs like cancan dancers, they show you the inside of their thighs, their breasts are hoisted up like—like—like missiles waiting for someone to push the button, they're wiggling their hips, they wear these skimpy outfits . . . you know what I mean."

Camille said, "I know what you mean, but I don't get it."

Edgar hesitated before saying, "They're the sexual reward—or they represent the sexual reward."

Running out of patience: "*Whose* sexual reward?"

"The athletes'," said Edgar, "or that's what they represent. Or maybe they actually are, too. I don't know. Anyway, this is an old, old custom. It goes back a thousand years."

"Cheerleaders?" said Roger. It was meant to be funny.

"No, what they represent," said Edgar. "When knights were victorious in battle, one of their rewards was random sex. But sometimes there were no battles to be fought, and so about eight or nine hundred years ago they started having tournaments. Two armies would come out on the field of battle, and it was supposed to be like a game. They weren't supposed to kill each other. They used blunt swords and lances and so on. The idea was to knock the other side's knights off their horses, and if you did, you got to keep their armor, their weapons, their horses, their tack, and all this stuff was worth a fortune."

Roger began twirling his forefinger in front of his chest, toward himself, as if to say *Let's speed it up*. "Get to the part about the cheerleaders."

"I am," said Edgar. "After the tournaments, the knights would have like a bacchanal, and everybody would get hammered and boff all the girls they wanted."

Edgar's attempts at campus vernacular were inevitably embarrassing. *Boff* was totally out of date, and *hammered* and the conjunctive *like* just didn't ring right coming out of his mouth.

"Sounds like an ordinary football weekend to me," said Roger.

For the first time, Edgar became animated. "Thank you—that's exactly the point! Nothing has changed in a thousand years! How do you think team sports like football originated? And ice hockey. With the medieval tournaments! What team sports did the original Olympic games have? None! It's really funny if you—"

"Wait a minute," said Greg. "How do you know all this stuff?"

"I *read*," said Edgar. "Anyway, it's really funny if you think about it. For a thousand years we've been having these watered-down versions of medieval tournaments, but with one big difference. The knights who fought in the tournaments also happened to be lord and master of everybody else. There was no such thing as a leader who wasn't also a warrior. But these 'sports heroes' we've got at Dupont, they're nothing but entertainers. What are they going to do when they leave here?"

"I never saw any figures for here," said Adam, eager to stay in the discussion in hopes of impressing Charlotte, "but nationally there are thirty-five hundred Division One college basketball players, and they all think they're gonna play in the NBA, and you know how many will actually make it? Less than one percent."

"Right!" said Edgar. Nobody had ever seen Edgar riding higher. "And the rest of them, they've spent four years at Dupont University doing alley-oops or sacking quarterbacks or whatever it is they do, and they'll leave here and they'll be . . . oh . . ."

"Sacking my mother and hijacking her car in the parking lot at the mall, is what they'll be doing," said Roger.

"Very funny, Roger," said Camille. "Why don't we be a little racist while we're at it?"

"Oh, racist my ass. Stop breaking my balls, Camille."

"You're telling me that remark wasn't based on a racist assumption?"

"Okay, I'm a racist," said Roger. "Let's have closure and put that behind us and move on. I've got a question that's so obvious nobody ever asks it. What is it with this sports mania in the first place? Why does anybody get excited because Dupont is gonna play Indiana in basketball? Either our hired mercenaries will beat their hired mercenaries, or vice versa. Why does anybody care? It's a game between two groups of guys who have no connection with our lives whatsoever, and even if they did, it's only a game! Why does a *game* get students so emotionally involved? Or anybody else for that matter. What does it *mean* to them? I don't see how it could mean *anything*, but obviously it does. It's a mystery. It's completely irrational."

Camille muttered, "I still say it was racist."

Charlotte was fascinated by Roger's transformation from just a few minutes ago. Up on this plane Roger Kuby was a different person, no longer the chronically off-key would-be wit, now an intellectual determined to get to the core of a psychological mystery. The serious Roger Kuby even *looked* better in her eyes. All at once she could *see* the handsome features hitherto hidden by his coat of fat.

"Irrational is right," Adam was saying. "It's a primitive ritual of masculinity, and girls just go along with it because that's where the boys are."

Oh, the Millennial Mutants were soaring now. Charlotte was enthralled. Maybe this was the group of students she had been looking for, the cénacle, students who, above all else, had a life of the mind, *la vie intellectuelle* she had envisioned back in Sparta as she looked out, at Miss Pennington's urging, across the mountains toward the distant, shimmering Dupont . . .

She was so enthralled, in fact, that she, like the others, had scarcely noticed the four students who had emerged from Briggs and were settling in on the other side of the steps, slightly above them. Like the Mutants, they wore the usual, the T-shirts, the shorts, the sneakers, the flip-flops. But their . . . aura . . . was entirely different. All four were lean and on the tall side, and even though their loose T-shirts and shorts obscured everything but their extremities, they were obviously "diesels," to use the Dupont word for boys who pumped up their muscles through weight lifting. The one in the foreground, about twelve feet from the Mutants, sat on one step with his feet on the step below. His legs were so long his knees came up practically to his shoulders, and his shoulders were *this* wide. His head, crowned by a baseball cap worn backward, and his angular face, beset here and there by acne scars, rested atop a preternaturally long, thick neck, with an Adam's apple that

T
O
M

W
O
L
F
E

stuck out like a rock formation. He kept pumping his heel up and down while his eyes roamed all over the place, as if he thought something or other was about to happen, God knew what. The other three were not quite so big, but they were big enough, and they had the same look of lounging on the steps while trying to figure out where the action was.

The contrast with the four male Mutants struck Charlotte immediately, although she couldn't have put a name to it. She cast a glance at Adam. He was built in the proper proportions and had a nice symmetrical face with a fine nose and nice lips—sensual, in fact—but now he seemed . . . slight. Greg was so sketchily put together, not even his height did anything for him. His mop of dark brown curls made his head look enormous and misshapen, stuck as it was atop that little pencil neck of his.

The newcomers turned their heads from time to time to check out the Mutants, turned back to their cohorts and twisted their eyebrows. Pretty soon all four were pulling dubious, ironic faces for one another's benefit, talking in low voices, chuckling, and then sizing up the Mutants again.

" . . . no mystery to it," Adam was saying. "I can *tell* you why. Lacrosse is one of the only two sports where white boys are the ones with the machismo. The other one's ice hockey. Basketball is totally a black sport, and football is mostly a black sport. It's just not as obvious in football, because the uniforms cover up their bodies and they wear face masks. Lacrosse would be all black, too, like *that*"—he snapped his fingers—"if black teenagers ever started playing it. They'd make the white players they've got out there now look like . . . like . . . like I don't know what . . . wusses, pussies . . . It wouldn't even be close. Same thing with hockey. A few body checks by the sort of black athletes who play basketball and football, and the toughest Canadian in the NHL would be a basket case. He'd be mush."

Oh yes, they were soaring, the Mutants were, *soaring*! And it was Adam who led the way. He was ramming home whatever he wanted to ram home. How could anyone even compete with him on this subject? He knew the athletes at Dupont, he tutored them, he had seen them up close. He could rip all mystery away because he had been inside their feeble heads. So absorbed was he in revealing all, he was the last to notice that trouble was nearby and staring at him.

The guy with the pumping flip-flop had risen to his feet. Sure enough, he was . . . *tall* . . . in fact, gigantic, as if from another species—rangy, lean, perhaps six-five or -six . . . and *big*. He rolled his immense shoulders and then started coming down the steps, his flip-flops slapping, toward Adam. The first thing Adam detected was Edgar, Roger, Camille, and Charlotte looking up. So Adam looked up. Leaning over him was a giant, or so he seemed from down here on the steps where Adam was sitting, a giant with immense forearms, a huge chin, an enormous Adam's apple, and acne on a face that now bore a look of such exaggerated seriousness—accompanied by such contortions of the forehead and eyebrows—that it oozed with irony and mockery of the hambone variety. And in that instant Adam knew, as surely as he knew anything in this world, that whatever happened next, it would not be pleasant. Then he caught a glimpse of the giant's three cohorts in the background, smirking, each an only slightly smaller edition of the giant himself. One had a brawler's grizzle stretching from the dome of his head, down his jaws, above his upper lip, over his chin, and under his chin to the itchy skin below, and Adam now knew that this was going to be unpleasant in a particular way.

"Don't mean to interrupt," said the giant with a ham actor's solicitude. "You guys having a seminar out here?"

Adam ransacked his brain for something . . . cool . . . to say, something to show that he got it, the big hambone's game, and that he, too, was into irony and could parry any such thrust. But all he came up with was, "No."

As soon as he said it, he realized he should just leave it at that, a curt, flat no. But what if the hulking guy took that as disrespectful? *That way lay disaster*—in an as yet unknown form, but inevitably, *disaster*! He heard himself adding, "We're just chilling, just hanging out."

The big interloper put on a hambone long face and began nodding over Adam with his eyes cast to one side and into an unfocused distance, as if he were pondering . . . pondering . . . pondering . . . Then he looked straight down at Adam and nodded some more before looking back over his shoulder and saying to his three comrades, "Says it's not a seminar. Says they're just chilling, just hanging out."

In a tone of mock contemplation, the one with the grizzle all over his head said, "Just chilling," and did some nodding of his own.

The Millennial Mutants grew silent. The high spirits of their intellectual romp through history, psychology, philosophy, and anthropology had—*poof!*—evaporated.

Adam knew he should stand up and not have the guy standing over him and looking down like this, but he was afraid that if he stood up, it would be perceived as a challenge . . . one that could only end badly.

T
O
M

W
O
L
F
E

"We thought it was a seminar," the big hambone said, "because you guys know so much about sports." His eyes suddenly seized upon Greg.

Greg tried a smile, then a shrug, then a sigh before attempting another smile and saying, "Well, not really," which came out *rilly*.

"No, you *rilly* do, rilly," said the guy, making it sound like the most effete locution he had ever heard. "We're *rilly* interested in sports, too." He motioned toward his sidekicks. "We play lacrosse."

Adam tried not to swallow or blink, but failed.

"—and you guys *rilly* know your lacrosse."

Silence. Implicit in all the *rillies* was: *you faggots*. The silence swelled up malignantly until Greg, the maximum Mutant, editor of the *Wave*, a supposed campus leader, realized he had to put up a defense. But how?

Finally, in only slightly more than a mumble, he managed to say, "Thanks. Nice talking to you. We have some things to go over."

"Hey, no problem," said the giant, lifting his hands up, palms forward. The hands were huge. "Go right ahead. You don't mind if we listen in, do you?"

In a faint voice Greg said, "Well . . ." Then he stopped. Something was happening to his lips. They were scrunching together into a little pink wad, as if gathered by a drawstring. Even more faintly he managed to say, "Well, no . . ." The muscles around his lips seemed to have an epileptic life of their own. He barely managed to croak out, "Wouldn't you rather"—his voice broke—"go play with your sticks?"

The lout broke into a wild, leering grin and just looked Greg in the eye until Greg broke. The giveaway was a big swallow and a frightened compression of the lips.

The giant turned toward his boys. "Says we oughta fuck off and go play with our sticks."

The boys went, "Wooooooooooo!" The one with the grizzled head said, "Play with our *what*? Did he say dicks or pricks?"

Greg said, "I didn't say—"

But the giant, leering at him once more, broke in. "We're not letting ourselves get"—he raised his right hand and let the wrist go limp in a hambone fashion—"rilly *pissy* here, are we?"

Greg opened his mouth, but the little muscles were playing such spastic tricks with his lips that he couldn't utter a word.

Inexplicably, the big lacrosse player turned toward Charlotte. He looked her up and down, smiled, winked, and said, "Hey, babe."

Then he turned back to Greg and began to leer in the most humiliating way, and the leer was the eternal leer of the playground, the one that says, "Come on, fag, think you can fuck with *me*?"

Greg had begun hyperventilating.

Suddenly Camille Deng sprang up, eyes snapping, lips pursed grimly. She looked about a third the size of their tormentor. She spoke in a low, rasping snarl:

"Let me put it another way. Take your lacrosse stick—bitch—and stick it up your ass net-first—bitch—and keep shoving until you shovel all the shit out of your mouth—bitch."

The giant's face turned bloodred. He took a step toward Camille.

Adam knew he should do something, but he remained rooted to the step he was sitting on.

Camille didn't retreat an inch. She thrust her chin forward and said, "Go ahead. Just touch me once. You'll be brought up on assault and sexual harassment charges so fast you'll be out of Dupont like a shot. You can go home and play with your all-American dick—bitch. And eat your buddies' ice cream"—she motioned with her head toward his comrades—"and drool their spooch from your filthy mouth, bitch."

The big athlete stopped in his tracks. The radioactive words *assault* and *sexual harassment* had jolted him. He knew them for what they were—career killers. He despised this woman—she was too grim and mean to be called a girl—as much as he had ever despised anyone, male or female, in his life.

"Oh, you little slit-eyed skank—"

"Slit-eyed!" cried Camille. "Slit-eyed!" It was a cry of triumph. "You heard that!" She was all but hopping up and down as her eyes panned over Edgar, Greg, Roger, Adam, and Charlotte. "Slit-eyed! You heard him!" Then she looked the bewildered giant right in the face. "You just had to go and do it, didn't you! You couldn't hold back! You just had to—" Whereupon she drew the edge of her hand across her throat like a knife and flashed him a vicious smile.

The guy looked as if he had been poleaxed at the base of his skull. He got the picture right away: *racial insult*. The poisonous skank had him. At Dupont that was worse than homicide. With homicide on your record, you had a fighting chance of staying in school.

"Let's go," he said in a barely audible voice, and they all got up and headed along the walkway toward the Great Yard. They looked back malevolently, but they kept walking.

Adam knew he should get up and congratulate Camille and whoop in triumph or something. And maybe say something to Greg. At least Greg had *tried*. But Adam still didn't move. He was paralyzed with shame and lingering fear. *I didn't do a thing . . . nothing . . . I just sat here.* (And what if they come back?)

At first none of them said a word. Then Camille, looking down as if at the steps, said, "Student . . . *athletes* . . ." As in herpes pustules. Then she looked up and said with great animation, "Hey, we gotta find out what that guy's name is! You can find out, can't you, Adam?"

Dispiritedly, "I think so."

Camille gave a humorless chuckle. "That moron is fucking *outta here*! He's history! He's a dried-up piece a shit! He's lucky if he's a student at Dupont—*student*"—another mordant chuckle—"forty-eight hours from now."

"Dja see the way they went skulking off with their tails between their legs?" said Greg. He had a grin of victory stretched across his face. "We *crrr*ushed those motherfuckers! They won't fuck with the Millennial Mutants again!"

We, thought Adam. You'd have caved completely if Camille hadn't stepped in. Yeah, well, Greg had put up *some* resistance, hadn't he. Couldn't very well deny him that.

"He won't fuck with *anybody* anymore!" crowed Camille. "Not at Dupont! That cretin is *roadkill*! And you're all my witnesses, right?"

She looked at each of them, including Charlotte, until all nodded yes. In fact, testifying in some kind of procedure against that lacrosse player was the last thing in the world Charlotte wanted to do. He had been sarcastic and mildly insulting, but Camille was a total . . . bitch. She was ready to bring the whole world up on "charges." Why? For what? The guy wasn't all that bad. He was virile. He was good-looking in a rugged way, acne scars and all . . . Beverly, on all fours: *Where are the lacrosse players?* Should he be expelled from Dupont, maybe have his life ruined, for calling a bitch like Camille a slit-eyed skank after what she said to him? Shoving a lacrosse stick net-first—

Camille's vulgarity made Charlotte queasy. No, it was more than that. It had shocked her in some fundamental way. In order to attack, Camille had abandoned all pretense of being feminine. Charlotte could still see the guy's stunned expression . . . It had shocked him, too . . . How anguished he looked as compared to a few moments before—

She glanced at Adam. He was looking straight at her, and she found herself in an eye lock. Adam was still sitting there on the step. He hadn't budged.

What was it he saw in her face? Adam wondered. It wasn't an accusation, in any case. Such a tender beauty she had . . . the purity of it . . . the innocence . . . the lithe legs, the sweet, delicate, lubricious curve of her lips . . . all in one. And she was as inexperienced as himself . . . forgiving yet intensely desirable . . . This was no mere observation. It was a feeling as real as any of his five senses. It suffused his body even unto the most remote nerve endings, suffused his body, his mind, everything within him—

Charlotte wanted to put an arm around him. He looked so forlorn and hopeless, sitting on that same spot where he had been sitting all along. He hadn't moved a muscle.

Reduce the world to a cocoon in which there were just the two of them. Just that, thought Adam, and he wouldn't ask for anything else.

I'm only eighteen, Charlotte thought, but I guess he needs *someone* to tell him everything is going to be okay. She broke the eye lock and departed that sad moment.

She thought the guy hadn't even noticed her, but all at once he had turned toward her, smiled, winked, and said, "Hey, babe."

15. THE TAILGATERS

As he and his family rolled into the Clarence Beale Parking Arbor in their Lincoln Navigator, a lawyer from Pittsburgh named Archer Miles got his first glimpse of the Bowl through the big old sycamores that stood in rows on the parking lot's landscaped dividers. The noonday sun was so strong, Archer had to squint. Would you believe it? More than four decades had elapsed, but it sure looked the same . . . an hour and forty-five minutes before the game, and already cars were pouring onto this vast arboreally umbrellaed asphalt plain and heading for . . . the Charlie Bowl . . . When was the last time he'd been to a game here? Must have been just three or four years after he graduated. Not one of Dupont's architectural gems, the Bowl, but awesome nonetheless . . . a stupendous tub of concrete, the equivalent of twenty stories high . . . officially named the Dupont Bowl . . . but back when Yale became the Bulldogs, and Princeton became the Tigers, Dupont, like Harvard, stood aloof from this cute vogue of naming athletic teams after animals with big teeth or sharp beaks. The students called them the Charlies, in jolly if ironic reference to the first name of the founder, Charles Dupont, and this became the Charlie Bowl.

Oh lore! Oh traditions! Oh Dupont! Who would have thought it would get to him like this, returning after all these years for a tailgate before a football game? I guess it's sort of like coming home to my youth, he thought. Although Archer could be profound and incisive before the bar, that was just about as deep as his powers of self-analysis ever got. Whatever, he wasn't going to express any such sentiment to Debby, his blond, twenty-two-years-younger, and—as he had noticed a lot recently—sharp-tongued second wife, who was sitting in the Navigator's other lofty leather-upholstered front seat. Debby was already bored and, in fact, had been bored ever since he thought up this trip. Nor was there any use sharing his tender thoughts with their two boys, Tyson and Porter, who sat right behind them in the Navigator's middle seats. They were Archer's second set of children and paragons of contemporary teenage cynicism. They enjoyed setting fire to the tails of tender thoughts.

"You sure you want to park here?" said Debby. "They all look like students to me."

That they did. From here to way over there you could see SUVs and pickup trucks parked in rows, with boys and girls milling about.

"Well, that's the whole idea, sweetheart," said Archer. "I want Tyson to see a little student life, too. These tailgates are always really fun."

Tyson was in his junior year at Hotchkiss. To Archer it was crucial that his boys go to Dupont. It had somehow become part of his conception of his own worth.

Archer gazed upon the great tableau again. It *was* a bit . . . odd. As far as you could see, the asphalt was littered with plastic cups, they looked like. They were even in the grass in the dividers beneath the sycamore trees. And the students . . . He knew, of course, that students were more casual these days, but the ones he was looking at—shorts, T-shirts, flip-flops—and *pickup trucks?* Things change, of course, but he couldn't get out of his mind the old picture of Ford and Buick station wagons with students—Dupont was all male then—hanging around the tailgates wearing button-downs, neckties, and tweed jackets or blazers.

Just in case—he wasn't sure of what—he parked the Navigator at the end of a row of spaces, three spaces from the nearest vehicle—an SUV with a bunch of students huddled about something at its back end.

Archer turned off the ventilation system and opened his window. A low garble of music was in the air, apparently from the radios of God knew how many vehicles, and a heavy, rich, sour, rancid odor. Archer could have sworn there were *two* odors . . . beer . . . and great fluffy fumes of human piss.

"Yuckamamie," said the younger boy, Porter, with a whine, "what's that *smell?*"

"Oh ho! I can tell you what it is," said Debby. "It's plain old—"

Archer nudged her thigh with his hand and cut her off. "I don't know *what* it is," he said. He gestured grandly out the window. "Now, *that's* a Dupont tailgate."

You could see quite a lot from up here in the high seats of the Navigator. Curious, but all across the great panorama of vehicles and students . . . *things* were bobbing up and down . . . *bubbling* . . . the way bubbles pop up on the surface of boiling soup, all over the place but in no discernible order. Archer squinted again. They weren't bubbles, they were . . . heads, shoulders, elbows, going up and down, up and down, on the asphalt by the SUVs and on the truck beds of the pickups. Why? From all over the place you could hear shouts of "Yo *something!*" . . . but Yo-*what?* . . . and high keening wails that went *Woooooo-ooooooo!*

From the huddle of students behind the SUV three spaces away came paroxysmal laughs. Then the huddle broke, and you could see a huge aluminum container standing on end in a plastic tub. One boy was furiously pumping a handle on top of it. Another had hold of the end of a sickly green hose that came from it, trying to fill a jumbo plastic cup, but something came foaming up out of the cap uncontrollably and went all over the boy's shorts.

"Fuck, Mark!" said the boy with the hose. "Lay off! Whattya think you're pumping, premium crude?"

The others were doubled over, spastic with merriment.

"A beer keg!" Archer announced, ignoring the word *fuck*. "I didn't know what it was! When I was here, they were all horizontal."

They descended from the heights of the Navigator. Archer stretched and then said, "Tyson, Porter, come here." Dutifully the two boys went there. He pointed. "See between those branches? That's the Charlie Bowl. It seats seventy thousand people. It used to be the biggest college football stadium in the country. When I was here, it was packed for every game. *More* than packed." He chuckled, smiled, and shook his head over what a wild time "more than packed" alluded to.

Tyson, the sixteen-year-old, couldn't have looked more bored, and the human capacity to look bored peaks at sixteen. Porter, the thirteen-year-old, feigned an interest by staring at the thing for a few seconds.

Turning toward Debby in hopes of getting some good old times going,

Archer said, "Mommy, did I ever tell you? We used to bring our dates over here the night before the game for a little . . . what you might call . . . nocturnal tailgating."

"Yo, Dad!" said Tyson. "What kind of tail?"

It genuinely annoyed Archer when Tyson acted as if he were now old enough to share off-color double entendres with adults. Of course, he himself had walked right into that one with his choice of words.

"Oh, *fudge!*" said Debby, who had not been listening to either one of them. Sweating, several wisps of hair pasted to her forehead, she was inspecting a tawny peach fingernail she had just broken trying to drag a wicker picnic basket out of the Navigator's cargo area and onto the tailgate.

"You can say the real word," said Tyson. "Everybody's heard it before, even the Hulk."

Tyson had taken to calling his brother, Porter, the Hulk, since he was skinny, reedy, small for his age, and wouldn't take his shirt off because his ribs showed. With a look of patient disdain, Porter changed the subject. In the best of whines—and, as opposed to looking bored, the human ability to whine peaks at thirteen—Porter said, "If the game starts at one o'clock, why are we here at eleven-fifteen?"

"Because I spent four hours stuffing these baskets full of food," said Mommy, "and you're going to have lunch right here. While Dad has his drinks and dreams about the old days, you can come back here and help me drag these things out there instead of standing around whining and complaining. Okay?"

"Yuckamamie," whined Porter. "I wasn't complaining, I was asking a question. I mean, yuck—a—mamie."

"What's 'his drinks' supposed to mean?" said Archer.

"You've got enough *bottles* back here," said Debby. "You must think you're nineteen again."

"And what's so terrible about that? Or dreaming, for that matter."

"Nothing—"

"Oh, this is just great, all of you," said Tyson with the sort of arch sarcasm boys acquire in northeastern boarding schools. "I can see why we got up at five-thirty and drove all the way from Connecticut for a tailgate at old Dupont. I mean like it's so *cool* and everything, and everybody's having such a *good time.*"

Archer wanted to strangle him . . . or at least punish him with some withering sarcastic comeback . . . but he didn't. He looked down at the asphalt and made himself cool off. It was maddening when children were sarcastic to adults, but it could be crushing when adults were sarcastic to children.

A sudden blast of music from a car radio. He looked up—

Tyson was no longer interested in him at all. His head was turned, his eyes were as big as saucers, and his mouth was agape and grinning at the same time.

"Oh wow!" he exclaimed. "Look at those guys! You see them?"

In the row of vehicles just ahead of them, some great, strapping young men were up on the truck bed of a pickup, engaged in a beer fight. There was no missing their "ripped" bodies, that being Tyson's term for lean, highly defined muscular builds, since practically all were naked except for the shorts that hung from way down on their hips. Barks of anger, cries of laughter, thrashing arms. One of them produces a punctured can of beer and sprays another in the face from two feet away. "Die, asshole!" the victim yells in a macho voice, whereupon he throws himself upon his assailant and they go crashing to the truck-bed floor. Knees, feet, legs, shoulders, grimaces, bloodred faces pop up and crash as they grapple. Over the pickup's radio, a throaty young woman wails in the pell-mell cadence of the new pop music craze, crunk: "—spears her haunches Dirty Sanchez dude what wants her nude and slutty pseudo-ruts her butt so rudely taunts her . . ." Others, including a regular young giant, maybe six feet six, rangy but with muscles everywhere, stand over the combatants, cheering ironically and egging them on. Behind the giant, another boy sneaks up, holding a jumbo plastic cup of beer in the air as if he were about to throw a baseball. "Hey, Mac!" he says. The giant turns about, and the boy hurls his beer bomb, cup and all, at his midsection. The beer goes all over Mac. It soaks his shorts clear down to the crotch. "Oh you dick!" roars Mac as he goes at him, but the boy dodges and vaults over the side of the truck bed and down to the asphalt. "Come on back up here, you wuss, and fight like a wuss!" And on it goes, as the crunk singer wails, "Gots the curse her pad her madder hearse her cold cunt cash her outta odor . . ."

Tyson was enjoying it immensely. Maybe this tailgate stuff wasn't as lame as he'd thought. Archer was trying to work it out in his mind that, after all, tailgate parties had always been about sheer exuberant fun, and this was different only in style, except that the next thing he knew, two of the great strapping lads were leaning out over the tailgate and hoisting a girl up by her arms. She was a big blonde, a bit heavy but good and chesty, wearing tight bootleg jeans and a lacy whisper of a camisole unbuttoned way down to *there*. She shrieked a shriek that wavered between protest and giddiness. As she twisted her torso this way and that, as if to escape, more and more breast bulged out of her flimsy top. They had just hoisted her, twisting and straggling, up to the truck bed itself when—*bango!*—the flimsy camisole popped open completely. She wore no bra. There were her breasts, her areolae, her nipples, big as life.

"Woooooooooo!" came the ironic but excited cry of the boys up on the truck bed and the others standing around the tailgate.

With a gasp of mortification, the girl stuffed them back inside her shirt and hopped off the truck's tailgate, smiling, but with eyes cast down, and going, "Ohmygod, ohmygod, ohmygod . . ."

From out of nowhere sprang a boy with a long but well-defined wrestler's gut, clad in low-slung plaid boxer undershorts—out of the fly of which protruded a two-foot-long plastic novelty penis with a clownishly large glans. A grizzle ran from the dome of this boy's head, down his jaws, under his nose, over his chin, and down under where it met a tangle of hair sprouting up from his chest.

"Where'd she go?" he howled drunkenly. He turned about in slow circles, his toy penis swaying in a variable lag.

Archer was stunned. What were Tyson and Porter supposed to come away with? Jesus Christ, collegiate was collegiate, but this was . . . indecent—*immoral* was the term that crossed his mind, but the very word had become obsolete. It had vanished from sophisticated conversation.

He cut a glance at Tyson and Porter. They were utterly absorbed.

The rich, sour odor rose up from the asphalt. Oh, it was beer, all right, four acres of sloshed beer. And those big white scraps littering even the sycamore islands? Mashed beer cups. And that bubbling panorama of bobbing heads, shoulders, elbows—four acres of America's college elite, Dupont students, pumping thousands, *thousands* of gallons of beer and hosing it down their gullets, and it comes out . . . where? And the result was—what?—piss, piss, great fluffy fumes of piss, four acres of it.

"I haven't seen a single freshman here," said Mimi. She motioned her head toward the group of guys clustered about the rear end of a black Expedition, jumbo cups in their hands, intently watching another guy trying to do something with the joint where the hose was attached to an aluminum keg of beer. The onlookers were being witty.

"Guess what, Griff. In America, things screw on clockwise! . . . Just a tip!" General laughter.

"Yeah, Griff, you SPED!"

"What the fuck's a sped? Not that I can figure out why the fuck I'm asking."

"Special Ed, you retard!" General laughter.

"Ecccchhhhh," said Mimi in a low voice, "frat boys."

"What fraternity?" said Bettina.

"Delta Handa Poka," said Mimi. "Oh, I don't know. I just know they're frat boys. They're already so wasted, they think if they tell their dumb jokes loud enough, that makes them funny."

"I don't see any freshmen, either," said Bettina. "No herds."

"The three of us are the herd," said Mimi.

"There's no way to like . . . blend in," said Bettina. "Every car is a like . . . private party where they all know each other. I never even heard of any tailgate. Tell me again how you heard about it?"

"I don't remember exactly," Charlotte lied. "I just remember somebody talking about it. It *sounded* like fun."

"Well, no offense, dahling," said Mimi, "but I think it kinda sucks."

Bettina lifted one foot and looked at the sole of her sandal. "Ucchhh. Nasty. There's beer *everywhere*. This parking lot looks like a fucking sewer. And all those crushed beer cups and shit everywhere. Looks like a bunch of those vinyl garbage bags broke open."

"Smells like it, too," said Mimi. "I'll bet you anything they *piss* out here. They're so hammered."

"I'm sorry," said Charlotte, "but I didn't know. I just thought it might be a way to, you know, meet some new people." It dawned on her how their roles had reversed. The night of the Saint Ray party, Mimi and Bettina had to practically drag her out . . . in the name of meeting new people. And now she had dragged *them* out. But she had stuck it out at the Saint Ray house, and she had met *some new people*, all right. "Why don't we just walk around a little bit more, since we're already way out here."

"I hope to hell they've got buses going back," said Mimi. "They had all these buses taking people *to* the game, but I never even thought of how the fuck we're supposed to get back."

That was Charlotte Simmons and the Saint Ray party, too, wasn't it! Except that she hadn't dared to be as testy about it as Mimi, for fear of being considered uncool.

Bettina said, "I think there's Chester buses that come along here."

"There better be. I'm not walking. I can tell you that much. I bet it's two miles back to campus."

Charlotte said, "It can't be *that* far. Let's just look around a little bit more. Maybe we *will* run into somebody we know."

"Okay," said Mimi. She rolled her eyes and pronounced the *o* in *okay* like a sigh.

Charlotte picked up the pace to lead Mimi on before she could change her mind. She felt a twinge of guilt. She hadn't prodded the two of them all this way out of a spirit of adventure and discovery. She didn't dare tell them the truth, which was that she hadn't wanted to wander around here by herself, like some clueless freshman social stray. As for why she wanted to wander around here—

At the moment the three freshmen were walking by a Lincoln Navigator, a huge thing, out back of which a man, a woman, and two teenage boys were standing around the tailgate, eating lunch out of a big wicker picnic basket. The man was pushing sixty at least, and he was sipping from a wide, squat glass with brown liquor in it and staring dolefully into the distance. *Had* to be an alum. What other grown-up would stay here ten seconds? The woman, a pretty blonde—his daughter?—was sitting on the edge of the tailgate, eating a sandwich and looking bored to death. The younger boy was walking backward in imitation of a moonwalk and whining. "Yucka-mamie . . . when does the *game* start?" The older boy, slouched back against the Navigator with his arms crossed, said, "What game? This is a Dupont *tailgate*, dummy."

Another SUV. Girls and boys were crowded around a keg on the pavement. Lots of ironic cheering. Right by the keg, two boys were holding a girl upside down by her legs. Her jaws were wide-open, and another boy had the nozzle of a hose literally inside her mouth.

"Eccchhhh," said Bettina. "That hurts just to watch. How do you swallow beer uphill with some guy hosing it into your throat?"

"Why should she care?" said Mimi. "She's got all she wants, guys at either end and more guys watching."

They moved on. Charlotte stopped in her tracks. They were coming to another pickup truck. Up on the truck bed was a startling sight, a hairy diesel of a guy clad only in a pair of plaid boxer undershorts with an enormous toy penis sticking out of the fly. His eyes were closed, he had his fists waist high in the disco dance style, and he was trying, and failing, to switch his hips in time to the music playing on the truck's radio: "Aching for your wan love, sister, shoving Mister Johnson gently when he's taking foreplay's lazy torpor bending his big woody could be making his stones sorer maybe . . ."

"Eccchhhh, crunk," said Bettina. "I can't stand it. It's like rap forced through bars of melody. I think it sounds contrived."

"Eeeyew, that guy looks so gross," said Mimi, looking at the one with the plastic penis sticking out. "Oh joy, another frat."

Charlotte said, "Maybe . . . ummm . . ." She had seen that grizzled head somewhere before.

"Hey! You! I know *you*!" It was a guy standing beside the pickup, on the pavement, pointing his finger straight at Charlotte. Tall, lean, wearing nothing but a pair of khaki shorts about to fall off his hips, the better to display his anatomy chart of a midsection. It was him, oh yes, Beverly's lacrosse player, Harrison. Charlotte shuddered as if from a chill. Here he was, her entire reason for manufacturing this "exploration" to a tailgate—and now?

He came toward her, grinning broadly and still pointing.

"You were at Lapham! What's her name's—something or other."

"Roommate. Beverly," said Charlotte. How tiny and timid her voice was.

"Now that you're here," he said, "come on up and party."

"Up?"

"Up on the truck. Come on."

"Up on the truck," said Charlotte. She looked at Mimi and Bettina and said, "You want to?" She said it in a small, conspiratorial voice with a wondering smile that was supposed to say, "Why don't we? It might be fun."

Mimi and Bettina just stared back at her. Bettina overbit her lower lip with her front teeth. Charlotte had no idea what to say to them. She wanted to stay, but could she possibly stay without them—or would they feel used or resentful of her as the one of their trio who attracts the cool guys?

"Hey, heyyy! Wuz up, babe?"

Up on the truck bed, standing beside the grizzled guy with the plastic penis, was a huge figure wearing only low-riding khaki shorts. Charlotte recognized him immediately. He was the gigantic lacrosse player who had confronted and frightened the Millennial Mutants on the steps of Briggs. And now she knew why she recognized the guy with the plastic penis. He had been with the giant. "I know *you!*" he said. "You're the . . . the . . . the . . ." He was so drunk he couldn't remember the end of his own sentence. "Come on up here with *me!*" He pointed at Harrison. "Guy's an asshole. Come on up here with me and do the shake." He began shaking his whole body violently, his arms hanging loose and his mouth open so that his big lower lip jiggled moronically.

Charlotte stared. He frightened her. He stopped shaking and staggered about with his immense frame stooped and his arms hanging way down.

She couldn't bring herself to say a word. She shook her head no.

Faster than it would take to tell it, the big stoop leaped off the truck bed, over the tailgate, landed on the asphalt beside her, keeled over, broke the fall with his hands, struggled up, and stood beside her, grinning manically.

"Come on up, babe. Time to *rock!*"

Her tiniest voice yet: "No." She shook her head slowly.

"Up we go!" said Mac, and in that same moment he clamped his big hands on either side of her waist and lifted her off her feet as if she were nothing more than a vase, up toward the grizzled guy and the monstrous glans of his toy penis.

"PUT ME DOWN! TAKE YOUR HANDS OFF ME! STOP IT! STOP IT! STOP IT!"

She was frightened—and affronted. She was rising toward the grinning face and outstretched arms and impudent faux-phallus of the grizzled ape.

"Come on, Mac, put her down. She doesn't wanna."

Harrison. Charlotte could get a glimpse of him only in peripheral vision.

"Fuck off, dick. You know what you are? A pussy. You know how you fight? You wanna know what I think of you, Harrison? You're a little girl."

"Dude . . . put her down. She doesn't wanna play."

"Oh—you—pussy," said Mac, trying to put Charlotte up on the truck bed and keep track of Harrison at the same time.

Harrison lunged, threw his arms around Mac's waist, and started jerking him backward, away from the truck. As Mac shuffled his feet to get his balance, Harrison kicked a leg out from under him. Mac began falling backward, still holding on to Charlotte by the waist. The moment seemed to stretch out stretch out stretch out in the most languid slow motion. Charlotte wondered almost idly, out of curiosity, what was going to happen to her. Mac let go of her waist and thrust his hands behind him to break his fall. Charlotte landed on top of him, sprawled across his chest and midsection.

She flipped herself off, rolled on the asphalt, scrambled to her feet, catching a glimpse of Bettina and Mimi looking on, bewildered. Bettina! Mimi! But no time! Mac was upright, too . . . groggy . . . He moved toward her, staring . . . His gaze went over her shoulder . . . In the next instant Harrison threw one arm around her and began pointing at Mac with his other hand.

"What the fuck, Mac? LEAVE HER ALONE! Use your fucking head! She's not a groupie! You got the skanks on your case already! You wanna get fucking thrown outta school?"

Mac said, "The fuck—" but the rest degenerated into a growl. He gave Harrison a stalking tiger stare and began a stalking tiger creep. Harrison let Charlotte go and got in a crouch. Mac was much more powerful, but he was also far drunker. Harrison began feinting one way and another and another and another with his shoulders. Mac lunged, and Harrison spun out of the way. Mac stumbled but managed to regain his footing and came after his adversary again. Quite a spectacle . . . Their shorts were lower than ever . . . You could see the gulleys that ran from the ilial crest down toward the groin . . . They were sweating . . . The sun threw their muscles into glistening swells and dark depressions. Mac was wary this time—stalking . . . stalking . . .

Gawkers were already crowding around, eager for loosened teeth, bloody noses, cut flesh, swollen eye sockets. In no time they had formed an impenetrable ring. Sheer adrenaline pumped cheers and animal cries out of their throats. All was uproar and pounding hearts . . . You couldn't hear the crunk singer anymore . . . The ring didn't leave Harrison room to use speed to any real advantage . . . Now Mac had Harrison backing up toward the truck with no place to retreat. Mac began closing in for the kill . . . from about twenty feet away. Fuck that! Harrison stopped retreating . . . He ran straight at Mac. Mac hesitated . . . Harrison dove . . . left his feet completely . . . hit the giant's knees from the side with the full momentum of his body. Mac fell like a tree. Both hit the asphalt.

"What the fuck's going on over *there*?" said Vance, who was standing on the truck bed of Julian's pickup. Not only could he hear all the giddy yammering and shouting of a crowd, but he could also just make out their heads, many of which were popping up in excited attempts to see better.

Hoyt, who was sitting on the floor of the truck bed with his back propped up against a side wall, drinking his fourth—or was it his fifth, and did it matter?—beer, said, "Beats the shit outta me. Sounds like a fight. Same old shit show."

Must have been his fifth beer, because he was trying to convince himself that it would be a more productive use of time to remain in this comfortable, contented position and get wasted than to go watch somebody fight.

Just then a huge collective groan welled up from over there in the midst of all the shouting. Another mass groan, louder yammering and cheering. Hoyt struggled to his feet, which was harder than it would have been if he could've used both hands. Right now he couldn't. Getting wasted, even in defeat, still had a grip on the big cup of beer.

"I'm gonna go see," said Vance. His blue eyes were flashing with anticipation. Boo-man, who had been diligently manning the keg for ten or eleven Saint Rays and their girlfriends, had stopped pumping and was craning his neck to try to spot the action. Even the Saint Rays and the girls down on the asphalt, who couldn't see a thing, were looking in the direction of the ruckus.

Hoyt was dizzy from drink and from standing up while drunk. But curiosity soon revved up his blissfully demolished willpower, and he clambered down from the truck bed with Vance and Boo-man.

The three of them were far from being the only students tramping through the beer and cups and converging on the fight scene. Once they got there, they could see that penetrating the crush of gawkers would be a tactical nightmare. But Hoyt, especially while drunk, saw no reason in the world why a Saint Ray should obey the rules of the mob, such as first come, first served. He began knifing through the gawkers with his most imperious, superior self on display. "Coming through . . . coming through . . . Hey! Coming through! Move! I said coming through!" In the case of the occasional jerk who wanted it known that he couldn't be fucked with, Hoyt would give the guy a certain accusing stare he had mastered, a veritable laser beaming undiluted blame, and say, "Don't dick around! I got the plasma!"

In no time he was in the first row of the ring. Holy shit . . . No wonder such a mob . . . Out in the middle of the ring were Mac Bolka and Harrison Vorheese . . . Mac Bolka and Harrison Vorheese! They were pumped, *pumped*!—and fighting for real. Right now they were both crouched, circling each other . . . breathing hard, pouring sweat . . . Their hides were covered in friction burns, cuts, and dirt. A stripe of bright red blood ran from Harrison's nose straight down to his mouth . . . He kept trying to block the flow with his lower lip . . . Mac Bolka's eyes looked like flashlight bulbs down in dark craters. They were both on their last legs, if Hoyt knew anything about it . . .

He leaned in close to the ear of some skinny dork who was standing right next to him. "What's all *this* about?"

"It's over some girl," the dork said without taking his eyes off the contest.

"What girl?"

"That girl over there on the edge." He gestured vaguely, eyes still pinned on the action. "The one in the dress."

There was only one girl in a dress amid the wall of gawkers. It was hard to make out her face, because she stood there hunched over, her hands pressed flat against her cheeks, her lips parted, her brow contorted, her eyes terrified, her cheekbones wet and glistening . . . Wait a minute. It was her, that girl—what the fuck *was* her name?—that little freshman, the one who gave him a hard time that night . . . But it was only that, a blip of random thought. Only one person was on his mind—Harrison, who was a brother. A brother! A Saint Ray! Not only that, but a lacrosse player . . . although he didn't actually think that thought in so many words. He *felt* it, that thought, as if he were wired to a circuit. And Saint Rays were those who *take no shit.* That thought he did think in so many words. If Harrison needed any help, *any* help, against that big ugly bear, he was going to get it. He, Hoyt Thorpe, was a warrior!—and took no shit where Saint Rays were concerned.

Harrison confronted Bolka in a crouch, his body heaving in search of oxygen. His eyes were glassy. He looked as if at any moment he would black out and collapse from sheer exhaustion. Bolka edged closer. With a cry barely louder than a whimper, Harrison charged, throwing his hands upward as if to force Bolka's arms apart and get a clean shot at him. In the next moment they were rolling in the dirt, and Harrison wound up on all fours with Bolka on his back. Bolka forced the smaller man's head onto the ground so that the left side of his face was mashed into the pavement. With some sort of wrestler's hold he clasped his huge hands behind Harrison's neck. The neck was bent at a frightening angle. *Bango!*—the very life seemed to depart Harrison. He was an inert piece of meat. Sure that his adversary was now, indeed, finished, Bolka rose upright on his knees in a fumid beer slick, his legs still straddling his adversary's body. He threw his shoulders back and looked about at the crowd and lifted his fists to chest level. Hoyt expected him at any moment to start pounding his chest and cut loose with a yodel. Still lying on his side between Bolka's legs, Harrison slowly rolled onto his back. His eyes were closed. His chest rose up and down in fast, shallow breaths. Bolka had a serious, almost sad look on his face, as if to say, "I didn't want to have to hurt him, but he insisted on picking a fight." Here at the perfect point on the graph of intoxication, Hoyt treated himself to a wave of sheer malignant hatred. He loathed the dumb fuck. Who was he? What was this Balkan mongrel diversoid doing at Dupont in the first place? The gale was blowing nicely. It was exhilarating. Just perfect. He was a Dupont man and a Saint Ray, and he knew. Loathing became something loftier and more refined: contempt.

Now the contemptible subhuman was rising to its feet. Bolka looked down at Harrison and shook his head as if he was sorry it had had to happen. Then he turned his back on the vanquished foe and began surveying the crowd. He had such a black scowl on his face, it seemed that at any moment he was likely to pick out someone else to slaughter. He stood stock-still and stared at someone. The scowl dissolved into a faint smile. "There's my girl . . ." He said it with a slow, sugary, cretinish drawl. *Theh's muh gul . . .* He began to move forward. It was *her*, the little freshman . . . He was heading straight for her.

He started to say it again: "Theh's muh gul—"

"Stay away from me!" It was a shout, a command, rather than a cry.

"Uhh—"

"I SAID STAY AWAY FROM ME!"

She was furious! Her face was stricken with fear and twisted with a flood of tears—but she was furious! She stood her ground!

Bolka, looking bigger and more gorged with muscle than ever, was now but a few steps away from her. He looked more rank, more frothy with sweat, more of a big ugly bear, more contemptible than ever. The gawkers were dumbstruck, paralyzed . . . tiny worthless creatures—

At that moment Hoyt *felt* it. That *point!* That point on the graph—the two lines *met* at that moment. The limbic and the rational were perfectly poised, in equilibrium. He loved himself as he watched himself detach himself from the ring of useless gawkers and enter the arena, a fellow warrior come to save and avenge a Saint Ray. And in that same moment a strategy came to him.

"Hey, dickhead!" Both hims loved himself as they heard the challenge, the note of unremitting contempt in his voice.

The giant turned about incredulously.

"Stay away from her, dickhead! She's my sister!"

Bolka cocked his head and produced a small sneer of a smile and said, "And who the fuck do you think *you* are?"

"If she's my sister, then I'm her brother, is what the fuck even a moron like you should be able to figure out, and what I'm telling you is, stay away from my sister!"

You could see the giant's scorn and fury dim down all at once, as if it were on a rheostat. Obviously he was beginning to process the implications in terms of public opinion, gawker opinion, if this was in fact the girl's brother. Hoyt and the giant were barely four feet apart. The graph! The point! He was *there*!

"I said . . . *stay* . . . *away* . . . from my *sister*!"

Hoyt could see the giant's rheostat dim a little further still. "How do I *know* she's your sister?"

Bolka had reduced things from the level of primal combat to the level of credibility. Hoyt knew he had him. With the steel of authority in his voice he said, "How do you know? Because it's documented. I have it right here."

With that, he lowered his gaze and dug into the left cargo pocket of his shorts and walked to within two feet of the giant. He produced a piece of paper from his pocket—in fact, a receipt for a DVD he'd rented at Mehr & Bohm Music Video—and said, "Here."

The giant took it in his hand and looked down at it.

Hoyt smashed him in the nose with his right forearm. Blood fairly exploded out of the big man's nostrils, but he didn't fall back. He scarcely budged. Amid the red flood down his face, his lips formed a savage leer. Before Hoyt knew what was happening—since he had no backup strategy—had never needed one—the giant had his arm around his neck and was squeezing with all his might. Hoyt became eminently aware of the fact that he could no longer breathe. Yet that wasn't as terrifying as the fact that he had now run into—this was—the dreaded hundredth man his dad had warned him about. He was all at once at the mercy of *one of those babies*. He felt no terror, not yet, only remorse over his own bad judgment, over his failure as a Dupont man and a Saint Ray.

Cries of rage! Shitfire! Flailing limbs! An avalanche! An incredible massive weight drove his whole body into the asphalt. He was buried beneath meat and rage. The other lacrosse players had come pummeling down from the flatbed. He was aware of the blows and the horrible pressure and the way the skin tore off his elbow and the horrible weight and smothering darkness of it all—but the pain hadn't registered. All he knew—felt—was that the giant's grip on his neck was gone. He might get beaten to death, but he could die breathing. He tried to curl up in a ball. He still couldn't feel the blows. He merely knew he was being hit. He didn't feel his left arm. He merely knew it was being bent the wrong way. He didn't feel the elbow that came smashing down on his skull. He merely thought it was lights-out. But in fact it wasn't. He could feel the beer all over his head because he could smell it. He could hear an old voice, a crude voice:

"Yo, laddy-buck, 'at's enough a that, you dumb shit!" *Laddy-buck.* That meant Bruce and the campus police had arrived. Bruce was a big old fat man who called guys "laddy-buck." It was as good as over. Hoyt didn't feel pain yet, not at this moment, not yet. He felt failure. He was a warrior cut down in the prime of youth. Hadn't done a thing wrong. Smashed the beast flush on the beak with his forearm, in the classic way. Shit! *One of those babies*: the hundredth man.

"Videotape the white apes with the badges and the blackjacks whacking a blood my blood yo' blood it's time you niggas get up off yo' ghetto asses shove the blackjacks up the Mister Brown back alleys of the po-lice thugs videotape the bloods my blood yo' blood the brothers getting bigger crack some white apes upside they own haids videotape the suckers laid out daid eliminated by the bloods my blood yo' blood videotape it motherfuckers"—until Jojo wanted to climb the locker-room walls and demolish the speakers and then crawl through the wires until he found Doctor Dis and twisted his head off for him. Why had Charles inflicted this rap so-called music on the entire team? All it was was ghetto noise. Why did he, Jojo, have to have Doctor Dis hammering his skull every second of every minute while he got dressed for practice?

As for Charles, he was sitting in front of his locker, four lockers down from Jojo's, changing clothes and enjoying his other favorite sport, which was giving Congers a hard time.

"Hey, Vernon," Charles was saying in a loud voice no one in the room could miss, "I see you got yourself a new whip." *Whip* was ghettospeak for automobile.

Congers, whose locker was opposite Charles's, said, "Yeah . . ." warily. He had long since learned that very little Charles had to say to him could be taken at face value, starting with the fact that Charles only spoke ghetto when he was being ironic.

"Whattaya call a whip like that?"

"A Viper," Congers said tonelessly.

"A Vipuhhh," said Charles. "Unnnhhhh *unnh*! You gon' be a playa now, baby! Whenja get it?"

Congers said nothing at first. Then, "A coupla days ago."

"A Vi-puhhh. How much it setchoo back?"

Another pause . . . "Somebody give it to me."

"Somebody *give* it to you?" said Charles. "Somebody sure loves you, bro. One a yo' peeps?"

"No."

"Then I hope the motherfucker's straight. That whip's worth fifty or sixty large. Don't you let the dude pat you on the ass or invitechoo in for a Slurpee when you say good night."

"A *Slurpee*," said Treyshawn. "*Hegghh Hegghhh hegghhh.*" He liked that one.

Congers's face clouded. He wasn't happy about the insinuation. "What the fuck you talking about?" he said to Charles. "I don't even know who give it to me."

"Don't even *know*? Some dude give me a whip like that, I'd remember his fucking name. Whatchoo mean, you don't know?"

"I don't *know*, man!" said Congers. "I'm getting dressed after practice, and I'm putting my pants on, and there's a set a car keys inna fucking pocket, and hanging off of it is this little thing"—he made a shape with the thumb and forefinger of his right hand—"about like this. Know'm saying? And on one side of it, it says Vernon Congers, and on the other side of it there's a number, a license plate number. Know'm saying? And so I be walking outta here, and right there at the curb's this car, and it's the one. Got the same number. Know'm saying? The doors was open, so I get in, and I be looking around . . . and there's the registration and this title thing, and both'm's got my mama's name on it. So—"

"Shhhhh!" said Charles with an exaggerated look of alarm on his face. "Don'tchoo be telling anybody about this—"

Jojo didn't listen to any more of it—Charles making fun of Congers . . .

What he had heard was already too much to take. Congers, a freshman—hadn't even played for Dupont yet, and the boosters had already given him a car . . . a *hot* car, no less . . . a Viper . . . Obviously the word was out everywhere, even among the alumni groupies. The ascension of the freshman phenom . . . the descent into oblivion of Jojo Johanssen . . . He had never felt lower in his life. His own teammates avoided looking at him, his oblivion was so embarrassing. Or was he being paranoid? He still couldn't believe it, but it had happened. His entire purpose for being on this earth was to play in the League. Jojo Johanssen's purpose had just been deleted. And yeah, yeah, don't give up, just play harder, suck up your guts, and the tough get going, and so forth and so on.

Over the next few minutes, no doubt, would come stage two of his decline and fall. The game was three days away, which meant that today and tomorrow the first team would scrimmage with the second team. The second team would be nothing but sparring partners, mimicking the Cincinnati offense, running Cincinnati's plays and setup patterns—in other words, serving as dummies for the benefit of the fabulous ones, the starting five. He would no doubt be impersonating Cincinnati's power forward, Jamal Perkins, known in the sports columns as "the Disciplinarian" because of his "physical" game, meaning rough and dirty. He would be playing against his nemesis, Congers, in the scrimmage, but if he got rough with him in Jamal Perkins–style, he would look spiteful and resentful. Roughhousing and rebounding—to sharpen up Congers's game . . . Great.

Out of the corner of his eye Jojo saw a shimmer of Dupont mauve enter the locker room. He didn't need to look straight at the man to know it was Coach in his starter jacket. Well—it would be okay to look at Coach, he decided. Besides, he couldn't resist. Nobody could. At any given moment Coach was about to explode with anger—or turn into a stern but loving father appealing to your better self. So Jojo turned his head. There he was, Buster Roth, in a deep mauve nylon starter jacket emblazoned with DUPONT in gold letters. Behind him were two assistant coaches, Marty Smalls, who was white, and Skyhook Frye ("Sky" for his height, "hook" for his favorite shot as a center for Dupont . . . back when), a towering black man. All fourteen players were looking at Coach. His eyes were narrowed, and he had folded his eyebrows in toward one another, but it was still impossible to read his face. He stopped a step or so from where his players sat on the benches in front of their lockers and put his fists on his hips, which was not a good sign. He rocked back on his heels and drew his chin down toward his clavicle, which seemed to widen his already thick neck and make his head look as if it had erupted from the throat of the canary yellow polo shirt he was wearing. That was not a good sign, either. Then he ran his eyes over his flock slowly, one by one. The silence became a mounting pressure.

He motioned to Marty Smalls to wheel the blackboard over to where everyone could see it, which he did.

"Marty, gimme some chalk." Which he did.

"And gimme a red, too." Which he did. "Okay. Okay. Cincinnati's got two new players. I've seen them at the camps. They're tall, and they're quick, but nothing's gonna make Garducci change his offense. For a start, he'll still run the back door."

Whereupon Buster Roth started drawing an elaborate diagram on the blackboard in white and red, showing the Cincinnati strategy of overbalancing its offense on one side of the court and then suddenly looping a pass to a forward or a guard driving toward the basket down the other side, coming in through "the back door."

"They've still got Jamal Perkins," Coach continued, "and he'll be down there holding, elbowing, stomping, and generally fouling the shit out of whichever one of you's closest to the basket."

Reluctantly, woefully, Jojo paid close attention to what Coach had to say about Perkins's role. Soon would begin stage three of the demise of Jojo Johanssen: the moment he stepped out onto the court playing the role of a dummy representing Jamal Perkins for the benefit and greater glory of the Viper-driving Vernon Congers.

Coach finally completed his discourse and turned away from his chalkboard and said, "Okay, you got that?" Nods all around. "Anything else you need to know?" Fourteen silent faces. "Okay. Let's get started. Charles, Mike, Cantrell, Vernon, Alan—you're Cincinnati. Marty?"

As Marty Smalls stepped forward with a freshly laundered stack of yellow practice shirts, Jojo sat catatonically on his bench, paralyzed by conflicting waves of wonder and belief. If Congers was playing for "Cincinnati," then Jojo Johanssen must be on the starting five—or had he missed something? Or once they got on the court, would Coach see he had gotten it backward and have them exchange shirts again? Now he couldn't resist looking at the others, although he did it sidewise. Mike was slipping his yellow shirt over his head, whereupon he looked straight at Jojo with his head cocked, his eyes popped open, and a twisted little smile on his face, as if to say, "You and all your blubbering about the end of your career. Are you happy now?"

Congers was on his feet but motionless, holding a pressed and folded yellow shirt absentmindedly and staring at Coach, not with hostility or even bafflement but with yearning, as if begging Coach to say, "Wait a minute, what are you doing with a yellow shirt?" But Coach was already leaving the room with Skyhook Frye. Marty Smalls was now busy distributing yellow shirts to the three swimmies—Holmes Pearson, Dave Potter, and Sam Bemis—and mauve shirts to Treyshawn, André, Dashorn, Curtis—and, without so much as a comment or a change of expression . . . to *him*. He still couldn't believe there was no catch to what was taking place.

By now most of the others had put on the shirts and were leaving the room. Oh, fuck! If he didn't get a move on, there would just be him and Congers in the locker room. That would truly be embarrassing. Jojo slipped the mauve shirt over his head and his torso as fast as he could. Congers's back was turned. He was facing his locker, looking straight ahead, and still holding the yellow shirt. Holy shit, the guy had some build. The muscles of his broad brown back seemed sculpted by light and shadow. His upper back was as wide as a door. Congers could annihilate Charles—or Jojo Johanssen—if he ever found the courage to do it. Jojo slipped out of the locker room. Congers hadn't turned around once.

When Jojo reached the floor of the Buster Bowl, the mauve shirts and the yellow shirts had already begun warming up. The sound of basketballs bouncing or rattling off hoops in a huge empty arena like this always stirred Jojo. The only lights were the fields of LumeNex floods at the bottom of the bowl.

Out of nowhere came Buster Roth, who motioned to Jojo to follow him to a shadowy stretch near the stands, directly behind the great goosenecked stanchion of one of the backboards.

He clapped Jojo on the upper arm and said, "Jojo, I've been riding you pretty hard for the past couple of weeks, haven't I?" Jojo didn't know what to say, but Coach didn't seem to expect an answer. "I wouldna done it without a reason." Buster Roth was in his stern but fatherly mode. "Jojo . . . you've been . . . tentative out there, preoccupied . . . worried about something. You don't have to tell me. That part don't matter. What matters is, I had to do something to get that"—he clenched his teeth and brought his right fist up in front of his heart and tightened it until it shook from the hyper-contraction of the muscles—"back into your solar plexus. You can't just tell a player he's gotta get his juice back. You gotta put him in a position where he either gets it back or he don't. Nobody's good enough—nobody—to be complacent at this level or so distracted that he loses that—" He did the shaking-fist semaphore again. "Okay. Don't think about it anymore. Just keep on showing me you got it. Now, go get 'em."

Jojo knew he should say thanks, Coach, but he couldn't get those words out. Thankful wasn't what he felt—not thankful, not victorious, not elated, not relieved, nor anything else he could put a name to. *Messed with* came close, but that wasn't quite it, either. This shirt he had on seemed in some way counterfeit.

He and his tainted shirt headed on out to the court. Thanks to the precision of the LumeNex lighting systems, the transition from the gloom to the court, with its futuristic backboard stanchions at either end, was like stepping out of the wings onto a stage on which awaited a glory the whole world could see. Or the whole TV-watching world, anyway. This is the only place I'm happy, he said to himself, and the weight of the past two weeks began to slide from his shoulders. If Congers himself came up to him right now, it wouldn't faze him for a second. Down at this end, the starters were warming up; at the other end, "Cincinnati." The percussion of innumerable basketballs bouncing became the only sound in the universe. Treyshawn was doing his Kareemas, as he called them in the name of Kareem Abdul-Jabbar, hook shots and fadeaways from just outside the lane. André was pumping in three-pointers from down in the left corner. Dashorn was indulging in the typical point guard's fantasy, pump faking a jump shot from beyond the three-point line and then slashing down the lane through all the giants and vaporizing them with a layup. The court was raining basketballs.

Without saying a word to the other mauve shirts or even looking at them, Jojo began practicing short jumpers. One clanged off the front of the rim. Jojo leapt up, took the rebound from below the level of the rim, kept ascending, and dunked it, stuffed it, all in a single fluid motion. He had just landed on his feet when he happened to look over and see . . . Coach . . . over there in the shadows . . . same place he had taken him aside . . . arm around a big man in a yellow practice shirt. Congers, of course.

The court was Jojo's refuge from all that was impure. There were rules, there were lines, and they couldn't be moved, twisted, cajoled, or flattered.

He had never before felt suspicious or cynical here on the holy golden stage. But at this moment he *just knew* what Coach was saying to his freshman phenom: "Look, Vernon, I can't humiliate old Jojo by not letting him start in the first game of his last season here, especially since it's at home. But don't worry, you'll be on the bench in name only. I've had you playing with the other starters for two weeks now, right? You already fit in better with them after two weeks than old Jojo does after two years. You're gonna get so many minutes, the only player who's gonna maybe get more is the Tower. And next year—hey, it's *all* yours. So don't worry about Jojo. You have to be gentle with a faithful old horse."

Jojo was standing stock-still on the golden stage holding the ball with both hands, the blond mesa atop his noggin a-dazzle in the LumeNex lights, when the word he was looking for came to him: *manipulated.*

16. THE SUBLIME

TATIC:::::::::: STATIC::::::::: STATIC::::::::: STATIC
::::::::: STATIC::::::::: STATIC::::::::: STATIC:::::::::
STATIC::::::::: STATIC::::::::: STATIC::::::::: STATIC
::::::::: STATIC::::::::: STATIC::::::::: STATIC:::::::::
STATIC:::::::::: STATIC choked the Buster Bowl, choked it here on the
LumeNex-floodlit polyurethaned blond wood floor of the court, choked it
up up on and up the cliffs of seats, choked it all the way to the dome—
choked it—but Jojo could hear every word the black giant, Jamal Perkins,
said as Perkins and his 250 or so pounds bellied him from behind.

"Yo, Token—yo' white ass better hope the man don't th'ow it to *you*,
'cause yo' token white ass gon' *fuck up*, Token! Yo' fucking fingers made a
china, and you shaking like a fucking cup, Token—"

So Jojo backed his own 250 pounds even harder into Perkins's midsection, all the while watching the orange ball, which was now the center of the
world, as Dashorn, the point guard, was dribbling it way out beyond the
three-point line, looking for an opening in the Cincinnati defense . . . and
the crowd, the full fourteen thousand, sold-out, was roaring, but Jojo no
longer heard it as a human sound. The roars ricocheted off the cliff until
they somehow fused and became sheer :::::::::STATIC::::::::: in Jojo's

ears, and the ::::::::::STATIC::::::::::: enveloped Jojo and the other nine players on the court and shut out everything else in the world—George III, resentful professors, smart but weak tutors, Sleeping Beauties who wouldn't give him the time of day, brothers barreling down the track to parent-approved success as lawyers and investment bankers ::::::::::STA-TIC:::::::::: Only when enveloped by the :::::::::STATIC did Jojo feel *alive* and *in his realm* and *fulfilled* in the :::::::::STATIC:::::::::: of battle, where the boundaries are clearly the boundaries and the rules are clearly the rules and the tally of battle is up on an electric board and is clearly the tally and smart mouths and the insidious strategies of weaklings mean nothing. Jojo's greatest dread was the sound of the horn, *the horn*, whose bray would signal a time-out, a substitution, the end of a quarter—and the play would stop, the static would turn back into human voices, and *just like that* he, Jojo the Athlete, would be back in the world where small people with shrewd purposes would once again have the power to humiliate him.

Still out there beyond the three-point line . . . bounced the orange ball. Dashorn passed it to André, who bent at the waist, holding the ball low with both hands about knee level, swinging it to this side and that, looking for a way to fake his man out and drive around him—gave up and passed it back to Dashorn, while Jamal Perkins was trying to get inside Jojo's head.

"Wuz all 'at wiggling yo' token white ass, Token? The *bitch* coming out? Hunnh?—the *bitch* coming out, Token? Four at home and five on the road— shit, you ain't gonna last five minutes in *this* game. This game rightcheer, right now! Old Buster gon' yank yo' white ass and put in Congers! Oh yeah, yank yo' flat-footed white ass and put *Congers*—"

Jojo was stunned. How did a Cincinnati player like Jamal Perkins know about his Vernon Congers problem? And if *he* knew, then the rest of the Cincinnati squad knew it, and if they knew it, then every team on the schedule knew it—

—and Jamal Perkins had now *done* it. He had gotten inside his head. He was messing up his mind . . . and now *all* the trash he'd been talking began to sting. Not that Perkins was some unknown black monster from the deep. Jojo played against him last year—played against him in the AAU leagues and at the shoe-company camps before that—but now this big bastard had gotten inside his head, and he couldn't remove him—which meant that now he couldn't let the bastard get away with talking about the *bitch* coming out, could he, since that was exactly the same as calling him a faggot, wasn't it, a *faggot*, and—that *bastard!*—you couldn't just *take* shit like that, could you.

Jojo blurted back over his shoulder in desperation, "Yeah, and outcho momma's ass, too, Jay*maulll*. Why she be calling you Jay*maullllll*? Yo' daddy a fucking Ay-rab? Or you even *know*, Jay*maulll*? Where yo' daddy at Jay*maulll*, out butt-fucking camels—Jay*maullll*?"

Jamal Perkins went silent, as if his breath had been knocked out ::::::::::: STATIC:::::::::::STATIC::::::::::: then a seething whisper: "Just keep on talking, you gray motherfucker. You got ass-rape on your fucking mind? We gon' *see* who's gonna get fucking ass-raped!" He dug the heel of his left hand into Jojo's left kidney.

A trill of delight! The black giant had wedged his way into Jojo's head, but now Jojo was inside of Jay*maulll*'s head, way inside, and that dumb fuck was never—but how did he know about *Congers?*

At that moment, Dashorn, dribbling with his right hand out beyond the three-point line, looked at Jojo and put his left hand up in the air. Then he turned his head toward André Walker, also out beyond the line, stopped dribbling, and held the ball in both hands. They had practiced this so often that Jojo didn't even have to think about it in any sequential way. He thrust himself back harder into Jamal Perkins's midsection in order to have the big man back on his heels when the ball came.

Dashorn faked a pass to André and, without looking, threw the ball inside to Jojo. The orange core of the world—Jojo had it in his hands in the :::::::::::STATIC::::::::::: of fourteen thousand cheering souls. Jojo's part was to pivot away, jump as if he were about to try a short jump shot, and instead pass off to André, who would come driving straight down the lane toward the basket—or to Treyshawn, who was to muscle his way around his man and drive toward the basket from over along the baseline.

Jojo jumped—both hands on the ball, Jamal Perkins up with him on top of him—André not in the lane—pick hadn't worked?—Treyshawn ramming his way to the basket, his man all over him but a fighting chance, Jojo lowers his arm to dish off to Treyshawn—now!—*whack*, Perkins chops Jojo's forearm, the ball pops out at a crazy angle, Jojo lands off balance on his back looking up at the LumeNex lights in the :::::::::::STATIC::::::::::: melee over the ball :::::::::::STATIC::::::::::: Perkins bulls his way in *got it* dismayed :::::::::::STATIC::::::::::: beaten! :::::::::::STATIC::::::::::: Jojo rolls over :::::::::::STATIC::::::::::: striped shirt referee's over him blowing his whistle swinging his arms in a scissor fashion to halt play ::::::::::STA-TIC:::::::::: calls a foul on Perkins. Jojo will shoot two.

STATIC:::::::::: dies down . . . He'd won . . . He'd gotten inside the big fuck's head and provoked him into a blatant foul . . . He wanted some way to announce it to the crowd . . . give them the whole trash-talking dialogue . . . explain how he obliterated the big fuck's delusion of domination . . . said unspeakable things to him . . . *out-niggered* him! . . . Yo! And you think it was just two big men fighting over a ball!

As he approached the free-throw line, a girl's voice shrieked, "Go go, Jojo!" A swell of cheers from all the cliffsides . . . Jojo tried to pick her out . . . The cry came from . . . over there . . . near the floor . . . but no luck, even though he could pick out individual faces now—

He'd never been calmer at the free-throw line in his life. He'd already won—if only everybody could know the truth of it. The others were lining up on either side of the lane. Treyshawn was giving him a big, goofy grin from down near the basket . . . In a falsetto voice: "Go go, Jojo!" Falsetto . . . Treyshawn knew how he'd won . . . Jojo could *feel* this confirmation by Treyshawn The Man . . . *feel* it, even though he wouldn't have dared explain it out loud to a living soul.

He sank the first shot *just like that*, without thinking about it. The noise of the crowd swelled . . . André walked up the lane toward him . . . Jojo met him, and they touched fists in the congratulatory way—

"Twenty-four! Twenty-four!" A girl's voice, again from courtside. A couple of beats before Jojo realized that was *his* number . . . He stared at the first courtside section of seats . . . You couldn't miss her . . . standing, beaming, red faced, miles of blond hair . . . Some sort of white thing . . . cardboard? . . . began to rise up in front of her until it covered her face . . . a poster with amateurish, inelegant, big, thick, unmistakable hand lettering: 24! I'LL BE YOUR WHORE! Great whoops from the other side of the arena, from those who could see it. The poster began to descend, and when it reached the floor of the stands—*poof!*—the girl was gone. More whoops, laughter, and mock but lusty cheers. A ribald buzz rose in the Buster Bowl, and heads were craning this way and that. 24! I'LL BE YOUR WHORE!

That warrior, Number 24, returned to the free-throw line, and the referee tossed the ten-inch orange core of the world to him. Jojo had never felt looser at the free-throw line than he did right now. The buzz had scarcely abated. The Buster Bowl moaned from the girl's salacious proffer.

Jojo bounced the ball four times, held it in a crouch, then rose to almost his full height before releasing it. The Buster Bowl went dead silent as the ball reached the apogee of its arc toward the basket . . . *Whisk* . . . It *snapped* the strings of the net, so clean was the trajectory and so steep the descent.

A roar—immediately rose to STATIC::::::::::: of stupendous intensity. It hummed in Jojo's very hide as he ran down to the Cincinnati end to play defense. He had to fight off the desire to smile for the crowd's benefit. As he passed the Dupont bench, in peripheral vision he could see Coach on his feet. Buster Roth in the tan gabardine suit, the shirt and tie he wore for games. The shirts were always white, custom-made, with some kind of go-to-hell high roll in the collar, and he always wore a Dupont tie, Dupont mauve with a print of golden basketballs emblazoned with small mauve versions of the Dupont D. Coach had his own unsmiling, clench-jawed look of triumph on his face and was leaning forward toward Jojo and yelling something to him. Whatever it was, Jojo wished he could hear it. His first name wouldn't be Fucking. Coach never used Fuck Patois in approval or triumph.

Over his shoulder he could see Perkins, whom he'd be guarding, coming up behind him . . . Not a good idea . . . asking for it . . . but he couldn't resist. As Jojo turned about to take up a defensive posture and play his man, he gave Perkins a sneer and a single dismissive wave of his hand. Perkins just stared at him with his lips slightly parted. No expression . . . Oh, Jojo had gotten inside the dumb fuck's head, all right, *deep* inside . . . Jay-*maulllll*, him and his "white ass" and "Token" and "bitch" . . . Jojo had *invaded* the dumb fuck's head and caused him to *lose it*, commit a foul so flagrant no referee in the world could have missed it.

Perkins played inside, the same way Jojo did, and Jojo took up his position between Perkins and the basket while the Cincinnati point guard, a black guy, American but named Winston Abdulla, not much over six feet but with prodigiously large hands—everybody who played against him talked about his hands—Abdulla dribbled about, looking for a way to get something going. Jojo immediately bellied into Perkins's back to reestablish dominance, get deeper inside the big fuck's shaved head. Perkins's delts and lats were so big, his upper back looked a mile wide through the shoulders and tapered down sharply to a narrow waist.

Jojo started in immediately. "Yo, Jay*maulllll* . . . What happened, Jay-*maullll*? You jes' plain-long fucking *lost it*'s what happened . . . Nome sayin', Bluhhhhhd? . . . The white man gitchoo all choked, Bluhhhhhhd?"—and on in that vein.

Perkins said nothing—*nothing*. He, Jojo, had crowbarred his way inside the giant's head, and the bullshit had hemorrhaged out of his fucking brain. Now Perkins was leaning back into him very hard, and Jojo began pushing back with both hands. The referees would allow that much as the big men went sumo to sumo inside. Winston passed to Cincinnati's great shooting guard, a willowy black guy named McAughton. Both Dashorn and Curtis moved in on him. Curtis covered him, and then Dashorn moved in from the side and almost knocked the ball out of his hands. Totally hemmed in, McAughton made a desperate bounce pass inside to Perkins. Jojo was all over him. Perkins held the ball up over his head out of Jojo's reach and seemed to be looking about to feed the other guard who was a step ahead of Curtis and cutting inside. Perkins brought the ball down and bent way over, as if to tuck it in his midsection—pushed off one foot, dribbled once, took two steps, wheeled about, and leaped as high as Jojo had ever seen anybody leap on a basketball court. Jojo jumped to block him. The next instant stuck in his mind like a photograph: the orange center of the world and Perkins's black arm in a corona of LumeNex light at an apogee a full foot above Jojo's own hopeless fingertips. Perkins rammed home a seemingly effortless dunk. He sailed over ::::::::::STATIC::::::::::STATIC:::::::::: the second tallest Dupont player on the floor and made it look easy.

How could it have happened? As Jojo ran back down the court, defeat registered with a pain real enough to be tactile ::::::::::STATIC:::::::::: STATIC::::::::::STATIC:::::::::: didn't want to so much as glance at Coach as he passed the bench, but his peripheral vision betrayed him. Buster Roth had his hands cupped around his mouth like a megaphone. He was leaning forward, a contorted figure emerging from the atomic fog of the ::::::::::STATIC:::::::::::

When Jojo got down near the basket to take up his position, Perkins was waiting for him, staring . . . but not saying a word. Instead, he had his tongue stuck in the big pocket of flesh between his gums and his lower lip. It created a bulge above his chin and a wholly mechanical smile in which his eyes weren't involved at all. Perkins had a pair of mean-looking eyes. He nodded up and down ever so slightly, as if to say, "Yes, white boy, that's how it's going to be. Get used to it."

Jojo felt fear. He wondered if Perkins could smell it. Jamal Perkins was not only big, he was quick and a plyometric marvel on top of that ::::::::::STATIC ::::::::::STATIC::::::::::

Perkins didn't say anything. This Jojo took as a bad sign. It was abnormal. Jojo backed into him, and Perkins shoved back, always with the heels of both hands over Jojo's kidneys. Not that it hurt particularly, but there was something . . . sinister . . . about it, something calculating . . . Out on the three-point line's semicircle, Dashorn and Curtis and André were shuttling the ball back and forth and trying picks that didn't work and getting generally frustrated by the Cincinnati defense. The shot clock was running down. Finally André faked a three-point jumper that was in fact a soft, looping feed to Treyshawn. Cincinnati's big Serb, Javelosgvik, was all over him. He was so aggressive and had such long arms that Treyshawn had to try a fadeaway with a high arc from ten feet out. It clanged on the cantilever that attached the basket to the backboard and bounced. Jojo and Perkins went up for the rebound ::::::::::::STATIC::::::::::::::STATIC::::::::::::: The ball took a lazy bounce almost straight up, and both men came back to the floor . . . had to jump again. Perkins shoved Jojo sideways with his forearm and beat him easily on the second jump, but the ball took a second clanging bounce on the rim and Perkins was already descending, heading back to the floor again as Jojo regained his footing and jumped up and seized the ball above the level of the rim and came down with it and, hemmed in by Cincinnati uniforms, fed it out to André, who immediately threw it back inside to him.

Perkins was all over Jojo's back. He growled out a single sentence: "Jes' give it up, bitch."

Jojo saw red—a red mist before his eyes. The Congers move popped into his head. He drew the ball in close to his chest and glanced back to gauge where Perkins's solar plexus was . . . *yes* . . . pivoted to his left and brought the ball up as if about to attempt a jumper—took his right hand off the ball, swung back to the right, and drove his elbow into Perkins's midsection immediately below the sternum with all his might—

Oooooofff!

—*hit home!*—swung around Perkins with a bounce and three strides and soared to *stuff* the ball—can't believe it! A black arm is already there, blocking the ball, which spins off his fingers. Jojo comes down off balance, stumbling away from the ball—the Serb has it, flailing his elbows back and forth and then shuttling it off to the point guard, McAughton—

What just happened couldn't have happened! He'd given Perkins a whack right in the solar plexus—and Perkins takes it and is somehow . . . *there* . . . to block an easy stuffer that was as good as *made*—

McAughton is already racing toward the Dupont basket on a fast break, feeds his shooting guard with a pass across court. Only an incredible leap by

André Walker deflecting the feed back to McAughton averts another conversion. Jojo lets out his breath and convinces himself: at least he couldn't be blamed.

The next—what?—minute, minutes?—went by in a delirium. He managed to get downcourt in time to intercept Perkins, but the next thing he knew, Perkins was feinting this way and that until he had Jojo flat-footed, and he drove to the basket along the baseline. With a lunge and a leap Jojo managed to get his hand up at least six inches above the rim as Perkins took off. But Perkins hurtled under the basket and did a twisting fall-away layup from the other side.

Jojo couldn't keep track of the sequences, but the same show was on, over and over. Perkins has Jojo so bottled up on offense that Dashorn, Curtis, and André give up going inside to him and seek out Treyshawn. Guarding Perkins—it isn't *guarding*. It's humiliation after humiliation. Explosions of quickness and power—and Perkins goes around him, over him, under him—three more baskets that seem to occur with such suddenness that Jojo—Jojo—Jojo—

And then the dreaded horn sounded. No longer inside the STATIC pearl . . . back into the world, where all was politics, judgment, and abrasion. The dreaded *horn* had sounded! The noise had not really died down all that much, but now the crowd was no longer dematerialized in an atomic fog. Jojo could see individual faces, even though he went to some pains not to look into them. He was conscious of the Cottontop Box at midcourt, the Pineapple Grove.

"Yo! Jojo!" A young voice from a section of the stands above the rich old people. "Which way'd he go? You're money, Jojo! Maybe a nickel!" Followed by a round of laughter.

Against his better judgment, Jojo looked up. There, in an aisle, was a clump of four guys—students by the looks of them—staring at him with smirks and crooked, slightly wary grins, waiting for him to respond.

Jojo looked away and headed on toward the bench. Only then did he look up at the scoreboard. He knew they were behind, but he didn't know it was that bad: 12–2. Jamal Perkins had scored eight of Cincinnati's twelve—all of them in man-to-man duels with Jojo Johanssen . . . the white boy . . .

He could already *hear* what awaited him at the bench. Coach was into full Fuck Patois. He wasn't even going to let the starters sit down . . . Fucking this and fucking that. He was letting Dashorn, Treyshawn, Curtis, and André have it . . . Even Treyshawn . . .

Just like that, the band, always installed throughout the game in the first eight rows of the stands at one corner of the court, broke out in a blast of brass and drums . . . the theme song from *Rocky* rendered in an insane arrangement . . . a convulsion of jazzy optimism. Lines of cheerleaders in clinging sleeveless V-necked mauve jerseys and pleated yellow miniskirts lined both sides of the court, wagging their fannies, making the music seem even fluffier. They were on the court before Jojo could even return to the bench. Where did they come from? It was as if they had flown down from the upper reaches of the Buster Bowl dome. Scampering right by Jojo came the dancers, the Charlies' Angels (Chazzies), in golden Lycra tights, cut almost as low as the top of the cleft in the rear declivity. The swath of flesh between their golden Lycra athletic bras and the low-cut golden tights was a twenty-first-century Venus bellyscape of winking navels and high-definition abdominals. Many was the time Jojo had found it arousing—this juxtaposition of the sharpness of the taut, ripped, shredded abdominals . . . and the soft, mysterious swells . . . But lust was completely foreign to him at this moment. *Just like that*, the dancers hurled themselves into modern dance choreography that turned the theme music from the movie *Rocky*, an anthem of martial determination, into a belly or, rather, abdominals, dance. At every corner of the court were acrobats and tumblers and gymnasts. Young men—with arms of steel, and mauve-and-yellow striped tights that clung to immensely muscular upper thighs—worked in pairs, launching lovely little cupcake gymnasts into the air above them, where the little lovelies did somersaults, half gainers, and back flips with yawning twists before they fell back into the young men's arms. The band, the cheerleaders, the dancers, the acrobats—an instant circus covering the court!—and this was nothing more than a time-out! The band exploded with giddily merry music, not stirring but . . . *giddy*, inexplicably joyous, aimlessly ecstatic. And hadn't the players, these giant men on campus, taken note of this hardwood platter of lithe and crazy little cupcakes? Oh yes, they had. To be sure. Some had gone through them serially. By now it seemed like a natural reward for the eminent warrior. Jojo had had his flings like the rest. It meant about as much as a nice cold beer . . . having a romp with one of these little cupcakes who bucked and humped and swiveled and swagged and worked so hard, shaking their bottoms from cliff to cliff.

The pandemonium was such that as Jojo neared the bench, he could no longer hear Coach raging in Fuck Patois. But it wasn't something that required hearing. Seeing it was quite enough . . . the way his upper teeth overbit his lower lip in order to spit out a *fucking* at maximum strength. All was uproar, and the band was playing "Love for Sale" at a tickled-pink tempo that longed for a drum major and six majorettes.

Out of the corner of his eye Jojo saw Dashorn and Treyshawn bending over at the waist to hear Coach better and, presumably, more privately, and Curtis and André were just joining them. Obviously Coach was gathering the five of them, as usual, for instructions before they returned to the court. He steeled himself. He knew he himself would get an earful, no doubt. He took a deep breath, joined the huddle—*Congers*—a visceral chill before his mind could fasten upon the logic—

Owing to Treyshawn's huge bulk, Jojo hadn't realized until this instant that sandwiched in between Treyshawn and Coach was Vernon Congers. He had bent over, his hands on his knees, like the rest of them . . . to get *the word* before play resumed. Jojo started to do likewise—but the logic kicked in, and he remained erect, his shoulders slumped and his lips parted.

Coach looked up at him with an expression that seemed to say, "Oh, hi, I didn't expect to see you here." To make it worse, his voice was kindly . . .

"Jojo, I want you to take a break." He motioned in a vague direction with his head . . . in a vague direction . . . but not so vague that Dashorn, Treyshawn, André, Curtis, and least of all Vernon Congers could fail to realize that it was toward the bench.

All except Coach turned their faces away from him, and Jojo looked away from them. Desperate to fix upon *something*, *anything*, his eyes found the scoreboard. Four minutes and forty seconds of the first quarter had elapsed.

It was as Jamal Perkins had predicted. His tenure as a starter for Dupont had lasted less than five minutes of the first game of the season—the season that would make or put an end to his career as an athlete, which is to say, the only career open, the only role imaginable, to Jojo Johanssen in this world.

He became acutely conscious of the band. Now the trumpets, the trombones, the clarinets, the French horns, the mighty drums, were playing "He Ain't Heavy, He's My Brother" with the unremittingly bubbly beat of "On the Sunny Side of the Street."

Two students who could care less about what was happening in the Buster Bowl were walking along in the rusky, dusky Monday night quiet of Ladding Walk. The Walk's ornamental streetlamps—feeble, all too feeble—cast the old buildings and trees on either side into grotesque shadow. One could *feel* it, the presence of so many architectural and arboreal hulks, stone-dead, dead still, in the dark.

"It does weird you out a little," said Adam, hoping to sound nonchalant. "Come to think of it, I don't even remember being on Ladding Walk at night before. But I also don't remember anything ever *happening* on Ladding Walk at night . . . or in the daytime, for that matter. Whatta you think there is to be scared of?"

"I'm not talking about . . . scared exactly," said Charlotte. "I just didn't want to walk all the way over here in the dark by myself . . . and then all the way to the end down there?"

Far ahead, the two edges of the Walk appeared to converge in total darkness, with only glimmering globes of light to mark the way.

"It's spooky, is what I mean," Charlotte was saying. "I was here one night with Mimi and Bettina. I don't remember why, I just remember how spooky it was . . . All right, I'm a plain-long scaredy cat! I'll admit it. I'm being silly— but I really do 'preciate you doing this."

She gave him a smile that made him want to throw his arms around her, lift her off the ground—*pop*. He just kept on walking. He was glad the light was too weak for her to see him blush. He felt noble; and more than noble, brave, or mildly so; and more than noble and brave, admired by the girl who was the answer to his prayers and, more than that, his virginity. It dawned on him that he had never seen her wearing jeans before. He motioned toward them. "Those new?"

"Sort of," said Charlotte. "Not exactly."

"Now, tell me again why you're going to the Saint Ray house?" said Adam. "To thank this guy who did *what* for you?"

As they walked along, Charlotte told him a rather long and involved story about this guy who had saved her from a terribly drunk and menacing lacrosse player. Why a girl like her would even go near a tailgate never became clear. Tailgates were idiotic Saturday afternoon blackout parties for cretins whose idea of a fulfilling weekend was to drink until they passed out Saturday night and then tell war stories about it on Sunday and Monday. He couldn't imagine a freshman, least of all a lovely little flower like Charlotte— who wouldn't even touch a beer—going near a tailgate.

"So this guy saves you from a drunk lacrosse player, and he doesn't even know your name?"

"He didn't then," said Charlotte. "I guess he does now."

She proceeded to tell him a rather boring story about how she and Mimi and Bettina had fled from the tailgate and how she felt bad because she hadn't thanked her savior. Adam tuned out at that point, and she rambled on. The gist of it seemed to be that she would feel remiss if she didn't thank him.

Adam said, "If he didn't know your name, how did you find out *his* name? How did you know how to get in touch with him?"

"I heard somebody call him Hoyt," said Charlotte. "That's kind of an unusual name, I guess, and when I told my roommate, she said her sister, who's a senior, knew a senior named Hoyt? Hoyt Thorpe?"

Adam stopped and just stood there in the middle of Ladding Walk and stared at Charlotte with his hands on his hips and his jaws agape.

"You're *kidding.*"

"You know him?"

"I've *met* him. You . . . are . . . *kidding* me! And now he's slugged *Mac Bolka*? Ohmygod, talk about insane—I cannot . . . believe this!"

"Believe what?"

"I've been trying to do a story on Hoyt Thorpe! Do you know about him and the Night of the Skull Fuck?"

"Well—Beverly told me something about it . . ."

"I want to do a whole takeout on it . . . everything, beginning to end. I mean, this involves a guy who could become President of the United States."

Feeble as the light was, he thought he could see Charlotte's eyes grow larger. Such a rapt look. She beheld him in dawning admiration, brighter, brighter, brighter, until the . . . glow on her face had become an aura, unmistakable even here in the gloom of Ladding Walk . . . and now maybe he could do it. Maybe it would be all right to try it. Not enfold her in his arms—well, no, but maybe put his arm around her waist? He tried to picture it. What the hell would that be, or supposed to be, about? He felt so amateurish . . . a pathetic virgin . . .

What could only be the Saint Ray house was just ahead. It was the only building alive on the entire Walk. Brass lanterns by the front door . . . lights in the upper windows, presumably bedrooms . . . all quiet and serene compared to the random Saturday nights he had gone to open-house fraternity parties . . . a thought that triggered a sinking feeling. He had had a uniformly miserable time at frat parties . . . all the hearty Big Man bellowing that went on . . . but then rational judgment, albeit wounded, returned.

Adam stopped again. They were barely twenty-five yards from the Saint Ray house front lawn. "Hey, I just got a great idea, Charlotte." His face had lit up with the excited smile that often comes with the *Aha!* phenomenon. "Why don't I go in there with you? You want to thank Thorpe, and I want to talk to him!"

Charlotte looked startled. For a moment she bit her upper lip with her lower teeth. "I . . . don't think that would be a good idea . . . I don't want him to think I came over to thank him just so a friend of mine could get a story for the *Wave*—you know?"

"All right," said Adam. "I won't try to interview him. I won't do that until some other time when he's not even going to think about any such connection. But in the meantime he would see me in a like . . . you know, personal light. When I finally *do* ask him for an interview, like down the line, he won't see me as just some—" He started to say "nerd," but caught himself. He didn't want her to know that frat boys or jocks or anybody else thought that way about people who worked for the *Wave*. "—just some guy from out of nowhere who wants to ask him some questions about the Night of the Skull whatever." He wasn't entirely sure why, but he decided he should lay off the word "Fuck" while he was asking her for a favor.

"Golly, I don't know . . ."

"It'll seem completely natural, Charlotte! I'm some guy who just happened to walk you over here in the dark." He turned his palms up and arched his eyebrows, as if to say, "What is there to object to?"

Charlotte grimaced and shook her head but didn't seem to be able to put her concern into words. "I can—that may be—I know what you're saying?—and I really am grateful?—but you said—when you write your story you said yourself this could be a really *big* story?—and what if he's upset? I mean, I already feel so guilty because I haven't thanked him up to now, and this is two days later?"

"But he *loves* to talk about it! He's *proud* of it!" Adam could feel his *Aha!* smile morphing into the excited beseeching of a beggar, but he couldn't do anything about it. The emotion was too real. "I know that for a fact! One of his fraternity brothers told me. He loves to sit around and talk about it. The other guy, Vance something, he's the one who doesn't want to talk about it."

Quietly: "Now you're making me feel guilty over *you.*"

"It's really not a big deal, Charlotte. It'll be so . . . easy!"

"I know," said Charlotte. "It's not *that*. It's just . . . I just want to thank him, and then—you know—like I just want to get it *done*? And leave . . . with no complications? Besides, if he likes to talk about it, why don't you just call him up and ask him?"

"I told you. I did. But he doesn't know who I am. I'm sure he'll talk to someone he feels comfortable with."

"I'm sorry, Adam." It was almost a whisper, and she averted her eyes when she said it. "I just want to get this done, and that'll be it." Then she looked up into his eyes and brought her raised face up to his with great earnestness and said, "Oh, Adam, I really am so grateful to you. You're *so* wonderful."

With that, she drew closer and put her hands on his shoulders and brought her face up to his and her lips toward his lips—and detoured at the last instant to his cheek, upon which she planted a kiss.

"Oh, Adam," she said again, "thank you. Thank you for doing this for me. When I get back, I'll call you. Okay?"

Now she was turning away to head to the door of the Saint Ray house. *A kiss on the cheek?* But then she looked back with the sort of smile that *tells you so much.* She seemed on the verge of tears . . . that would flow from the eyes of love . . . Tears . . . Tears of joy? But what exactly *were* tears of joy?

Tears for the protector? He had quite an interesting theory he was developing about how all tears, at bottom, have to do with protection. We cry at birth because we come naked into this world and we *need* protection. We cry for those we love who were desperate for protection and *didn't get it in time.* We cry with gratitude for those historic souls who *have protected* us at critical moments, with great risk to themselves. We cry for those who are voluntarily heading off into the valley of the shadow of death in order to protect us and who *will need protection* themselves as they do so. We cry for those who needed protection so very much and, with it or without it, have fought the good fight against great odds. *All* tears had to do with protection. *No* tears have to do with anything else.

The whole theory had matured nicely in these few minutes—moments?—in the dark on Ladding Walk. Could bliss come any better than this? . . . afloat in one of the loveliest and most prestigious university settings in the world, gazing down upon old bricks laid in a herringbone-and-diamond pattern created by the sorts of masons who no longer exist in our world, buoyant on the verge of two triumphs . . . conquests of the heart and of the head . . . a second major contribution-in-embryo to psychology— was there any greater happiness? Yes! The sublime was called Charlotte Simmons.

17. THE CONSCIOUS LITTLE ROCK

harlotte stood alone in the cavernous entry gallery of the Saint Ray house, waiting. Over there was the staircase with its massive, majestically carved and curved railing. The lumpy coats of paint made this triumph of American woodworking seem even shabbier tonight than it had in the dim light of the frat party.

The odd-looking guy who had let her in—his ferocious pair of eyebrows had grown together above his nose, and his hips were wider than his shoulders—had gone off to fetch Hoyt. The guy's uncool, un–Saint Ray appearance triggered a vaguely unpleasant recollection she couldn't pin down. So did the odor of the place—full-bodied, putrid, with a thin sweetness running through it, like a wooden floor rotting because of leaking radiators. It had in fact been marinating for many years in spilled beer.

A mere transient sensation. Mainly she was feeling guilty about the way she had treated Adam . . . and awed by the prospect of seeing Hoyt . . . Why hadn't she told him the truth about the jeans? Maybe because she didn't even want *herself* to know what she had done this morning . . . gone to Ellison, the high-end clothing store, and bought a pair of Diesels. *Eighty dollars!*—and she'd had only $320 left for the entire semester. Now she was down to less than half of her entire allowance—all so she could go "thank"

Hoyt Thorpe! Why hadn't she at least given Adam a decent kiss on the lips, a mercy kiss—the way Beverly bestowed her mercy fucks, or so she claimed—instead of that pathetic little vesper-service peck on the cheek? Why hadn't she let him come inside to meet Hoyt? Hoyt!—a grown man, not a boy! She kept trying to figure out what it meant—beat up the governor of California's bodyguards when they attacked him—what had Beverly called it—the night of the . . . some kind of fuck? . . . and then utter bewilderment. The governor of California . . . She could see his florid face and thick white hair as she watched him on television last spring—the Dupont commencement address . . . which had given her strength, renewed her courage after Channing's raid on her house after commencement . . . out in the *Grove*, did Adam say? Adam—

Worse guilt. Now she knew exactly why she wouldn't let Adam come in. Hoyt would see her in the company of a *dork*—Adam!—who was merely trying to bring her into what she had dreamed of, a cénacle, as Balzac had called it, a circle of intellects equipped and ready to live the life of the mind to the fullest . . . and here she was in the . . . First Circle of Hell, the entry gallery of the Saint Ray house.

Somewhere beyond the entry gallery, frat-boy voices exploded with laughs and mock cheers and then calmed down. Evidently some sort of game was in progress. Somewhere else, perhaps upstairs, somebody was playing a rap song with a snare-brush drumbeat and a saxophone in the background.

Hoyt appeared. He came toward her, limping. He had a bandage plastered down one side of his jaw almost to his chin. His eye on that side was black and puffy. There were stitches above the eye that closed what must have been a gash. His nose and his lower lip were swollen.

As he limped closer, he appeared quizzical, as if he had no idea who she was. But when he reached her, he smiled and said, "I must look great," and started a laugh—abruptly halting it with a wince that squeezed his eyes shut. When he opened them again, he was smiling warmly and blinking, and tears showed up in the corners of his eyes. He pointed to the side of his rib cage. "Sorta fucked up."

So moved was she by the dreadful wounds, the awful beating he had taken for her sake, that she barely noticed the incidental bit of Fuck Patois.

He cocked his head, looked into her eyes with the smile of one who has lived . . . and said, "So you're . . . Charlotte. At least I know your name now.

If you wanna know the truth, I never thought I'd see you back in this house again."

"Me neither." Her voice was hoarse all of a sudden.

"I never even got to ask you why you ran away."

Charlotte could feel her face turning red. "I didn't. I—they *pulled* me." She almost swallowed the words, she felt so ashamed.

Hoyt started to laugh, then winced with pain again. "Don't make me do that," he said. "It didn't look to me like anybody was pulling you. By the time you got to that door, you were practically knocking the door down. You were sprinting, is what you were doing." Confident smile: "Like what did you think I was?"

It dawned on her that he wasn't talking about the tailgate but the night of "We've got this room." She had no idea what to say. Her face was ablaze with embarrassment.

Hoyt delivered a philosophical-sounding sigh. "H'it don' matter none. That was then."

H'it don' matter none? Was he mocking her accent? She didn't know what to say to that, either. So she just blurted out, "I came to thank you. I'm so sorry about what happened to you. I feel like it was my fault." She lifted her hand as if to raise it and caress the battered side of his face, but then she withdrew it. The sight touched her all over again. He had gone through all that for *her.* "I wasn't even there when it was over. I feel so bad about that, too. I just had to come . . . thank you."

"It wasn't—" He abandoned that sentence and paused—for an eternity, it seemed to her. Finally: "You don't have to thank me. I did it because I wanted to. I wanted to *kill* that asshole."

"I hope somebody told you I called yesterday? All they said was that you couldn't come to the phone. They didn't tell me about . . . any of this."

"Well, it could've been worse. I twisted my knee, but it's not too bad."

"I'm so sorry. I really am. And I'm so grateful."

"Hey!" said Hoyt. His face brightened. "Come meet a couple of the guys."

Another yawp of laughter, convulsive this time, and mock-cheering. Charlotte looked up at Hoyt quizzically.

"That's just a bunch of guys playing Beirut."

"Beirut?"

With great relish he described the game and the Pantagruelian beer-drinking it involved. "We can go watch if you want to, but first come meet a few guys."

Limping, Hoyt led her toward a room that opened off the entry gallery. As they neared it, she could see flares of TV colors within, followed by a collective groan and some guy saying, "Ho-lee shit! Mo-ther-fucker-er!" As they reached the doorway, Hoyt put an arm around her shoulder. Charlotte considered that a bit forward, but she was immediately distracted by the sight of six, eight—how many?—guys sprawled on the leather furniture, their faces blanched by a flare of white from a football jersey that filled the screen of a TV set on the wall.

"Gentlemen!" said Hoyt in an arch way, as if to admonish them to clean up their language, "I want you to say hello to, uh, uhh, uhhh, my friend"— he gave her a quick glance, as if to remind himself who she was—"uh, Charlotte."

Ironic applause and attaboys. They were all staring at her with big grins on their faces. Charlotte knew she must have looked bewildered, because a guy in khakis and a white T-shirt that showed off his muscles said to her in a kind way, "We're laughing at Hoyt. He has trouble remembering names."

More laughter.

"Come on, you guys," said Hoyt. "Charlotte doesn't want to see a bunch of assholes give a brother shit."

Groans and laughter.

Charlotte felt Hoyt give her shoulders a squeeze. It all came back . . . his constant *touching* that night, but she had too many conflicting emotions to make an issue of it. She also felt she was at the center of a stage.

"Just pretend they're gentlemen," said Hoyt. "Charlotte, this is Vance."

"Hi," said a slim, handsome guy with an open, friendly face and tousled blond hair, sitting on the arm of a fat leather-upholstered easy chair, his arms around his knees.

"I think we met," said Charlotte. Her voice seemed so tiny. Oh, she wasn't likely to forget *his* face. He was the one Hoyt had chased off that night because *We've got this room.*

"Oh, yeahhh," said Vance, obviously not remembering at all.

"And this is Julian . . ." Hoyt took his arm off Charlotte's shoulders—to her considerable relief . . . she didn't want to be presented to this room full of boys as *his*—and introduced her to them all, one by one. In fact, they did prove to be gentlemanly . . . hospitable, friendly . . . lots of welcoming smiles.

Vance insisted that she have his easy chair, and Hoyt eased himself into the chair next to it.

Charlotte couldn't imagine what she could possibly talk to any of them about, but it was a moot point, as it turned out. Everybody returned to watching the screen. The flaring light lit up everybody's face in colors. On the screen . . . a seemingly interminable series of collisions . . . smacks, clatters, thuds, *oooofs* . . . of football players tackling one another, ramming each other headfirst, colliding torso to torso in midair. Charlotte's pulse was rapid, but it had nothing to do with the TV screen. She was excited . . . the only girl in a room in a fraternity house with a whole bunch of cool boys. What did she look like to them? Terribly young and immature? They were all upperclassmen. Hoyt and Vance and Julian seemed a generation older than she was. Sunk this far down into an easy chair, she became terribly conscious of how tight her jeans were on her thighs. Her legs—were they really as great as she thought they were? Without moving her head, she glanced about to see if any of them were drawn irresistibly . . . to taking a look. To her disappointment, none seemed to be, not even Hoyt, who seemed to be watching TV and not watching it. He looked as if he had an appointment somewhere else.

On the TV a voice said, "Wait a minute, Jack, you're not saying teams are *instructing* players to go out there and wreck the other guys' knees—"

The roly-poly boy called Boo said, "You ever see those old-timers' introductions before the Fiesta Bowl? Guys look like they got two-by-fours for legs." He hopped off the arm of the couch and did a rocking, stiff-legged walk across the floor. "Fucking look like they just got a five-hour furlough from the rheumatoid arthritis ward."

Much laughter. Even Hoyt smiled, Charlotte noticed out of the corner of her eye. But how could they find it funny? To Charlotte, what she had just seen was sickening. It filled her with alarm and pity. What was it about boys? These boys were *rich*, rich enough to pay dues, on top of everything else, just to belong to a fraternity. They were smart. They had to be, just to get into Dupont at all. But they were no different from the boys at Alleghany High. She glanced at Hoyt—and Channing popped into her head. They were all crazed on the subject of manliness, and manly violence was the manliest thing of all. Seeing an athlete being crippled—it didn't drown them in pity, not for a moment. It *intrigued* them. They identified not with the victim but the assailant. Being here frightened her—and thrilled her. She was no longer on the outside desperately denying that she wanted to be inside. *I'm Mr. Starling's rock,* she thought to herself, *and I only think I have free will.*

She felt three pats on her knee. Without looking, she knew it was Hoyt—*three* times? She tried to translate that as affection. *Touching* her again.

Now everybody's eyes swung to the doorway. A beaming couple was peering in—a very tall, rawboned guy with a high forehead—Harrison!—and a much shorter blond girl, the cute sort, in jeans and a baggy sweatshirt.

"It's the hairy man!" said Boo. "And the Janester!"

"Hi-i," said the girl, the Janester presumably, with an up tone and a down tone. She obviously knew them all.

Harrison was so tall that when he put his arm across the girl's shoulder, it came down at an angle.

"Hoyt," said the girl, "what happened to your head?"

Hoyt, without a smile: "Comes from banging it on the floor every time you hear the same question." He still didn't smile.

Recovering from a paroxysm of laughter, Boo said, "How bummed out is Hoyt, Jane?"

While Jane was saying something to Julian, Boo began singing a ditty under his breath: "CDs are a-coming, their tails are in sight . . ." He immediately looked to Hoyt for his reaction. Hoyt just looked back at him.

For the first time, Harrison noticed Charlotte. "Yo! Hey, uh . . . uh . . ."

"Charlotte," said Hoyt. He still wasn't smiling.

"Have you noticed?" said Boo. "Hoyt has a way with names."

"Everybody knows that," said Harrison. To Charlotte: "Wuzz good?"

"I just wanted to thank Hoyt." She sounded so tiny and weak to herself.

"Thank Hoyt?" said Harrison, genuinely puzzled. Then he seemed to get it. "Oh yeah . . ."

Everybody was looking at the screen again.

Harrison said to Hoyt, "Hey, Dawg, I'd love to stay and shoot the shit and all, but we gotta bounce." He looked at Charlotte. "Nice to see you, uh, uh—"

"Charlotte," said Hoyt.

"Right, good going," said Harrison. "Later." Harrison and his little friend began climbing the shabby grand stairs.

Charlotte felt a tap on the outside of her leg, just above the knee. *Touching* her—

Alarmed, thrilled with alarm, she turned. Hoyt had withdrawn his hand but was still leaning toward her. He wasn't smiling, and he didn't have his cool, ironic gleam in his eye. If anything, he looked tired. He motioned toward the doorway with his head and stood up. So she stood up, too, and they headed out of the room. No one seemed to notice except Vance, who said to Hoyt, "Real nice, Clark."

Hoyt said, "You need to hit manual reset, Vance."

"Rock on, Clark."

Once they were back in the entry gallery, Charlotte said, "Why does he call you Clark? He said, 'Real nice, Clark.'"

"It's from some movie." Then he shrugged phlegmatically. "How about if I show you a little of the house without hundreds of people dancing and boozing all over it?"

Thrilling alarm! She felt as if her nervous system were doing millions of computations per second. Finally: "I have to get back. I just wanted to come by and thank you."

Hoyt looked at her blankly for a moment, then began slowly nodding okay. "I'll give you a ride home."

It was a relief, and yet . . . he hadn't even asked twice! What was wrong? The way she looked? Something she said—or all the things she hadn't said, hadn't been mature enough to know how to say—after he had introduced her to all his friends?

Hoyt insisted on driving her back, and she said no, he really shouldn't, considering how he must be feeling, but he insisted, which pleased her.

Once they were outside, he took her hand as they walked toward his car, but he did it gently. Their conversation was one that any two students meeting for the first time might have had. He asked her how she happened to come to Dupont. Charlotte took great pleasure in describing Sparta, how small it was, how far up in the mountains it was, what hard times it was going through, all of which lit her up with a certain amount of underdog's glory, she thought. Just an ordinary college conversation . . . made electric by the fact that their fingers were intertwined. She asked him the same question, and it was just as she suspected from the confident way he carried himself . . . a fancy suburb of New York . . . his father the international investment banker, the private schools he went to . . . Charlotte became almost giddy with the realization that she was walking along in the ancient, romantic grandeur of Ladding Walk with a sort of young man she had never known before, a wealthy, preppy, sophisticated young man who was a man through and through, a man willing to risk his life—that was what it had *amounted* to—for her, for a girl he barely knew!

Hoyt's car turned out to be a huge SUV—tan?—gray?—she couldn't tell in the dark—old and rather the worse for wear. On the side it said "Suburban." To Charlotte it seemed somehow just right, even glamorous in an inverted way, that he would drive this . . . well . . . sort of *bohemian* old truck as opposed to something new and flashy—and ohmygod, he squeezed her hand . . . not for a second but five seconds, ten seconds before he released in order to get into the SUV.

"Oh—no, Hoyt . . . I can get back by myself all right." This was the first time she had ever spoken to him by name! There was something profound about it, and thrilling.

He had squeezed her hand—

"No, it's cool," said Hoyt. He smiled.

"I really shouldn't let you do this, Hoyt." Was using his name again going too far?—*and he had squeezed her hand—*

As they drove to Little Yard, neither spoke.

Charlotte's mind began churning. Was he going to drop her off on the sidewalk by the gateway or was he going into the parking lot? And if they stopped in the parking lot, was he going to suggest going in with her . . . or would he look at her with a look that makes the same suggestion without words . . . and if he did, what would she say? Or would he park in the parking lot and turn the engine off and, without a word, put his right arm around her shoulders, gently, look into her eyes—and what would she do if he did?

Hoyt drove straight to the main gateway . . . and he put an end to that dilemma: he never turned the motor off. He looked at her with the sort of warm, loving smile that says . . . everything . . . and said to her, "Okay?"

Okay? The loving smile remained, radiant, upon his lips. It meant—meant—meant in one second I'm going to slide my arm across your shoulders and kiss you before you leave . . .

Charlotte looked more deeply into his eyes than she had ever looked into any guy's. Her lips were slightly parted, and it was an eternity of her making before she finally said, "Oh yes, this is fine. This is perfect." But she didn't budge. She just kept looking at him, and part of her realized she was forcing . . . the issue . . . but how could it end with her just getting out and pushing the door shut. Then she heard herself saying, "Hoyt"—called him by his name again!—"I just want you to know . . . I really mean it. That was the bravest thing I ever saw anybody do. You were so wonderful, and I'm so grateful."

With that, the conscious little rock moved her head ever so slightly closer to his and ever so slightly parted her lips. To Charlotte the moment was pregnant to the point of bursting. But Hoyt's arm didn't move, and his head didn't move. Neither did his smile, which was so warm, warm, warm, loving, loving, loving, so warm and loving and commanding, all commanding, she couldn't move.

"Come on, now," said Hoyt. "I wasn't being brave. You're embarrassing me. I got in a stupid brawl, that's all, but I'm glad it got you out of there. Lax boys are crazy. I guess you know that now."

Her eyes still locked on his, Charlotte leaned forward and caressed the unbattered side of his face and put her lips upon his. He returned the kiss gently . . . and briefly . . . without trying to put his arm around her. They disengaged quickly.

Hoyt! Your smile! Brimming with love, isn't it?

"Good night, Charlotte."

Charlotte! Good night, *Charlotte!* The first time he had used her name . . . actively, with feeling.

She gazed into his eyes for just a second longer, then hurriedly opened the door and got out without saying a word and without looking back. *Without a word . . . without a look back . . .* Somehow that was what the moment demanded. She had a vague, fleeting recollection of having seen it in a movie.

She floated through Mercer Gate and into the courtyard. The lights in the windows around the quadrangle seemed like the Chinese paper lanterns in a painting by Sargent. In all of Little Yard, only she would know about that painting by Sargent. As she floated across the quadrangle, she could see exactly where the picture had been positioned on the page, a right-hand page it was, although she couldn't remember where she was when she saw it. Only she would know about that painting by Sargent. In all of Dupont College, only *she* was Charlotte Simmons!

18. THE LIFEGUARD

harlotte had never been in a building like the Dupont Center for Neuroscience before, although she had seen pictures of such places, all lean and clean and bare and spare and white and bright and sharp and hard, with glass walls. In Mr. Starling's office, two glass walls came together to form a right angle on a corner without benefit of any column or other structural support. Mr. Starling, wearing a white lab coat, sat at a sci-fi outer-space-movie desk. Charlotte found all this glamorous and awesome, awesome in the more literal sense of wonder commingled with fear.

This was his, Mr. Starling's, building! It wouldn't even exist except for his pioneering at Dupont! He was chairman of the Neuroscience Department, father and ruler of this entire shining twenty-first-century Xanadu of Science! She was sitting not three feet from him in the presence of . . . the Future! An entirely new millennium in the life of the mind was in birth here! Yes . . . but just why had he—summoned her here by e-mail to go over the paper on Darwinism she had turned in? Her hopes were high—*He loves my paper!*—and fears of the worst made her highly anxious.

Mr. Starling's eyes were lowered, peering through a pair of tortoise-colored half-glasses perched way down on the ridge of his nose. He was scanning her paper and adding notes in the margin to ones already there. The door to the room was wide open. Charlotte could hear the four women who worked in the outer office answering the telephones ("He's in a meeting"), complaining about the coffee ("What do they make this with, Fantastik?"), complaining about men ("Why would I want to go to this reunion and have to grin at a bunch of old men I've been introduced to three times in the last hour, and they still wonder why I look familiar? . . .")

Mr. Starling put Charlotte's paper down on his desk, took off the half-glasses, put them in the breast pocket of the lab coat, and leaned so far forward in his chair that his forearms rested on top of his thighs. *Why such an extreme posture?* He smiled. Whether that smile expressed warmth, pity, or cynical mistrust of the wiles of the human beast, Charlotte didn't know. She couldn't decode it.

"Ms."—*Miz*—"Simmons," said Mr. Starling, "I want to ask you something. Did you by any chance think the assignment was to disprove the theory of evolution in fifteen to twenty pages?"

The irony cut her to the quick. "No, sir." She could barely make her voice rise above a gasp.

"The assignment," he continued, "was to assess the theory with regard to the conventional requirements of the scientific method. Perhaps you remember our discussing the fact that in science, no theory merits consideration unless you can provide a set of contraindications, which, if true, would prove it wrong."

"Yes, sir," mumbled Charlotte.

"From this standpoint," said Mr. Starling, "evolution has to be considered as a special case. You may remember our talking about *that.*"

"Yes, sir."

"Because of the immensely long intervals between cause and effect—hundreds of thousands of years being 'the short run' and millions of years being the norm—and because of the relative lack of paleontological evidence spanning such vast intervals—there is no way of stating what would prove it wrong."

"Yes, sir."

"But you chose to leave that minor-league ballpark and go to work dismantling the entire theory . . . in fifteen to twenty pages."

"No, sir," said Charlotte in a strangled voice.

Mr. Starling picked her paper up from the desk, put his half-glasses back on, and riffled through to the last page. "Twenty-*three* pages," he said. "You overshot the mark slightly . . . in more ways than one."

This time, a completely incoherent gasp.

Mr. Starling was smiling at her in a kindly but devastating way. It was the kindly smile you bestow upon a child to show that even though you are compelled to give her a dressing-down for something very wrong that she's done, that doesn't mean you *dislike* her or *blame* her for still being a child.

Shot through the heart, she was! An abject failure for the first time in her life as a student! Unable to comprehend the most clear-cut of guidelines for a major assignment! A student's performance on the class's two term papers would account for two thirds of her grade! Even if she got an A-plus on the second term paper and in everything else in the course, she couldn't possibly receive more than a D for the entire semester! *D!—and I am Charlotte Simmons!*

"No, sir!" she said in a voice made hoarse by fear and occluded by shock, but audible. "I would never do that! I would never be that presumptuous, Mr. Starling! I wouldn't even know where to begin!"

"No?" said Mr. Starling. "Let me summarize your argument very briefly." He peered at her over the half-glasses. "If I wreak undue damage to it at any point, you won't hesitate to speak up, I hope."

"Yes, sir—I mean, no, sir." The triple negative had her dazed. The additional irony—sarcasm?—was like a punch in the stomach.

"All right." Mr. Starling began going over the notes he had made in the margins of the paper. "Right off the bat you argue that the human beast—" He peered again. "That's the term you use, 'the human beast.'" Drily: "I can't speak for Darwin, but Zola would have liked that, I suppose."

Hoarsely: "Yes, sir. *La Bête Humaine.*"

"Ah. You've read it?"

"Yes, sir."

"In translation or in French?"

"Both."

"Ah." That seemed to stymie him for a moment. "In any case"—his eyes returned to the paper—"you say that Darwin shared a common frailty, almost a superstition, of the human beast. He couldn't conceive of anything in the world, or the world itself, for that matter, not having had a beginning. And why? Because the human beast's own life had a beginning—and would have an end. Every living thing, the plants and animals he lived on, even the trees in the forest, had a beginning—and an end."

Ever so meekly, Charlotte interrupted. "Sir, I didn't say 'frailty' or 'superstition.'"

"All right, we'll strike 'frailty' and 'superstition.' Now . . . you say that since human beasts, including Mr. Darwin, I presume, believe that everything must have a point of origin, then everything must start out very small . . . like a baby at birth or, if you'd rather, at the moment of conception—that's a political question, I suppose—or the cosmos at the moment of the Big Bang—or Darwin's single cells 'in a warm pool somewhere.'"

He looked up. "I'm glad you remembered the warm pool. Oh, and incidentally, Darwin died in 1882 and never learned about the Big Bang, but I get your point."

Blow after blow to the pit of the stomach!

"This you call 'original fallacy.' After the point of origin, the newborn—the human beast, the cosmos and everything in it—grows larger and larger and more complex. It progresses. So the human beast believes that progress is normal and inevitable. This you call 'the progression fallacy.'"

Barely audible: "Yes, sir."

"All right. Now you introduce a bit of intellectual history. Darwin was alive at a time when progress was on everybody's mind. It was a time in which modern industry was developing and changing the face of England. Also technology, mechanical invention, modern medicine, and the first widespread distribution of printed materials—books, magazines, newspapers. On top of everything else, and on every Englishman's mind, was the spread all over the world of the British Empire. Darwin, you tell us, was swept up in this general belief in progress, and long before he went to the Galápagos he intended to show that all animals, all species, had progressed from a single cell"—Mr. Starling looked up, smiling—"or those four or five cells in our famous warm pool."

He returned to her paper. "In fact, you inform us"—he lifted a declamatory forefinger into the air in a gesture of ironic bombast—"that *nothing* begins, and nothing ends. No physical or chemical elements, no particles, ever leave the biosphere. They merely change in their combinations. Your 'life,' which you say is merely another way of saying your 'soul,' is over, finished, but all of the materials that comprised your body and your brain remain, destined to be recombined. In other words, 'dust to dust.' Correct?"

Defeated: "Yes, sir."

"Oh—and I mustn't forget this." He had his forefinger on one of the pages of her paper. "You also inform us that time is nothing but one of the human beast's inventions. Your term is 'mental constructs.' Other animals react to light, darkness, and climate, but they have no sense or awareness of time."

Mr. Starling put the paper on the surface of the desk. He leaned back in his chair and stared at Charlotte, smiling, inexplicably, for what seemed like a minute at least but was probably only a few seconds. She waited for the coup de grâce.

"Ms. Simmons," he said, still smiling in that certain way, "people, scholars and laymen, have been trying to undermine the theory of evolution for almost a century and a half. That aspect of your paper doesn't interest me at all, frankly. What impresses me about what you've done is your extraordinary use of the literature, some of it highly technical, even esoteric—"

Impresses?

"—and the nuanced way in which you are able to project the ramifications of a theory, whether Mr. Darwin's or your own. Just to cite one example, I'm a bit bowled over by the fact that you found and were capable of digesting and using Steadman and Levin's study of the lack of time sense in animals. That's a very elegant, very sophisticated—methodologically, very exhaustive, highly technical—in terms of brain physiology—it couldn't have been done before the development of three-dimensional electroencephalography in the nineties—and obscurely published paper. It appeared in the *Annals of Cognitive Biology*. How on earth did you find it?"

Could this actually be? A bit breathlessly, "Well, I went to the library and I went online, and one thing led to another?—I guess." Had she regressed to *I geh-us?*

"And Nisbet's lecture on how Darwin had seized upon Russell's theory of progress, not to mention his theory of evolution." Mr. Starling snorted a laugh. "How did you come upon that? Hardly anyone seems to cite Nesbit anymore, and in my opinion he was not only the greatest American sociologist of the last century but also the greatest philosopher."

Is what seems to be happening—happening for real? A small voice—*but a-wing . . . like a swallow!* "I was sort of lucky? That didn't take so long."

Mr. Starling tapped the paper lightly with the back of the tips of his fingers. "This is an *outstanding* piece of work, Ms. Simmons . . . and despite what I just said, I did rather enjoy the sheer *nerve* of your taking on the old man."

A-wing and soaring: "I didn't mean to be doing that, Mr. Starling. I'm sorry it—it—"

"Don't be sorry! Darwin hasn't been *beatified* yet. He's close, but it's not a done deal."

Charlotte didn't really absorb all the things Mr. Starling had to say after that. What he seemed to be saying was . . . he didn't know what she was thinking about majoring in, but whatever it might be, she should consider working a few hours a week here in the Center for Neuroscience. Work in the laboratory with animals and with humans, using brain imaging, was the frontier. This sort of work, as he had mentioned in class, had already begun to re-create humankind's—"the human beast's, if you'd rather, Ms. Simmons"—conception of itself.

Yes! she said to everything and all of it—*Yes! Yes! Yes! And Yes!*

When she departed the Center for Neuroscience, it had become a sunny afternoon, and she flew like a swallow over the campus of Dupont University, with amazing speed and exhilarating swoops and dives, in Heaven, but with no destination. The *flight* itself . . . was the thing.

Charlotte, along with Mimi and Bettina, was standing in a long, loud, nervous line, made up mainly of Dupont students, on the sidewalk in front of the I.M. The sulfur streetlights turned their faces a chemical yellow and killed whatever color existed in their *nostalgie de la boue* gear. It didn't do much for the I.M. itself, either. It made the red paint on the clapboard façade look like dried blood. The place could have used a nice big backlit electro-plastic sign as a distraction from its itchy appearance. Instead, in the interest of indicating that this establishment was for those in the know, there was only an ordinary address plaque over the entrance, reading "I.M. 2019"—2019 being the street number. In short, the I.M. was as fashionably seedy and worn-out as its young patrons' clothes.

Fear and desire reigned here in the line: the desire to be *where things are happening*, on the one hand, and fear of what would happen if the gatekeepers caught you using a fake ID, which was illegal, on the other. At least three quarters of the line was underage. As usual, their nervousness took the form of the Fuck Patois, which they thought gave them a front of cool and confident twenty-one-year-old moxie.

SOME GUY: ". . . because she was wearing a miniskirt with nothing on underneath it and doing fucking keg-stands, that's why."

ANOTHER GUY: "The beaver smiles! That's her best fucking feature. Don't look at her face in the morning or you'll get awfuck's disease."

SOME GIRL: "Oh shit, this ID says I'm thirty-fucking-one!"

GUY: ". . . won't give me *skull?* Shit, she won't give me her fucking digits."

GIRL: ". . . yeah, and all he'll fucking ever be is an ass-wipe."

GUY: ". . . one dodgy fucking be-atch, if you ask me, yo."

GUY: ". . . so why the fuck not? . . ."

GUY: ". . . don't give a rat fuck, personally . . ."

GIRL: ". . . dis the fucker hard-core . . ."

GIRL: "The *fuck* she's keeping it real!"

GIRL: ". . . can just go fuck himself . . ."

CHORUS: "I say fuck that!"

"I say fuck this!"

"I say fuck all."

"Fuck off!"

"Oh, fuck."

Momma. If Momma showed up right now and saw her, thought Charlotte, saw her in a line full of people talking Fuck Patois, about to sneak into a *bar* with a *fake ID* . . . Everybody does it, Momma . . . *Everybody?* The *contempt* Momma had for that creature of the herd, "everybody"! Everybody and their everybody-does-it violations of Christian teachings and the law! But Momma, I'm not going into the bar to *enjoy* it . . . An exploration is all it is . . . It was important that she see this legendary I.M. place for herself and find out what people got so excited about. Besides, it wasn't *her* idea. It was Mimi's. Mimi still played the role of the sophisticate among the three of them, but she was no longer patronizing. She no longer treated Charlotte as the clueless mountain girl. The status of Charlotte Simmons had risen another gradation after the two lacrosse players fought over her at the tailgate. Mimi had been more the benevolent mentor this time, as she told Charlotte and Bettina how they could fake their way into the bar. Mimi had had her own ID manufactured—she mysteriously declined to say how—and she could probably pass for twenty-one anyway. Once inside, she would find girls with real IDs, drivers' licenses most likely, who looked more or less like Bettina and Charlotte. The pictures on drivers' licenses were always distorted anyway. Then she would come back out and slip the bogus IDs to them. Yes, she said, since Charlotte wanted to know, fake IDs were technically illegal, but everybody uses them. If they went after everybody who used a fake ID, everybody at Dupont would have a record.

T O M W O L F E

Everybody! A rush of guilt . . . Momma had not merely told her to obey every law, every rule, every regulation—she had *conditioned* her. Obedience in all things great and small was next to godliness. Sparta had three stop-lights, all on Main. One Saturday when she was twelve, Charlotte was walking with Laurie, and Regina happened along. Without thinking twice about it, Regina crossed the street against the light. So Charlotte and Laurie did, too. Charlotte hated herself for days. She hadn't had the courage to say, "You do what you want. I'm waiting for the light to change."

By now Mimi, Bettina, and Charlotte were only nine or ten places back in line. Charlotte's heart began banging away. She could see the gatekeep-ers, two men, standing out in front of the glass door. The one actually scru-tinizing the IDs was short, wiry, swarthy, thirtyish, hawk faced, wearing a black turtleneck sweater and black pants. The other was a young giant—early twenties?—with closely cut, curly sandy-colored hair atop a great melon of a head supported by an even thicker neck . . . curiously tiny eyes and mouth. Charlotte knew that face . . . from where? The Saint Ray house! He had been the bouncer guarding the door to the stairway that led down to the so-called secret room! Now he was guarding the portal of the I.M., arms folded across his vast chest, expressionless as a mountain, towering over his little hawk-eyed colleague.

A piercing whine at the head of the line. "Whattaya mean? I've been in here a hundred times!"

It was a tall boy wearing a quilted vest and a T-shirt with the arms cut off—the better to reveal his Cybex-maxed upper arms. He thrust his head down belligerently toward the lithe hawk of a gatekeeper. The hawk's moun-tain of a sidekick unfolded his arms—just that, unfolded them—and the protest was over. The tall guy with the Cybexed biceps left the line, he and two pals, muttering imprecations and threatening retribution.

So the guardians of the gate meant business! And the humiliated boy looked a lot older than Charlotte. A chill of fright and chagrin; she felt guilty, humiliated—revealed before all the world—and her time hadn't even come yet.

But for the guilty, time speeds up. Now Mimi was before the hawk and the giant. Charlotte held her breath, hoping he would turn Mimi back, since that would bring their entire scheme to an end. But Mimi breezed on in, as she had predicted.

Charlotte and Bettina hung back to wait for her return. It seemed like no time before Mimi emerged, faking a jolly laugh as she slipped Bettina and Charlotte bootlegged IDs and hurried back in. Charlotte studied hers . . . a driver's license, New York State, in the name of Carla Phillips, 500 West End Avenue, New York, New York, 10024. The picture didn't look like Charlotte Simmons at all! . . . Well, maybe vaguely . . . Why don't I just leave while there's still time! I'm about to break the law! A grim Momma was eyeing her.

All too soon they were at the head of the line, approaching the hawk. Bettina went first. Charlotte's face was already on fire. The man studied Bettina's ID and then Bettina, the ID, and then Bettina again, oh so dubiously!—Charlotte's heart was a panicked bird trapped in her rib cage—before waving Bettina through.

This pointless risk of her entire moral self . . . and she was standing before the Man. He was not as young as she had first thought. The pupils of his eyes were BBs deep within lids thick and wrinkled as walnut shells. His head was no bigger than a cantaloupe. The turtleneck of his sweater seemed about to swallow the head whole. But above all there was his mustache, a bushy thing curled upward at either end. There was a minute orange crumb—nachos?—lodged in it. He looked up from "Charlotte's" driver's license with an insinuating twist of his lips that caused the mustache and its tiny orange crumb to swing an inch or so. He held the laminated card in one hand and gave it a contemptuous flick with the other.

"This your driver's license?"

Her throat had gone dry. She was afraid to try speaking. So she nodded yes. Unspoken—but nevertheless a lie.

"Where's home for you, 'Carla'?"

She was sure the way he had pronounced *Carla* was sarcastic and as much as said, "You liar." She croaked out, "I'm from New York City?" Fear had thrown her right back into Down Home locution. The question-mark rise at the end made it sound like this lie was one she had tried to swallow but couldn't keep down.

"I can't make out this address, Carla."

Thank God she had memorized it, but she was so hoarse. "Five hundred West End Avenue."

The little inquisitor gave her a hideous wink and said, "That's a helluva Brooklyn accent you got there, 'Carla.'"

"We just moved to New York?" A lie, uttered so faintly it was obvious she was just lobbing it and ducking.

"Hey, Carla, I know you. You're Hoyt's friend, right? Remember me?"

It was the big Saint Ray bouncer. He had an oddly high-pitched voice. Smiling like this, he looked like a different person, not rough and tough at all.

Charlotte said, "Sure do"—*sher do*—jumping at a chance to ingratiate herself. "You were—" She didn't know how quite to put it. "—at the Saint Ray house?"

"A*wright!*" the bouncer said, as if he had just been paid a great compliment. Then he leaned over and whispered something to his colleague.

The little hawk let a big sigh out through his teeth, which gave it a whistling sound, and looked into the distance. "Okay, Miss New York, go on in." He motioned toward the plate-glass door. Sardonically: "If you can make it there, you'll make it anywhere."

Charlotte hadn't the faintest idea what he was talking about. She hurried toward the door for fear he'd change his mind.

The front door of the I.M. led into a small vestibule with a plate-glass inner door, through which Charlotte could make out a nightclub dusk with just enough light to reflect off the white faces of a mob of students. She could hear a low, numb thundering of sound and the muted percussion of drums and an electric bass. She pushed the door open, and—*bang!*—squalls of noise and waves of noxious odors engulfed her, the sweet, rotting smell of beer, huge tides of it faintly laced with the putrid smell of vomit amid a bilious nightclubbed gloom, the bangs and wails of a band, and the victorious roar of students ecstatic over having made it into the right place. The mob of students looked like a single drunken beast with a thousand heads and two thousand arms, scratching and itching and itching and scratching at the pustules of a fiery pox, which turned out to be the tips of all the cigarettes. The whole place looked . . . itchy . . . filthy . . . infested . . . the floor, the walls, which were covered in wide, rough planks painted purplish black, even the splintery rip-cut edges. Deep within the gloom, two gashes of light, two long, glowing troughs, were just bright enough to reveal all the smoke in the air and throw the beast into silhouette. The nearer one must be a bar; the one in the back the bandstand. As Charlotte's eyes adjusted, the beast began to resolve into individuals packed shank to flank, from here to all the way back . . . there. One of the first fine details she noticed was the perfect white crescents of the teeth of girls in jeans—prayers answered by the goddess Orthodontia—as they looked up into the faces of boys in jeans, eyes glistening, lips smiling, as if never in their lives had they heard such mesmerizing wit or wisdom.

Charlotte's eyes were darting about, looking for Mimi and Bettina. They were standing off to one side, near the door. Charlotte hurried over to them, and they put their heads together and began laughing, all three of them.

"What happened?" said Mimi.

"You know the man with the face like a hawk? He didn't believe me!"

Great sieges of laughter, giddiness upon giddiness, as Charlotte regaled them with the story. She had seldom been so elated in her life. She had succeeded in a subterfuge! Cool! (No longer lying and cheating.) She had proved she was among the worldly ones who know how to handle things! (No longer committing an illegal act.) She had risked and dared . . . *pour le sport!* (No longer the shameless waste of spirit of a Regina Cox.) She was the brave girl who had gone into battle, been shot at—and survived! (Without the bother of dwelling on the purpose.) She laughed and chattered more animatedly than at any time since she arrived at Dupont.

Mimi indicated that she wanted to go to the bar and get a drink. The roar, the shrieks, the wailing, pounding music were so overwhelming that if you weren't within a foot of one another you couldn't make yourself heard. The three girls slithered and squeezed through the crush of students. Charlotte brought up the rear. She had no intention of getting a drink, which might cost a dollar or more, but it seemed terribly important to stay in her little freshman herd and keep moving . . .

Nearing the bar, she became separated from them by an impenetrable knot of boys and girls. The girls were shrieking—the usual shrieks to indicate excitement over the presence of guys. Charlotte couldn't get by them.

She felt a tug on her arm. It was Bettina, who had a bottle of beer in her hand. She motioned toward Mimi, who had a big glass of something. They headed toward the band, in the back. Charlotte followed as they made their way through a bewilderingly excited crowd. The odors—rotting malt, vomitus, cigarette smoke, bodies—became worse and worse. The sheer mass of bodies—it was so hot in here! Reminded her of the Saint Ray house that night . . . the heat, the smoky nocturnal gloom, the yowling drunks, the music that never stopped, the putrid air, the drunken cries of the male animal on all sides.

"Kiss muh bigguh-fwy booty!" *Kiss my biggie-fry booty!*

"Luke, I am your father!"

"Sucka sucka! Who the fucka's gonna steal a Sonicare toothbrush?"

"They can take away our lives, but they can't take away our freedom!"

In the back, five musicians, glistening with sweat, were an apparition of highlights that were too bright and shadows that disappeared into a black wall behind the bandstand. They looked not so much like three-dimensional forms as twitching slicks of light. The drummer was fat and bald as a Buddha, banging away at an extraordinary battery of drums, cymbals, bells, blocks of wood, triangles. In front of the bandstand was a small dance floor. It was as itchy and beat-up as the bar area. Jammed in around the floor, in virtual darkness, was a gridlock of cocktail tables—small, round, cheap, painted black, mobbed with white faces bawling as they sucked smoke down into their lungs. A young singer, caramel colored, fragile as a stalk, head shaved except for a pair of enormous sideburns, which created a poodle effect, was singing to a leisurely reggae beat.

A dank gloom . . . cigarette smoke invaded Charlotte's nose to the point where she could have sworn it was also burning her corneas.

Bettina and Mimi were making hurry-up gestures. They had spotted a guy and three girls—upperclassmen, apparently, since they actually looked twenty-one—getting up from a cocktail table not too far from the dance floor. Already Mimi and Bettina were rushing pell-mell to claim the table, jimmying their thighs between back-to-back chairs and sprinkling 'scuse me's over the cross faces of the students they jostled. Charlotte did her best to keep up. As soon as they sat down, Mimi lit up a cigarette to show that . . . *she belonged*! Bettina began moving her torso languidly to the reggae beat to show that . . . *she belonged*! Cigarette in one hand, Mimi brought her bottle of beer near her lips, looked at Charlotte, and arched her eyebrows, pantomiming, "Don't you want something to drink?" which really meant, "Don't you want to *belong*?" Charlotte shook her head no, and leaned forward with her forearms braced on the edge of the table, and looked right past Mimi at all the young bodies clumped together. Why? Belonging to—what? What was the point of this clump of humanity eagerly pressed against one another in a beaten-up place like the I.M. on a Friday night? She immediately answered her own question with another. What if I were in my room alone right now? She could *feel* it . . . sitting at her desk, staring out the window at the uplit library tower while loneliness *scoured* out all semblance of hope, ambition, or simple planning. Charlotte Simmons!—removed from all family, all friends, every familiar terrain, every worn and homely object . . . Did a single other student at Dupont feel as lonely as she had felt?

Her eyes lit upon five girls who were about to squeeze in at a table by the dance floor, just two tables away. They looked just as young as she did, all desperately grinning and laughing. *That* one—the one sitting practically *on* the dance floor—the blonde—the one with all the cleavage—the superior air she had, her chin up in the air—the very picture of *I'm hot*—oh come on, Charlotte! Be honest with yourself! You know she's hot! The girl had the kind of long, straight, silky blond hair that makes every non-blond female in the world—every one of them without exception—wring her hands over the careless, pointless, offhanded unfairness of Fate.

Bettina had noticed the new arrivals, too. She leaned close to Charlotte, gestured toward them, and said rather superciliously, "Why don't they just wear a sign around their necks saying, 'Fuck me, I'm a freshman'?"

Charlotte laughed, but her spirits sank. Why was Charlotte Simmons here? What was this thing the three of them were involved in—herself every bit as much as Bettina and Mimi? The *hunt*! The *hunt*! The boyfriend! Necessary as breathing! What academic achievement, what soaring flight of genius, even a Nobel Prize in neuroscience, could ever be as important?

The band had broken into a soulful Bob Marley–style number. The singer was tilting his head way back, so that the microphone he held seemed to be diving right down his gullet. Half a dozen couples were grinding on the dance floor. Specimens, lab animals they were, in a neurobiological environment that triggered certain stimuli, causing them to infuse their mucous membranes with alcohol and nicotine, so overwhelming was the urge to . . . *belong*—

For the first time in her two months at Dupont, Charlotte felt like her old self, independent, aloof—aloof from the customs other freshmen accepted as the natural order of things in college life and surrendered to without a peep. Why was it so important for these bright, rich kids—fourteen-ninety average SATs—to buy into what was primitive? This itchy, dilapidated dump as opposed to something stylish or at least slick and spick-and-span . . . this Caribbean music . . . Charlotte Simmons was above them all. They were specimens for her to study. The I.M. was a terrarium full of rich boys and girls in rags, and she was peering down into the terrarium and studying them . . . the male and female of the species grinding genitals . . . the swollen . . . thing, under cotton, searching for . . . the crevice, under cotton . . . the Buddha drumming, flailing everything in a nine-foot radius . . . the caramel singer eating more microphone . . . but then here was an aberration! A guy was coming onto the dance floor by himself. No, he was merely using the dance floor as a shortcut. Thatchy hair, open button-down shirt, sleeves rolled up, shirttail hanging out over his khakis, limping, but with an arrogant gait, as he strode between the grinding two-backed beasts. He turned his head. A surgical type of bandage was plastered down one side of his jaw, from his ear almost to his chin—

Hoyt.

He was heading toward her. She was acutely conscious of how frantically her heart was beating. He must have been at a table on the other side of the floor all along. How had he even found her in this smoky darkness? How long had he—

Mimi leaned across Bettina and said to Charlotte, "See who's coming? It's your lifeguard from the Saint Ray house."

Charlotte looked up as if she hadn't noticed him before. Her face was burning. She only hoped it was too dark for Mimi to notice.

Mimi leaned across Bettina again. "What are you going to say to him?" She looked excited.

"I don't know." Charlotte's voice was shaking.

Now he was barely six feet from her, but he didn't seem to be looking directly at her. Closer and closer—and right past her, without a glance. He was closing in on the table with all the five freshmen crammed in about it. He leaned over the blonde with the cleavage and the Hair. The girl was sitting right on the edge of the dance floor with her back to it. Hoyt tapped her on the shoulder. Charlotte—all this was happening right in her face. The blonde swung her head about with a flourish of all that silky hair. Hoyt's smug smirk dissolved into a puzzled but sincerely concerned look.

Charlotte couldn't begin to hear what he was saying to the girl. The band and the increasingly drunken roar of the place drowned out everything else. Nevertheless, a name bubbled up her brain stem: Britney Spears.

The blonde was giggling, giddy with excitement, and blushing—giddy with embarrassment, if Charlotte knew anything about it. Hoyt pulled over one of the small cocktail lounge chairs from the table beyond and sat down beside the blonde. Now Charlotte couldn't even pretend not to be looking. Hoyt was talking and smiling at the same time, and his quarry was still giggling. Hoyt was leaning in, pouring soul into her eyes with the look that says, "We're both feeling something we can't talk about yet, aren't we."

Then he began tapping her on the outer surface of her arm, starting up near the shoulder and progressing netherward.

The way Hoyt's eyebrows were arched, it was obvious he was asking a question. He and the girl stood up. The girl turned her head and displayed an embarrassed, somehow regretful smile at the other girls at her table. Out onto the dance floor they went, Hoyt and the blonde. They locked pelvic saddles, and he began thrusting . . . himself, grinding . . . grinding . . . The band was playing with a slow, hypnotic, syncopated beat. The singer kept repeating the same two lines:

> "You must use your strength—
> Very sen-si-tive-lee . . .
> Yes, you must use your strength—
> Very sen-si-tive-lee . . ."

Hoyt kept his mouth slightly open in a way that said, "That's it . . . that's it . . . Just stay in the groove . . . you've got it, baby . . . yeah, baby . . . and you're starting to love it . . ."

The girl was red in the face. Anybody could see that, even in this smoky, reeking, shrieking, beer-humid, vomit-tangy electro-night-light. But a smile of dawning naughtiness was beginning to steal across that red face, overriding all embarrassment and foreboding.

Hoyt and the blonde left the dance floor and headed through the mob toward the entrance, holding hands; he chattering, she staring straight ahead, unfocused, contemplating the immediate future.

"Ohmygod," said Mimi, reaching across Bettina again, this time to show Charlotte the watch on her wrist. "Your lifeguard is too much. Look at *that*. Who *is* that stupid little frostitute?"

"What's a *fros*titute?" said Bettina.

"You've never heard frostitute?" said Mimi. "You know 'frosh,' like freshman?"

"Hmm, I think so," said Bettina, "I guess so . . ."

"Frosh . . . frostitute," said Mimi.

Charlotte tried to be the picture of nonchalance, but it wasn't going well. She had to turn away from both girls. There was no way they wouldn't see how close she was to crying. She couldn't believe this, and yet she could, which made it worse.

Ohmygod, all the bodies . . . it was soooo hot . . . The smoke from other people's rotten lungs burned her rhinal cavities. The Buddha drummer was walloping everything he could reach with his sticks. He obviously thought he was putting on a great show.

You . . . bastard! Sharp intake of breath—she had never used that expletive before, not even in her thoughts. Hoyt had done this just to torment her! Comes over as if to see her and veers off to some little . . . slut! Never even thought that word before, either . . . or had she once, about Beverly . . . A ray of hope: if he went to all that trouble to torment me, then I must really be on his mind. Fog rolled in: or maybe he was heading for me and then saw something better, a little . . . frostitute . . . fresher fresh meat, which is all he cares about, obviously . . . Or maybe he never saw me at all . . . That was possible, wasn't it, in the darkness, in the stench, the heat, in all the Buddha noise . . .

Dream on, Charlotte . . . Look at it any way you want. He disdained me, hurt me, humiliated me . . . He *betrayed* me, right under my nose! In front of my friends!

The caramel-colored singer's head was still way back.

> *"You, mon, can bring down the house—*
> *Very sen-si-tive-lee . . .*
> *And wo-mon can bring down the house—*
> *Very sen-si-tive-lee . . ."*

Charlotte was conscious of the way Mimi was staring at her; Bettina, too, less obviously. They wanted to see how she took in *that*. She shrugged and tried to be insouciant. "He was a Good Samaritan. That doesn't mean he has to—"

She didn't complete the sentence. She didn't want to get caught trying to put into words what she wished he had wanted to do. She would merely reveal how hurt she felt, and she knew Mimi—damn you, Mimi—would enjoy, in her tarantula way, every second of that.

19. THE HAND

Welcome, O sage of Athens," said Buster Roth. Coach was reared back in his swivel chair with his fingers interlaced behind his head and his elbows winged out on either side. "What news from Marathon?"

"From where?" said Jojo. Coach had a big friendly smile on, but Jojo detected mockery in the air.

"Marathon," said Coach. "Twenty-six miles and change from Athens. Big battle going on, and there's this runner they got. It was in the A—uh, the time of Socrates. Old Socrates—" Coach broke off the sentence and made a gesture as if he were shooing flies. "It don't matter. I was just kidding, Jojo, just kidding . . . So here we are . . . I'm liable to get used to these mystery visits of yours. I hope you got better news than last time."

With those few words Coach's demeanor changed. His eyes narrowed, and Jojo had the uneasy feeling that Coach looked upon him as a specimen to be studied. He gestured toward a fiberglass bergère. "Whyn'tcha have a seat?"

"I'm—" Jojo had thought out what he was going to say this time, but it was all breaking up and slipping away. He lowered himself into the chair, stared at Coach, exhaled laboriously, and finally managed to say, "It's not about Socrates, Coach. It's not—it's not good. In fact, it's bad, Coach. I got my—I'm in a jam."

Coach narrowed his eyes even more.

"The thing is," said Jojo, "I'm in this American history class. Mr. Quat."

Coach took his hands from behind his head and put them on the arms of the chair and turned his head and let his eyes climb the wall, and he cut loose with a big sibilant sigh that came out as "Shiiiiiiit . . ." Then he turned back and hunched forward in the chair and uttered another noisy sigh. "Okaaaaay . . . let's hear it."

So Jojo began recounting the story, all the while studying Coach's face for some nod or wink or God knows what that would indicate that he, Coach Buster Roth, monarch of the Buster Bowl and the Rotheneum, would take care of it, would protect his boy. From time to time Coach interposed a question. "*When* did you remember? Did you say *mid*night?" . . . and a few moments later: "Whaddaya mean, had to get him to help you?"

"Well—you know—I needed a lotta help, it being so late and every-thing."

"Whaddya mean, a lotta help? And spare me the bullshit."

"I gave him a sort of a rough outline."

"What's a sort of a rough outline supposed to mean, for Christ's sake?"

"I told him what it was supposed to be about."

"You told him what it was supposed to be about."

"Yes . . ."

"And that's all you told him?"

"*About* all . . . I guess."

"About all, you guess . . . Well, I'd call that one rough fucking sort of a rough fucking outline, Jojo. Wouldn't *you*?"

Coach swiveled ninety degrees in his chair and let his eyes climb the wall again. "Jesus H. Christ," he said to the wall. Then he spun about and ran Jojo through with his eyes. He began softly. "Jojo . . . first you come in here and you tell me you're no dumb jock, you're fucking born-again Socrates, and you wanna take Philosophy 306 and rationalism and animism and a whole load of other shit . . . and now you come back here and inform me, as if no one would ever guess, that you're a . . . FUCKING IDIOT! A MORON! AN IMBECILE! HOW MANY TIMES HAVE I TOLD YOU MEATHEADS, 'WE'RE HERE TO HELP YOU BUT KINDLY DO NOT ABUSE THE SYSTEM!' WHAT IS IT ABOUT THE WORD 'HELP' YOU DON'T FUCKING UNDER-

STAND! 'HELP YOU' AIN'T THE SAME AS 'DO IT FOR YOU,' YOU SIMPLEMINDED SHIT! SOCRATES! HOW DARE YOU COME IN HERE AND BREAK MY BALLS ABOUT SOCRATES WHILE YOU'RE HAVING A TUTOR WRITE A FUCKING TEN-PAGE PAPER FOR YOU?"

Jojo was abashed—and then he sensed that Coach was already inventing an I-told-him-so defense in case this thing blew up into something serious. But that merely made him feel hopeless on top of abashed. He was aware of sounding almost babyish as he whined and squeaked out, "But that was *before*, Coach—"

"Before my ass."

"—before I made my turnaround, Coach! I wrote—that paper was back—"

"Turnaround." Sarcasm dripped from the word. "THE ONLY WAY YOU NEED TO GET YOURSELF TURNED IS INSIDE OUT! I CAN'T FUCKING BELIEVE . . ."

"Coach! Please! I'm begging you! You gotta listen to me, Coach! That was before . . ."

Coach returned to the soft, menacing voice: "What the fuck difference do you think 'before' makes? You think I can intercede with this guy Quat and say that was before old Jojo said, 'By the moons of Minapoor'"—he thrust his right hand upward mock-dramatically—"'Behold! You now see Socrates before you!' Do you by any chance remember me telling you about the *pricks* on the Dupont faculty? DO YOU?"

Jojo, six feet ten, 250 pounds, nodded as contritely as a second-grader.

"NOW do you know what I'm talking about?"

Nod, nod, nod. A first-grader.

"Somebody made a mistake with this Quat. Somebody—I know who, but it don't matter. Well, welcome to Prickdom. HE'S A FUCKING PRICK! Curtis was complaining about him. Curtis wanted to twist his head off and shit down his windpipe. You didn't hear the way he treated Curtis? You skipped that class or something?"

"I know," said Jojo. "I was right there, Coach. I swear to God! But I wrote—uh, the paper—that was before—"

"SAY THAT ONE MORE TIME, JOJO, AND I'M GONNA SHOVE 'BEFORE' DOWN YOUR THROAT UNTIL IT COMES OUT YOUR ASS! Your balls are on the frying pan, in case you don't know it, and 'before' don't mean shit." Coach dropped the look of contempt and

T
O
M

W
O
L
F
E

began to eye Jojo shrewdly. "Did you actually confess to Quat and say, 'Yeah, the tutor wrote it for me'?"

"No-o-o . . ."

"You're sure? Don't fuck with me now, Jojo."

"I'm sure, Coach."

"Okay, and who is this tutor we're talking about?"

"Adam . . . Gellin, is his name."

"And you and him, you're on good terms?"

Jojo stared off and compressed his lips . . . and decided, in a flood of shame, he'd better not fuck with Coach now. "No, not exactly. I could've treated him better, I guess." The picture of Adam's face when he had paged him at midnight that night came to mind.

"Does that mean you're on *bad* terms?"

"Well . . . I don't know, but Coach, it don't matter. The guy don't have enough here"—Jojo tapped his sternum with his fist—"to do anything about anything anyway. You know that kinda guy, Coach. You told me about 'em."

"Yeah, well, I'm still gonna want to see him."

Jojo's spirits edged upward for the first time in days.

Coach was calming down and thinking about ways to do something. "He just might find it instructive to know that if *you* get into deep shit over this, he will, too."

"He already knows that, Coach. That was the first thing he thought about when I told him what Quat said. He's saying, 'I didn't actually *write* it, Jojo,' and 'I was just helping you polish the rough edges, right, Jojo?' Like I told you, he's not what you'd call a ballsy little guy." Jojo smiled for the first time since they had started talking. It pleased him to think that he and Coach were two stand-up guys in a world full of weaklings.

Over the next few weeks, Charlotte didn't know what to do about Adam. She was obviously on his mind all the time now. He'd call her room, he'd go out of his way to intercept her on the campus, he'd check by the treadmills in the gym to see if she was there, he'd leave notes saying why didn't she come over and "hang" or "chill" with the Mutants, who would be getting together at such and such a place at such and such a time, and finally he had taken to doing the unheard-of at Dupont: he'd ask her out on "dates," out to real restaurants even—and he'd pay for it!

At Dupont, nobody asked anybody out on a date unless they were already spending most nights in each other's beds, and even then the boy would word it along the lines of "Whatcha doing tonight? Wanna chill?" Or: "Wanna go over to the I.M. and hang out for a while?" Adam had gone far beyond that. He'd come right out and asked her to a restaurant in town, like Le Chef, at a particular time . . . and then insisted on coming by and taking her there. Sometimes he would borrow a car from Roger, so he wouldn't have to take her on a bus through the City of God.

Charlotte could no longer kid herself that she was going out on these dates just so she could have some decent food for a change. She was also willingly dropping by from time to time to hang out, to chill, with him and the Mutants. No—she literally did not know what to do with Adam. She didn't know whether to encourage him or not encourage him . . . or, since in fact she was encouraging him, going on these dates, just how far to go with him. He obviously wanted more than just dinner, talk, and looking into her eyes and holding her hand on a checkered-tablecloth tabletop at Le Chef. Oh yes, she had allowed him to do that, hadn't she . . . He kept trying to get her to "come by" his apartment, which she wasn't about to do, or let him come up to her room, in which case she would talk about Beverly as if Beverly were tethered to the wall in there. She *had* taken to giving him good-night kisses, however—long mercy kisses—

Or was calling it a mercy kiss just another way of kidding herself? The truth was . . . she *wanted* to fall in love with Adam. If only she could! How much tidier life would be!

One night Adam took her to an event at the Phipps—it was hard to say what to call it, a concert, dance performance, or what—featuring a group called the Olfactory Workers. Charlotte had never even heard of anything like it. She guessed not many others had, either, because the Phipps was only about a quarter full. But Adam was eager to go. He didn't know exactly what it was about, but he had read a reference to the Olfactory Workers somewhere. He had such a curiosity, it was infectious.

The Olfactory Workers were six young men and four young women, all dressed in black tights—even the four sort of fat ones—black tank tops, and black vests with mandarin collars and no buttons. Six of them played musical instruments, two trumpets, a French horn, an oboe, a bassoon, and drums. Four of them were dancers who did a kind of modern dance, Charlotte guessed it was, the kind of dancing she had seen in movies, very close to gymnastics, except crazier. But strangest of all were the four big black kettles with lids, up on black metal legs, two on this side of the stage and two on the other. The kettle lids were outfitted with nozzles and a series of levers. Two performers, one on each side, operated the braziers, spraying some sort of odor-bearing mists from the nozzles up into the air . . . musk, sandalwood, pine knot, cedar, tannery leather, rose, lily, lime, saltwater spume, and some that were not exactly noxious, but disturbing all the same. A system of blowers, exhaust fans, and olfactory "mops"—Charlotte took this on faith from the program . . . she couldn't see them, although she could hear the blowers and exhaust fans—cleared the atmosphere between numbers—or mostly, it wasn't perfect—and the odors created, or were supposed to create, a beyond rational harmony between the dancing, the brass, the woodwinds. The music was not definable, at least not by Charlotte. It would start off with what sounded like Roman Catholic chants—but always with rolling trap drums behind it—and dissolve into jazz, which would dissolve into disco music, or so Adam whispered to her, and the oboist and the bassoonist, both women, would lower their mouthpieces and sing mindlessly happy disco rhymes (Adam informed her) in soprano harmony—"It's a disco evolution . . . Got to risk a revolution"—and then dissolve into a high-pitched a capella as the trumpets and the French horn were drummed up into something that had no name, or at least Adam didn't know it, and the sublime geysers of sandalwood filled the air, although not all the nutmeg and cinnamon were out of the air yet—

A small matter, very small, for Charlotte was now transported! . . . not so much by the Olfactory Workers and their odors and music and dancing and singing as by the fact that this was something experimental, esoteric, cutting-edge (she had picked up that term in the modern drama course), one of the exciting, sophisticated things Miss Pennington had assured her awaited her on the other side of the mountain, the things that would open up her eyes to harness and to achieve great triumphs with . . .

As they left Phipps, Charlotte felt so transported that she voluntarily hooked her arm inside of Adam's and leaned against his shoulder. Adam, she might have known, immediately misinterpreted the source of her excitement and sought out her hand, finally got it, and leaned his head against hers just as she was attempting to disengage.

There was an absolute blaze of light as they emerged from the opera house lobby and went out onto the portico, a blaze strong enough to light up the trees in the Grove—and what if someone saw her cuddling with a . . . dork?

She immediately hated herself for even thinking such a thing, but the worst of it was that it wasn't even a fully formed thought. It was a visceral reaction.

And she *wanted* to want Adam! She *wanted* to want to kiss Adam good night in a deeply committed way. Adam had an *interesting* mind, an *exciting* mind, an *adventurous* mind, as did his friends, the Millennial Mutants . . . I mean ohmygod just compare them with an evening at the book-denuded "library" at the Saint Ray house . . . with its huge plasma TV screen tuned to ESPN and conversations in which wit, if any, consisted of smart, knowing remarks about sex and drinking and sports, featuring comments on the limitations of the metabolically swollen athletes they never tired of watching and sarcastic insults of one another. They would explode with laughter because Julian told I.P. that "Poison people" never got laid—they just got drunk and "blew chunks." Oh, man, how funny was that! Julian could be counted on to make cracks like that, while Hoyt—but she refused to let herself think about Hoyt and the way Hoyt looked. She forced herself completely into the here and now—

—and here and now, Adam had an *interesting* mind, as did all the Millennial Mutants. Their conversations were exciting. They flared and gave off sparks and ranged from the highest—"You can't ascribe 'meaning' to life," Adam once said, "only purpose, which is reproduction, obviously"—to the lowest, or, Charlotte guessed, belly buttons were low enough. The other day Camille Deng had said, "Boys don't grow up to be men; they shrink back into childhood. They look at the scar tissue inside all these bare belly buttons and think they're looking at labia majora and labia minora. They think if they hook up with a girl with a bare belly button, they get to put their dicks in there."

Even putting dicks in labial belly buttons was a more complicated thought than anything Charlotte was likely to hear at the Saint Ray house. She was there once or twice a week now, when Hoyt made the usual "invitation": "If you want to, why don't you come on by . . ." She didn't end the evening by saying good night over her shoulder as she walked up the stairs with some Saint Ray's arm around her, like most of the other girls who showed up that late. It was acknowledged, or assumed, that she was Hoyt's "girlfriend," which made her feel triumphantly cool, but he hadn't pressured her to . . . hook up. She alternated between being grateful for that and wondering what was wrong. Each night he drove her back to Little Yard. They kissed for longer and longer times, in the front seat of the car.

Naturally, it was not something either of them ever said out loud, but since Hoyt knew they were going to kiss good night, he began driving into the parking lot instead of up to the entryway to Little Yard. There were never any parking places, so Hoyt would just pull over to the side of one of the lanes and stop and leave the motor running and the lights on. That reassured Charlotte and at the same time worried her. The running motor and the lights meant he wasn't planning anything more than a kiss. The last one had been a pretty long kiss, but at the same time, she wanted him to want—but not have—more. She wanted it both ways.

And then came the night a car was actually backing out of a space.

"I don't fucking believe this!" said Hoyt. "I thought they had the fucking things bolted to the pavement!"

Hoyt put the Suburban in gear, shot forward and cocked the wheel, and turned so sharply that Charlotte felt as if they were about to roll over. She let out a shriek—"Hoyt!"—and the next thing she knew, they were in the parking spot just vacated by the other car. Cars were parked on either side of them and in front—long rows of cars. Hoyt was laughing.

"That wasn't funny, Hoyt! You liked to get me killed!" That had just slipped out. She sounded just like Aunt Betty.

"Liked to gitchoo killed, hunh?"

Charlotte hoped he wasn't laughing *at* her. Perhaps he thought she was talking mountain talk for humorous effect.

In the next moment, that was no longer the thing to worry about. Hoyt turned off the engine and the lights. Now, in the dark, they were as much as hidden from sight, with rows of empty cars on either side.

Hoyt sank back into his seat and looked at her with a . . . *significant* . . . little smile. Signifying what, she couldn't quite make out. She decided it was a smile of complicity, as if to say, "Well, here we are, Charlotte, here we are, just the two of us, inside the steel-and-glass shell of this vehicle, and we have an understanding we two." But an understanding of precisely what?

It wasn't a fully formed thought, but Charlotte could picture him giving her a long, loving kiss and then pulling her close to him, and the two of them would feel closer and closer, somehow part of one another, and gradually he would begin to tell her how much he loved her. Not in so many words, of course . . . but the accumulation of his musings would add up to that, and after a while she would say she had to go now, and they would have one last long, profound kiss, and she would open the door and descend from the Suburban and hurry through the Gothic tunnel of Mercer Gate and into Little Yard without looking back, and he would gaze longingly at her slim, athletic, perfect form until she disappeared from view. It was like a movie in her head.

In fact what he did was recline still farther in his leather bucket seat and stick his tongue sideways into his cheek, saying, "You know, you look a lot like Britney Spears."

"Don't you think it's time you got a new line, Hoyt?" It gave her immense and inexplicable pleasure to use his name like that, in that natural, casual way.

"Line? Me? What line?"

Charlotte couldn't tell whether he was just having fun, or what. "*What* line? I bet you were saying the same thing to that girl at the I.M."

"What girl at the I.M.?"

"That freshman with the long blond hair and the skintight jeans. You came straight across the dance floor and headed right for her."

"Boy, a blond freshman with tight jeans. That really narrows it down."

"Oh, excuse *me*. I guess you go after so many girls with blond hair and tight jeans, it's hard to keep them straight." All the while, Charlotte was appraising her abilities at repartee. She found herself not too bad.

"How would you know, anyway?" said Hoyt.

"Oh, it wasn't very hard to tell," said Charlotte. "You weren't exactly subtle about it."

"No, I mean, what were you doing at the I.M.? You're not twenty-one. Don't tell me you *lied* about it. I hope you didn't use a fake ID. I hope you know that's a felony. I hope you haven't *told* anybody about it. Now they've got you in the palm of their hand."

Hoyt looked so serious she was afraid for a moment that he really meant all that. And Hoyt must have detected that moment on her face, because he all at once returned to his smile of . . . understanding . . . but much broader this time, and he held out his arms without giving up his deep recline and said, "Come here, Miz Spears."

It crossed Charlotte's mind, as she thrust her body toward him, that her pitching forward from her bucket seat, while he remained in his casual, kingly position, as much as said, "I can't resist you." Nevertheless, she found herself lunging, canting her torso into his arms. *Found* herself . . . oh sure . . . in the very moment that she had to halfway lurch out of the bucket seat—it was so deep—and over that stupid armrest-cupholder-cubby thing between the two seats—she tried to tell herself it *just happened*—it wasn't really what you would call volition.

Now she was more or less on top of him, since he was . . . receiving her advances . . . and he had his arms around her and lifted one hand and placed it gently behind her head and pushed it toward the undamaged side of his face and launched into a kiss. Hoyt began moving his lips as if he were trying to suck the ice cream off the top of a cone without using his teeth. She tried to make her lips move in sync with his. The next thing she knew, Hoyt had put his hand sort of *under* her thigh and hoisted her leg up over his thigh. What was she to do? Was this the point she should say, "Stop!"? No, she shouldn't put it that way. It would be much cooler to say, "No, Hoyt," in an even voice, the way you would talk to a dog that insists on begging at the table. On the other hand, for days and days and days she had wanted him to want to do something like this. All the while they were kissing, and Charlotte decided, well, she guessed the leg was all right—even though the hem of her dress, which she had already shortened in the first place, was pushed up toward the hip socket—because he wasn't doing anything *with* the leg. Instead, his hand was now rubbing her side, from up around the shoulder down to the waist and up from the waist to the shoulder . . . and now down from the shoulder, past the rib cage, and slightly *below* the waist . . . and then up to the shoulder, which it began to rub in a slow, profoundly caressing way . . . and then it made a slow and profoundly caressing trip down the side and then slipped clear off the track just below her armpit, which also was the level of her breast, but then got back on the track and caress caress caress caress it began working on her waist—and thank God she ran and worked out and everything, because if it had found even a garter snake's worth of a tube at her waist, she would have been mortified . . . uh-oh, it was caressing caressing caressing caressing down her side *below* the waist, where it found the big bone that was the summit of her ilial crest caress caress caress caress, but what if it came inland, moving toward *there*—what would she do then? . . . And it *did*! It moved *down* the crest and into the gulley formed by the leg meeting the lower abdomen, the gulley that leads down *there*—and she twitched in the gulley, involuntarily—

—and the hand *leaped* back up to the side of her hip while they continued kissing, and now it was working its way back up, toward the shoulder presumably, or could it—

—he put his tongue in her mouth . . . Uh-oh, it—the hand—had jumped the track and was heading inland toward her rib cage until it reached . . . *there*! But no, it stopped at the side of the breast and began caressing that, the flesh on the side . . . *Streak!* Suddenly it had leaped to the upper outside of her thigh, where the flesh was bare, until she felt the hem of her dress move up on her skin until the hand was only inches from her panties and creep creep caress caress a finger—or was it two fingers?—two, perhaps even three, were *under* the elastic band of her panties where they fit around the leg and were now traveling down the gulley, and any moment, any millisecond, she would have to say "No, Hoyt"—but this was what she had wanted him to want to do—and she was caught between excitement and panic, and it—the tongue—she felt as if she were swallowing it and she didn't mind it anymore because Hoyt had begun to moan softly—he couldn't very well *say* anything with his tongue in her mouth—*streak* the hand had leaped back up to the rib cage, no longer on the side but going up the front, inland. Slither slither slither slither went the tongue, but the hand—that was what she tried to concentrate on, the hand, since it had the entire terrain of her torso to explore and not just the otorhinolaryngological caverns—oh God, it was not just at the border where the flesh of the breast joins the pectoral sheath of the chest—no, the hand was cupping her entire right—*Now!* she must say "No, Hoyt" and talk to him like a dog—and oh God, what was she supposed to do *now*—inasmuch as it, his hand, was at this instant passing over her entire right breast and she could feel the pressure—light pressure, but pressure—*Now!* the *No, Hoyt*—but it was as if the cord between her will and her central nervous system had been cut and there was even something about the big slug that had entered her mouth that now seemed part of *her*, so much so that she began running her own tongue over the intruder tongue and sought to put her tongue inside *his* mouth, although things were getting congested and she *couldn't*, under any circumstances, let the hand slip inside her bra—and in the next instant it was *gone* from up there—it had leaped again!—from up here perilously close to down there, sliding up her bare thigh to the elastic of her panties—the fingers went *under* the elastic of the panties moan moan moan moan moan went Hoyt as he slithered slithered slithered slithered and caress caress caress caress went the fingers until they must be only eighths of inches from the border of her pubic hair—what's *that*!—her panties were so *wet* down . . . *there*—the fingers had definitely reached the outer stand of the field of pubic hair and would soon plunge into the *wet mess* that was waiting right . . . *there*—*there*—

Without conscious decision she withdrew her tongue from Hoyt's mouth, pulled her head back—and snapped, owner to dog, "Hoyt—no!"

"No—*what?*"

A bit shortly: "*You* know what."

"I know *what* what?" The voice was combative but the face was a dog's, the dog that has been caught in a forbidden act and reprimanded and lowers its head and looks up at its owner with sad eyes, distrustful lest it be reprimanded again or else swatted.

But he quickly recovered his Cool King Hoyt of Saint Ray authority and said in a calm voice, oozing with the accusation of contemptible violence against cool code: "What are you doing?"

"I'm going to my room, Hoyt."

Her voice was faltering. Only the would-be confident tacking on of the *Hoyt* at the end gave it any semblance of confidence whatsoever. So she reached out and stroked his uninjured left cheek.

"I'm sorry, Hoyt, but I have to go."

She tried to plant a light kiss on his lips, but he turned his head petulantly to put his lips out of range.

Now afraid she'd gone too far—by not going far enough—and ruined everything: "I'm really sorry, Hoyt."

"Roger that," said Hoyt with a devastatingly kind smile that as much as said, "This is the last good-bye."

"It's just that—"

"You have to go." He shrugged and then smiled the devastating smile again and shrugged again.

Charlotte got out and stepped over a railroad tie marking the perimeter of the parking lot and walked up a small grassy slope toward Mercer Gate. A flash of recall—her father with his mermaid tattoo beaming like a red alert from his forearm, shooing off the student porter because he thought he was going to demand a tip . . . the ratty camper shell on the ratty pickup truck . . . the Amorys at the Sizzlin' Skillet—which is to say, the defeats, all the defeats . . . and how they began . . . She was all at once overcome by the possibility that what had just happened was the worst defeat of all—giving up a cool coup—a boyfriend, a *senior*, gorgeous-looking, a victory in and of himself—how she would stand out!—and she had let him go *that* far . . . before her little Sparta girl panic set in—but she just couldn't let him do what he was about to do . . . It hadn't been a *decision* at all, had it. It had been a reflex, as natural as drawing your hand away when the griddle plate on top of the woodstove is red-hot—she'd seen it when it was truly red-hot. A group of boys and girls was just entering the tunnel of Mercer Gate, girls screaming the scream of excitement from being with boys and one boy shouting in a mock-serious deep voice, which you'd think was the funniest voice in the history of the world from the way the girls were screaming. The old-fashioned lights up on stanchions near the tunnel made them all a sickly jaundice yellow until they disappeared into the shadows in the tunnel. She could hear the throaty roar of Hoyt's Suburban starting up, the roar of a rusted-out muffler, if she knew anything about it—Daddy would have repaired it himself in no time—and she was dying to look back, *dying* to, even though she wouldn't be able to tell whether Hoyt was looking at her or not, given the darkness and the sick, jaundiced, moribund light from the useless, fussy old-fashioned light fixture reflecting on the windshield—she wanted desperately to look at him, as if to say, "I didn't mean that to be final, Hoyt!—please, you mustn't take it that way!"

"Charlotte."

She looked about. Bettina was just coming in, too.

Bettina, in a concerned voice: "Hey, what's up?"

"It shows, hunh?"

"Well . . . yeah," said Bettina. "You're not too hard to read, you know."

Now they were in the gloom of the tunnel, where a couple of lamps gave off a sickly, feverish glow that was worse than no light at all.

"I just did something *so-o-o-o* stupid," said Charlotte. She said it louder than she had meant to, and the words echoed slightly in the tunnel. For a moment the *so-o-o-o-o* lengthened like a moan and a whimper and a stifled wail of grief.

"You did *what* so stupid?" said Bettina.

But Charlotte wasn't listening. An impulse had begun wriggling inside her central nervous system, a tiny impulse, which, if it could have spoken, would have asked: was there some pretext, any pretext, on which she could call him without seeming to be begging?

When Hoyt returned, only Vance and Julian were left in the library. Vance said to Hoyt, "You're not back as soon this time, playa. Getting any sump'm sump'm?"

Hoyt sank into the Hoyt easy chair and said, "Welllll . . . I wouldn't call it genuine *pink* sump'm sump'm, but we work at it. You know? We persevere. We'll get there. In fact—you know what? I'm going to invite her to the formal."

"*That* little girl?" said Julian. "What about Whatshername? I call her

Whatshername because it took you about two months of cum dumping"—
he motioned upstairs with his thumb—"before you learned her name. If the
Guinness Book of Records had a category for anonymous cum dumping,
you'd be in the fucking book, playa."

Hoyt stared off toward nowhere and said, "She was good sump'm
sump'm, man. She really fucking was. But she's given me the big fuck-you.
She won't even fucking talk to me on the phone anymore. Ungrateful—she
claims I'm nothing but another *frat playa*—her words."

Vance and Julian howled. "A *playa*!" said Julian. "Fuck! You shouldn't
even *associate* with a girl who's no better judge of character than that!"

"Julian's right!" said Vance. "You don't go bringing an imbecile like that
to a *Saint Ray formal*! I mean, shit!"

They had a good time with that for a while, but they finally ran out of
wit, and Hoyt said, "The fact remains, how the fuck can I even *go* to the formal with no date? I can't just call up some girl right on the verge of the thing
and say, 'Hey, gorgeous, how about coming with me to the Saint Ray formal,
so I can have some sump'm sump'm like everybody else?'"

"You can always hijack I.P.'s date once you get there," said Julian.

"What are you talking about?" said Hoyt.

"You know this girl Gloria—she's a Psi Phi? She's bangin'! She's awesome. I'd give my left nut for some a that. How fucking I.P. ever talked her
into being his date, I don't fucking know."

"Well . . . shit," said Hoyt. Pause. "Nawwww . . . I'm gonna take a chance
and invite Charlotte."

"Hey, dude!" said Vance. "You know her fucking name! This must
be love!"

20. COOL

ou keep saying 'cool,'" said Edgar, "but what does that mean, somebody's cool?"

"If you have to ask," said Roger Kuby, "you're clearly not cool."

"I wouldn't have it any other way," said Edgar, "but what does it *mean*? If somebody came up to you and said, 'What's the definition of cool?' what would you say? I've never heard anybody even try."

Edgar only took charge like this when the Mutants met in his apartment. They loved to meet here. For all of his mild manner, Edgar lived a good eight blocks deep into the City of God in a small 1950s apartment building. Most of the other tenants were Hispanic or Chinese. The elevator was loud, rickety, and mysteriously dented. Edgar's hallway was drab to the verge of decrepit. It had eight identical metal-clad flush doors, all with more than one lock. But when Edgar's door opened—magic!—inside was a wonderworld of taste . . . and expense, at least by Dupont undergraduate standards. None of the rest of the Mutants' living quarters rated any classification more exalted than "bohemian." Edgar, by contrast, was more like "cutting edge." He had modern leather and stainless-steel furniture, brass lamps from some place in Nebraska, and a rug—a huge, real woven rug in a rich camel's-hair color, woven God knows how many tufts to the square inch so that it looked as smooth and luxurious as cashmere. Edgar himself was holding court—in an authentic Ruhlmann "elephant chair" from the 1920s. His father, a distinguished biologist, was CEO of Clovis Genetics, an heir to the Remington munitions fortune, and an art collector and patron.

Camille said, "Well, I can tell you one thing. 'Cool's' got nothing to do with women. Nobody ever calls a woman cool."

"That's 'cause guys like you'n'me, Camille, we like 'em *hot*," said Roger. That got a laugh. Thus encouraged, Roger looked at Randy, he who had come out of the closet, and said, "Right, Randy?"—and gave him a mock grin and two fast-pumping thumbs-ups.

Randy's face turned red. He was speechless. Adam felt terribly embarrassed for him. He glanced at Charlotte. She was engrossed, smiling slightly.

Camille shot Roger a scorching look, but not, Adam realized, because of what Roger had said to Randy. It was because he was interrupting her point, her insight. Any Mutant would feel the same way.

Adam jumped in so that Charlotte wouldn't think he was out of it. "That's not really true, Camille. I've heard girls called cool. Think of—"

"Yeah, if they're the frat-hag, buddy-girl type," said Camille, breaking back in, fire in her eyes. "It's a male thing. Not that I give a good fuck. The guys they call cool are all a bunch of fratty dickheads, if you really think about it. They're guys who demonstrate their ignorance in some approved way."

Greg jumped in. "Actually, I think Camille's right."

"Oh, wow, thank you," said Camille. "*Actually* . . . you *think*."

Adam could tell by the way Edgar was leaning forward over the table, swollen with a lungful of air, that he was primed to begin the discourse he no doubt had in mind when he first introduced the subject. But no-oh-oh, old Greg wasn't about to let that happen, was he. He was also leaning forward. He had his torso twisted until it was vertical to the table, as if he were a knife primed to thrust.

Edgar began, "When you think—"

Sure enough, Greg cut him off. "I *like* Camille's idea." His eyes swiftly panned the table—no doubt, thought Adam, to indicate that he himself the leader was running the show and that his remarks were for the illumination of one and all. "I wouldn't go so far as to say cool equals stupid, but being a dim bulb doesn't disqualify you, either. Treyshawn Diggs is cool, right? Nobody's gonna say the Tower ain't cool, and he's got like the mental faculties of that . . . that . . ."—his eyes darted about, trying to find something brainless enough.

Randy Grossman and Camille gasped simultaneously. "Why don't we be a little racist about it!" said Camille.

"Racist?" said Greg. "What's racist about somebody being a fucking moron?" Smart comeback, Adam thought with gloomy envy. They weren't about to contradict him on that. "All you're saying is, you were never in a class with Treyshawn Diggs. I *was*. I was in his seminar section of Economics 106, and we're learning about how you measure the GNP. The T.A.'s talking about how you arrive at a gross sum for wholesale transactions and how you divide that into two sums and subtract each sum from the sum of gross manufacturing output on the one hand, the sum of gross service costs on the other, and you take the resulting sums and divide them by this and that, and I mean it's a *beast*, and hands are going up all over the place, and one of them's Treyshawn Diggs's. The T.A. can't believe it. I mean, Treyshawn hasn't raised his hand for *any*thing the entire semester, and so the T.A. calls on Treyshawn, and you know what the Tower says? He says, 'What's a sum?'"

Greg himself was already laughing by the time he got to *What's a sum?* And then some vivid memory of the actual scene must have bubbled up into his brain, because the laugh turned into a manic cackle, an uncontrollable yawp, and Greg began beating his fists on the arms of his chair with his head down and his eyes shut, and he tried to repeat the words *What's a sum?* but tidal waves of mirth came rolling up from his innards and slammed the words against the roof of his mouth. Adam glanced at Charlotte. She was smiling, shaking with chuckles, practically laughing out loud, Greg's hysterical seizure was so infectious. She was *absorbed* with Greg.

Head still down, eyes still squeezed shut, Greg brought his hands up in front of his face, palms toward Camille, in a defensive gesture—"I know . . . I know"—before giving way to new paroxysms of laughter. Adam's envy turned to resentment, and resentment reached the threshold of anger. The basketball team was *his* terrain! Treyshawn Diggs and company were *his* exclusive conversational nuggets. The sonofabitch was *poaching* on *his* preserve! One of the few compensations for the hours and hours he had to waste on these imbeciles was his status among the Mutants as *the* reigning expert on big-time collegiate sports, and here was Greg, right in front of Charlotte, using *his* material and captivating her with some shamelessly purloined spiel about Treyshawn Diggs!

Now—before Greg could get hold of himself—while he was still in the thrall of his self-amusement, *now* was the time to take back the subject and *ram it down his throat*.

"You're absolutely right, Greg . . . up to a point." Suavely masking his anger . . . "But there's a more fundamental principle here. Being a basketball star doesn't guarantee you're cool. I'll give you a good example. You know this freshman, Vernon Congers? He's taken Jojo Johanssen's place on the starting five away from him. You'll see why when we play Maryland next week."

The Mutants never admitted to being sports fans . . . *themselves* . . . but this bit of news had their attention.

Edgar said, "But I saw him—"

Adam quickly pulled a Greg and cut Edgar off once more. "I know, you saw him start the last game. That's only because Buster"—first name familiarity—"still starts him in the Buster Bowl because he doesn't want to start an all-black team at home. But Congers plays twice as many minutes as Jojo even at home, and Buster's already starting Congers on the road." Peripheral glance: good; now Charlotte was absorbed in *him*.

He proceeded to regale them with an account of how Charles Bousquet made life miserable for Congers and how pathetic Congers's attempted comebacks were. "But you wanna know the reason they don't think Congers is cool? This gets down to the underlying principle I'm talking about. It's not because he's stupid, it's because—"

Camille broke in: "Is this Congers by any chance black?"

Warily: "Unh-hunh . . ."

Camille said, "So here we go again, right?"

"Whattaya *talking* about, Camille? Bousquet's black, too!" said Adam.

"Oh, that really does make a huge difference, doesn't it."

Not about to let this degenerate into a squabble with Camille, Adam raised his voice and bellowed right on over her: "IT'S NOT BECAUSE HE'S STUPID! It's because he's *defensive*! Charles"—*I'm on a first-name basis with him, too, of course*—"asks him what's the capital of Pennsylvania, and the poor bastard freezes up. He knows he's doomed. He starts to say Philadelphia, but he knows Charles would've never asked him if it was that easy. You can see the humiliation in his face. He knows he's been reduced to a 250-pound loser. He wants a trapdoor so he can fall right through it and disappear. So the main thing is confidence . . . confidence and insouciance." He hoped the big word impressed Charlotte. "All he had to do was act like he didn't give a shit about what Charles"—first-name basis—"or anybody else thought of his intelligence. Confidence plus a little roughhousing isn't bad, either. Next time he ought to grab Charles in a headlock and say, 'This is an

IQ test, Chuck, and the question is, how you gon' get your head back.'"
Without meaning to, Adam had put so much emotion into saying "This is
an IQ test, Chuck" and the rest of it that he half realized he was actually acting out a revenge fantasy. He had involuntarily made a fist and lowered his
shoulder and cocked his arm into a choke-hold clamp as if it were *he* who
wanted to crush somebody's windpipe. Actually, Bousquet would be about
the last member of the basketball team he would want to finish off. The anabolic bastard he *really* had in the grip was Jojo—no, Curtis Jones, who had
gone out of his way to be rude and humiliating—no, it was *every* big-time
athlete he held in that lethal lock, every lacrosse player—*those* cretinous
bastards—every jock, every bully who had ever walked over him as if it were
in the natural order of things that little Adam Gellin was a weakling.

Already, with peripheral vision, he could see Charlotte looking at him
in a funny way—

—and so he quickly tried to cover up his hatred of the Curtis Joneses
and Jojo Johanssens of the world by amping up his insight's brilliant light.
"Of course, a guy like Congers, he got into Dupont with three-figure SATs.
We're talking low seven hundreds, maybe—"

"Aw, that can't be true," said Greg. "They couldn't *afford* to take a
chance like that."

"Wanna bet?" said Adam. "What's the average SAT at Dupont now?
Fourteen-ninety? They'll knock off five hundred points for a basketball or
football player—"

Greg broke in. "Yeah, and that's not even close to low seven hun—"

Gamely, Adam overrode Greg. "But the point I'm making is confidence
or putting on the appearance of confidence. That's at the core of being cool,
and I don't care who you're talking about."

"Confident about what?" said Randy.

"Everything," said Adam. "Taste, status, appearance, opinions, con-
frontations—you know, like dealing with other students who are trying to
fuck you over or professors who are reprimanding you—"

"Shit, the professors don't reprimand anybody at Dupont," said Randy.
"I wish they did. What they actually do is, they tell the T.A. to give the guy a
bad grade, and they hide in their office."

Camille sighed, as if about to fire another Deng rocket, probably because of the word "guy," but she said nothing.

"Did you ever have Ms. Gomdin in psych—" Randy began.

But Adam wasn't about to allow the subject to change to the eccentricities of Dupont pedagogy, so he walked right over Randy: "THE OTHER SIDE OF BEING CONFIDENT"—Randy looked startled— "IS NEVER TO PLEASE PEOPLE"—Randy was vanquished, so Adam lowered his voice—"or not obviously. The cool guy doesn't flatter anybody or act obsequious or even impressed by somebody—unless it's some athlete, maybe, maybe—and you don't act enthusiastic unless it's about sports, sex, or getting high. It's okay to be enthusiastic about something, like Dickens— although if you want my honest opinion, I don't know how anybody could be *enthusiastic* about Dickens—"

Randy smiled and raised the first two fingers of his right hand and said, "Peace," which Adam took to be approval, and so he couldn't resist dilating upon this extraneous obiter dictum: "I mean, you can be a lot of things about Dickens, but I don't see 'enthusiastic' being one of them—"

"You really can't see being enthusiastic about *Great Expectations* or *Dombey and Son?*" said Greg.

Fucking Greg again. Nothing to do but walk right over him again: "OKAY, I CAN SEE IT, but the point I'm making is, sure, you can be en-thusiastic about Dickens or Foucault—or Derrida, for that matter—but if you want to be cool, you don't show it, you don't say it, you don't even let on. A cool guy—and I've seen this happen—can secretly work his ass off five— no, four—nights a week at the library, but he has to make light of it if any-body catches on. You know what the favorite major of the cool guy is? Econ. Econ is fireproof, if you know what I mean. It's practical. You can't possibly be taking it because you really *love* economics."

Greg had to be heard from, of course. "You're leaving out the most ob-vious thing, Adam."

"Which is what?"

"Size and build. It's a hell of a lot easier to be cool if you're tall and you spend half the week pumping yourself up on the Cybex machines. That's what makes me laugh, all these guys—"

Goddamn Greg. "ANOTHER THING IS IF YOU START SOME CLUB—" said Adam, but Greg was not one to let himself get walked over.

"—who go around campus walking like this." He stood up and started— "—THE ADMINISTRATION APPROVES OF—"

The others were laughing—and ignoring him. Greg was walking across the floor with his thighs straddled and his chin pulled down and his trapezius muscles flexed up, to make his neck look bigger—"as if they're, you know, like so . . . *hung* . . . they can't get their legs any closer together—"

"—LIKE SOME ENVIRONMENTAL—" It was no use. Fucking Greg had the floor, and the others found him *so* amusing . . . laughter laughter laughter. Well, he, Adam, had held the floor for a good stretch, and he, Adam, had established the basic concept of cool, the theory of confidence. Although he hadn't dared look at Charlotte for more than an instant at a time, she had been . . . engrossed . . . so he chanced a glance now. She was engrossed, all right, but with Greg's stupid act, smiling and chuckling—

—and then she spoke up! To Greg! "You know Jojo Johanssen? He's on the basketball team? He walks just like that except he also sneaks looks at himself in reflections in the windows? And he straightens his arm . . . like this?—and all these *things* pop out back here." She put her hand on the triceps of her straight arm.

Hawhawhaw. Greg was delighted, of course, and Randy, Roger, and Edgar joined in the merriment, and Charlotte was mighty pleased with herself. Her implied approval of Greg's puerile form of humor bothered Adam, but there was something else as well. He had never seen Charlotte make fun of anybody before. Somehow this was an opening breach in her purity, her innocence. He didn't want her to be like other people, mocking, cutting, cynical, even though he didn't hesitate to be that way himself. But Charlotte was different. She had a different order of intelligence and charm.

"I thought you liked Jojo," he said. It was actually a reprimand.

"I *do* like him," said Charlotte. "I can comment on the way he walks and still *like* him, can't I?"

"Yeah, what's the matter with you, Adam?" said Randy. "You know Jojo. You're not saying Charlotte's *wrong*, are you? I've noticed that you have the occasional comment about Jojo, and I wouldn't exactly characterize them as flattering, and you're his tutor."

Adam shook his head with exasperation. Somehow he couldn't stand Randy's referring to her as "Charlotte" that way, as if she was *theirs*, too, now.

"Adam Gellin and the mouths of babes," said Camille.

So she knew exactly what he was thinking . . . He wondered if everything he felt about Charlotte was obvious.

He had no way of knowing it, but he was filled—*suffused*—with a love for a woman that only a virgin could feel. In his eyes she was more than flesh and blood and more than spirit. She was . . . an essence . . . an essence of *life* that remained tactile and *alive*—his loins certainly remained alive at this moment, welling up beneath his tighty-whiteys—and yet a . . . a . . . a *universal solvent* that penetrated his very hide and commandeered his entire nervous system from his brain to the tiniest nerve endings. If he could only embrace her—and find that she had been *dying* for him to do just that—she, her tactile *essence*, would come flooding into every cell, into all the billion miles of spooled DNA—he couldn't imagine a unit of his body so minute that she would not *suffuse* it—and they would . . . *explode* their virginities in a single sublime ineffable yet neurological, all too neurological, moment! They would—

"—the flip side of it, Adam? Does that mean it's cool for athletes to do that?"

Pop. It was Edgar. Edgar had just asked him a question—about what? His mind spun.

"Except for athletes!" said Greg. Dependable old Greggo—immediately taking advantage of his lapse in attention in order to leap back into the ring.

"What do you mean, except for athletes?" said Edgar.

"Treyshawn Diggs does good works," said Greg. "Or they show pictures of him in the newspaper, and he's down in 'the ghetto' helping 'the youth'—and as long as it's *him*, that's cool."

"What's wrong with that?" said Camille.

"There's nothing *wrong* with it—"

"Then why are you saying"—she mugged a prissy expression and minced out the words—"*the ghetto* and *the youth?*"

"Stop breaking my . . . scones, Camille. All I'm saying is that if you're a sports star, you can act enthusiastic about some charity and still be cool, because you're precertified macho, and in that case you can show your tender side—like feminine side. Somebody like Tower, it even makes him look more macho by contrast."

"Okay, I'll grant you that," said Edgar, "but first you've got to be a *big* athlete."

"Yeah," said Greg. "Or else you've got to have—"

Adam glanced at Charlotte. She was looking from Edgar to Greg and from Greg to Edgar. She was *absorbed* in what they were saying. The urge overcame him. Got to break back in—

But Greg beat him to the punch: "I'd describe cool in an entirely different way. I'd say cool is . . ."

At this point Greg made the mistake of rolling his eyes up and hesitating as he searched for *le mot juste*—

—and Adam slipped in a counterpunch: "Includes nobody at this table"—as if he were finishing Greg's sentence for him. He sped up and raised his voice before Greg could recover: "I MEAN, FACE IT. BY OUR OWN DEFINITION—MILLENNIAL MUTANTS—we're flaunting our enthusiasm for academics. We're all out to get Rhodes scholarships—"

"Oh ho—the boy bleeds ego!" said Greg.

"DON'T GIVE ME THAT SHIT, GREG! Are you really gonna sit there and pretend—I mean, this is *me* you're talking to and a table full of self-professed Millennial Mutants!"

"There's goals, and there's bleeding fucking egos, and yours—"

"Oh, shut the fuck up," said Camille. "You guys are giving me a pain in the crank."

"The *crank*?" said Randy Grossman with a whoop of delight. "Please, Madame Deng, be so kind as to show us your crank!"

"You wouldn't know what it was if you saw it," said Camille. It was a snarl.

Randy's face, which he had lifted in majestic hauteur when he came out of the closet six months ago, fell and turned red. His eyelids were brimming with tears. In a low, hoarse, beaten voice he said, "I never expected that—from *you*, Camille."

So womanish! thought Adam. He immediately hated himself for the thought. After all, coming out wasn't like switching a light, probably. There must be a painful period during which someone like Randy remains terribly sensitive. But he looked like a woman, all the same. He looked like Adam's mother, like Frankie, on the brink of one of her crying jags after his father informed her that she hadn't "grown." Adam felt guilty all over again.

But not Camille. "The fuck, Randy? Suck it up, Randy. I didn't say cunt, I said crank."

Randy averted his eyes, turned his anguished face away, covered his eyes with his hand, and started pouting.

"Come on, Randy," said Edgar solicitously, "Camille said crank. She was joking. Who *would* know what a crank was, even if they saw one? *I* wouldn't."

After that, the weekly meeting of the Millennial Mutants deteriorated rapidly. Adam kept glancing at Charlotte. She was obviously fascinated by the whole thing. Her eyes jumped from one combatant to the other. Adam was not fascinated. He was no longer even thinking about Randy and Camille—or not in the sense of Randy versus Camille. He, if not they, had put it behind him and moved on to another question entirely. How had he performed in her eyes—Charlotte's? Was she saying to herself, He's weak. He let Greg break in and ram his own point about the Rhodes scholarship competition right down his throat . . . and then just sat there like a dummy and let Camille and Randy take the conversation off on a whole other tangent about pariahism. Or would that be more than offset by the fact that it was he who had actually defined cool. It was he who had developed the concepts of confidence, defensiveness, the suppression of enthusiasm for anything or masking of enthusiasm for anything adults might want to pat you on the head for—

He kept torturing himself with Doubt, swinging back and forth from the positive to the negative. Had she shown any signs at all of becoming comfortable with the Mutants? She was fascinated by the whole Mutant mission in an intellectually barren era, wasn't she—but what was she to make of Randy or Camille? The evening died a whimpering death, and Edgar drove them back through the City of God and to the campus in his Armor My Baby tank, the Denali.

Adam insisted on walking Charlotte back to Little Yard, and she was glad. She felt euphoric. She had just been witness to the sort of conversation she had just *known* Dupont would be thriving with—back when Dupont was an . . . El Dorado, a glow, a vague but glorious destination on the other side of the mountains. The Millennial Mutants didn't just *use* this word cool like everybody else at Dupont, they analyzed it and broke it down into . . . to . . . to intellectual components that would never even occur to indisputably cool guys such as the Saint Ray house was full of, such as Hoyt himself first and foremost . . . while the Mutants were openly, brazenly, proudly uncool . . .

They had barely reached the Great Yard when she felt Adam's hand snaking down the inner surface of her wrist. She let him. Then she let him intertwine his fingers with hers. He was so bright . . . so much the sort of person she had hoped would become part of her life when she went off to Dupont. She suddenly felt so grateful to him, she leaned her shoulder against his arm as they walked. He looked at her with searching intensity now, as opposed to all the little glances he kept flashing at her when they were at Edgar's.

Adam tightened the hold on her hand, and that plus the look he was giving her somehow made the silence hang heavier and heavier.

"Well, Charlotte . . ." he said finally. His voice sounded funny—nervous, in fact. He paused, as if he really didn't know what he was going to say next. Then he said, "Did you have a good time?" His voice was a little clearer but still almost half a croak.

Charlotte said, "You know . . . I really did." She consciously prevented herself from pronouncing "did" *dee-ud*. "Everybody was so inter—resting." Likewise, she had almost let "interesting" loop up into four syllables with a question mark at the end, but she caught herself after the first syllables.

"Like who?" Adam's voice sounded a little better now.

"Oh, like Camille. You'd never know, the way she talks like a . . . a . . ."

"A blitzed frat boy?"

"Yeah! But she's really got a sharp mind. Everybody at the table was so . . . quick. You know?"

"Such as—give me another example."

"Well . . . like Greg. Greg was funny, wasn't he? The way he was imitating an athlete walking—it's so true! That's Jojo all over! I mean, I just love the way you all know how to . . . to *isolate* a part of something, and then when you're able to see that, you're able to see the whole thing in a different way, in a—I don't know—a more analytical way, I guess. I loved all that."

Now it was Charlotte who intensified her grip on Adam's hand. She was thrilled. This evening was a real adventure of the mind. Right over there, in the weak antique glow of its streetlamps and immense shadows that all but swallowed them up, was the beginning of Ladding Walk. And far, far down Ladding Walk, deep, deep in the darkness, was the Saint Ray house—the library, which had no books . . . the big plasma TV set, always turned on to ESPN SportsCenter . . . There were Hoyt, and Julian and Vance and Boo . . . and the sluts who feigned an interest in their dumb comments. She could *see* Hoyt . . . so comfortable in his listless cynicism, which, in any event—just like Edgar had said!—never had to do with anything but sports, sex, drink . . . and contempt for people who weren't cool . . . en route to the destination, which was always to get trashed, wasted, hammered, crunked up, bombed, wrecked, sloshed, fried, flapjacked, fucked-up, or get plainlong fucked, laid, drained, get some ass, get some head, some skull, a lube job, get your oil changed, get some brown sugar, quiff, goo, pussy . . . pussy . . . *pussy* . . . when hardly a step away was a world of ideas—about everything from the psychology of the individual to the cosmology of—of—*everything*!

Charlotte found herself holding Adam's hand tightly and once more leaning against his shoulder. He stopped. He released her hand and turned to face her. It was obvious what should come next. She experienced such a tender feeling for him, and she wanted to let him know that—and in that same instant she wished . . . he just wouldn't. He slipped an arm around her waist and pulled her toward him and at the same time pulled his head back so as to look into her eyes, she guessed . . . and what *was* that look?—that little smile? Mainly he looked nervous. And then he took hold of one of the temples of his glasses; and he pulled it up slightly, abandoned that activity, returned the hand to the back of her waist, and then cocked his head slightly and brought it closer and closer to hers. He was blinking rapidly, and it dawned on Charlotte that he had been trying to figure out whether to take his glasses off first or not. He brought his lips down to hers, and she parted her lips the way she had learned to do it with Hoyt—and her lips landed above and below Adam's. She brought her lips closer together in order to engage his, but in that same moment he had opened his wider, seeking out hers, and when the two sets of lips finally met squarely, it was more like a . . . mash . . . than a kiss, and so she, with a mixture of sympathy and guilt—why guilt?—uttered a little moan. He pulled his head back just far enough to mouth the words, "Oh, Charlotte!"—then mashed her lips again.

Charlotte was too embarrassed—embarrassed?—but that was the way she felt!—to look at his face again. So she pulled her head downward from his lips and rested it on his chest, to spare his feelings. Big mistake. This merely spurred him on to more passionate moaning. He began rocking her body from one side to the other, saying, "Charlotte, Charlotte, Charlotte," and then moaning some more. Now he seemed to draw her even closer, and he pressed his hip bones up against hers. And then—Charlotte couldn't be absolutely sure—he seemed to be thrusting his mons pubis in search of hers. She stuck her buttocks out far enough for that to be impossible. She took her head off his chest and looked at his face. Fog was developing on the lower part of his glasses, which made his eyes appear to be peering over a wall. "What are you thinking?" she said. She knew she shouldn't have—but how else to evade, gently, the quest of his rocking mons pubis?

Sure enough, he stopped rocking, although he kept an arm around her waist. He looked into her eyes and said, "I'm thinking—I'm thinking I've wanted to do this, to hold you like this, from the very moment I first laid my eyes on you."

His throat had gone dry, and his voice was so hoarse and low and raspy it was as if he were pushing it on a sled on a dusty road.

"From the very first moment?" She pulled her head back so that he could see she was smiling. She thought she'd try to lighten the tone of this tête-à-tête. "You sure didn't *look* that way! Matter of fact, it looked to me you weren't very happy to see me sitting at that computer there in the library."

"All right, then why don't we call it the *second* moment."

He was smiling, but it wasn't what you would call a merry old smile. It appeared to be underwater, in a pool of the tears of a happy but terribly poignant recollection.

"It didn't take me long to change," he said. "I hope you remember that, too. Don't you remember how I all of a sudden changed and introduced myself? And asked you your name?" The same dry voice, but this time with a certain extra note, a note of tender hush that one adopts when revealing lovely secrets that lie just below the surface. "I guess I can tell you this now. Afterward, I was sorry I had introduced myself to you as just Adam. You know how you get in the habit here of introducing yourself just by your first name? So naturally you just said Charlotte. Did you know there are *five* freshmen named Charlotte?"

This gave Charlotte an opening to break free of him by jumping backward and putting her fists on her hips and her arms akimbo in the look of mock reproof a girl adopts when her boyfriend reveals emotions he couldn't very well have confessed to before now . . . "You actually *looked it up?*" She went up to the coloratura level on the *up*. "You went through the whole list of freshmen?"

Adam opened his eyes very wide, compressed his lips, and began nodding yes in the way lovers do when they admit to a euphoric guilt over something irrational the obsessiveness of their love has driven them to do.

"I don't—*believe* it!" cried Charlotte with the same smile and her eyes wide in wonderment. Above all, she wanted to keep things . . . out of the mush.

But his face went very serious. "Charlotte—" His voice was as dry and constricted as could be. "Why don't you come to my apartment, where we can really talk? I have so much to tell you. I don't live very far from here. I can walk you back."

This caught her unprepared. He could probably read the dismay on her face, but she managed to say, "I can't." She just blurted it out, and yet, oddly, she said it correctly, *can't* instead of *caint*. Then she began ransacking her brain madly for the answer to the question that was bound to come next.

"Why not?" said Adam.

"I've got to study. I've got a neuroscience quiz in the morning"—which she didn't—"and I should've been studying when we went over to Edgar's."

"Not even for a little while? It's really not very far from here." The way he said it, he was all but begging.

"No, Adam!" she said, managing to smile at the same time. "It's a hard course!"

"Well . . . okay. I just wish—" He broke off the sentence. He came toward her with an uneasy expression on his face—the opposite of confident, it occurred to Charlotte—fiddled with his glasses, and this time took them off. It was like printing an announcement.

Charlotte mashed her lips against his for a moment, then adroitly slid her head forward until they were cheek to cheek and let him hold her for a few seconds. He started the rocking business again, so she broke free and smiled at him as if giving up the bliss of that embrace was the hardest thing in the world for her, but she had to be stern with herself.

"I've just got to go, Adam. I wish I didn't." She had already turned and started walking toward the entrance of the Little Yard by the time the *didn't* passed her lips.

"Charlotte."

From the grave, beseeching tone, she knew she'd better stop. She turned about. Soundlessly but unmistakably, his lips, tongue, and mouth formed the words "I love you." He opened his mouth so wide on the *love* that when he snapped his tongue from the roof of his mouth to just behind his lower teeth, she could see his glottis guarding the descent into the larynx. He gave her a little wave and a smile of sweet sorrow. He had his glasses back on. Being nearsighted, he used them for distance.

Charlotte gave him the same sort of wave back and some sweet sorrow along with it and hurried through the deep archway.

For the first time since she had come here, the courtyard seemed like a marvelously cozy, comforting, and at the same time luxurious haven. The luxury was in the way the lights here and there lit up the extravagantly leaded casement windows and brought the incisions of the brick and stonework into deep shadows.

Had she ever felt this confused, this delightfully confused, in her entire life? Being with the Mutants and feeling the . . . *lift* . . . of their intelligence and their *ravenous appetite* . . . for knowledge and their ceaseless . . . *quest*— even in light moments—to find the very structure, the very psychological and social structure, of the world . . . What a rush the evening had given her! She *wanted* to fall in love with Adam. He was the best looking of the boys in the group. Actually, Edgar was basically the best looking, but he had a baby-ish coating of buttery flesh, and he was so unrelentingly serious, which only made it worse when he tried to be cool—leaning back aristocratically in his bulbous "elephant" chair—the insouciant way Hoyt settled himself into the leather upholstery of the Saint Rays' *liber*-less library. Insouciance was the word. It was as if some Frenchman had coined it knowing that Hoyt Thorpe was coming into the world. But Hoyt did care about things if they were important enough. He had assaulted a brute twice his size . . . for her.

She felt so confused—yet she was soaring!

21. GET WHAT?

The next morning was one of those damp, chilly, gloomy, gray affairs, and windy on top of that. The wind got to you when you walked across the Great Yard, especially if, like Charlotte, your only pair of jeans was dirty and you didn't have tights or boarding-school-girl high wool socks or even a pair of panty hose. The wind invaded her shanks, flanks, and declivities as if her skirt wasn't there. Much of it wasn't, since she had hemmed it so high—and sloppily, since Momma had never insisted that her precocious little genius reduce herself to such Alleghany County housewifely toil as sewing and darning. Didn't matter; showing off her athletic legs was the main thing. She no longer thought of it as vanity. It was a necessity.

That being the case, the chill that gripped her nether parts scarcely bothered her. At the moment her consciousness was centered in the Broca's and Wernicke's regions of the brain, home of the higher mental functions—as she had learned in the class she was heading for, Mr. Starling's.

She was feeling quite intellectual this morning. The evening with the Millennial Mutants had put her in that mood, which at the moment seemed glamorous. Mr. Starling would be lecturing in his peripatetic and Socratic way about José Delgado, the first giant of modern neuroscience, as he called him. This business of hanging out at the Saint Ray house and indulging in long workouts at the gym and whiling the time away puzzling over Hoyt . . . and Adam . . . had begun to take its toll. Ordinarily, she would be heading for Mr. Starling's class knowing José Delgado's book *Physical Control of the Mind* backward and forward . . .

So caught up was she in thoughts of the higher things that she scarcely noticed the big figure rushing down the steps of Isles Hall and hustling toward her on one of the walkways that converged on the Saint Christopher's fountain. Charlotte was walking right by the fountain when he seemed to drop from the sky to right in front of her: Jojo, big as life.

"Hey, Charlotte!" Jojo's smile didn't seem so much one of happiness or surprise as of ingratiation.

"Oh, hi." She stopped, but gave him a flat smile and some body language that said, "I really have to be somewhere."

"Stocks for Jocks just let out," said Jojo, "and you know what? This is the truth. I was just saying to myself I hope I'd run into you."

His eyes were wide open in an attitude of supplication. "Can I—I gotta talk to you for a second. Can we go somewhere?"

"I can't." It occurred to her that she at last had "can't" under control. Without even thinking first, she had pronounced it *can't* instead of *caint*. "I don't want to be late for class."

"It'll take two seconds." Jojo's face turned serious. What was it that was different about him? Ah, he was wearing a shirt with a collar and some sort of loose warm-up jacket. He wasn't giving the world an eyeful of his muscles. "It's important," he said.

"I *can't*, Jojo."

"It'll only—" His face fell. "Okay, I'm not gonna lie to you. It won't take just a second. When do you get outta class? I've got a real problem."

Charlotte breathed a deep breath of frustration. Whatever problem Jojo had, it wasn't going to be on a very high level, and she was primed for a high level—the highest, Victor Ransome Starling. But not knowing how to parlay the question, she said tonelessly, "In an hour."

"Can I meet you somewhere—then? Please?"

With such a begrudging reluctance it didn't even sound like a question: "Where."

"How about out front of Mr. Rayon?"

By the time she nodded a down-in-the-mouth yes, she was already on the move around him.

The huge athlete looked whipped, the way his eyes tracked her as she went. It gave her an odd sensation, having the upper hand with this enormous sports star and campus celebrity. As she turned away, there rising above them both, Jules Dalou's statue of Saint Christopher carrying the infant Jesus across a stream. The great French sculptor had rendered the figures so dramatically that Charlotte had the sensation that they were actually moving. It stirred her. She was capable of *experiencing* art, not just looking at it. The rest of the world, or most of it, was like Jojo; which is to say, cut off from the life of the mind.

The lights were down, and on the amphitheater's stage an eight-foot-high slide screen gleamed with a photographic portrait of a swarthy white man with a grand mustache and a trimmed beard that swooped down from his temples along a pair of strong jawlines to the thick but carefully coifed beard on his chin. The widow's peak of his hairline was by now, in his middle years, well out in front of the rest of the stand of hair on his pate, but the avant-garde strands on the peak had been combed back with such blow-dry bravura that the overall effect was of a unified flowing mane. He looked rather like one of the Three Musketeers, except that at the bottom of the picture you got a glimpse of the knot of a necktie and the collar of a white smock.

Mr. Starling was saying, "Delgado was one of those scientists who faced death—or so it seemed to other people—by using themselves as guinea pigs to test their own discoveries."

The lectern was off to one side of the stage so that everyone in the class could see the screen. A beam of light from above illuminated Mr. Starling's slim figure and his heathery blue-green tweed jacket ever so romantically, in Charlotte's eyes. She found it easy to imagine Victor Ransome Starling as one of those death-defying heroes of discovery, even though she knew that aside from cat scratches, he had been in no danger during the experiment for which he had won science's highest award.

"I'm not mentioning this so you'll admire their courage," he was saying. "In fact, it's quite the—well, not the opposite, but the obverse, I suppose is the word. Friends and colleagues were terrified for them, but here we have two men, Walter Reed and José Delgado, and one woman, Madame Curie, who had such faith in the empirical validity of their physical knowledge and their own powers of logic—such faith in rationalism, which was barely two centuries old, to touch upon that theme again—they had no more fear than the conjurer who swallows fire, although even if you take that into account, I think you may be impressed by how Delgado proved his point."

Now the picture on the screen was a long shot of a bullfighting ring. There were no more than a couple dozen people in the stands. On one side of the picture, in the ring, was a charging bull. On the other side was a man in a white smock standing stock-still and holding a small black object in his hands at waist level. Other than Mr. Starling's voice, there was not a sound in the amphitheater. Charlotte was completely absorbed in Mr. Starling and the slide screen. There was no periphery, not in this hall, not in this world. Hoyt and his hand and Adam and his anxious lips and Jojo and his hangdog face no longer existed. The El Dorado that Charlotte Simmons had come to Dupont to find was at last the entire known world.

"That's José Delgado," said Mr. Starling, "and *that's* a two-thousand-pound Andalusian bull . . . and those . . . sticks . . . you see sticking out of his shoulders are the *picas* the picadors—you know *picador?*—have stabbed him with to make him angry."

"Oh—my—God!" It was an indignant yelp from a girl somewhere below. Charlotte had no trouble interpreting it. Animal rights was one of the issues some people on campus really got heated over. "That—is—horrible! It's—so—wrong!"

From the lectern Mr. Starling said sharply, "*That's* your reaction to a culture different from your own? I'm sure I mentioned that José Delgado was Spanish, and in case I didn't mention it, that's a bullring in Madrid. Spanish culture is far older than ours, by a factor of millennia. You are perfectly free to object to it. You are free to object to *all* cultures different from your own. Would you favor us with a list of alien cultures you find most objectionable?"

Laughter spread slowly through the amphitheater. Clever parry, Mr. Starling. Denigration of another culture, especially one whose people are less well off than your own, and referring to anything as evil, which would indicate you might very well have religious convictions, were more socially unacceptable at Dupont than cruelty to animals.

Mr. Starling returned to his discourse. "Now. What is about to happen in this picture is actually not as important as what leads up to it." He gestured toward the screen. "This photograph was taken in 1955. In 1955 Delgado was known not as a neuroscientist but as a brain physiologist." He moved out from behind the lectern. "Can anyone tell me what the status of brain physiology, the physical study of the brain, was at that time?"

No takers. Charlotte silently berated herself. If she had studied harder—had gone to the sources, as Mr. Starling had advised—had been the student she was supposed to be—she would be able to star at this very moment. Mr. Starling was still surveying the class . . .

Finally he gave up and said, "It barely *existed* at that time, brain physiology. It had been rendered irrelevant medically by Freudianism. If psychoanalysis was the ultimate cure for dysfunctional mental capabilities and behaviors, why waste time on the taxidermy of the matter? That was the idea. Freud stopped the study of the brain cold for half a century, especially in this country, which by the 1930s had become the very headquarters, so to speak, of the Freudian method. Delgado was a rare creature. His contention was that you couldn't understand human behavior without understanding how the brain worked. Today that seems obvious. It seems axiomatic. But it didn't then. Delgado had found a way of mapping the brain—which is to say, determining which areas of the brain controlled what behavior—by using stereotaxic needle implants and stimulating them electronically."

A loud gasp, probably from the girl who had yelped when Mr. Starling mentioned the picadors' handiwork. But she said nothing, and this time Mr. Starling ignored her.

He gestured toward the screen again. "In this case Delgado has implanted an electrode in the bull's caudate nucleus, which is just under the amygdala. As you can see, the bull was charging full tilt. When it came close enough to make it interesting, Delgado pressed a button on the little radio transmitter in his hand, and the bull's aggressiveness vanished"—he snapped his fingers—"like *that*. The sheer momentum brought the bull all the way to Delgado. You have to imagine a ton of beef with horns coming at you."

Another slide, a close-up. "The bull appears to be a foot or so on the other side of Delgado. The animal's legs are bent in the attitude of a lazy canter. But you'll note that the anger has vanished. The bull's head is up, and it appears to be loping. This picture doesn't show it, but in fact the bull actually altered its course to *keep from* hitting Delgado."

Mr. Starling seemed to be enjoying himself, perhaps because he knew he *had them all*, even the animal rights girl. "Now, what was the lesson of this experiment? The instantaneous lesson was that an emotion as powerful as a raging urge to kill can be turned off"—he snapped his fingers again—"by stimulating a particular area of the brain. The more profound lesson was that not only emotions but also *purpose* and *intentions* are *physical* matters. They can be turned on and off physically. Delgado could have turned a perfectly peaceful, bashful bull—there used to be a children's book called *The Bashful Bull*—or a cow, for that matter—he could have turned either one into a raging killer by stimulating the amygdala itself. As I've mentioned, Delgado was a physician as well as an experimental neuroscientist, and he hoped to find a way to improve people's health and behavior through 'physical control of the mind.' That was the title of the one book he ever wrote—although he must have written a hundred scientific monographs recording his various experiments—that was the title of his book, *Physical Control of the Mind.* The philosophical implications were enormous, and he recognized that right away. His position was that the human mind, as we conceive it—and I think all of us do—bears very little resemblance to reality. We think of the mind—we can't help but think of the mind—as something from a command center in the brain, which we call the 'self,' and that this self has free will. Delgado called that a 'useful illusion.' He said there was a whole series of neural circuits—most of which the human animal isn't aware of—that work in parallel to create the illusion of a self—'me,' an 'individual' with free will and a soul. He called the self nothing more than a 'transient composite of materials from the environment.' It's not a command center but a village marketplace, an arcade, or a lobby, like a hotel lobby, and other people and their ideas and their mental atmosphere and the Zeitgeist—the spirit of the age, to use Hegel's term from two hundred years ago—can come walking right on in, and *you* can't lock the doors, because *they* become *you,* because they *are* you. After Delgado, neuroscientists began to put the words *self* and *mind* and, of course, *soul* in quotation marks. Delgado's conception of the self as a product of a physical mechanism has begun to turn philosophy and psychology upside down. It's occurring right now, in our time. The most influential theories of the self throughout most of the last century were *external* theories. Marxism was a philosophical theory that said that *you,* your*self,* were the product of the competing forces in the class struggle between the proletariat—or the working class, including the *lumpenproletariat,* the term for what we now call the 'underclass'—and the bourgeoisie and the aristocracy. Freudianism was a psychological theory that said each of us is the product of the oedipal conflict within our families. In both theories we are the product of external forces—social class, in one case, the family you're born into, in the other. Marxists prided themselves on being materialists—realists who faced facts and didn't fall for the usual idealism peddled by the philosophers. But the Marxist notion of materialism is sheer whimsy compared to that of the neuroscientists. Neuroscience says to us, 'You want materialism? We'll show you the real thing, the material of your own brains and central nervous systems, the autonomous circuits that operate outside of what you conceive of as "consciousness," the behavioral responses you couldn't change even if you trained for a lifetime, the illusions you will never—'"

—Charlotte was transported. The way the downlight cast Victor Ransome Starling's face into planes of bright light and deep shadow struck her as something ineffably noble and majestic. Every time he gestured, his white fingers flashed with highlights, and she caught the glint of yet another heathery tone in the weave of his tweed jacket. He who would lead her to the innermost secrets of life—and to the utmost brilliance of the glow on the other side of the mountains Miss Pennington had called her attention to four years ago—

In that moment, in the theatrical darkness, as the sublime figure down on the stage moved in an electrifying succession of planes of chiaroscuro whose light, plus the light of the screen radiant with the image of the man who revolutionized the way the human animal sees herself, cast a glow upon the very crest of the heads of all the students—just that, the very crest, where here and there wisps of hair spun into pale golden gauze—Charlotte experienced a *kairos*, an ecstatic revelation of something too vast, too all-enveloping, too profound to be contained by mere words, and the rest of the world, a sordid world of the flesh and animals grunting for the flesh, fell away.

As she emerged from Phillips and out upon the Great Yard, Charlotte could see out of the corner of her eye that Jill, the girl who sat next to her, was barely a step behind her, but Charlotte didn't want to have to talk to her. She didn't want to descend long enough for even the most perfunctory so-long. She was too high for that, high in an important way, high on ideas—no, high on the excitement of discovery, of seeing the future from the peaks of Darién. O Dupont!

It was even gloomier and more on the raw side out here than it had been when she went into the building an hour ago, but the walls of the Gothic buildings across the way were built to withstand any threat . . . with an imperious confidence . . . O trefoil tracery! O ye buildings such as will never be built again! O ye fortress of language—and therefore memory—and therefore ye key to the ideas that move a people, a society, and thereby history itself—ye key to prestige compounded by the prestige and authority of its origins! O Dupont! Dupont! O Charlotte Simmons of Dupont—

Pop. The great hulk of Jojo Johanssen was heading straight toward her on the sidewalk, giving her an ingratiating grin again. Where had he come from this time? But . . . of course . . . he had been waiting for her somewhere down there, like a dog tethered outside a grocery store.

Bigger smile from the giant: "Well—how was it?"

Charlotte merely nodded okay. It would be silly to treat it as an actual question. What could she say about what she had just experienced that he would even begin to understand?

"Where can we talk?" said Jojo. "Mr. Rayon?"

Charlotte gave him a look of frustration and a sigh of resignation—and they went to Mr. Rayon. The lunchtime mob had already begun to assemble. From the moment they entered, heads were turning toward Jojo. A couple of boys piped up with low *Go go Jojos*. Jojo's reaction was not to look at them.

He was craning his head this way and that, looking for a spot quiet enough for a serious discussion. He led her to a table for two in a corner next to a wall just beyond the cafeteria's Thai food section. No one looking on could help but know he had chosen this spot not for convenience or ambience. It was in the dim corner formed by the restaurant's white blank wall and a five-foot-high salmon-colored LithoPlast room divider at this end of the steam counters and stainless-steel railings of the Thai section. The divider did not protect the tête-à-tête from rice and pulpy vegetables steamed with too much water and salt. The smell wafted here and wafted there, but it never went away.

Jojo had Charlotte sit in the seat in the very corner, looking out on the lunch crowd, while he sat across from her with his back to the room. What earthly good did he think that would do him? The back he had to the room was enormous.

Mischievous smile, or mischievous by the up-country reserve of Charlotte Simmons: "I like your shirt."

"You do? Why?"

"I don't know—the collar."

Jojo tucked his chin down and squirmed, trying to tuck it in deeper in a hopeless attempt to see the collar. When he finally looked up, he shrugged with his eyebrows and one corner of his mouth, by way of making it clear he didn't care. He put his elbows on the table and said in a low voice, "I've got like—a serious problem."

He let this revelation hang humid in the air while he stared at her.

Charlotte said nothing. Jojo had folded his eyebrows in so far toward his nose, it made his nostrils flare. Somehow . . . he looked ridiculous, this huge campus celebrity with his little scrunched-up features. He hadn't roused her curiosity much more than an eighth of a degree. She didn't *care* what basketball star Jojo Johanssen's great problem was. She didn't even so much as nod her head to encourage him to continue. Of course he was going to anyway.

"Lemme put it this way: I'm like"—searching for the right expression—"fucked."

How illuminating, and how gross. She knew she should be used to students talking to each other that way by now, but she wasn't, and having some giant male talking to her like that only made it worse. She just looked at him with an expression that intimated nothing at all.

Jojo soldiered on. "It's this mother—this professor I got in American history, this guy Quat. You ever heard of him?"

Charlotte shook her head no, ever so slowly and ever so briefly.

"Well, he's a hard-ass—he's got a thing about athletes. How we ever ended up in that class, I'll never fucking know."

Gross and grosser. Charlotte purposely didn't ask who "we" were.

Jojo provided the information nonetheless: "André and Curtis are in the same class."

Charlotte looked at him blankly.

"You know . . . André Walker and Curtis Jones."

Still a blank.

"Anyway, Quat assigns us this paper, and everybody's paper's on a different subject, and there's no book . . ."

Charlotte tuned out. What particular form of malingering or shiftlessness Jojo had indulged in didn't interest her . . . until he got to Adam, and she realized that this was the very paper Adam had been writing for Jojo when she first ran into him in the library.

Her expression came alive. "Do they *know* Adam wrote it for you?"

"I don't know what they know," said Jojo. "This guy who calls himself a judicial officer showed up today. Do you know Adam?"

Warily: "Yeah . . ."

"How do you know him?"

Warily: "I know some friends of his. They have this sort of club."

Jojo said, "Yeah, well, he's not exactly the type who . . ." He didn't complete the thought. "I left a message on his cell . . ." He averted his eyes and shook his head gloomily. "If the guy gets to Adam, I don't know if it'll make any difference if I *do* talk to him . . ." Forlorn, eyes still averted.

"What guy," said Charlotte, "and make a difference in what?"

"This guy came by today. He calls himself a judicial officer. Coach says he's just like a cop. That means they're not gonna just drop this thing with a warning or something. They're cranking up for a fucking trial. If the guy gets enough evidence, they'll put my ass in front of some panel."

Sharply: "Please don't talk like that."

Genuinely surprised: "Like what?"

"Stop cursing. Must you curse every other word? I can't even understand what you're saying, much less help you."

Jojo studied her face and attempted a little beginning of a smile, to see if she just might be joking.

"What's the worst that can happen?" she said.

"They can suspend me for a semester."

"Well, that wouldn't be the end of the world, anyway."

"The hell it wouldn't! It'd be the end of *my* world," said Jojo. "The next semester is *the* basketball season! The postseason games are in March! The NCAA tournament! Everything!"

"So what are you going to do?"

The hangdog sag of the supplicant was in his face. "You can help me."

"Me?"

He shook his head yes. "Remember when I came to you and said I wanted to turn myself around academically?"

"Yeah—yes."

"And you said I oughta start by studying Socrates? Remember how you told me that?"

"Yes . . ."

"I *did* that. I switched into Philosophy 306, the Age of Socrates."

"You did? You really did that?"

"Yeah, and it's the hardest course I ever took. I could spend the whole week reading and still not read enough. Mr. Margolies. He's a serious fuh— guy. I don't know what he's saying half the time, and I don't think the others do, either, but nobody's got the nerve to put his hand up and say, 'What's *agon* mean?' or 'Why do you say Socrates was the first philosophical rationalist?' What the fuh—what's *that* supposed to mean? I actually go to the library after class and look up stuff. I never even went in there before, except for a couple of times Adam took me there. I always had the feeling I was standing in there blinking and everybody was laughing at me. Now I go in there because I don't want to just sit there with my mouth open in Margolies's class. I don't know if I can even pass the course, but you know what? I'm sorta proud of myself." Jojo's face lit up for the first time. "Do you know the difference between Socrates's 'universal definitions' and Plato's 'Ideas'? You don't—right? Well, I . . . *do*." Jojo had the smile of a child proud of an accomplishment. "Plato thought 'Ideas' exist, actually *exist* in the world, independent of human beings, meaning no matter whether anybody uses them or not."

Charlotte nodded and said, "That's very good, Jojo."

Then his face darkened. "I know it's good. That's what makes this damn 'judicial officer' shih—stuff such a ball-buh—makes me so mad. It was after that paper Adam wrote for me that I started . . . turning around—and being a student—and taking a lotta shih—catching a lotta hell for it. Coach started yelling at me when I told him I was gonna take the Socrates course, and then he started laughing, like it was a joke, me thinking I could pass a course like the Age of Socrates, and then, in practice, he started calling me Socrates, fuh—effin' Socrates this and effin' Socrates that. It's like . . . he's calling me a retard, right in front of everyone. But I'm putting up with all that. I'm gonna stick with Socrates. The hell with Coach. Socrates said you have to look to yourself for 'virtue and wisdom.' That's what he said, 'virtue and wisdom,' and I'm living by that now. And so it's now, after I've become a different person, it's now they're siccing this like . . . cop on me, over one fuh—one freaking paper from before! There's Before Socrates and After Socrates, B.S. and A.S.—" He barked a rueful laugh. "That don't sound right, but you know what I mean."

Charlotte, but not Jojo, could see the panorama of the crowd in Mr. Rayon. Students at the tables and in the Thai food line were turning their heads to look at the two of them. At first Charlotte was embarrassed. But now she saw their little table in this dim, dismal corner the way all those celebrity-hungry and celebrity-gossip-hungry, prurient swiveled heads saw it. There was the great Go go Jojo with his hulk stretched halfway across the table and his huge head thrust practically into the face of that—pretty?—girl and talking ever so earnestly and intently. Who is she? Something that intense—a tête-à-tête was what it was, if any of them knew the term. Who is that girl? The thought made Charlotte smile in spite of herself.

"—know what I mean," Jojo was saying. "What's funny?"

"Why do you say *don't*?" said Charlotte. "Nobody ever told you what the third-person singular of the verb *to do* is?"

Petulantly: "You think that's funny, don't you—and I'm trying to tell you something serious. Since you asked—everybody on the team says *don't*—he don't, she don't, it don't."

"Why?"

"I don't know. If you say *he doesn't*, everybody thinks you're fronting."

"Why do you care about that?"

"I don't . . . anymore," said Jojo. He smiled a tight, grim little smile. "Not A.S."

"After Socrates," said Charlotte.

"Fucking A," said Jojo. He held his palms up in front of his face in mock defense. "It's just an expression, just an expression. It don't—doesn't mean anything." This time he smiled a little smile of resignation, as if resigning himself to the way the world was. "That's why I need you. You're the only person who can testify for me."

"Testify?"

"If they take me in front of this panel. You're the only person who can say something like I came to you on such and such a day, *after* I handed that paper in and *before* Quat started breaking my—giving me a hard time."

"You think they'll believe you? You went to a *freshman* for advice?"

"That's the way it happened! Will you do it? Will you testify for me?"

Charlotte didn't know what to say. Jojo—a trial—testify?—questions?—whose?—something told her it was a mess well worth avoiding. But she was already experiencing the guilt she would feel if she refused.

"Yes." Flatly, in a put-upon voice.

Jojo lurched still farther across the table and grasped both her small hands with his big hands and held them as if he were making a snowball. He squeezed them.

"Thank you! I owe you one! Good girl! Good stuff!"

His big smile was not so much a smile of happiness and relief as happiness and victory, as if he had talked her into something. That made her uneasy. She didn't much like this "good girl, good stuff." It was patronizing. Did he think he had put one over on her?

TOM WOLFE

On the other hand . . . the way it must have looked to everybody in the room . . . Jojo has a real *thing* for this girl. She looks so young! Who is she?

"Did anybody ever tell you you're beautiful? And different? You're not like the other girls on this campus."

It being Monday night, Hoyt and eight or nine other Saint Rays had gravitated to the library couches and easy chairs, cracked leather upholstery and all, to chill, i.e., drift through the evening in as aimless and effortless a manner as possible, bolstered by the presence of others like themselves. Naturally ESPN SportsCenter was on the big plasma TV screen. Hot colors and orangey slices of postadolescent flesh flared in a Gatorade commercial . . . and now four poorly postured middle-aged white sportswriters sat slouched in little low-backed, smack-red fiberglass swivel chairs panel-discussing the "sensitive" matter of the way black players dominated basketball.

"Look," the well-known columnist Maury Fieldtree was saying, his chin resting on a pasha's cushion of jowls, "just think about it a second. Race, ethnicity, all that—that's just a symptom of something else. There's been whole cycles, every generation, whole cycles of different minorities using sports as a way out of the ghetto. Am I right? I mean, like boxing. A hundred years ago or whatever it was, you had the Irish, John L. Sullivan, Gentleman Jim Corbett, Jack Dempsey, Gene Tunney. Then here came the Italians: the Rockys—Marciano, and Graziano—and Jake LaMotta and so on. Or take football. Way back, you had the Germans, like Sammy Baugh. So now you get to basketball. In the 1930s and 1940s, you know who dominated professional basketball long before the African Americans? Jewish players. Yeah! Jewish players from the Jewish ghettos of New York! Oh, there was—"

"You notice that?" said Julian. His voice rose up from out of a canyon of leather, he had sunk so far down into the couch. The question was for the room, but he looked first at Hoyt, who had settled into the easy chair that was, by silent consensus, *his*, as Saint Ray's heroic fighting man. His assault, even though unsuccessful, on a huge all-American lacrosse player, coming on top of the Night of the Skull Fuck, had dramatically increased the awe factor.

"Notice what?" Hoyt said—idly, as befitted his status. He immediately turned and tilted his head back on the leather to take another swallow of his fourth—fifth?—can of beer. He was losing count again.

"The way they always say 'Jewish players' or whatever it is," said Julian.

"They don't say 'Jews,' they say 'Jewish players.' They call Irishmen, 'Irishmen'; they call Italians 'Italians,' Germans 'Germans,' Swedes 'Swedes,' Poles 'Poles,' but they don't call Jews 'Jews.' They say 'Jewish players.' It's like saying 'Jew,' even if the guy *is* a Jew, is like a—a—an insult. It's like automatically anti-Semitic."

"Anti-Semitic?" said Boo McGuire, who was sitting on the arm of a couch with his roly-poly legs hanging down either side, as if he were riding a horse. "Maybe, but the fucking Canadians themselves won't say 'Jew,' either."

General laughter.

"Whattya mean?" said Julian. "I don't get it."

"That guy, Maury Fieldtree"—Boo gestured toward the TV screen— "he's a Canadian himself."

"Aw, come on," said Julian, "Maury Fieldtree."

"You didn't know that?" said Boo. "His real name's not Fieldtree. It's Feldbaum. I'll bet you anything. And Maury—you know where that comes from? Moishe . . . They make it Maurice, which is where Maury comes from, or Murray or Mort. So that's old Moishe Feldbaum you're looking at."

"How do you know all that?" said Heady Mills, who sat on the couch on the base of his spine. "You a fucking Canadian yourself and not telling us?"

Laughter all around.

"No, I'm just naturally smarter than you," said Boo. "Besides, some of my best friends are Canadians."

More laughter. Hoyt was automatically laughing along with the rest of them, as befit a cool brother, but in fact he felt irritable and anxious, and the four—or five?—beers had not helped any. It was just dawning on him what a catastrophe his college transcript was going to be . . . Coasting along for three years just assuming that somehow he would drift into investment banking in New York when he finished at Dupont. That's what you did when you graduated from a university like Dupont. You went to work for an investment bank in New York. Nobody had a clue what investment banking actually was. The main thing was, once you got the job, you were making two hundred, three hundred thousand a year by the time you were twenty-five . . . It was just dawning on him that the guys who had done that had two sides to them, the cool side and the secret side. They had a lot of secret dork in them, these guys. When they went over to the library at midnight, they weren't just going over there to hit on girls, the way he did. They went over there and nerded down for the night, like Vance. It had taken Hoyt a long time to realize that half the time when Vance came back to the room at three or four in the morning, he'd been over at the library hammering the shit out of econ and statistics. Even if he, Hoyt, hammered the shit out of econ and statistics and everything else for the rest of the year, he'd still have C's and B-minuses that were already on his transcript . . . and reports coming back from guys who graduated last year said the i-banks went over your transcript with a vengeance. Even B's made you a questionable case, and B minuses and C's might as well be F's. Being cool meant nothing; being handsome with a cleft chin meant nothing; beating the living shit out of buff bodyguards, all-American lacrosse players, and school bullies meant nothing. The whole thing made his head hurt, and this time the beer wasn't giving him a lift or even ordinary numb relief. In fact, this time it had him bloated with self-pity.

Julian was saying, "It's the same thing with fags. Like they don't want to hear the word 'homosexual.' It's like there's something dirty about the word."

"They got that right," said Vance. "It's the medical term for buncha brown-dick ass-bangers."

Laughter laughter laughter.

"Yeah," said Heady. "If you say homosexual instead of gay, then that makes you a bigot."

"I love this fucking word 'gay,'" said Boo. "You got some fucking faggot weighs ninety pounds and's got AIDS maggots crawling in and out of his asshole, and he's 'gay.' Gimme a fucking break."

Another round of laughter.

"Yeah," said Julian, "and they got Queer Studies listed in the fucking course catalog. For some fucking reason, 'queer' is okay. But just let some professor call it by its right name, Homosexual Studies, and he'd get fucking canned."

Hoyt wasn't listening any longer. Lying back on his easy chair, pissing away the time . . . When he thought of all the evenings he'd diligently pissed away in this broken-down room—

Another commercial was on, and more hot, slick colors flared . . . girls on a beach at spring break, squealing with laughter from being high, or maybe embarrassed by the way they're hanging out of their bikinis—

Julian was in the middle of saying something when Hoyt stood up, stretched without looking at anybody, and started walking out of the library. The group went silent and watched him, as if wondering if anybody had said anything he didn't like.

Vance spoke up. "Where you going, Hoyto?"

Hoyt stopped and stared at him in a distracted way and finally said in a tired voice, "Come on, dude, I'm going over to the I.M."

So Vance got up, and they headed over to the I.M.

The I.M. was pretty dead. There was no live music on Monday nights. Some melancholy country rock CD was playing over the sound system. It was early on the daily club-and-saloon circadian cycle, the prime hours being 11:30 to 2:00. Without a crowd to animate it, the place looked as gloomy and shoddily constructed as it actually was. The black lengths of splintery rough-cut lumber that covered the walls didn't look so much Collegiate Bohemian as ineptly designed and assembled. Most of the round black tables were empty; and, empty, they looked battered and cheap. It was hard to believe that just two nights ago hundreds of students were vying and lying, trying to pry their way into this place, dying to be where things were happening.

Tonight Hoyt didn't even want a table. He found it a relief to be hunched over the bar in this quiet, decrepit joint with yet another beer in front of him. A gale had begun to kick up inside his skull, and he knew the line had moved up pretty far on the graph, and he knew he could always deal with that, except that he kept losing track of what Vance was saying.

". . . the fucking Inn at Chester?" was the end of the sentence.

"No shit," said Hoyt, hoping to extract some details that would put him back in the picture. "The Inn at Chester?"

Vance gave him a funny look and said, "Hoyt—what the fuck, dude, I just *told* you the Inn at Chester is where they'd stay if they came . . . looking."

Despite the rising gale and defective information, Hoyt picked up the scent of Vance's usual paranoia. So he said, "They come look for you?" He was vaguely aware that he sounded like a movie Indian. Incipient diction impairment.

"That's the problem," said Vance. "I don't know."

No, Hoyt said to himself, the problem is bad drinking. You feel lousy, you can't halfway sleep, and you dread the clarity of morning . . . or even early afternoon . . . which in turn made him think of the dreaded Afternoon Hangover—

At first he was only vaguely aware . . . A couple had taken seats at the empty end of the bar, seven or eight seats away. They were young, but they weren't students. The guy had the face of a twenty-year-old, but he was bald

T
O
M

W
O
L
F
E

on top, which made him look weak and pathetic. Despite the turtleneck sweater the guy wore, anybody could tell he had a scrawny neck underneath. In short, a nonentity. Hoyt paid no attention to them until he caught the girl—woman—staring at him. He turned away for a few seconds, then glanced at her again. She was still staring at him.

He nudged Vance. "Theh girl"—he motioned toward the end of the bar with his head—"theh girl staring at me?"

Vance stole a look. "Yeah. Probably at me, though. She's hot."

The girl—woman—was, indeed, hot. She had quite a head of straight dark brown hair, trimmed to just above her shoulders, more *done* than any student's. She had a lean face but a full lower lip, with some dark lipstick smooth enough to create little highlights, and a long, slender neck with a tiny gold necklace that also picked up the light . . . in such a delicate, defenseless way. She wore a black sweater with a V-neck. She wore a short black jacket on top of the sweater, but mainly there was . . . the V in the V-neck. The point came down so deep that Hoyt could see . . . could see . . .

"Def'ny me," he said to Vance. "Well . . . fuck." He got up from the stool.

"Yo, da playa gits up," said Vance with as close to a ghetto accent as any Phipps was likely to get. "Da playa makes his move. Be cool, Hoyt. What about the guy?"

"The fuck, I'm gon' be nice't motherfucker." Oh shit, he hadn't even meant to talk ghetto. It just came out that way because Vance had said "playa" . . . The diction problem . . .

As he walked toward the girl, the gale was . . . up. He glanced at himself in the big mirror behind the bar . . . Could see only his head and shoulders, but that was enough. Both hims took a good look at him. With his head turned that way and tilted slightly back so that his cleft chin came to the fore, a small, confident smile playing on his lips—the objective him wondered if maybe that smile wasn't too much like a smirk, but both hims agreed he looked awesome and awesomely cool. Also, with his head turned this far, his neck looked a mile wide, like a column rising up from out of the open neck of his polo shirt. The gale was blowing.

Only when he was practically right there did it occur to Hoyt that he didn't really know what he was going to say to the girl. He couldn't very well say the usual, because the closer you got, the more she looked like an actual woman. She must have caught him in her peripheral vision, because she turned her head toward him. Her face was like her hair, which is to say, perfect . . . *done* . . . The way that full and glossy lip of hers played against her lean face . . . the high cheekbones . . . the brilliant eyes . . . Like most males, Hoyt knew nothing about the subtleties of makeup. Not that it mattered. Nothing could challenge his confidence, not at this point on the graph. He was now quite close to her, and he leaned on the bar with his forearm and spoke with the utmost certainty.

"Excuse me, don't mean to interrupt . . ." He gave her the most charming of smiles, and then he looked at her companion and gave him one. ". . . but I just had to ask you"—now he was looking straight into *her* eyes—"you must—I swear, where I'm sitting, you . . . get tired of people saying you look just like Britney Spears."

The woman—holy shit, she was good-looking! She didn't giggle. But she didn't look annoyed, either. She smiled, but in a cool way, and said, "Britney Spears is blond. Do you get tired of people telling you you look just like Hoyt Thorpe?"

The great playa was speechless. The playa's light in his eyes went out. "Hey . . . How'd you do that? You know my name?"

"I wasn't sure," she said, "but you do look like Hoyt Thorpe." She glanced at her companion, and he nodded in confirmation. Then she looked back at Hoyt, still smiling. "We were looking at a photograph of you this afternoon. I hope you didn't notice me staring at you just now."

Hoyt tried a chuckle and gestured with his hand casually—cool—and said, "Well, I mean . . ." He didn't know what to say beyond that.

"This is quite a coincidence." She glanced toward her companion again. As before, he nodded confirmation. "I'm Rachel Freeman," she said. She extended her hand in a businesslike way.

Hoyt shook her hand and, feeling exceptionally smooth all of a sudden, gave it an extra little squeeze before they disengaged. He looked deep into her eyes and said, "Dya have a ride back?"

"A ride back?" said Rachel Freeman. She didn't seem to find the question worth answering. Without a pause she gestured toward the man. "And this is my associate, Mike Marash."

So Hoyt shook hands again. The bald, baby-faced Mr. Marash smiled politely.

"We're with Pierce and Pierce," said the most gorgeous woman in the world.

"Pierce and Pierce?"

"We're an invest—"

"*I* know," said Hoyt. He didn't want this Rachel to think he was so inexperienced as not to know what Pierce & Pierce was. Even somebody who had cut as many econ classes as he had knew what a position Pierce & Pierce occupied in the investment banking industry. He was merely surprised. The crummy I.M. was not the sort of place you expected to find people from Pierce & Pierce knocking back a couple of drinks on a Monday night.

"We're in town on a recruiting trip," said the rutrutrut-eyed Rachel. "That's why this is such a coincidence. You're on our Dupont list! I'm supposed to call you! That's why I was so surprised to see you. We were supposed to call you up tomorrow and arrange an interview."

"Me?" He meant to say it coolly, without the one-octave-up note of surprise.

She assured him yes and suggested they meet for lunch at the Inn at Chester. The Inn at Chester . . . he'd bet anything that was where she was staying. He looked into her eyes. They were glistening . . . sizzling . . . aflame . . . with the inner fire you couldn't see at first, thanks to the perfectly composed façade of her *done* hair, high cheekbones, glossy lips, swan's neck, tiny twinkling chain of gold . . . What were those eyes saying? . . .

"In at the Inny!" said Hoyt. He was aware that the diction problem was getting worse.

"What?"

"In and out, in and out at the Inn!" This was so bad he laughed to cover it up. He was saying stupid things, but so what? Score! Victory! He nodded yes and gave her a smile, a sincere smile.

Pop.

—he'd been pouring lust into her eyes for many beats longer than he should have . . . before he walked away and returned to where Vance was sitting.

The diction problem getting worse, but he was able to get across to Vance the gist of the business side, the Pierce & Pierce side, of his conversation with the gorgeous V-neck brunette.

"I'll be damned," said Vance. "That's great, Hoyt. Pierce and Pierce . . ."

Hmmmmm . . . Vance's voice sang a note of happiness for his brother Saint Ray and comrade-in-arms. He knew how bad Hoyt's grades were. Hoyt had moaned about them many times. Then Hoyt felt so sad. He was overcome with sympathy for the Vancerman. Sure hoped he wouldn't get jealous. If the sexy little i-banker had Vance Phipps on her list, she obviously hadn't been studying *his* picture . . .

The objective Hoyt, the one looking over his shoulder, had begun to wonder if this wasn't just a stroke of dumb luck . . . but the inner Hoyt made sure the sound of the gale drowned out and overpowered the outer Hoyt and his chronic case of the Doubts.

Over the speaker system, a country rock singer named Connie Yates was singing. The drums, the bass, and the electric guitars were banging and sloshing away. Hoyt sang along with Connie Yates for a while. Vance was looking straight ahead into the mirror behind the bar. Vance Phipps of the *Phipps* Phipps . . . It would be just like Vance not to get it, listening to someone who can't sing, sing. Get what? Hoyt felt like some essential part, the part that made it all clear, had blown away in the gale. So he cast a sideways glance at Rachel, who would get it . . . but she and the guy weren't there anymore.

22. SHAKING HANDS WITH FORTUNE

uch excitement! The Lounge Committee had never before convened in Charlotte's room, where the boarding-school-cool and aloof Beverly ruled. But these were special circumstances. A senior, a member of the coolest fraternity of all, Saint Ray, had invited Charlotte, a freshman, to be his date for a Saint Ray overnight "formal" in Washington, D.C. The questions before the committee were two: should she or shouldn't she go—and what was a "formal," anyway?

Bettina and Mimi gawked at this side . . . and the other side . . . and this side again, where Beverly's galaxy of electronic wonders rose up from a jungle of cords plugged into big cream-colored junction knuckles . . . a plasma TV that turned on a stainless-steel base, a recharger stand on the desk, a refrigerator, a fax machine, a makeup mirror framed in LED lights—there was no end to it all—compared to what the other side of the room looked like . . . well, abandoned . . . plain wooden Dupont dorm-issue desk, straight-backed chair, the bureau, and a single electrical device, an old, rusting gooseneck lamp on the desk.

"Which side is yours?" said Mimi.

"Take a wild guess," said Charlotte.

Beverly's clothes and towels were strewn across her unmade bed and its twists and tangles of sheets and covers, and down on the floor in a field of dust balls were vast numbers of shoes, not always matched up, littered this way and that.

"Where's Beverly?" said Mimi.

"I don't know where she goes," said Charlotte, pulling the straight-backed chair over a few feet, facing the beds. "She never comes back until two or three in the morning, if she comes back at all."

Thus assured, Mimi sat in the techie-looking swivel chair at Beverly's desk, gave it a spin, and came rolling over beside Charlotte, who was sitting on her wooden chair. Bettina sat on Charlotte's bed.

Charlotte was beginning to regret that she had told Bettina or Mimi about the formal. But how could she not? They were her closest friends; and the unspoken, taboo function of the Lounge Committee was to boost one another's morale until they figured out a way to ascend from loser status. Besides, one thing she really wanted to hear them all say was that there was nothing wrong with going off on a fraternity party like this . . . and if it showed everybody that she was already on the ascent . . . that was all right, too.

"I've heard of formals," said Bettina, who was sitting on the foot of Beverly's bed, "but I don't really know what they are. What are they?"

Charlotte said, "I don't really—"

"Wait a minute. Back up. Rewind," said Bettina. "I want to know how this all happened. The last thing I remember was that brawl at the tailgate. And so now he invites you to his fraternity's formal? You must have seen him since then—or something."

"Oh, sure," said Charlotte, as if it were both obvious and insignificant. She kept looking at Mimi—to avoid looking at Bettina, who was her very closest friend. She hadn't told them . . . anything about seeing Hoyt after that. "Afterward, I went over to the Saint Ray house to thank him. I mean, he could've like . . . gotten himself killed."

"You went over there *that night*?" said Bettina.

Now Charlotte was forced to look at her. Oh God, the consternation on her face! Charlotte read it as not merely a look of surprise, but rather, the surprise of one who has been betrayed. "We brought you back here and stayed with you for two hours while you lay down on that bed and cried."

"I don't mean that night," said Charlotte. "It was a couple of days later."

"So that was *before* he hit on that blond girl at the I.M.?" said Bettina.

"I guess—I don't know."

"Funny, you didn't get around to telling *us* that."

Charlotte felt so guilty, she *knew* her face was crimson. "I was just being polite. I felt like I just owed him—I mean, if it hadn't been for him . . ." She didn't try to complete the sentence. The more words she uttered, the more guilt oozed out.

"Wow," said Bettina, "that was a nice thing to do. You neglected to tell us what good manners you have."

That made Charlotte feel so small she couldn't even muster the strength to combat the sarcasm. "It didn't seem like a big thing at the time." Her voice sounded worse than defensive. It sounded fugitive.

"And so *then* he invited you to the formal," said Mimi. Her face wore an expressionless mouth below a pair of big, guileless eyes, the classic attitude of Sarc 3.

"Noooooo," said Charlotte, just as fugitively as before. All the while her brain was crunching prevarication equations. "I've like . . . hung out with him a few times since then."

Bettina and Mimi must have said it at once: "What does *that* mean!"

"We sort of—you know—hung out."

"Oh, you *hung out*," said Mimi. A pause. "Where?"

"Mostly at the Saint Ray house, I guess. But nothing happened. I swear! There were always a lot of people around. Everybody was just hanging out. I never went upstairs in that building. I pledge you my word."

"*I* don't care if you went upstairs," said Mimi.

Oh God, thought Charlotte. I've betrayed them. Why didn't I tell them anything, any little thing, about seeing Hoyt? Aloud: "Well, anyway, I didn't. All these girls—they're *fools*, the way they just go *hook up* with guys. It's so . . . so *demeaning*. I've straightened Hoyt out on that point."

"Are you saying you've never hooked up with him?" said Mimi.

"Noooooo . . ." As soon as she said it, she realized it was about as indefinite a no as anybody ever came up with. "I was never *alone* with him in the Saint Ray house." She emphasized the *alone* to draw attention from the rhetorical flexibility of the rest of the sentence. Already her amygdala—or was it the caudate nucleus?—was aflame with the memory of the explorations of *the hand* in the Little Yard parking lot.

"And he never *tried*?" said Mimi.

"I guess he sort of *tried*," said Charlotte. "I guess they all do. But I was very *clear* about that?" She could see Bettina flicking a Sarc 3 glance at Mimi. "I don't think you believe me, but he's been a gentleman ever since that first night at the Saint Ray house?" Why was she reverting to statements accented like questions? Part of her knew she was beseeching them to accept all this at face value and say that going off on this fraternity formal sounded like fun. "He already knows how I feel. But does it look terrible to go off to Washington with him like that?"

"Hah," said Bettina without mirth. "What *does* look terrible around this place anymore?"

That wasn't the answer Charlotte wanted.

"But what exactly's involved in a formal?" said Bettina.

"Oh, the fraternities and sororities have them," said Mimi, who prided herself on being knowledgeable in such areas. "The idea is, the guys wear tuxedos, and the girls wear party dresses, and they have a party away from the campus at some place like the Inn at Chester. Or they go out of town overnight, and that's supposed to like make it really special."

"Yeah," said Bettina, "but what do they do at a formal?"

"I don't know," said Mimi. "I've never been to one. But I bet they do what they do at every party. The guys get drunk and yell a lot, and the girls get drunk and throw up a lot, and the guys try to get a little somethin' somethin', and the next day the girls claim they can't remember what happened and the guys remember all kinds of shit, regardless of whether it happened or not—except that the clothes and the food are better."

All three of them laughed, but even amid the trilling merriment, Charlotte knew she heard a voice—talking on a cell phone—outside in the hall, which could only be—

The door opened, and in came Beverly, her head leaning into the cell phone she held up to her ear, and right behind her was Erica. Beverly stopped in her tracks, the cell phone still at her ear, glowering, especially at Mimi—in *her* room—in *her* chair. Mimi sat up very straight on the edge of the chair—Beverly's chair—as if ready at any moment to depart the nest, like a barn swallow.

Beverly now stared at Charlotte. Into the cell phone she said, "Jan . . . Jan . . . I know . . . Gotta go. Call you back."

She took a few more steps into the room, staring at Charlotte but saying nothing. Erica came in behind her, and Charlotte seized the moment to stand up and sing out, "Hi, Erica!" Mainly she didn't want Beverly to advance into the room looking down at her—and she didn't want to stand up as if out of respect.

Erica gave Charlotte a stone-cold smile. Charlotte thought of it as the Groton smile. Before Beverly could say anything, Charlotte said, "Sorry,

Beverly. I just didn't think you'd be here. We . . . we're having a sort of meeting." She didn't dare get into what for.

Charlotte said, "This is Erica?—Mimi? Bettina?"

Erica at least looked at everybody long enough to freeze their bones with a withering, bone-dry preppy smile. Beverly glanced at Mimi and Bettina, just those two, and that was it.

"Well—" said Beverly, looking at Charlotte with a neutral expression. Charlotte decided it must be Sarc 2. "So what's going on?"

Charlotte had no idea what to say, but Bettina piped up, "It's major, Beverly."

Charlotte could tell immediately, from Bettina's loud tone and the ultra-familiar way she used Beverly's name, that she was tired of everybody giving way before this supposed paragon of the boarding-school elite—and that her anger actually came from her realization that despite all the ways the Lounge Committee had of dismantling the status, the worth, of this elite, down deep she still regarded them as . . . the elite.

"Wow," said Beverly in a completely careless, Sarc 3 tone of voice. She was not looking at Bettina, either, but straight at Charlotte. She flipped her palms upward in an idle fashion and said in the same tone, "Must be big news. So what is it?"

Rather than appear to Mimi and Bettina that she was ducking from Beverly, Charlotte just blurted it straight out. "I've been invited to a formal, and I'm trying to decide whether to go or not."

"Really? Who with?"

"Hoyt Thorpe."

It was Erica who chimed in, "Hoyt—Thorpe?" She had a big, incredulous smile on her face and popped-open eyes. "Are you *serious*?" It was the first time she had ever responded directly to anything Charlotte said or did.

"Yeah . . ."

"Where is this going to *be*?" The same popped eyes and an expression on a crest between laughter and astonishment.

Charlotte's voice cracked slightly as she said, "Washington . . ." This stuck-up . . . bitch . . . rattled her.

"D.C.?"

"Yeah . . ."

"How on earth did this happen to you?" said Erica, whereupon she broke into a chilling boarding-school laugh.

Beverly said, "Oh, Charlotte *knows* Hoyt Thorpe." Not even Sarc 3; straight-up-front Sarc 1.

Erica put on a Sarc 3 look of seriousness and concern. "You know who they invite to formals, don't you—especially the Saint Rays and . . . *Hoyt Thorpe*."

"Hope you get along with all the Saint Ray frat whores."

"I'm not the least bit worried about Hoyt," said Charlotte. "Not for one second. Hoyt knows beter than to try—to—whatever you're talking about— with me. And I don't know anything about any . . . 'frat whores.'"

Erica said, "Okay, just make sure you don't become one of them."

Beverly said, "Ha! Charlotte! A frat whore? She'll probably bring her pajamas and bathrobe with her and insist on sleeping on the couch!"

"You know I'm still in the room," Charlotte said. "Plus, it's none of your business where I sleep."

"Ooh, getting a little testy, aren't we?" said Beverly.

"Well, sorry if I don't broadcast where I sleep like you do," said Charlotte.

"Oh, please!" said Beverly. "Not that I'd tell *you* anything, but at least I do get some play every now and then. Be careful at the formal, Charlotte. No one likes a goody two-shoes."

So anxious was he to be on time, Hoyt got to the lobby of the Inn at Chester, where he was to meet Rachel—Rachel—Rachel—he couldn't remember what she said her last name was—nobody had last names anymore anyway—Rachel—she of the lips—he could close his eyes and see those teasing, serpentine lips—so eager was he to make this stroke of luck pay off, he got to the lobby fifteen minutes early and sat down in a commercial knock-off Sheraton armchair in a lobby cluster, as hotel franchise decorators called them—clusters of couches, armchairs, side tables, and polyurethaned coffee tables, all calculated to domesticate the lobbies, which these days were usually like this one, cavernous spaces caked with marble and plasticized-shiny showy-grain wood.

The lobby vista at eye level, to anyone sunk down in a chair, seriously subverted whatever glamour the place might have conjured in the mind of a twenty-two-year-old who lived in the give-a-shit squalor of a fraternity house. Everywhere he looked . . . potbellies, sagging paunches—an entire field of them, as far as the eye could see—an entire tableau of men whose abdominal walls had given way. Disgusting . . . certainly to any male who had attended Dupont for going on four years—Dupont, where buff and dense bodies had become a part of fashionable male dress, and flat, cut, ripped, cobblestone body-armor abs were Buff at its best. These innumerable disgusting guts befouling his line of sight hung from middle-aged and even mid-thirties men, scores of them, perhaps hundreds, apparently attending some sort of business conference, by the looks of the name cards pinned to their shirts. Their shirts were no small part of the problem. Obviously the invitations, or instructions, had gone out marked "Dress: Weekend Casual." They were wearing short-sleeved sport shirts, polo shirts, V-neck cashmere sweaters with T-shirts showing in the V, the occasional huntin'-n'-fishin' khaki twill shirt—without jackets—all guaranteed to reveal not only their ponderous guts but also their stooped shoulders, double chins, wattles, and etiolate arms. Did it bother them? Not for a moment, judging from the roaring surf of conversation, the cackles—such hearty old-folks cackling as you never heard!

Hoyt was floating in this pool of blissful superiority, a hard frat guy in a world full of blubber, when he felt a hand on his shoulder. Startled, he swung his head about—

Looking at him with a bemused expression from behind the chair was the hottie from Pierce & Pierce, Rachel. "Ohmygod—I frightened you."

Her smile! Her smooth white flesh glowed. She looked even more lubricious than she did the other night—the same businesslike black suit and the black V-neck sweater—but it wasn't a sweater, it was black silk—reached even deeper, revealing an expanse of bare white flesh—with the tiniest of gold chains circling her lovely neck, bearing only a single small pearl that whispered in its small pearly way, *This tiny strand is all that stands between you and all my fair white flesh—if—if!*—and it was no mere happenstance that her eyes were made up to suggest the mysteries of the night and that her hair was now so silken, shiny, and blown full—

Pop. Before he could say another word, she had come around the chair and extended her hand in a perfectly businesslike way. They shook hands.

Chester was not noted for its restaurants. In fact, the Inn's main dining room, officially the Wyeth Room, was about as good as it got in Chester cuisine. The place was packed, and the maître d' said there was no table for two available. Rachel of Pierce & Pierce produced a scalding hiss and said, "Then we'll take a table for four or six . . . or eight . . . or twelve. I made this reservation . . . right here . . . in this very spot . . . twenty-three hours ago, and I *want* . . . our table."

Her imperiousness worked magic. In no time the perfect table for two materialized . . . by a window looking out on the Inn's terrace and garden, with swaths of flowers lit up even this late in the fall in exuberant blues, yellows, mauves, and magentas beneath the midday sun. Rachel was no more than twenty-four or twenty-five years old . . . and a woman . . . but she had exerted her will to power in a restaurant stuffy and stiff enough to intimidate any girl Hoyt knew at Dupont.

In the center of the restaurant the buildup of ricocheting voices was deafening, but here by the window they could hear each other and at the same time be sure that no one nearby could hear them.

"I wish I could show you the reports we have about you," said Rachel, "but I can't." Big smile.

"Reports? How could—what reports?"

"Perhaps I shouldn't tell you this in so many words, but you come very highly recommended."

It was against his better judgment, but Hoyt couldn't resist pulling his chin down into his neck and opening his eyes very wide and saying, "I do?"

"Unh—hunh." The smile—the maroon lips—the eyes that said so much more than her voice! She looked away in order to fish two or three or four sheets of paper, stapled together, out of a leather portfolio. She put them on the table and scanned the first sheet.

"Let's see . . . 'unusually mature for a student his age' . . . 'refuses to be intimidated' . . . 'decisive and quick-acting in critical moments' . . . 'character traits should more than compensate for lagging academic performance' . . .'"

Not even trying to conceal his astonishment, Hoyt touched the middle of his chest with the fingertips of his right hand. "That's me?"

"Yes, and the source carries a lot of weight with Pierce and Pierce." She gave him a profound if indefinable look, waited a few beats, and said, "The governor of California."

Alarm seemed to spread throughout the lining of Hoyt's skull with a feverish heat. He desperately ransacked his meager knowledge of the wiles of politicians to figure out the origin of what he had just heard. A prank? A warning? A threat? The maroon-lipped woman before him didn't actually work for Pierce & Pierce? She was some whore doing the bidding of the damnable governor? Many things churned in his brain far faster than it would take to catalog them, and none of them was good.

TOM WOLFE

It seemed an eternity before he was able to summon the presence of mind even to say the limp and the predictable: "You're joking. Like hell that's the governor of California."

"I assure you it is," said Rachel. "Or it's from someone on his staff speaking specifically for him."

She held the top sheet close enough to Hoyt for him to read the letterhead. "The State of California." And beneath that "Office of the Governor" and "Sacramento" and so on.

"He's quite a fan of yours, the governor is." Seeing Hoyt's consternation, she said, "Hoyt! Don't be so skeptical! This didn't just come from out of the blue, you know. The state of California has 224 billion bonds outstanding— forgive the Wall Street–speak—I mean 224 billion dollars' *worth* of bonds. They're one of our most important clients. They'd be one of *any*body's most important clients. So when we get a recommendation like this from the governor of California, we take it very seriously." She gave Hoyt her warmest smile yet. "I wish you could see the look on your face. I don't know how you could be *that* surprised. Obviously you know each other, or he's seen you at work firsthand. I mean, this is a very detailed report." She looked down at it again. "I mean . . . like here: 'He also shows his maturity in the way he handles sensitive information. He doesn't divulge the nature of complex or delicate situations simply to call favorable attention to himself.'"

She looked up again. "I mean, nobody in my office has ever heard of a student recommended this highly before, or not by anybody in a position like the governor's. Not to be blunt about it, but coming from him—I probably shouldn't tell you this, either—it's more like an instruction than a recommendation."

Hoyt studied her face again, this time as much perplexed as aroused. "Be straight with me, Rachel—is this some kind of a joke?"

Rachel gave him another of her sophisticated smiles, and practically convulsed with suppressed chuckles. "One of the original Pierce brothers— Pierce and Pierce?—Ellis Pierce—used the word 'loser' in a sentence, and somebody asked him what he meant by loser, and he said, 'A loser's just like everybody else, except that he won't shake hands with good luck.' Or so it says in their biography, the one by Martin Myers? You know the book?"

Hoyt shook his head no.

"It's called *Fierce and Fierce*," said Rachel. "Cute . . . Stop staring at me like that! We're talking about a job that pays ninety-five thousand to start. I don't think that's bad, to start."

"Doing what?" said Hoyt as disinterestedly as he could manage, seeking to regain his much-vaunted cool.

She explained that there was an eight-week training program, after which one was assigned to sales, analysis, a trading desk, or whatever.

"All right," said Hoyt. "Let me ask you something else I'd like a straight answer on. Aside from the fact that he considers me an awesome guy, why is the governor of California going to all this trouble for me? Or is this just some generous streak he's got?" He searched her face for any hint of knowledge she wasn't owning up to.

Completely deadpan: "I don't know. It seems self-evident to me. I assumed you'd know the context and everything."

Hoyt gave her a slanted, ironic smile, calculated to make her smile in complicity if she, too, was aware that this had to be a bribe. But she didn't smile. She seemed genuinely puzzled by his expression. Then he surveyed her lips, the little ever-so-fragile gold chain with the tiny pearl, the only thing standing between him and . . . and . . . and this time such things didn't resonate with his loins at all. It was the rational poker player in him that was inflamed now. No more irony . . . He sat there staring at her and nodding ever so slightly, but over and over and ever so sagaciously . . . Pierce & Pierce and $95,000 a year to start . . . He kept on nodding, ever so significantly, expressionless, in a gambler's way.

Wait'll he tells Vance about this! Unfuckingbelievable.

Rachel set her glistening dark lips in their most concupiscent smile yet. "I'm waiting, Hoyt. Are you going to shake hands with Fortune or not? She's a much-maligned lady. That's from Evelyn Waugh."

Hoyt extended his hand, and Rachel took it. They looked into each other's eyes, and Hoyt gave her hand a certain squeeze, but the hand he held was all business. The hand didn't give him its room number, much less its key. All it said was, "It's a deal, big boy."

On the way up in the elevator, Adam said to himself—out loud, "Whoa-oh-oh . . . pull yourself together" . . . Not even Buster Roth was so brutish, he'd dare have somebody do something physical . . . but there were other ways of eliminating him, weren't there? Somehow—they'd blame the whole thing on *him*. He wrote the paper for Jojo and pressured him into handing it in . . . Maybe they were going to tape what he said to Buster Roth . . . Why hadn't he brought someone along . . . like Camille . . . She'd happily tell Buster

Roth to stick his head up his descending colon until his shoulders disappeared. Camille! The very thought gave him a few volts of courage.

Before he knew it, the elevator door had opened and he was in Buster Roth's lair . . . He was conscious of four or five men sitting on the leather and stainless-steel furniture . . . not students. Who were they?

He approached a fence made of panels of glass . . . seemed like a reception area . . . Four lean, sleek veal-gray workstations in a row and, at each, a lean, sleek young woman perched on a lean, ergonomic word processor's chair. Adam could hardly believe it. They were gorgeous. As opposed to all the plastic veal in the place, they were definitely flesh and blood. Two of them, one with long dark hair parted down the middle, the other with long light brown hair parted down the middle, happened to swivel about, to get up. Adam felt inadequate to even approach these girls. They weren't much older than he was, if at all, but they seemed to be from another order of human, in which everyone was glamorous and sex-savvy.

He caught the eye of the one with dark hair. Adam could barely croak out his appointment with "Coach Roth." The girl turned to another young woman, whom she called Celeste, seated at a workstation, and Celeste turned to her computer and then to Adam, gave him a polite smile, assured him that Coach Roth would see him shortly, and gestured toward all the postmodern leather and stainless steel. Polite smiles they gave him, that and nothing more. They had written him off after the first glance. Each had sized him up as someone incapable of flirting . . . precisely because he had never even . . . gotten laid. They could tell! It showed! And the older he got, the harder it was going to be to do it, to admit he'd never done it before or demonstrate the same thing through his ignorance of technique and clumsy attempts at learning.

So he sank into a couch, and the rich tannery smell of the leather rose and befuddled him. He knew he should be concentrating on what he was going to say to Buster Roth, but the same vision kept dissolving his powers of logic: Charlotte, running on the treadmill, her face free of makeup or even thoughts of artifice—innocence in the flesh—and the dark line, the juice of her own body, down the cleft in her buttocks.

This strange state, with lust wafting through logic, lasted a long time, for Coach Roth did not see him shortly.

At last, "Mr. Gellin?" It was the same girl. She led him down a narrow arched passageway. He emerged into a room as bright as day. A big, middle-aged man wearing a polo shirt rocked back in a swivel chair behind an enormous postmodern desk—rich wood—walnut?—pointlessly curvy as on Philadelphia channel news shows. Buster Roth.

As Adam entered, Roth didn't get up. In fact, he rocked back still farther in his chair. He eyed Adam for a moment with a slightly sly smile before he said, "Adam?"

Adam heard himself saying, "Yes, sir."

Roth gestured toward an armchair near the desk. As Adam approached, Roth squinted his eyes at him and turned one side of his lips up in a smile that wasn't so much a greeting, as Adam saw it, as a conclusion: I know *your* kind.

Adam sat down, and Roth, still rocked way back in his desk chair, said, "How long you been with us, Adam?"

"You mean tutoring?" said Adam.

Roth nodded yes.

"Two years, sir." Why was he adding all these sirs? But he knew why. It was fear. He also knew viscerally that Roth was one of that breed of men who was totally unlike himself, the kind who welcomes a fight over anything whatsoever, the better to demonstrate his dominant nature, the kind who, in fact, couldn't wait to show you how much he liked to tangle, the kind who, as a boy, dared you to take him on and then made sure you caved in immediately, perhaps by bullying but more often subtly, through "good-natured" roughhousing in which you always wound up as the "mock" victim and through a condescending obliviousness when you went out of your way to flatter him or curry favor. Adam, like so many others, had grown up knowing that the male sex was divided into these two types, those who seek to impress by their willingness to fight and who abide no insinuations that they might not have it—and those who, like himself, know from age six on that they don't have it and who seek to avoid all situations where the distinction might be made. He would live out his life knowing which breed he was. He would be aware of it every day until the day he died. His shame would be profound, so profound that he would never mention it to a living soul, not even the intimate soul to whom he had divulged . . . *everything* . . .

"Two years . . ." Buster Roth was saying. He began nodding, as if ruminating over this interesting piece of information. "Well, I'm sure in two years you've gotten to know a lot more about sports and athletes than most students."

Adam couldn't figure out what the right answer to that might be. One answer might indicate that he knew more about it than was good for him. Another answer might indicate that he had a negative attitude.

T
O
M

W
O
L
F
E

Finally Adam said, "I can't really tell, sir. I don't know how much other students know. Other students certainly talk about the sports program a lot. I know that."

"Well, you're talking about *fans* now, Adam. I'm talking about—but by the way, since we're on the subject, would you call yourself a fan?"

Adam didn't know the right answer to that, either. "Yes" seemed like the better part of wisdom, but his pride wouldn't let him say that, not even in front of an audience of one—one who had committed his entire life to sports. So he said, "Sort of, I guess, but I guess not in the way"—he wanted to say not in the way you mean, but that didn't sound tactful enough—"not in the way most fans are fans."

"Sort of but not in the way most fans are fans . . ." said Buster Roth with an unnatural drawl. Irony? "What would you say yours is?"

"Well, I'm like interested in sports . . . as sports, I guess you'd say. I mean I think it's really interesting that millions of people become completely absorbed in sports, emotionally involved."

The tactician in Adam—which is to say, his powers of logic—told him to drop the subject and act dumb or ask Coach Roth some humble question that would flatter the man's sense of mastery of the world of sports. Neutralize yourself! Make *him* the subject! Why didn't you just say, "Oh, yes, I'm a fan . . ." But the intellectual exhibitionist in him brushed the tactician aside, and he said, "Well, I guess I mean I'm interested in what makes fans *fans*."

He wanted to say, "Why on earth do Dupont University students with average SATs of fourteen-ninety get excited, scream their hearts out over 'their' basketball team—which is made up of a bunch of hired mercenaries who probably wouldn't average nine hundred without the swimmies—who live a life completely apart from the real students, who feel infinitely superior to them, who eat better food in a better dining room, who have tutors to do their schoolwork for them, who say *you ain't, he don't,* and *nome saying?*, who look upon friendly student fans as either sluts or suck-ups—why are they *fans* of such people?" But not even the egoist in Adam could push him that far, so he settled for, "I keep wondering why people in Boston, where I'm from, get so excited over the Red Sox. I mean, there's not anybody on the team who's from anywhere near Boston. They don't set foot in Boston, most of them, except to go to Fenway Park. But that doesn't matter. Red Sox fans are the most loyal fans in the world."

He sensed that he was already getting too wound up. This was not the time, if ever, to try out the theory of championism on Buster Roth. "I mean, that's the sort of thing that interests—that I'd like to figure out, I guess."

"I see," said Buster Roth with a tuned-out expression on his face. "What about the athletes themselves? You've gotten to know some of the athletes pretty well by now, I'd imagine."

Adam hesitated. "I don't know. I guess there are all kinds."

Buster Roth smiled, which Adam took to be a good sign.

"Well, let's talk about our mutual friend, Jojo. Jojo's got a serious issue on his hands here. Whattaya think he ought to do?"

Adam had never thought of it from that point of view. It confused him. "Well . . . I don't know . . ."

"If I were you, Adam, I'd give it some thought. If Jojo is penalized over . . . whatever has happened . . . you could run the risk of the same penalty."

The idea stunned Adam. His brain churned, finally settling on a single consideration. If that was true, if any such thing happened, he could say good-bye to the Rhodes scholarship, to any and all scholarships, to any and all consulting jobs, and to the pretension of being a Millennial Mutant.

He croaked out, "I don't understand."

"Let's suppose," said Buster Roth, "that you wrote the entire paper for Jojo, and all he did was hand it in. I'm just saying what if." He paused and squinted at Adam. "I'm not saying that's what happened. Jojo doesn't say that's what happened. But if the panel decided that's what happened, then Jojo would be suspended for the next semester, which happens to be the basketball season. And so would you."

Adam felt an adrenal flash flood. "The panel?"

"Oh yes. If things got pushed far enough, there would be a panel of four students and two faculty members, and there would be what amounts to a trial, and if the panel found Jojo guilty of any such thing, then anybody who knowingly aided and abetted him would be considered just as guilty."

Adam didn't know what to say. He had the terrifying feeling that the brute behind the desk—with his arms as big as Adam's thigh, with his look of domination over . . . *the other breed*—was ready to swat him like a fly. "I—" He didn't know how to word what he wanted to say. "But—the Athletic Department *hires* the tutors and makes it clear that we're supposed to give the athletes all the help they need. That's what we're told—all the help they need."

"Oh? Did anyone in the athletic department ever tell you to write an entire paper for an athlete and all he had to do was hand it in? If so, I want to know that individual's name. Not that I'm saying that's what happened. All I'm saying is that's what Jojo's teacher thinks. The actual truth could be something else entirely. Only you and Jojo know."

Adam could feel his pulse galloping in the carotid artery in his neck. The next question would be, "So what *did* happen?" and he hadn't a clue as to how to answer it. He waffled as best he could: "It's hard to give like a . . . yes-no—"

Buster Roth held up his right palm in the halt mode. "I'm not asking you to go through the whole thing right now. What I want you to do is take a day or two and try to remember everything you can about what happened . . . or didn't happen. You understand what I'm saying? Make sure you haven't forgotten anything."

Adam's mind was spinning. He immediately feared the worst. He was being set up—although exactly how, he couldn't imagine. He was being tested—but for what? Loyalty? Coolness at conniving? He was being made to *look* as if he were lying—by accepting the suggestion that he take a few days to "remember." He was being toyed with—because the warrior breed, eating spareribs, bones and all, loved to torment the *other* breed. On the other hand, suppose he just blurted it all out, as he could right now, without forgetting one speck of detail—could it be that Buster Roth was offering him a way out by "remembering" what happened . . . in a certain way . . .

And then he couldn't resist: "What does Jojo say happened?"

As soon as he asked, his heart fell. A question like that—he was as much as admitting his willingness to cook up some kind of story in order to wriggle out of the jam he was in.

Buster Roth looked him in the eye and said in a level, almost monotonous voice, "Jojo says he wrote it himself. At the last minute he realized there was some important material he needed, so he called you up and you showed him the books where he might be able to find it. So he used those books, and by now it was the last minute and he'd run out of time, and he didn't know exactly what all the terms meant, but he used them anyway. That's what Jojo says happened."

Buster Roth stopped talking but continued to look Adam right in the eye. The atmosphere was now humid with the matter of whether Adam remembered it that way or not. But Roth never asked.

Adam wouldn't have known what to say if he had.

As soon as Vance came into the library, Hoyt jumped up and steered him into the billiard room. "You wanna hear something incredible, Vance-man?" With great gusto, he told him about Rachel and Pierce & Pierce.

"Shit, Hoyt," said Vance, "that's fucking awesome!" He looked toward the doorway. There was I.P., saying, "Anybody got—"

"Nobody *got*," said Hoyt. "Saint Rays only fuck around for *real*."

23. MODEL ON A RUNWAY

I know they'll be older than I am, I know they'll be better dressed than I am, cooler cooler cooler oh so much cooler than I am, but please, God, don't let them be blond and skinny, don't let them be cute and bitchy, don't—please, God!—don't let them be the sort of boarding school Sarc 3 girls like Beverly or Hillary or Erica, who can cut you open before you even know the knife has gone in—

Oh, please, God!

By now, three-thirty p.m., the sun was already low in the sky, and the rays came slanting through the trees here on Ladding Walk, breaking every-thing—the old buildings, the antique lampposts, the cobblestones—into dancing flecks of shadow and flickers of light so bright they made Charlotte avert her eyes. She didn't expect there to be many students on Ladding Walk on a Saturday afternoon, but the ones she saw were walking toward her, toward the bosom of the campus, which all knew by heart, sounding so care-free and happy, chattering away on their cell phones . . . as they, too, broke up into dappled dancing shadows and lights before her averted eyes. It struck her as . . . ominous. They were heading *toward* the bosom of Dupont. She was the only one heading *away*, toward the edge, destined for someplace shady—namely, the Saint Ray house. If Marsden Hall, the main classroom building on the Walk, weren't in the way, she could see the house from here.

It occurred to her that she had never seen it in daylight. The Saint Ray house had always been that dangerous, that tempting Devil's nest of the night.

Beverly—Beverly, who knew about such things!—had warned her not to go off with Hoyt or any other Saint Ray to another city for a formal. But how could she pass up a chance at such eminence, a freshman invited to a formal all the way down in Washington, D.C., by a senior, the coolest guy in the coolest fraternity at Dupont? I am Charlotte Simmons! Besides, that was two weeks ago, when the formal wouldn't be until "two Saturdays from now," and two Saturdays was a long way off, wasn't it? But this . . . is *that* Saturday. A frightening look at herself as if from above, in astral projection: nothing but a little girl, all alone, just recently come down from the mountains, clad in a red T-shirt, a pair of tight jeans, and an ugly, puffy khaki-colored synthetic-down-filled jacket from Robinson's in Sparta, which made her look about seven when it was zipped up like this—a round, puffy bundled-up seven, carrying a canvas boat bag containing everything she was taking for the dinner and the dance in a fancy hotel. That was her luggage! A boat bag Bettina had lent her, which, she now realized, only made it worse! She could just imagine what Vance's and Julian's dates, whom she had never met or laid eyes on before, were going to think about a canvas boat bag, the warm and toasty little girl's coat—

Oh dear God, don't let them be blond and skinny!

Now she could see the Saint Ray house. It looked so much smaller . . . and shabbier . . . in daylight, more like just some old house, albeit with columns before the front door—not like the Devil's nest, in any case. SUVs were parked out front—illegally—on the Walk itself. Guys were going back and forth from the SUVs to the house. Vance was in the front yard. He was making exaggerated gestures to someone on the porch and yelling something Charlotte couldn't make out. Quite a show he was putting on. She was willing to bet anything it all had to do with a girl.

Charlotte hurriedly unzipped her puffy jacket and thrust it back until it was barely hanging on her shoulders. Godalmighty, this wind! But make sure she doesn't look seven, make sure they all get an eyeful of her body. That was the main thing . . .

She wasn't worried about Vance, Julian, and Hoyt. It was all . . . the dates. Julian was taking his regular frat-house girl, named Nicole, who had never been there when Charlotte was there. Vance was taking his regular girlfriend, whoever she was. Charlotte had never heard of her hanging around Saint Ray at all. She knew they would both be upperclassmen—and

TOM WOLFE

female upperclassmen, she kept being told, resented "fresh meat" in the first place.

Two girls stood next to each other on the porch. Surely, God—not those two! One was blond and the other almost blond, so light was her long brown hair—and both were skinny. The almost-blond one . . . Charlotte could have sworn she had seen her before. Where . . . she couldn't imagine. Two other girls, one blond and the other dark-haired and skinny, were sitting down on the edge of the porch.

Vance was looking straight at the light-brown-haired one and barking, "Come on, Crissy, how about giving me a fucking hand? Where'd you put the thirty-rack? And what the hell'd you do with the handle?"

The girl cocked her hips in a mocking way and said airily, "That's not my job, Vance. You're the one who's going to get sloshed the second we get there." She turned to the blonde and, not lowering her voice in the slightest, said, "My boyfriend's a fucking alcoholic, Nicole."

With a cry that was half shriek and half laugh, the blonde, Nicole, poked her thumb into Crissy's side—a big twitch and a *Heyyy*—and said in a merry coloratura, "Oh, you little hypocrite!"

Vance motioned toward an SUV, which turned out to be Hoyt's Suburban, and said, "All right, then where's the rest of your shit? Your shit's your job, right? I don't know if we have room for all this girl stuff. You think we're going away for a week or something? Why'd you need a duffel bag?" *Stern*— and Vance wasn't the stern type.

Charlotte began to get the picture. Vance was rolling out all the gruff stuff to show Julian, Boo-man, Heady, and the other guys just who wore the pants in this relationship. God help him if he indicated in some unguarded moment that he felt *tenderly* toward her.

Now Charlotte remembered where she had seen this Crissy before. She was the girl Vance had tried to bring into the bedroom that night at the Saint Ray party, prompting Hoyt to say, "This is *our* room." She obviously had him whipped. And why not? She was merely perfect. Wide jaws, smooth jawline, model-girl face, big blue eyes, long good-as-blond brown hair, a suede jacket so soft it made you want to bury your head in it, a brown leather belt that matched it, a button-down shirt with the top four buttons undone, absolutely the right jeans, pointy-toed boots polished to a mellow glow, as opposed to a sharp shine, and a little bright brown leather bag that probably cost more than everything Charlotte had on put together. The blonde had the pointy boots, the jeans, the same little brown bag, and a tight T-shirt with bright yellow and light blue horizontal stripes that made her chest look bigger.

And here came Charlotte Simmons in her mousy outfit, half of it borrowed, a ratty red T-shirt—a pair of still not-quite-right jeans, and sneakers—*sneakers!*—no handbag at all, no garment bag, not even a duffel bag, but rather—a shapeless canvas boat bag.

Amid all this scurrying around the front yard, however, no one had even acknowledged her arrival. And why should they? Some droopy little freshman standing there in rags toting her miserable sack. Julian was busy trying to jam more "girl stuff" into the rear end of the Suburban. Vance was busy trying to stare down the good-as-blond Crissy, who stood on the porch with her hips cocked insolently and the rest of her body Cybex-machined, treadmilled, and de-carbohydrated to near perfection. Boo-man, Julian, and Heady had lowered their voices an octave in order to sound like manly rakes. They bantered, they bellowed, they ribbed one another with hawhawhaw-haws. And Charlotte just stood there in social oblivion. Where was Hoyt? Should she start looking for him? But she couldn't . . . too demeaning . . . too demeaning . . .

"Crissy!" the blonde, Nicole, was saying. "You are *so* bad! How can you say *he's* an alcoholic? I mean, I wish I had a little video of you at the *after-party* last night. You don't remember how you like . . . got down on all fours—"

"*Hahhhhh!*" Crissy soared into a trill of laughter, "Oh, puh-leeese! Give—me—a—*break*! Do you honestly think you could have like . . . *aimed* a camcorder? How many times did you go throw up?"

"Ohmygod," said the blonde, rolling her eyes, "don't even *mention* that ohmygod . . . that bathroom was *so-o-o-o-o* disgusting. Did you go in there? *Eccccch.* I woke up with *such* a hangover this morning. I'm not talking about a *hangover*, I'm talking about like a *toxic* hangover."

"Tell me about it."

"But I mean *poisonous*. I got up and I was walking like . . . what are those birds that have one leg shorter than the other?"

"The dodo bird?"

"I guess. Whatever. I could like hardly make it downstairs to the dining room. I stuck my head in the kitchen, and I said—"

While Charlotte stood there like an invisible waif, the two girls regaled each other with "hilarious" accounts of how each, unbeknownst to the other, had gone to the kitchen of their sorority house and implored the cook,

Maude, evidently black, judging by the way they mimicked her accent—
"Maude took one look at me . . . I didn't even know I still had Vance's
sweater on . . . the fucking thing comes down to *here* . . . and my hair was all
like . . . plastered down over my face . . . it stuck like fucking *Velcro* . . . and
Maude, she's like, 'Lawd God in Heaven, Crissy, lookitchoo! Whatchoo girls
be up to now!'"—how they implored her for "grease," greasy omelets, greasy
French toast, biscuits glopped with butter, which made Nicole feel like she
had just swallowed a basketball afterward, but how the fuck else could you
deal with a hangover except with grease?

"I need some grease right now," said the blonde. "I need some *serious*
grease. I mean, like french fries. You know the really *nasty* kind, like they
have at the Sizzlin' Skillet?"

Both laughed and laughed.

To Charlotte, this bit of repartee could scarcely have been more deflating. They had to make the *Sizzlin' Skillet* the lowest and most disgusting of
all cheap food . . . The two were upperclassmen, great pals, members of
what was known as the hottest, most socially luminous sorority at Dupont—
Delta Omicron Upsilon, or DOU, affectionately—even reverently—called
the Douche—blessed with an aura of northeastern private schools, fair,
straight hair, and sophistication. And they were such lovely little liars. Charlotte couldn't imagine an ounce of grease going down the gullet of either
one of those two perfect skinny bodies.

"Hey, babe! Put your stuff in the car?"

It was Hoyt! Coming out the front door of the Saint Ray house, beaming a big, hearty smile at her! Thank God! She felt saved from *utter* oblivion.
He bounded down the steps toward her, as perfect in his frat-boy way as the
two Douche girls were in their way. He had on a well-worn tan hunting
jacket over a light blue shirt unbuttoned down the front to just above the
sternum, the shirttails hanging out over a pair of chinos frayed at the bottom
of the pant legs, and flip-flops.

"Put your stuff in the car?" he said again as he came closer, still smiling.
Charlotte hung on to that smile for dear life. It was her validation. No matter what she looked like to them, she was under the aegis of the coolest of the
cool, Hoyt Thorpe.

But she didn't know how to answer him. She couldn't just hold up the
boat bag—

So she said, "Not yet."

What a sad, weak *not yet*! She couldn't get a word out with the careless ease, the perfectly at-home insouciance of the two girls standing near her on the porch.

"Well, we can't keep dicking around or we'll be late," said Hoyt, pleasantly. "We got a band to make connections with, the hotel's got waiters and shit lined up for us. I see Vance. Is everybody else here?" He turned that way and saw Julian. He turned this way and saw Vance's date, Crissy, and the other one. "Djou meet Crissy and Nicole?"

Charlotte looked at the pair with a sinking heart. *Crissy and Nicole.* On top of everything else, they were both *–ey* girls. All the *cool* girls at Dupont, the ones who were *with it*, were *–ey* girls—Beverly, Courtney, Wheatley, Kingsley, Tinsley, Avery, and now Crissy. Of course, there was Nicole . . . and Erica . . . but thinking of Erica made her sink still farther—

She croaked out a miserable little "Hi"—just that, all the while realizing that her stricken, frightened face spoke volumes concerning her confidence, maturity, strength, social competence, *bon vivance*, charm, wit, knowledge of the ways of the world—*volumes!*

"And this is Charlotte," said Hoyt, gesturing toward her.

Oh God, it was too much. The two *–ey* girls merely waved to her—no, not so much a wave as a half a wrist tick . . . and that *dead smile* . . . the same one Beverly's chum Erica had given her . . . The lips widen and even turn up slightly at the corners, but the eyes die and the brow ages twenty bored years and the lights go out.

"Don't anybody move," said Hoyt. "I gotta get one more bag"—he motioned toward the house with his head—"and then we gotta get the fuck on the fucking road. Wait a minute"—now he was looking at Charlotte—"where *is* your bag?"

Charlotte stood there with her mouth half open and her face growing hot and crimson. But there was no way out. Timidly she lifted the canvas boat bag and mumbled—she couldn't even make her voice *work*—"This is all I have."

She didn't dare look at the Douche sisters. She knew they would be cutting proto-sniggering glances at each other.

Hoyt held it up chest-high for a moment, as if weighing it, but, thank God, made no comment. Instead, he jogged the fifteen or twenty feet to the Suburban, tossed the canvas boat bag through the window and onto the backseat, wheeled about, yelled to Charlotte and the two Perfect girls, Crissy and Nicole, "Remember, nobody moves a muscle!" and jogged toward the house.

Charlotte was dying to move somewhere, anywhere. What was she to do? The two sorority girls were already brow to brow in whispery, giggly conversation. Was she to approach them and somehow wedge her way into their conversation—which was no doubt about *her*? Was she supposed to stand there like a homeless urchin and wait for them to deign to include her in proper cool Douche society—and have everybody in the yard look at her, this . . . this . . . this totally socially inept little urchin, this totally clueless little freshman who had no business even being among us?

So without a word—she knew very well she couldn't even speak—she walked to the SUV and leaned back against the rear door and crossed her arms under her breasts and looked at her wristwatch every ten seconds or so to indicate that she was waiting for someone—which would be Hoyt, obviously, since she was attached to his car—and therefore was *not out of place here* . . . But how long could she keep this pose?

Sure enough, when they finally headed off, Hoyt was driving, Charlotte was in the bucket seat next to him, Vance and Crissy were in the second row, and Julian and Nicole were in the third, which meant the whole bunch of them, except for Hoyt, would be looking at the back of her head, whether they meant to or not, and therefore would be aware of her alien presence for the entire trip.

They were barely under way when they drove past the erupting fields of lightbulbs, the big long handle vibrating in shocking-pink neon outline, the gaudy name being written in script as if by an unseen hand: THE SIZZLIN' SKILLET.

"Last chance for serious grease!" Crissy sang out to Nicole. Gales of laughter, as if there were nothing more low-rent than stopping for a bite at the Sizzlin' Skillet.

Looking out the window at it was the last thing in the world Charlotte wanted to do at this particular moment. The last thing in the world she wanted to recall was that horrible hour, which seemed like twenty-four hours, in which the planets of Momma and Daddy, on the one hand, and the Amorys, on the other, collided . . . and this ride was going to be *hours* of it.

A voice behind her said, "Ohmygod . . . I don't believe this . . . Charlene! Tell your friend his name is Hoyt, not Heeshawn!"

Charlene!

Charlotte turned away from the window. On Hoyt's head was a . . . *do-*

rag . . . just like the ones the black ghetto boys in Chester wore, a swath of black cloth wrapped around his head all the way down to his eyebrows and a flap of it hanging down the base of his neck. He swiveled his head as far as he could to the right, and he was grinning—not at her, however, but for the benefit of Crissy in the seat behind, she who had shrieked the mock shriek—

And called her *Charlene*!

Hoyt said, "Her name's not Char*leeeeeeene* . . . It's Charlotte."

Her.

He said it in a merry voice and seemed to sling the words out the corner of his mouth and back over his shoulder to make sure they reached their intended, Crissy. As he turned back in order to see the road, he gave Charlotte a split second's worth of smile.

Charlene! Her! Hoyt's *her* hurt almost as much as *Charlene*—

Crissy, from behind: "Oh, *I'm* sorry, I'm *so* bad with names—Vance! This I *really* don't believe! Look, everybody, this is little Master Vance Phipps of the *Phipps* Phippses! My little Goldilocks."

Charlotte looked back despite herself. Vance had on a black do-rag, too, exactly the same as Hoyt's—and so did Julian. They were both grinning foolishly.

Nicole, from the third row: "Ohmygod, you guys—thank God you're here, Crissy. Can't we get a little fratty-er?"

Hoyt, eyes on the road, sang out merrily, "No prob, Nicole!"

Vance and Julian laughed.

Nicole said, "You think maybe we've got something on our little brain, Hoytsy?"

Crissy said, "I'd like to see you guys wear those things on campus. The AfrAm Solidarity—they gon' *lynch* yo' ass, motherfucker!"

Hoyt, Vance, Nicole, and Julian laughed.

Meanwhile, *Charlene* . . . *Her* . . . a sound like steam turning into fog filled *her* head. They all, Hoyt included, acted as if Charlotte Simmons didn't exist.

After that, as the Suburban rolled down Interstate 95, Crissy and Nicole and Julian and Vance and Hoyt had a rare old gibefest, songfest, witfest, and what-the-fuck-shit-asshole-motherfuckerfest for themselves, but not for Charlene Simmons. If one of them broke into song, all five of them always knew the words. At one point, one of the countless allusions to sexual perversion—perversion in Charlotte's book, in any event—inspired Julian to break into song, a rap song that included the lines

TOM WOLFE

Yo, you take my testi-culls,
Suck 'em like a popsi-cull.

The very same disgusting "lyrics" somebody down the hall had been playing on a stereo in the middle of the night when Beverly sexiled her! And all five of the frat and sorority girls knew the words. They couldn't have sung along with Julian more lustily! The three guys, still sporting their black do-rags, rocked back and forth in their seats to the stupid beat, caroling away while their black neck flaps flopped this way and that. Crissy and Nicole were fairly wailing with delight, as if there was nothing more joyous in the world than the thought of sucking testicles. The highway was ten lanes wide at some points, and people in adjacent cars would look at the Suburban incredulously, trying to make some kind of sense out of the sight of three white boys wearing black do-rags and rocking their shoulders in an exaggerated fashion. The five brothers and sisters enjoyed the hooples' bewilderment enormously.

They recalled hilarious moments of hilarious parties past. Halloween—that girl Candy, wearing a silver lamé thong bikini, underneath the strobe lights with a spiked leather collar around her neck and a heavy chain as a leash in the hands of that greasy Goth, all dressed in black, the one with the slimy black ponytail and hoop earrings and his two front teeth with gold caps, each inset with a little diamond or rhinestone or whatever the fuck they were. Gales, roars of laughter over *that* precious memory.

Crissy said, "You think she's really into S and M?"

"I don't think so," said Nicole. "She just blows too many lines, is her problem."

With that, Hoyt lifted his chin way up and slightly to the right, vaguely in his little seatmate's direction, and cleared his throat in a loud manner. The car went quiet. Charlotte had the impression that he was telling Nicole and the rest of them not to get on *that* subject with his date sitting there, although just what the subject—"blows too many lines"—was, she hadn't the faintest idea.

Hoyt leaned over, put his hand on her forearm, smiled charmingly, and said, "I wish you'd been there. Too much Halloween was that girl's problem. What did *you* do for Halloween?"

A nervous jolt hit Charlotte's solar plexus. She could literally feel it. She was obliged to . . . say something in this alien company gone suddenly silent.

With a hoarse croak: "I guess—I don't remember."

That was so weak and lame she couldn't possibly leave it at that. She had to say something more. She began hyperventilating. "I guess—I don't exactly hold with Halloween?" Ohmygod! She had blurted out an old mountain countryism, the "hold with." Her face was on fire.

More silence. Then Crissy said, "I've been meaning to ask you, Charl-*uuuuunh*"—she quickly swallowed the second syllable because, obviously, she knew she had gotten it wrong the first time, or had chosen to get it wrong, but had already forgotten what it actually was . . . or had chosen, with Sarc 3 finesse, to forget what it was—"where are you from?"

Fury overwhelmed the nervousness of inferiority. *I am Charlotte Simmons*. Without turning her head, Charlotte sat rigidly, looking straight at the road ahead. Since it had worked once before, she snapped, "Sparta, North Carolina—Blue Ridge Mountains—population nine hundred—you've never heard of it—don't feel bad—nobody has."

As soon as the words left her mouth, she realized that this exhibition of peevishness and defensiveness had only made things worse. Hoyt began laughing in a vain attempt to turn it all into a little joke. Charlotte looked back at Crissy and forced a grin and a spastic laugh, as if it had been all in fun.

Crissy wasn't sitting still for that. "*I'm* not worried at all. I certainly hope *you* aren't."

"Oh, no, Crissy. I was just kidding?"

Waves and waves of humiliation . . . Even her "Crissy" seemed to hang in the air like an impertinence. You?—presuming to be on a friendly basis with a Douche like Crissy?

She was aware of Hoyt looking at her out of the corner of his eye. A tremor of suppressed sniggers from both rows behind her. She began to feel it—the puncture wound at the base of her skull.

Hoyt said, "Remember that guy Lud Davis? They used to call him Lud the Stud? Played when I was a freshman. He was the only good *white* running back we've ever had, far as I know. He was from the Blue Ridge Mountains, too, someplace called Cumberland Gap. I don't know why I remember that. Cumberland Gap." He looked straight at Charlotte and in a voice stuffed full of intense interest, said, "Do you know Cumberland Gap?"

A subdued little voice: "No . . . I don't think so . . ." She tried to think of some amiable way to expound upon the subject.

Silence.

"Well, he was a really cool guy," said Hoyt. "He practically *lived* at the I.M."

Oh, how encouraging. You could be from the mountains and still be cool . . . and how condescending.

"Then I'm sure you saw him a lot," said Vance.

"No prob when you're sobriety personified and you got maturity to burn."

Julian said, "Well then, if I were you, I'd check the fucking gauge, because you sure burned up a lot of it Monday night."

"Whattaya talking about, Monday night?"

"Over at that thing at Lapham, that reception. You were there, Crissy. It was eight fucking o'clock, and Hoyt's so wrecked he's asking the fucking master's wife how many men she's slept with in her life. She's looking around like 'Help! Somebody get this . . . *thing* off me!' and Hoyt's like, 'Bottom line! Bottom line! How many!'"

Hoyt said, "I don't know how you can sit back there and lie with a straight face." He put his hand on Charlotte's forearm again and said, "Don't listen to him. What's that story about the island where nobody tells the truth?"

"It's not a story, Hoyto," said Vance, "it's some kind of math problem."

"Bullshit," Julian was already saying. "You must've yelled 'Bottom line' at that poor woman a hundred fucking times! Tell the truth, Big Dog."

"Well . . . they do say she's hot," said Hoyt. "Guys at Lapham told me that. I doubt that old Wasserstein can get it up to her standards."

The frat boys and the sorority girls broke up over that, and everything was back on course again. Nicole was saying, "I know for a fact that . . ." and she was off on a story about some other master's wife.

Hoyt leaned over toward Charlotte again, and this time he grabbed her left hand as he bathed her in a smile of warm charm and said, "Wasserstein is the master of Lapham College. You know Lapham, the one with the gargoyles."

"Oh, yes, I sure do!" said Charlotte with incredibly more joy in her voice than the topic could support. She added a merry little laugh, as if she sure had to admit it was amusing, bringing up those gargoyles. She began laughing at anything that seemed intended as funny—how-drunk-I-was stories, guy's-such-a-loser stories, can-you-believe-what-a-slut-she-is stories, flaming-queen stories, vulgarisms delivered with a burlesque Italian accent— "Uppa You Ess" (Julian).

She didn't realize what a fool she was making of herself until Vance said that I.P. had a date for the formal and that she was very hot, believe it or not, a girl named Gloria.

"Holy shit!" said Julian. "Does that mean he's cheating on his hand?"

That broke everybody up, Crissy and Nicole included. But when Charlotte, who hadn't the faintest notion what I.P.'s "cheating on his hand" meant, joined in with her own wail of laughter—the others abruptly went silent. She turned about, and they were all casting *significant* glances at one another. Obviously, the "hilarious" phrase was some sort of inside joke. An outsider pretending to understand it was merely revealing how frantically, how fawningly, she wanted to be one of the gang.

It was all too shaming. By now all of them thought of her as a wretched little misfit. To make it worse, Hoyt felt like he had to lean over and pay attention to her periodically, to reassure her that she actually still *existed* in their Cool company, and then he'd rejoin the fun. So many idiotic stories . . . so much idiotic gossip . . . so much enthusiasm for such smutty humor and vulgar language . . . from rich girls who obviously spent hundreds of dollars on a jeans outfit, and rich boys, pampered boys, wearing black ghetto do-rags because the incongruity, the irony of it is so . . . smart and delicious—

—but how could she possibly quit! She had been so visibly proud of this "triumph"—being invited by a senior, an indisputably cool senior, to his fraternity formal. Mimi and Bettina had been impressed to a degree that was well beyond envy, because it was in a realm they couldn't begin to qualify for. They could only wonder. And of course they had made her promise to tell them everything afterward . . .

The rest of the trip fell into a regular pattern. The frat boys and the sorority girls sang songs—all of them seemed to know all the words to everything—they shared gossip—the two bitches were superb at filleting people's reputations while seeming to be merely adding little details—they turned whatever they could into sexual innuendo—they indulged their predilection for Shit Patois. Charlotte had been aware of Fuck Patois from the day she arrived at Dupont, but it was not until spending hour after hour after hour cooped up in this SUV that she realized how cool it apparently was to use *shit* in every way possible: to mean possessions ("Where's your shit?"), lies or misleading explanations ("Are you shitting me?" "We need a shit detector"), drunk ("shit-faced"), trouble ("in deep shit"), ineptitude ("couldn't play point guard for shit"), care about ("give a shit"), rude, thoughtless, disloyal ("really shitty thing to do"), not kidding ("no shit?"), obnoxiously un-pleasant ("he's a real shit"), mindless conversation ("talking shit," "shooting the shit"), confusing story ("or some such shit"), drugs ("you bring the shit?"), to egest ("take a shit"), to fart in such a way that it becomes partly egestion ("shart"), a trivial matter ("a piece a shit"), unpleasantly surprised ("he about shit a brick"), ignorance ("he don't know shit"), pompous man ("the big shit," "that shitcake"), hopeless situation ("up Shit Creek"), disap-pointment ("oh, shit!"), startling ("holy shit!"), unacceptable, inedible ("shit on a shingle"), strategy ("oh, *that* shit again"), feces, literally ("shit"), slum ("some shithook neighborhood"), meaningless ("that don't mean shit"), et cetera ("and massages and shit"), self-important ("he thinks he's *some shit*"), predictably ("sure as shit"), very ("mean as shit"), verbal abuse ("gave me shit"), violence ("before the shit came down" or "hit the fan," "don't start no shit," "won't be no shit"). Still, they didn't neglect Fuck Patois, and they talked some more about how many shots they had at the after-party after the party at the Deke House (Delta Kappa Epsilon), and they philosophized about how you shouldn't party much past four a.m. because you risked get-ting the dread afternoon hangover. Hoyt was as absorbed in all this as the rest of them. He'd be looking straight ahead to keep his eyes on the road, but Charlotte could practically see his brain rotating 180 degrees so he could be in back with them. Periodically he would turn toward her and put his right hand on her left forearm and smile and look oh so deeply into her eyes, as if there were something . . . profound . . . going on between them. All of this took ten seconds at most. She tried to work it out in her mind that this was his way of saying that no matter whatever else might be claiming his atten-tion, he was always thinking of her. Sometimes he would lean toward her and sing a line or two of a song in her ear, a song he and the other four were having such a merry time singing, which she obviously didn't know. A cou-ple of times he put his arm around her and leaned over so far that their heads touched, and a couple of times he placed his hand gently on the midpoint of her inner left thigh. Ordinarily she would have pushed it away, since Vance, Julian, and the two Douche girls might be able to see it, but Hoyt's affection was the only thing that included her in the trip at all, any chance of social redemption for her Sparta rat-tat-tat at Crissy. That gaffe hung in the foul air of the Suburban like an odor. Hoyt's attentions were like maintenance. He had to feed the pet periodically to keep it calm until they got to Washington.

She ransacked her brain for conversational gambits . . . and invariably wished she hadn't tried. Vance happened to mention that it was no use trying to talk to the president of the Deke House unless you brought along your shit detector. So Charlotte piped up, "They actually have such a thing in neuroscience now. You attach—I think it's about a dozen—electrodes to somebody's scalp? And you start asking questions? And a certain part of the person's brain lights up on this screen they have if they're not telling the truth. It has nothing to do with emotions and nervousness and all that, the way an ordinary lie detector does. It's called a PET reporter gene slash reporter probe—"

By the time she got that far, she could read the numb, torpid expression on everybody's face, and her voice trailed off feebly: "I know that's kind of a long name, PET . . . reporter . . . gene . . ." She tried to smile to indicate that she realized it all sounded kind of . . . nerdy . . . and that that was what made it funny . . .

Vance's response to this conversational nugget was a single "Hmmmh," whereupon he turned to Julian and said, "So yesterday I ask this big shitbird, I ask him—"

Once more Charlotte crashed and burned.

They came around a big bend . . . and there it was . . . the Potomac . . . and on the other side, Washington . . . The nation's capital!—and she, Charlotte Simmons, from Alleghany County, North Carolina, was arriving as one of the hundred best high school students in the nation, a Presidential Scholar—to be honored, to meet the President, to have made public what she already knew inside: Charlotte Simmons, emerging from the hollows on the other side of the mountain, was destined for great things. The nation's capital! She made Miss Pennington drive her around the circle past the Lincoln Memorial four, maybe five times so she could get a look at Daniel Chester French's statue of Lincoln, which *stirred* her as he looked down from way up there in his majestic chair in a way that not all the photographs or films in the world could have prepared her for. And now she approached that same great city in a barren gray gloaming, with a frat boy named Hoyt Thorpe at the wheel and four sarcastic, foulmouthed strangers who had no interest whatsoever in her presence—in fact resented it and made fun of it—and what was it that stirred her now? At best, anxiety; at worst, dread.

Traffic on the bridge was heavy, and when they were about two hundred yards from the Lincoln Memorial, a galaxy of red taillights lit up in front of them, and traffic came to a dead halt. Charlotte felt an overwhelming urge to get out of the car—to just open the door without a word, get out, give

them all a little wave good-bye, and disappear. She had—what?—thirty seconds? twenty seconds? before the traffic started moving again. But she had
only twenty dollars. How could she possibly get back? Never mind that!
There's the Lincoln Memorial! You *know* that grand figure! It is wonder,
ambition, honesty, purity of purpose made manifest in marble! Go! Literally
sit at his feet! The rest will take care of itself! Yes . . . but how could she just
come trooping back to Little Yard and announce that she had aborted her
big triumph . . .

I am Charlotte Simmons, she who is willing to face risks . . . and take
risks! For I am not like the others . . .

Too late. The traffic started moving again. The Vietnam Memorial—
couldn't see it from here; too dark out, in any case. The Washington Monument—a vague silhouette in the distance . . . not stirring . . . dim, dying,
shaming . . . Did *any* of this mean *anything* to *anyone* else in this car? They
were on Connecticut Avenue, crossing Pennsylvania Avenue, meaning the
White House was only a couple of hundred yards . . . that way. She had
been there! She had shaken hands with the President of our nation! Charlotte Simmons! A Presidential Scholar! Miss Pennington, one of her inevitably all-wrong print dresses covering her stout form, honored as her
mentor! All that—just seven months ago! What is tonight—

Now the lights of commerce on lower Connecticut Avenue were the fir-
mament. They came to Dupont Circle—what grim irony . . . *Dupont* Circle—and took Massachusetts Avenue to the northwest—and Charlotte
could see it in her mind's eye—and there it *was*—the British embassy!—
such a grand Georgian palace!—the Scholars had been given a special
tour—the amazing breakfront with a palm motif from the palace at Brighton
Beach—a world was opening up! The memory tempted her, but somehow
she knew it would end up like the PET reporter gene/reporter probe, so she
said nothing, and if anybody else knew that they were passing one of the
great architectural gems of our nation's capital—or even *thought* of this city
as "our" anything other than the location of our hotel—they certainly contained their excitement successfully.

The hotel, called the Hyatt Ambassador, looked new. It was a tower with
an absolutely sheer face, absolutely identical ribbons of anything-but-grand
windows up above, and a spectacular parabolic arch of concrete serving as a
porte cochere over the entrance.

As they drove up, Crissy startled Charlotte by saying in a loud voice,
close to the puncture wound in the back of her head, "Char*lunngh*"—she

completely vagued out the second syllable again—"please tell Heeshawn there to take that stupid thing off his head." She looked at Vance. "You, too, Veeshawn. I wish you could like see how lame you look. Your little goldilocks creeping out from under that *thing* . . ."

Nicole, sitting next to Julian in the back row, said, "Right on, sister." Then to Julian, "How about it, Jushawn?"

Hoyt turned around to look at Vance, and then all three boys looked at one another. Hoyt glanced out the window at the bellman . . . a young black guy, not big, but with the kind of sunken eyes and sunken cheeks that look . . . hotheaded . . . wearing a short-sleeved military tunic of tan and palm green, like a Caribbean colonel's, pulling a tall baggage cart with a lot of shiny brass tubing. Hoyt did a little dismissive shrug and took his do-rag off, and Vance and Julian followed suit.

Then Hoyt, still looking back at the others, nodded toward the bellman and said, "Fuck *him*."

The overt meaning was, "We don't need to use this guy and give him a tip." But Charlotte realized that the real meaning was "I didn't remove my do-rag because I was intimidated by the presence of this mean-looking black kid" . . . although she bet anything he had . . .

Crissy and Nicole went inside, into the lobby, and Charlotte, not knowing what else to do, followed them while the boys, who had waved the bellman off, unpacked the car. Why didn't they hurry up? Charlotte already felt awkward and incompetent and superfluous. Crissy and Nicole ignored her and fell into conversation about what they were going to wear to dinner.

Charlotte had a burning desire to be somewhere else, so she walked away from them and strolled across the lobby, as if to take an idle look around. Soon it became not so idle, this look-about. She had never seen such a lobby in her life. She walked perhaps forty feet—and the lobby had no more ceiling. Her eyes swept upward. The entire core of the building was a vast empty space, circular, bounded by rings of balconies and windows, reaching all the way to the top—she couldn't even imagine how many stories high—where there was an enormous skylight dome. One level below the lobby, at the base of the enormous cylinder, was an enclosed interior courtyard. Charlotte could see its terra-cotta-colored tile floor between the foliage of tropical trees and shrubs—enormous trees and shrubs, considering the fact that they were planted in ceramic tubs. Somewhere down there . . . a piano, bass, and drums playing Latin music amplified to overcome the rushing sound of a waterfall and the pings and clatters of silver-

TOM WOLFE

ware and dishes. Now she could make out, beneath the trees, tables and walkways and little bridges and tiled stairs that led up to the lobby in leisurely, meandering segments, with big tiled landings where they turned.

She had never seen a building like this. She and Miss Pennington, like most of the scholars and their mentors, had stayed at a hotel on N Street called the Grosvenor, paid for by the government. They had shared a small room with twin beds, and Miss Pennington snored all night. All the same, it had been exciting. She had never spent a night in a hotel before. For breakfast they had waffles—she had never had waffles before, either, not with real maple syrup instead of artificially flavored Karo. But that was nothing . . . compared to this! She had an idea. Crissy and Nicole hadn't seen what she had just discovered.

She hurried back to them. They were still talking away and didn't notice her or didn't care to notice her, whichever. She walked right up to Nicole, who seemed like a marginally easier nut than Crissy, and with a smile and bright, wide eyes said, "You have to come see this *ho*-tel! Right over there"— she pointed—"you look down on this courtyard, with *trees* and a *water*fall, and above it there's this . . . *space*, this empty space, and it goes all the way up to the roof, but it's all *inside the building*! Y'all oughta come *see* it!"

The blond Nicole broke off her conversation and gave Charlotte a patient look, bordering on annoyed. "You mean an atrium?"

"Oh," said Charlotte, "I hadn't *thought a they-at*. You mean like in one of those Roman *houses*? It's sorta like they-at, but this one goes up—maybe like thirty stories? You oughta come see it!"

"I've seen about a dozen of them," said Nicole, deadpan. "Every Hyatt has one." Then she turned back to Crissy. "Well anyway, I figured the heels are too high, but like so what? Guys don't know how to dance anyway, and by the time these guys reach the dance floor, they'll be like *so-oh-oh* drunk . . ."

Charlotte was still staring at Nicole, her mouth slightly open. She felt as if she had just been kicked in the stomach. Her big architectural discovery— it had only revealed, if any further revelation was needed, what a clueless little hick she was. Nicole and Crissy were right in front of her in their perfect jeans, perfect shirts, perfect pointy-toed boots, perfect cocked hips, ignoring her corporeal existence with perfect efficiency.

Hoyt, Vance, and Julian, loaded down with luggage, were walking toward them. Thank God for that. She wouldn't be left standing here, the lone wayfarer.

Hoyt said cheerily, "Okay, gang, we got the keys. So let's go on up." Then he looked at Charlotte. "And oh, hey, babe"—he swung his left side toward her . . . swung it because he must have had three bags under his left arm—"could you take yours? I feel like my fucking finger's coming off."

And there it was, her canvas boat bag, hanging off the crooked little finger of his left hand. She took it. She was too embarrassed to say a word.

"Thanks," said Hoyt. And then he addressed Crissy and Nicole and laughed. "I thought my fucking finger was coming off!"

And there *she* was, standing in the lobby of this . . . this . . . palace of a hotel—in sneakers, jeans, T-shirt, and cheap, puffy polyurethane-chip-filled jacket that made her look like a tiny walking hand grenade, the complete urchin from the hills, lost in the midst of all this luxury, carrying her belongings in her sole piece of luggage, a little boat bag. In a small, defeated voice she said to Hoyt, "Did you get my key, too?"

"Your key?" He looked nonplussed. Then: "Oh, sure. We got everybody's keys. Let's go."

Crissy looked at Charlotte and gave her the dead smile. Then she said to Nicole, "She's smart. I don't know why I brought so much like . . . stuff."

Not "Charlotte's" or even "Charlunnh's," but "She's."

Charlotte was still sifting all that for Sarc 3—and finding none, although she felt certain it must be there—when Nicole said to her, "What are you wearing tonight?"

Automatically wary, Charlotte didn't know what to say. Somehow it would come out that she borrowed the dress from Mimi. She didn't even want to show it to her, either, rolled up—balled up was more like it—in the bottom of her bag. She finally said, "Just a dress and some shoes."

"A dress and some shoes . . ." said Nicole. She nodded several times in a ruminating fashion. Then she turned to Crissy and said, "That's not a bad idea."

Both sorority girls began nodding, with eyes downcast and serious expressions, as if ruminating upon a remarkable profundity. Charlotte felt devastated. She *knew* this was classic Sarc 3.

Then Crissy said, "I hope you don't mind my asking . . . but what *kind* of dress?"

What did she care! Obviously she didn't. She was only interested in more material to nod at Nicole with in mock sagacity. But it didn't matter. Charlotte had no more fight left. She felt defeated and sad—sad about her own amateurishness, her shortcomings as . . . a girl. In that respect she had gotten absolutely nowhere since Alleghany High. Self-disappointment, self-pity, abject capitulation to a stronger foe, and that pathetic form of inverse aggression that goes along the lines of *Now don't you feel guilty for what you have reduced me to?*—some of which she was quite conscious of—commandeered Charlotte Simmons—she who had been sent forth to do great things—not only to give herself up to an ignorant Lost Province but, with conscious inverse aggression, to exaggerate it: "What kind of dress?" *Dreh—ess?* "I don't know what kind." *Kiii—und.* "A dress, is all." The self-abasement gave her what she wanted: a perverse thrill. Was the word masochism? She didn't know. Up to now that had just been a concept she had picked up when Miss Pennington was telling her about what psychologists were saying way back in the early twentieth century—Freud, Adler, Krafft-Ebing, and all that.

Being on the elevator with Hoyt, who was joking about all the bags he had under both arms, lifted her spirits a bit. Her room turned out to be taken up mainly by two queen-size beds. The beds, plus two side tables, a low wooden bureau, a little commercial reproduction Louis writing table with two chairs, and a big freestanding wooden armoire—housing a gigantic television set—left very little space to walk. Hoyt came in behind her and dumped the luggage on a bed with a big sigh.

"This isn't too bad," he said.

"Where's your room?" said Charlotte.

Blithely: "I'll be in here, too."

"But I thought—"

"Hey, we were lucky to get any room at all, Charlotte."

He couldn't—it couldn't be that way—but on the other hand, he had called her by her actual name for the first time on the entire trip.

"Julian and Nicole are rooming with us," Hoyt said, as if it were the most natural thing in the world.

A start of panic—but then she realized that it would be better that way. It would be sort of like an encampment. Certainly nothing funny would go on with everybody in the same room. Sort of like an encampment . . . she kept hanging on to this word *encampment*, with its overtones of a campfire and a good, tuckered-out sleep in a sleeping bag made from rubber ponchos and blankets.

Soon Julian and Nicole arrived, and Julian dumped his armful of bags on the other bed. Same sort of sigh. "That's a shitload a luggage. *Girl stuff,*" he added, smiling at Nicole.

"Where are Vance and Crissy?" said Nicole.

"A couple of doors down the hall," Hoyt said. Hoyt and Julian and Nicole started chatting, but Charlotte was busy checking out the room. She tried to figure out where the hotel could put the cots. The room was so crowded with stuff already.

"Ohmygod, it's five-thirty," said Nicole.

That was another thing, now that Nicole had raised the subject. Dinner was at six-thirty. Where were they all going to change? How were they going to take showers? Four people in a small space, boys and girls, changing clothes, taking showers, fixing their hair—making sure they looked right—

Charlotte sat down on the edge of the bed where Hoyt had dumped all that luggage and crooked her forefinger around her chin and pondered the situation.

"Then I say we better get started," said Julian. "Hey, Nicole, hand me that handle. It's in my red-and-black bag, the tennis bag."

"*You* get it Julian," said Nicole. "Those things are heavy."

Julian sighed.

Hoyt said, "I'll get it." He reached inside the bag and withdrew a huge plastic bottle, more like a jug really, with a big plastic handle. It was so heavy you could see Hoyt's forearm trembling as he handed it to Julian. A yellow label on it said ARISTOCRAT VODKA.

Then Hoyt delved into one of his bags and produced a bottle of orange juice and a stack of eight-ounce paper cups, and Julian arranged them on top of the low-slung bureau—setting up a bar, Charlotte deduced. She immediately went on alert. Five-thirty in the afternoon!

Julian set about removing the plastic seal around the mouth of the big jug of vodka, and Hoyt went to work removing the one on the bottle of orange juice. They were so *intense* about it, as if they couldn't wait another second to get at their alcohol. Charlotte tried to work it out in her mind that this was an adventure. She could hear Laurie's voice on the telephone: "College is the only time in your life when you can really *experiment*—and when you leave, everybody's memory evaporates." That didn't make her feel a whole lot better, however.

As Charlotte sat on the bed, Julian's back was to her, but she could hear a voluble, voluminous plummet plummet plummet sound as Julian poured the first ration of vodka out of the great brimming jug into a paper cup. Then he added some orange juice, although it couldn't have been much, because all that plummeting must have meant a lot of vodka.

He handed the cup to Nicole, sitting on the other bed, who immediately tilted it back, then rocked forward, her eyes squinted and tears forming, and let out a demonstrative half moan, half sigh: "Shit, Julian, you think you like put enough vodka in it?"

"You can handle it."

Nicole hurried to prove him right, knocking back another gulp and then rocking forward and smiling and lifting her eyebrows way up and opening her eyes wide in a look to convey the notion that it was a little strong but hit the spot.

Julian set about pouring two more cups practically full of vodka.

Hoyt sat on the bed beside Charlotte and began stroking her back. Part of her wished he wouldn't, not in front of these two people she barely knew, but at least it *included* her. Nothing else did.

Meantime, Nicole had drunk another gulp and picked up the telephone between the two beds. By the chummy, confidential way she spoke, Charlotte could tell she had called Crissy in her room.

"Oh, we're just, you know, pre-gaming." She cupped her hand over her mouth and lowered her voice, but Charlotte was so close she could still hear what she said: "Where's what? . . . Ah. You mean the tumor?" She laughed at something Crissy said. "I'll give you three guesses, and the last two are not eligible for this competition . . ." She laughed again. "Right . . . *right here*, if you know what I mean."

Charlotte knew what she meant. They were talking about *her*. She was a tumor, a sick condition that just wouldn't go away.

By now Hoyt had advanced from stroking her back to rubbing her shoulder with a circular motion. That was even more embarrassing; but as long as Hoyt wanted her—Hoyt, the best-looking, coolest guy in the entire fraternity—whatever the likes of Nicole and Crissy thought of her was nullified, she figured.

"What do you want?" he asked her. "Hey, relax."

Only then did she realize how stiffly rigid her whole body was as she sat there. "Want?" she said.

"To drink."

"Oh, nothing, thanks. Maybe some orange juice."

"Orange juice—come on now, want me to put a little vodka in there for you?"

"No, it's really okay," she said.

He started rubbing her shoulder again, rubbing harder yet with tender concern, and that started to feel good, and not only good but important, important for Nicole and Julian to notice. His hands were big . . . and relaxing . . . and nice to have on her body. Her shoulder started feeling warmer, and she couldn't resist looking up at him. She loved the way he was looking down at her. The tenderness and warmth of his smile—and he was so handsome! The cleft in his chin, those flashing hazel eyes that were totally absorbed in *her*—he was asking of her something she would not be comfortable doing, but she didn't want him to stop looking at her with that impish expression, that mysteriously lascivious yet loving mien . . . The look on his face was her inviolable protection against the smirks, the Sarc 3 glances, and the mock ruminations of Nicole and Crissy.

"Well, just a little," she said finally.

Hoyt reached over and took the jug of vodka off the bureau, and as if he, like Julian, couldn't control the flow, he practically filled a cup with it and added a splash of orange juice.

"Not a little orange juice—I meant a little vodka!" She added a laugh so they would think she really was entering into the spirit of things . . . and was *not* sitting stiffly and anxiously on the edge of the bed.

No way could she keep that laugh from sounding nervous, however. They were all watching to see what she would do with the drink. She was holding it like an as-yet-undetonated explosive. She forced herself to put it to her lips. She swallowed and made a face. Julian and Hoyt laughed, but in a way that said this was all good fun. It tasted terrible. It went down sour and burning and hit bottom, whereupon a sickly sweet aftertaste bloomed. But she could see Nicole already polishing off the rest of her cup and apparently passing it back to Julian for more. It became terribly important that Nicole not seem cooler than she was, more fun, more grown up, on a different planet when it came to sophistication. She took another sip. It didn't taste any better, but this time she didn't make a face.

Instead, she looked up at Hoyt again and said, "Actually, it's not that bad!" and added a smile in hopes he'd think she meant it.

Maybe if she could just finish it, she really would feel better. After all, alcohol was supposed to relax you. In any case, maybe tonight she wouldn't feel so much like she was on the outside looking in. Maybe she would stop feeling like the little freshman misfit from the sticks sitting down there at dinner tonight . . . the bump on a log . . . at a big table full of older, livelier, cooler, perfectly blond boarding school girls who belonged to the best sororities. Why should she let herself be reduced to what Nicole and Crissy thought she was? After all—I am Charlotte Simmons! . . . and things were not so bad, were they . . . She was still a freshman so attractive that the hottest guy in Saint Ray, the hottest guy in *any* fraternity maybe, had asked her to his formal . . .

The hottest guy was now massaging the back of her neck, and it made her feel secure . . . inoculated against the others . . . and each time she looked up at him, he was still looking down at her with a wonderful smile that changed from tender to mischievous and back to tender before she knew it, and she drank some more . . . How bad could it all be? And it wasn't just Hoyt . . . Look at Julian . . . Look at Nicole . . . Julian was a very good-looking guy, too, and if she could look objectively at Nicole for a moment, she was a gorgeous blonde. Charlotte took another swallow of vodka and then another. And you had to say the same thing about Crissy, if you were objective . . . and about Charlotte Simmons, unless she was way off the mark about the face in the mirror . . . If other people could look on . . . they'd say Charlotte Simmons was part of the most glamorous crowd at Dupont . . . and the coolest guy at Dupont was shining his face down at her as if she was what he wanted close to him more than anything else on earth . . . She took another swallow . . . The thing about drinking was, it wasn't really about the taste. It wasn't the way the vodka went down, it was the way it hit bottom and then bounced up in . . . a bloom . . . that left like your whole torso abloom with a warmth that really did make you feel more relaxed. Once you knew you were drinking not a *drink* but a *feeling*, it stopped tasting so awful . . .

When she passed her cup back to Julian for another, nobody took notice of it. Nobody did any mock cheering, no attagirls or that's-more-like-its. That was a good sign. It meant she *looked* more relaxed. The fact was, she really felt more relaxed.

She realized that she had just consumed more alcohol in these past few minutes than she had ever consumed in her entire life, even counting the beers she had nursed along at the Saint Ray house. And the effect? It wasn't at all what she was afraid it would be. She felt less frightened by the situation . . . but otherwise she was completely herself. As long as Hoyt was nearby, she really had nothing to worry about. In fact, once she got going on the second drink, everybody, even Nicole, seemed to accept her as a valid part of the "pre-gaming," to use Nicole's word, which no doubt came from tailgating.

By and by Nicole picked up her garment bag and a bunch of things and disappeared into the bathroom to get dressed for dinner. And she stayed in there and stayed in there.

To Charlotte's astonishment, Julian and Hoyt began taking off their pants.

"Don't mind us," said Julian with a cheery smile. "We try not to be too formal at these formals. Right, Hoyt?"

"We're just getting changed," said Hoyt. He shrugged in the general direction of the bathroom, indicating that they didn't have much choice.

Before she knew it, both boys had taken off their shirts, too, and were just standing around in front of the bureau in their plaid boxer shorts and T-shirts. Charlotte's eyes must have been the size of plates, because Julian cocked his head at her in a mock-serious way and said, "Or I think that's all we're doing . . . Whatta you think, Hoyto?" He smiled in a mock-lascivious way.

—or was it merely mock? But she wasn't alarmed the way she would have been ordinarily. She merely felt that something bizarre was going on and she was watching attentively to find out what it was.

"Oh, I don't know," said Hoyt, looking at her in such a way that she would realize he was only kidding. "Seems to me the ball's in Charlotte's court now."

"Wanna try for a threesome?" said Julian. The question ended in a scream of a laugh. His two big belts of vodka were kicking in.

"You're such a fag, Julian," said Hoyt. "Two guys and one girl isn't what they mean by *ménage à trois!*"

Charlotte felt bold enough to attempt a witticism. "It means housework for three?" she said.

"*What's* housework for three?" said Julian.

"*Ménage* means housework in French," said Charlotte.

"Housework?" said Julian. "Whattaya talking about, Charlotte?"

The witticism lay there, dying.

On the other hand, Julian, after being in her company for the last four or five hours, had finally addressed her by name.

"Housework . . ." said Hoyt, seeking to rescue the moment. "That's actually pretty funny. If you weren't such an animal, Julian, I'd try to e-lu-ci-date you."

"*Elucidate.* Who's a fag now?" Julian said to Charlotte, "Me, I've got something for you." He began lifting his eyebrows up and down, acting clownishly suggestive. He had speedily reached the level of . . . drunk.

He broke into a hip-hop dance, jerking his hips and shoulders this way and that, all the while looking deep into Charlotte's eyes . . . and she *knew* he meant some of it. She began to feel sexy in her own skin.

He was still dancing for Charlotte's benefit when Nicole finally emerged from the bathroom. Charlotte noticed her, but Julian's back was to the bathroom. Nicole's face was perfectly made up, perhaps a little too made up, and she wore a knee-length black tube dress and black stiletto-heeled shoes. Charlotte's entire conception of the world at that moment narrowed down to a single question: how would she compare with the worldly blond Nicole. Thank God! The suede jacket Nicole had been wearing masked a rather straight torso, a boy's torso, one Charlotte knew she could outdo. All that Charlotte's brain calculated in an instant. In the next instant, Nicole's perfect face fell. There was her date, Julian, dancing around in his underwear for the benefit of somebody else's—Hoyt's—date.

Hoyt, who happened to be facing her, said, "Hel-*lo*, Nicole. You look hot!"

Julian stopped in his tracks.

"Please don't distract him," said Nicole. "I've never seen Ju folk dance in his underwear before."

Julian spun about, lifted his palms up in a gesture of helplessness, and said, "We were just waiting for you to finish in there."

This was not the Cool Julian of the Saint Ray house. No, it was the standard man caught with his pants down.

Charlotte found this deeply satisfying. The guilty response told her that Julian *had* been more than kidding around. On the other hand, she had a sudden desire not to be in the room for whatever happened next. So she stood up, picked up her canvas boat bag, and headed straight for the bathroom.

As she approached Nicole, she said, "You're through in there?"

Nicole looked past her, as if she weren't even there.

The bathroom was a cramped space done in sad pale tones of—what?—stale cheese. The bathtub and the toilet were the color of stale mozzarella. The shower curtain looked like rubbery stale mozzarella. The counter where the basin was ran the width of the wide plate-glass mirror. That counter was a thick piece of plastic with fake bluish veins in it. It was supposed to look like marble. Instead, it looked like Roquefort—and then the cheese conceit began to make her bilious, so she abandoned it.

She slipped off her jeans and T-shirt and stood before the mirror appraising herself . . . in a bra and panties . . . A young face white as snow stared back.

Time was going by! Hurriedly she took the mascara, the eyeliner, the eye shadow, the brush, and the lip gloss, which Bettina had given her, out of the bag—but she couldn't make her hands apply the makeup. Momma's condemnation of painted women had sunk in far, far too early. She settled for a little bit of clear lip gloss. But then she saw the mascara . . . A *little* wouldn't hurt. So she put on a little . . . Not bad!

She slipped Mimi's red dress on over her head and stepped into Mimi's meretricious stiletto-heeled shoes. Wow! She seemed to rise up a foot higher in the mirror. "You've got to be *kidding*!" she said to the snow-white face, which smiled at her mischievously. She got a good look at the tops of Charlotte Simmons's thighs now, because—ohmygod look at that!—the red dress hung barely four inches below her underwear line. It was a lot shorter than she remembered from when Mimi showed it to her! Hoisted way up on the high heels like this, the girl in the mirror looked like an ice-skater. She swirled left and right, dancing with Charlotte Simmons. Every time Charlotte Simmons swished her dress, she, on this side of the mirror, caught a flash of her panties and a bit of the taut, upward curve of her taut, perfectly curved bottom. Ordinarily, if Charlotte Simmons looked like this, it would scandalize her and make her shrivel at the thought of what people would think. But tonight she was giving Charlotte a pass. The girl had been through enough today, constantly worrying about what others were thinking. "Who *cares* what other people think?" the Charlotte Simmons in the mirror said out loud.

When she left the bathroom, she felt like a model on a runway, although she didn't do anything foolish like trying to walk the way the models did. Sure enough, Hoyt and Julian looked stunned. They looked like they wanted to eat her up in one bite. They didn't dare say anything, however, because of Nicole.

Nicole was getting an eyeful, too. Creases formed in her forehead. But she put on a cheery, friendly voice when she said, "Well, that's awfully short! How are you going to sit down, Charlotte?"

Good sign! Now Nicole, too, had felt compelled to call her by her name!

"Oh, I'll be fine," said Charlotte.

She felt slightly bare—but also slightly careless, insouciant, as the French said. No, the word was not insouciant. The word was sexy. Not even when she wore her little white shorts and sandals, showing her legs from all the way up here to the tips of her toes, did she feel this sexy.

Hoyt became so attentive it was almost embarrassing. Anywhere she sat, he sat next to her, rubbing her shoulder, her back, her leg—just the outer flank, which didn't seem so awful, since she had so much leg showing in the first place—stroking her cheek, stroking her hair where it cascaded down the back of her head and neck—

Nicole was not very talkative. For one thing, every now and then Julian, who was getting good and drunk, would direct his frat-boy one-liners to Charlotte instead of her. With Hoyt, there was no contest. He was rapt. Funny how rapidly things could turn around . . . and the last shall be first.

Finally the four of them went downstairs to dinner.

24. TO . . . US!

The party was in a section of the vast interior court that could be reserved for such affairs. Charlotte and Hoyt walked hand in hand down one of the country-tiled stairways that meandered lazily from landing to landing, down through a forest of trees in tubs. Mimi's high heels were not made for walking downstairs. Charlotte had never even had a pair on before. Each step caused an ultra-contraction of the calf muscle . . . and yet there was something sexy about that, too. Up on their floor, before they descended, she had sneaked a look at her legs in the full-length mirror by the elevators. Propped way up as they were on a pair of heels as high as . . . as . . . as high as *her feet were long*, practically, and revealed as they were by a red hemline that barely cleared her hip sockets, those were a pair of . . . *legs* she had. She couldn't help wondering what the view looked like to men, if any, coming down the stairs behind them.

Through the leaves of all the trees she could see a dusk lit up ever so romantically by candles on regular regatta tables with white tablecloths. Had she been told that the dusk was created by a maintenance man turning rheostat dials in a bank of light switches, it would not have diminished her awe. In this lush, romantic setting, she was meandering down a picturesque terracotta stairway hand in hand with the coolest guy in all of Dupont—who caressed her hand now and again with light squeezes. She couldn't help but wonder who was looking—and she hoped that Crissy was one of them, although she no longer nursed a resentment against her. After all, even Crissy was a part of *this*, this magic moment.

The section of the court Saint Ray had booked was walled off by shrubs planted in the inevitable tubs and trimmed so that they looked like seven- or eight-foot-high privet hedges. At the entryway to the section, white stanchions had been embedded in the hedge tubs, and they reached a good fifteen feet above the floor. From one hung the mauve-and-gold flag of the university, with the famous coat of arms featuring a stylized cougar rampant. The cougar was mostly lost in the folds, thanks to the dead, still air of the atrium, but there was something grand about it all the same. Dupont! From the other stanchion hung the flag of the Saint Raymond fraternity, consisting of the Raymundus Vox Christi cross of royal purple and scarlet—against a field of deepest aubergine, embroidered with small corn-yellow stars. As every Saint Ray was told at the time of initiation—and forgot within a week—the scarlet represented the blood of Christ and the martyred Saint Raymond. The royal purple represented the martyred saint's special place in the kingdom of Christ the King. The bent ring was a symbol of the loop of iron driven through Raymond's lips to silence the evangelical voice with which he had begun to convert his Roman captors themselves to Christianity. At the moment, all that was lost in folds, too, but no one could help but be drawn to the brilliant swaths of scarlet against the royal purple and the deepest aubergine.

So gaudily rich were these two flagpole tapestries that the entryway between the hotel's hedges in tubs came close to being a grand entrance—at least close enough for a group of Dupont men and their dates, who already felt swell about themselves. As Charlotte and Hoyt, still holding hands, made their entrance, a hundred, a thousand, pairs of eyes seemed to turn toward them. The place was packed with Saint Rays and their dates, and obviously most had done their share of pre-gaming. The usual rumble of party conversation was already shot through with cackles and hoots. Somebody deep in the pack cried out in a voice that strove to be deep and manly, "You can't get any tonight, you might as well tie it in a fucking knot!"

Charlotte barely even noticed the Fuck Patois any longer. What riveted her were all the faces turning toward Charlotte Simmons and her date of all dates, the cool and handsome Hoyt Thorpe. There was Harrison the lacrosse player and there were Boo-man and Heady and—yes! Vance and

Crissy—Crissy in a very low cut black dress, looking dumbfounded, eyes fixed on Charlotte Simmons of the lissome legs exalted upon four-inch-stiletto-heeled red satin pumps with toe cleavage—Charlotte Simmons of the waist so tiny, her upper torso rose up in a V, making the cleavage of her bosom look more formidable than it really was.

Harrison came toward them, beaming, eyes lit up with alcohol, lit up so brightly the scars on the side of his face from the brawl didn't look sad at all, looking not bad in his rented tuxedo with his big neck swelling up out of a too-small winged collar, no doubt also rented, singing out to Hoyt, "Yo! Dawg!" He began running his eyes up and down Charlotte. "Where you been keeping our Charlotte?"

It was the first time *he* had ever called her by name, too!

"Away from you fucking predators, is where, if you really wanna know," said Hoyt.

"Well, well . . ." said Harrison, still giving Charlotte the once-over. "Welcome to the feast of Saint Raymond. What can I get you to drink? Wait a minute, I don't remember—you don't drink or something like that?"

"Tonight Charlotte's breaking training," said Hoyt. "Just this one night. In honor of Saint Raymond."

"Awesome," said Harrison. "What'll you have?"

Charlotte hesitated. She knew her head had what they were always calling a buzz, but it was only that—a buzz. It didn't change anything, except that it seemed to make everybody else more comfortable.

"An orange juice with vodka?"

"Okay, one orange juice with vodka." Harrison beamed again and started to turn away.

"Hey, tiger," said Hoyt, "what about *me*?"

"I'm here to take care of the ladies, Dawwwg," said Harrison with a hyped-up attitude and smile.

"How about a little fucking show of gratitude?" said Hoyt. "Who was it that brought"—he gestured toward Charlotte—"to this event?"

"Ahhhhh," said Harrison. "In that case, whattaya fucking want?"

"Same as Charlotte. With vodka. You know *with vodka*?"

Charlotte began reflecting, giddy with triumph, upon what had just taken place. Sure, she knew she couldn't take at face value the two of them going on about how pretty she was and how smart she was and all that . . . *but* . . . they were *attentive*! They were *really* attentive! And on the way down, the whole carload couldn't have ignored her more completely. Hoyt had paid *some* attention, but he did it as if he were feeding quarters to a parking meter. But now—it wasn't just the flattery either . . . There was no mistaking the looks that not just Harrison but also Boo-man and Heady and Vance and their—

Vance and Crissy! Had to talk to Hoyt and Harrison or laugh or do *something* to show Crissy what a great time she was having with them. Well— she'd laugh, that's what she'd do, but she put so much energy into it, she actually crowed out a sharp yawp. Hoyt and Harrison looked at her.

"Oh, I'm sorry," she said, maintaining a smile. "I just thought of something."

Hoyt shook his head and said, "Uhh . . . riggghhht . . . thought of what?"

Charlotte laughed again and pushed off of his shoulder with her fingertips as if he were ribbing her in the most hilarious way imaginable. In her mind's eye Crissy was standing there drinking it all in and saying to herself, "Wow! And I thought she was just some hopeless little thing from the sticks—but now these two cool guys—"

Pretty soon Harrison returned with two orange juices with vodka—or vodka with barely enough orange juice to discolor it, as it turned out once more. Practically straight vodka like this was awful. It tasted like some chemical, but it wouldn't hurt anything, and it certainly did help her bond with everybody.

Standing here in the court of a soaring atrium amid trees in tubs and little candle glows in a rheostated dusk in a private section attended by waiters dressed like Caribbean army colonels behind walls of hedgerows in tubs was so-oh-oh cool. Saint Rays were all around her, unformed Prometheuses, self-wrestled into tuxedos, all ululating and doing red yodels of unbound vulgarity, but Prometheus was not vulgar—so they're not Prometheuses but . . . Bacchuses . . . a photograph in—what book?—Michelangelo's *Bacchus*, the lower belly swollen with wine . . . she felt dizzy, all right, but it wasn't affecting her mind at all. How else could she have thought of . . . of . . . whatever it was . . .

Hoyt was no more than a foot away from her, talking to Vance, and Crissy was behind them. Charlotte laughed out loud. Crissy was tête à tête with Nicole, and they were both stealing glances at her—Nicole in her tube dress, Crissy revealing as much breast as she dared. Charlotte had nothing against these girls any longer—but what were they and *their* looks? Harrison wasn't looking at *them* the way he had looked at *her*. He had looked her

up and down! He had always sort of given her the eye, hadn't he, but . . .
tonight!

Hoyt turned, and ohmygod, the smile he gave her was like a warm
current flowing over every nerve in her body that was beneath the epi-
dermis—

"Your glass?" One of the Caribbean army colonels was right there,
pointing toward the empty glass in her hand.

"Oh—thank you!"

As he put the glass on the tray, he said, "You like an other?" *Oh-therr*. It
was funny the way he broke *another* in two and pronounced other "other"
with a long *o* and such a vocal *r* at the end.

"Uh . . ."

"Yes, she does." Hoyt, putting his big hand on her waist and drawing her
close to him.

"What you like?" the waiter asked Charlotte.

Charlotte looked at Hoyt, whose face was now close to hers—ohmygod,
the magical, melting look he was giving her! Hoyt turned back to the waiter
and said, "With . . . *vodka*."

Charlotte had to laugh at that. "You and your *with . . . vodka*."

Hoyt squeezed her close to him again, and she laughed some more. She
wanted to make sure that Crissy and Nicole *saw* what a wonderful time she
was having, *saw* her mesmerizing guys with her looks and, now that she felt
more confident, her personality. In a short time she had *woven* herself into
the very *fabric* of the formal.

Charlotte roamed the party slyly with her eyes. Julian certainly wasn't
anywhere near Nicole. *There* he was . . . way over *there* . . . completely out
of sight of Nicole—*hitting on that girl* as hard as he could! That girl's hair
was dark, and it came only down to her shoulders, but it was very full, and
her mouth was too wide, but her lips were sooooo sexy, and her smile and
the way she squinted her narrowed eyes within the brushed, dark debauchery of her eye sockets was sooooo suggestive, and Julian was leaning over her,
his face not a foot away from hers, with his *smooooooth* smile on his face, just
pouring himself into her straight through her optic chiasmas. She had on
just a slip of a black dress that plunged in front, and any moment Charlotte
expected Julian to put one hand on the small of her back and draw her close
and kiss her, ravish her the way that guy does in the ad for—she couldn't remember what the ad was for. For an instant she wished Nicole would go
over there and stumble upon that scene—but in the next instant she didn't

want any such thing to happen. It was mortifying to think how much a girl could be hurt, even Nicole—

—whereas Crissy, who had behaved much worse toward her than Nicole—Crissy had Vance whipped. Whipped. Vance was so handsome, too. She had loved his shock of tousled blond hair from the first moment she had seen it. Vance looked like a young British aristocrat, insofar as she had any idea what such a person looked like. And Crissy didn't let him out of her sight. She was *right behind* him.

The waiter, the little Caribbean army colonel, was at her shoulder again with her drink. She tasted it. It was *awful!*—so awful it made her laugh.

"Hoyt!" Her eyes were tearing, but she was laughing and holding the drink up before him. "What did you *tell* that man? This is *sooooo* strong! I don't think this drink like . . . like ever knew an orange from . . . like . . . an *orangutan!*"

She found that a very funny remark—then realized she was shrieking, her words laced with laughter in a way that had seemed like so . . . *overdoing it* when other girls did it. But it probably didn't matter, because it was so noisy here.

The conversation was roaring, and the boys were bawling out drunken cries. Charlotte looked up at Hoyt—who still had his arm around her waist—to get his reaction, but he didn't seem to notice. He just kept beaming down at her in such a loving way. She beamed up at him. She did let her eyes dart past his right ear just once. She wanted to see Crissy and Nicole watching the two of them. Barely six feet away, Heady, in his solemn tuxedo, threw his head back, thrust his arms to the heavens as if supplicating God's mercy, and cried out, "Oh, yessss! Woohooooooo!"—which Charlotte realized was the cry of a television animated cartoon character, Homer Simpson, when he opened a can of beer, tilted his head back, and took his first gulp. Only then did she notice the can of beer Heady held in one of his heavenward hands. Hoyt poured his . . . his . . . Dared she even let the word "love" into her mind as Hoyt looked at her that way? But the two Douche sisters were talking to Boo-man and his date and laughing . . . as if they were having a wonderful time.

Now Julian was coming toward them, and the cute brunette he had hit on was right by his side. Wait a minute . . . if Charlotte's eyes weren't deceiving her . . . Julian had his left hand down against his left thigh, and the brunette had her right hand down against her right thigh, and the two thighs were pressed practically flat against one another, and sandwiched in between the thighs, where they no doubt thought no one could see it, they had their fingers intertwined and—and what on earth were they *doing*? And they thought no one could see them doing it! It was so-o-o-o funny! She looked up at Hoyt to tell *him*—he would get such a laugh out of it—but he had been distracted by Vance. Uh-oh . . . Julian had spotted Nicole, who was no more than ten or twelve feet away, and his face became long, solemn, and guilty, and he disengaged fingers with the brunette and moved about a foot away from her, as if he were the most innocent boy in the world and on top of that a shade sad, and Charlotte had never seen anything so funny, and what was it Julian had kept saying to Hoyt—"You dawg, you"? Julian was now heading straight for Hoyt, with the girl tagging along a discreet half step behind, also with a *who me?* deadpan look on her face.

Now they were barely three steps away, and Charlotte, on impulse, rushed toward Julian, grinning—she couldn't help it—and heard herself saying, "Why, Julian, you old playa, you, where have you been?" *Bee-ehn*— but she was laughing so hard she didn't worry about a little hickism sneaking in, and she gave him a little touch on the posterior of his upper right arm, and two things happened. He gave her an astonished "Who me? What are you talking about?" expression, and simultaneously something swelled up under the hand she had on the back of his arm. She was mystified for a couple of heartbeats, and then she figured out what it was: his triceps muscle. Charlotte laughed and laughed. She removed her hand from his arm and held up a forefinger and wagged it and said, "Julian, you're so *vaaaiin!*"

Julian looked at her as if he couldn't understand what had come over her, and she laughed some more. For an instant she entertained the thought that maybe he really was mystified by this new "front-busting." That was one of Julian's favorite words, front-busting. It flew through her mind herky-jerky as a dove, and that only made her laugh some more. So-o-o-o vaaaaiin! She began laughing so hard she had to lean over and put her hands on her knees and ride it out.

Hoyt came over and said, "Hey, wuz up, babe?"

"Wellll," said Charlotte with a big sigh before catching her breath, "Julian's so-o-oh *vaaaain!*" The very word *vain* threw her into another doubled-over paroxysm of laughter.

Hoyt said, "If you say so, babe," and put his arm around her and pulled her tight against his side.

Charlotte decided that the new Charlotte Simmons was a big hit.

Presently, after much imploring by the little Caribbean army colonels, the roaring crowd headed for the part of their section that was beneath the lobby floor. There dinner awaited.

There were six round tables with about ten chairs at each one. One table was in the center, and the other five were clustered about it in more or less a circle, but you would have thought there were twice that many if you judged by the noise. As long as they were out in the open court, some of the racket dissipated in the thirty stories of empty air above it. In here, however, there was a ceiling, and even though it must have been twelve feet high, the Saint Rays were by now so drunk—and excited—they had reached that stage at which everything sounded funnier if shouted or cried out or yodeled with a manly, sex-obsessed red laugh, and the shouts, cries, and yodels hit the ceiling and bounced back until all was uproar. They sure looked better, the guys did, in their tuxedos and clean white shirts and all—even I.P., who had a date. She had beautiful dark hair. Charlotte couldn't see her face from here. The black tux made his hips look not so gigantic. He made many jesting gestures for his date's benefit, one of them being a funny snakelike thing he could make his huge, grown-together eyebrows do. Charlotte suddenly felt sentimental about I.P. He took such abuse from his fraternity brothers, it was nice to see him really happy, with a pretty girl at his side. Charlotte was happy herself and had enough goodwill to go around.

Once the boys took their seats and went to work on the lobster or some appetizer, the noise level dropped ever so slightly, just enough for Hoyt, sitting next to her, to shout across the table and introduce her to everyone. Out of the corner of her eye she saw I.P. come to a chair a few seats beyond Hoyt. She was disappointed to realize that aside from Hoyt, she didn't know a soul—because she was feeling *social*, more so than at any time in her life. She recognized a couple of the guys, whom she always saw playing quarters or Beirut in the entry gallery outside the library at the Saint Ray house. One was sitting right next to her, a lanky guy with thatchy hair, like a thatched roof, good-looking in a bit of a gawky way, and she could even hear in her mind's ear the peculiar way he groaned over disappointments at those stupid beer games and his ironic cheers and the clapping he did when someone on his team "scored" by arcing a Ping-Pong ball into a cup of beer, but she didn't know him and didn't even catch his name.

The last person Hoyt introduced her to was I.P.'s date, who was sitting on Hoyt's other side. "Charlotte?—this is Gloria."

This Gloria turned her head toward Charlotte, and—ohmygod, it was *her*, the girl she had caught Julian holding hands with. She didn't seem to recognize Charlotte, but Charlotte sure recognized her. She stared at her as if saying hello, but actually trying to find some fatal flaw. She tried and tried and finally had to face facts. Yeah, her mouth was a little wide—but her upper lip had a curve like a bow, as in a bow and arrow, and her bottom lip was full. Her face had the sort of dark-lady cast that promises *forbidden love*. Her eyes were so over–made up they looked like a pair of black craters with big gleaming white orbs at the bottom, but Charlotte had to face facts: it was a look guys probably went crazy over. Her hair was a lush, silky, shimmering black, and the little black dress—"little" didn't begin to describe it. It plunged so low in the front that when the girl was leaning over the way she was at this moment . . .

The eyeballs of the two Beirut players seemed to be popping out of their heads in multiples, the way they did in animated cartoons.

Just then an odd chiming sound began at the center table. The guys and a couple of the girls were tapping silverware against their big balloon-shaped wineglasses, so far empty. Then it spread to every table until all the guys, even Hoyt, and of course I.P., were banging away for all they were worth, and laughter erupted and mock cheers and whistles and more laughter, until the entire room was filled to bursting with the sheer animal exuberance of young manhood, accompanied by a confused storm of rhythmless *pings* from what sounded like half the wineglasses in the world being used by a demented mob as a glockenspiel.

Then there arose a cry from out of these young male gullets, indecipherable at first but then in unison:

"Sexy—prexy!"

"Sexy—prexy!"

"Sexy—prexy!"

"Sexy—prexy!"

And then a tall, slender figure rose up at the center table, looking perfect—*perfect*—in a tuxedo and a crisp, high-wing-collared, stiff-bosomed white shirt that looked like they had been made for him (in fact, both had). A tumultuous applause broke out, clapping such as Charlotte had heard only once before—for Charlotte Simmons at graduation last spring—and cheering laughter, whistles of the sort in which the boys put two fingers in their mouths and shot amazing piping rockets of sound into the already bursting air.

It was Vance, looking absolutely patrician . . . tall, straight as a column. His blond hair, instead of flopping all over the place, was combed back. It

TOM WOLFE

was parted in the middle, but his hair was so full, the part was like a tiny roadway down in the bottom of a canyon. He looked like a picture of F. Scott Fitzgerald that Charlotte had seen on the cover of a paperback of *This Side of Paradise*.

She had never dreamed he could look so handsome, the very image of dignity, yet glamorous at the same time. Ahhh . . . so he was the sexy prexy, the president of Saint Ray.

With only a slight smile on his face, a calm smile, a confident smile, Vance raised his glass of champagne to the level of his chin, and in a voice stronger than any she had ever heard him speak, he said, "Gentlemen!" He paused. He raised his chin slightly. There wasn't a sound in the room, aside from some sort of steam jet back in the kitchen. He was practically looking down his nose as he ran his eyes over every Saint Ray at every table. Somehow his presence made the whole bunch of them seem like golden youth, frisky young men in formal dress black tuxedos, white dress shirts, and black bow ties, with golden sunburst medals of Saint Raymond's cross pinned to their breast pockets and tiny ribbons in their lapels—frisky young men on the very brink of a bacchanal, but at this moment cognizant of the roles Destiny would call upon them to play someday.

Then he raised his glass from the level of his chin to the level of his lips and, tilting his chin up even slightly higher, said, "To the ladies!"

Hoyt, I.P., the two Beirut players, Oliver the oboist—every Saint Ray in the room—rose up. They lifted their glasses to their lips and as if with a single voice boomed back, "THE LADIES!" and in a single choreographed motion tilted the champagne glasses way up and drained them down their gullets.

Then they all sat down laughing and cheering, half of them also lavishing physical attention upon "the ladies." Charlotte spotted Julian slipping his hand beneath Nicole's hair at the base of her neck and lifting her head toward him as if he intended to devour her face. He did kiss her briefly on the lips. Heady, who must have been pretty far gone, made a foolish grinning face and then plunged his head into his date's lap. The girl didn't know whether to be amused or annoyed. She settled for looking at everybody at the table and arching her eyebrows and shrugging as if to say, "What do you do with a guy like this?"

I.P., on the other hand, was the soul of propriety and tenderness. As he sat down, he gave Gloria the most sentimental of admiring looks and brought his glass to his lips in a silent toast especially for her. And once he had taken his seat, she gave him a lovely smile and reached over with her right hand and took his left hand and lifted it slightly and gave it a squeeze. So perhaps she didn't have eyes for anyone but I.P. He smiled and smiled. He was so proud of his lovely little Gloria, and Charlotte yielded to a moment of sentimentality herself and felt very happy for him. At that sweet moment she felt Hoyt's big hand rubbing her back with the circular motion as before, and then he leaned toward her, and giving her as loving a look as a girl could possibly ever dream of, he put his lips near her right ear and said, "To *a* lady . . ."

Then he leaned still farther and gently kissed the nape of her neck.

The *feeling* . . . ohmygod! Shivers and fire all at once! Hoyt pulled back just far enough to give her a look that washed like a gentle wave over every nerve ending in her body . . . Ohmygod . . . and then he leaned forward and kissed the nape of her neck again . . . Ohmygod! . . . She placed the fingertips of her left hand on his neck—since his head was practically behind her back—just the fingertips, ever so tentatively, but then she withdrew them because it would be just too crude to make Hoyt think she wanted some deep kiss or something right there at the table. Frankly, Julian and Nicole looked sort of gross to her. If they wanted to play tonsil hockey . . . fine . . . hooray for *them* . . . and as if resonating to the same thought, she and Hoyt sat up straight at exactly the same moment. Without touching her at all, he turned his head and gave her that same . . . look . . . his loving look . . . and that look was worth more than all the kisses in the world.

More bangaway chiming of the wineglasses at the center table. Vance was still on his feet, standing with his courtliest posture. He intoned, with a noble gravity, "Ladies, we salute you, we pay you homage, we open our enlarged Saint Ray hearts to you, because you're who we got all these rooms for." He pointed upstairs.

Much appreciative laughter and a few drunken whistles and catcalls over Vance's show of grandiloquence.

"And because we feel so honored by your presence," Vance was orotunding, glass of champagne aloft once more, "your every wish is our desire. If you want something, you need but ask, and if you want something something you don't even have to ask—Ladies!—We give you . . . ourselves!" Whereupon he knocked back the rest of the champagne in his glass.

All was pandemonium. The Saint Rays sprang to their feet, glasses aloft, laughing, cheering, and chanting, "Sumpin' sumpin'! Sumpin' sumpin'! Sumpin' sumpin'! Sumpin' sumpin'!"

This time, as they took their seats, they commenced pawing their dates with a drunken ardor. Even I.P., who had been so proper with his gorgeous Gloria, now leaned over and flopped an arm around her shoulders and started tugging. She ducked her head, winced, then put on a calm smile and pushed him away.

"Ivy . . . down boy," she said gently.

Then the Caribbean colonels arrived with the main course, some sort of slices of meat covered with gravy. Charlotte didn't even bother to find out. She was too excited to worry about food. Red wine had materialized in the big balloon glasses . . . just like that. She hadn't been aware of anybody pouring it. Wine was something of a relief. It went down so much easier than vodka, and of course nobody ever actually *got drunk* on wine.

Hoyt had turned to talk to Gloria on his right. The tall Beirut player was talking to his date, on his left. Spotting Charlotte sitting there with no one to talk to, the other Beiruter shouted a couple of questions to her. Nice of him, but the questions were where was she from and what year was she in. Great—you strike me as some child from the sticks. She zapped him with the Sparta rat-tat-tat, not out of anger—she was in too good a mood for that—but to show him she was too cool to just sit there answering duh-duh questions. The guy pulled in his head like a turtle.

So she was right back in the same state of social isolation. Well, what did she care? She was Charlotte Simmons . . . She tried to make her expression suitably insouciant, chin tilted up. She let the music flow through her head like a breeze. The D.J. was playing an odd piece of music called "The Politics of Dancing," judging by the lyrics. *Very* odd, this number . . . It built up layer by layer like a symphony. It kept doubling back on itself to gather up all momentum that had been left behind, building up strength, more and more strength, like Beethoven—well, maybe not exactly like Beethoven—but maybe it was the *equal* of the classical symphonies, the symphonic sound of today. She had the makings of a theory—

But how much satisfaction could you derive from analyzing "The Politics of Dancing"? The fact was, Hoyt was paying an awful lot of attention to Gloria, whose breasts were spilling out of the gap plunging down the front of her dress. What if he started hitting on her, the way Julian had? What if he—

Thank God this formal actually had something formal about it. The fraternity brothers dressed up in actual tuxedos and brought dates—they actually used that word, "dates"—with them, special dates, because inviting a date to a formal meant there truly existed something between the two of you. It wasn't the sort of context in which the guys would be playas and fool around . . .

Charlotte rose from her chair the poli-tics of dan-cing *unhh-unh* her red dress from Mimi felt shorter than ever of dan-cing *unh-unh* she took two steps the poli-tics not really sure of herself way up on these high heels of Mimi's *unhh-unh* but try it anyway *unhh-unh* kept her legs straight and bent over at the waist the poli-tics of *unhh-unh* reached way down and pretended to flick something off the right toe of Mimi's toe-cleavage dan-cing dan-cing ohmygod the dress felt like the hem was only an inch or two *above* where the buttocks meet the legs –tics of dan-cing her legs her *bare* legs anybody any guy Hoyt wrapped up in Gloria *unhh-unh* could see the erotic dip where her calf muscle inserted into the back of her knee the poli-tics of dan-cing she straightened up ohmygod the hem of the dress seemed to remain way up there *unhh-unh* she walked slowly out of the room in a circuitous route to make sure Hoyt got the full rear view of dan—

The ladies' room was the most elaborate thing . . . a lounge with chairs and side tables and vases of flowers . . . from there into the toilet area, in which everything looked brand-new, even the floor, where tan diamond-shaped tiles were inset at all four corners of the white tiles. Charlotte headed straight for the big plate-glass mirror over the basins, and there she was, Charlotte Simmons. Since there was nobody else in there, unless somebody was in one of the stalls behind one of the brushed aluminum doors, she was alone, and so she pulled some faces—haughty, angry, bored, come-hither—and put her hands on her hips, which she rocked and cocked to this side . . . and then rocked and cocked to the other side *and* pulled faces and—ohmygod!—the clatter of a latch, and someone *was* coming out of a stall! Could the girl have possibly seen her carrying on in front of the mirror? Charlotte quickly turned on the water at a basin and pulled down the lower lid of one eye as if looking for some irritating speck.

Soon she was prancing back from the ladies' room—and right there . . . Hoyt. No more Gloria in his eyes. He was looking straight at her and smiling, and it wasn't a snarky smile or a smile of amusement or a polite smile, but a smile just for her, the same loving smile he had given her ever since they arrived in Washington. She was tempted to look back and see if Miss

Chrissy Snob Sarc's eyes were still fixed on her—riveted by the look the coolest guy in Saint Ray was giving her. Hoyt with his wide jaws and the cleft in his chin . . . he was so-o-o-o handsome.

Hoyt talked to her continually now and left Gloria to I.P. He called her Babe and stroked her shoulders and her arms a lot. The room was very noisy now . . . *squalls* of laughter, a roaring *surf* of conversation, the yells of young men drunk on the rising sap of youth, like Bacchus . . . like Bacchus— hah!—Hoyt poured her some more wine—it wasn't that you couldn't actually *tell*—but after vodka . . . whew . . . what was wine? And once you understood that guys like the Saint Rays *were* the Bacchuses of modern times—but Bacchus Bacchus Bacchus sack us crackers—this whole working it out in terms of Bacchus was making her dizzy. What did she really know about Bacchus—other than that—had the D.J. turned up the volume or was it *her*? The music seemed so *loud* now . . . a song by James Matthews playing his guitar.

> "*I've been alone before,*
> *So it's all right . . .*
> *I've learned to know the score,*
> *So it's all right . . .*"

It made her laugh out loud.

"Wuz funny, babe?" said Hoyt.

"The—" Charlotte stopped and started laughing again. The truth was, she couldn't remember whuh wuz funny, dude.

Her spirits slipped for an instant, but she couldn't think of that now—

The Caribbean colonels were bringing dessert in big bowls glazed in swirls of many colors with big, big silver spoons, and you took however much you wanted. It was a frozen chocolate mousse with frozen strawberries on top. She meant to take just a little bit, but the spoons were so big and so long—the handle was like a lever, and the shovel part got stuck in the frozen mousse and—*oops*—she catapulted a glob of it up in the air, and the instant seemed stretched out forever as the glob descended, descended, descended and fell into her lap, on her dress, right in the middle, up close to the top of her thighs, since the dress didn't fall much below there anyway. She was appalled. A frozen brown chocolate glob *right there*, right near her crotch—it was horrible!

"Here, use this!" It was Gloria, who was leaning toward her in front of

Hoyt. She held up a glass tumbler, which seemed to be full of soda water, and lowered a wad of her napkin into it.

"Let me get it off with this!" Hoyt had a spoon and was heading right down *there*—

"No, Hoyt!" Charlotte said, giggling, and pushed his hand back.

"Then you do it," he said, handing her the spoon.

Mortifying. She was spooning a messy glob right out of her . . . crotch . . .

More chiming of the glasses at the center table, quickly picked up by Saint Rays at every table and even some of the dates until there was a mad crystal uproar—accompanied by banging on the table—thank God! She could complete this shameful business of swabbing the stain on her dress while they were all absorbed in banging their glasses in paroxysms of drunken laughter and—*smash!*—somebody at that table over there had rapped his wineglass so hard it shattered and—*smash!*—another one, over *there*—and *smash! smash! smash! smash!* glasses were shattering all around—*smash!*— I.P. was laughing convulsively, and then he held the blade end of his dinner knife and swung the heavy handle like a club at a big balloon-shaped wine- glass—*smash!*—he hit it so hard that Gloria and everybody else in the vicin- ity, including Charlotte, ducked from the flying shards, and he said, "Oh shit—I didn't mean to—yo! You wanna see something fucking incredible?"

With his forefinger and thumb he lifted up the base and the stem of the glass, which remained intact.

"Didn't—fucking—move!" His eyes panned around the entire table to show everyone this physical marvel . . . and the fact that he was such a high- spirited rake.

The little Caribbean colonels were suddenly everywhere—also a forty- ish man with a paunch, shirt and tie, and no jacket—and Vance was on his feet, standing tallest and waving his upstretched arms back and forth over his head like a football referee signaling "no good" or "out of bounds," and fi- nally the uproar subsided to ripples of drunken laughter here and there.

Vance assumed his official presidential pose. "I've just had a conversa- tion with a distinguished gentleman from the Hyatt Ambassador Hotel whom I reminded of the words of Saint Raymond himself, which, translated from the Latin, mean, 'Fucking put it on the bill.'"

Laughter, applause, whistles. Julian started yelling, "Saint Ray! Saint Ray! Saint Ray!" hoping to get a chant going. A couple of guys joined in, but it fizzled.

Vance remained standing. "Gentlemen . . . let me recall our all-too-eloquent toast to the ladies, which I would gladly repeat . . . if modesty and the impatience of Saint Ray's resident crystacidal maniac, I.P., did not prevent me."

Gales of laughter, clapping, whistling, unintelligible shouts. By this stage of the evening, the brothers were drunk enough to believe that Vance's verbose buffoonery actually gave the brotherhood an aura of elegance. I.P. was in Seventh Heaven. He kept beaming at Gloria and then around the room and back at Gloria, honestly believing that Vance was paying him a great compliment as a rake among rakes of coolness and social wattage.

"But now," Vance continued, "it is time for me to propose a toast to *you*." He paused. The ensuing silence, in a roomful of drunks in an advanced stage of wreckage, was a tribute to the periphrastic performance he was putting on. Charlotte wondered if anybody in the room other than herself knew the adjective "periphrastic." She doubted it. A smile of superiority stole over her face. And the coolest guy in all of Dupont, who has fallen in love with me, is massaging my back, and everyone in this room can see that.

"Ladies," Vance was saying, "you happen to be in a roomful of men who this year have turned Saint Ray into a brotherhood as awesome and . . . and . . . and tight" — "tight" came off a bit lamely, since "awesome" meant the same thing, but everybody was still with him — "as Cy's Lamborghini." He smiled approvingly at Cyrus Brooks, whose daddy had given him the most expensive sports roadster in the world, a Lamborghini Leopardo, then added, "Or at least after Tully's has repaired it for the we're-not-fucking-countingth time, and before Cy takes it out again and eats the transmission because he's still wondering what the fuck this manual shift shit is."

Laughter, catcalls at Cy's expense. Vance continued smiling at the young Lamborghini owner. "No, I mean it, you guys have been fucking amazing. This is my fourth year as a Saint Ray, and this frat gets more solid by the year. The house of the Lip-locked Saint" — burst of laughter — the guys found that extremely funny-elegant — "has never been so completely one for all and all for one before. It's been the biggest honor of my life, being president of Saint Ray, and I want to thank you, and I want you to know I love you guys — hey, wait a minute, 'All for one and all *on* one' . . . that's the fucking Hell's Angels' motto!"

Vance had just barely pulled himself out of the pool of bathos as he was going under for the third time.

"Come to think of it, we've got a Hell's Angel. We've got a guy who makes national political big shots piss in their pants." He was looking at Hoyt. Charlotte had to twist her neck and look up to see Hoyt's expression. He had a small and rather cold smile on his face. He stopped massaging her back.

Vance lifted a champagne glass halfway up and declaimed, "Gentlemen, to you, the brothers of Saint Ray." He raised the glass up high, then extended it toward his brethren and panned about to all six tables. "You've made me proud, you've made yourselves and every single one of us proud, you've . . . uh . . . you've"—uh-oh, he was running into tricolon trouble again—"you're . . . the shit! To . . . *us!*"—whereupon he tilted his head back and propelled the whole glassful down his gullet.

More pandemonium. The Saint Rays rose to their feet again. On top of the shouts, cries, and clapping came *ooo-ahs* and ferocious foot-stomping, which would have rocked the floor had they been in a building fifty years older. The floor here in the atrium court was a synthetic country tile set in concrete.

The guys had totally forgotten their "revered ladies," so enchanted were they by the notion they were the best there ever was. The ladies, for their part—Charlotte could see Crissy and Nicole and, right here, Gloria slumped back in their chairs, gloriously bored and casting knowing glances at one another, trapped, as they were, in this hot tub of sentimentality. But Hoyt, still on his feet, clapping, looked down at Charlotte and gave her a big wink—and the loving smile! She felt like leaping up and giving him a kiss on the mouth right in the middle of this supreme moment of male bonding.

They began to take their seats again, all but I.P. He stood by his chair, lurching slightly as if from a psychomotor malfunction, the glass of red wine in his hand sloshing about so perilously it was hard to keep your eyes off it. He was eagerly trying to get Vance's attention. Somebody else at another table was tapping his glass, primed to make a toast. I.P. began lurching and shouting, "Vance! Yo! Hey, Vance!"

Vance ignored him at first, but then gave in, saying, "Okay, I.P. Mr. I.P. has the floor."

I.P. hoisted his sloshing glass up almost to lip level and said in a bellowing voice, "I just want to say—I just want to say . . ."

He appeared to blank out. He was still holding the glass aloft, but his eyes seemed to be fixed on . . . nothing . . . somewhere in the middle distance.

Julian began applauding. "Well said, Ipper! *Next!*"

I.P. wasn't having it. Still louder he shouted, "I just wanna say . . . I just wanna say . . ."

"Then just fucking say it!" yelled Julian. "You—" He didn't complete his characterization.

Laughter and whistles.

"I JUST WANNA SAY . . . this place is the fucking greatest place, the fucking best house on campus, and I just wanna thank all you guys for such a fuckin' amazing time this year, and that fuckin' goes for you, too, Vance— you're the fuckin' greatest . . . uh . . ." I.P. blanked out again. He couldn't seem to remember Vance's title at Saint Ray.

"Bullshitter?" suggested Boo-man.

Laughter, applause, catcalls.

I.P. had his mouth open, ready to say more, but an unbelievably loud whistle came from a table beyond Vance's.

"Yo! Hey, yo!" It was Harrison, who was on his feet, pumping his fist straight up and down. He was so drunk and was punching the air so hard that he seemed about to dislocate his shoulder.

Laughter . . . which Harrison interpreted as encouragement. He beamed a smile and declaimed, "I just wanna say one thing, but like . . . that's the most important thing, and I just wanna say, this frat gets the hottest fucking chicks on campus!"

Convulsive laughter, sarcastic whoops and howls. *"Good job, Harrison!"* . . . *"Real smooth, baby!"* . . . *"It's Don Juan!"* . . . *"From now on you gotta play with a helmet, dawg!"*—insinuating that Harrison suffered too many head injuries playing lacrosse—and the guys began looking around at the girls to see how they took that one. Crissy, sitting next to Vance, was doubled over and laughing so hard she finally held her own head, her palms over her temple.

Harrison, taking it all at face value, assuming they were laughing *with* him, grinned foolishly and tried to lean on the shoulder of his date—who was seated—to steady himself, but he overshot his target and fell into the edge of the table. When he righted himself, he continued to smile foolishly and aimlessly at everyone, then sat down on his chair with a thud.

More toasts . . . each more incoherently reaching for superlatives than the one before. The event was rapidly falling to pieces. Charlotte drank some more wine.

Dinner was over, and the D.J. got the music going in the dance section out in the atrium itself. The guys stood around the edges telling each other outrageously funny but mainly loud things. It was that time of the evening . . .

Three girls ventured out onto the middle of the floor and began to dance, facing inward toward one another, as if they were in a circle, shaking their fannies and letting the boys get an eyeful. It struck Charlotte as oddly like the school dance she went to at Alleghany High. A group of girls on the dance floor by themselves, waiting for the boys to work up their nerve . . . two of them Nicole and Gloria! Nicole was the perfect blonde, and Gloria was the perfect brunette, exotic, provocative . . . dark . . . the dark lady . . . with lips that curved like a bow and promised . . . God knew what. Then Julian went out to join them . . . and then I.P. came floundering out, screaming, "I need some—" and clamping his hand over his mouth as if to prevent himself from announcing what he wanted . . . or said he wanted. Somehow Charlotte just couldn't match up I.P. and Gloria. But she could see Julian and Gloria, and obviously Julian could, too, because he kept flashing looks at her as they jerked and hopped onto the middle of the dance floor, three girls and two guys making a clumsy effort to dance hip-hop style. Now lots of couples were out on the floor—and the guys all paired off with their dates and began—it looked like . . . *grinding*—even I.P., with his wide hips and his perfect brunette date.

The next thing Charlotte knew, Hoyt was pressing his palm into the middle of her back and steering her toward the dance floor and saying, "Let's dance, babe." He said the "babe" with a smile that ended with his lips slightly pursed in the way that indicates, "What I just said is merely a cue for something much more profound." Charlotte felt as if the music were filling the atrium of the hotel with a fine, drizzling haze that crackled with electricity, and Hoyt was firmly pushing her onto the dance floor with a look that just . . . *melted* her. She glanced up for a moment—the world! The world was up there on the lobby floor, where there was a railing, and people—old people, people forty years old at least—were leaning against the railing and looking down at all of them, as if from a balcony. How sad they must feel, cut off from youth, from beauty—from a love like Hoyt's—and how fascinated they must be, and how envious—and Hoyt pulled her close to him until her torso was flat against his—she had *never* been so physically close to a man's body before—and Hoyt began moving—

—and she could feel the bone of her mons pubis pressed against his and she realized they were *grinding*, which she wouldn't do at the Saint Ray party that time, but she didn't even *know* Hoyt then. There was Julian with

Nicole, and he didn't just press his mons pubis against hers, he kept thrusting it thrusting it thrusting it thrusting it, which was gross—but he wanted her, and just think what it must mean to have someone as handsome and cool as Julian wanting you that much!

Hoyt had both of his hands on her back, and she had her hands on his shoulders, and he slid his hands lower on her back, and now he was *really* pulling her pelvic saddle up against his, because below his mons pubis there was definitely . . . definitely . . . but it didn't really mean what it really meant—it just showed that he *wanted* her, madly, just the way Julian wanted Nicole—so that he was now totally in her thrall—so much so that he moved one hand still lower until it was right on top of her buttocks—

—and now he was moving her buttocks back and forth with that hand, holding her still closer, until she could also feel her crotch rolling back and forth over . . . over . . .

She didn't so much think about it as give way to it without calling it anything. She glanced about. *Every* Saint Ray, everyone was doing it. They were sweating. She could see *creeks* of sweat running down Julian's face as he undertook the task of keeping Nicole's crotch locked to his. All over the floor—black tuxedos—grinding groins—black-and-white Holstein bulls doing it . . . It made Charlotte smile, because now she was on the *inside*. She knew they weren't bulls at all, but vulnerable males. Poor I.P.! Poor Vance! He had seemed so sure of himself, standing up in a martial pose and declaiming stentoriously—and all the while he lived whipped by a woman, by Crissy. Some of the Saint Rays were thrusting their montes pubis—who in this room would know the plural of mons pubis . . . other than . . . Charlotte Simmons?—thrusting them so hard into their dates, the girls were practically lifted off the floor. Boo-man was grunting inside of his coat of fat—*Ungh! Ungh! Ungh! Ungh!*

Charlotte started laughing.

"What's . . . fuh-ney?" Hoyt was working so hard, holding her body flat against him with one hand and manipulating her buttocks with the other, his very words came out like grunts.

That made her laugh even harder.

"Whunh? Whunh?" said Hoyt.

"You don't see it? Black-tie Holstein bulls—" She realized she wasn't making any sense—but it was so funny. "Black-*tie* black-and-white Holstein bulls"—which threw her into a regular convulsion of mirth.

Hoyt's response was to remove his hand from hers, up in the conventional ballroom-dancing position, and place it on her buttocks, so that he now had both hands on her buttocks. He began pulling her buttocks and her entire pelvic saddle in toward his groin with all his strength, until his breathing became stertorous and he was exhaling little grunts himself. He was getting so carried away, intoxicated by her, Charlotte Simmons!—she tilted her head back and took a look at his face. He had his eyes closed. His entire being—the coolest being of all the cool beings at Dupont—was now consumed by his desire for her—Charlotte Simmons! Then he slid one hand up to the small of her back and, keeping her body up against his, brought the other hand up and slipped it under her long hair at the back of her neck, cocked his head—and went in for the kiss, the tonsil-hockey kiss, not just pressing his lips upon hers but *devouring* them—and he thrust his tongue inside her mouth. It practically choked her but at the same time gave her the delicious feeling that he had overpowered her, and her entire *self* now consisted of his tongue inside her mouth and the oscillating groin joint—although now she began to feel the presence of his belt buckle—why such a big metal belt buckle?—felt like the lump of metal had torn straight through her thin dress—she was overwhelmed. This kiss seemed to last forever. He took his hand away from the back of her head and began sliding it up and down her body, first along the side, down to her ilial crest, and up to her armpit and then more toward her abdomen down to the gully that ran from her ilial crest to her crotch and then up to her breast, which he cupped from the side, outside her dress, drawing it closer to him. When he withdrew his hard-munching lips and his behemoth tongue, she felt dizzy, and the scene broke up into slices and flakes—the black-tie Holstein bulls rutting rutting rutting rutting—a flash of I.P. rutting rutting not with but against Gloria, whose face was as calm as a statue's, whose eyes were directed forty-five degrees from I.P.'s panting mouth—a slice of Vance rutting rutting rutting with his lips an inch away from Crissy's ear, no longer maestro of the Saint Ray's, now Crissy's whipped whipped whipped whipped *whipped* boy—while Hoyt's adventurous hand slid from the channel and onto the delta of Venus, as Anaïs Nin called it—and she *wanted* Hoyt's hands there, wanted him holding her up against him, wanted him to choke her with that big rolled salami of a tongue, wanted *them* to see it, the Crissys, Hillarys, all the *–ey* snobs—just get an eyeful of a cool guy—the coolest—falling in love—she wanted to keep moving like this eternally, dancing, loving—in this deliriously dizzy spin in the dark as light reflected white off the faces of the old people up on the balcony consumed by envy and regrets.

Every—what?—half hour?—saline-depleted, sweating, she and Hoyt would sit down at one of the tables on the edge of the dance floor and have some more drinks. One thing she had come to realize about wine: it tasted so good. Wasn't like vodka at all, and even if you were dizzy, as she was, with the roar of the bottom of a waterfall inside your head, it didn't make you any dizzier, the waterfall didn't roar any louder, it just kept you so *alive* to your body and unashamed of your love, proud of it, in fact, and she had overcome all the shyness of a little girl from 2,500 feet up a mountain.

Vance and Crissy sat down at the table and ordered tequilas from a little colonel. Vance was sweating so much, his collar was wet and wrinkled. Even the perfect Crissy's face was flushed, and she didn't look so disdainful. And the first thing Vance said was not to Hoyt but to *her*—by *name*!

"Charlotte, you ever had a date with a shit-faced Hell's Angel before?" He nodded toward Hoyt.

She didn't feel mousy and at a loss for words at all! "He's not a Hell's Angel, he's a black-tie Holstein!"

Vance and Crissy looked blank at first. But then they turned toward one another and arched their eyebrows and pulled funny oh-I-get-it faces.

Vance said to Hoyt, "Hoyto, and that—whatever the fuck it is—is—fucking—that."

The three of them—Vance, Crissy, and Hoyt—laughed, but without looking at her. Charlotte couldn't help but smile. *Beam,* in fact. They *got* it! She had a wit that snuck up on people and—*gotcha!* All the while, Hoyt never took his hand off her. Every now and then, while he and Vance were talking, Hoyt would reach way over and wrap his hand around her shoulder and pull her toward him—practically pull her whole chair over!—and lean way over toward her and, from out of nowhere, apropos of nothing, say to Vance and Crissy, "Is this girl cute or what?" He always said the same thing, so she took to pulling her head away and looking at him crossly in a fake way, as if to say, "Why are you always so mischievous?"

Then they'd go back onto the dance floor and Hoyt would press her body against his and fondle . . . that and that and them and those and this . . . and he would overpower her with more tongue insertions.

The entire atrium was slowly turning clockwise. Then it stopped and began turning slowly counterclockwise. The flashes and slices came faster. The D.J. switched to a slow number, "Dear Mama" by Tupac Shakur. Charlotte remained pasted up against Hoyt, who was still visiting those and them and that and that, when she thought she heard someone wretching convulsively, a girl, if she had to guess, over near the privet-hedge entryway to this section. The putrid smell of vomit came wafting by but soon dissipated, probably thanks to the fact that there was no ceiling, unless you counted the skylight thirty stories above. Then came the familiar bracing smell of a mop bucket full of ammonia . . . Charlotte was in a . . . delirium . . . but a *perfect* delirium . . . and the perfection made her realize that she was superior to every other girl on the floor—being, as she was, Charlotte Simmons—and what she thought and what she felt physically had never been in more perfect accord as Hoyt's body became a part of her central nervous system.

Tupac Shakur was still plaintively adoring his momma when Hoyt whispered in her ear, "Want to go upstairs?"

"But I'm not tired yet. What time is it?"

"Ohhh . . . twelve-thirty. I'm not tired, either. Let's just go up for a sec, before Julian and Nicole get there."

Charlotte knew what he was getting at, but there was also the fact that she wanted to hook up, without going all the way, of course. She wanted to please him, to run her hands through his hair, make him smile the way he smiled at her all night, but more intensely and ecstatically, have him eager for her, like an animal. That was what made her . . . *thrill* inside. He was a beautiful animal at the peak of his rude animal health. And yet she could always control him. "All the way"—that was exactly what she wanted him to want! To know that this beautiful animal named Hoyt—the coolest and sleekest and most beautiful animal, the elite animal of the elite Dupont—to know that she had reduced his world to a single obsessive thing—wanting *Charlotte Simmons*! That was what *she* wanted! He was the animal, and she was the hunted. He was in love with her. That she knew. He lusted for her. That she knew. To see his love and his lust and his very mind, for that matter, turned white-hot and forged into a single super-concentrated alloy—whose shape *she* would determine—that was all she wanted!

She followed him into the elevator.

25. YOU OKAY?

They were alone in the elevator. Hoyt didn't even wait for the doors to close before he started kissing Charlotte, pushing her up against the back wall, caressing her breasts, pressing his body against hers from chest to groin. She kissed him back in a spirited fashion and felt cool doing it, let her body go limp against the wall, wrapped her arms around his neck, allowed him to do whatever he wanted with his hands.

In no time at all, the elevator came to a stop. It was the lobby floor. The door opened, and a yahoo of drunken frat-boy noises welled up from the courtyard below. Hoyt had Charlotte flattened against the elevator's back wall. The fact that his lust was now on display upon the most public floor of the Hyatt Ambassador Hotel didn't hold him back for so much as an instant. So obsessed was he by his animal quest, he kept his hands cupped about her buttocks rutrutrutrutramming his mons pubis into hers. A man and a woman in their forties or fifties started to enter the elevator. Charlotte looked right into their faces. She smiled, hoping to assure them that this was not at all what it looked like—she and Hoyt just happened to be young and alive—but the couple wheeled about and retreated into the lobby, where the adolescent ululations of drunken Dupont students enveloped them all over again. Then the door closed, and the college-boy yawp vanished. The elevator was heading up. The known world consisted of Hoyt, his head buried in her hair, his mouth kissing her neck, his groin bucking and grinding, and him going from grunt to groan and back to grunt*ungh ungh ungh ungh*—

They reached their floor, and Hoyt intertwined his fingers and hers and led her down the hall. His hand was so *hot*. He looked at her only once. It was his loving smile—but nervous this time. He didn't say a word.

As soon as they entered the room, he threw the door latch into the locked slant so hard it was like a gunshot, and he closed some sort of metal hasp up higher on the door. Without a word, just a lot of passionate *ohhhh-ungh*s, he started kissing her again and cupping her buttocks and pulling her toward him—*ohhhhhhungh*—and then he entwined his legs in hers, as if otherwise she might go away, while he struggled out of his tuxedo jacket with a lot of twisting and thrashing about. His face was red, his shirt was dark in the armpits, clouds of odor rose, but his chest swelled out, and it was manly, and once he got the jacket off, inside out, he began maneuvering the entwined legs to walk her backward to the bed. She felt the edge of the bed touch the back of her dress. Hoyt reached down, lifting her dress up on one side, feeling about for her underwear, and now she could feel the bed on her bare thighs. She pushed his hand away with a sharp thrust, only to find herself falling back on the bed, with him on top of her. He said nothing, and neither did she. She was excited, a bit frightened, but more than anything else curious. What exactly would he do now? He put one thigh between her thighs, practically smothered her with the heft of his body, and began kissing her again. He kissed her lips and then stuck his big tongue *waaay* down her throat until she thought she was going to gag, and then he began kissing her upper chest, where the cleavage was. She was afraid he might try to move lower, but instead he began kissing her shoulder, and then he began trying to pull the dress down and off that shoulder. She gave his wrist a good whack with the heel of her free hand, and all of a sudden he was halfway on his back. She hadn't hit him that hard—and she realized that he had rolled himself over, keeping his leg between hers, however, and was now practically ripping his black bow tie off and unbuttoning his shirt and wriggling for all he was worth, getting out of it, and then going to work on his T-shirt, which got caught upside down and inside out on his head. With a mighty thrash and jerk he tore it off his skull. Neither of them said a word. She was amazed how well defined his abdominal muscles were. In the course of all this struggling, with his shoulders sinking into the bedspread, his abdominal muscles contracted and writhed and contracted some more. Amazing! She knew he worked out at the gym, but he seemed so slothful about everything, it had always seemed to her—but he hadn't been slothful about his abs! He was wonderful all over again!—and she couldn't help running her fingers over his wonderful abs and lingering in the crevices between the units, which must have driven him wild, because with another *ohhhhhungh* he rolled on top of her, flattening her entire body into the bedcovers and the mattress. He started lifting her dress up slowly and methodically, all the while kissing her mouth, her neck, her shoulder, her chest, only lower down this time, and then he returned to her neck—oh God!—it sent shivers through her body when he kissed her neck that way, and she wasn't going to stop him quite yet as he kept edging, edging, edging the dress up her body, because she *wanted* his hands on her, the way they were now as the dress slipped up, up, up as high as her breasts—where they stopped—and he embraced her around the chest, awkwardly—what was this all about, these two little fists he was making under her back? He was *unhooking her bra*! Was *this* what men did?—and pulling the straps out from under her and slipping the bra *and* her dress up, up, over her head—the *feeling* as his hands slid over her areolae and her nipples—she found herself—just so!—found herself!—naked except for her white cotton panties. Time to say something—but Hoyt's bare chest and awesome abs were coming down on her to meet hers, and she wanted this, the feel of his skin on hers, which was not all *that* serious because he still had on his tuxedo pants and shoes, but even through the pants she was aware of how swollen his groin was. He started moving rhythmically on top of her, and she was so physically titillated—how *wet* she was all of a sudden!—and she arched her back so that it would titillate her more, and she wondered what she was supposed to do in this situation—maybe lift her loins up to meet his coming down?—go in the same rhythm so they moved together in a kind of dance?—thank God he still had his pants on, but should she say something *now*, before he had notions of going any further—or should she wait a little longer, so as not to destroy what she had now, which was his entire life, his entire being, his entire soul—but she didn't know about the soul, how it figured in—

He rolled off her! He sat beside her but not looking at her, his back arched, his hands reaching down to his feet—he was taking his shoes off! And now he was leaning back and unzipping his pants and leaning forward slipping them over his hips and abandoning them on the floor—and was *this* the point at which she should *say* something, just so he would be straight about the limits? Yes, it probably was, and so she started to say—but the *smile!*—he was straight above her now, supporting his weight with his arms, the heels of his hands pressing down on the bed on either side of her shoulders—smiling his smile of . . . love!—and she had her lips parted, about to say—but how could she say it at precisely this moment when his *smile*—and only his plaid boxer shorts remained—not that she could see—but the contour of it forcing the plaid way out—no mistaking it—and she became very conscious of her bare breasts, which she couldn't very well clap her hands over and be Miss Modesty all of a sudden—since that would be so little-girlish. He was bringing that smile down closer and closer to her face. She thought he was going to kiss her on the mouth, but instead he kissed her neck, nuzzling away with his lips. Ohmygod! She went from being dizzy to being deliriously dizzy. His smile! His kissing her neck! She couldn't very well—although she should—not at this moment, however—not even as he lowered his mouth and began kissing her upper chest and then stuck out his tongue and then massaged her skin with his lips. And now he was on her right breast—right on it!—doing the same things with his tongue and his lips—and then the left breast—the same thing—was this what men did? And then he moved lower, down the midline on her upper abdomen, down to her belly button, which he stuck his tongue into briefly—was *this* something that men did?—and down, down—until there was no more when and if about it. Now she had to speak up. Suppose he went—but surely men didn't do *that*—and he didn't. Instead his tongue veered off to the side and worked its way down the gulley from her ilial crest down to where her panties began. He put a forefinger under the elastic at the top on this side and slowly ran it across her lower belly just above the level of the mons veneris to *that* side, where he used the forefinger to pull the panties down over her hips and low upon her buttocks, and then he put his other forefinger under the elastic and slowly slid it back toward *this* side, but the latitude was much lower now, and his finger slid slowly through the hair on her mons veneris and not a shiver but a tremor ran through her—a muscle in her lower abdomen actually convulsed—and inside her—and ohmygod she felt so *wet*—and he pulled the panties down below the buttocks on this side—she was just *flowing* out—she didn't even know that *existed*!—as he pulled the panties down over her thighs and knees and then all the way *off* her, and now she was stark-naked, and he was still kissing her lower abdomen where it was so soft and unprotected and then swirling his big old tongue around—

Hooking up. So now she'd really done it, *hooked up*. This maybe qualified as *heavy* hooking up—although not *really* heavy, since they were still on first base, or maybe on the way to second, even though it was heavy, it was just an experience, an experiment, and Laurie's words sailed, verbatim, through her brain: "College is the only time in your life when you can really *experiment,*" even though Laurie had gone all the way . . . So congested down there . . . so sensitive . . . so many warm secretions—seemed like pints—*now!*—she couldn't wait any longer!—she was too vulnerable—certainly he *knew* . . . but now it *was* time to make *sure* he knew the limits. She lifted her head so that she could look at him. She was staring right at the top of his head and could see his thick, thatchy hair bobbing ever so slightly as he kissed and licked and licked and kissed—only now he was running his tongue over her skin in sort of spirals that were looping lower and lower on her abdomen until—had his tongue just brushed the top of the hair on her mons?—*now!*—*act!* She summoned up her will and tried to give his head a jolt with the heels of both her hands, but lying flat like this on a soft bed, she couldn't get the leverage she wanted and it certainly was a mild jolt, if it was a jolt at all, and he acted as if she were *signaling* him to slide his head down a few inches farther and his mouth and his tongue—ohmygod!

"Hoyt!" She said it sharply.

He immediately stopped and rose up, supporting himself on the bed with the full length of his arms, and he looked down at her with his most wonderful look of love, only the nervous version, which was all right because he *did* know the limits and he was stopping voluntarily. In fact, he slid back down the bed and completely off it. She let out her breath. But what?—he was unsnapping his shorts at the waist—

"Hoyt?"

"Yeah?"

Obviously his mind was not on what she was saying, because he was looking down and stepping out of one leg of the shorts and then the other, and—ohmygod! In her whole life she had never actually seen such a thing in such a state—although she could tell—dear Brian!—she had only seen her little brothers' when they were smaller and her father's once when he stepped about a foot out of the outdoor shower looking for a towel—but . . . *that* . . . ball-peen hammer . . . it looked like a heavy *ball-peen hammer!* . . . a ball-peen hammer with a translucent sheath over it, and now his knees were on the bed and he was crawling toward her on all fours—

"Hoyt!"

"Whuh."

It wasn't even a question! It was a grunt half turned into a word. Words didn't register with him any longer.

On all fours—and he kept crawling. Did he actually expect her to sleep with him? *Sleep with* was the actual phrase that blipped through her brain, and in the next instant the absurdity hit her. *Sleep* with? Ball-peen hammer? She was naked. He was naked.

"*Hoyt!*"

"What?"

Charlotte smiled nervously and said, "I don't know about this." She was so hoarse all of a sudden.

"It's okay," he said. "I have something." Whereupon he reached over to the bedside table and took a condom out of his wallet and held it up in the air for a moment. *See?*

"Uhhh . . . I don't mean that. I mean I don't know if we should do this." Very hoarse. Couldn't even *make* herself smile any longer. Hoyt's arms had already crawled as far as the midpoint of her thighs. He already *loomed* over her . . . a hulk with a big ball-peen hammer . . . But he stopped. He looked as if he had been poleaxed at the base of the skull. He looked stunned . . . and beyond stunned, devastated.

"But I really want to make *love* to you." Oh, what a pleading warble was lodged in his throat! "I've wanted to make love to you from the moment I first saw you."

"But you don't understand—"

"I understand what I felt—and what I feel!" Quite dramatic, he was. "I came up to you as soon as I saw you at our party. I knew! There were so many—but there was only you. There *is* only you!"

"But you don't understand—I've never—I've never—"

"You're a virgin?"

Charlotte lay there, her lips parted in a stuporous way and her mind racing and racing before she finally let the damning admission out: "Yeah."

"Well, I'll be really slow, then," said Hoyt. A certain smile was on his face, the reassuring buck-up, won't-hurt-a-bit smile, not just of a physician but of a healer whose devotion to her well-being—to her joyful flight through this trial—ran deeper than the very oath of Hippocrates, "First, do no harm."

"It's okay. Don't be scared. I've wanted this for so long. It'll feel good. I promise."

That smile! The problem of protocol was overwhelming. What would it look like if she said no—*now*? What would it look like—after letting him go

T
O
M

W
O
L
F
E

this far? Would it look like—was this what people do at a formal, the way Mimi said? Would he feel hurt, and after hurt, angry, and call her a teasing bitch? Did she dare become known as the teasing bitch who lets a guy get worked up, worked up, worked up, and lies there naked as a jaybird, legs parted, and then waves a finger and says no-no-no-oh? Ohmygod what would that look like—would that bury Charlotte Simmons for good? Dead in the ground at Dupont with Loser and Prude and Tease on her headstone? She, Charlotte Simmons, who could have had it all! He's so ardent! Wants to make *love*—he loves me!—

::::::A terrible undertow of the Doubts::::::*But I can't do this*::::::

—but, popping up again, her spirits said, Maybe he *does* love me! Maybe we'll be a couple after this—wait'll Mimi and Bettina—and Beverly—hear about it—*I'll* be the one with experience—I'll no longer be the one who has to hop around like a mouse when people talk about all this—

::::::trying not to look at him::::::the condom, the ball-peen hammer ::::::the undertow again::::::the Doubts::::::more time::::::can't think spinning like this!::::::Look, Hoyt::::::just wait a second, okay?::::::::::

Before she could murmur "Look" or "Okay" or "Wait" or anything else, he thrust the ball-peen hammer right into her—and it went nowhere. He thrust again, with a grunt this time. Got nowhere. A wave of pain rose. Another thrust. Nowhere. "*Ehhhhhhuhhh.*" It hurt. He didn't stop for an instant. He was as earnest as a battering ram. He *thrust* and broke through. She let out a yelp of pain and, more than pain, surprise, and more than pain and surprise, insult. This big *thing* was *stuffed* into her innards—her very *innards!*—and insult upon insult!—*moving*—in, out, in, out—

"Ow!" The insult, the insult!

Hoyt and the thing paused. "Are you okay?"

"Mmnnnnh," she said, her eyes watering, wanting to say, "NO, IT'S NOT OKAY! THIS HURTS, THIS HURTS, THIS HURTS, THIS HURTS"—but he kept moving in, out, in, out to THIS HURTS, THIS HURTS. Animal grunts, animal grunts. She looked at his face, blearily, her eyes were watering so. *His* eyes were closed. He was sweating, groaning, biting his lower lip. She *couldn't* tell him to stop, couldn't even tell him to slow down, because . . . because that look of rapture on his face was what she wanted, was what she had wanted from the beginning, and what she did not want to go away. She was at this moment all that life could hold or mean for him. He was . . . Charlotte Simmons's, down to the last molecule.

His pace started to quicken. Rut rut rut rut rut her body shook shook shook shook shook and bounced bounced bounced bounced bounced from his jolt jolt jolt jolt jolt his eyes tightened his face turned red and scrunched scrunched scrunched scrunched scrunched his teeth clenched clenched clenched clenched clenched clenched from deep in his throat a grunt grunt grunt grunt grunt until finally he let out a loud, prolonged moan and slowly eased back off her, out of her, and lay there half on his side and half on top of her.

"Ahhhhhhhhhhh," he went, in a tone of immense satisfaction as he rolled over completely on his back. And then he said, "You okay?"

He wasn't looking at her. His face was aimed straight up at the ceiling, and his eyes were closed. No part of his body, not even a finger or an ankle, was any longer touching her.

His eyes were still aimed at the ceiling.

Now he would hold her in his arms, curl up next to her and, in the softest, most intimate of voices, thank her, tell her it was okay, that she made him happy, that what they had just done fulfilled a great yearning of his . . . had brought alive for him what he had feared was an impossible dream . . .

Instead, he got up off the bed, went into the bathroom, and yelled out, "You need a towel?"

"No thanks," she said in a trembling voice.

She was shaking inside. She didn't hurt anymore, but what had happened inside her? She needed him close to her. He would return to her, tell her something wonderful had just occurred, something neither of them would ever forget, something that made any temporary pain inconsequential. He would tell her that she had been a beautiful girl when they entered this room and now she was a beautiful *woman*.

Hoyt came out of the bathroom and, without looking at her, immediately set about putting on his boxer shorts. As he snapped the shorts closed at the waist, he suddenly raised his head and stared at her with a puzzled frown . . . not at her face, however, but at her still naked loins.

"Shit, is that blood?"

Charlotte looked down and noticed that underneath her groin was a circle of blood droplets. She looked at Hoyt, but he didn't look at her. He seemed possessed by the droplets of blood.

"Sorry," she said quietly. "What should I do?"

"I don't know, but if they want to make us fucking pay for it, they've got a big surprise coming." He kept staring at it.

He picked his shirt up off the floor, his wad of a shirt, the one he had just wriggled out of, looked about for the T-shirt, found that on the floor at the foot of the bed—

Why was he still standing—when he should be close to her? What was he doing getting dressed? Where did he think he—they?—were going to go?

She was stark-naked and very conscious of it. She pushed herself up, swung her legs over, and sat on the edge of the bed. She felt woozy, dizzy— very dizzy now—bilious. She leaned way over to lower her head and get more blood to her brain. The contortion sort of cramped her . . . She brought her head back up. Hoyt, absorbed in buttoning all his buttons, pulling up his pants, and fastening his belt with the incongruously big buckle, didn't look at her once.

She wanted to do nothing so much as lie back down on the bed, on top of her own guilty, loathsome, inexcusable blood droplets, and sink through the mattress and the floor and vanish into the fourth dimension, the fifth dimension . . . some dimension where no one would ever be tempted to search . . . She felt so horrible. She realized that her body was still very drunk. All along she had known, consciously, that she had drunk an awful lot, but only now did she admit to herself that alcohol could ever make her, Charlotte Simmons, drunk . . . *this* drunk.

So horrible, so horrible—but she couldn't just sit there slumped naked on the edge of the bed. Her panties—a wet, crumpled little mess at the foot of the bed, but what did it matter, the filth? She put her feet through them while still sitting, but she stood up to pull them over her hips. Her head felt so heavy, there was such pain deep behind her eyes—her brains had shifted. They were piled up against the right side of her skull. She was going to pass out! She sank back to sitting position on the bed and lowered her head between her knees again. She'd just have to endure the pain. Mustn't pass out—certainly not like this.

There was a rap on the door. "Dude, you in there? Open up, I need the room!" It was Julian.

Afraid to stand up again, Charlotte reached over and grabbed her crumpled dress and her bra from where they were mashed against the headboard. She put on the bra and unfurled the dress this way and that, searching desperately for the hem so she could slip it over her head.

To her dismay, Hoyt, who now had on shirt and pants, shoes and socks, unlatched the door, opened it, and with a grand, sweeping gesture of welcome, said, "Wuz'up, bro?" and ushered in Julian and—it wasn't Nicole but Gloria, I.P.'s date.

The two of them flicked the briefest of glances at Charlotte but didn't so much as nod to her. Charlotte was as mortified as she had ever been in her life. She had managed to squirm into the dress until it dropped down as far as her lap.

With a sly smile, Julian said to Hoyt, "Hope I didn't interrupt."

"Not at all," said Hoyt with a casual, ambiguous laugh. "We were doing some more shots. Want some?" He was already walking toward the bureau, where he poured himself a shot of vodka and then poured another, which he held out toward Julian. Gloria stood there erectly, chin up, shoulders back, chest thrust forward, an inchoate smile on her sensual lips. Hoyt swung his arm to hand Gloria the shot and gave her a little wink, just a here's-to-you, down-the-hatch wink, but a wink all the same. It began to register with Charlotte . . . Other than the "we" in "We were just doing some more shots," Hoyt had not acknowledged her existence since Julian and Gloria arrived— not by word, not by gesture, not by so much as a roll of the eyes. She still sat on the edge of the bed, stunned by what was unfolding before her, unable to move. But then she felt tears rising in a flood, and she sprang from the bed and ran, literally ran, past the three of them, within inches of them in the narrow space between the foot of the beds and the front of the bureau—she had no choice—to reach the bathroom before she broke down completely and started sobbing in front of them. The last thing she heard before she shut the bathroom door was Julian saying, "O-kaaaaaay . . ."

The bathroom was a slop of sopping towels and washrags flung on the floor, over the edge of the tub, over the shower-curtain rod. Even with the door shut, she could hear Hoyt and Julian laughing about some girl—her!— no, it was some girl with glitter on her dress . . . and about how dumb Harrison's toast had been and how it was a good thing he could play lacrosse because "he can't speak on his feet for shit." The beautiful dark lady, Gloria, was laughing and giggling along with every syllable of it.

Charlotte felt dirty and sore. She stepped out of her dress, her bra, and panties. She wet a washcloth and lathered it with soap and washed between her legs and washed some more and then washed again and repeated that and washed a few times more—no sign of blood—until she began feeling woozy. She was listing to the right. She had to do a quick little step to keep from keeling over. Her brain began to throb. She sat down, naked, on the toilet lid, shivering . . . and weeping . . . heaving convulsively but determined not to make a sound . . . and reveal how profoundly wounded she felt. After a while she made herself stand up. She stood before the mirror over the basin. She had to brace herself on the basin's countertop with both arms. This time she didn't appraise her body for a second. It was nothing but a weak, contemptible, corrupted piece of flesh. Her skin looked clammy and pale; sickly was the word. She was puffy and red about the eyes. Her entire brain felt inflamed. Her pulse was like a mallet. She saw double images of herself. Her hair was as disheveled as a dove's nest, but she wasn't about to go back out there and retrieve the canvas boat bag where her brush was. That would be another thing they could have a good time for themselves with—how she came out of the bathroom barefooted, looking like an automobile wreck, to fetch . . . her boat bag.

Well . . . she couldn't stay locked up in here forever. She picked up her panties from where she had thrown them on the basin counter. Ohmygod they were disgusting . . . sodden to the touch, which, it occurred to her with the oddly fond lash of self-flagellation, was only appropriate for what she had now reduced herself to. She had to sit down on the toilet lid again in order to put them on without passing out. She fondly indulged the self-abnegating clamminess of them, their formerly lubricious, now merely unsanitary, wetness. She lowered her head and sniffed a few times to make her self-abnegation complete. How very foul they smelled . . . the sweat, the urine, the shit, the sheer filth, all the secretions that made them . . . slimy. Yet she wasn't about to go back into that room without them. She snapped on the bra . . . and slipped the red dress over her head . . . No comb . . . Her hair was wild . . . mashed here . . . sticking out tangled there. She ran her fingers through it to push it all back at least . . . horrible . . . She gave up, gave in, left the bathroom, and reentered the bedroom barefooted to surrender herself, totally, to humiliation.

With her very first barefoot step onto the synthetic carpet, she began to feel bilious . . . There they were, Hoyt, Gloria, Julian, acting as if nothing had happened, still drinking their beloved "shots" . . . Hoyt and Gloria sitting next to each other on the low part of the bureau. Hoyt's back was to Charlotte. He didn't even look up . . . He was engrossed with Gloria . . . his head had the cool tilt he used when he was flirting . . . Oh, the dark lady had her breasts right out there first and foremost and an oh-so-sensual curl on her lips . . . Julian was on his back on the other bed in some sort of acrobatic or gymnastic position, with his hips and buttocks up off the bed, supported by his hands, and his feet directly up over his head. He was giggling, and then he went into a fake laugh, and then he began giggling again and kicking his feet up in the air as if he were dancing upside down. He was very drunk. Charlotte walked to within six inches of Hoyt and Gloria. Gloria flicked her a glance but immediately returned to Hoyt's face. She was giving him a . . . suggestive . . . Dark Lady smile and holding a small paper cup with probably vodka in it, as if about to make a toast. Hoyt didn't even look up. Gloria cocked her head back and threw the shot down her gullet. He acted as if he didn't know Charlotte Simmons was there.

Only Julian took notice. He stopped giggling and dancing in the air and rolled forward to a sitting position on the edge of the bed. "Hey, Charlotte, are you okay? You don't look so great."

"Uh, yeah, I'm fine. I think I just had too much to drink. I feel a little sick."

"You feel like you gonna puke?" said Julian. "'Cause I gotta sleep in this room tonight, and it better not smell rank and shit."

With that, he started laughing and rolled back on the bed and started kicking his feet in the air over his head again.

About to cry, Charlotte lowered her head and brought her hand up over her eyes, but she managed to swallow her sobs and lift her head. In peripheral vision she could see Hoyt looking at her. He said, "You okay?"

She started to look at him but decided not to, for fear she might start boohooing and blubbering.

"I think I just have to lie down for a second, and I'll be okay," she said. The "I'll be okay" part trailed down into inaudibility, and she collapsed onto the other bed at a 45-degree angle, her back to the room.

Her fondest hope was that Hoyt would come to the rescue and at least sit on the bed and rub her back and ask Julian and Gloria to go somewhere else. She didn't want to talk to him, for she would surely burst into tears. She just wanted him to be with her.

She wanted to curl up on the bed, but Hoyt's red-and-black bag was in the way. She pushed it toward the foot of the bed—and saw why he had put it on the bed in the first place: to cover up the bloodstain. There they were, a few dried-out drops of blood . . . now just inches from where they came from in the first place, the Charlotte Simmons reproductive tract . . .

She curled herself up into a ball. She took a self-destructive, self-hating pleasure in wrapping her body about such a filthy, sordid memorial, a shrine not only to a little fool but also to a little fool's illusion that men fell in love. Men didn't *fall* in love, which would be surrender. They *made* love—*made* being an active, transitive verb that rhymed with *raid*, the marauder out for blood, *laid* the raider who got laid, *daid* as a bug I got my killing ov'ere'at the Hyatt Ambassador *Ho*-tel in Washington, D.C.

She discovered that even though her back was to the room and she was rolled up in a ball with her eyes closed, the angle she had collapsed in enabled her to see the others. If she parted her eyelids ever so slightly, a mere millimeter or so, her upper eye could make out Hoyt, Gloria, and Julian in a blurry outline. She went "Ooooonuh," as if sinking into a coma. She began breathing deeply and slowly, as if asleep. Four or five minutes later . . . Hoyt was coming over! He was *leaning* over her!

He whispered ever so softly and from ever so deeply in his throat, "You okay?"

Now he was leaning over *farther*! She could tell from his breathing. There was something in front of her face. She didn't dare open her lids any wider. After a couple of beats she deciphered the shape. It was his forefinger . . . Now there were two fingers . . . now three . . . now four . . . And now all four were waving back and forth in front of her face like a fan . . . Then — nothing.

A few seconds went by, and Charlotte could make out the shapes again. Julian and Gloria had also gotten up from their seats on the other bed. All three were near the armoire, and Hoyt was facing the other two. They spoke in low, she's-asleep voices.

"Whattaya think?" said Julian. "Is she okay? Should we find another room?"

"Yeah, probably," whispered Hoyt from down there low in his throat. "It looks like she's not moving again for the rest of the night." A pause. "I had to knock the dust off her."

Julian's voice: "You're *kidding*! You're shitting me?"

Silence — broken by the piping wheeze of a couple of laughs, Julian's and Gloria's being suppressed, contained in the lower lobes of the lungs only by the most intense and self-denying of pressures. Hoyt was whispering, "Yeah" . . . inaudible . . . "sorta, freaks" . . . inaudible . . . "fucking formal" . . . inaudible . . . "haven't seen a hillbilly beaver like *that* . . ."

Julian's voice: "You're terrible, Hoyto."

Julian's laughter and Gloria's came out in spurts of air through the nostrils. Charlotte thought of bullets going through a silencer. *I had to knock the dust off her.* Hoyt's whisper again: ". . . like fucking Astroturf . . ."

She could see just well enough to make out Julian giving his buddy-bro a good-job jab on the arm.

"I heard Harrison has booze in his room," said Julian. "Why don't we go up there? I bet everyone went up there after the D.J. stopped."

Julian and Gloria started walking toward the door, and Hoyt followed. Julian opened the door, then stopped. He motioned toward Charlotte. "So you think she'll be okay."

"Yeah, she's passed out," said Hoyt. Whereupon he clicked off the lights. He became a silhouette against the light from the hallway for a moment—and then the door slammed shut from its own hinge-spring mechanism.

Charlotte propped herself up on one elbow and looked around the room in the dark. It wasn't *completely* dark. A vertical line of noxious sulphur-yellow light from the parking lot below seeped in where the white plastic wands used for closing the curtains failed to bring the two halves together truly across the ribbon of plate glass that served as a window.

Lifting her head proved to be a perilous decision. The room was spinning, and she felt nauseated. She stood up and staggered—something was seriously wrong with her vestibular system—to the bathroom, clicked on the light, which she found blinding. There was the slop of sopping towels and washrags. She knelt before the toilet bowl, hiccuped once, and then vomited. Some of it got all over the rim of the bowl, and some of it got all over the bodice of Mimi's dress, which had hung down when she knelt. Still on her knees, she reached up and flushed the toilet, then crawled on all fours toward the bathtub. She had the distinct feeling that if she stood up, she would pass out. She fished a washrag from out of the slop on the floor by the tub and crawled back to the toilet and wiped off the rim and crawled back to the tub and retrieved another rag and a hand towel and crawled back to the toilet bowl and dipped the rag into the now more or less clean water in the bowl and tried to scrub the bodice clean and dipped the towel and washed off her face and wiped her mouth. She was all right as long as she stayed on all fours, like an animal, and didn't have to raise her head. She crawled out of the bathroom, leaving the light on, and crawled on the carpet all the way back to the bed and crawled up on the bed on all fours and pulled the covers down and crawled under the covers, puked-on wet dress and all, and curled up on her side and sobbed herself to sleep.

She didn't know what time it was when she halfway woke up and could hear something on the other bed . . . *unnhh unnhh unnhh unnhh unnhh* . . .

T
O
M

W
O
L
F
E

and could make out—who? Gloria?—on her knees and elbows and somebody mounted on her from behind and going *unngghh unngghh unngghh
unngghh unngghh*—and then she lost consciousness again.

It must have been about five a.m. when she hazily heard people stumbling into the room and some clumping and clunking about and some muttering, male, along the lines of "Aw shit." Charlotte pretended to be fast
asleep and kept her eyes shut tight, since from the position she was now in,
she couldn't see anything anyway without lifting her head or turning over.
The odor of vomitus on her own dress was sickening.

A muffled *thunk* . . .

"Ow! Fucking—"

Hoyt's mutter. "Fuck. What died in here?"

He got into bed with Charlotte and never budged from the outer edge
of his side of the bed, and neither their skin nor their clothing touched for
the rest of the time they spent together in that queen-size bed, which must
have been five hours, because it was shortly past ten in the morning when
Charlotte woke up to someone banging on the door—smelled like puke in
here—and an angry girl shouting, truly *shouting*, "JULIAN, YOU
FUCKING DICK, OPEN THE DOOR! I NEED MY BAG!"

This time Charlotte didn't bother feigning sleep, and she rolled over
and lifted her head to see what was happening. She was alone in the bed,
and she could hear the shower running in the bathroom.

Bang bang bang bang. "I KNOW YOU'RE IN THERE, YOU
LITTLE SHIT! YOU EITHER OPEN THIS FUCKING DOOR
OR I'M GETTING THE HOTEL TO OPEN IT! I NEED MY
BAG!"

Sunlight was pouring into the room through the gap in the curtains. In
the other bed—Julian. He rolled himself over halfway and was resting on
one shoulder, eyeing the door. Then his head, just his head, keeled over
toward the floor.

Slowly he lifted his head and muttered in a hoarse voice, "Aw, fuck." He
closed his eyes and clamped the thumb and middle finger of his free hand on
his temples and massaged them. Gloria's head popped up on the other side
of the bed. Her mouth hung open slightly, and her eyes were the very picture
of alarm. Julian swung his legs out from under the covers and over the edge of
the bed, sat there for a moment with his head hung way down, then stood up,
emitting a profound sigh. The sigh set off a phlegmy cough that came dredg-

ing up from the deep recesses of his lungs. He trudged toward the door with a conspicuous lack of psychomotor control, squinting against the sunlight.

He opened the door just a crack and said, "Sorry, Nicole, which one's yours?"

"I can get it myself, thank you very much."

"No, I'll get it for you. No problem."

"YOU MEAN I CAN'T FUCKING COME IN AND GET MY OWN BAG?" Nicole was really screaming now. "YOU ARE SUCH A SCUMBAG, JULIAN! YOU KNOW WHERE I SLEPT LAST NIGHT? OR DO YOU EVEN GIVE A SHIT! I SLEPT ON CRISSY'S FUCKING FLOOR!"

Julian clenched his teeth and stretched his lips out very wide in a grimace. Charlotte could see all sorts of little tendons or whatever they were popping taut on the surface in his neck. Sheer feminine intuition told her what that was all about. Julian wasn't worried about Nicole's predicament. He was worried that her shit- and fuck-laced screams would rouse other people in the hotel and thereby Create a Scene.

"Oh, hey, wait a second," he said.

Stiff-arming the door against invasion with one hand, he reached way down and way over with the other and picked up a sleek navy leather-trimmed nylon bag with chrome zippers. He hoisted it so Nicole could see it through the crack in the doorway.

"Isn't this it?"

"Yes, but I need my fucking makeup case. It's in the fucking bathroom!"

Julian froze for what seemed like thirty seconds—but couldn't have been—while his brain churned, trying to choose between Creating a Scene and the Sordid Truth. The Sordid Truth evidently seemed the less horrible of the two, because his shoulders slumped in resignation and he opened the door all the way and admitted his date. Nicole pushed past him without so much as a glance. She was wearing the same black tube dress. It couldn't have been more wrinkled if she had balled it up and thrown it on the floor in the back of a closet and forgotten about it for a year. Her perfect blond hair looked like a forkful of hay in a sheep trough. Her face was bleary, puffy, bereft of makeup except for a smear of last night's mascara that had somehow reached her cheekbone. Her skin was the color of a tombstone.

Gloria now had the covers pulled up over her head. Nicole looked at the great lump and spat out the side of her mouth, "You're such a slut, Glo-

TOM WOLFE

ria!"—and opened the door to the bathroom, magnifying the noise from the shower.

"What the fuck?" That was Hoyt's voice from behind the shower curtain. "Oh, hey, Nicole babe, it's you! Whyn't you jump in here with me? I give a great soap job!"

"Fuck you, Hoyt! Whyn't you soap up your fist and stick it up your ass."

Leaving the bathroom with her makeup case, she craned her head into the bedroom and lasered a look at Gloria, who by now had eased her eyes, forehead, and matted mop of dark hair out from under the covers.

"So long—Miss Community *Cunt!*" said Nicole.

Then she stormed out, slowing down only long enough for a farewell to Julian, who was still standing, stricken, near the door. In a frigidly calm voice she said, "You know, Ju, you really *are* a puny, pathetic little limp dick."

On the drive back, everybody was too hung over to say much. Gloria was stretched out on the entire third row of seats, sleeping. Vance, Crissy, and Charlotte were crowded into the second row—Charlotte mashed up against the window, Crissy in the middle, and Vance in the third seat, behind Julian, who was in the passenger-side bucket seat up front. Hoyt drove.

Hoyt and Julian talked to each other, laughing about how drunk they'd gotten and how great Harrison's after-party had been and how they now felt like a pile of bricks had fallen on top of their eyeballs. Charlotte was sitting directly behind Hoyt, so he could have easily explained to her who So-and-so was or asked her if she wanted to stop for a drink or to go to the bathroom or told her any of the words to the songs, but he didn't.

Dreadfully hung over, a malady she had never experienced before, Charlotte had a brief coughing spasm in Maryland, and Hoyt said, "You okay?"

She went, "Mmmnh," just so he would have a response, and she wouldn't say anything more. A couple of hours later, as he let her out in front of Little Yard, he said, "You okay?"

She didn't so much as glance at him. She just walked away with her boat bag. He didn't ask twice.

26. HOW WAS IT?

ike a fool—and she knew it—Charlotte glanced back at the Suburban just before she reached the archway tunnel into Little Yard. She knew it wouldn't happen, but somehow it had to happen—he would be standing beside the driver-seat's door, looking across the roof of the Suburban, shouting, "Hey! Yo! Char! Come here!" Instead, what she saw was Gloria, risen from the back row, where she had lain motionless and soundless for the entire trip—staring at her. *Right at her.* Her nose was practically up against the window. Her dark hair was a big, messy wreath around her face. Her eye sockets were a pair of mascara sinkholes. She didn't smile, wave good-bye, or betray any other sentiment. No, Gloria was . . . studying little Charlotte Simmons, still clutching her canvas boat bag . . . a specimen of . . . what? The Suburban started pulling away just as Charlotte saw Gloria turn her head toward the front seat. She was grinning and saying something . . . about what?—and then the Suburban was gone . . . But Charlotte already knew, didn't she . . .

By the time Charlotte took her first few steps into the tunnel, she had an ache in her throat, the ache a girl gets after a long period of trying to hold back tears. Rejection and dismay turned into an all-enveloping fear of imminent doom. She who had departed soaring, she thought, in social ascension, she who knew how to handle herself, she who had been so aloof from girls who just lay down and gave it up, she who had announced that she had Hoyt Thorpe trained like a dog—Charlotte Simmons had returned. Oh, yes, *she*, Charlotte Simmons, the girl of the hour. What was she going to tell everybody? Above all, Beverly—of the boarding school elite she professed to have only contempt for—who had warned her not to go off on an out-of-town fraternity formal with Hoyt Thorpe, of all frat boys on God's earth . . . I am not a good liar, thought Charlotte. I am not even a half-decent actress. In our house nobody ever showed you how to deceive. Momma—but I can't let myself think about you right now, Momma.

Momma!—Before she had even made it through the archway tunnel, the ache in her throat became so severe that she truly didn't know if she could make it all the way back up to the room without bursting into tears. If Beverly was in the room—she'd die.

She approached the courtyard with such apprehension that she could actually hear her heart beating whenever she opened her mouth to take a deep breath. It made a rasping sound from down deep, as if the wall of her heart were scraping against the underside of her sternum with every beat. Thank God . . . practically nobody around, just a few people on a cross-walk . . . over there . . . She wanted very badly to run to the door of Edgerton—but someone might look down and wonder what's wrong with her. Inside, she didn't take the elevator, because everybody took the elevator. She walked up four flights, opened the fire door—

The Trolls . . . What were they doing at this end of the hall? It was as if some sadistic god really had created them specifically to make Charlotte Simmons suffer. Why? Why else would they be here *now*? A sunny Sunday afternoon—why had the Trolls set up their gauntlet . . . for this moment? At the less-traveled end of the hallway? She had never seen so many of them . . . eight? nine? ten Trolls? *Don't even look at them. Act as if they—do—not—exist.* But once again she felt powerless . . . against the strange little shrimpy Maddy and those huge E.T. eyes of hers. "What's the matter, the elevator's not running again?" Charlotte got away with just shaking her head no—but there were so many more of them to go. The knees ahead began pulling up to the chests one by one, as if choreographed specifically to drive Charlotte Simmons mad. And once more, Helene said, "Hey, how was your weekend?"—and Charlotte couldn't think of any way to answer *that one* with a gesture, either, and once more guilt convinced her autonomous nervous system that she *had to* respond to black girls—and she responded as brightly as she could—"Good!" *Good* came out at such a high, frantic pitch, she prayed to God the Trolls would take it as meaning it had been such an amazing weekend, she was ecstatic—or would they divine the truth and realize it was the first flash of a flash flood of tears?—which nothing could hold back now. Sure enough, Maddy again, from the rear: "Anything wrong?"

She barely managed to get to the door, duck inside, close it—take one look about—no Beverly!—thank you, God!—and dive onto her bed and put the pillow over her head—to muffle the sound—and give way to sobs sobs sobs sobs sobs sobs racking racking racking racking racking racking convulsive sobs sobs sobs sobs sobs with a polyester down pillow muffling her head. Far from disliking the pillow, she wished it were bigger, big enough to enclose her whole body, muffle her existence at Dupont University, where there was nothing left for her. How could she possibly face all those girls she had so proudly lorded her virginity over—had so proudly shocked with her contempt for Dupont's easy virtue—had bragged to about her ability to control guys and keep them at bay, most specifically a guy named Hoyt Thorpe? What had she done? How could she have allowed herself to do it? She was unclean, she had let herself be used in the filthiest way, she was a ratty hotel washrag, a cum dumpster. That was what Charlotte Simmons was, a filthy cum rag that had been tossed onto the floor of a hotel bathroom with the rest of the slop. Here she was, trying to hide from herself under a pillow, from her Diesel jeans, on which she had spent one fourth of her money for the semester, and her red T-shirt, which she had thought looked so cool and now seemed so juvenile and tacky . . . And that wasn't the end of it, was it. This was *Bettina's* T-shirt, and those were *Mimi's* dress and heels in that pathetic boat bag . . . and she would have to *return* those things, tomorrow at the very latest, and there was no way she could face either one of them and proceed to lie about what had taken place. They would want a minute-by-minute description of the formal—and they were not to be denied. She *might* be able to lie to Beverly, but she would become such a nervous wreck doing it, Beverly would *know* she was lying.

Hoyt . . . *hah*. She said the *hah* to herself with such force, it popped out of her mouth in the form of a rueful sigh. Right now, at this moment, Hoyt was probably smoking pot with Julian and Vance and some other brothers of "the best fucking fraternity at Dupont," mellowing his way through his hangover, listening to Dave Matthews or O.A.R., mellowing mellowing mellowing the afternoon away while she lay here with a pillow around her head and the Trolls whispering and sniggering about her on the other side of the wall.

Oh . . . let them whisper and snigger all they want. The best she could hope for from them was that they would maintain their delusion that she considered herself too cool to talk to them. She wasn't about to confide in them and give them some inkling of what had taken place over the past twenty-four hours, the past twenty-four hours of debasement and humiliation, of floundering in muck and slime. Every time she closed her eyes, she flashed back to that fitful sleep . . . in which she was lying there on a hotel bed . . . while the rest of them were playing drinking games, talking about her, talking about her body—about her old-fashioned hillbilly *beaver*—about knocking the dust off her. That was what her losing her virginity in such a squalid way meant to them: a few chuckles about knocking the dust off a musty up-country *beaver*, a little stray that somehow had wandered down from the hills.

She took the pillow off her head and rolled over onto her back. Doing so must have raised dust from the pillow, because the sun was coming into the room in such a way that she could see the particles suspended in the air above her, stuttering and jittering every which way in the light—and she flashed back to the day Channing and the others invaded the yard for the sole purpose of humiliating her and showing the world their contempt for her fine airs . . . and she had lain down on the bed in her little slot of a room . . . watching dust particles dance in a shaft of afternoon sunlight and thinking of how impossible life would now be in Sparta—now that the whole county knew about Daddy threatening to castrate Channing if he so much as laid a finger on his perfect little girl again. And oh God the memory of how she had been revived by the sight, on television, of the most-talked-about politician in American, the governor of California, possibly the next President of the United States, giving the commencement address at this place that was to be her salvation, Dupont University, the most magnificent setting in which the great man could address the nation last spring, a Gothic tower soaring behind him, a pageant spread out before him, a field of mauve and gold robes—a rich mauve that had entered the language as "Dupont mauve"— the flags of forty-eight nations represented by the graduates, heraldic banners representing God knew how many mysteries of Christendom a thousand years ago, kept alive on the looms of the twenty-first century because they went so well with the compound arches and rib-rife vaulted ceilings, the random Chaucerian casement windowpane etchings of ancient Gothic buildings erected en masse in the 1920s. This great eminence, who had so stirred and girded her loins—her *loins!*—was known at Dupont as the ridiculous, fat-flanked cottontop stooge of a fellationic farce known as the *Night of the*

Skull Fuck, starring a drunk frat boy named Hoyt Thorpe, with Master Vance Phipps of the *Phipps* Phippses in a supporting role . . .

Charlotte got up—it made her dizzy—could her body still be drunk?— trying not to see what she couldn't help but see out the window, which was the highest-soaring of Dupont's many soaring tributes to the glory of God, the library tower, and went over to Beverly's side of the room—what did "Beverly's side of the room" matter any longer?—and rifled through her heap of CDs until she found the Ben Harper CD and brazenly lifted the lid of Beverly's CD player—what did "brazen" mean any longer?—and flipped to song number 3, "Another Lonely Day," and sank back onto her own bed and listened to Ben Harper's sentimental young voice sing about how the whole thing wouldn't have worked out anyway and how all that's left is just another lonely day. She couldn't help it . . . she couldn't keep her face from scrunching up or the tears from bursting forth from her eyes, from her aching throat, from the deepest reaches of her lungs, her solar plexus, her convulsively contracting abdomen. She put the pillow over her head again so the Trolls couldn't hear, but not so forcefully that she herself couldn't hear the slow, sad ballad of the inevitability of loneliness. Her entire nervous system was depressed by her hangover, in any event, and it became a relief, bordering on joy—the feeling was so near the absolute limit—to give up, let all her defenses collapse, capitulate, wallow in the hopelessness of her ru- ined life at Dupont. On the other hand, she made sure the Trolls couldn't hear her—

Would Hoyt ever call? She knew he wouldn't. She knew he'd never speak to her again. He'd already dumped the cum rag into the slop. She could never set foot in the Saint Ray house again. Never again in the Saint Ray house . . . What will Bettina say about that? It was ironic. Bettina was the one who had first led her there that night, which now seemed so very long ago. What would Mimi say? No doubt they had had conflicting emo- tions when they learned that Charlotte Simmons was going off on a formal with a senior, a very cool senior. It didn't take much imagining . . . They were envious. But her ascension also gave them hope. She had seen it in their faces when the three of them met in this room and Beverly and Erica had barged in. They *wanted* to see her on that bridge, the bridge to the frat world, where sorority girls would be apprised of your presence at Dupont and cool guys would regard you as hot and hookupable and you would be invited wherever the cool and the hot and hookupable went to have their fun and display their status . . .

Charlotte Simmons wasn't going to be invited anywhere. She had gambled. She had let her classes slide, she had let Adam and the Mutants and her dreams of a cénacle slide . . . and her promise to Miss Pennington, the one and only thing she had asked of her—yes, that, too—so sure had she become that Charlotte Simmons was about to ascend from clueless public school hillbilly girl hidden up-hollow in the Blue Ridge Mountains of North Carolina to the summit of female competition at the great Dupont. How foolish, how egotistical, how shallow her goal, how low her aim, how twisted her priorities—

O Hoyt! O Hoyt! She wanted that smirk again! She wanted him to press her against the back wall of an elevator again! She wanted him to *want* her! He would *call* her any moment now—

With that one, she realized just how crazy she had become. He would never call. The very idea would make him recoil. No, he wouldn't even recoil. Recoiling presumes an emotion, and nothing about Charlotte Simmons would any longer rouse an emotion in Hoyt Thorpe.

As she lay there on her back, the flood tide rose again, and she could feel the tears spilling from the corners of her eyes and pooling inside the lids, and so she opened them—and the particles were no longer dancing in the air, or at least she could no longer see them. The light had dimmed. A cloud must have passed across the sun. She looked toward the window, and her eye hit on the library books stacked up on her desk—oh God she didn't need *this*! She had a paper due in the morning in modern drama on Susan Sauer's interpretation of the work of the performance artist Melanie Nethers—which was so convoluted and lit'ry and tortuously dull and lifeless . . . what little she had read of it . . . she would have to read every word of it from the beginning and staple every word into her brain—they were such floating little wisps of thought, those words. There was no way she could possibly concentrate on any such task. There was no sense even beginning. She'd have to get up tomorrow early and do it before class, and she knew that would never happen. There was no holding back the inevitable. What *use* was it?—what earthly use? Why struggle with the metaphysical idiocy of something Susan Sauer wrote?

She was so wretched, so completely ruined, the only possible course left was to stop resisting in this doomed struggle with misery. O how knotted her throat was! Not just sore but *twisted into a knot*! Surrender, Charlotte—even though she could tell that this crying jag would be different from all others, this jag would have its own head, this jag would rack and wrench her body and soul beyond all hope of relief through surrender—and here they came, the tears, *scrunching* the muscles of her lips, her chin, her neck, her brow, *bursting through* her optic chiasma to force their way out between her eyelids, *flooding* her nose, her entire rhinal cavity, in a stinging rage—

What was that!

She could swear she heard a girl's voice syncopating in the sort of one-sided conversation you overhear during other people's cell-phone calls—

Never was there a quicker-acting antidote for a crying jag. Off went the waterworks. Charlotte rolled toward the wall and pulled her knees up into the fetal position, feigning sleep, barely in time—

The door swung open and, "Ohmygod! . . . Yeah, totally—" Good and loud.

Charlotte could see every inch of her roommate in her mind's eye, the very angle at which she canted her head into the cell phone, the way her eyes lolled, focusing on nothing, the cockeyed dip her new Takashi Muramoto bag took as it hung from the crook of her elbow, with all this *stuff* about to fall out of it—

"Yeah . . . yeah . . . yeah . . . like *totally*! I can't wait to hear about it!" Beverly shrieked into the phone. "Where are you studying tonight?—wait, hold on a sec—Charlotte, you bitch! That's my CD—ohmygod, sorry, babe, my roommate's playing my fucking CDs now"—as she simultaneously yapped into the phone and went to the CD player and stopped Ben Harper and switched the CD to Britney Spears's *In the Zone*—"Okay, yeah, going to the café tonight, definitely—oh, wait, he'll be at the library? Maybe we should go there—ooooh, we can sit next to them! Awesome, okay, meet you at seven."

Whereupon she clicked the phone shut and let her bones collapse on her swivel chair, by the sound of it.

"Hung over?" Beverly said in a hearty voice not to be denied.

"Yeah," croaked Charlotte, as if Beverly had interrupted an afternoon hangover nap. She didn't dare turn over and let Beverly see . . .

Beverly's response to that was, "So—spill it!" She really barked it out. She wasn't about to let her roommate hide behind this nap shit, as she would have no doubt put it.

Charlotte could hear Beverly making little breath sounds in time to Britney Spears. *Britney Spears!* No doubt Beverly's head and shoulders were bobbing to the beat, too. Part of her was deep inside the music, half whispering, half singing, "Come on, Britney, lose control!" The rest of her was right here in the room with a real lungful: "I can't hear you, Charlotte!"

"It was fun," Charlotte said, extra-foggily.

"Fun? What else? What'd you do?" Under her breath: "Shake it, Britney, shag and roll . . ."

The groggy fog who faced the wall: "Do? We went to dinner and went dancing and stuff."

"You must have stayed up all night! You sound like shit! You're all curled up on the fucking bed in the middle of the afternoon with the sun shining—ohmygod, I can't believe you! You! Of all people—*hung over! My* roomie! Got fucking ripped with Hoyt Thorpe! I mean where did little Miss Charlotte Library Stacks go? What were you doing all night, anyway?"

"I told you, Beverly."

"You didn't tell me anything! I want details. Come on! Ohmygod, I never thought I'd be fucking living vicariously through *you*! I mean, you have to tell me everything—I mean everything!"

"There's nothing to tell. I'm so tired, really, I just have to take a nap."

"Well, I mean, you shared a room, right?"

Awkward pause . . . Charlotte wanted to lie, but she couldn't even imagine what the lie would be. She now realized that no Saint Ray, least of all Hoyt, would be caught dead providing a private room for a date. It wouldn't be so much the cost as the . . . whipped, unmanly wussiness of it. Beverly would see right through that one.

So she gave in and said, "Yeah."

"Welllllll . . ."

"There were other people in the room, too."

"So?"

"So there were four of us in the room. It was like a . . . a . . . an encampment. So there's nothing to tell."

"Wow, an encampment. You mean nothing happened? You're such a fucking prude!"

"I didn't say that. But nothing really major or anything."

"Ohhhhhhh! So something did happen!"

"Look, I don't even remember. I got so drunk I can't remember anything."

"Ahhh, a blackout baby. Our Miss Charlotte! Who'd a fucking thought it! Don't you realize that every blackout baby tries to cop out with this can't-remember shit?"

"I'm not copping out. I can't remember."

"You're not going to tell me, you little bitch." Beverly giggled. "You're not going to tell your own roommate? Come on!"

The fog, closing in thicker: "No . . . I just have to get some sleep; then I have to go write a paper. I'll tell you another time."

Silence. Long pause. Sarcastic sigh with much musical expelling of the breath between the teeth. Finally: "You know what I say to that, Roomie? That blows. *Eccccchhhhh*. Pardon me while I take my finger out of my throat."

Beverly departed. She didn't slam the door, she merely gave it a smart *clack*.

Charlotte lay there with her eyes closed, trying to dream up better evasions, smoother lies, credible lies, nimble lies, numbing lies, tranquilizing lies, and then she fell into the arms of the Sandman.

The telephone was ringing. It was dark! She felt disoriented. What time was it? It was dark outside and dark in here. No Beverly. The whole thing descended on her. Was it Hoyt? He's apologizing! She knew inside that was—was—but she rolled off the bed and leaped for the phone. "Hello?"

"Hello-o-o-o-oh!" sang Bettina's voice. "So-o-o-oh? How was it?"

"Oh, hi," Charlotte said in a dead, toneless, obviously disengaged fashion.

"What's wrong with you? If it was anybody but you, I'd say you sound hung over. Was it fun?"

"Yeah, it was fun."

"You don't exactly sound excited."

"Well, I'm just so tired."

"What happened?"

"You know, I just can't talk about it right now. I'm in the middle of an English paper."

"Oh, come on," pleaded Bettina. "I'm calling from the library. I'm dying to know."

"Seriously, I'm so late getting to this paper. I can't talk to you now."

"Okay. Fine. See you later, I guess." Bettina hung up, obviously offended.

The phone rang several times that evening, but Charlotte didn't answer it again. All she wanted to do was sleep and forget Dupont ever existed, or go home to Momma and Daddy and forget Dupont ever existed. Forget? Forget about forgetting in Sparta. The one and only thing everybody in the county would want to talk about would be Dupont. What grand lie could she dream up to explain away Charlotte Simmons's dusty, scuffling, bungling hangdog retreat from the other side of the mountain, where great things had awaited . . . Charlotte Simmons's return to Sparta and the three stoplights . . . Up her brain stem bubbled Lucien de Rubempre's ignominious return to Angoulême from Paris on the outside baggage rack of a carriage, hidden beneath a heap of suitcases, carpetbags, and boxes in *Lost Illusions* . . . which in turn detonated a startling reminder of the paper she had to hand in tomorrow morning. Susan Sauer's interpretation of Melanie Nethers . . . She didn't agree with the stupid thing in the first place, but the seminar leader, a T.A., meaning not a real teacher but a graduate student, meaning her knowledge of pedagogy was nil—the T.A., the irritable Ms. Zuccotti, regarded Susan Sauer on Melanie Nethers as a piece of critical genius. She had gone so far as to hand out a pamphlet *about* Susan Sauer on Melanie Nethers. Charlotte had scanned it and sized it up immediately as metaphysical sentimentality multiplied by itself, and how was anybody supposed to derive the square root of metaphysical sentimentality taken to the second power and hidden behind a veil of cynicism? . . . The whole thing was a whiff of some old lady's breath . . . She was *damned* if she would devote another second of her concentration to some old biddy's gauzy exegesis of another old biddy's gauzy exegesis that no one needed in order to understand that Melanie Nethers was a sick joke. So she sat down at her desk and took some lined loose-leaf notebook sheets and a pencil and wrote out a hasty, half-baked attack on both of them. Who was this Sauer idiot, anyway? And who was this ponderous old Renee Sammelband who wrote the pamphlet? When she finished, she picked up her three pages—she had never turned in a paper shorter than six or seven before—and read them over. She knew immediately that she had written something witless that gave every indication of having been slung together in a rush. But it was done. That was the main thing. In any case, it was the limit of her energy and patience. All she wanted right now was a little oblivion. Of course, she'd have to go over to the library before she crashed, to the computer cluster, and transcribe and print it out. But first she needed a break. She lay down again. In no time, the Sandman carried her back to the Land of Nod.

Some hours later—she had no idea how many—she was aware of Beverly returning to the room in the dark . . . aware, and that was all . . . This time she didn't have to feign sleep, and Beverly didn't contest the matter.

The next day, Monday, Charlotte couldn't get out of bed. Her alarm clock sounded its grating buzz over and over again, and she kept hitting the snooze button. Beverly? Gone, thank God. What was the point of getting up? What was there to look forward to except a lot of uncomfortable questions from Bettina, assuming she would speak to her again, and Mimi, plus, sooner or later, the inevitable interrogation, inquisition, by Beverly, who had picked up the scent of blood. Between now and the beginning of Thanksgiving break—Friday after this-coming—she didn't have a great many choices. In fact, it came down to one: hide in the library, do the schoolwork, and avoid everybody—

Ohmygod, it was already 9:50—and modern drama started at 10:00! Well—might as well just blow it off. For a moment, she was Self-destruction on a pedestal, smiling at Grief. But cutting a class and sleeping would only make her feel more depressed later on. She jumped out of bed. Her jeans were still on the floor where she had left them last night. Diesel . . . *the* jeans she just had to have . . . She couldn't abide the sight of them. She pulled her wrinkled old print dress over her head, and over that a heavy old pale blue sweater her aunt Betty had knit for her ages ago, and put on her sandals. She didn't even have time to brush her hair. She darted toward the door. Wait a minute—the paper. She wheeled about—*damn!*—she'd never gone to the library and typed it in and printed it out! She retrieved the three loose-leaf sheets from the desk. Once outside, she started to run—sprint—to the library. *Damn!* Couldn't run in sandals! So she took them off and put them in her left hand. She had the sheets of paper in the other. *Now* she ran, she flew, across the courtyard, out onto the sidewalk, across the Great Yard toward the three-story-high majesty of the entrance to Dupont Memorial Library tower. Students laughed at the spectacle as she rushed past, distressed sheets of loose-leaf paper in one hand, a pair of sandals in the other, barefoot, hair wild. *O-kaaaaaaaay* . . . She came barreling into the library and sprinted to the computer cluster—*sprinted* across the grand lobby, beneath the great Gothic-beribbed dome, barefoot. She heard students laughing. A lot. The soulless carcass of Charlotte Simmons, her frantic bones, her pale, pale hide, her bare feet, were a scream, so far as Dupont was concerned.

By the time she finished furiously typing the pages into the computer and printing them out, sweat was running down her face from her temples and her forehead. She knew she must reek from the frenzy of it all. No time for a stapler. She sprinted as fast as she had ever run in her life to Dunston, where the class was, clutching the flapping printout pages in one hand and her sandals in the other. It was chillier out than she thought. She reached the classroom door almost twenty minutes late. She hastened to put the sandals back on, opened the door, and entered. *Damn!* The strap of the left sandal had twisted so that the sole was half on her foot and half off. But how could she stop now and correct it? So she came limping in, as if crippled. She was breathing with huge, audible heaves, and she shook spastically as a chill hit her. Sniggers all around. Her face was splotched with red and streaked with sweat, which continued to pop out on her forehead and stream downward. Her hair was mashed flat on one side, from sleeping on it, and shaggy as a patch of ragweed on the other. She had obviously thrown her clothes on with no other aim than to cover her body rapidly. The sweater turned out to have a particularly unfortunate stain that made it appear as if she had just dribbled something down the front. A big moth hole on the side made one wonder if she were wearing a bra, which she wasn't. More sniggers. Her face was a picture of fear . . . of what everybody else in the room must surely think of her. Every inch of Ms. Charlotte Simmons gave off waves and waves of shiftlessness, incompetence, irresponsibility, sloth, flabby character, and the noxious funk of flesh abloom with heat, sweat, fear, and adrenaline. Then there was the . . . thing . . . the splayed-apart piece of paper she clutched . . . crumpled thanks to her fierce grip, wet from sweat. It looked like something the cat dragged in. Sniggers and more sniggers. Ms. Zuccotti broke off in the middle of a sentence and said nothing more until the embarrassment settled herself into a chair at the seminar table. The other twenty-five or -six of them had ample time to concentrate on the creature as it sat there sweating and heaving and gulping air. *Ecce* Charlotte Simmons! — she who was about to turn in a paper that was purposely, angrily calculated to offend every critical and aesthetic standard she knew Ms. Zuccotti to possess, and was whipped off in an archly juvenile display of cynicism unalloyed by wit, mellifluousness, or pertinent content. Down at the other end of the table, one boy was writing a note for the amusement of another, and the recipient glanced her way and then grinned at the note writer. Who was he? Charlotte was certain she had seen him once at the Saint Ray house. Monday morning — and he already *knew*!

At that moment the paranoia factory opened for business, tooled up for a day of capacity output.

Charlotte sat slumped over in her chair throughout the class, taking notes and then turning them into doodles and looking out the window, failing to laugh when the rest of the class laughed, because she hadn't been listening, nodding off, jerking alert, like any other morning zombie, shivering occasionally. She was no longer hung over, but however inadvertently, she was accomplishing a pretty good impersonation of someone who had gotten wasted the night before . . . and this was Monday morning. So bleary was she with self-loathing and paranoia, the only positive thing she could think about was going over to Mr. Rayon and getting a cup of coffee. Fleetingly, since it wasn't really an important thing, it occurred to her that she had never drunk coffee until coming to Dupont. Momma didn't think children should drink coffee. Until she left for Dupont, she had been Momma's good, good girl. That ran through her mind without irony or cynicism or regret. It was the way things had always been.

No sooner had she gotten in the coffee line at Mr. Rayon than she noticed, sitting way out in the cafeteria's mob of tables, a senior named Lucy Page Tucker, who seemed to be—she was pretty far away, but she *seemed* to be staring at her. She was sitting with three other girls. "Everybody," meaning a lot of girls from the sorority set, "knew" Lucy Page—who was from Boston but went by this Southern-style double first name—because she was president of one of the two hot sororities, Psi Phi, the Douche being the other. The Psi Phi girls were known as the Trekkies, after the old sci-fi TV series, *Star Trek*. Lucy Page was hard to miss, even from a distance like this. She was a big girl, with broad cheekbones, wide jaws, a curiously pointed chin, and a prodigious mane of blond hair that she combed straight back, which made her look like the lion in *The Wizard of Oz*. Charlotte looked away for a few seconds, then stealthily cut a glance at her. Lucy Page Tucker still seemed to be staring at her—even though she was now bent way over the table, as were the other three girls, their heads barely eighteen inches apart. Charlotte felt her heart revving up. She looked away and inched forward in the coffee line a yard or two before stealing another look. Thank God! Lucy Page was no longer staring her way. At that moment a brunette whose back was to Charlotte, sitting across from Lucy Page, waved to someone off to the side, and Charlotte caught her profile. Lightning struck Charlotte's solar plexus. *Gloria!* Even at this distance Charlotte knew that face! How could I be such a fool! she thought. Showing up at Mr. Rayon's like this! The very crossroads of the campus!

She abandoned the coffee line and hurried into the women's bathroom and went into a cubicle. She locked the door and sat down on the toilet lid,

T
O
M

W
O
L
F
E

breathing too hard . . . so stricken with fear that she had to lock herself in here—inhaling ammonia fumes that were battling it out with the egestive funk of the place. Ohmygod—*Gloria!*

For the rest of the day, Charlotte went from class to class in fear. She desperately wanted to know what Gloria had told Lucy Page and if Lucy Page would tell Erica and if Erica would tell Beverly. Every time she passed someone vaguely familiar on the campus, she wondered if they *knew* . . . and then the dimensions of *what* they might know would grow and grow into something even more vast. She wasn't the first girl at Dupont to be summarily dumped, she assumed. But no girl in the history of Dupont or any other college had ever been dumped under circumstances like these. She had been dumped by a member of the hottest fraternity at Dupont— and not just "a member" but a demi-celebrity, hero of the Night of the Skull Fuck, the lionhearted boy who would stand up to any man—even an ox like Mac Bolka—the frat boy who was every frat boy's definition of Cool, as handsome a boy as ever existed—O Hoyt! How could you!

She kept her head down, in hiding and in shame, as she walked across the Great Yard. Stealthily she scanned that tableau, the vast lawn, the majestic tower at one end, that vista known all over—the world?—as the very portrait of higher education's highest aspirations in America, and she saw bobbing ponytails and swishing manes, and bottoms going this way and that way within jeans tight as skin and worn through to perfection, the better to reveal every cleft and declivity . . . Had any of them ever done what she had done? Had Hoyt maneuvered them to bed, too? But they had probably lost their virginity in private, not in front of an audience of meat-show strangers, long before it was her turn. Why him? Why did an utterly callous, affect-less male possessed by the Casanova syndrome have to be the one? Had she mocked God? Momma's God? Had she called His wrath down upon herself? Life and the Soul had departed her body. She was a pillar of salt that hadn't blown away yet.

When classes were over, at two-thirty, Charlotte hid in the DeLierre Museum of seventeenth-, eighteenth-, and nineteenth-century Chinese and Japanese art over on the other side of Lapham—not much risk of running into anybody she knew in the DeLierre—until after dark—a little after four-thirty, now that it was December—before chancing a return to Little Yard to pick up books and notebooks and hide out in the library, become Miss Charlotte Library Stacks again. Beverly . . . she couldn't face Beverly. Beverly would either let loose another barrage of questions—or she wouldn't, meaning she had already heard about it all . . . as it blew from Gloria to Lucy Page to Erica . . . to the world. She could count on Beverly to add a few Sarc 3 or even Sarc 2 or 1 comments, just to let Charlotte know she knew.

She entered Edgerton with consummate stealth, removing the sandals once again lest they slap on the floor. She peeked into the lounge to see if Bettina or Mimi was in there. The coast was clear. There was the elevator. The door was open, and no one was on it. So she got on and took a chance instead of resorting to the stairway. She made it to the fifth floor without anyone seeing her. She walked down the hallway once more, toting her sandals, silent as an Indian. She slowed down to practically a tiptoe when she got near Bettina's room . . . just in case Bettina was . . . lying in wait. As she padded past on the balls of her feet—"Charlotte." Someone inside was using her name in conversation. She paused, opened her mouth to take a deep breath—and heard her own rasping heart again. *They would hear her!* It seemed so loud, she closed her lips and forced herself to breathe only through her nose.

"I mean, this is *Charlotte* we're talking about." It was Bettina's voice.

"Who'd a thunk it!" A merry schadenfreudish voice, followed by giggles. That was Mimi.

"I can't believe she slept with him!" said Bettina.

"Yeah," said Mimi. "She's always like such a goody-goody. All those little like . . . homilies, she gives us . . . That the right word?"

"She gives us shit, is what she gives us," said Bettina. "She makes you feel like shit if you hook up with a guy—and we don't even do *that*."

"She thinks she's so smart, but you have to be a fucking moron to sleep with fucking Hoyt Thorpe at a fucking frat-house formal," said Mimi in the campus-wise, all-knowing, been-there manner she had.

"I *know*! He may be hot, but I mean, your fucking *first time*, and *he's* the one?"

Mimi, laughing: "And the bed—holy shit, lotsa luck going to another Saint Ray formal."

"Well, I mean, that wasn't her fault," said Bettina.

"Yeah, but you don't bleed on the bed! You just don't! And this girl Gloria—Gloria Barrone?—you know who I mean? She's a Psi Phi? She *saw* it."

"How did she see?"

"Hoyt showed her!"

T
O
M

W
O
L
F
E

"Wow, he's an asshole. What a dick. Was it her period?"

"No. What I heard is—I heard that Hoyt told Gloria it was her first time, and he like totally didn't know what to do. He like freaked out after."

"What do you mean, freaked out?" said Bettina.

"I don't know, I mean like he couldn't deal with it. Why should he? I mean, it wasn't like it was their wedding bed. It's probably a little awkward to be some random girl's fucking first time . . . at a frat formal!"

"That's so awful. How did you find out?"

"My friend Sarah Rixey told me."

"Sarah Rixey?—how did *she* know?"

"I don't know. I think she said this girl Nicole told her. She's a junior. I know they went to the same school in Massachusetts. I met her once."

"And how did *Nicole* know?"

"She's hooking up with this guy who's a Saint Ray," said Mimi. "I guess that's how."

"I still can't believe Hoyt is such an asshole that he'd show Gloria Barrone, though. She's like best friends with Lucy Page Tucker, who's the president of Psi Phi."

Charlotte had heard enough. She kept on walking . . . past her room. She couldn't even deal with the remote chance that Beverly was in there. If a couple of freshmen as low down on the grapevine as Bettina and Mimi knew, then certainly Beverly, who seemed to be already wired into the sorority scene, would know. It was Monday evening, not even forty-eight hours . . . later . . . and who *didn't* know! Her own friends were having a merry old time trashing her behind her back. Everyone knew! Hoyt had told two people, Gloria and Julian—and no doubt Vance, who no doubt told Crissy, who no doubt told Nicole as soon as they got together to tell war stories about the weekend—and now everybody she could possibly care about knew, and God knows how many others, as well, who might enjoy the incidental schadenfreude of pointing out the little hillbilly freshman from the mountains who "lost her pop-top" at a frat formal in a hotel.

How could he have told Gloria? Julian would have been bad enough, but *Gloria*? Was he utterly heartless, utterly cynical? Did he have a sadistically cruel streak? Was he so completely lacking in empathy for others—never mind sympathy—that he thought it was funny? She wanted to strangle him, *kill* him, *obliterate* him from the face of the earth. *Yell* at him . . . but in person, which meant she would at last *see* him again—look into his face. His hazel eyes, his smile, his cleft chin, his expression, which was not heartless at all but capable of such . . . love, and maybe if she had told him as soon as he invited her that she was a virgin, everything would have turned out differently, and he wouldn't have freaked out—that must have been all that really happened—he just didn't *know*, and the surprise freaked him out—yes, she had told him . . . just *before*, but by that time he was so aroused—after a certain point the male can't restrain himself—and if he saw her, looked into her face again, he would sob an apology—O Hoyt!—

So caught up was she in this fantasy that she wasn't aware of the Trolls just around the bend in the hallway until she was right on top of their ratty legs sticking out like a row of logs. She could scarcely believe it. Didn't they ever move? Didn't they have *anything* else to do? What were they, buzzards? The vile-looking, scrawny little Maddy turned her eyes up at Charlotte in the eerie way she had. Charlotte felt frustrated, but she steeled herself to the task of maintaining whatever cool she could. She smiled slightly, whispered "Hi," and kept walking. Scrawny Maddy was already drawing her knees up to let her pass, when she piped up. "Hey, there." She began giggling. "How you holding up?"

Another shock in the solar plexus—not so much the fact that the girl *knew*, which meant the whole bunch of them knew, as the fact that she dared to be so casually *impudent* about it.

"Fine," Charlotte said curtly, as if to maintain the fiction that she still existed on a plane far above them. She continued on through the gauntlet, panicked over the possibility of other fish-eyed stares and impudent—

"You know you're barefoot?" It was the big black girl, Helene. Giggles ran up and down the Trolls.

Charlotte rushed to the fire door and headed down the stairs toward—she had no idea where. Even the Trolls felt superior to her now! They didn't talk to other freshmen who actually had lives. They only observed them, used them as gossip fodder, envied them, resented them, sought to tear them down like tarantulas—*tarantulas*. It registered on her that Miss Pennington had introduced her to the term in a moment as unpleasant as this one, although she couldn't recall what it was. Maddy—that little limp-haired weasel-faced crone-in-embryo—even Maddy knew she had lost her virginity in the most public way—even Maddy was gloating over the fact that Charlotte Simmons and her aloof ego had gotten screwed over and plunged into the depths of campus loserdom.

She stopped at the next landing to put the sandals back on—they had dared to make fun of her bare feet! She was starting to sweat again. She was breathing in a rapid shallow fashion. She looked down the four flights of stairwell below. They were lit only by a single 22-watt circular fluorescent bulb at each landing. The walls were old-fashioned plaster, hard as rock, painted institutional green. The stair rail was some sort of molded metal painted black. When she tried to see all the way to the ground level, the stairwell became a narrow shaft full of tight right angles leading to a small terminal gloom.

It dawned on her that she had no idea what she was going to do when she reached the bottom . . .

Ordinarily, President Cutler received visitors not at his bombastic eight-foot-long desk, but at one of the office's two furniture clusters. Over here was a bergère, two cabriole-legged armchairs, and an Oxford easy chair, all upholstered mauve morocco leather. Over there was the richest chestnut brown leather sofa you ever saw, a long coffee table, and chairs upholstered in cloth of assorted mauve-dominated designs—all resting on a vast custom-made tawny yellow rug with a repeat pattern of Dupont-mauve cougars, taken from the Dupont family coat of arms. The clusters provided important visitors with an intimate, personal setting—"intimate" as in inside the royal chambers and "personal" as in VIP. That, plus a festival of Gothic interior decor—windows within intricately compounded arches, a ceiling painted in elaborate medieval motifs, and so on—seemed to work wonders with prospective donors. Perversely, the breed appeared to be stimulated more poignantly in the lap of conspicuous consumption than in settings of ascetic self-denial.

But the President didn't feel like getting intimate and personal with either of the two men he was looking at across his desk right now. They were the two worst extremists he had to deal with on the faculty, and their Weltanschauungs couldn't have been more at odds. No, he preferred to have the immovable heft of his desk between him and them.

Where the two hotheads were seated, they were facing a painting on the wall behind the President, a famous larger-than-life full-length portrait of Charles Dupont in his riding outfit, his glossy black left boot in the stirrup shimmering with highlights as he prepares to mount his champion four-year-old, a glossy black stallion named Go to the Whip. Dupont's stern face, broad shoulders, and mighty chest are twisted toward the viewer, as if someone has just been so foolish as to utter something impertinent. The artist,

John Singer Sargent—it was his only known equestrian painting—had made the Founder's riding crop oversize and placed it in his right hand at such an angle that he appears on the verge of whipping the offender across the mouth twice, forehand and then backhand.

But if either of the two extremists, Jerome Quat or Buster Roth, was intimidated, he hadn't shown it yet.

Jerry Quat—a butterball clad in a tight sweater—V-necked with a white T-shirt showing in the V—was saying, "Yeah, but I don't give a damn what the coordinate search showed, Fred! The fact remains, there is no way in the world that anabolic moron wrote that paper—and you know what, Fred? I'm not going to shut up about this until somebody"—pause, long enough to suggest that Somebody just might be the anabolic caveman sitting about three feet away from him, Buster Roth, uncharacteristically clad in a blazer and tie—"comes clean."

Oh you little pisser, thought the President. Jerry Quat was ratcheting his impertinence up to the point where he would be forced to reprimand him or else lose face in front of Roth. Fortunately, he had already told Roth what to expect where Quat was concerned, which was free-floating resentment. But look at Roth. He's clenching his teeth. At a certain point he's going to explode over cracks like "anabolic moron." That's as much as accusing him of feeding his team steroids. Either of these hotheads was too much to have to deal with, and having both on his hands at the same time . . . how was he going to butter up Jerry Quat—whose life was one long, inflamed itch for revenge against the Buster Roths of this world—without detonating Buster Roth, who regarded the Jerry Quats of this campus as unsexed subversives out to sink "the program"?

Well, here goes: "Now, Jerry," said the President, "I hope you realize that I don't *want* you to shut up. I really mean that. One of your greatest contributions has been calling things by their right names, which makes it very hard to just finesse or bury the issues." He smiled warmly. "Perhaps I shouldn't say this—I may be asking for more than I'm bargaining for—but I want you to keep on calling a"—he started to say "a spade a spade," but that was not acceptable any longer, even though it was an old, old expression and had nothing to do with "spade" as a piece of vulgar slang for African American— "calling things as you see them. You're an outstanding history scholar, Jerry, but right now that's one of the most important things you can do—keep everybody's eyes open and thinking clearly, as only Jerry Quat can do it."

The President was relieved to see that Quat's grim frown failed him just long enough for a smile of childish pleasure to flicker at the corners of his mouth. Just a flicker, of course; he immediately returned to looking every inch a bitter and obnoxious little shithead. Look at him . . . in his late fifties . . . him and his Lenin goatee, his shapeless, baggy, unpressed khaki pants and a grim gray sweater so tight it hugged every fold and flop of flab of his upper body, making his chest look like breasts lying on a swollen gut. Nothing under it but a T-shirt, the absence of a collar fully exposing his frog's swell of a double chin . . . into which has settled a round face whose fat smoothness is interrupted by the bags under his eyes, a pair of age-narrowed lips, and gulleys running from each side of his nostrils down past his lips, almost down to his jawline . . . and the goatee . . . all of which is topped by a thinning stand of black hair turning scouring-pad gray, cut short with no part, like an undergraduate's. What is this look, this getup, supposed to represent? His aloofness from the Neckties and Dark Blue Suits (such as the President was wearing) who still run the world? His solidarity with rebelling youth (if any)? Or just a simple eternal adolescent bohemian poke in the eye? A combination of all that, probably.

Oh, the President knew the type very well by now, being Jewish himself. Only a fool would ever talk about it, of course, but there was more than one type of "Jewish intellectual." The President, like Jerry Quat, probably, was three generations down the line from a penniless young immigrant from Poland named Moiscz Kutilizhenski. Immigration changed his last name to Cutler, and life on the streets of New York changed his first name to Mo. Mo became an electrician, started out on his own in New York as Cutler Commercial Wiring, and flourished in the building boom following World War I. Under his son, Frederick, a City College of New York graduate, the firm became Cutler Electric, which grew so big during the building boom of the 1950s and 60s that Frederick began to mix easily—on a business-social level—with the old Protestant establishment, and he became a member of the Ethical Culture church, one of two churches of choice for Jews who decided to completely assimilate, the Unitarian Church being the other. Frederick named one of his four sons Frederick junior, which was a true gesture of assimilation, since no traditional Jew ever named a child after a living person. By now the Cutlers were so well off that he enjoyed the luxury of packing Fred junior off to Harvard to study the higher things, as certified in due course by the boy's B.A. from Harvard and Ph.D. in international relations from Princeton. After a brief teaching stint at Princeton, he became a career diplomat, serving for years as first secretary to the American embassy in Paris.

Fred junior's son, Frederick Cutler III, B.A., Harvard, Ph.D., Dupont, had a sterling academic career as a Middle East historian and at this moment, sitting at this vast desk, was the president of Dupont.

The man sitting across from him, the butterball grotesquely squeezed into a dark gray sweater, was of another sort entirely, despite the fact that they were both Jewish and agreed on practically every public issue of the day. Both believed passionately in protecting minorities, particularly African Americans, as well as Jews. Both regarded Israel as the most important nation on earth, although neither was tempted to live there. Both instinctively sided with the underdog; police violence really got them steamed. Both were firm believers in diversity and multiculturalism in colleges. Both believed in abortion, not so much because they thought anyone they knew might want an abortion as because legalizing it helped put an exhausted and dysfunctional Christendom and its weird, hidebound religious restraints in their place. For the same reason, both believed in gay rights, women's rights, transgender rights, fox, bear, wolf, swordfish, halibut, ozone, wetland, and hardwood rights, gun control, contemporary art, and the Democratic Party. Both were against hunting and, for that matter, woods, fields, mountain trails, rock climbing, sailing, fishing, and the outdoors in general, except for golf courses and the beach.

The difference, as the President saw it, was that Quat was a resentful petit bourgeois Jewish intellectual, as the Marxists used to say. Not that Frederick Cutler III had ever enunciated this insight to a living soul, other than his wife. He hadn't lost his mind, after all. In the Cutler theory, the Jerome Quats of the academic world were born to parents in the middling strata of American society who told them from as far back as they could remember that life was a Manichaean battle—i.e., the forces of Light versus the forces of Dark, of "us" against the goyim, with white Christians, especially the Catholics and White Anglo-Saxon Protestants, being the most powerful and most treacherous. Every incoming Jerry Quat on the Dupont faculty immediately established the fact that despite the last name, Buster Roth was not Jewish. He was of German stock, stone German and stone Catholic. In Fred Cutler's taboo theory, the parents of the Jerome Quat types had never reached the business and social elevation where non-Jews at that altitude very much *wanted* you in their orbit, and your self-interest and theirs became interdependent. In the eyes of Jerome Quat, whose father had been a mid-level civil servant in Cleveland or some such place, there could never be a true accommodation. The WASPs and Catholics could make all the

T
O
M

W
O
L
F
E

protestations they wanted, but they would forever remain insensitive, powerful, treacherous, and by now genetically anti-Semitic. Or to put it another way, the Quats were the usual little people with limited vision. The Cutlers were men of the world.

Figuring he had lubricated little Jerry with enough praise and acknowledged his position as leader of the forces of Light at this great university, the President now cupped both hands and brought his palms within inches of one another and twisted them this way and that as if he were making an imaginary snowball and said, "At the same time, Jerry—"

"Don't you start at-the-same-timing and but-on-the-other-handing and still-neverthelessing me, Fred!"

The President couldn't believe it. The little shitbird insisted on putting him right against the wall.

"You know, I know, and Mr. Roth here knows that Jojo"—uttered contemptuously—"Johanssen, whose SAT scores, if we had access to them, which we don't"—he gave the President a sharp look—"and why not, Fred?—would no doubt prove to be lower than his hat size, assuming he knows what a hat is, other than an adjustable baseball cap, which he wears sideways—"

"That's not true, Professor! You're dead wrong about his SATs."

Buster Roth couldn't hold back any longer, and the President knew he had to jump in fast lest the whole meeting turn into a pissing match. Merely being called "Professor"—just that, Professor rather than Professor Quat or Mr. Quat—was enough to set Jerry Quat off, since Jerry would know that in the mouths of coaches and recruited athletes the title Professor, all by itself, carried the connotation of Pretentious Fool.

"Oh yeah?" Quat snapped. "Then why won't anybody—"

"Mr. Quat! Mr. Roth!" said the President, "Please! Let's remember one thing! Whatever any of us may think, Mr. Johanssen retains some basic rights here!"

He knew the word "rights" would get to Jerry Quat. To Jerry, rights would be the civic equivalent of angels. Sure enough, Quat shut up, and Buster Roth was shrewd enough to shut up, too, and let the President argue the case for Jojo's "rights." The President continued: "Now, I gather we all agree that Mr. Johanssen's paper was suspiciously far above the rhetorical level of any other work he had submitted."

"*Rhetorical* level?" said Jerry Quat. "He doesn't even have a clue what the *words* mean!"

"All right, it looks suspicious in terms of vocabulary, too. But that is prima facie evidence, which presents us with a problem. No one has less tolerance for plagiarism than I do. No one is more of an absolutist when it comes to the penalties for plagiarism than I am. But the language of the judicial code is very clear on this point. Plagiarism must be proved by discovering the source of the material in question. Stan Weisman has done the best job he could, it seems to me." He was careful to use the man's name, which was Jewish, rather than his title, judicial officer. "He did a coordinate search of all the usual suspects, all the rogue Web sites that offer to provide students with papers. He did a coordinate search of every other paper submitted for that assignment, including those from three of Mr. Johanssen's teammates. And he came up with nothing. He interrogated Mr. Johanssen, who denies receiving any help other than the books cited in his bibliography. He interrogated Mr. Johanssen's tutor, a senior named Adam Gellin, who denied writing the paper or even assisting on it."

"Adam *Gellin*?" said Jerry Quat. "Why do I know that name?"

"I believe he works for *The Daily Wave*," said the President, who by now knew very well that he did.

"Well, I've seen the name somewhere."

"Professor—"

Oh shit. Buster Roth was piping up again with his *Professor*.

"We're very firm about that with the tutors. That's the first thing we tell them. They're there to *help* the student-athlete"—Quat's lips and nostrils twisted sarcastically at the very term—"but they're *not* there to do their work for them. Writing a paper for somebody—no way." He shook his head and slashed the air with the edge of his hand, to emphasize the "no way." "This is Adam Gellin's third year working with student-athletes, as fine a young man as I ever met, and I never heard a him doing nothing that wasn't strictly by the book. I talked to him myself after this thing came up, and he got mad at me for even *suggesting*—you know what I'm saying? I never saw him lose his temper before, but *this*? . . . No way!" He slashed the air again. "I know Adam—and Adam? They don't come any more decent and honest than Adam Gellin . . . No way!" Another slash for good measure.

The President let out his breath. Bravo, Buster. He could have used a little help in the grammar and syntax department, but he had managed to be pretty convincing. This was all very tricky stuff for the President. Circumstances had forced him to become a temporary ally of Buster Roth. Roth had approached him and warned him—although not in so many words—that if

Johanssen was forced out for even one semester, the scandal would hurt not merely "the program" but the entire university. It wasn't that Buster was so concerned about losing Johanssen himself—he was gradually being replaced by a hot freshman named Congers, anyway—but such a turn of events would make "the program" look so sleazy and hypocritical. For years the university had built up and promoted its reputation of being a national power in football, basketball, ice hockey, and even minor sports—track and field, baseball, lacrosse, tennis, soccer, golf, squash—without compromising academic standards by so much as a millimeter. A case indicating that Dupont had tutors who wrote the athletes' papers for them would explode all that in the public eye. It might, he had hinted in guarded terms, open up a whole can of worms. Where did the players' new SUVs come from? What about this list of "friendly" courses? What about these rumors that four of the team's players had SAT scores of under nine hundred? The President thought about that. For a start, it would knock Dupont from second, behind Princeton, in the *U.S. News & World Report* rankings down to . . . God knew where. *U.S. News & World Report*—what a stupid joke! Here is this third-rate news weekly, aimed at businessmen who don't like to read, trying desperately to move up in the race but forever swallowing the dust of *Time* and *Newsweek*, and some character dreams up a circulation gimmick: Let's rank the colleges. Let's stir up a fuss. Pretty soon all of American higher education is jumping through hoops to meet the standards of the marketing department of a miserable, lowbrow magazine out of Washington, D.C.! Harvard, Yale, Princeton, Stanford, Dupont—all jumped through the hoop at the crack of the *U.S. News* whip! Does *U.S. News* rate you according to how many of the applicants you offer places to actually enroll in your college and not another? Then let's lock in as many as we can through early admissions contracts. Does *U.S. News* want to know your college's SAT average? We'll give it to them, but we will be "realistic" and not count "special cases" . . . such as athletes. Does *U.S. News* rate you according to your standing in the eyes of *other* college presidents? Then a scandal indicating that all our lofty pronouncements about the "student-athlete" at Dupont are not only a joke but a lie—well, anybody could write the rest of that story.

But there was no instructing the faculty to keep mum about such things and cooperate. You had to become a college president to realize how powerful the faculty could be when aroused. We *are* the university, was the attitude of the Dupont faculty. Consequently, they resented not only the vast amount of money that went to sports, they also resented the glory. Why should a collection of anabolic morons such as the Dupont basketball team, led by a man who goes by the ridiculous name of Buster, be idealized at one of the world's greatest institutions of learning? The President had wondered about the same thing himself, for years; and when he was a young faculty member, he had been resentful and contemptuous the same way Jerry Quat was, although not with such bitterness. It wasn't until he was promoted from chairman of the history department to provost of the university that he began to understand. Contrary to what most people believed—himself included in days gone by—big-time sports did not make money for the university, did not help to underwrite the academic departments, etc. National championship teams receiving big postseason television fees lost still more money, more than all the minor sports, baseball, tennis, squash, lacrosse, swimming, the lot put together. Big-time sports were a *stupendous* drag on the financial health of the university. In a practical sense, they were like sticking a .45-caliber revolver barrel in your mouth and pulling the trigger. Nor did alumni donations increase or decrease with the fortunes of the teams. It was something subtler and grander at the same time. Big-time sports created a glorious aura about everything the university did and *in the long run* increased everything sharply—prestige, alumni donations, receipts of every sort, as well as influence. But why? God only knew! These great athletes—Treyshawn Diggs, from a lower-middle-class black neighborhood in Huntsville, Alabama; Obie Cropsey, all-American quarterback, a redneck from rural Illinois—none of the athletes in the major sports resembled the vast majority of the real students, not intellectually, not socially, not temperamentally. Nor did the two groups mix at Dupont. The athletes were received with awe wherever they went, but few real students had anything to do with them personally, and vice versa. Part of it was that the other students thought the athletes existed up on a plane so far above them, they shouldn't presume to intrude. And in truth, the Athletic Department saw to it that they spent so much of their day in mandatory physical training, mandatory practice, mandatory dining at training tables, mandatory study halls in the evening, and certain "suggested" "athlete-friendly" courses that their contact with real students would be minimal in any event. They were alien mercenaries paid in kind and in glory. So why would the real students, the alumni, the parents of prospective applicants, the world at large, *care* how *our* aliens performed against *their* aliens? Fred Cutler had no idea. He had puzzled over it for more than ten years now, and he had . . . no idea . . . But one thing he did know for sure: a winning coach like Buster Roth, Low Rent grammar and all, was . . . a demigod. He was a far bigger figure than President Frederick Cutler III or any Nobel Prize laureate on the faculty. He was known across the nation. He now had his own castle, the "Rotheneum." Officially he, Frederick Cutler III, had authority over Roth. On paper, in the catalog, Buster Roth was on the faculty. But he also made more than two million dollars a year. Because of his private deals with sports equipment companies, his television product endorsements, lectures, and other public appearances, it was hard to determine how much with accuracy. The President's salary was four hundred thousand a year, one fifth as much or perhaps less. And there you had it. He had the official power to oppose Roth at any juncture. But he could only do so gingerly, with his own job in his hands—because there was one thing he couldn't do. He couldn't fire him. Only the board of trustees could do that—and they could also fire the President.

Ironically, only someone much lower down the ladder—some faculty member with tenure—dared speak out, dared cause trouble. And who was the hothead, the firebrand, who did the most to inflame the entire faculty's resentment of how the natural and rightful order of things had been turned upside down? That hothead, that sorehead, was the blob sitting right across the desk from President Frederick Cutler III.

"Jerry," said the President, "there's one thing that makes this case a little different, and I thought I'd run it by you. Stan Weisman"—I'll keep that name front and center, he said to himself—"discovered an interesting thing. After Johanssen turned in his paper, but before the question of plagiarism came up, he seems to have undergone something of a conversion, as it were. He decided—or so he told his friends—to become serious about his academic work. He shifted out of a one-hundred-level survey course of modern French literature to a two-hundred-level course on the nineteenth-century French novel with Lucien Senigallia, where all teaching and discussions are in French. He shifted out of a one-hundred-level Philosophy of Sports course into a three-hundred-level course Nat Margolies teaches—the Age of Socrates, I believe it's called. And Nat, as you may know, is pretty demanding and cuts no slack for anybody—*anybody*."

Buster Roth spoke up, looking at Jerry Quat. "Oh, I've never been prouder of any of my boys than I was when Jojo came to me and told me he wanted to take that course, the Age of Socrates." Buster Roth smiled at the recollection and shook his head, as if to say that was really *some* turn of events. "I wanted to make sure he understood what he—the commitment he was making. I said, 'Jojo, have you ever taken a three-hundred-level course before?' He said he hadn't, and so I said, 'These are advanced and very serious classes. They can't wait for you if you fall behind,' and I'll never forget what Jojo said. He said, 'Coach, I know I'm taking a risk, but I feel like I've just been grinding out credits up to now. I'm willing to take a risk to get *myself* to a higher level. The way we look at the world today'—he said, or something like that—'it all starts with Socrates and Plato and Aristotle, so that's where I want to start.' And then he's telling me about Pythagoras, I think it was, and how he was great in math but pretty backward in philosophical thought—I mean, I had no idea he was into all this stuff. I was really impressed, but it was more than that. I was *proud* of him. Here was the kind of young man you're always looking for. Oh, I know people get excited over sports *qua* sports, the competition and all that—"

Qua? The President couldn't believe it. Buster Roth was sitting here saying "sports *qua* sports"? He wondered if he'd planned it.

"—but I like to think of my role as an educator first and a basketball coach second. You know? I think it might a been Socrates himself who said, '*Mens sana in corpore sano*,' a sound mind in a sound body, and a lot of people forget—"

Oh shit, Buster, thought the President, *you just blew it*. Socrates, he don't speaka the Latin. You just buried that beautiful *qua* of yours. And you didn't have to translate *mens sana in corpore sano* for a Jerry Quat.

"—that that's the ideal. There's a beautiful synergy there, if we can only make it happen. And there's a guy like Jojo, the kind a big, plainspoken guy people are gonna call a 'dumb jock'—you know what I mean?—and he's coming to me on his own to tell me he don't wanna miss the chance he's got to make that synergy work at a great university like Dupont."

The President studied Jerry Quat to gauge his reaction to Buster Roth the Greco-Roman scholar. He expected the worst, but Quat was actually studying Roth. He didn't look convinced—but neither did he have the typical Jerry Quat sarcastic look, turning his face away from the speaker and tilting his gaze upward as if bird-watching until the mindless boor shuts up. He was trying to decide—the President devoutly hoped—if there was more to this great side of beef with a Dupont-mauve blazer on than he had thought.

"I've never been prouder of one of our athletes in my life," Buster Roth was saying. "This was all Jojo's idea. It's one thing to take chances on the court. Jojo is used to that. He's a kid who's used to doing the unexpected un-

T
O
M

W
O
L
F
E

der pressure. But it's another thing for a kid to take a chance in a thing that's just as important where he don't qualify as a star."

The President was beginning to get nervous. The *he don'ts* were piling up. All it would take would be the notion that Buster was just blowing smoke up his tail.

"So how is our newborn scholar doing in the Big Risk?" said Quat.

Buster Roth and the President looked at each other for a moment. "I've checked with Mr. Margolies," said Roth, "and he says Jojo's struggling a bit, but he's working hard and getting his assignments done, and he's been taking part in class discussions and so on."

The President jumped in and said, "I've talked to Herb myself, and that's pretty much the same thing he told me. This is an unusual situation."

"It's not unusual," snapped Jerry Quat, "and it's not even a situation, if by situation you mean some state of affairs that is not easy to interpret and deal with. Unfortunately, it's not 'unusual' for 'student-athletes'"— pronounced affectless felons—"to engage in the most egregious cheating. Your Mr. Jojo is lazy, ignorant, and a simpleminded *cheater*. Let's keep our eyes on *that* ball. What he has or hasn't done for Herb Margolies couldn't interest me less. I've looked your Jojo's callous, contemptuous disregard for the core mission of this university in the face, and I don't like what I've seen, and I don't intend to put up—"

Oh shit, oh shit, oh shit. The President could see the Cutler-Roth strategy tanking right before his eyes.

"—with any such thing ever again." The hotheaded little ball of fat, resentment, and revenge wasn't addressing his tirade to Buster Roth, however—he didn't dare look that force of nature in the eye—but to the President. "If Mr. Roth wants to deal with a bunch of seven-foot bab—uh— brainless athletes, that's his business, but I think—"

The President was positive that Quat had been on the verge of saying "baboons."

"—he has an obligation to do what he can to keep them out of courses where teachers are serious about—"

Buster Roth's face had turned red. He leaned toward Jerry Quat, trying to get him to look him in the eye. "Now, you hold on! You don't even know what you're talking about!"

"I don't?" said Jerry Quat, although he still wasn't looking straight at Buster Roth. "I've got *four* of your 'student-athletes' in my class, and they all sit together side by side like lengths of lumber. I call them the Four Monkeys: See No Evil, Hear No Evil, Speak No Evil, and Comprehend Nothing Whatsoever."

A pissing match. The President had to step in and break this thing up. "You sure you want to say monkeys, Jerry?"

"What? Am I sure—" He halted.

The President looked on with some satisfaction as it dawned on the butterball that three of the four athletes he was referring to were black.

He began sputtering, "I didn't mean it—I mean, it's just an old expression—a cliché in a way—I mean it's totally removed from—I mean, I retract that. It was just a manner of speaking . . ." He began backpedaling as fast as he could. "One of them, a Mr. Curtis Jones, *does* wear a baseball hat to class, on sideways, and when I—" He paused. His face turned redder than Buster Roth's. He was boiling with anger again. He looked straight at Roth. "The bottom line is, I want your student-athletes out of my class, all four of them! I don't intend to teach your fucking 'Jojo boys' ever again! They belong in fucking junior high school! Jesus Christ, you guys are such a fucking disgrace! I don't want to have to fucking think about it again!"

He stood up abruptly, and the globs of fat on his body oozed this way and that beneath the sweater, and he glowered at Buster Roth and the President, both. "Nice chatting with you . . . about pediatrics." With that, he turned his back on them and walked out of the room.

Speechless, the President and Buster Roth looked at one another. The President wondered idly why so many Jews of a certain age used the expression "Jesus Christ." You never heard it from undergraduates anymore, Christian or Jewish.

Only Adam and Greg and the usual Jolt stains, empty pizza boxes, crumpled straw sleeves, and abandoned white plastic forks and spoons were to be seen in the office of the *Wave*. Adam was excited enough for a whole office-full.

"Now Thorpe calls me and says he's changed his mind. He doesn't want to run the Skull Fuck story after all. As if *he's* running it."

"What did you tell him?" said Greg.

"I said I'd tell you that. So I've told you—and *fuck him*. I didn't say we *wouldn't* run it. Don't you see, Greg? Something's up, and he's scared all of a sudden, and the story's hotter than ever."

"Well . . . I don't know," said Greg. "This is *still* something that happened last spring . . ."

You don't know? thought Adam. Or you're still as scared shitless as he is?

Beverly had already left, and even with the door closed Charlotte could hear others on the floor yodeling cheery good-byes and rolling their wheelie suitcases down the hall as the great Thanksgiving exodus began. Thank God! Solitude! No one around to look cockeyed at Charlotte Simmons. Thank God she and Momma and Daddy had long ago agreed that the Thanksgiving break and the Christmas break were so close to each other this year—barely two weeks apart—that she shouldn't take two trips and spend all that money.

It turned out there were quite a few other freshmen who had made the same decision. And thank God she didn't know them. They all smiled at each other in a same-boat fashion as they ate their three meals a day in the gloomy Abbey. The Abbey drummed up a roast turkey dinner on Thanksgiving Day for all the holiday orphans. For the next four days, all she had to worry about was Christmas. There was no way around that one.

27. IN THE DEAD OF THE NIGHT

The last six miles up Route 21 are what makes a person realize just how high up in the mountains Sparta is. The old two-lane road winds and winds and remains so unremittingly steep the whole way, it makes even a passenger feel, in her gizzard, the car or the truck struggling struggling struggling to make it—any car, any truck. In a bus, particularly a full bus, it used to make Charlotte feel as if at any moment the clutch would snap and they would go careening backward down the mountain; but buses no longer go to Sparta, not because of the steep grade—although 21 can become impassable pretty quickly when it snows—but because of a grim slide in demand. Ever since the factories moved to Mexico, and the movie theater, the only one in all of Alleghany County, shut down, Sparta hadn't been what one would call a prime destination, except for vacationers and tourists who loved the county's beauty, which was pristine, undefiled by the hand of man.

On those last six miles up Route 21, on this particular December night, all was pristine. The first real snow of the season had just begun to fall, and the way the wind blew it—in a darkness made yet darker by the towering woods that came right up to the edge of the road and obscured most of the sky—the two-lane hand of man would suddenly vanish before the driver's eyes as great skiffs of snow came rolling across it; and then it would reappear, and Daddy would keep hunching forward, squinting and muttering imprecations, since he knew the road would only disappear again. The old pickup was struggling struggling struggling, and once or twice it had skidded slightly on a curve. Daddy had become so single-minded he was no longer asking Charlotte, who was squeezed in next to him in the front seat, all sorts of questions about Dupont. Momma, who sat on her other side, had stopped talking, too. Momma was looking ahead as intently as Daddy, and she had begun shadow-braking the car with her right foot an instant before Daddy did it for real and then twisting her torso an instant before Daddy turned the wheel to navigate the next curve; and as Daddy switched from low beam to high beam and high beam to low beam to see if there was any angle of light that would help him define the road amid the skiffs and swirls of snow, she would hunch over and lean forward the same way he did, as if moving their heads closer to the road's surface was actually going to help them see it better.

Only Buddy and Sam, jackknifed into the little excuse for a backseat, remained oblivious enough of the driving conditions to continue the ebullient family fusillade of questions about the awesome college *their own sister* had come back from on her Christmas break.

"Charlotte," said Buddy, eleven years old last week, "What's Treyshawn Diggs like?"

"I don't know him," said Charlotte. She said it flatly, tonelessly, even though she knew the least she should do was say, "I'm afraid I never have met him, Buddy," and say it with a congenial lilt. But she couldn't. She couldn't manufacture any lilt.

"You don't?" Both surprise and disappointment were in Buddy's voice. "But you've met him."

"No," said Charlotte in the same dead voice, "I never have."

"But you've seen him, I bet. What's it look like, him being seven feet tall?"

Charlotte paused. She knew this performance was inexcusable, but she was so depressed that Self-destruction couldn't come down off her pedestal, so enamored was she of Grief.

"I've never seen him, Buddy."

"You've seen him *play*." It was spoken like a plea.

"I've never seen him at all. It's almost impossible to get a ticket for a game, and it costs a lot of money. I haven't even seen him on television."

Sam said, "How about André Walker? He's really cool." Sam was only eight, and he knew who André Walker was. It seemed so odd and sad somehow. "I've never seen him, either," she said. She couldn't have said it more lifelessly.

"How about Vernon Congers?" said Sam.

"Nope."

A groan of disappointment in the backseat—Buddy's. A slightly whining sigh, Sam's.

After all other emotions have died, guilt survives. To her own surprise, Charlotte found herself saying, "I do know one of the players. Jojo Johanssen."

"Who's he?" said Sam.

"I think I heard of him," said Buddy. "Which one is he?"

"He's a forward, I think," said Charlotte. "He's white."

"Oh, yeah," said Buddy. "Dupont's got this white guy. They were playing Cincinnati. Is he any good?"

"I guess," said Charlotte.

"Is he big?" said Sam.

"Yeah, he's very big," said Charlotte. Poor Jojo, she thought. Even my little brothers know about Vernon Congers, and nobody knows about you. It was merely that, however, a thought. There was no emotion attached to it. It all seemed so pointless.

"How big?" said Sam, persevering.

"I don't know." She started to leave it at that, but guilt intervened. "When I stand next to him, he might as well be ten feet tall. That's how big he is."

"Wow," said Sam.

More guilt. Jojo's height was the only "colorful" detail about Dupont she had volunteered since she got off the bus in Galax. Galax was just over the state line, in Virginia. Eleven-thirty p.m. the bus had arrived, and all four of them, Momma, Daddy, Buddy, and Sam, had been there waiting for her, beaming smiles of joy—no, more than that, excitement!—that lit up the night. *Our daughter—our sister—is home for the first time in four months from the legendary Dupont. Just imagine! Our little girl—our big sister—goes to Dupont! And here she is!*

Charlotte had forced herself to smile, but she was aware that the smile didn't involve the rest of her face. And God knows how her face must have looked. She hadn't been able to sleep for two nights now. Maybe she should have gone to the Health Center. Maybe they would have put her in the hospital . . . Maybe God would have come to take her away in the night. She couldn't imagine a better solution.

Daddy as well as Momma had immediately begun spraying her with questions about Dupont. Their blissful assumption that she would be as excited as they were to talk about it—that she would react with the same joy of triumph with which she had approached Dupont in August—struck her as naïve and irritating. How irritating, how childish it was of them to stand there with big smiles, displaying enthusiasm concerning something they knew absolutely nothing about. In other words (which she never said to herself), how uncool was that?

It made her extremely nervous, all these questions. How was Beverly? Were they getting along? What was living in the dorm like? They were so proud of her grades, even though they had just known she would set Dupont on fire. What courses did she like best? Then Buddy chimed in and asked her, teasingly, if she had a boyfriend. And Daddy said, teasingly, *he* wanted to hear the answer to that one.

Only Momma noticed that her little girl was deflecting the questions, saying she just didn't know, even acting dumb, but Momma obviously wanted the weariness of the ten-hour trip to account for it. She wasn't yet ready to consider the fact that her little genius might be moody or, as it happened, worse than moody.

The fact was, Charlotte had not minded the length and the grind of the trip at all. The trip had been the sort that people refer to as "endless." The depressed person wants trips to be literally endless, because as long as she is in transit from one point to another, her worries, her despair, are removed from where they originated . . . and where they will inevitably resume. Under the circumstances, what could be better than being in a soft reclining chair in a spaceship with strangers, a spaceship in that it moves fast and makes you feel detached from earth (way up here in this chair) as you behold, from behind big sheets of thick plate glass so darkly tinted that no one outside can even see you, blissfully alien landscapes drifting by . . . Please, God, let it last forever—or else come take me away in the night.

In the here and now, in the struggling old pickup, Charlotte peered out at the snow, which now looked wild and demonic, lit up the way it was by the headlights. Maybe they would skid, turn over, plunge into the darkness over there on the left, down that nearly sheer incline, tumbling end over end until the old vehicle burst open and came apart. A crash—her consciousness departs, there is *nihil*; and *ex nihilo*, God comes and takes her away in the night.

Such plunges, such fatal wrecks, had occurred before on 21—but what would happen to Momma and Daddy and Buddy and Sam? No one would emerge unscathed from such a crash. She wasn't so far gone as to wish anything to happen to their lives just to create an acceptable end to hers, one that would provide no satisfaction, no super-delicious schadenfreude for the Beverlys, the Glorias, the Mimis . . . and no frat-boy notoriety for . . . for . . . No, nothing must happen to Daddy and Momma, who loved her, loved her unquestioningly, Dupont or no Dupont, who would undoubtedly take her back into their bosoms, as unclean as she was. She tried to think of ways the wreck could occur so that God would come take only her away in the night.

Hours from now, when daylight came, it would be too late. Oh what a genius Charlotte Simmons is, but the little genius would not be nearly smart enough. How long would it take Momma to see clear through her and know that something fundamentally wrong had occurred—that her good girl had committed moral suicide? How long, Momma? Twenty minutes? Thirty? A whole hour? And what was she to say to Miss Pennington? That everything was fine? That she had never felt more vibrantly alive in her life—alive with the life of the mind?—and in that way allow her, the teacher who saw Charlotte Simmons as the justification for the entire forty years she had spent toiling at a country high school up in that Athens of the Blue Ridge Mountains called Sparta—allow her to have three and a half or four more weeks of illusions before little Justification's grades for the fall semester come home in a letter to Momma and Daddy? They didn't comprehend Rhodes scholarships and cénacles and matrices of ideas, much less Millennial Mutants. They didn't know how nearly perfect your grade point average had to be to go to graduate school at any major university in America. But Miss Pennington would know about such things.

Daddy didn't plunge off the road into the void. He didn't even take as long as a depressed girl might have reasonably hoped for. In no time, there they were in the middle of Sparta, stopped at one of the three stoplights, the one where 21 crossed 18. The stoplight, which was suspended over the intersection, was rocking in the wind. The snow was really beginning to stick. There was nobody walking along the street, nobody anywhere on the street. There was the old redbrick courthouse, looking suitably ancient and mute in the darkness and the drifting snow. Could have been a movie about the early 1800s, except for the big, modern polished granite marker that had been erected on the Main Street side. They moved on . . . past the spot where she had jaywalked behind Regina because she didn't have the fortitude to refuse to break the law . . .

"Recognize that?" said Momma, pointing to the right.

The snow was coming down so hard, it was hard to see it at first, but there it was, about two hundred feet from the road, on the upslope of the hill, looking as ghostly as the courthouse . . . the high school. Charlotte leaned forward, almost across Momma, and peered into the darkness and the snow. At first she felt nothing. There it was, that was all . . . There was the extension where the basketball court was, where *the young woman who* had held forth as valedictorian. There it was—it was just a building, a dark, dead building in the middle of a storm. The tears caught her unaware. They seemed to be pouring down from the sinuses beneath her cheekbones. Thank God she had a handkerchief. She stifled them by burying her head in it and feigning a coughing fit, and Daddy inadvertently helped by saying, "Look't the motel." *Mo*-tel. "All I see's three automobiles."

They were already beyond the town. The only lights now were the old pickup's headlights reflecting off the snow, which was coming down in great gusts and spinning crazily before the dusky rusky forests.

"Well, good girl," Momma sang out, "know where we're at?"

Charlotte pretended to come awake with a start.

"Look familiar?" said Momma. "You been away for four whole months!"

Charlotte managed to croak out, "It's good to be home, Momma," whereupon she pressed her face against the shoulder of Momma's rough work jacket so that Momma would just think she was being sweet and loving and not see the tears rolling down her cheeks.

She managed to hold herself together until they entered the house and went into the living room and Daddy clicked on the light . . . and there it was, the picnic table, only there was a nice, freshly pressed white tablecloth over it and an arrangement of pinecones, pine sprigs, and red holly berries in a little wicker basket in the middle of it. There were some light next-to-nothing bentwood chairs she hadn't seen before. There was the Christmas tree, as usual. There were little holly wreaths, brilliant with the red berries— must have been six wreaths—hung about the room at eye level on the walls. That was something new. The floor had been waxed. Every square inch of the room was spick-and-span. Momma had done all this . . . for her. Daddy was already stoking the grate in the potbellied stove. Charlotte took a deep breath. The countrified odor of a room saturated over the years in coal fumes rushed in—suffused all of her, it felt like.

A burst of laughter and a strange bray of music—the TV set was on. On the screen—a man dressed in black with a pale, totally bald head shaped like a bullet clamped by big black earphones was standing, laughing at what must have been the funniest thing in the world and pressing both hands into some sort of electrified keyboard. The keyboard was making the braying sound. Buddy and Sam, of course; first things first; turn on the TV.

Daddy stood up from the potbellied stove and went over to the boys. "Hey, turn that off! It's after midnight! This iddn' TV time. It's bedtime. The Sandman's who you boys best be turning on."

The Sandman . . . Charlotte couldn't hold back any longer. She burst into tears, although quietly. Momma put an arm around her and said, "What's wrong, little darling?"

Thank God, Daddy and Buddy and Sam were involved in the TV set and its imminent fate. Charlotte managed to stop crying, but she could tell her eyes were red, puffy, and bleary.

"It's nothing, Momma. I'm just so tired. That bus ride . . . and I had to stay up so late studying all week . . . "

The TV set—off. Momma still had her arm around her, the good girl. Charlotte was ashamed to look at Daddy and her little brothers, because there was no hiding the fact that she had been crying.

Momma said, "She's just tired."

Jes tarred. It was all Charlotte could do to keep from crying again.

When she got into bed in her old room, that little five-foot-wide slot of a room, she lay there unable to sleep, which she knew would happen. Her mind was a machine turned up high, and it wouldn't slow down. She kept thinking about the day, her trip back home, but not the way a calm person would, in terms of sequences in the flow of time or incidents. The whole day was like scenes on a stage—dark scenery, a forbidding backdrop for the . . . dreaded thing, which was closing in on her still—no exit, only the end, which was inevitable. When was Momma to learn that she was unclean, polluted beyond all redemption? When was Miss Pennington to learn that her special creation, the girl who was the glory of her career, anointed in her name to keep her eye on the future and create a glory that would light up the world—when was poor Miss Pennington to learn that her prize pupil had thrown away her future, wrecked it in four short months in the most sordid and juvenile way, besotted with a frat boy—a frat boy!—the epitome of all that is immoral, mindless, childish, cruel, irresponsible, affectless, and vile among American youth?

Perhaps she should tell everybody . . . everything . . . first thing in the morning and get it over with. But what would that change? These were not matters you "put behind you and moved on" from. She was no closer to knowing what to do than she had been at the bus stop in Galax.

The wind was howling now. Good. Please make this storm long and dark, dear Lord. If morning must come, let it be grim and gray. Let the snow pile deep and paralyze the world.

She lay there listening to the storm and trying not to feel her heartbeats, which she knew were too rapid again, and praying that the moaning and keening of the wind would put her to sleep at last. Would she ever be able to sleep again? Here in her old bed, the snug harbor . . . where Daddy used to get on his knees and lean over her and say, "Warm, toasty, cozy, comfy, safe, and secure—*ahhh*," and she always fell asleep before he could complete the crooning three times, "Warm, toasty, cozy, comfy—"

She decided to chant it to herself. In a tiny, low voice she said, "Warm, toasty, cozy, comfy, safe, and secure—*ahhh* . . . Warm, toasty, cozy, comfy, safe, and secure—*ahhh* . . . Warm, toasty, cozy—"

She stopped and slid out from under the covers. It was freezing, but that was the least of her worries. She got on her knees beside the bed and closed her eyes and pressed her palms together and let her fingertips touch her chin. She said to herself in a very low voice:

> "*Now I lay me down to sleep.*
> *I pray the Lord my soul to keep.*
> *If I should die before I wake,*
> *I pray the Lord my soul to take.*
> *Bless Momma, Daddy, Buddy, and Sam and tell them, after —*"

She paused. She wanted to get it right.

> "*—and after, dear Lord, you descend in flight*
> *and take a soulless one away this night . . .*"

Charlotte remained stricken with insomnia throughout the storm, which began to let up around three or four a.m. She would have never known she had slept at all except for the fact that she had a dream shortly before she woke up. She was in the City of God, and it was unpleasant. Beyond that she couldn't retrieve a thing.

Daylight created a blazing frame around the shades—whereas she had prayed for, counted on, heavy gray skies . . . as a shield. She could hear children romping in the snow. She got out of bed and pulled the shade back. The snow was a blinding white sheet of light that ran into the woods. There were Buddy and Sam and little Mike Creesey from just down the road, him and Eli Mauck, all of them bundled up in puffy quilted jackets that made them look like four hand grenades, playing some sort of game that had them feinting this way and that on either side of a tarpaulin-covered hulk out back.

She wanted to stay in her bed forever; but with the sun up that high, it must be well into the morning, and the dread of Momma having to come back and pry her out of bed and thereby sense how depressed she was—that was even worse than her dread of facing the world. She forced herself to rise and get dressed . . . in the tapered jeans and cardigan sweater she had brought from home to Dupont and worn exactly once. She hadn't dared come home with the Diesels—on which she had blown twenty-five percent of her allowance for the semester. All were incriminating evidence . . . of her self-degradation. Her mind was racing again. Her head felt like the ashes from the coal grate.

She went into the kitchen and found Momma, who seemed to be puzzling over a recipe. Please, Momma, don't say a word. Just keep on doing what you're doing. You're not obliged to make any fuss over me whatsoever. Only a girl who has experienced it herself has any idea of how conversations *pain* girls who are depressed. She vowed to summon up the willpower to act like a normal girl home for Christmas—but could she even remember?

Momma looked up from her book and smiled ever so cheerily and said, "Well! She is arisen! Did you have a good sleep?"

"I did,"—*dee-ud*—said Charlotte, forcing a smile. "What time is it?"

"Oh . . . pert' near ten-thirty. You slept nine and a half hours. Do you feel better?"

"Sure do," said Charlotte. "I was so tired last night." She slipped a little bit of down-home *tarred* into the word and then figured she'd establish a hedge against whatever might be . . . crushing . . . later on. "I still feel sort of . . . like woozy. I don't know what the matter is. What are you fixing, Momma?"

"Remember once, when you were nine or ten—might a been your birthday—I been trying to recollect—and I fixed something I'd never fixed before—and you called it 'mystery,' and it was the first mixed vegetables you ever did like? You always wanted things plain—plain-long mashed potatoes, plain-long boiled snaps, and you hated things as had carrots in 'em, but you liked 'mystery'? Well, we haven't had mystery for a long time, but I thought we oughta have it tonight, you being home."

"Tonight?" Charlotte just said it as a response. Whether they would have mystery tonight or not was not something her mind could tarry on.

"I didn't tell you last night, you were so tired"—*tarred*—"but tonight—" Momma halted and broke out a big smile. "You notice something new in the living room last night? I don't think you did."

The conversation was already such a burden, so heavy, inexplicably heavy, such an *invasion* of her mind, but Charlotte soldiered on. "No, I don't think I did, either—oh, wait a minute. You mean the holly wreaths?"

"I reckon they are *new*," said Momma, "but I'm talking about something bigger'n holly wreaths." Big, beaming smile again. "Come on!" She headed toward the living room. Charlotte followed.

The light reflecting from the field of snow across County Road 1709 was dazzling. It lit up the living room brighter than Charlotte remembered ever seeing it. The very *air* in the room seemed to be lit. It was magical . . . but in a terrifying way to a depressed girl who sought refuge in light dimmed, in the snuffing out of the light—as they called it in Momma's Church of Christ's Evangel—the light at the apex of every human soul.

"You see it yet?" said Momma. "It's practically under your nose!"

Snapped back into the here and now, Charlotte concentrated on—what was practically under her nose . . . But of course! The chairs, eight of them, old bentwood like the ones they used to have at the little tables near the soda fountain in McColl's drugstore, with wooden seats and the simplest sort of bent rods of wood as the backs—all of them newly sanded, oiled, stained, and polished, by the looks of them, and drawn up close to the picnic table in neat ranks, so that the backs almost touched the white tablecloth.

"The chairs?" said Charlotte. "They really were here last night?" A wisp of memory of chairs from last night . . . during that terrible moment of tears and agony.

"The chairs and what else?" said Momma. "What do the chairs go with?"

Charlotte studied the chairs again. "The chairs are right up against the top of the picnic table? You took those big old benches off?"

"Look at it real close."

Charlotte lifted up the end of the white tablecloth—and there was no picnic table at all, but a real table. She looked at Momma in a wondering way. Momma's smile was as happy as a smile could be. Charlotte pulled the cloth back farther. It was a very plain old table, with no carved ornamentation and made of loblolly woods at best, the kind of table they used to refer to as a kitchen table. It must have actually been a worktable, because there was a line of drawers with metal pulls beneath the top on both sides. But like the chairs, it had been restored to within an inch of its never-elegant life, arduously waxed and polished until a certain luster had been coaxed out of its close, bland grain.

"Where'd it come from, Momma?"

"Over't the Paulsons' in Roaring Gap." She proceeded to recount, with considerable pride, how the Paulsons had wanted Daddy to take it to the dump, but he hauled it home and worked on that table for mighty near a week solid and took it all apart until the whole thing was in pieces and then put it back together until it was true and steady as a rock and got new pulls for the drawers—the ones on them when he got it were all rusty—and sanded and oiled and waxed and polished the whole thing until it was a new table.

"And don't tell him I told you, but you know why he did it? Because his little girl was coming home from college. He knew what you must've thought about eating on that picnic table. He wanted to surprise you. Your daddy dud'n say a lot, but he sees a *whole* lot."

"What happened to the picnic table?"

"It's out back where it ought to be. They're made for outdoors."

Whereupon Momma led her back to the kitchen door and pointed out the covered hulk out in the snow. Buddy was chasing Mike around it, and Sam and Eli were laughing at them. "It'll be real nice to have it out there in the spring."

As soon as they returned to the living room and Charlotte laid eyes on the "new" table again, she began weeping, without even realizing it was going to happen. She forced a smile through the flowing tears and threw her arms around Momma's neck and sobbed out, "Oh, Momma, Daddy's such a . . . good . . . person . . . and you're such a . . . good . . . person . . . and you all are . . . so . . . good to me . . . " She buried her face beneath Momma's chin.

Momma evidently didn't know what to say, because she just held her close for a bit. Finally she said, "There's nothing to cry about, my little girl. I think maybe *part* of you's still my little girl."

"A whole *lot* of me is, Momma. That's one thing I learned, and I had to go all the way to Pennsylvania to learn it." Pennsylvania. For some reason she didn't want to utter the name Dupont. "I don't care about everyone else. I just don't want to let *you* down."

"How could you let me down? I can't figure out what's going through your head, my good girl. Ever since you got off that bus last night, I've been wondering."

Well—would there ever be a better moment to tell her everything, to confess to everything and beg forgiveness? But what would *that* solve—forgiveness? Momma would never be able to call her "my good girl" again, never look at her as the same person again. Knowing it would mortify her, no matter how she found out, what were the proper words for the confession? Could she possibly look Momma in the face while she told her—and watch the face of her mother change before her very eyes as she realized what her good girl had become? But this was the moment—

—and how was she to seize it? "I'm fine, Momma." She gulped back some tears. "It's just this past week. If I didn't know better, I'd say it's been . . . awful, Momma. I've been under so much stress?" She regretted "stress." She knew Momma would spot it right away for the trendy term it was. What was stress, when you got right down to it, but just plain weakness when it came to doing the right thing? "We had tests all week—and I never got half the sleep I needed—I've been lonesome, Momma. I never thought I'd get lonesome. Miss Pennington was always telling me how independent I am and how unique and everything. I'm not unique, Momma. I get lonesome like anybody else. I had to go all the way to Pennsylvania to realize how many folks I've always had around me here at home, folks who will do about anything to help me."

Momma disengaged from the embrace, although she kept an arm around Charlotte's waist. She smiled and gestured toward the table Daddy built. "Then you're going to love tonight."

"Tonight?" A shadow passed over Charlotte's face, but Momma didn't notice that.

"Tonight we're going to get a chance to see just how good Daddy's table really is. I—we've invited some folks over for supper, folks I know you'll want to see—"

Horror at the thought: "You *have*?"

Momma didn't pick up the horror, merely the surprise. "Just a few special folks . . . Miss Pennington . . . Laurie . . . Mr. Thoms and Mrs. Thoms. They're all *dying* to hear about Dupont and all."

"*No, you can't, Momma!*" It just burst forth from her throat before she even considered how it might sound.

Momma looked at her, baffled.

"Not tonight, Momma! I just got home. I need a little time—" She couldn't dream up what for.

"But you *know* you like them all. I invited them *special*."

Charlotte realized that her reaction had revealed exactly what she wanted to hide. On the other hand, that didn't relieve the pain of such a prospect at all. With a manufactured calm she said, "I know, Momma, but you never *asked* me or anything."

"Well, darling, I'm real sorry. I was thinking it would be a nice surprise. Laurie? Miss Pennington? Mr. Thoms? You want to tell me why you're so upset?"

"I'm not upset, Momma. The only thing is . . . " She couldn't think up what the only thing was. She couldn't dream up a serviceable lie. It occurred to her that never before had she had to dream up lies in this house, other than little white lies. On the other hand, deep down she realized that lying was not foreign to her nature. Anyone—or certainly she—who has been praised so highly so regularly and for so long keeps within her the means of patching up punctures on the road. "I guess I was surprised, that's all."

She knew she didn't have it in her to ask Momma to call it off. But ohmygod, Laurie and Miss Pennington. She wasn't actress enough to fool them even if there were nothing serious to fool them about.

How could she possibly get through it? The machine was racing again, punched up to maximum power with the heat on HIGH. It didn't slow down even when it had stretches of nothing to do. It dug out and inflamed shortcomings that had been in a dormant state. At graduation Mr. Thoms had announced her as the winner of Alleghany High's prizes for French, English, and creative writing. At supper tonight there would be nothing to indicate to him that she had kept any special interest in these fields at Dupont. She knew there had always been a self-centered side of her character that showed itself publicly as thoughtlessness in her treatment of others.

After last night it was obvious that she should have brought Buddy and Sam some kind of souvenirs of Dupont for Christmas . . . T-shirts or, if they cost too much, photographs of Treyshawn Diggs and André Walker, any little thing—or for Momma and Daddy, for that matter, maybe Dupont coffee mugs or something . . . but had she? Ohhhh no; and there was no way to get them now. Instead, she'd have to get the boys the usual piece of junk from Kyte's . . . which always looked like it came from Kyte's.

Just give her time. There would be many more things she would root out to torture herself with. She was in that state.

All day she manufactured reasons why she shouldn't leave the house—the snow . . . town would be a mess (of people she didn't want to see . . . they would be ringing out like bells with questions about "Dupont") . . . on a day like this she should just do some reading to prepare for finals . . . *the finale* . . . She should be on hand in case the angel decided to come during the day . . . She puzzled over what *would* look like an accident . . . If she stumbled and fell before a car or, better, a big high pickup barreling along 1709, fell in such a way that the driver himself wouldn't even be able to tell that she "threw herself" in front of his vehicle . . . But nobody was barreling along 1709 today in a pickup truck or any other vehicle—1709 hadn't been plowed yet, and even the biggest pickups were just inching along like everybody else.

Fortunately, Momma was so busy getting ready for the supper—she insisted on calling it supper, because having four people over for "dinner" sounded suspiciously like a party—that she didn't pay all that much attention. When Charlotte told her she was studying for her final exams, it didn't seem odd. The truth was, Charlotte couldn't read in her present state. To a depressed girl, words on a page become irrelevant, impertinent, as do images on a screen. She had brought home a barely two-hundred-page book Mr. Starling had recommended, *The Social Brain*, by Michael Gazzaniga, who was famous for studies of patients in whose brains the neural pathways connecting the two halves of the brain, the corpus callosum, had been severed. A month ago she had found Gazzaniga's work fascinating.

Sitting on the "easy chair," she opened the book at random. "Why is it the more a human (brain) knows, the faster it works, while the more an artifact (computer) knows the slower it works?" The sentence did not connect with her mind. She would find no reason to answer the question. What on earth did it matter whether the brain worked faster than the computer, or vice versa? Who in God's name had the luxury of caring? How irrelevant it was! What did it have to do with her *getting fucked*—there! there you had it—*getting her pop-top popped*—by a known twisted serial sex offender, a callous frat boy who then broadcasts the delicious news to the entire Dupont University campus—*and it fucking freaked him out because she was a virgin!* In a delirium of juvenile boyfriend madness she had sacrificed everything—virginity, dignity, reputation, plus her ambitions, her mission, her promises and obligations to everyone who had stood by her, educated her, served as her mentor—and tonight she would have to look Miss Pennington in the eye.

She sought to slow down the passage of time by breaking the afternoon into half-hour segments. For the next half hour I have nothing to fear. No one will invade my life. I can do what I want, which is to lie back in this chair and do nothing, not even think. (Fat chance of that, of course. She knew the machine would not slow down for a moment, would not cool down even *this* much in the next half hour any more than it had in the last half hour.) I have the entire half hour, and after that, another one, but I'm not going to look ahead. Ahead, in due course, about four-thirty, the sun will go down, but I do not exist in the period from now to four-thirty. I live only in this half hour, which is entirely removed from the rest of time.

The boys—Buddy and Sam and their friends Mike Creesey, and Eli Mauck—came into the kitchen from outside, breathing hard, giggling, taunting each other—"Here's the way you throw!" Sounded like Buddy.

"Buddy—" That was Momma.

"You throw that way your ownself, Pants on Fire Girl!"

"Buddy! You boys take your boots off before you come in the house. Look at you!"

"Awww . . . "

Buddy, Sam, Mike Creesey, Eli Mauck . . . the machine was racing so fast . . . racing so fast so fast so fast . . .

How could it be? The half-hour segment was already over, used, spent fruitlessly—and she was ten minutes into the next! There weren't many left. By five o'clock, there might as well have been none. The guests were invited for "supper" at six, and in Alleghany County, people were on time.

Ordinary vanity disappears when a girl is depressed. In fact, for most girls, that is the only time after they reach puberty that that particular unnatural state is ever encountered—i.e., when they are severely depressed.

The depressed girl wants only to disappear. The notion of "looking her best"—she doesn't *deserve* to look her best. Looking her best is a mockery of what she really is. She put on the same old print dress she graduated in (and first went to the Saint Ray house in!), taking the precaution of letting the hem out, which brought it down practically to her knees.

Momma called out from the kitchen, "Charlotte! You about ready?"

"Yes, Momma!" It irritated Charlotte to have to report in for duty like that. For someone who didn't give parties—merely had folks over for supper—Momma was awfully nervous. The rich smell of roast turkey was in the air . . . and mashed sweet potatoes whipped up with mashed carrots, plus white raisins, if Charlotte wasn't mistaken—the wonderful "mystery" that had been the delight of her childhood—and the sharp odor of the vinegar that would be poured over chopped onions to put on the boiled snap beans . . . The smells brought back all the wonderful Thanksgivings and Christmases of her childhood, those moments of special excitement— which she now experienced all over again with the poisonous residue of nostalgia. How much more completely delusional could those peaks of childish well-being have been? What warning did the little genius have that her first stop beyond the olfactory heaven that Momma created would lead in a few frantic blinks straight to sheer rot, sheer animal rutting, to spiritual as well as physical debauchery, to the present moment, when she dared not show her shamed face to the world, not even to lifelong friends—especially to lifelong friends?

Momma said, "Now, Charlotte, I'm counting on you to remind me that Mr. Thoms's wife is named Sarah, not Susan. I'm always about to call her Susan. Don't see her very often."

Momma was smiling, but Charlotte could see that she was nervous. She was insecure about having the Thomses over. There were no what you might call social classes in Alleghany County; there were just respectable people and people who weren't respectable. Respectable people were churchgoing, devout, took education seriously even if they weren't well educated themselves, didn't go out drinking where people could see them drinking, were hardworking—assuming they could find work within a fifty-mile radius of Sparta—and were neighborly in a good old country way.

Nevertheless, within the ranks of the respectable, there were different levels of status, and wealth and position did not go unnoticed. Mr. Thoms had no wealth, or none that anybody knew of, but he had position. He was a good-natured man who always acted like Just Folks, and he had taken a real interest in Charlotte; but his wife, Sarah not Susan, was something of an unknown quantity. Neither was from hereabouts, but Mr. Thoms was from Charleston, West Virginia, and he fit right in. Both were college graduates with M.A. degrees. Mrs. Thoms was hired right away, as soon as Martin Marietta opened their plant. She was from Ohio or Illinois or one of those states and was considered a bit standoffish, or reserved, depending on how much it mattered to you. Charlotte would have bet anything that Mrs. Thoms's presence was what Momma was nervous about.

Headlight beams swept over the two front windows and then slid to the side as a car pulled into the driveway.

"Somebody's here," Momma sang out cheerily . . . and began looking about the room as if giving it one last inspection. Cheerily, yes, but it wasn't like Momma to simply say the obvious. Charlotte took it as another sign that Momma was nervous. But what was *nervous* compared to *petrified, doomed*? Who would it be? Please God, don't let it be Laurie and Miss Pennington! Laurie was supposed to pick up Miss Pennington and drive her over. Let it be Mr. and Mrs. Thoms! They know less! Please, God, just one more segment, I beg of you, just fifteen minutes! Fifteen minutes with only the Thomses to deal with! I beseech thee—for so little, for only fifteen minutes with those who are only mildly threatening, which is to say, ever-so-slightly more innocuous! Is that too much to ask?

Presently, a rap on the front door, where Daddy had rigged up a home-made knocker. Charlotte's heart was kicking up again, beating far too fast. Daddy opened the door—

—the beaming face of Mr. Thoms (the way he smiled at her at graduation as she mounted the stage!). As he shook hands with Daddy, you could see the plaid liner of his raincoat, his navy blazer and necktie, his dark wool pants—the thought flashed through Charlotte's mind: how unusual wool pants were—you could go for weeks at Dupont without laying eyes on a pair—and he backed up against the doorway to usher his wife in—very pretty she was, a brunette, beautiful in a way, a strong but perfectly formed nose, lips that seemed to be curved into a continual flirtatious smile, drowsy eyes, rather heavily made up for Sparta, but she had a chilly look about her, a lean, grim set to her jaws and the faint vertical line of an ever-incipient frown in her forehead. Her clothes were not at all unusual or fashionable, a plain slate-blue dress and a magenta cardigan sweater with a somewhat prissy line of pearl buttons down the front. Momma was greeting the Thomses with great animation.

"Well, hel-lo, Sarah!" she sang out. She obviously had been fixing that Sarah into her memory . . . to last.

Mrs. Thoms took a deep breath and quickly scanned the room. Charlotte was sure the funk of coal and gas fumes had shocked her and made her look about the poor little room in a judgmental fashion.

Charlotte had instinctively hung back. So Momma introduced Mrs. Thoms to Buddy and Sam first. The boys shook her hand and said "Yes, ma'am" to whatever it was she had asked them. Meantime, Momma was busy making a fuss over Mr. Thoms, who was too polite to take a deep breath and investigate the premises, even though he had never been here before, either.

"Oh, Land o' Goshen, Mr. Thoms, you're so nice to *come!*" She called him, whom she knew fairly well, Mr. Thoms, and her, whom she barely knew at all, Sarah. Charlotte started to try to figure that out—but for what earthly reason did it matter? All that mattered was—when would they leave?

Mrs. Thoms approached by herself. "Charlotte," she said, "I don't think I've seen you since graduation last spring. I never did get a chance to tell you what a wonderful speech you gave."

Charlotte could feel herself blushing. It wasn't from modesty in the face of praise. "Thank you, ma'am," said Charlotte. Then she tensed and blushed, expecting the next words out of her mouth to be about Dupont.

"Right after your speech, I told Zach"—it seemed so strange, this Zach— Charlotte had a recollection that Mr. Thoms's full name was Zachary M. Thoms, but it had never occurred to her that there might be people who called him Zach—"he ought to have a public speaking program at the high school. I think every student ought to be able to do what you did—maybe not as well, but they ought to not be *afraid* to. You didn't even look at a note."

Charlotte felt herself turning crimson all over again, not so much because of Modesty's proper embarrassment as because she couldn't think of any appropriate reply. Should she say thank you again? Somehow it didn't fit. She just wanted this whole evening to be over.

Seeing Charlotte stuck, Mrs. Thoms filled the conversation vacuum. "Oh, I wanted to ask you, Charlotte. My brother married a girl from Suffield, Connecticut, and one of *her* sister's daughter's best friends—she met her when they both went to Saint Paul's School in New Hampshire— you know Saint Paul's?"

Charlotte hadn't followed any of this genealogical excursion, but she did get the part about Saint Paul's, and she said, "Yes, ma'am."

"Well, her friend goes to Dupont—I think she wanted to go to Dupont, too, but she ended up at Brown. I shouldn't say 'ended up,' I guess—she's a senior now, and she can't say enough good things about Brown. Anyway, her friend is a senior at Dupont—"

This conversation, innocuous though it was, was already weighing down on Charlotte, already an immensely heavy burden for a depressed girl. The last thing in the world she wanted to chitchat about was somebody's daughter at Brown's former friend at Saint Paul's who is now a senior at Dupont.

"—and she—I'm talking about my brother's wife's . . . sister's . . . daughter's friend"—she started laughing at herself—"What does that make her? If my brother's wife is my sister-in-law, then what does that make *her* sister—*also* my sister-in-law?—or my sister-in-law once removed—" She laughed again. "I think I've been in the South too long! I can't believe I actually said that, 'brother's wife's sister's daughter's friend'—anyway, she's a senior at Dupont and she says she knows you."

"Knows *me*?" Charlotte was startled—frightened. Her amygdala had removed the safety and was primed in the fight-or-flight mode.

"That's what she said. The girl's name is Lucy Page Tucker."

The blood began draining from Charlotte's face. She stared at Mrs. Thoms with a ferocious intensity, looking for . . . even the slightest tip-off to—

"You know her?" said Mrs. Thoms.

"No! Not at all . . . " Charlotte realized that her voice was weak and shaky and terribly wary, but she had no control over it. "I mean, I think I like . . . know who she is. But I've never met her? Golly, I don't think I'd know her if I saw her. And she says she *knows* me?"

I'm being too defensive! she thought. Now she'll know she's onto something! Charlotte's brain was boiling, and the steam rose.

"That's what my sister-in-law said. I just talked to her this afternoon. I got the impression that you and this girl were in the same crowd."

Now Mrs. Thoms seemed to be studying *her* face for . . . any little giveaway. Charlotte knew she should be . . . cool . . . but it wasn't in her.

"Oh, not at all!" she said. "I mean, I think she's like . . . president of a *sorority* or something! I don't even have any crowd. I'm just a freshman. I'm not even—" She didn't try to complete the sentence. She shrugged.

"Well," said Mrs. Thoms with a cheery smile, "maybe she's considering you as a candidate!"

Was that smile fake . . . ironic? How much did she know? All of it? Gloria talking to Lucy Page at Mr. Rayon . . . the lioness . . . She wouldn't forget that big face and its mane of blond hair in a thousand years.

"Oh, she wouldn't be considering *me*. I'm just—I mean, nobody's ever even *heard* of Sparta or Alleghany County or the Blue Ridge Mountains, most of them. They went to private schools? I mean, like . . . we're completely different? I'd *never* join a sorority. I mean, I might as well like . . . join the . . . uh . . . uh . . . Afghanistan *army* or something—"

Mrs. Thoms laughed at that, but Charlotte didn't even have it in her to laugh along with her. She hadn't even meant it as funny. *Nothing* is funny to a depressed girl. She had to spit *all* of it out.

Even as she did so, Charlotte was aware that she was out of control, and she only hoped that all the question marks in her declarations had neutralized their—desperation. How much Mrs. Thoms knew, which also meant how much Mr. Thoms knew—boiling, boiling, boiling, boiling, Charlotte scanned Mrs. Thoms's face square millimeter by square millimeter—

A drop in the noise level of the little room as the front door opened—

"Why, Miz Simmons"—gasp—"land's sakes, it's just real nice"—gasp—"to see you!"

The unmistakable good-hearted contralto of Miss Pennington. She and Momma had always remained Miss Pennington and Mrs. Simmons to each other, and more than once Charlotte had wondered if it was because of her. Charlotte could hardly believe it, but Miss Pennington went up and gave Momma a hug, and Momma hugged her, too. Charlotte knew intellectually that the very sight should fill her with happiness. The two most important women in her life had closed whatever gap there was between them—but ohmygod, think of the peril! What one knew, the other would know, too! And what Mrs. Thoms knew—they would soon know, too!

Behind Miss Pennington came Laurie. She immediately frightened Charlotte—because she looked so radiant—actually radiant it was, her complexion; actually winning it was, her smile; actually contagious, they were, her high spirits—Laurie lit up the room.

"Mrs. Simmons!" she said. "It's been a month of Sundays!" Whereupon she gave Momma a big hug.

"Merry Christmas!" The jolly contralto of Miss Pennington as she shook Daddy's hand and then put her other hand on top of Daddy's hand, creating an affectionate sandwich.

Daddy was beaming over such a merry and sincere expression of fondness, and his eyes followed her as she embraced Mr. Thoms and then made a fuss over Buddy and Sam.

The boys had been smiling and dancing a little jig ever since she and Laurie came through the door.

"This is for you and the family!" said Laurie, hoisting her other hand, two fingers of which were looped through the neck handle of a half-gallon plastic jug of apple cider, non-fermented, one could be sure. There was a green-and-red plaid Christmas ribbon about the neck. "This is from Miss Pennington, too. Merry Christmas!"

Momma took the jug in both hands. "Well, I'll be switched," she said. "You all surely did bring this to the right house. Buddy and Sam are sort of partial to apple cider themselves!"

She looked at them. Buddy put on a comic grin, and Sam copied him, and everybody laughed.

"What do you say, boys? 'Thank you, Miss Pennington, thank you, Laurie! And Merry Christmas to *you!*'"

Charlotte stood where she was, next to Mrs. Thoms. She was fully aware of what a marvelous Christmas moment this should have been . . . the family assembled round the potbellied stove . . . dear friends arriving on a snowy night bearing gifts . . . cheeriness so rich and thick you could cut it like fruitcake . . . Laurie looking absolutely glorious, a girl in the prime of youthful joy, generosity, and love for the folks around her . . . and Charlotte Simmons, on her first trip home from the field of triumph—*she goes to Dupont*—in a state of panic over what somebody right here in the room knows. She *wanted* to rush forward and hug her beloved mentor, who had plucked her out of obscurity in the Lost Province and sent her off to the great world arena "where things happen." She wanted to shriek "Laurie!" in unrestrained, girlish camaraderie upon seeing her best friend from high school—the one constant when she took her stand against Channing and Regina and all the rest of the Cool clique—and rush toward her and embrace her with the sheer uplifting joy that gladdens the heart of every grown-up looking on, because she knows she's witnessing a bond of sisterhood that will last a lifetime, regardless of their fates in terms of wealth, the status of their husbands, or anything else. But Charlotte could barely force herself to put a civil smile on her face, and a rush toward anyone was out of the question.

Charlotte could see Momma coming about. "Where's Charlotte?" she said. "Charlotte! Look who's here! Oh, there you are! I can't see for looking!"

From the expression on Momma's face you could tell that she was just waiting for her daughter to come forward, rush headlong, and put on the show of affection the moment demanded. And so was everybody else. Charlotte made the gravest smile one could imagine—and she knew it—and could do nothing about it—and moved forward, away from Mrs. Thoms, ever so slowly. She wanted to move faster . . . *con brio* . . . but she couldn't command her legs to do it. She could feel her smile growing steadily more feeble by the moment.

In the few seconds it took her to reach Miss Pennington, *something* must have happened to her poor feeble face, because she saw Miss Pennington's big Christmas smile grow puzzled. She threw her arms around the big woman's neck and said, "Oh, Miss Pennington, Merry Christmas." The words were right, but the music was off, the notes, flattened by panic and something more, which was guilt.

Miss Pennington must have detected something herself, because this wasn't the kind of homecoming embrace in which both parties rock this way and that before finally stepping back to make a beaming appraisal of one another. No, they parted pretty quickly, and Miss Pennington sounded as if she were speaking in some official capacity as she said, "Well, Merry Christmas to you, Charlotte. When did you arrive?"

Charlotte told her when she arrived and what a time they'd had driving up the mountain in the snowstorm. What on earth had the woman seen in her face? Then she turned to Laurie and tried hard to do better. "Laurie!"— and she held out her open arms.

"Why, it's the Dupont girl!" said Laurie.

They hugged each other and even put their cheeks next to one another's; but as hugs go, it felt like sheer protocol. Whatever it was about her expression—her manner—

"Merry Christmas, Mr. Thoms! Mrs. Thoms!" Laurie had already turned to the Thomses. Her ebullience had immediately returned. Her cheeks were rosy. Her smile was sunshine itself. Youth! Joy! Hope! Rude animal health! Beauty! Laurie wasn't *really* beautiful, but her radiance made up for any flaw. What did it matter, the faintly puffy quality of the end of her nose? She was the girl—the confident, warm-spirited, buoyant, loving young woman— any parents would love to see coming home from college. Charlotte didn't envy her, however, because envy was irrelevant. Envy was a luxury of those who still had hopes for the future. No, Laurie merely made Charlotte pity herself all the more. She forced her to see in the most graphic way all the qualities Charlotte Simmons no longer possessed. She no longer had the strength to pretend, either. Anything anybody said, any look anybody gave her—for that matter, the mere presence of anybody in this room—bore down on her with an abominable weight and made her anxious to be somewhere else. The entire planet now orbited menacingly around her deep worries. All else was irrelevant.

Momma wasn't the sort who was given to having people stand around talking and drinking refreshments—not even unfermented cider or lemonade or branch water—before sitting down to have supper. Charlotte decided she was just going to have to find the strength to get through it. There would be some pretty good talkers at the table, Momma, Miss Pennington, Mr. Thoms, and, as she now realized, Laurie (who had gotten *fucked*, same way she had) and Mrs. Thoms wouldn't be bad at it, if she had to guess. That left only her and Daddy. So she would just let all the talkers talk and talk and talk, and she would get through it by forcing a smile and nodding a lot, and if anybody asked her about something at Dupont, she would just turn it over to Laurie and ask her how that thing is at N.C. State.

She was stunned when Daddy—*Daddy*—said, "Charlotte, we're gonna put you right"—*riot*—"here at the head a the table, so's you can tell everybody"—*everbuddy*—"about Dupont. Everybody's gonna be real interested"—*innerested*. He looked about at the Thomses, Miss Pennington. "Isn't that right?" *In'at riot?*

Murmurs, burbles of confirmation, and Laurie's "Like totally!"

Charlotte experienced a pain that wasn't physical but might as well have been. A great pressure squeezed her head from either side and bore down on the top of her skull. There was no worse fate than the sentence Daddy had just meted out. In the same instant it struck her just how countrified Daddy's speech really was, Momma's, too—and just how collegiate Laurie's had become: Laurie's with all the *like totallys* and *cools* and *awesomes* and *ohmygods*.

Charlotte blurted out, "No, Daddy!" She knew she should demur in a calm, somewhat light way, but she was long past wily levity. She was in pain. "Nobody wants to hear me go on about—school!" *School.* She avoided the name Dupont at all cost; too painful. "Laurie—please!—you sit here. I want to hear about N.C. State!"

Friendly protests all around, as if her reluctance was mere modesty. So she found herself sitting at the table on one of the drugstore bentwood chairs Daddy had brought back to life. The inquisitors stared at her down both sides of the table. On one side were Mr. Thoms, sitting closest to her, Laurie, and Momma—or rather, that's where Momma would be sitting—right now she was in the kitchen—and on the other side were Miss Pennington, sitting closest, Mrs. Thoms, and Daddy. *Mrs. Thoms!*—she was Death, sitting there with a hypocritical smile on her face, waiting for the perfect moment in which to cut her down. And Miss Pennington, barely twenty-four inches away from her—Miss Pennington was . . . the Betrayed . . . a pending broken heart as big as the moon . . . in a word, guilt. The rest were merely eyewitnesses to the self-destruction of Charlotte Simmons. Merely? Two of them were Momma and Daddy, still ignorant of the truth, whom she had made the proudest parents in Alleghany County . . . before her hollow, sham character revealed itself . . . One was Mr. Thoms, the elder who had officially and sonorously proclaimed her to all of Alleghany County as *the young woman who* . . . and the other was the young woman who . . . had scarcely been noticed because Charlotte Simmons's eminence had cast such a long, deep shadow—Laurie, the runner-up who had proved to be everything the illustrious Presidential Scholar wasn't. She had taken her inevitable *fucking* and come back from it as a whole person who was a delight to have around, a young woman who . . . was ready to head forth, promising as the dawn, into a limitless future.

Thank God, Momma arrived in no time, bearing a tray with the aroma of a freshly roasted turkey, which she set before Daddy along with an old carving knife and fork and a sharpener. The aroma! A single look at the crisp but still moist skin covering the bird's mighty breast, and even a person who had never seen such a thing before would know that here was perfection. Then came Daddy's part, thank God, providing a further reprieve. Daddy stood up and started sharpening the knife on an old-fashioned sharpening rod. It made a rasping sound that brought Buddy and Sam right out of the kitchen to catch the show that Daddy was so very deft, so precise at, the way he first cut the skin that held the thighs and drumsticks tight against the carcass and then found precisely the crucial point where the thighbone joined the hip. He severed the joint with a single, seemingly silken strike, causing the thigh to fall away cleanly, and then he began carving the breast into slices as big and intact and yet as thin and even as you could possibly ask for. The boys were agog at the craftsmanship of it and couldn't wait for the part where Daddy started on the other side of the breast, because he would always sharpen the knife on the rod again, and they loved to hear the rasping sound and see the way Daddy flourished the sharpening rod and the knife like a performer. Laurie said, "Bravo, Mr. Simmons!" and the others oohed and laughed and clapped, which made Daddy smile. Meantime, Momma brought out the "mystery," which had a sweet, exotic aroma, and the boiled snap beans, which didn't have much of an odor themselves, but the diced onions in vinegar that went over the snaps had a smell that was sharp and sweet at the same time, and then came the cranberry jelly that Momma made herself and the pickled peaches she always pickled herself late in the summer—and the aroma of the peaches was sublime, and their taste was "ambrosial," which was a word Momma loved—and everybody was making a big fuss over Momma and her cooking.

No sooner had the applause for Momma as chef crested than Mrs. Thoms turned to Charlotte and said, "Charlotte, how is the cuisine at Dupont compared to *this*?"

Charlotte said, "It's—it's—" She was trying to think of the right word, *le mot juste*, but it wasn't that at all. It was the pain it caused her to have to enter the conversation, to have to emerge from the shell she thought she had begun to create about herself. The words she sought were whatever would answer the question and shut it down and not suggest any follow-up. "It's— there's no comparison. Nothing compares to Momma's cooking." She smiled to try to show that she was keeping things light—and she herself could tell that somehow the smile flopped about, disconnected from lightheartedness or amusement.

Mrs. Thoms was not to be put off, however. "Oh, I can understand that. I'm sure nothing actually does compare to home cooking, not when it's *this* good. I guess what I mean is, how would you rate the food in general at Dupont?"

"It's not bad."

Silence. Her response, or lack of one, had created an awkward silence.

"Just not bad?" said Mrs. Thoms, soldiering on.

Charlotte thought and thought, mainly about how toilsome it was to have to talk . . . to anybody about anything, especially anything to do with Dupont. Aloud she managed to say, "More or less."

"More or less?" said Mrs. Thoms.

Silence. It was so bad that Charlotte realized she had to force herself to do something . . . anything. She finally managed to say, "I eat all my meals at the Abbey—the dining hall."

She didn't want to mention even the name of a building at Dupont. Everyone at the table wore a look that said, "And therefore?"

It was torture, this being forced to talk. "I mean, it's mostly the same."

Everyone looked baffled. With an agonized frown she said, "What about you, Laurie?"

"What about me what?" said Laurie.

"I don't know . . . Do you eat all your meals in the same place?—I guess."

Laurie gave her an ironic cross-eyed look of the sort that asks, "Are you trying to mess up my mind—or wot?" She drew a blank from Charlotte's face. After a dreadful pause Laurie said, "Well, our dorm has its own cafeteria, but there are a lot of restaurants."

"There must be a lot of restaurants around Dupont, too," said Mrs. Thoms, looking at Charlotte.

"There are," said Charlotte—it was so painful, forcing the words out—"but they aren't included in my meal plan, not even the one in the middle of campus. I always eat in the dining hall." *Please!* I don't *want* to talk about Dupont!

Mrs. Thoms looked across the table at Laurie, Momma, and Mr. Thoms, and said, "Now, I think Charlotte's getting around a lot more than she lets on. A sister of a sister-in-law of mine has a daughter who has a friend who goes to Dupont, a senior—as a matter of fact she's the president of one of the big sororities—and *she* knows who Charlotte is. In fact she seems to know a lot more about Charlotte than Charlotte knows about her, and Charlotte's a freshman."

Charlotte saw Momma break into a smile, no doubt because this meant that her little genius had already established a presence on campus. A presence, all right—Mrs. Thoms was looking at her and smiling, too—but could it be with some sort of twisted Sarc 3 cruelty? Could it be that . . . *Death* was speaking? This woman was now going to tell it all . . . for the perverse joy of watching the insect squirm!

The reply came from the mouth of a panicked girl. "I don't see how! I mean, I've never even met her. I've heard of her—she's the president of her sorority and everything, but I don't *know* her. I wouldn't know her if she came walking in that door. There's just no reason in the world why she would even know my name! I don't have anything to do with her or any friends of hers or the kind of people who would—"

She stopped. Too late, she realized they were all looking at her in a funny way. Now they would all think there was . . . definitely something going on here, wouldn't they? She had to say something that showed that this wasn't important and didn't disturb her. "She must have me mixed up with somebody else."

Of course that didn't help at all. Mrs. Thoms said with a chuckle, "Well, is there somebody else from Sparta, North Carolina, who's a freshman at Dupont?"

Charlotte was speechless . . . and in greater panic. Why would Lucy Page ever mention Sparta? Because *they* had told her about this naïve hick freshman who kept snapping at people with her "Sparta—you never heard of it" put-down. And why would Mrs. Thoms say that? Because she knew the whole story and was set to torture her with it, drop by drop—in front of her family.

Charlotte looked at Mrs. Thoms in sheer fear. Consciously she realized that she should hate this woman who had come into her home for the perverse pleasure of humiliating her in front of her parents and her two little brothers, who were probably listening in from the kitchen. But Charlotte Simmons no longer had any right to take the moral high ground. She was too worthless to pass judgment on another person, no matter what she was doing.

The silence lengthened in a baffling way that made everybody at the table, the panicked one was sure, realize that they had all at once been confronted with some unspeakable state of affairs.

"I just don't know," Charlotte said finally. But why had she said it in such a timid little voice? So she added a smile—which made things still worse! What had she done but call yet more attention to her guilt?

She slogged on. Everybody was dying to hear all about the fabled Dupont, which to them obviously was Olympus, Parnassus, Shangri-la, and the peaks of Darién all rolled into one. What were the teachers like? "They're fine," said Charlotte. She wanted to leave it at that, but she saw six people staring at her with shortchanged looks on their faces. So she added, " . . . except for the T.A.s." She immediately regretted the emendation. Who were they? What was wrong with them? "They're graduate students. There's nothing wrong with them. They just don't know very much about the subjects." Surely—there must be some brilliant teachers there? "There are," said Charlotte, and that was the end of that. How did she find living in a coed dorm? "You sort of get used to it—" And that was the end of that. And the girls shared bathrooms with the boys? "You just sort of deal with it the best you can." And that was the end of that—in her mind—but the grown-ups wouldn't let it alone. Wasn't it embarrassing sometimes? "Not a whole lot, as long as you keep your eyes on the tiles in the floor and the enamel in the basin and don't look in the mirror and don't listen to anything"—and that was as much as she cared to say about that. Did she see much of the athletes on campus? "No." And that was that, except Momma reminded her that she had told Buddy and Sam that she knew a basketball star. "That's true, I do know one, but I wouldn't call him a star." She left it at that—but who is he? What's his name? "He's called Jojo Johanssen." What was he like? "He's nice." That was all, nice? "Well . . . he's about as bright as the bottom of an old skillet." She declined to elaborate. What was her roommate like? "She's all right." Just all right? "I hardly ever see her. We have different schedules." Daddy put on a big grin and said that Buddy wanted to know if she had a boyfriend, but he never did hear the answer. Polite chuckling all around the table.

"Charlotte!" Laurie piped up. "Spill it!"

Bitterly, Charlotte saw Hoyt in her mind's eye, then said, "No, I don't."

She said it deadpan, without humor, without regret, as if she'd been asked whether she had an electric blender in her room. Momma wanted to know where students went on dates. "Nobody goes out on a date, Momma. The girls go out in groups, and the boys go out in groups, and they hope they find somebody they like."

Momma seemed appalled and wanted to know if Charlotte did that. "I did one time—I went out with some of my friends? But it was so stupid, I never did it again."

Mrs. Thoms wanted to know what she did instead. By now she was feeling so despondent, so unworthy of human company, she said, "Nothing. I don't go out. I'd rather read a book." Saturday night—on the weekend—she didn't go out at all? "No, I never go out." Same disengaged poker face. Unconsciously she was beginning to enjoy misery and misanthropy, just the way you'd hear people in Alleghany County say, "Cousin Peggy? She's enjoying poor health."

Had she been going to the football and basketball games? Dupont was having a great year in sports. "I can't go, because they charge too much money for the tickets? But I wouldn't go if they gave them away, I don't reckon. I don't know why anybody gets excited. It's got nothing to do with them—and it's got nothing to do with me? It's stupid, is what it is."

What *did* she do for amusement? "Amusement? I guess I—I go jogging or I go to the gym and work out." For amusement? "Well . . . to me it's more amusing than all the stupid things other students do. They all act like they're in the seventh grade or something, and all that matters is —" She broke the sentence off. She had been about to mention drinking, but she didn't want to make Momma go ballistic. "Going around acting like idiots."

Miss Pennington seemed concerned. "Now, Charlotte, surely . . . the academic side of things must be exciting." She said it in the tones of an entreaty. She was all but begging for it to be so.

Charlotte suddenly felt guilty for letting Misery out for a romp. "That's true, Miss Pennington. I have one class—" She started to talk about Mr. Starling's, but she decided that she shouldn't call attention to him in view of the catastrophic grade Momma and Daddy and, ultimately, Miss Pennington would soon lay eyes on. *I have one class* remained suspended in the air.

"A class in what?" Miss Pennington stared at her, still in an attitude of supplication.

"Neuroscience," said Charlotte. Awkward silence—it was such . . . *agony* . . . making conversation. "I never thought it could be so interesting." She realized that her face must not have looked as if she was interested in *any*thing. Another awkward silence. "My teacher, Mr. Starling, says the year 1000 was just forty sets of parents ago. He always puts it that way."

Mrs. Thoms said, "Starling . . . Isn't he the one who won a Nobel Prize?"

"I don't know," said Charlotte.

"I didn't mean to interrupt," said Mrs. Thoms. "You were saying, 'just forty sets of parents ago'?"

"That was what *he* said. Mr. Starling." With that, Charlotte dropped the subject. She no longer wanted to talk about the "sets." Her voice would sound as if every set weighed a ton and she was lugging them out one by one.

Silence. Ten or fifteen seconds of it seemed like an eternity.

Mrs. Thoms plunged into the vacuum. "But I'm curious. Why did he say that?"

"I don't really know," said Utter Loganimity on a monument, smiling at Grief.

Silence; a gruesome silence this time. But guilt intervened. Guilt wouldn't allow her to remain *that* dead. "I'm guessing, but maybe he meant the year 1000 isn't all that long ago, but the way human beings look at themselves—in the West, anyway—has totally changed?" Not only Miss Pennington but also Momma seemed preternaturally attentive to this revelation. Then it dawned . . . for the first time all evening, they were getting a little of the Great Dupont from her, something deep. Charlotte became hyperaware of all sounds in the here and now, the muffled, low-crunching combustion of the potbellied stove . . . Daddy chewing—he didn't always keep his mouth closed . . . Buddy trying to order Sam around in the kitchen in a low voice, because if Momma heard it she'd set him straight and mean it . . . *fwop fwop fwop fwop* a car with a flat tire gimping along outside on 1709 . . . a chunk of snow sliding off the roof . . .

Mr. Thoms said there was certainly a lot written about multiculturalism and diversity in colleges these days. How did they manifest themselves in everyday life at Dupont?

"I don't know," said Charlotte. "I just hear about them in speeches and things."

Laurie piped up again. "At State, everybody calls diversity *dispersity*. What happens is, everybody has their own clubs, their own signs, their own sections where they all sit in the dining hall—all the African Americans are over there? . . . and all the Asians sit over't these other tables?—except for the Koreans?—because they don't get along with the Japanese, so they sit way over *there*? Everybody's dispersed into their own little groups—and everybody's told to distrust everybody else? Everybody's told that everybody else is trying to screw them over—*oops!*"—Laurie pulled a face and put her fingertips over her lips—"I'm sorry!" She rolled eyes and smiled. "Anyway, the idea is, every other group is like prejudiced against your group, and no matter what they say, they're only out to take advantage of you, and you should have nothing to do with them—unless you're white, in which case all the others are not prejudiced against you, they're like totally right, because you really *are* racist and everything, even if you don't know it? Everybody ends up dispersed into their own like turtle shells, suspicious of everybody else and being careful not to fraternize with them. Is it like that at Dupont?"

Laurie was looking at Charlotte. They *all* looked at Charlotte. Charlotte drew her breath in through her teeth with a sharp sigh, focused her eyes at Nowhere in the distance, as if contemplating the question, and then began nodding yes with a pensive frown. She was contemplating all right, but not Laurie's question on her "dispersity" theory. No, she was thinking of the gusto with which Laurie delivered it, her high spirits concerning the human comedy that was college life, her youthful joy in adventure, her eagerness to impart what she was learning in the great outside world. In short, she had all the qualities they had hoped to see in Charlotte Simmons—the dour little taciturn mope now sitting at the head of the table.

She didn't envy Laurie. Not at all; from the very beginning, she had hoped Laurie would assume the role she had been designated to play. All this . . . talk . . . was so painful. Laurie's wonderful spirit—venturing forth and exploring the world—made Charlotte realize that she herself had become worthless. Her sitting here at the head of the table was a dreadful fraud. Although Momma's, Daddy's, Miss Pennington's, Mr. Thoms's, and Laurie's intentions were only the best, every question they asked her about her college "experience" was de facto mockery. Part of Charlotte wanted to spring it all—*now*. Get it over with! Go ahead, show all that was left of Charlotte Simmons's world, which was the handful of souls at this table, how completely she had corrupted herself in a mere four months. She had no ill feelings toward Mrs. Thoms. You have to think yourself worth saving before you get angry at someone who wishes to kill you. She felt like leaning back in this poor drugstore chair, rocking back on its two rear legs, spreading her arms like Christ's on the cross, looking straight at Mrs. Thoms, and saying, "Come, Death, take me. I have no desire to struggle any longer. Save me the trouble of doing it myself." Being so young, she had never thought of what Death would look like. It had never occurred to her that Death might be a woman. Now, after eighteen years, the day had come, and Death was a pretty, fortyish brunette with provocative lips, posing as the wife of a country school principal. She stared at Mrs. Thoms, and Death stared at her, pretending to be puzzled.

Laurie was holding forth—very amusingly, too—about how at State, girls never used words of more than three syllables when boys were around. "You'd never talk about dressing appropriately because 'appropriately' has five syllables. Instead, you'd say, 'dressing the way you ought to,' or 'dressing the way people expect you to.' You'd never say 'conversationally,' because that has six syllables. It's not that a boy won't understand a five-syllable word, it's that it makes a girl sound too—oh, efficient, I guess—or too bright, as if she might be able to take care of herself. She won't seem vulnerable enough. She won't seem like she needs *the big brave man* enough." And Laurie was having such a good time! A delightful smile played about the corners of her lips every time she opened her mouth.

Before dessert, Laurie and Mrs. Thoms got up to help Momma take the dishes off the table. Miss Pennington started to get up, too, but Momma said, "No, Miss Pennington, don't you move. Many hands make light work, but we've got too many hands already. Kitchen's not big enough." Miss Pennington didn't protest very hard.

Mr. Thoms was busy talking to Daddy about something. Miss Pennington said to Charlotte in the sincerest of voices, "It's just so good to see you, Charlotte. I've thought about you a thousand times since you left. I've had so many things I was dying to ask you."

"It's so good to see *you*, Miss Pennington," said Charlotte. She tried to smile but wasn't a good enough actress, and that was that. She just stared at her old mentor and idly took note of the reticulated veins in her face.

"You're awful quiet this evening, Charlotte." Miss Pennington cocked her head slightly and smiled in the all-knowing way she had. "In fact, I can't figure out if you're here in this room or someplace else."

"I know," Charlotte said. She sighed, and as she let her breath out, she felt as if her whole bone structure were collapsing. "But it's not that, Miss Pennington. I just feel so tired." She slipped a little *tarred* into the pronunciation, and only afterward did she consciously face the fact that she was talking Down Home solely to solicit pity as a little country girl. "I had so much to do last week—we had a test in neuroscience that was worse than a final exam. I didn't hardly get any sleep all week." The implicit double negative was on purpose, too.

"I see," said Miss Pennington in a tone that indicated she didn't see at all.

The strategist in Charlotte figured this was the moment to start laying out some excuses to cushion the blow that was coming. "It was terrible, Miss Pennington. I found out at the last minute that a whole topic I thought wasn't going to be on the test—about the relationship of the amygdala to the Wernicke's and Broca's areas of the brain and things like that?—was going to be on the test after all?—and I didn't have any time left?—I mean, the way he teaches—Mr. Starling?—he introduces a subject, and then you're supposed to do your own research on it?—and I misunderstood. I mean, I'm real worried, Miss Pennington. It was about forty percent of the test." *Tay-est*—likewise calculated.

Miss Pennington looked at her for a few beats beyond the ordinary . . . her head still cocked to one side . . . ironically? . . . before saying, "I'm your *former* teacher, Charlotte, but I hope you know I couldn't be any more interested in how you're doing than if you were my own daughter. I haven't heard from you in quite a little while now."

"I know . . . I'm sorry, Miss Pennington, but I get so caught up—and I don't half know where the time's gone . . . "

"If you want to—if you *want* to—why don't you come by to see me while you're here. Sometimes it helps to talk to somebody who knows you but now has a little distance, a little better perspective. If you *want* to."

Charlotte lowered her head, then looked at Miss Pennington again. "Thank you, Miss Pennington. I do want to. That would be—I'd like to do that." Try as she might to make it otherwise, the words came clanking out like empty bottles in a bag.

"Just give me a call, anytime you want," said Miss Pennington. She said it a bit drily.

Dessert was a big hit: homemade pie and ice cream. Momma had baked the pie herself, mincemeat apple it was called, made of apples, raisins, cloves, and a couple of spices Charlotte didn't know the names of, and Momma served it hot from the oven, along with some ice cream she had churned by hand, vanilla with bits of cherries in it. The aroma of the cloves and the apples was intoxicating. Even Charlotte, who had hardly touched the rest of the dinner, lit into the pie. Compliments from all around; Momma was beaming. It was so good that Daddy became very much the Man at the table and was saying things like, "Better have some more, Zach"—he and Mr. Thoms were Billy and Zach now—"it's right out the oven—gon' be better now'n it'll ever be again!" It became a blissful hiatus, a time removed from all troubles great and small. Charlotte abandoned herself to the three irrational senses, the olfactory, the gustatory, and the tactile. She wanted it to last forever.

When it didn't, the ladies got up again to help with the dishes, Miss Pennington among them this time—all but Charlotte, who remained in her chair trying to *will* the interlude to last longer. Mr. Thoms had moved down the table to talk to "Billy," and Charlotte was gazing at them idly, trying to *will* her disasters from reoccupying her mind. She jerked alert to find Laurie slipping into Miss Pennington's chair and leaning close to her with a big smile on her face.

Staring into Charlotte's eyes from no more than eighteen inches away, she said, "Well? . . . "

"Well what?" said Charlotte.

"Well, I haven't heard from you since we talked on the phone—it was almost three months ago. I believe we were talking about a certain subject." Her smile grew even brighter.

Charlotte could feel her face turning scarlet, but she couldn't think of a thing to say.

"I think I'm owed a little report," said Laurie. "That's my consulting fee."

Laurie had put on some pounds, which made her cheeks and her chin, where it settled into the turtleneck of her sweater, look full. Somehow this made her prettier than Charlotte had ever seen her. She was happiness personified.

Blushing terribly, Agony Personified said, "There's really nothing to report."

"Really nothing?" said Laurie. "You know what"—her eyes seemed to brighten to about three hundred watts, and her smile became two weeks and three days wide—"I don't *believe* you!"

Charlotte was speechless with panic. Mrs. Thoms had said something to her when they were both in the kitchen! Was Laurie now one of Death's instruments—Laurie, who had always been her friend through the worst of times?

She spoke fearfully. "I don't—there just *isn't* anything . . ."

In a singsong voice Laurie said, "I don't bel*ieve* you, Charlotte . . . and I *know* you, Charlotte. This is your old friend *Laurie*, Charlotte . . . You can't be gaming *me*, Charlotte . . ."

"Gaming me"—*college slang*.

Paranoia had a gun at her temple, but she wouldn't just lie outright to Laurie. "Practically nothing," she said with a dreadful tremor in her voice.

"What's with you tonight, Charlotte? You are *not happy*. What's going on?"

Just then everybody returned from the kitchen. Before she got up to return to her seat, Laurie said, "You and I have got to have a talk. Seriously." *Seriously.* "Call me tomorrow," said Laurie, "or I'll call you. You and I've got to sit down and talk about life. Okay?"

"Okay," said Charlotte. She nodded yes several times, dourly, as Laurie turned to walk away.

"Now—who'd like some coffee?" said Momma. "Miss Pennington—how about it?"

Part of Charlotte intended to call Miss Pennington and Laurie—she owed them that much, at least—but another, franker part of her, stiffened by fear, knew she wouldn't. Laurie called Charlotte several times, and she put her off with this excuse and that, and a lifeless, moping voice, until she gave up. Day by day her guilt concerning Miss Pennington accumulated. Many evenings she vowed to call her in the morning, but in the morning she would inevitably put it off until later. That evening she would go to bed early to get away from the sidewise looks Momma and Daddy and even Buddy had begun giving her. She knew she would be lucky to get two hours' sleep all night, but lying in bed immobile was better than being stared at or talked to.

So the next morning she borrowed Momma's old parka with a hood and drove to Sparta . . . to kill time. She was strolling past the Pine Café when a good-looking boy in a waist-length trucker's jacket came out.

Ohmygod—"Well, I'll be switched! The Dupont girl!"

Caught flat-footed, Charlotte said, "Hello, Channing."

"How *is* old Dupont?" he said.

"It's fine." Not a trace of emotion. "What's up with you?"

"Well, hell," said Channing. "Ain't any jobs around here. After New Year's, me and Matt and Dave's going down to Charlotte and join the Marines. You know, I kinda hoped I'd run into you sometime. I always felt real bad about what we did over't your house. You must've hated me."

Charlotte pulled the hood away from her face. "I didn't hate you, Channing. I never hated you. I think of you a lot."

"You're blowing smoke up—"

"No, I always liked you, and you knew it."

Channing broke into a big smile. He reminded her of Hoyt. "In 'at case . . . I say let's get it on, gal!" He motioned toward the café.

Charlotte shook her head no. "That was a long time ago, Channing. I just wanted you to know." With that, she pulled the hood up over her head and hurried away.

One morning she was making one of her fifteen-foot excursions from the living room to her bedroom when Momma put her arm around her and said, "Charlotte, now I'm your momma, and you're my good girl, and far's I'm concerned, that's the way it'll always be, no matter where you are and how old you are or anything else. And right now your momma wants you to tell her what's wrong. No matter what it is, if you'll just let it out, it won't be as bad as it was. That much I can guarantee you."

Yes! Tell Momma—now—everything—and get it over with! Charlotte was on the verge—but how could she form the words and make them pass her lips—"Momma, I lost my virginity"—actually Momma, I didn't exactly *lose* it, I let a frat boy get me dead drunk because I wanted to be "one of the crowd"—and then I let him grind his genitals against mine on a public dance floor, because, you have to understand, *everybody* was doing it, and then I let him grope and feel and explore practically my whole body on a public elevator because I *did* want him to *want* me—you can understand that feeling, can't you, Momma?—and then we got to the room—oh, that's right. I didn't mention that we were staying in the same room, did I, with two beds, one couple in one bed and another couple in the other—I forgot to mention that, too—and it was interesting in a dirty way, because in the middle of the night I got to watch the other couple *fucking*, naked as a pair of jaybirds, and they did it the way a bull does it to a cow?—from behind?—with this really crude thrust thrust thrust?—but the drunk boy I tossed my virginity to wasn't like that—he rolled a condom down over his erection—for some reason, it reminded me of a ball-peen hammer—and then he went thrust thrust thrust rut rut rut, but it wasn't really that much like a bull and a cow, because he was facing me—and after it was done, he rolled off me without even looking at me—and then all he said afterward was that I had gotten some blood on the bedspread, and he acted pissed off at me—"pissed off"—that's the way they talk, Momma—anyway, that's about it. I haven't even laid eyes on him since then, not counting the four-hour drive back to Dupont—Oh, I didn't tell you we drove to Washington to do this? Anyway, that's about it, I guess. That's *one* reason I'm so depressed, but there's also this thing that happened with my schoolwork while I was so wrapped up with this frat boy—

Ohmygod, she wouldn't be able to complete the first sentence! Momma was an absolutist on this subject! When she said you'll feel better right away if you let it all out, she didn't have the *faintest notion* of the particular cat she was beckoning out of the bag. Momma wouldn't hear a word after "virginity," or even "I was staying at a hotel with a boy." Charlotte went numb with fear and guilt at the very thought.

So what she said, in fact, was, "No, Momma, it's nothing like that. I think I'm just exhausted. I hardly got any sleep the last two weeks before the break."

Momma didn't show any signs of actually swallowing that. She just gave up asking.

On Christmas morning, Buddy and Sam, as always, got up before dawn. That was no imposition on Charlotte, since she hadn't slept all night in any event. She was in the living room with the boys, who were down on all fours wondering what was in the packages under the tree, when Momma and Daddy came in, looking half asleep. Charlotte summoned all the resources she had left and put on a pretty good impression of someone excited by Christmas morn.

It became clear that the day's major excitement was the biggest package under the tree, which had a tag on it saying that it was to Charlotte from the whole family. They always took turns opening Christmas presents, with the youngest, Sam, going first and the oldest, Daddy, going last. This time everybody, even Sam, made sure Charlotte opened her two little presents first— and that her big one be the last present opened, even after Momma's and Daddy's last one.

All four of them, Sam, Buddy, Momma, and Daddy, waited in breathless silence as she commenced removing the wrapping paper.

"Go ahead," said Momma, "and just rip it off. It won't matter."

Inside a box that a set of manual lawn-mower blades had come in . . . was a computer with a full-size screen. Charlotte had never heard of the brand name before: Kaypro. She was surprised, and she put on a pretty good show of being deliriously surprised and moved.

"Well, I'll be switched!" she said. "I can't hardly believe what I'm looking at!" She turned toward each of the expectant faces before her, professing profound gratitude.

"We *made* it!" said Sam, and it turned out that was pretty much the case. Daddy had got hold of this old, discarded machine, and he and Sam and Buddy had cleaned and repaired it and hunted down some replacement parts—which was not an easy thing to do, since Kaypro went out of business years ago—and rebuilt it. It seemed that Daddy had included the two boys on every single part of the project, so that when Sam said, "We *made* it," he wasn't far off the mark.

"It's because you got all A's!" said Sam. "We figured you ought to have your own computer!"

Charlotte took Sam into her arms and hugged him and then Buddy and Daddy and Momma. She would have broken down crying, but she had no tears left. Tears, no matter how sad they might be, were a sign of caring about something and therefore a sign of a functioning human being. She was admirably patient as Sam and Buddy and Daddy explained to her, with infinite Christmas delight, how it worked. Kaypro had gone under so long ago, there were no instruction manuals. They had had to learn all about it from scratch. Daddy said Sam and Buddy were much better at it than he was. He was an old dog that couldn't learn new tricks, but they took to it like a duck takes to water. And did that make them proud! She hugged them all over again and said she just didn't know how she had gotten along this far without it, and the best Christmas present of all was knowing that they had made it themselves, just as Sam said. Which was, in fact, true, since she had no idea where or if she could install it in her room and it was easy enough to use the ones in the library. The thought of staying in her room—where Beverly could come walking in at any moment—chilled her. The very fact that she would be returning to—that place—at all seemed remote to the point of impossible.

Nevertheless, there came a day when Momma and Daddy and Buddy and Sam drove her back to the bus station in Galax. Daddy personally oversaw the placement of the computer—cushioned inside the lawn-mower blade box with all manner of rags, Styrofoam, balled-up newspapers, and an old, ratty rubber bathtub mat—into the belly of the bus.

Charlotte *wanted* to cry when she said good-bye to them, but she was parched with a fear of the unknown that went far beyond the nervousness she suffered the first time she set out from the Blue Ridge Mountains for— that place. One thing the trip home had shown her: She could never make Alleghany County home again; nor any other place either—least of all, Du— the college to which she was heading. The bus was home; and let the trip be interminable.

28. THE EXQUISITE DILEMMA

irls at Dupont quickly learned the protocol of the Dupont Memorial Library's Ryland Reading Room, where on any given night except Saturday the largest concentration of boys on the campus could be found. Long, stout, medievalish study tables filled the vast space from front to back. In the back, Gothic windows rose up God knows how high before exfoliating into ornate stone lobes and filigrees filled in with stained glass. It was perhaps the second grandest study hall in the country, after the main reading room of the Library of Congress.

Practically every boy in the Ryland Reading Room was there to study. Girls came to study and to scout for boys. The boy-scouters sat at the tables in chairs facing the entrance, the nearer an aisle the better. If a girl sat with her back to the entrance, that meant she was there solely to study. If she sat with her back to the entrance at the midpoint of one of the study tables way down there beneath the exfoliated lobes and filigrees—i.e., as far as she could get not only from the entrance but also from the aisles—it meant she would just as soon be invisible. Or so it meant to Charlotte Simmons, who occupied that particular spot at this moment.

At the entire table were only two other souls: a reedy, nerdy boy, also with his back to the entrance, busy hiding the fact that he was mining for gold in his nose with the fingernail of his little finger, and a skanky girl facing front at the far end of the table. "Skanky" had slipped into Charlotte's vocabulary by social osmosis; and this girl was skanky. She was thin, wan, pimply, with curly black hair bobbed short but scraggly all the same, wearing a meat-gone-bad-green T-shirt that emphasized the flatness of her chest and a mannish green Dupont Windbreaker. Charlotte could tell she was a stone loner.

And Charlotte was so wrong. In no time she heard a concert of stifled giggles and the rustle of plastic bags. She cut her eyes toward the skank—

Pastel cashmere pullovers! Three girls, one of them blond, two of them with light brown hair, had materialized at the skank's end of the table and were leaning over talking to her in the dreaded cluster whispers. One wore a lemon-meringue-yellow cashmere sweater; another, a hike-in-the-heather blue cashmere sweater; the other, an ancient-madder-pink cashmere sweater. Charlotte recognized none of them, but pastel cashmere sweaters in the Reading Room at night screamed out . . . *sorority girls!* So did the little bags they held in their hands. The girls were back from what sorority boy-scouters called a "candy run."

The hike-in-the-heather-blue blonde whisper-exclaimed to the skank, "Blood-sugar run, be-atch!"

"Ohmygod—do I see Sour Patch Kids?" whisper-exclaimed the skank.

"Fill me in on that Zurbarán shit, and there's some strawberry gummies in it for you, too."

Soon all three cashmeres were standing around the skank, and the whisper party had begun. In these Reading Room whisper parties, girls whispered entire conversations, they whispered chuckles, they popped consonants and sighed vowels until everyone within earshot wanted to cry out "Shut the fuck up!" Nothing could be any worse than these whispered conversations, which got under your hide like an unreachable itch. Charlotte put her hand up to her eyes like a blinker, to make sure *they* didn't recognize *her.*

Now the skank and her friends were chewing away on Sour Patch Kids and gummies and making a sound like cows chewing their cuds and whisper-giggling over the sound they were making.

"Why don't we smack our lips a little . . . Dover?" (Had someone really named a daughter Dover?) "You sound like you haven't had a sugar fix in a month."

"I haven't—not Sour Patch Kids. You know how everybody says they're junk? They are junk, but there's junk and there's thrilling junk."

"Woooo—don't look around, but isn't that Whatisname Clements, on the lacrosse team?"

"Where?"

"You're right!"

"I told you not to look around!"

"I had to! He's the hottie with the body!"

Whisper-laughter, whisper-laughter.

"Maybe he'd like a Sour Patch Kid."

"Or maybe he's lost. I never saw a lacrosse player in the library before. Somebody better go see if he knows where he is."

Whisper-laughter, whisper-laughter.

Charlotte was dying to lift the hand that hid her face and look around and see if *she* had ever seen him before. After all, *she* knew her way around the lacrosse players—

And all at once she was back at the formal, down in the court during the drinks, and Harrison was making a fuss over her and calling her "our Charlotte," and Hoyt was beaming because she was such a hit with Harrison, and she had never been so happy in her life, because she felt so pretty and cute and witty and popular, and Hoyt gave her a loving look—

O Hoyt! That look was *sincere*! You're not a good enough actor to have merely pretended to—to *love me*—

Before she knew it, the terrible flash flood had returned, her eyelids were spilling with tears, and the sting of it filled her rhinal and laryngeal cavities. She couldn't let anyone see her crying, especially not in this huge public room, and most especially not the skank and the three cashmere pullovers who were almost certainly sorority girls—

Gulping air and trying to stem the tide, she lifted her hand—just to spread the fingers in the hand beside her face—and peeked through her fingers. All four girls, the three cashmeres and the skank, were now facing the entrance. As she looked at their faces, she saw four . . . raccoons . . . black rings around their eyes . . . four raccoons foraging at night, not for food, but for boys—and now one of them was looking her right in the face! In her curiosity, her hand had slipped entirely from her face—and they could see her!

Just that. She didn't dare look again. The flood was raging. Any moment—

If she left the library now, she didn't have a prayer of doing well on the neuroscience exam, and if she didn't do well, an already bad situation could become a disaster. She had so much reading to do in books she could only find here—

It was only by contracting her abdominals as hard as she could that she was able to stem the wave of convulsions that were coming to take over her lungs, trachea, chin, all of her body from the solar plexus upward, in point of fact. That *could not occur* in this very public place . . . She stood up and shoved—just so, shoved—her books and papers into her backpack, pushed her chair back with a jolting noise she didn't mean to make—it echoed throughout the great room—and quickly walked down the aisle to the door. If they had had ray guns, those four pairs of raccoon eyes could not have bored into her back more painfully; and if she had eyes and ears in the back of her head, she couldn't have seen the sheen on those Stila-glossed lower lips more clearly, or been scalded any worse by the rising steam of their whispers.

Blind with the tears that were about to rage, Charlotte burst through the swinging doors at the entrance—jolted—padded, *collided*—

"Aw, man!"—a male voice on the other side—

Gingerly, Charlotte eased one of the two doors open—and found the way blocked by a boy on his hands and knees, facing away from the doors. Books—on the floor—all over the place. Two of them had landed wide open, facedown; on one the spine had torn loose from the hard backing of the covers. Others had landed this way and that. The boy looked back over his shoulder, his face the very picture of anger—

"Ohmygod! Adam!" she said. "I didn't know anybody—I'm really sorry! It just never occurred to me!" She stood there shocked, mindlessly keeping the door ajar.

He twisted himself about into a sitting position and looked up at her warily. It seemed to register on him for the first time that it was Charlotte. He managed a smile of sorts. "Why don't you just come barging on through?" He shook his head in the manner that implied *You idiot*, but he managed to hang on to the smile . . . more or less.

"I swear, Adam, I had no idea anybody was there! I'm so sorry!"

"There's a window in the door, Charlotte."

Shhhhh! Came the sibilant chorus from inside the Reading Room. A boy's voice: "People are trying to study in here!" Another angrier: "Haul it outside and fut the shucking door!"

Charlotte let the door swing closed. Adam struggled to his feet and looked about at the books on the floor.

"Well, that's one way to run into you or you to run into me . . . or something . . ."

"I'm so sorry! I was in such a rush!"

"No, it's fine, nothing's hurt, don't worry." By the time he got to "don't worry," he was bending over to collect the scattered books. "I haven't seen you in forever." Then he looked up at her. "What have you been doing with yourself? Where've you been hiding?"

Charlotte shrugged and looked down, as if at the books, because the tears had started.

"They're all about Henry the Eighth and England's break with the Church of Rome," he said, nodding at the stack of books he now cradled in his arms.

Charlotte couldn't hold the flood back any longer.

"Charlotte! What's wrong?"

She lifted her head and, feeling the tears rattling down her face, lowered it again. "Oh nothing, just a bad day, that's all." The first little convulsions began silently.

"I think it's more than just a bad day. Can I help?"

The full convulsions overwhelmed her. She put her head on Adam's shoulder and began sobbing.

"Let me put these down." He placed his stack of books on the floor up against the wall. When he stood up, he put an arm about Charlotte. She nestled her head on his chest, and the convulsions came in waves.

"Hey, it's okay, shhhh," said Adam. Students were staring at them. "Want to go downstairs? Why don't we go down to the stacks so we can talk."

The best she could do was nod yes as her head lay on his chest, so uncontrollable were her heaving lungs.

Adam left his books where they were and led her toward the stairs ever so slowly, with his arm around her. "Oh, Adam," she said in a weak, congested voice, "I don't mean for you to—what about your books?"

"Hah. Don't worry. Nobody'll touch them. They're all full of arcane religious history. Nobody will know what a *matrix* is in those books. Henry's break with Rome was the most important event in modern history. All of modern science flows from that. People don't get the point of all the pioneers of human biology being Englishmen and Dutchmen—*oh*."

He stopped when she put her arm around his waist and leaned her head against his shoulder. Her head fell forward now and again as the sobs rolled on and rolled on.

"It's going to be okay," said Adam. "Just let it out, honey. I'm with you."

Even in the watery depths of her misery the *Honey, I'm with you* struck her as an off-key . . . dorky . . . expression that assumed too much . . . And "just let it out." What trendy, sappy theory was *that* based on? In the mountains everyone was raised to "hold it in," on the theory that emotional disintegration is contagious . . . In the mountains men were strong . . . but at the same time she had . . . only Adam.

She had been back at Dupont for less than twenty-four hours and was already ravaged by a loneliness more desperate than anything she had felt as a little girl from the mountains arriving at the great Dupont for the first time five months ago. She had been living under the illusion that she had *made friends*—Bettina and Mimi. The bitter cold but utterly clear light of schadenfreude—Bettina- and Mimi-style—had proved otherwise. They were merely three girls who had found themselves thrown together in the first circle of loserdom. The Lounge Committee . . . They had huddled together for warmth, all the while resenting the fact that fate had cast them out among the losers, namely, one another. What Charlotte suffered from now could not be given any diagnosis so benign as homesickness. She had just *been* home, only to learn that Sparta, Alleghany County, and County Road 1709 were no longer a retreat she could return to.

There existed on this earth no home, no peaceful place where she could lay her head. After a twelve-hour bus trip, counting the two hours she had to wait at the bus station in Philadelphia for the bus to Chester and the half hour she had to wait for the local bus to the Dupont campus, Charlotte had arrived at Edgerton House, room 516, at midnight, praying to God that Beverly would not be there. God answered her prayers. Beverly was back—her half-opened luggage was on her bed where she had left it—but she was out. Charlotte unpacked, undressed, got into bed, lights out, at a frantic pace, and was lying there in the now implacable grip of insomnia when Beverly came in at about three a.m. in a drunken stupor, talking incoherently. Charlotte pretended to be asleep. She lay awake all night listening to Beverly snoring, talking, bubbling, belching, crepitating in her stuporous sleep. Charlotte got up in the dark at six a.m. It took a tremendous exertion of will. A depressed girl seeks total inertia and never wants to get up, but with Charlotte the fear of humiliation and its obverse, pity, overcame it. Above all, she wanted to make sure she could get dressed and get out of the room while her alien roommate was still unconscious. The thought of having Beverly look her up and down, ask questions, make insidious Sarc 3 comments—or ignore her, the way she had for the first month—was more than she could bear.

As soon as she stood up, her head had felt like a desiccated husk. Splashing water on her face in the bathroom had done nothing to revive her. The ordinary motions of getting dressed only made her yearn more for sleep. All the while she was terribly anxious lest Beverly wake up. How morbid it all was! How desolate! To be mortified by the very possibility that your roommate might become conscious of your presence! To have no old friends, no new friends—to be afraid of the most elementary gestures toward making friends—how very hopeless was her life! Why wouldn't God come take her away in the night?

She had made sure she was there waiting the moment the dining hall opened. Very few students had breakfast that early. The moment she finished, she put on her old quilted jacket, pulled the hood up over her head until it covered most of her face, and hurried to her two classes, medieval history and French, saying nothing in either class. From French, her face still stashed away beneath the hood, she rushed to the library, seeking refuge and anonymity. She had skipped lunch. The idea of being abroad on the campus in the middle of the day made her too anxious. In the afternoon, when the Reading Room was its quietest, she sought to concentrate on a monograph entitled "Neuroscientific exigeses of 'self,' 'soul,' 'mind,' and 'ego,'" and she began trembling. She—who had been studying the illusion of free will all semester with the calm and comfort of the conceptually enlightened observer—was cornered! Here! There was nowhere to go, no new direction to consider . . . nothing to aim for except the Big Inertia. She took advantage of the early nightfall to scurry to the dining hall the moment it opened for dinner, at five-thirty. She bolted down some pasta and departed before other students had even begun arriving in any numbers. Briefly buoyed by carbohydrates, she had returned to the Reading Room resolved to concentrate on neuroscience truly conceptually, to keep its insidious hands off her own central nervous system and that chemical analog computer known as her own brain—and had collapsed into the arms of Adam, who called her Honey but whose bony embrace was all she had.

Adam kept his arm around Honey as they reached the basement stacks. These were stacks of the venerable sort, cliffs of metal shelves supporting rack after rack of books. The cliffs were so numerous and crunched so close together, floor to ceiling, the sensation that they were about to fall over on you would have been overwhelming if the ceiling hadn't been so low, no more than seven and a half feet. Floor to ceiling, with no more than thirty inches between cliffs, in a windowless space so vast and so miserably lit—by trays of fever-blue fluorescent tubes hung from the ceiling—that on the far side the cliffs seemed to recede into a terminal gloom choked with the dust of tens of thousands of dead books. In fact this soaring tower of academe had been retrofitted with the latest twenty-first-century HVC (heating, ventilation, and cooling) systems in an age of particulate matter phobia. Adam maintained his one-armed savior's embrace, which forced them to squeeze together as they made their way through the narrow spaces between the cliffs.

They walked until they had traveled deep, deep into the vast space. Far from the world, they sat down in a corner where two cliffs of books met.

Charlotte had managed to contain her tears, and Adam said, "So what is it?"

"Nothing really, just a stupid thing I did. You don't want to know . . . or do you already know?"

"Already know? Know what?"

"I guess not."

"What happened, Charlotte?"

"Well, have you ever done anything that, I don't know, was totally out of character or totally against your morals and everything you believed in and then really regretted it afterward?"

"Well . . . whoa . . . okay, yeah, I'm sure—go on . . ."

"Even more than that, like . . . done something so awful that turned into—it just shames you whenever you think about it, and you just keep thinking about it over and over?"

"Charlotte—stop beating around the bush. I have no idea what you're talking about."

"Well, I had an interesting weekend just before Christmas break." She did not say it with a smile.

"What did you do?"

She turned her head so that she was looking straight into his eyes. "Adam?" she said softly. "Don't hate me."

"Why would I? What are you talking about?"

Whereupon, sitting there on the floor, she poured out the whole story. She told him everything.

Afterward, Adam said nothing. He put his arm around her. She rested her head on his shoulder and closed her eyes. He put his other arm around her, too, and held her for a long time without saying a word. She felt good in his arms, bony though they were. She trusted him totally. He wasn't going to try to turn this into an opening to slide a hand here . . . and there . . . and there . . . He wasn't going to stroke her leg in the guise of comforting her. There was no guile to him. He was calming her and protecting her. He began rocking her, ever so gently—just that, rocking her like a baby. Had she not been aware that she was, in fact, on the floor deep within the stacks of a nine-million-book library, she could have nodded off into a peaceful sleep.

Finally, still holding her, Adam said, "Oh, wow . . ." Long pause. "That's pretty intense, Charlotte. But that guy's a dick! You're so much better than he is! Frat guys are losers, Charlotte. They're misogynists. They are the most sexist—they're animals. They haven't evolved. They're afraid to climb out on this new branch of the tree of life marked hominid. A bunch of filthy shit-heads—what happened was not your fault. I hope you can see that. It's that sort of—that whole mentality the frat guys have. I've been around them. It's a group mentality, and it's dangerous because as long as you're in their midst, they try to create an atmosphere of . . . of . . . of, you know, our way is the only cool way, and you're a total loser if you won't laugh at the moronic rubbish we laugh at. I can't see you even hanging out with them. It makes no sense. They're such wastes of time, wastes of mental capacity, wastes of every-thing!—and that includes the space they occupy and the air they breathe." He made a contemptuous sound deep in his throat. "You have to dumb yourself down just being in the same room with them. Their idea of witty repartee is like . . . grunting out insults. They are so below you, Charlotte! You can do anything you want, *be* anyone you want. Look at you. You're gor-geous, you're smart, and most of all, you're curious about life! You need ad-venture!—and I'm talking about real adventure, not *fraternity formals*."

Adam's voice rose and rose, and he became more and more fervent in his exhortations, to the point where he began gesturing for emphasis, and his glasses fell off and he tried to put them back on properly, but that interrupted the flow, the beat, of his apostrophe, so he held them in his hand. "You're dif-ferent from them. You're a different species. I take that back—you're not a part of *any* species! You're unique! There's nobody like you! How could you possibly lower yourself to the level of the herd? You're—you're Charlotte Simmons!"

I am Charlotte Simmons. Without knowing Miss Pennington, not even her name, Adam had arrived at the very same declaration, the very same argument. That didn't encourage her in the slightest. There was nothing in her worth encouraging and never had been. The two of them, Miss Pennington and Adam, had merely managed to hit upon the same sickly sweet gob of verbiage. Charlotte was far beyond the reach of genuine praise, never mind witless flattery. The worthlessness of the depressed girl is complete and across the board. I am Charlotte Simmons—what a pathetic, what a feeble piece of self-delusion . . . and so forth and so on . . . Only the bony nest of his embrace brought any solace at all.

After *You are Charlotte Simmons,* she heard nothing but the light and abstract ramble of his voice, even though he talked on and on. She curled up until she was all but cradled on his lap. Her head and upper torso lay on his chest. She had found an interlude—no, not a mere interlude—but a state of being, a steady state at a blessed remove from the world, below ground, in a tubercular blue light, neither day nor night, two creatures safely hidden deep within an endless, endless metal forest of dead books no one would ever touch again.

They remained that way for what seemed like a blessed, timeless eternity, she in his arms and he bathing her nerve endings in the warm flow of his words . . . about . . . what did it matter.

Adam said, "Look"—Charlotte braced herself for "Honey," but it didn't come—"this *is* Dupont, and it's the same Dupont you dreamed of, but you haven't let yourself find it. There *is* a whole other life here. There *are* people here—you once used the phrase 'life of the mind,' and you've already been face to face with it. Let me tell you something. Edgar Tuttle is going to be a *great* figure in the not too distant future. His mind is—he has such a conceptual power—do you remember the afternoon he suddenly gave us the social history of . . . the *cheer*leader? Right in the middle of a casual conversation? I can't remember a moment when he wasn't worth listening to. And Roger—he makes such bad jokes—and he's so brilliant at the same time. And Camille—don't be fooled by her dirty mouth. She claims she's some sort of flame-throwing lesbian. But I think she's like Camille Paglia. She establishes some ultraradical position way out to the left of everything else, and from out there she can cut down anybody on the left or the right. Okay, she loves to go for the throat, but with her you can be sure that nobody—

nobody—is going to be able to get away with the usual arrant bullshit. Charlotte, these are the sort of people who will do a country's thinking for it."

Edgar Tuttle . . . conceptual power . . . Camille . . . ultraradical . . . Adam's words became a nice warm bath. Charlotte relaxed and curled up into his embrace once more . . . She wanted nothing more than to float and bob in perpetuity in this lukewarm current.

"I mean, just think what feminism did and how it happened. A lot of businessmen woke up one day in the twentieth century, not really that long ago, and a lot of congressmen and senators and public officials—but it's businessmen that amuse me the most—they woke up one day and said, 'Well, golly, I guess we have to make way for some women in our executive ranks and pay them real money—and stop treating them like women. I just don't know how it all happened, but it's happened and I guess we have to get used to it.' Or right here! Dupont! Thirty-five, forty years ago there were no female undergraduates at Dupont—or Yale or Harvard or Princeton—and like overnight, the next day, they've all gone coed—and there was never any debate! The big business corporations never started a debate! None! Nobody—Congress, the Pennsylvania Legislature, the universities, the press—nobody debated women's rights. It all happened because of an *idea* that spread because of its own intrinsic power. A handful of people with no power of their own, no money, no organization, came up with an *idea* that just sailed right over politics, economics, and . . . and . . . and everything else, and it caused this huge change! And that idea was, women are not a gender, a sex, except mechanically. What they are is a class, a servant class slaving away to make life easier for the master class, namely, men. That was all it took! Here was an idea so obvious—an idea so big that nobody had ever backed away far enough to see it before. But a handful of women *did*—Simone de Beauvoir, Doris Lessing, Betty Friedan, and . . . and . . . I forgot . . . a few others—and the way everybody, women *as well as* men, looked at women changed fundamentally. You can call these women intellectuals, if you want, but they were above mere intellectuals. They were a . . . a . . . I guess the word is *matrix*, as in mother of it all. They created the *idea*, and your everyday intellectuals—they were like automobile dealers selling this new model that the manufacturers, the matrix, shipped to them. *That's* what every Millennial Mutant intends to be, a matrix. We're already at a level frat boys and all that element—"

Something about the Pennsylvania Legislature . . . and gender . . . and sex . . . and a servant class and the master class . . . and automobile dealers . . .

debris from the waters, and every now and then a bit of it lodged in Charlotte's brain, but mainly she just kept floating and bobbing with her eyes closed in Adam's gentle, earnest swell of words in 98.6 degrees Fahrenheit . . . same as her body . . . perfect state of sensory deprivation. She could feel the tension draining out of her nerves, the toxins draining out of her brain . . . time vanishing . . . her body, at last perfectly relaxed, sinking into Adam's bones bathed by the flow, the flow, the warm bouillon flow of his words . . . Tawny, his words were, tawny as oxtail bouillon, and warm . . .

So fluent—not to mention convincing—did Adam feel, it was quite a spell before it occurred to him that the girl in his arms, the beautiful girl miraculously in his arms, was no longer listening. He craned his head down in order to look directly into her face. Had she fallen asleep? Her eyes were closed and her body was at last relaxed, but she wasn't breathing like someone asleep.

He stopped talking, even though he hadn't gotten to the point he wanted to make about how the "intellectuals" were ignorant of what Darwin actually said. He knew she was interested in Darwin. Well, it was enough, wasn't it, that at last she was in his arms. What a weird place for it—sitting on a concrete floor deep in the bowels of the stacks. Talk about gloomy . . . and yet here she was in his arms . . . He had dreamed about this, but not in such a weird place . . . What if he gave her a soft and tender kiss on the lips, sort of a consoling kiss after what she has been through? . . . Bad idea. For him to make a move after everything she had just told him—she might not interpret that as consoling. Besides, it was physically impossible in this position. Her head was lying on his chest. When he bent his head over to look at her, he had barely been able to see her face. To get his mouth all the way to her mouth, he'd have to rearrange her whole body, and that might bring her out of the spell she was in. He'd have to remove his glasses and put them . . . where? For about the three thousandth time he thought of laser corrective surgery. But what if he was that one in five thousand who rolled his eyes a sixteenth of an inch at exactly the wrong moment and the laser beam fried his eyeballs?

He stared into the biblioglutted gloom. He should be grateful enough just to be holding her in his arms . . . which he was, for a while. The two pressure points where his pelvic saddle rested on the concrete began to annoy him. One of his legs was going to sleep in the thigh. It was damned frustrating to have your loved one in your arms . . . and she's off in . . . a spell, a trance, the Land of Nod, a stress coma—he had heard of such a thing. He looked at his watch. He'd been down here for more than an hour! *She* didn't seem aware of *where* she was . . .

He held her some more, but it was becoming tedious . . . He tightened his embrace a bit . . . Nothing . . . Then he began rocking her again . . . Nothing . . . Finally he bent his head over as far as he could and said, "Charlotte . . . Charlotte . . ." For a moment . . . nothing—but then she lifted her head from his chest and gave him a look of weary disappointment.

"I'm sorry," he said, "but I think we ought to get up from here. We've been sitting on this concrete floor for a long time."

For an instant she looked annoyed on top of disappointed, but she began to get up, nonetheless. He sprang to his feet in order to experience the ineffable joy of extending his hand and helping her up. She thanked him in a distracted, perfunctory way—but then, without a word, hooked her arm inside his and leaned her head against his shoulder as they walked toward the stairway.

When they reached the grand Gothic lobby, she took her head off his shoulder but clung more tightly, if anything, to his arm.

"You feel any better?" he said. "Maybe a *little* better?"

"Yeah."

Outside, the Great Yard was covered in seven or eight inches of snow, with an icy crust that looked somehow corroded where the walkway lamps washed it with wan coronas of light. A penetrating wind swept across it. In the darkness, the great stone hulks of the Gothic buildings facing out on the Yard appeared frozen in place, like ships trapped in ice.

Adam didn't want . . . this . . . to end. He absolutely thrilled to the look she had in his arms. He ransacked his brain for some way—"I'm kind of hungry. Why don't we stop by Mr. Rayon for a second? It's on me."

"No!" It was more of a startled cry than a rejection. "I just want to go to sleep."

Her head was buried deep within the parkalike hood of her quilted jacket.

Once more she leaned her head, now deep within the hood, against his shoulder. Once more he thrilled to the pressure of her extremities against his arm. Every conceivable strategy churned in his brain—and all were stymied by the fact that she had come to him already traumatized, literally in tears, because of the sexual predations of a frat boy like Thorpe. He *hated* that smug bastard.

Adam began walking in the direction of Little Yard, where, feeling once more thwarted, he would no doubt be unable to come up with any comment tender enough and cool enough and Lothario enough to . . . to . . . to . . .

They couldn't have gone a hundred feet before Charlotte held on to his arm tighter than ever and stopped and looked up at him, her eyes two little orbs reflecting light from deep within the recesses of the hood, and said in a little voice, "Adam—please—don't leave me."

Adam stood there still and speechless—petrified lest he overinterpret what he was now hearing.

"I can't go back to my room," she said. "I can't stay there with my room-mate. It's like being cooped up with—I can't do it, Adam, I can't do it . . ." She was on the verge of tears. "Can I stay with you?"

"Of course." His imagination was feverish and yet not big enough to comprehend what on earth he was hearing. Ever fearful of disappointment, he decided to assume a cavalier air. "Whatever your"—then he caught himself. It wasn't his métier, cavalier. He would just be himself: "Whatever you want."

Her eyes narrowed so far, the lights went out. She turned her head so far, the hood popped up in front of him like a wall. He would never understand her. But then she turned the mouth of the hood back toward him and the eyes were lit once more.

"Just anyplace to lie down, Adam. A couch, the floor, anyplace. I can't be alone. I can't explain it. You're my only friend—" She began sobbing. Her voice came out in little tremulous cries: "My . . . on-ly . . . fri-end!"

She buried her face, hood and all, into the breast of his North Face jacket, racked with sobs, and he wrapped both arms about her. "Of *course* you can stay at my place." She abruptly stopped crying. How brave she was. "I won't *let* you be alone. You can stay there as long as you like. I have a futon. I'll always be there for you. *You* can have the bed, and *I'll* take the futon."

"No—no—" She began sobbing again. "Just put me"—sobs—"where I'll be the least trouble. I don't"—sob—"deserve—" whereupon the "erve" in "deserve" broke up into racking sobs: "erve-erve-erve-erve." Adam, essentially a literary intellectual, didn't realize he was listening to the typical depressed girl who has made the appalling discovery that she is worthless.

She put her arm around his waist and her head against his shoulder, and he put his arm around both her shoulders and hugged her upper body tightly against his own. It was a bit awkward, since his stride covered more ground than hers, but they walked that way out of the Great Yard for seven blocks until they reached the old town house in the City of God where Adam lived.

They spoke very little. Most of the way Charlotte continued sobbing softly, while Adam interjected his *There theres*, *It's all rights*, and *Don't worry, I'm not going to leave you, honeys*. The *not going to leave you, honeys* did more to quiet her than anything else. Otherwise they barely spoke at all, but Adam's brain and central nervous system were making the circuit at a furious rate.

One moment—euphoria! His fondest dream had come true *just like that*! Charlotte was moving in with him—and it was her idea! She wouldn't take three steps without clinging to his body—holding his arm, putting her head on his shoulder! She beseeched him not to leave her. She did everything but say "Take me! I'm yours!" He was giddy, delirious, here in the dark from the radiant happiness soon to be his. Dupont, society, the world, the cosmos, all of existence was now compressed into two people, himself and Charlotte Simmons. It was that blissful suspension of disbelief called love.

The next moment—the Doubts. It was all *too* good to be true. He happens to bump into her, literally, in the library, and—*bango!*—all at once she's *his*?—but specifically because she's disgusted and chagrined by sex?— and suffered a trauma in losing her virginity? Where did that leave him— and his burning desire to lose *his* virginity to this girl, because she was as innocent as he was and wouldn't look down on him for his lack of experience?

The next moment—she'll be with me in my apartment all through the night, in the same room, because there *is* only one room, and it's a small room and her body will be there and there's only one real bed, and one thing leads to another in life, doesn't it?

The next moment—but how do you get a girl into bed with you when she has come to you in flight from a frat-boy sexual predator? The next moment—

—and on it went and off it went on/off/on/off/on/off and the binary circuit burned and burned.

As they drew near Adam's building, he began to tremble, aroused by the thought of what might possibly, miraculously, now be his . . . and anxious about how the dump might look to his beloved. What would she think? Place reeks from dirty, moldy clothes and shit lying around . . . The house itself was in a moldering old district full of brick houses with wood trim built way back in the early twentieth century as one-family residences on tiny lots.

Each house was barely seven feet from the next, creating dank alleyways that never saw daylight and always felt damp. The bricks had long since turned five shades darker from grime and coal soot. The wood trim in the cornices, corbels, overhanging eaves, shutters, window frames, architraves, front doorways, and small front porches—everything was dry-rotting, warping, flaking from poor paint jobs or else too few. Generations of black wires slopped with white paint ran from top to bottom next to the gutter pipes, which had their own problems. Most of the houses, like the one Adam lived in, had long since been cut up into small apartments.

But tonight Charlotte was no sightseer. She whimpered and held on to him for dear life. The staircase up to his apartment was a steep, narrow, dingy shaft painted brown. It clattered from the aged metal strips on the leading edges of the steps. It was too cramped for them to ascend side by side; so as he led the way, Adam extended one hand behind him for Charlotte. She desperately insisted on holding on to him. The four-story climb was disorienting enough even when you did it every day. And this time Adam was dizzy with love. His hands trembled as he unlocked the three dead-bolt locks on his door. He opened it, clicked on the light—and his spirits plummeted—

—for he now saw his apartment through his loved one's eyes. This was no "apartment"! This was a slot!—one of four created by cutting an ordinary front bedroom and rear bedroom in two. Three graduate students rented the other slots. Adam's was ten feet wide and felt even smaller because it was beneath an eave whose slope eliminated half the ceiling and nearly all of one wall and threatened to pound your head down into your thoracic box from the moment you entered. The "kitchen" consisted of the smallest "stove," "sink," and "refrigerator" ever made squeezed into what had been a closet in a former, better life. The quotation marks spread like dermatitis in Adam's brain as he thought of what must be going through the mind of the girl of his dreams. The "bed" was a mattress on a cheap, unfinished flush door from a lumberyard, supported at the corners by cinder blocks. And the blankets, sheets, and pillow on that "bed"? A rat's nest! And from that rat's nest and the dust-ball-filthy floor—both strewn with dirty socks, sneakers, underwear, handkerchiefs, sweatpants, sweatshirts, sodden towels—there arose such an odor that it overwhelmed even him, he who breathed this foul air day in and day out. And the answer to his prayers couldn't even see the worst of it yet: the bathroom . . . was in the hall . . . and the wretches in all four slots had to use it!

He glanced fearfully at her. She was looking at him with a pained expression.

He said, "I know it's not what you—"

"Oh, Adam!" she exclaimed. "Thank . . . ank . . . ank . . . ank . . . ank"— the "thank" broke up into sobs—". . . ank you . . ." Whereupon she threw her arms around him and pressed her head against his chest. She began talking weirdly, her voice muffled by his North Face jacket. "I'm so tired, Adam. I feel so terrible. Please stay with me. There's no way you can know how I feel. I can't be alone tonight. I'll—I can't, Adam, I can't . . . I just canh-anh-anh-anh-anh-anh't." She tightened her embrace of his rib cage.

A hail of thoughts blipped through the Wernicke's area of his brain, one of which was that she no longer said *caint* for *can't*.

"Don't worry, honey," he said, "I'm right here with you, and I'm going to stay right here with you."

She stopped crying, released her embrace, and stood up straight. "Adam, Adam, Adam," she said, shaking her head in an expression of starry-eyed wonderment. "There's just no way I can thank you—"

But there *is!*

"—enough. I'm so anxious and so tired." Pause. "Could you show me where your futon is?"

"I'll get it out, but you're not sleeping on it. You're my guest. You get the bed. I'm going to change the sheets and make it up for you."

"No—"

"No no's, Charlotte. This is my place, such as it is, and that's the way I want it."

"You don't have to—"

"I *do* have to, because that's the way it's got to be."

She acceded, lowering her eyes and nodding Yes. Then she looked up at him, her eyes big and starry; she fixed them upon his face for what seemed like a very long time. His anticipation rose rose rose rose rose—

"Where's the bathroom?"

Adam braced for this one. *Oh, the bathroom's out in the hall. Everybody else uses it, too.* He tried to speak in a cool, offhand manner: "Oh, you just go out the door"—he nodded toward the entrance to the slot—"and it's right next to it?—the first door on your left?" He failed. It occurred to him that he sounded like Charlotte, turning declarative sentences into questions.

In fact, she seemed oblivious to the sketchiness of his voice and the geographical implication of his instructions. She was long past caring about such things.

"Uhh . . . you might want to lock the bathroom door while you're in there? Just in case?"

As soon as she went out the door, he hurriedly stripped the bed, throwing the random clothes in a pile on the floor, and made it up. His brain and nervous system were once again off in a wild synaptic and dendritic scramble. Yes . . . but what should he do? What dare he try?

He was in the same state of confusion when she returned. When he turned toward her, she gave him a tender, almost fearful—glorious! glorious!—smile, then once more threw her arms around his rib cage and pressed one side of her face into his chest, and eagerly, eagerly, he embraced her. He took a stray shot at pressing his mons pubis against hers, but he couldn't find it.

"Oh, Adam, Adam, Adam"—he could feel her jaw muscles moving on his sternum—"someday I'll know how to tell you—I'll know how to explain . . . Last night I prayed to God. I prayed to God to come take me away in the night. But I couldn't sleep, and God will only come take you in your sleep. You're a good person, Adam. I'm sure you don't know what it is like to have so led your life that you will never sleep—"

"Shhhhh. Come on, Charlotte, don't keep flagellating yourself. You haven't done anything *wrong*! You've been done wrong *to*, that's all."

She released her grip around him and straightened up. But he still had his arms around her, and she was looking up at him. This was the moment—for a soulful, lingering kiss—but that wasn't a *take my lips* look she was giving him. She was shaking her head.

"I'm sorry, Adam," she said. "I didn't mean—I can't let myself fall to pieces like this and expect you—"

"Don't be silly."

"I wish I could explain it all. I'm like . . . desolate, Adam. You've pulled me back from . . . like an edge. Thank God it was you I hit with that door." That made her smile . . . oh so wanly.

"Then I guess we both thank God," said Adam. He figured that gave her an opening as big as the moon.

She looked up into his eyes searchingly. "I need to try to sleep." She glanced toward the bed. "I'm so tired. But you don't have to turn the lights off. If you want to stay up, that's okay. It won't make any difference."

If you want to stay up, that's okay—it won't make any difference? Adam took this poorly. He abandoned his embrace. "Oh, by all means!" he said, gesturing toward the bed with his palm up, as if making a formal presentation. "Your bed awaits you."

He said it with just a shade of irony, which she didn't get, obviously. She immediately turned, headed for the bed, and got in without undressing. She pulled the covers way up.

Pouting a bit, Adam proceeded to slide the futon out from under the bed and prepare to turn in. The damned thing was covered in dust, which he instinctively blamed on Charlotte, who had accepted the bed after first saying she wouldn't.

He made a point of not looking at her, but then she said, "Adam? Oh, Adam, I'll never be able to thank you—you've saved my life tonight—saved—my—life, Adam . . . I'll never forget thi-i-i-i-i-"—she was sobbing—"i-i-is . . . Oh, Adam! Don't leave me . . ."

He said, "Everything's okay, Charlotte. I'm right here. Try to sleep." He didn't say it as warmly, let alone as lovingly, as he might have.

He turned away, swept the dust off the damned futon, threw a couple of ratty old blankets on it, folded up his damned North Face jacket to use as a pillow, turned off the damned lights, stripped down to his T-shirt and shorts in the dark, stretched out on the damned futon, expelled a big, noisy hangdog sigh, and went to sleep . . .

The clinic! Great honor! Poor, anorexic girls—pale, bony girls with barely any mammary capacity at all—reaching out to him with their paper-pale, bony arms . . . Before him: a pale, pale starveling with a potbelly the size of a cantaloupe—asking why? Why? Why? Simple, said the distinguished consultant—who was himself! You're beginning to eat now, and your body is storing fat where it can draw upon it fastest, which is there—your belly. A beautiful girl behind him—he couldn't see her but he knew she was beautiful—said in a soft, kind voice, "But that's not true, Adam . . . Adam? . . . Adam? . . . Adam! . . . Adam!"—

He woke up in the dark.

"Adam!"—such anguish in her voice. As he ascended from the hypnopompic depths and reached the surface, he realized that it was Charlotte, and she was up on the bed and he was down here on the floor, on the futon.

"Adam!"

"What is it?"

"I—don't—know—what's happening!" The words were coming in spurts. "Please—hold me! Please—hold me!"

What time was it? Here in the dark of the night, he had no idea. He threw back the blankets on the futon and knelt by the bed. He could feel the mattress shaking as soon as his chest touched it.

"What's wrong?"

"I don't—know . . . Hold me—Adam."

She was lying on her side, facing him. That was all he could make out in the dark. He leaned forward and slipped one arm under her neck and wrapped the other around her shoulder. She was shaking like someone with a fever.

"Adam, I'm so—get in beside me. Lie next to me. Please! I'm so frightened!"

"Next to you?"

"Yes! Hold me in my skin! I'm trying to get out of my skin! Please!"

Baffled, excited, bewildered, thrilled, he got into the bed, and his knees pressed against the undersides of her thighs. She had rolled over, so that her back was to him.

She continued to shake terribly. "Hold me! I don't know what's happening! Oh God, please! Put your arms around me!"

So he did. His chest was pressed up against her back. He could feel the snap of her bra. His head was behind her. She kept shaking.

"Oh God—closer . . . Put your legs under my legs—please!"

She had curled into a fetal position. He had to lift his knees to make contact with the undersides of her thighs again. It was as if he were a chair lying on its side, and she was sitting in it.

He felt no more lust at all. She was finally in his bed, and she was a wreck. Her body was rigid.

"Hold me tighter, Adam . . . Keep me in my skin . . . Tighter . . ."

It was some time before the shaking stopped and her muscles relaxed and her breathing became normal, more or less. During that time, his thoughts raced. Hoyt Thorpe had done this to her. Adam reduced the guy to a coward begging for mercy in a variety of ways. One time he had him in a full nelson, which was illegal in college wrestling, and he gave him a choice of surrendering or having his neck broken. *You don't believe me, you pathetic little shit? Try a little of this . . .* His fingers intertwined behind Hoyt Thorpe's neck, he forced his head down down down until he screamed, begged, and whimpered for mercy.

Meanwhile, he held the girl he loved in his arms and pressed his body against hers, to keep her inside her very hide.

They stayed that way for a long time. Even after he ran out of ways to maim Hoyt Thorpe, Adam continued to think of what the frat boy had done . . . the barbarity of it . . . the evil. It was not cool for a Millennial Mutant to regard Evil as an absolute, but as he held this girl in his arms, he knew that in fact it was.

At that very moment, about 2:45 a.m., that very person, Hoyt Thorpe, was in the library with Vance and Julian. He was in his chair knocking back a can of beer, but mainly he was riding into the night on a few lines of cocaine he had sucked up into his nose through a straw. The exhilaration always made him feel more than ever like a born leader of the warrior class. It also did wonders for his imagination, he was convinced, like those French poets who smoked hashish or something, although he never could think of their names. The one sure thing was that it made him very voluble.

". . . fucking Stand Up Straight for Gay Day. Straight Up the Brown Canal Day is more fucking like it . . . and they want everyone on campus, 'straight or gay'—*gay* . . . which is spelled 'straight up the Hershey highway'—they want everybody to wear blue jeans to show 'solidarity.' So I say, let's show 'em some solidarity." He extended his middle finger. "I say we all turn up at Stand Up Straight for Gay Day wearing khaki shorts. Can't you fucking picture that?" Eyes aglitter, he looked to Vance and Julian for approval of this inspiration.

"Oh, great fucking idea," said Julian. "You ever heard of the middle of winter? It's about fifteen degrees out there right now."

"But that's the whole point!" said Hoyt. "That's the whole point! It won't kill you—and they'll get the fucking message!"

Vance and Julian looked at each other.

29. STAND UP STRAIGHT FOR GAY DAY

Adam now saw his apartment, his lopsided little slot, as a sanatorium for a single patient, the girl he loved . . . the love of his life. He wanted to proclaim his love! He literally wished he could go up on a promontory with Charlotte at his side and put one arm around her and lift the other to the heavens, saying: "Behold! Gaze upon her ineffable beauty! This is the girl I love! She . . . is my very life!" But who was there to proclaim it to? He knew the Mutants better than anyone else, but to proclaim to this intellectual cabal, "I'm in love!"—even the thought of all the stupid laughter and sidewise glances was more than he could bear.

At the same time, he had a deep worry, which he imagined was lodged in some posterior lobe of his brain. Jojo's plagiarism case was unresolved. Nothing seemed to be happening. The case was dormant, to all outward appearances. But he had lied to the judicial officer . . . on the advice of Buster Roth, who was not his friend. He could be thrown out of Dupont! He couldn't imagine it. It was as unreal as the thought of death. Yet there it was! He had dug the grave himself! This unimaginable thing . . . could happen!

Every possible moment he spent with Charlotte. He slept next to her in his little twin bed, elated by her dependence on him—she could get no sleep at all unless he held her for a couple of hours or more—and frustrated by the fact that sleeping next to her was a different preposition from sleeping with her. "Different preposition" was the very word that formed in his thoughts. "Witty," he said to himself, without the faintest tinge of amusement.

In any case, he couldn't spend *every* moment with her. This was final exam week for the first semester, and he had to ace these exams in order to be in the running for a Rhodes scholarship. At the same time he had sworn to himself to revive "The Night of the Skull Fuck" . . . for the *Wave* in some way that would make Hoyt Thorpe realize: Vengeance is ours, saith Charlotte Simmons and Adam Gellin, and we shall be paid. On top of that, a mundane but time-consuming matter: four hours of pizza deliveries every night. He was paid by the hour for tutoring athletes. But the Athletic Department had stopped giving him assignments. He, Adam Gellin, Millennial Mutant and prince, Prince of Love in a fairy tale, had to hop in that decrepit Bitso-sushi and hustle PowerPizza pies.

Charlotte had taken to lying listlessly in bed during the day. If she got up, she never wore anything but Adam's synthetic School of Hudson Bay lumberjack shirt. Obviously, she had no intention at all of leaving the apartment. One of Adam's most urgent duties was making sure she *did* pull herself together, at least long enough to get dressed—in the same clothes she arrived in—and go take her exams. She protested that she couldn't take them, because she hadn't been able to study. Adam assured her she was a genius, that she had worked so hard and brilliantly during the first half of the semester, the momentum she already had would be enough. The past was the past, it was time to put it behind her and move forward into the billion-volt future that awaited her and her unparalleled life of the mind, and so forth and so on—dreadful, dutiful mouthfuls of clichés, in short, but he could tell that his flattery and optimism were gradually beginning to work.

Inwardly, sympathy, money, and charity were battling it out with an incessantly smoldering, smoking, smitten lust for virginiticide at the hands of and the mouth, breasts, and loins of his beloved. One moment charity would be telling him he should take her to the Health Center and put her in professional hands for treatment of depression. This girl wasn't merely unhappy, he realized after the first day, she was depressed. But lust rebutted: that would *really* finish her off . . . sinking into the theory-quacking innards of the twenty-first-century versions of the madhouse—being perhaps declared "clinically" depressed and sent home—he couldn't let that happen. What she needed was love, caring attention, encouragement, praise, visions of a radiant future . . . and order. He needed to establish a positive routine for her. Yes!—you *must* take your exams. Yes!—you *must* have a neat appearance whether you leave the apartment or not. And to himself: Yes!—this miserable poverty-rotted slot I live in must have the appearance of order.

The first day Charlotte went out, quaking, for an exam—neuroscience—Adam inserted the eyes of a movie drill sergeant into his head and saw this place for what it was: an inexcusable rat's nest. And the bathroom . . . in a common hall . . . since all four apartments, meaning four boys who were little more than nodding acquaintances, used it, nobody ever found it worth his while to keep it clean. The filth, the foul odors, the grime in the crack where the tile floor met the tub, which had corroded green copper stains stretching out a foot or more from the drain, the shaved beard stubble hair accumulating in a sludge in the bottom of the basin, the virulent ring of sludge near the top of the basin, the grit on the tiles, which were the old-fashioned tiny octagonal kind, cracked here and there, the black mold that was spreading over the shower curtain, which was an ancient sheet of plastic the color of intravenous feeding tubing that drooped where three curtain-rod rings were missing, the paint blistering and peeling on the ceiling thanks to lack of ventilation—Adam had never seen all this with real eyes, Charlotte's eyes, before. Bringing *order* to this disgrace became a mission. He found a snow shovel, an old gray wood-backed scrub brush and a one-fourth-full bottle of ammonia in the cellar. He *scraped* the pox-erupted paint off the ceiling . . . got down on all fours and *scrubbed* the mold and paint poxchips off the shower curtain, the scum from the basin, the corroded copper stains and poxchips out of the tub and—on hands and knees—the tile floor, nearly asphyxiating himself with the ammonia . . . *picked up* all stray garments and other detritus in his slot . . . *made* the bed with hospital corners the way his mother did . . . *swept up* the underbrush of dust balls, hair balls, mashed Band-Aids, ATM receipts, dead Snapple bottles of diluted fruit juice concoctions, black plastic caps with pocket clips from thrown-away throwaway ballpoint pens, junk-mail flyers, and magazine insert cards. It took him more than three hours.

No sooner had he put all random objects, his sneakers, the heaps of paper on his desk, his glasses cases, his medicine kit, and his Community Coffee mug, which he had to carry back and forth to the bathroom, into neat rows and piles, than Charlotte returned from the neuroscience examination. She entered the slot with a miserable look on her face. Adam waited for it to brighten when she noticed the new shining order of the place. He smiled, opened his arms wide in a comically exaggerated fashion, and said:

"Welcome to the new, brighter life *chez* Gellin!"

Charlotte rushed into his arms, threw her arms about his waist, lay her head on his chest, and burst into heartrending tears.

"Oh, Adam, I butchered it, I butchered it, I buh-uh-uh-uh-uh-uh. . . ." The convulsions came so fast, she couldn't even complete the word.

"I seriously doubt—"

"I didn't halfway study enough! It was so horrible! Now everyone's going to give up on me! I've let everybody dow-ow-ow-ow-ow-ow-ow-own . . ." She gulped for breath. "Mr. Starling, Miss Pennington . . . everyboh-ah-everyboh-ah-ah-ah-ah-ah-ah-ody . . ."

Relentless tears. Adam wondered who Miss Pennington was. "Come on! Pull yourself together! Everybody feels that way after a tough exam! I can guarantee you've done better than you think you have."

"Ohgod, it was bad enough as it was! Mr. Starling won't even look my way anymore! He thinks I've turned into he doesn't know wha-uh-uh-uh-uh-uht . . ."

"*Stop it! Stop it!*" Adam barked it out like an order, surprising even himself. "*I won't have it!*"

Charlotte abruptly stopped crying and stared up at Adam with her mouth slightly open and her tearful eyes shining . . . with respect bordering oddly on pleasure, as women sometimes do when a man claims the high ground and rebukes them.

The team pulled up to the CircumGlobal Lexington in a brand-new Mercedes SuperLuxe charter bus, white with stylized blue speed lines on the sides. Jojo was sitting halfway back, next to Mike. The seats were like first-class seats on a Boeing 767. The windows were tinted dark as sunglasses, so that at first he couldn't make out anything. But then he saw them. Like the other players, he never consciously admitted to himself how satisfying the sheer presence of the gawkers and the groupies was. Quite a crowd outside the entrance to the hotel . . . He was surprised that Lexington, which he had always thought of as a Kentucky college town, was big and big-time enough for a CircumGlobal . . . A lot of well-to-do white Necktie types he was looking at . . . probably waiting for cabs to go out to dinner or whatever, and . . . there they were, six, eight, maybe ten groupies . . . white. The groupies were always white, although at least 85 percent of the stars of big-time college basketball were black. Strange business, the groupies.

Jojo rose with alacrity, or rose insofar as a man six-foot-ten could rise up in a bus. No matter what his troubles were, no matter if a freshman hot dog had taken his starting position, no matter if an athlete-hating history professor had sworn to have him expelled from Dupont, no matter what—the ten minutes it took them to enter some grand hotel and stand around the lobby waiting for the student managers to sort out their luggage for them and check them in at the desk were ten minutes of Heaven on Earth. He knew damned well that every member of the team, including the swimmies, got the same rush, even though nobody, including him, was ever going to be fool enough to say so out loud. For those ten minutes, they were giants bestriding the earth.

The moment they, the players, emerged from the bus, descending the steps, ducking way down to avoid hitting their heads on the doorframe—

The onlookers held their breaths, lest these giants crack their skulls. They let out their breaths as the giants cleared the door and stood up straight, like gigantic jackknives unfolding.

The groupies pranced forward, pretty white girls whose faces, had they chosen to leave them unpainted, could have been those of the sweetest, most dedicated day-care-center volunteers. As it was, their eyes shone from way down in Night Life black occipital craters. Their eyelids bore cantilevered store-bought lashes, their lips gleamed with an astonishing range of hues, the waists of their jeans were below the tops of their hip joints, and the jeans were so tight, their belly buttons so conspicuously pierced with silver rings from which hung a short string or two of pearls . . . that they looked like hookers. They obviously looked that way to the adult hotel guests, who had never seen such a troupe in their lives. But they weren't. They were volunteers. They were offering their bodies for nothing more than the honor of having these famous giants use the fissures in their loins and faces howsoever they chose. They were like the temple harlots in Buddhism—or was it Hinduism—or what the hell was it? The name Left-handed Shakti blipped through Jojo's brain . . . The course had been called The History of Religion in Asia and Africa, but all Jojo could remember were the temple harlots. The idea had made him feel perversely concupiscent at the time. But in his current mood Jojo felt sorry for the groupies. Whose little girls were they? Did their parents have so much as the faintest knowledge of all this? Jojo had had enough of these volunteer hardwood harlots. Such an empty, decadent pleasure, devoid of any emotion higher than an animal's, unless you counted smug satisfaction as an emotion.

"Treyshawn!" piped up one of the groupies, a little blonde whose breasts looked like a pair of small round gym balls that could be removed or reattached at a moment's notice.

"Hey, sugar," said Treyshawn out the side of his mouth, in a gloriously bored fashion.

"Hi, Jojo! Remember me?" Jojo took a look out the corner of his eye. Not bad, actually. A tall white girl, brunette, delicate features, great legs revealed by a skirt hiked all the way up to . . . *there*. Jojo not only didn't "remember" but also was not going to lower himself by responding. On the other hand, he *was* the second one to be solicited, preceded only by Treyshawn. So they hadn't forgotten him!—despite the fact that he never started on the road anymore. He was just beginning to savor that little boost in status when—

"Vernon!"

"Vernon!"

Two of them, two juicy little groupies crying out for . . . the man who had cost him his starting position on the team of the national champions.

As the boys went through the revolving doors and into the lobby of the CircumGlobal Lexington, it started all over again, the awe, the *ahhhs*, the unabashed gawking. They towered above the hooples in the hotel lobby. They were like an entirely new and advanced order of humanity. Buster Roth required his boys to wear jackets and ties on road trips. The white players—Mike, the swimmies, and himself—all wore navy blazers with khaki pants, except for one of the swimmies, who wore a pair of gray flannels. But the black players were into styling, voguing. Styling and voguing this year meant three- and four-button single-breasted suits. Treyshawn wore a five-button, custom-made. The top button buttoned way up high. The bottom button seemed to be about six feet lower. The suit made Treyshawn look like a chimney. Coach knew what he was doing. When the team came walking into a blingy hotel lobby like the CircumGlobal's, they weren't mere giants. They were ready to . . . rule. That much you could read in the gawking faces of all the swells staying at the hotel.

Jojo had exulted in that feeling many times. Tonight, however, too many problems were converging at once. He was no longer a starter. The humiliation of it right now was bad enough. But what about the long-term meaning, his dream—no, more than his dream . . . his *assumption*, the basic assumption of his life, that he would play . . . in the League . . . the League! The elevation that would give his whole life meaning! It was merely that, a baseless assumption. There was still a chance of his changing all that. But he wasn't going to change anything if he got thrown out of Dupont. It had taken a long time for the truth to sink in concerning this history teacher who was bringing him up on a charge of plagiarism, Mr. Jerome Quat. He had never for a moment allowed for the possibility that Coach couldn't take care of the situation. Why, Coach was a Dupont legend; but it now developed that not even Coach plus the president of the university could budge this prick Quat. The fucker knew very well Jojo Johanssen could have never written a paper like that, and sooner or later he would find a way to prove it. Eventually, if it dragged on long enough, that wuss Adam—was it Tellin?—or Kellin— what the fuck *was* his name?—whatever it was, he'd cave. The guy wasn't built for hanging tough under pressure. No, Go go Jojo was fucked. The mildest penalty would be suspension for one semester—the one in which most of the basketball season and the NCAA tournament, the March Madness, occurred.

Or he could get an F in the Age of Socrates. He was in way over his head, just as Coach said he would be. He had gotten wrapped up in Socrates and Plato . . . Socrates's equation of knowledge and virtue, his "universal definitions" as distinct from Plato's Ideas, but he wasn't used to all the reading, the way the real students were, or doing the papers, which involved insights and analogies and a lot of other things he'd never had any practice in, or using big words, "the dialectic," "eudaemonological ethics," "intellectualist and over-intellectualist attitudes." When he had the chance, he'd be in front of his computer. Mike would want to play Grand Theft Auto or Stunt Biker, or NBA Streetballers, but Jojo would be there at midnight online, looking up words. An F in the Age of Socrates would have the same consequence: he would be banned from athletics for a semester.

There must have been at best a half-dozen groupies in the lobby, even though the CircumGlobal wasn't the sort of place that was going to let them hang around volunteering their perfect pink lamb chops for long. Coach had ordered everybody to ignore the girls. Even smiling at them created a trashy impression, and he wasn't going to stand for them besmirching the program's reputation. Yeah, yeah. Jojo could see the boys checking the cutie-pies out with sidewise glances and then sniggering to one another and trying to foresee the future, i.e., life after bed checks.

Mike and Jojo shared a big room with a pair of queen-size beds. Jojo couldn't have isolated the details for you himself, but he could tell . . . this was a luxury hotel. A pair of great fluffy white terry-cloth bathrobes in the closet with the CircumGlobal family (dating back to 1996) crest embroidered on the breast pockets . . . likewise upon the matching bath sandals . . .

Mike didn't waste a minute. He immediately went to the inevitable School of Mahogany armoire, housing the television set, picked up the remote, settled back into an easy chair, and turned on one of the hotel's own vast in-house selection of Pay-per-View hard-core pornographic movies. Jojo, on the other hand, retrieved two books and a spiral notebook from his Dupont duffel bag and headed straight for the desk, where the lamp had a bulb brighter than forty watts, this being one of the not immediately visible amenities of a luxury hotel, and began poring over Aristotle's *Metaphysics*, which contained a lot about Socrates.

From the television set came the usual whinnying and *unnghhhs*, those two sounds being the outer limits of acting ability in the adult movie genre. Jojo glanced over. From his angle all he could see was a linguini of shanks, flanks, paunches, haunches, swollen nodes, pendulous melons, and stiffened giblets writhing with spastic jerks and spurts on a hotel bed.

"How the fuck can you sit there watching that shit, Mike?"

"That's not the question," said Mike. "The question is, how can *you* sit *there* reading that . . . whatever the fuck you're reading?"

"Well . . . I got to study, man. I got the finals in this"—he paused, not wanting to say the name Socrates —"this history of philosophy course I'm taking."

"Whoa-ho!" said Mike, lifting his hands and contorting his face in a mock show of surprise. "I forgot! I'm now rooming with—"

"You say the name Socrates, dude, and I'm gonna cut your fucking nuts off for you."

"Hey, anything but that, Soc—I mean, old roomie of mine. There's some fine, fine jiner waiting for us down there after bed check."

Jojo emitted a philosophical sigh. "You know, I was wondering when we came into the hotel. Why do groupies do what they do? Why do they come fuck a bunch of basketball players they don't know and will never see again? I don't get it. It's not as if they're busted or something. Some of them are really pretty. They don't *look* like sluts. Well, they *sort* of look like sluts. But I still don't get it."

"To tell you the truth, I don't think about it. It seems to make *them* happy. Why look a gift horse in the mouth, is what I say."

There was something curious about what Mike had just said. Jojo couldn't put his finger on it. Provided with a printed transcript, he probably would have, eventually. Sooner or later it would have dawned on him that his roommate had spoken three consecutive sentences without using the words *fuck* or *shit* or any of their conjugative or compound variations.

Bed check was usually just before midnight, and, sure enough, at 11:55 the telephone rang and Jojo answered the one on the desk. The assistant coaches, Skyhook Frye and Marty Smalls, made the calls.

"Hey, you're getting good, Sky," said Jojo. "Yeah, it's me."

"We got a rough game tomorrow, Jojo," said the voice of Skyhook Frye. "So don't you guys fuck with me. Okay? Now, where's Mike? He better be fucking *there*. Or *not* fucking there, as the case may be."

Jojo handed the phone to Mike.

Mike listened to Skyhook, all the while giving Jojo the upward roll of the eyeballs that says, "Tedious motherfucker, ain't he."

"Me?" said Mike. "I'm in bed. You woke me up . . . Would I shit you, Sky? . . . Okay, peace."

Mike hung up and said to Jojo, "Whatta we do—wait—fifteen minutes or what?"

"I'm not going out. I got too much homework."

"Are you fucking serious?"

"Yeah, I'm serious! I can't fuck around. I've got an exam coming up in this . . . Age of Socrates course."

"What the fuck is it with you and—"

Jojo cut him off. "Watch it! It's like I told you, I can say 'Socrates' but you can't. It's bad enough hearing it from fucking Coach."

"Even with that hottie"—Mike motioned toward the lobby—"waiting for you?"

"What hottie?"

"'What hottie' . . . the one who's all legs and no dress. She practically lay down on the floor and spread 'em as soon as we got off the bus . . . I saw you checking her out . . . 'What hottie' . . ."

The recollection stirred Jojo. He couldn't help it. He fantasized her standing before him . . . those fabulous long legs . . . that little hint of a skirt barely covering her hip sockets . . . and she has on nothing underneath . . . and she has shaved her pubic hair . . . *Get ouddda here!* He forced the tumescent-making thoughts out of his mind.

"Oh, that girl," he said. He pulled a face, as if to say she was just another groupie, and so what was the big deal? "I gotta pass this fucking course, is what's on my mind right now. All I got to do is get an F, and I'm truly fucked."

Mike tried this way and that way to coax him out of his righteous abstinence from life after bed check, but Jojo would not be moved.

"Well, that's okay," Mike said finally, ". . . if you wanna be like that . . . But don't give me a hard time if some Dupont . . . fan . . . happens to insist on joining me when I get back to the room."

"Yeah, yeah," said Jojo. He made a point of turning to the books he had on the desk before he had completed uttering the first *yeah*.

Once Mike had gone, Jojo began to enjoy the bracing virtue of self-denial. This was in fact the perfect time to focus upon Aristotle's *Metaphysics* and get that out of the way. He could just imagine Mike and probably André and Curtis and Treyshawn, maybe Charles, heading off to some bar with their little cum dumpsters and having the same birdbrain conversations they had in Chicago and Dallas and Miami . . . just long enough to chat them up a little before scrogging . . . all so sad and weary and shallow . . . for, as Socrates himself put it, "If a man debauches himself, believing this will bring him happiness, then he errs from ignorance, not knowing what true happiness is."

Jojo began taking notes. He had hardly ever done that before; but this course, the Age of Socrates, and this teacher, Mr. Margolies, had actually gotten to him. "Concepts" . . . it was all about "concepts" and "conceptual thinking." . . . The age of Socrates was the age of the first systematic thought. By the very *way they thought*, the Greeks changed the world. Socrates believed in Zeus. Whether or not he believed in the others, too — Hera, Apollo, Aphrodite, and . . . and . . . Jojo never could remember all of them — there was no record anyway. But Socrates believed in Zeus . . . Jojo wondered if people used to get down on their knees and pray to Zeus or hold hands around the dinner table and thank Zeus for the meal, the way his great-aunt Debbie did . . . but whatever. Socrates was a fiend for logic, all the "inductive reasonings" and "ethical syllogisms" . . . Jojo had Aristotle's *Metaphysics* in front of him, and Aristotle was saying, "Socrates did not make the universals or the definitions exist apart; Plato, however, gave them separate existence, and this was the kind of thing they called Ideas." . . . Jojo was sure that would be on the exam, and so he decided to read that section over again . . . "Socrates did not make the universals or the . . ."

Jojo had a picture of Socrates and his students in his mind, although he really didn't know where he got it from . . . They're all sitting around in to-gas . . . Socrates has long white hair and a long white beard and a white toga, and his students all have laurel wreaths around their heads . . . and the to-gas . . . He wondered how they carried anything in the togas. They were just sheets, as nearly as he could tell. But maybe they didn't have so much . . . stuff . . . to carry . . . no car keys, cell phones, ballpoint pens, credit cards . . . Yeah, but what about money? They must have had to have money. Or maybe they didn't, at least not every day. What the hell was there to buy? They didn't have CDs or cars to buy gas for or Gatorade and Powerbars and all that . . . Then he wondered about what you did with your toga when you had to go to the bathroom . . . He could imagine all kinds of difficult situa-tions . . . For that matter, if the students wore laurel wreaths every day, where did they get them from? Who made them? Women, he reckoned, but what women? Socrates didn't say much about women . . . Who did the dishes? Or the laundry? Maybe they had slaves, or was that just the Romans? Well, he didn't have time to go off on all these tangents. Back to the *Metaphysics* . . . This shit was hard to read . . . What'd he mean, "As man's body is composed of materials gathered from the material world, so man's reason is part of the universal Reason or Mind of the world"? It gave Jojo great satisfaction to fig-ure this stuff out. If only he had started taking all this stuff seriously when he was a kid . . . or even when he was in high school. "Socrates overlooked the irrational parts of the soul," Aristotle was saying, "and did not take sufficient notice of the fact of the weakness of man, which leads him to do what he knows to be wrong." Jojo thought that over. Socrates just got through saying man's reason is what it's all about, not false happiness like going around fucking groupies, and all of a sudden here's Aristotle saying moral weakness, such as fucking groupies, is what it's all about, too. He wondered if Aristotle and Plato and Socrates had groupies. Just how well known were they? When they went away and checked into—but they probably didn't even have ho-tels then, or not this kind, where—

There was a rap on the door, which was evidently metal, even though it was painted like wood.

"Who is it?" yelled Jojo.

"*House*keeper," . . . accenting the first syllable and sort of singing the whole word, the way they did in hotels.

With a sigh, ticked off at being interrupted, Jojo went to the door and opened it.

"Jojo? I'm Marilyn." Fair young face, lots of eye makeup—

—long legs, fabulous legs, looking even longer, since her foot was tilted up at a forty-five degree angle upon a pair of sandals with the most negligible of little slip-on straps and heels that must have been close to four inches high. They rose and rose, those fabulous legs, up to the most negligible little skirt in the world—it was her, all right.

Demurely: "Can I come in?"

"Oh . . . sure, sure," said Jojo, ever the courteous giant. As he held the door open for her, he started trying to figure out how to tell her she couldn't stay. How did she even know what room he was in?

She came in and stood right in front of him as he let go of the door, which closed by itself.

"Wow!" she said with big eyes and a lovely girlish smile. "You look tall on TV . . . but you're really *tall!*"

Jojo was confused. She was one of those people you can just tell right away are nice and well-mannered.

"How did you know what room I was in?"

"Your teammates told me." She continued to smile in the nicest, sunniest fashion. "They said you've been studying very hard and feeling lonesome, and you needed a break . . . and here I am."

Jojo shook his head. "Oh, those—" He stared at the floor and shook his head some more. Then he lifted his head, and she hadn't moved. Her face was no more than eighteen inches from his, and most of that was due to his being a foot taller than she was. "Look—Marilyn—it's Marilyn, right?"

She nodded yes with the same simple, adoring look as before.

"You're nice to come give me a break and all, but I got to study. Don't listen to my—" He caught himself as he was just about to say "fucking" but caught himself. "—teammates, especially the guy—the white guy. Mike."

Her expression never changed: cheery, lovely, straightforward, utterly non-ho'-like. "Well . . . could I just watch?"

"Watch? Whaddya mean, could you watch?"

"Watch you study."

He searched her face for irony—and found none. She was different from most groupies. She didn't gush with all the *likes* and *seriouslys*. She didn't flirt with her eyes.

"Why would you want to watch me study?"

She looked up at him in the same open, guileless way, still smiling. But now her smile had a slight cant to it, as if to tell him he still didn't understand, did he.

"I won't stay long," she said.

No sooner had the word *long* left her lips than—*bango!*—her hand cupped his crotch. She was still looking straight into his eyes with the same smile, which kept saying, "Oh, I wish you understood." Now she had unzipped his khakis and put her hand inside.

Jojo shook his head . . . but without conviction. Now she had her hand inside the fly of his boxer shorts, and Jojo involuntarily closed his eyes and in an odd, trancelike way began saying, "Oh shiiiiit . . . oh shiiiiit . . ."

By the time they reached the bed, she had somehow managed to unbuckle his belt and undo the top button of his khakis. Like many a man before him, his brain had dropped like a stone into his groin.

He was barely cognizant of the next few hours . . .

Rising up toward an opening from out of some sort of dark shaft into a blinding light . . . For an instant he had absolutely no idea where he was. From deep darkness into excruciating light, it hurt his eyes, was all he knew, that and the odor of spilled beer.

In the next instant Mike's voice: "Aw, shit, roomie, didn't mean to—" He emitted a high-pitched whistle, using his tongue and upper teeth. "So that's what your friend Soc—uh, your Greek friend looks like. Not bad. Go go, Jojo. If I'd known the Age of Soc, uh, uh, was like that, that's who I'd be studying, too."

Groggily, Jojo propped himself on one elbow. Mike and some sort of blond bimbo were standing about five feet inside the door staring at him—at *them!*—him and Whatshername? Marilyn? Whatshername was lying facedown, stark-naked, the inside of his right thigh lay athwart her bare bottom, and his foot was hooked beneath *her* thigh. They had fallen asleep! Jojo couldn't think of what to say. He lay there sprawled and speechless, still deep in the hypnotic state. He tried to figure out which was worse, lying there like he was or removing his thigh from the girl's naked bottom, giving Mike's groupie an eyeful of his genitals.

"Jojo," said Mike, "I want you to meet Samantha."

Jojo just stared. The girl's blond hair was so short but so curly, it reminded Jojo of ivy grown amok. She had on a lacy top, resembling a peignoir, with jeans, at the moment a fashionable teenage clash of chords deemed provocative.

"Samantha, say hello to Jojo."

"Hi, Jojo," the girl said.

"And Marilyn," said Mike.

"Hi, Marilyn," the blond groupie said, even though the naked girl in the bed looked dead to the world.

"It's 'Marilyn,' right, roomie?" said Mike, with a mocking smile. "She looks wiped out."

Jojo said nothing. He was staring groggily at Mike's blond groupie. She was smiling at him flirtatiously—*flirtatiously*—and so broadly, it brought out the dimples in her cheeks and forced her eyes into squints. She had on such long, mascara-laden false eyelashes, they looked like rows of charred matchsticks. She wanted to *flirt?*—and him stark-naked with one leg wrapped around a stark-naked girl?

Now the girl, Marilyn, was beginning to stir. She rolled toward Jojo, so that his leg enclosed yet more of her body. She lifted her head, puzzled, then spotted Mike and his groupie. She turned back toward Jojo and gave him a kiss on the lips, then said, "I have to go tinkle."

With that, she got up and sauntered stark-naked to the bathroom, as if this were the most natural social situation in the world.

Mike stared at her approvingly. "Whattaya been studying, Jojo, Helen of Troy?"

Jojo sat up on the bed, conscious of the fact that this laid his flaccid but still-swollen penis out flat on the undersheet, then retrieved the covers, which were bunched up at the foot of the bed, and got a glimpse of his and Whatshername's clothes abandoned all over the floor in the first rush of lust.

"He's really big!" Mike's groupie whispered to Mike, nodding at Jojo.

"Yeah, he's big in many places," Mike said in a full voice obviously aimed more at Jojo than at the groupie. "But that don't mean he's big every place."

Jojo didn't so much as look at them. He just reached down, pulled the covers up, got under them, and rolled over on his side, turning his back on Mike and the groupie.

Pretty soon Whatshername Marilyn returned from the bathroom. For some reason she had a towel around her waist. It covered her up down to the knees. But she sauntered toward Jojo with her shoulders back and her breasts rampant, then abandoned the towel upon the floor along with everything else and climbed into bed. He hadn't really taken it in before, but she had shaved her pubic hair, too. How *did* the word get around?

Mike finally shut out the lights. Jojo could hear him and his Whatshername Samantha undressing and getting into bed amid a lot of giggling and teasing and *Oh-no-you-don'ts*. The next thing he knew, Whatshername Marilyn's hand was between his legs.

She whispered in his ear, "Hmmm . . . I think *he's* awake, too." The sensation of her breath blowing across the stand of little hairs in his ear aroused him.

"Oh shiitt . . . oh shiitt . . ." Since he had already been about as totally embarrassed as you could be, there was no longer anything left to act discreet about, much less proper, was there . . .

The last thing he remembered, before failing asleep again, was himself scrogging his groupie with complete moral abandon—"moral" was the unwelcome word that crashed the party in his central nervous system—and listening to the *unnghhhs, Yesyesyesses, notyetnotyetnotyets* (the groupie), and *Yeahbabyyeahbabyyeahbabies* from the next bed. In the nearly but not altogether total darkness he could make out Mike's groupie straddling his hips and bouncing up and down.

It made Jojo think of a rodeo. All she needed was a cowboy hat to wave in the triumph as she scored her animal.

Later on—he couldn't have said when—he woke up again. This time it was dark, and Mike was saying in full voice, "Jojo! Jojo! Yo! Jojo!"

"Uhhhht?" Jojo managed to say, meaning "What."

"Wanna swap?"

"No."

"If you change your mind, let me know. You'll love Samantha, I'm telling you. Say hello to Jojo, Samantha."

"Hi, Jojo," the groupie said.

"See?" said Mike. "Nice girl."

Even in his groggy state, Jojo was appalled. By the light that came in under the door, he could see Mike and his groupie head to the bathroom.

He rolled toward Marilyn and embraced her, this time with pity and guilt and an urge to . . . save her. Something about her made him think she really was a nice girl.

She misinterpreted Jojo's intentions. She put her hand between his legs again.

This time he was not aroused. Embracing her more tightly than ever, he whispered into her ear, "I can tell you're a nice girl. Why do you do this?"

"Do what?" she whispered.

"Well—" He didn't know how to put it . . . "Wh . . . be so nice and obliging to somebody like me. Like . . . make yourself available and everything. You don't even know me, and that girl—she don't know Mike."

"You're *serious?*" She said it in such a way that obviously he was either making a little joke or was a little dense.

"Uh . . . yeah. Why?"

"You really don't understand?"

"No."

"You're a star." Most obvious thing in the world.

"And therefore?"

"Every girl wants to . . . fuck . . . a star." She said it in the same sweet, sincere voice she said everything else. "Any girl who says she doesn't is lying. Any girl."

Try as he might, Jojo could not think of a cogent reply.

A moment later she added, "And *every* girl."

In the morning—she was gone. Jojo loathed himself.

A pair of speakers boomed out over the length and breadth of the Great Yard.

"*Think* about it! . . . you know? . . . Think about it . . . Freedom of expression extends only to conventional expression? Is that the message the university is sending but doesn't have the guts to come right out and say? Or should I say *straight* out?"

Got a small ripple of laughter from the throng with that one. "How come straight writers can write about straight intercourse from the lubricant secretions of the vaginal ducts—which they call 'juicy'—that's what they call it, 'juicy'—and then they bury their faces in this juicy pie, and that's supposed to be romantic passion—"

Got a big laugh with that one, did Randy. Namby Pamby Randy Grossman was at the podium up on a jerry-built dais on the plaza at the entrance to the Library Tower, the same place presidents and dignitaries spoke at commencements and convocations. A crowd of what?—four hundred?—five hundred?—students wearing blue jeans stood upon the grass facing Randy. On Stand Up Straight for Gay Day every student was supposed to wear blue jeans to show support for gay rights. Adam had his blue jeans on. Not only that, he stood on the ground in front of the dais, a good ten feet below the level of the microphone, along with nine other students supporting lengths of raw pine lumber bearing placards. His read, FREE SPEECH IS QUEER, TOO! In other words, he had become one of Randy Grossman's spear carriers. He wondered if it would look odd if he held the placard over his face.

"But just let *us* write on one of Dupont's sacred walkways in chalk about Eskimo pie juice, in which—if you haven't tried it, don't trash it—a guy puts an ice cube in his mouth and then your cock and massages your prostate with two fingers, and you're telling me that's weirder than the straight guy with his face in the pie lapping up bodily fluids plus every bacterium and virus known to STD plus the odd streak of urine?"

Oh, Randy got whoops, screams, yodels of laughter with that one—and Adam, in his heart of hearts, wanted to drop through a crack in the Library Plaza and disappear. Morally, politically, he felt not only duty-bound and righteous in what he was now doing, but courageous as well, a bit noble, if the truth were known. The Gay and Lesbian Fist, and specifically Randy, had challenged all progressives on campus, students, faculty, administrators, employees, all and whomever, to join the Stand Up Straight for Gay Day demonstration, so that no longer could anyone dismiss it as Oh *them* again. One progressive cause was everybody's progressive cause. Otherwise, they would never build up the momentum they needed. Randy had caught him and Edgar in the *Wave* office and left them no room to wiggle out of it. So here he was, on the plaza in front of the Library Tower, the most prominent spot in the Great Yard—there were TV crews—he could see the cameras, and their red lights, showing that the camera was on, were aimed right at him—or at least they couldn't miss him.

". . . call it graffiti if you want to. That's okay." Puffed up by applause and laughter, Randy was booming out like Jesse Jackson or somebody.

"But graffiti can also be art, and art can be vandalized, as this university has vandalized one of the great calligraphic achievements in its history—"

Adam didn't know Randy had it in him. But it didn't really help that when he wanted to emphasize a point, he would throw up his hands . . . with his elbows pressed against his rib cage. Not that there was anything wrong with making effeminate gestures—gestures and walks and body language generally shouldn't be categorized that way—but Randy *made effeminate gestures*, when you got right down to it, and none of the hundreds who had gathered here in the Great Yard could miss it. And nobody watching those videotapes they were making—which would be shown where?— to how many thousands?—millions?—on network television?—but they couldn't broadcast references to fellatio and cunnilingus on TV, could they? Much less Camille's placard—she was in this same lineup of spear carriers, down at the other end, with a placard aloft reading, FUCK A DUCK! FUCK A CUCUMBER! FUCK ANYTHING! FUCK ALL! The same sign company had produced all the placards, including hers, but she had no doubt composed this piece of polymorphous perversity herself. But those millions or however many would pick up on Randy's effeminacy immediately—

—and what else would they pick up? Adam Gellin as one of the Gay and Lesbian Fist's loyal fellatiotic troopers, FREE SPEECH IS QUEER, TOO!—in short, Adam Gellin, gay—in plain, noneuphemistic English: Adam Gellin, queer, lover of anal sex and Eskimo pies. He hated himself for even thinking such a thought, having any such faintness of heart. He could tell Edgar felt exactly the same way. Edgar was at one end of this lineup of spear carriers—or placard carriers—at the foot of the podium and the feet of Randy Grossman. Edgar's placard read SUPPORT GAY MARRIAGE — NOW! From the moment he picked it up and shouldered it, he looked ashen. The two of them had the same problem, and he bet Edgar, like him, was ashamed to talk about it. Edgar, like him, had no obvious sexual involvement with women. He had often wondered if Edgar was gay, and Edgar had probably wondered the same thing about him. Maybe Edgar *was* gay. How was anyone to know? Why was everybody so obsessed with the labels? What was wrong with the neutral term "bachelor"? Why had he given in and allowed Randy to shame him into coming—so the entire campus could conclude he . . . was homosexual? Not that he hadn't done exactly the right thing, what so many others who gave lip service to gay rights wouldn't have dared do—and his thoughts began to race around in a circle again.

"—beloved 'truth,' as they probably think it is," the amplified leader of the people was saying, "they don't even know *their* truth! Made to order *by* them—*for* them! What kind of 'truth' is that?—the ultimate delusion! The self-scam! The *self*-scam! The so-called 'trustees'—the *ring* that controls Dupont—they're so retro, they won't stop at conning you and me, they're—"

Adam couldn't believe it. Randy was getting louder and more shrill. Now he thought he was an orator. He was turning rhetorical . . . *figurae repetitio, figurae sententiae* . . . Namby Pamby Randy Grossman, leader of the people—

"Boooo . . . Boooo . . . ." A chorus of *boos* was rising from somewhere in the rear ranks of the crowd. Adam, standing at ground level, couldn't see.

But Randy, up on the dais, could. He started screaming. "Yo! You! Yeah, you! You repressed queens in the back there—"

"*Boooo!* . . . . . . *Boooo!* . . ." The chorus was mounting in volume.

"—you in the short pants! That's cute! It's so butch! The Eskimo pie got you all turned on, didn't it? You can't wait to get back to the *frat* house and try it, can you!"

The blue jeaners in front loved that. They cut loose with the sort of cries and yodels of adrenaline-pumped people bloody ecstatic over grievous wounds inflicted upon the enemy.

But the *boos* of the agitators rose to the level of a roar, then broke into a chant. Adam couldn't hear what they were saying at first, but then he got it. "COCK—SUCKERS! COCK—SUCKERS! COCK—SUCKERS!"

It was so blatantly bigoted, he couldn't believe it. Students had been expelled or suspended for an entire year for less, especially when it was antigay.

Then he could see them. Some were bulling their way through the blue jeaners as if they were about to storm the dais and seize the microphone. Others had come around the flanks of the crowd. Now he could understand Randy's reference to "You in the short pants." To a man, they wore shorts, mostly khaki shorts, the kind commonly worn with flip-flops in the spring and early fall, except that they were wearing construction boots—and it was freezing out here. At first Adam didn't get it, the short pants, but in the next moment he did. "You want everybody to wear jeans to show support for gay rights? We'll show you something—utter mockery—even if it means freezing our asses off!" There must have been dozens of them, and as they came to the fore, their chant overwhelmed the attempts of the crowd, taken by surprise, to shout them down.

"COCK—SUCKERS!" they chanted. "COCK—SUCKERS!"

But wait a minute—now that they were close, Adam realized it wasn't COCK—SUCKERS at all. "GOD'S YUCCAS! GOD'S YUCCAS! GOD'S YUCCAS!"

Randy was shouting into the microphone: "Stuck on sucking cocks! You're stuck on sucking cocks! You're queerer than we are!" he boomed out over the Great Yard. "Admit it—"

"GOD'S YUCCAS! GOD'S YUCCAS! GOD'S YUCCAS!"

"—you wanna suck each—" Randy broke off his analysis in midsentence. All at once he realized they were shouting "GOD'S YUCCAS!"

Some of them were no more than fifteen feet away—and big. What did they intend to do?—Adam leaned forward and looked this way and that at his fellow placard holders. He didn't want to be the first to break ranks—nor did he intend to be the last.

He glanced up. Randy was no longer at the podium. The little shit must have bolted, fled. Adam brought his placard—FREE SPEECH IS QUEER, TOO! in front of his face. But what good would that do? None. So he peeked around the placard . . . In the immediate foreground—Hoyt Thorpe! He was the one leading the chant!

"GOD'S YUCCAS! GOD'S YUCCAS!"

Fear and hatred descended upon Adam's amygdala with equal force. Tormentor of the woman he loved!—physical threat to his very hide in the here and now! He worked it out by concluding that if he now confronted the bastard physically, it would play right into the counterdemonstrators' hands— and besides, Thorpe would recognize him—and the Night of the Skull Fuck story would be compromised, and—

What? A woman's voice raged over the Great Yard: "FUCK YOU IN THE ASS, YOU CLOSET QUEENS! YOU FUCKING HIV VAMPS! WHAT'S THIS SHORT PANTS SHIT? YOU HOPE SOME CHILD MOLESTER WILL STICK A WEENIE UP YOUR HERSHEY HIGHWAY?"

Camille. Could only be. Adam didn't even have to look up to be absolutely sure. But he did anyway. Her face was as contorted as he had ever seen it.

"WANT IT THAT BAD? WHYN'T YOU PULL YOUR LIT-TLE PANTIES DOWN AND LEAN OVER AND TAKE IT LIKE A MAN! YOU FUCKING SHIT-FACED MAGGOT MOTHER-FUCKERS!"

Camille's raw-throated rant breathed life into the blue jeaners. They broke into a roar of their own. Thorpe and the other frat boys—there was Vance Phipps, too!—their lips were still moving in the chant

:::::GOD'S YUCCAS:::::GOD'S YUCCAS:::::but they could no longer be heard. Hoyt Thorpe held up his hand, as if to restrain his boys and avoid a pitched battle, then slowly led them away and back toward the other end of the Great Yard. Nobody could hear them, but they kept chanting

:::::GOD'S YUCCAS:::::GOD'S YUCCAS::::: Hoyt Thorpe looked over his shoulder, smirking coolly at Camille as he retreated.

Others in the lineup of placard bearers were turning this way and that, talking to each other excitedly and casting glances in the direction of the departed frat boys. Adam took advantage of the moment to slip away. He strolled nonchalantly toward the library, letting the shaft of the placard lean against his shoulder at the angle of a rifle . . . looked about . . . laid the placard facedown on the plaza . . . and walked as casually as he could into the library, through the front entrance. Just what to do next . . . he had no idea. Stop standing out on the Great Yard holding a sign above his head saying QUEER, that was the main thing.

He stood in the lobby, just stood there, looking up at the ceiling and taking in its wonders one by one, as if he had never laid eyes on them before, the vaulted ceiling, all the ribs, the covert way spotlights, floodlights, and wall washers had been added . . . It was so calming . . . but why? . . . He thought of every possible reason except for the real one, which was that the existence of conspicuous consumption one has rightful access to—as a student had rightful access to the fabulous Dupont Memorial Library—creates a sense of well-being. But as one fear subsided, that gave another fear room to rise. Adam's deep worry rushed to his forebrain. The plagiarism case. It wouldn't disappear. He didn't want to see Jojo again, and he dreaded seeing Buster Roth again. Getting out from under the corrupting pressure of "the program" had proved to be an enormous relief . . . except that he really wasn't out from under it yet . . . Jojo and "his" paper on the psychology of George III . . . Just how did they think someone like Jojo was *ever* going to write a paper on the psychology of *anything* . . . unless somebody wrote it for him? A wave of paranoia . . . he was following a strategy laid out for him by Buster Roth. He could *see* Roth right now, as if he were right in front of him. What did Roth care about the fate of Jojo Johanssen's ex-tutor? *Nothing.* Roth would impale Adam Gellin's carcass on a spit if he thought it would benefit "the program" . . . He began to drive himself crazy . . . trying to imagine how Buster Roth could use his statement . . . that he hadn't helped Jojo on the paper in any way . . . to improve Jojo's chances in this case. He closed his eyes. So there he was, standing in the lobby with his eyes closed, torturing himself with his thoughts, listening to a thousand footsteps echoing off the stonework of the grand space—

"Adam, what are you doing? Why aren't you out there?"

It was Randy Grossman. He had a frantic, accusing look on his face. Adam knew the more pertinent question was why wasn't Randy out there, why he had disappeared—but Adam was too overwhelmed by guilt to even mount the argument. The truth was, he *did* want to get away from the demonstration. Randy and the Gay and Lesbian Fist were 100 percent right in their cause. Gays and lesbians deserved not merely to have equal rights, they deserved also to be welcomed, *embraced, hugged to the bosom*, as sisters and brothers, the moral and social equals—in many cases, the moral superiors—of straight people. Absolutely no question about it! But to be *labeled* as one of them? *Yuchhhh.* The thought made his flesh crawl. He couldn't imagine anything more ruinous or disgusting. That made him feel even guiltier as he stood here in the soaring sanctum of the Dupont Memorial Library looking at Randy's appalled expression. Randy had done a brave and noble thing. He had come out. He had put his reputation on the line. He had overcome many fears and limitations and girded his loins . . . even unto the task of ascending to a podium in the Great Yard to lead the people on Stand Up Straight for Gay Day. And he made Adam's flesh crawl, which made Adam feel guiltier.

He began sputtering and making imaginary snowballs and trying to explain to his moral superior, Randy, that he wasn't *leaving*—by no means!—it was just that he . . . uh . . . he'd had a . . . *muscle spasm,* yeah, a muscle spasm, from holding the placard in place for so long, and he'd had to put it down for a moment and he was heading right back into the fray and so forth and so on.

Thus morally cowed—by Randy Grossman!—he sheepishly left the library and picked up the placard—Randy Grossman, his superior here at the Masada of our times, watched him suspiciously every step of the way—and headed back to the ruckus, the rhetorical mayhem of the sound system, which made twerps think they were leaders of the people, to the battleground—for that was what it might become! Suppose Hoyt Thorpe had retreated merely to regroup and—attack!—*assault!* He could see the cool smirk on his face! Yet shame proved to be more powerful than fear. Adam found himself back in the line of Praetorian guards in front of the dais, with a big sign over his head saying QUEER.

"—not even by pushing the envelope of their at once bulked-up and refined hypocrisy can they find a basis in case law or morality or simple human decency for their opposition to same-sex marriage. Not only that—"

This time it was the voice of a man, not a student, thundering out of the speakers and the Great Yard and echoing off the stone façades of Dupont's most venerable buildings. Adam put the placard over his face so he could look back up over his shoulder at the podium and see who it was. It was a fat man in his fifties, probably, wearing a V-necked gray sweater that was too tight and brought out many unfortunate folds in his flesh. Adam didn't recognize him, but considering his elocution, it was a good bet that he was on the faculty.

"—so that the religious right chooses to stress the premise that marriage is all about children. But if we look at *their own holy text,* how often does *their own holy prophet,* Jesus, dwell upon children? He doesn't dwell upon children . . . *at all.* In fact, he only mentions them *once,* and that's in response to a question. It's in what the religious right refers to as the New Testament, the Book—their name for a chapter—the Book of Mark, verse forty-two, in which Jesus says, 'Suffer the little children to come unto me, for of such is the kingdom of Heaven.' That's their own prophet on the subject of children. That's it! Let'm come shake hands with me here in public! That's it! It's a photo op! On the basis of *that* they're telling us their religion is opposed to same-sex marriage? They don't *know* their own religion! We've got a knowledge gap here, and we'd have to build a bridge for them to ever get across it!"

Whoops, howls of laughter, as the wise man outed the philistines.

"Now, my wife and I have two children, and we love them, we're extremely close to them, and we'd do anything in the world we could for them. But do we think our marriage is 'all about' them? We both have careers, and we happen to think our marriage is also 'about' our work. I'll go further. We happen to think our work is meaningful. My wife is an attorney, and she is always on call, by her own choice, for the court to appoint her to represent indigent defendants in criminal actions. I teach here at the university, and I happen to think—of course, I can't guarantee that my students don't think otherwise"—big smile, hearty chuckle—"I happen to regard teaching as— to use words I hope the religious right will be comfortable with—a 'holy calling,' and our marriage is 'about' those things, too. Is there any reason why partners in a same-sex marriage could not rear children, could not adopt and raise children from among the literally millions of children in this country who are without parents, with the same love and dedication my wife and I try to give our children? Of course not. The two things, the gender composition of the marriage and the rearing of children couldn't have *less* to do with each other! Couldn't have *less!* To have to deal with such a nonsensical argument at all . . . *stuns* the normal mind!"

That brought a burst of approval from the crowd of blue-jeaners and spurred the speaker on to greater heights.

"The sheer *ignorance* of it actively victimizes those who are the most vulnerable and defenseless, the children of this country! Victimizes them and subjects them to unspeakable abuse!"

A roar of approval, but Adam put the placard in front of his face again. He wasn't joining in. Whoever this old guy was, he was a foxy old bastard. He had just *happened* to have to divulge that he was married and had two children. Oh, of course, to be gay was 100 percent terrific, maybe it was far, far *better* to be gay, but he just *happened* to let it out of the bag that he was a *straight* cat, he was, he was. Adam resented that. This faculty member, whoever he was, could score big points by appearing at the Stand Up Straight for Gay Day rally—but with a microphone to let the world know he *himself* was no fucking faggot . . . while Adam Gellin had to stand here stock-still and silent, holding a sign up over his head that said QUEER in big letters. Why couldn't he have a microphone, too, or at least add a line to his sign? Now it said,

FREE SPEECH
IS QUEER,
TOO!

Why couldn't he add,

AND NOT JUST
STRAIGHT
LIKE ME!

Damn, that was longer than what was already there . . . The damned placard by itself would have to be six feet high. With the stick . . . the thing would end up eight or nine feet tall . . .

The old guy was really soaring now, barrel rolls, outside loops, power dives, inverted spins . . . There was no holding him back . . .

Who was he, though? Overcome by curiosity, Adam sidled over to Camille, who was once more a Praetorian guard. He was careful to keep his sign facing front and his face behind it.

"Who *is* that?" he said.

"Jerome Quat," said Camille out the side of her mouth. "He's one of the few faculty members with guts. The rest just sign petitions."

"Jerome *Quat?*" Adam was startled. "Teaches *history?*"

Camille nodded yes. A tremor went through Adam's solar plexus. His heart started banging as if it had an appointment somewhere else. Jojo's history professor!—the very one who had him and Jojo trapped inside a box like a couple of insects! This was *him!*

Adam's every instinct told him to vanish—*now*. But he couldn't very well bolt in the middle of the guy's talk . . . Randy and the guilt factor . . . So he just stood there with the QUEER placard over his face, thinking . . . Gradually his mind caught up with his amygdala . . .

Mr. Jerome Quat came down, at length, from the heights of oratory and stood at the podium accepting the applause and cheers—real cheers—and one of the current undergraduate chants of approval, which went, *Wooo wooo wooo wooo!* Camille had joined in and was going *wooo wooo wooo wooo* as she put her placard down and hurried from her post to go back behind the dais and congratulate him. Adam followed her. Quat had descended from the dais at last and was currently thronged by Fist leaders and fans . . . and seemed to feel no urge to hurry away from their flattery and gratitude and more flattery.

Camille was elbowing her way to the great man with typical Deng doggedness. Adam stayed on her heels, even elbowed his way past an odd body or two the way she did. He put his hand on her shoulder. She spun about angrily but then saw who it was.

"He's awesome!" he said to Camille. "He's the Man! I never heard him speak before! I gotta meet him!"

"I'll introduce you!" said Camille. "He's the only one with any fucking guts!"

When she reached Quat, she raised her hand to give him a high five, and he slapped her palm with gusto. "Mr. Quat, you're the only straight professor on the whole fucking faculty with any fucking guts!"

Far from being taken aback, Quat threw an arm around her, squeezed her to him and said, "It's Jerry, Camille . . . Jerry. You're the one with guts! The way you sent that bunch of frat boys packing—that was golden!"

They proceeded to do quite a duet in that fashion before Camille was aware Adam was planted right in front of them, barely thirty inches away.

"Mr. Quat—"

"Jerry."

"—this is my friend Adam Gellin."

"Adam Gellin . . . ," said Quat, as if ruminating . . .

"I told you about the Millennial Mutants?" said Camille. "Adam's one of us. There's supposed to be all these liberal straight guys who are going to stand shoulder to shoulder with the Fist? A lot of them are going to—but they're dicks—"

"'Dicks'? Camille, I love you, kid!" said Quat with a great chortle.

"—and they don't show, but Adam did. He was right down there in front of the podium with a placard."

Quat shook hands with Adam and began ruminating again. "Adam Gellin . . . Why do I know your name? Just the other day . . ."

"Adam writes for the *Wave*," said Camille. "He wrote the story about the trustees and their Buddy Club. You see that?"

"*Everybody* saw that! Congratulations," he said to Adam. "The way you made those pompous—but that isn't what I was thinking about . . . It was something else . . . It was just the other day, too . . ."

Adam took a deep breath—and held it. Odds . . . evens. Acey-deucey . . . He thought of Charlotte . . . waiting for him. Damn it! This time he wasn't going to let himself be frozen with timidity.

"Mr. Quat," he said, "I think I can tell you why. Until recently I was a tutor for the Athletic Department. I was the tutor for Jojo Johanssen."

He pursed his lips and stared straight into Quat's eyes. He tried to resist swallowing, but he couldn't. He'd said it—and now he was in play.

Quat didn't say anything for a moment. Then he began nodding his head. "Ahhh," he said. "I see." More nodding.

He seemed as unsure of what was happening as Adam did.

Later that afternoon Adam opened his cell phone with such a feeling of elation that it even dispelled—for the moment—his fear of the Quat situation. He immediately called Greg at the *Wave*.

After keeping him hanging—for about five minutes, it felt like—Greg came on the phone and said, testily, "What is it, Adam? We're on deadline here."

"This'll take two seconds," said Adam. "You know the Skull Fuck story?"

"Holy shit, Adam!" said Greg. "How many times—"

"Just one thing, Greg, just one thing. I've got the angle! This makes it news! I just got off the phone with a source deep . . . *deep* . . . within the Saint Ray house. Hoyt Thorpe just took a bribe from the governor of California to keep quiet about the Skull Fuck story. And just thirty minutes before this call I got a call from Thorpe saying he's changed his mind, and we can't run the story. A bribe, Greg! A Dupont student gets fucking bribed by the likely Republican nominee for president! . . . Greg . . . Are you there?"

Finally, wearily, Greg said, "Yeah. I'm here."

"Greg, this source is ironclad. We're talking iron-fucking-clad."

TOM WOLFE

30. A DIFFERENT PREPOSITION

dam assumed a role completely foreign to him. He became Charlotte's "bad" camp counselor, the one who couldn't care less about being known as "a good guy," the one who insists that the campers not only obey the rules but also realize that the rules have the force of righteousness, which is to say God, behind them.

Charlotte was like many another depressed girl before her. Come the dawn she would still be wide-awake, all too alert, all too alarmed by the thought of having to get out of bed. There was the drag of inertia and the fatigue of insomnia and, worse than either, fear. The insomniac's period of sleep, whether she falls asleep or not, is like Charlotte's eight-hour, nine-hour, ten-hour interstate bus ride. In that period she has no duties, no obligations, no responsibilities, no one to confront, because there *is* no one to confront. She has official permission from God to take care of *nothing* for the duration.

The morning of Charlotte's modern drama exam was the worst. Adam had set the alarm for eight, because the exam was at nine-thirty and he intended to make sure she took a shower, yes, in the hall bathroom, and *did* her hair, and dressed neatly. The alarm went off, and Charlotte didn't budge, even though she was clearly not asleep. She responded to Adam's exhortations with indecipherable grunts. He climbed over her and got up and turned off the alarm. She lay there the next thing to comatose; her eyes were open, but the lights were not on.

"Damn it, Charlotte!" said Adam. He stood before her in T-shirt and boxer shorts, elbows akimbo. "I've gone to a lot of trouble for you! I didn't want to get up at eight, either, but I did. And you're going to, too. You've got an exam ninety minutes from now, and you're going to take that exam, and you're going to arrive at that classroom looking like a person who cares about herself, and you're going to eat enough to provide enough blood sugar to be able to concentrate on that exam. So let's . . . *hop—to it!*"

Charlotte didn't move a muscle, but her lights turned on dimly. In a tiny, groggy voice she said, "What difference does it make? I stay here, I go there . . . either way I get an F." With that, she moved a muscle, two muscles, in fact, the frontalis muscles, which enable a girl to lift her eyebrows in a shrugging manner.

"Oh, really?" said Adam. "Now, why is that? And please provide some pity for yourself in your answer."

The little voice said, "It has nothing to do with self-pity. Mr. Gilman is absolutely—I don't *think* the way he does. I *can't* think the way he does. He thinks this poor all-messed-up little woman, this 'performance artist,' Melanie Nethers, is the most important thing there is in modern drama. Shaw, Ibsen, Chekhov, Strindberg, O'Neill, Tennessee Williams, they're all passé? They're not cool? He thinks 'cool' is a *concept?* What am I supposed to—"

Adam wouldn't let her finish. Gesturing at her inert, horizontal form with both hands, he said, "Charlotte—this is not right!"

"It's not a matter of—"

"It's simply *not right!* Do you hear me?"

"Whether it's right—"

"You can't just *blow off a final exam!* Who do you think you are? How *dare* you be so thoughtless?"

"Well, the plain truth is—"

"You have *no idea* what the plain truth is!" This time Adam clenched his teeth and gestured at her with both hands, fingers curled as if they had claws on the tips. "WHAT YOU'RE DOING IS PLAIN WRONG! YOU'RE THROWING AWAY A GREAT MIND AND A GREAT OPPORTUNITY! WHO GAVE YOU THE *RIGHT* TO DO SUCH A THING! WHO THE HELL DO YOU THINK YOU ARE?"

"I think—"

"THIS IS *NOT RIGHT!*"

"I—"

"GET UP! GET UP! THIS IS NOT RIGHT, YOU JUST LYING HERE LIKE THIS!"

"Will you—"

"NO! I WON'T! THIS IS NOT RIGHT! IT'S WRONG!"

"Will you let—"

"NO! I WON'T! WE'RE ON THE EDGE OF A KNIFE HERE AND WE'VE GOTTA JUMP ONE WAY OR THE OTHER, THE RIGHT SIDE OR THE WRONG SIDE! THERE'S NO MEDIAN STRIP!"

Something about Adam's avalanche of implacably moral stuff got to her, resonated with some of Christ's Evangelic creed she had brought to Dupont without meaning to, sewn, as it were, into the very lining of her clothes. There was also, unbeknownst to either of them consciously, a woman's thrill!—that's the word for it!—her delicious thrill!—when, as before, a man expands his chest and drapes it with the sash of righteousness and . . . *takes command!* . . . upon the Heights of Abraham.

That moment was a turning point. Charlotte pulled herself together, did as she was told, and made it to the exam with time to spare. She returned to Adam's apartment convinced that she had butchered this exam, too, and complaining about the weird, warped mentality of Mr. Gilman. She did not break into tears; she did not despair. Scorn, contempt, and hatred were her métier. She registered not woe but anger, a deadly sin perhaps but a positive sign in this case.

Adam continued to go to bed with her every night. He pressed his body upon hers every night, at her bidding. As the night wore on and Charlotte finally drifted off into two or three hours of sleep, he slept with her—ever more bitterly conscious of the irony of that little phrase. If he had ever uttered such a thing in the company of, let's say, Greg or Roger or Camille, any of them would have assumed Charlotte was draining his testicles for him every night. "Draining his testicles" was Camille's term for a girl's "living with" some boy. Camille wouldn't say, "That little idiot has been living with Jason for a month now." She would say, "That little idiot has been draining Jason's testicles for a month now." If the truth be known, the kinetics of Adam's "living with" Charlotte hadn't changed in the slightest. He still embraced her like a mother holding a five-foot-four baby on her lap. Charlotte never lay facing him in bed. He held her from behind, not as a lover, but as that vapid soul, the loving friend who sees to it that a poor troubled girl feels protected and secure—and not alone in this trough of mortal error where all mortals must abide. Many was the time the loving friend had an erection beneath his boxer shorts. Many was the time that stiffened giblet had the urge to thrust itself forward—two or three inches would have been enough—and let her know it was there . . . that was all . . . merely acquaint her with that pertinent fact. But how could he risk it? What had chased her into his bed but . . . somebody else's mindless, wandering erection, a battering ram who had knocked her door down and ravaged her.

Irony, irony, all too exquisite, the irony—and then one night something entirely unexpected happened. Charlotte fell asleep within one minute after they had climbed into bed and he had put his arms around her.

She had her first full night's sleep in six weeks or more. She awoke refreshed and even betrayed signs of optimism. The same thing happened the next night. The next morning she *wanted* to get up. The end of insomnia was pretty solid evidence that she was pulling out of her depression.

After a few days, Charlotte suggested that they return to the original arrangement, with him on the futon and her on the bed, or vice versa, since she felt much better and was no longer afraid at night. Adam was of two minds. How could he give up the tantalizing, if so far frustrating, prospect of having her body next to his every night and in the fullness of time sleeping with her in the metonymical meaning of the expression? At the same time . . . it was damned uncomfortable, two people in that one narrow bed; and besides, playing nurse without compensation in kind or in money was impossible to enjoy much beyond ten days.

And so there came a day when the second semester began, and Charlotte decided she should return to her own room in Edgerton and rejoin her clothes and other belongings. She and Adam were by no means splitting up. In fact, Adam walked her back to Little Yard and went up the elevator in Edgerton with her right to the door of her room on the fifth floor. She opened the door—it wasn't locked—and invited him in. So he went in.

A big blond-streaked head of hair—filled up the room. Spectacular! Such a tall, slender girl! On second thought, the word was . . . *skinny* . . . and her *nose* and her *chin*—Charlotte's roommate. Adam knew immediately from Charlotte's description.

"Hello, Beverly," said Charlotte. It was about as cold and wary a greeting as Adam had ever heard, especially in light of the fact that this was a roommate she hadn't seen or spoken to, so far as he knew, in ten days. Then Charlotte added in the same cold voice, "This is Adam." Still looking at her roommate, she said in the numbest of tones, "Adam, this is my roommate, Beverly."

Adam forced a big grin, a very big one, and said, "Hi. Nice to meet you."

Beverly gave him as dead a smile as he had ever seen in his life. Her lips extended about ten millimeters on either side, but the rest of her physiognomy was having no part of it. In that same half second her eyes gave him the once-over, head to toe and back up to his head. *Enough of him*—she devoted the rest of that second to Charlotte.

"So . . . the roommate returns," said Beverly. Her expression said, My, how you do amuse me. "I thought you must have turned right around and gone back to North Carolina. But then I saw you on campus a couple of times during finals. So then I figured you must be staying out on Ladding Walk or someplace."

Charlotte's face turned absolutely scarlet. She was speechless. Adam was afraid she might cry. The silence stretched out out out out before Charlotte responded. "I've been staying at Adam's."

"Oh," said Beverly. Her voice struck *le chant juste* of fake sarcastic surprise and interest. She gave Adam another flick of the eyes, going head to toe and back to his head again with an expression that couldn't have said A PERSON OF NO CONSEQUENCE any louder if she had shouted it. Adam felt wounded and furious before his mind could even process the particulars.

Pretty soon, in due course, at the doorway, Charlotte gave Adam a hug good-bye, but it wasn't the hug he had come to cherish—and live for—the one in which she threw her arms around him and laid her head on his chest. In fact, it wasn't much more than a social hug. She gave him a kiss, but he could only imagine it touched his cheek. It was definitely not more than a social kiss. Whispering, she said, "Call me? Or I'll call you? Promise?"

As the Edgerton House elevator descended, Adam weighed the pluses and minuses and decided the result was very much in the plus column. *Of course* she hadn't given him an ardent embrace as he departed . . . not with that *snobbish bitch*—the bitch had deigned to look at him exactly twice and speak to him not even once and clearly found him A PERSON OF NO CONSEQUENCE—no preppy pink button-down, no creaseless Abercrombie & Fitch khakis—was *that* it, you *bitch?*—no fratty swagger, no fratty smirk?—no inchoately flirtatious fratty twist of the lips and significantly too-long eye-lock, as if to say if the circumstances should happen to change, *let's fuck?*—was *that* it, you *bitch?*—you sorostitute . . . you *Douche* in the larval stage, you cum dumpster for Saint Rays and Phi Gams only—*discriminating* anorexic bitch, aren't you—you pus-boil lump of conventional thought, conventional taste, and stillborn conventional passions selected like one of those whatthehellsthename handbags from some giddily expensive pur-veyor—too true, isn't it!—*that's* what we have here, isn't it!—and ten years from now, as you sit in your summer place in . . . in . . . in Martha's Vine-yard with your Saint Ray clone consort watching a *60 Minutes* segment with Morley Safer—he'll be about a hundred, it occurred to him—Morley Safer interviewing Adam Gellin, creator of the New Matrix of the Twenty-first Century—that will be the title of the segment—you'll turn to the big cloned jut-jawed titanium head—big but very light—sitting beside you and say, "Oh, I've known him for a long time—he was my roommate's boyfriend at Dupont"—not with *that* snobbish bitch looking on was Charlotte going to demonstrate the depths of her . . . her . . . her feelings for him. That would be too much to expect. *But!*—she had said frankly, openly, "I've been *living with Adam*—and I don't care for a minute if you know . . . you snobbish bitch . . . I'm proud of it! That's the way things are! Get used to it!" And she had whispered—he could *feel* that angelic whisper of hers as well as hear it—"Call me? Or I'll call you? Promise?" Promise, oh yes . . . promise me, promise me.

Adam departed Edgerton, the Little Yard, and the Mercer Memorial Gate with visions of loamy loins dancing in his head.

The telephone exploded, and Charlotte woke up from way down deep, won-dering where she was. That became clear soon enough.

"Who the fuck is *that?*"—from beneath a roil of bedclothes, Beverly, groaning, surly, angry over being awakened by *your* fucking phone call. Groggy voice: "What the fuck time is it?" *Whuh the fuck time'sit?*

Eight o'clock on the dot, it was. Charlotte picked up the receiver in the middle of the second ring.

"Hello?"

"Hey, it's—"

She didn't get the rest of it, because Beverly's growl rose up so loudly from her winding sheet of covers. Her head remained mashed flat into a pillow and her eyes remained closed—but I *command you* to hear my voice: "Drag it the fuck outta here! I mean, shit, it's the middle of the fucking night!"

Charlotte cupped her hand around the receiver and said, "Hello? I'm sorry?"

"It's me, Adam. Who *was* that? Beverly? Want to grab some breakfast at the café before you go to neuroscience?"

"I guess I—I have to think a second."

Going to the café, which meant Mr. Rayon, would cost her three or four dollars, and she remembered how fast her five hundred dollars had melted away during the first semester. On the other hand, eating alone in the cathedral gloom of the Abbey . . . More than that, she was feeling guilty about the way she said good-bye to Adam last night . . . the sort of hug and non-kiss you'd give a cousin . . . He had clearly been hoping for something more, but she hadn't wanted to show any more emotion than she did. Why? Well . . . Beverly was looking, and embraces are intimate . . . Oh sure! You *wish* that were the reason! It was because Beverly was looking on, all right—but specifically because Beverly didn't think much of Adam. She made that clear without saying one word. Adam—one glance, and Beverly ranked him very low on the Cool scale and the Up scale, that being the measure of how much one understands about the higher life, the Up life, the circles where people live a style of life that revolves about the protocols of being rich and the sophistication that wealth can subscribe to, play with, and afford—and she, Charlotte—face facts!—did not choose to be seen throwing her arms around a guy that low on the scales of Cool and Up . . . She was immediately overcome by guilt . . . and contempt for herself and her lack of backbone . . . after Adam had just about saved her life . . . and for her snobbery—unfortunately, that was the term for it—where Adam was concerned. She was guilty! As guilty as Beverly! . . . guiltier—inasmuch as she knew Adam, knew how wonderful and charitable and loving he was, and owed him so much.

All of that went through her mind in a rush, and she put maximum enthusiasm into her voice and said into the receiver, "That would be *great!*" But she hadn't said, "That would be great, *Adam*"—because that might arouse Beverly's contempt all over again.

It aroused her wrath, in any case. She started doing one of her classic bed-thrashing numbers.

Adam's voice in the receiver: "How soon can you be ready?"

Charlotte, aloud: "Fifteen minutes?"

From the bed: "Shit, Charlotte, drag it the fuck *outta* here!"

In the receiver: "Okay! I'll swing by in fifteen minutes."

Charlotte, aloud: "Thanks! Bye."

"Goddamn it, Charlotte!" Beverly had now propped herself up on one elbow and was looking right at her. Her head had canted over at such a groggy angle, it rested on her shoulder, and her hair was in her face. "I asked you nicely! I'm trying to fucking sleep!"

Charlotte looked at the big woozy face before her—and she surprised herself. She wasn't intimidated or even timid. She wasn't sorry, and neither was she angry. She didn't even feel like pointing out the absurdity of the word "nicely." She looked *down* on the face before her. She existed on a different plane. She had risen from the ashes. I *am* Charlotte Simmons again, but a Charlotte Simmons who has walked over the coals and through the flames and emerged with the strength to *let you know that* and, for the first time, to be candid.

"Beverly," she said, "there's something I want to ask you." She said it with such a calm, unapologetic voice and with such a level gaze that Beverly's expression went from cross to wary. "You said you wanted details about what happened at the Saint Ray formal. Since then, have you heard what happened? Has anybody told you about it?"

A trace of alertness stole into Beverly's face. "I *heard* something . . ." She shrugged.

"What you heard was true," said Charlotte. "And if you heard any details, they were true, too. And if you didn't get enough details, any details you can imagine, they're true, too. So now you know everything? Probably more than I do myself? I gotta meet somebody for breakfast. I'll see you later."

Beverly stared at her with as blank a look as Charlotte had ever seen on her face. Whereupon Charlotte went into her closet and found her old bathrobe, the one she had been cowed out of wearing soon after she got to Dupont. She put it on with a flourish of the belt, stepped into her banished old fuzzy slippers, picked up her old vinyl kit, and headed for the bathroom. Beverly slowly sagged down off her elbow prop and sank back into her bed without another word.

When Charlotte and Adam reached Mr. Rayon, the breakfast crowd was just beginning to build. It always built slowly because the typical student didn't wake up before ten a.m. if he could possibly avoid it. Charlotte still felt strong. She *was* Charlotte Simmons again. All the same, she looked around to see what she could see. She and Adam got in line. How shiny and slick and light and bright and white the walls were! And overhead, what fierce martial colors the banners had! The laughter of girls and the pings of stainless-steel table utensils against earthenware crockery spiked up through the doggedly manly roar of boys in the season of the rising sap. Charlotte was relieved to be with Adam rather than alone in this crowd. She dreaded the thought of somebody seeing her alone and knowing the story and pitying her.

Adam was right behind her, and she turned to him and said: "Adam—I hope I don't start crying when I tell you this, but you've done so-o-o-o-o much for me. I didn't think I could ever show my face again. I felt like I was caught in a . . . in like the maelstrom in the Edgar Allan Poe story, and there was no way I could get out of it. But you got me out, Adam. I feel like a human being again. You really—well, I'm more grateful than I can ever put into words."

Even as she said it, she realized it was for two reasons, and one of them made her feel devious. She said it because she meant it—but she also said it so that if any Crissy or Gloria or Nicole or Erica or Lucy Page or Bettina *was* looking at her, she would see her in animated conversation, indicating that Charlotte Simmons had *not* been reduced to a little forlorn and universally scorned cum-rag of a country girl.

Adam slipped his hand around the inside of her elbow, gave it a gentle squeeze, and brought his mouth close to her ear and said, "Thanks, but I really didn't do anything for you. All I did was remind you of who you actually are and what you can become. I just *reminded* you."

For an instant, when Adam drew so close to her face, Charlotte was afraid he was going to plant a kiss on her cheek or maybe even shoot for her lips or intertwine arms or put his arm around her or make some otherwise embarrassing expression of his ardor. She didn't want *that*. But he withdrew his hand after the little squeeze and was as decorous as you could ask for.

A big joyful smile spread across her face, and she said, "You didn't just *remind* me of anything. You absolved me. You really did. You got me back on my feet."

Her beaming, tickled-pink smile didn't go with the gravity of the sentiment. Puzzled, Adam drew his eyebrows together, and his head twitched. Her harmless—well, wasn't it?—duplicity was accumulating. Once more she meant it—but at the same time she wanted anyone who happened to be watching to see that not only did she have company but she was also in excellent spirits, not at all laid low by anything that had happened. The resurrected Charlotte Simmons . . . a *happy* girl.

And someone *was* watching! As she moved ahead in the line, she felt a tap on her shoulder and turned about to see Bettina.

"Hey! Where've you been?" An upbeat, sunny Bettina.

"Around," said Charlotte, moving forward and picking up a tray.

"Hey, what's wrong? You pissed at me?"

"No," said Charlotte in a noncommittal tone, and she kept moving forward.

"Well, Mimi and I are sitting over there if you want to sit with us."

"I'm already sitting with someone, thanks."

"Who?"

"Adam is his name."

"Who's he?"

"He's right back there — plaid shirt."

Bettina glanced back and took her time about it and then said to Charlotte, "What is he, a T.A. or something?"

"No, he's my friend." The way she said it cut off any further discussion.

"Ohhh," said Bettina. Her nostrils flared slightly and curled, as if Adam gave off an odor from afar. "Okay, then, whatever. See ya later." Bettina left, miffed, presumably to rejoin the other snake, Mimi.

Charlotte was offended by Bettina's tacit verdict on Adam — and worried by it. Was he that obviously dorky? She tried to work it out in her mind. Even if he was, it wouldn't take much to change that. Some contacts or laser corrections . . . and get rid of those glasses. That would be the first thing. Cut back on all that curly hair and shape it and get rid of that part. That would focus attention on his face. He had fine features. In fact, he would be handsome, if only he would let himself be handsome and un-dork — such a word? — un-dork his clothes. What are those dark blue wool pants with the pleats and cuffs . . . *wool?* . . . no guys wore wool pants . . . and that old man's belt with that sort of fake-silver sleeve instead of a normal belt buckle, and the plaid shirt with green and tan and rust-red stripes going this way and that on an oatmeal-gray background? She had the sneaking feeling that he had decided to get dressed up for breakfast with her, and this was the result. Those plaid shirts gave off whiffs of Engineering Geek or Chem Major. And those brown moccasins with soles like rock ledges — what was this unerring eye for just the wrong thing? Some simple, plain button-down shirts, some khakis, some jeans, some flip-flops, some loafers, although she would have to choose the loafers—nothing to it, and he'd be a different person!

Charlotte's breakfast came to $3.25 for orange juice, cereal, berries, and toast. Much too much—did she really need toast? Could she conceivably return it and get her money back? Not she. She knew she wasn't the sort of person who could pull something like that off . . . Her rehabilitated spirits were sinking. Tray in hand, she led Adam over to the same out-of-the-way table behind the Thai food wall divider where she had her first talk with Jojo; only this time she sat with her back to the room. As to why she had done so, chosen this table, chosen this chair—she knew but fought its rising to the level of conscious knowledge.

They sat down, and Adam looked very happy. She had never seen him look so happy. She had seen him in a good mood before—but only after an odd and in its way exhausting form of combat. He loved to compete with Greg and the other Mutants in conversation—but it was a struggle, because they were good at it. He had a passion, obviously, for *her*, but he didn't know what to do with his glasses if he was going to try to kiss her—another struggle. He got all balled up trying to figure out some way to sound passionate without sounding dorky—yet one more struggle. No one on earth would call Adam laid-back, but that was what he seemed to be at this moment.

"I don't know if I ever told you," he said, rocking back on two legs of his chair and smiling like a man who just shot the moon, "but I went to Japan the first semester of my junior year, and I spent a week with a family in a little fishing village two hours from Tokyo by train, way out by the ocean. For breakfast they didn't have an entirely different menu the way we do. For breakfast, you know how we—or most people—have things we never think about the whole rest of the day? Juice, cereal, sliced bananas, eggs, pancakes, French toast, English muffins, cheese Danish." He chuckled, quite delighted with himself. "Hmmm! Never noticed all that pan-European breakfast terminology before! That's completely American, using all those foreign names for simple food. Greek coffee? Nahhh. I don't know anybody who has Greek coffee for breakfast. Anyway, we have our special breakfast foods, and we never think about them again until the next morning. But you know what they have for breakfast out in a little village like the one I was in? They have leftovers from dinner the night before. Fish soup, warmed-over rice, stir-fried dumplings if there are any left; they're really good. Now in that *one thing*, breakfast, you can read the story of the difference between two peoples, two cultures. For a start—"

And off he goes, thought Charlotte. It was endearing, this tendency of his . . . for the most part . . . after all, he *did* have the most wonderful intellectual curiosity.

". . . things we're trying to deny ourselves"—she realized she had lost track of what exactly had led to things we're trying to deny ourselves.

". . . the calories, the carbs, the bread, the butter, the cheese Danishes I mentioned, the eggs, whereas in Japan there's nothing 'scientific' about it—"

A delicious aroma was wafting over from the other side of the salmon-colored LithoPlast divider. With the extraordinary power the olfactory sense has—Mr. Starling had talked about this—it went straight to a receptor in her memory, bypassing her "logical mind"—the very way Mr. Starling pronounced the words "logical mind" put them in quotation marks—the aroma summoned up a vision, in detail, from the time she and Jojo had sat at this very table and the same aroma had come wafting over from the Thai food counter on the other side of the LithoPlast divider. It was absolutely "ambrosial," the adjective Momma used for food that was out of this world—in fact, Momma used to serve a dessert she called ambrosia, slices of orange with white coconut shavings and a little bit, no more than a sort of glaze, of molasses covering the bottom of the bowl—Momma used cereal bowls—but why was she putting ambrosia . . . and Momma . . . in the past tense? Did this—

". . . and the yang of life, the passive and the aggressive, broadly speaking. As a result, the Japanese have the lowest incidence of—what's the matter?"

He was looking at her quizzically.

Oh God, she must have let her eyes wander. Had she really been staring at a blank wall of LithoPlast?

"Oh, I'm sorry," she said, already centrifuging her brain to try to force some little white explanation to the surface . . . Got it: "What you said about different cultures and different foods? It made me think of—in neuroscience, you'd be surprised—or maybe you wouldn't—by what a hard time the neurophysiologists have trying to figure out exactly what neural pathways like . . . you know . . . what's the word?—*convey!*—it's *convey*—convey the sensation of hunger from the stomach to the brain."

Adam just stared at her with his upper teeth overbiting his lower lip in puzzlement. The wonderfully happy look he had a moment ago was gone. That made her feel guilty all over again. He was sweet, and he really was smart—and why was she *glad* nobody else was here listening to all this? She consciously wanted to be Adam's friend, his close friend—no, it was more than that . . . she wanted to *love* him! That would solve so many problems! She could live the life of the mind and the life of romance in one and the same person! All things that really counted would come together! She would once again be on the high road. She could return to Sparta and report to Miss Pennington without fear, without guilt, without . . . lies . . . but she *didn't* love him, and she couldn't *force herself* to love him . . . She didn't feel butterflies in her stomach at the very thought of him . . . If she did, she was convinced, love would drive all the cheap, smug standards of Cool out of her mind. But Adam did have his blind spots, after all, such as trying to turn ordinary things into his beloved "matrical ideas," and he didn't even realize it was a form of showing off.

After breakfast, he insisted on walking her over to Phillips, to the very door of Mr. Starling's amphitheater—and then he stood there smiling at her until she turned her back to climb up the amphitheater stairs to the top, where she sat. When she took her seat and looked down—he was still standing there, smiling. Then he gave her a little wave that halfway resembled a salute. To top it off, he mouthed, in a heavy, overripe mime, the words :::::I:::::LOVE:::::YOU:::::HONEY::::: Charlotte was embarrassed to the core—what if somebody *saw* that?—but she felt obliged to give him at least a nod and a little white smile, which she did, and he *still* stood there— so she looked down at the desk arm of her chair, as if studying something with maximum concentration. Why couldn't he leave, like a normal person? Practically all the students in the class were juniors and seniors, and she didn't know any of them, except for Jill, her seatmate, and she barely knew Jill—nevertheless she was glad Jill hadn't arrived and wasn't witnessing Adam mooning over her like this—and there were definitely some cashmere types in this class, and she could just *hear* them saying, "So now the country bumpkin is banging a loser, a nobody, an independent . . . She definitely makes the rounds"—and above all she could hear the sniggers sniggers sniggers sniggers sniggers . . . She lifted her eyes as covertly as she could, which is to say, without lifting her head . . . Thank God! No Adam; he had finally left. But why the "Thank God"?

"Good morning, ladies and gentlemen."

It was Mr. Starling, at the lectern. He was wearing a tweed jacket that would have looked almost gaudy if the amphitheater's stage lighting hadn't brought out its colors so richly—orange, yellow, chocolate brown, luggage brown, and a certain light blue that sang harmony and brought them all alive . . . perfectly, in Charlotte Simmons's eyes . . . Yet another stab of guilt and regret . . . She could have been so close to this man . . . and his pioneering in humankind's understanding of itself . . . in the new *matrix*, as Adam would have it, except that Mr. Starling had already created a matrix, for real, not in dreams . . . and she could now be living on the very frontier of the life of the mind. He had given her her chance.

Her heart sank. Any day now, the final grades for the first semester would be out, and Momma and Miss Pennington would finally . . . find out . . . and she, the little mountain prodigy, could not think of any way to give them a little white forewarning that would soften the blow.

In his peripatetic, Socratic fashion, Mr. Starling was moving about the stage, lit up so resplendently by the lights overhead, talking about the origins of the concept of "sociobiology," developed by a zoologist from Alabama named Edward O. Wilson. Wilson's specialty had always been ants—ants and the complex social order and divisions of labor within ant colonies. He had been a newly minted Ph.D., a young assistant professor teaching at Harvard, when he went to an island in the Caribbean known as "Monkey Island" to help his first graduate student launch a study of macaque rhesus monkeys in their natural habitat. They talked about certain similarities—despite the enormous differences in size, strength, and intelligence—between ants and apes.

"And Wilson experienced what every research scientist lives for," said Mr. Starling, "the *Aha!* phenomenon, that flash of synthesis that will revolutionize the field. If there were similarities—analogies—between the social lives of ants and apes, why wouldn't Homo sapiens be part of the same picture? The analogies came flooding to his mind." Mr. Starling paused, then looked about the amphitheater with a mischievous smile. "But just as Nature abhors a vacuum, Science abhors analogies. Analogies are regarded as superficial, as 'literary,' which to the scientific mind—and certainly to Wilson's—means impressionistic. Now . . . since Science abhors analogies, just how did Wilson go about showing that from ants to humans the social life of all animals was similar—and more than similar, in fact, since in all animals it was part of a single biological system?" Mr. Starling scanned the hundred and fifty students before him. "Who will be so kind as to provide us with the answer?"

Charlotte, like so many others, craned this way and that to see if any hands were up. She herself didn't have the faintest idea. She had scarcely even looked at Wilson's book, which was called *Sociobiology: The New Synthesis*—not *A New Synthesis*, but capital-T *The New Synthesis*. How could she have, given all she had been through for the past two months? So many students were craning about in their desk chairs to see if any brave soul was going to tackle that one, their chairs made a creaking, shuffling choral sound.

A hand went up barely three feet away from Charlotte . . . a girl two rows directly ahead of her. Long, straight light brown hair she had brushed until it absolutely shone. Oh, Charlotte knew about such things.

Mr. Starling gazed upward. His line of vision was such that Charlotte could have sworn he was looking straight at *her* . . . but of course he wasn't. He pointed, and it was as if he were pointing straight at her.

"Yes?"

The girl with the shining light brown hair said, "He used allometry? If that's the way you pronounce it? In all my born days" — *bawn days* — "I never heard a living soul say that word out loud."

Laughter and chuckles all around. *All miii bawn days.* Countless faces were smiling at her. She had not only a Southern accent but a quite coy, little-ol'-me Southern accent.

"Would you define allometry for us?"

"I'll certainly try." *I-i-i-i'll sutney try-y-y-y.* Appreciative chuckles. "Allometry . . . allometry is the study of the relative growth of a part of an organism in relation to the growth of the whole. It's a really — what's the expression — *bangin'* way to describe morphological evolution . . . is the way Iiiii'd put it."

Renewed laughter, wholly *with* her! Such learned, esoteric material pouring forth in a flirtatious, Savannah deb-party Southern accent! This Dixie chick knew what she was doing!

"Very good," said Mr. Starling. He had a big smile of his own. "And perhaps you can tell us why this allometry was so useful to Wilson."

"Well," said the girl, "it's like this new dance?" Laughter, laughter, before she could even name the dance. "Allometry enabled Mr. Wilson to like . . . do the submarine?" Laughter, laughter, laughter. "He went down . . . *under* the anecdotal level, the surface level? . . . and found mathematically corroborant first principles?" — *fuhst principles* — "and that way he doesn't" — *dud'n* — "have to say an ant is like a human being or that a . . . a . . . I don't know . . . a baboon is like a sea slug? — because he can show that behavior at *that* evolutionary level is demonstrably — or I reckon I should say allometrically? — the same as behavior at *this* evolutionary level . . . seems like to me."

Laughter, laughter, laughter, even scattered applause — and some boy shouted out, "You go, girl!" Another round of laughter—and then all eyes turned to Mr. Starling to get his reaction.

He was smiling right at the girl—and right in the direction of Charlotte. "Thank you," he said. A pause, during which he continued to smile at his new discovery, the Savannah-drawling, flirtatious little prodigy. "Seems to *me*," he said, "absolutely correct." Laughter, laughter. He gazed out on the entire class. "Science abhors analogies. But science loves—or accepts—allometry, even when it finds its equations insoluble. But that problem needn't detain us." Then he turned back to his little star comedienne, smiled at her once more. "Thank you."

As it beamed up, the smile had hit Charlotte Simmons, too . . . and gone right through her. His former star, the one with the hillbilly Southern accent, was no longer even there. It was as if God had devised a little skit to show Charlotte Simmons how far she had fallen . . . replaced by another Southern girl, who had materialized right in front of her . . . same size, same long, straight, shining light brown hair . . . astounding the class with her brilliance . . . in a Southern accent . . . from the sophisticated coastal lowlands. Why hadn't Charlotte Simmons done the same reading? Why hadn't *she* kept up? Why hadn't *she* found time to think about these things . . . and have a life of the mind? She knew she shouldn't dwell on the answer. She couldn't afford to lapse back into tears. Adam was right. Tears, all tears, starting at the moment of birth, were cries for protection. But she didn't want to dwell upon Adam and the matrical dialogues of the Millennial Mutants, either.

Outside, after class, it was a cloudy, dark day, as if it were about to rain . . . Once more the mystery of why this light made the grass of the Great Yard look so richly green . . . In any case, the gloom was fitting for any girl as morosely self-loathing as Charlotte was at this moment, and she was thankful for that.

There was a more immediate concern, however. She gave the Great Yard a quick, surreptitious once-over . . . for fear Adam would be waiting, here, there, somewhere nearby, and reattach himself to her. He was becoming her . . . personal tumor :::::I:::::LOVE:::::YOU:::::HONEY:::::

Ohmygod!—how could she think that way? Adam was the only friend she had left. But it wasn't something she was thinking. It was something crawling beneath her flesh . . . *Honey* . . . How could she help it?

"Hey, yo! Yo!"—right behind her, but it wasn't Adam's voice.

TOM WOLFE

She turned about slowly. She was in no rush. Who on the entire campus could be shouting at her in order to bring her good news?

And there was Jojo . . . not much improvement over Adam, if any . . . hustling toward her with big strides. He wore the would-be ingratiating smile he seemed to think would make one want to do something for him. Charlotte was already familiar with that. At least he didn't have one of his disgusting muscle shirts . . . instead, a navy shirt, maybe flannel, with regular buttons and a collar . . . beneath a vast, wide-open puffy North Face jacket . . . made him look like a behemoth, it added such width and bulk to his frame . . . How did he—but of course . . . he remembered from the last time when neuroscience let out.

Now he was right in front of her, looking down at her with his transparently manipulative smile. Charlotte refused to smile back.

"Wuz up? Wuz good?"

Charlotte said nothing. She just lifted her eyebrows in order to wrinkle her forehead, which delivered the message, "Don't be tedious."

"I haven't told you the big news," said Jojo. An even bigger, merrier smile.

Perfunctorily: "What big news, Jojo?" She started walking on the sidewalk beside the Great Yard, hoping to get away from Phillips in case Adam did show up looking for her.

Jojo tagged along. "I'm taking French 232 this semester." His little eyes opened as wide as they could, as if this news would register in a big way.

Idly: "What's that?"

"Nineteenth Century Poetry: the Courtly, the Pastoral, and the Symbolist—and we read it in French. I'm not kidding. And she teaches it in French. Miz Boudreau. She *is* French, Miz Boudreau. This isn't Frère Jocko French. I'm through with all that stuff." He gave Charlotte the child's smile that invites praise.

She was, in fact, impressed. She even gave him a small smile. "Wow . . . You're getting brave, Jojo. You know about the Symbolists? Baudelaire? Mallarmé? Rimbaud?"

"No, but that's the point. I *will* know. I haven't told anybody, not even my roommate, Mike. And Coach—no fuh—freaking way! He's never gotten over Socrates. And that's the other thing."

He stared at her with wide eyes and the expectant grin of a child, lips slightly parted, and Charlotte couldn't help but want to play the expected part.

"What is?"

"I got a C-plus in the Age of Socrates! I just saw it online!"

"Congratulations," said Charlotte. The word came out flat, because the news had given her a start. "Grades are posted?"

"Yeah, this morning."

Charlotte frowned without knowing it. She would have to go confront her own . . . news . . . on the computer . . . the one in her room, the one Momma and Daddy scrimped and saved and slaved over, Buddy also, to give her for Christmas. Oh God, how could she have let what had happened . . . happen?

Jojo misinterpreted her expression. "You don't think that's good? They all thought I'd crash and burn!"

"No, you just reminded me of something. My grades must be posted, too."

"Yeah, but you don't have to worry about grades! I do. Coach'll still be piss—uh, he'll still be mad at me. He doesn't wanna know about the Age of Socrates. He still calls me—"

—still says "He don't," doesn't he—

"—Socrates, Fuh—Freaking Socrates is my full name. But I'm gonna tell him anyway. I got a C-plus, Charlotte!"

For Charlotte—sheer gloom. C-plus was pathetic, given the grade inflation at Dupont and everywhere else. But she would consider herself fortunate beyond all hoping if she got a C-plus in neuroscience . . . after that paper, that test, and that horrible wreck of an exam—

"And I wrote my own course paper, too. Nobody helped me, *nobody*. 'The Ethical Life: Socrates versus Aristippus and the Post-Socratics.' I blew 'em up with that one, dude!" He looked about and started zipping up his North Face jacket. "Muh-thuh-fuh—damn! It's getting cold out here. Come on over to Mr. Rayon."

"I don't—"

"I know, you don't have any money. It's on me. Don't tell anybody about that, either. Guys think you're a pussy—sorry!—they think you're some kind of a . . . a . . . a *wuss* or something, but that don't matter. Come on!"

Jojo was in a very good mood—him and his wonderful C-plus. He'd take her to Mr. Rayon . . . Charlotte had the sort of feeling a girl tries to keep from becoming a full-blown thought . . . Maybe she should take Jojo up on it. In her mind, her breakfast with Adam at Mr. Rayon this morning made an announcement to . . . everyone who mattered. Here she was, a vain and foolish little girl who had lost her virginity to a notorious playa at a formal, and the playa, in classic playa form, had let the world in on it. Poor little proto-slut! Her reputation was so ruined, she was now reduced to hooking up with random dorks like Adam. But if she reappeared with the cool-by-definition Jojo Johanssen . . .

"Okay," she said, "but I really don't have any money."

It being late morning by now, Mr. Rayon was not quite half full. Jojo chose the BurgAmerican line; and as he and Charlotte slid their trays down the stainless-steel cafeteria rails, people came over to say hello to Jojo as if they really knew him. Jojo got an Everything bagel, as it was called, encrusted with God knows how many kinds of seeds and bits of this and that. Charlotte got some oatmeal with sliced strawberries on it. Jojo looked at the oatmeal dubiously—and then began to lead her to that same old corner, next to the Thai section and the salmon-colored LithoPlast divider, but Charlotte balked. "Not there, Jojo. How about over here?"

Whereupon she led him to a table—a table for four out in the middle.

"Kinda noisy," said Jojo.

"It's not noisy *now*."

Jojo shrugged, and they sat out in the middle. Noisy here or not, Jojo remained in an excellent mood. "I got a C-plus! A C-plus in the Age of Socrates! A three-hundred-level course! I did it! Can you believe it?"

Charlotte congratulated him all over again and continued eating her oatmeal while it was still warm. The strawberries weren't much. They were out of season. A cloud stole across Jojo's face. "But I'm not gonna kid myself," he said. "I still got a problem. I got two problems. Coach and the President—I'm talking about the President of the whole fuh-reaking university, Cutler—yeah!—they both went to see this muhthuh—this bastard—well, I'm sorry, that's what he is, a real bastard!—Quat, and he won't budge, the little fat . . ." He decided not to supply a noun. "If I have to go through a . . ." He decided not to supply an adjectival participle. ". . . a hearing or whatever they call it . . . well, I mean . . . *shit!* I'm sorry, I'm sorry—but it makes me so damn mad. I mean, here's—"

Charlotte cut him off. "You said two problems." She didn't feel like listening to a rant about Mr. Quat, especially since Mr. Quat happened to be right.

"Yeah," said Jojo with a long, sad sigh. "You gotta help me on both of them, Charlotte. I told you how I'm taking French 232 this semester. I'm proud of myself. Frère Jocko French and all that stuff . . ." He gave Frère Jocko French and all that stuff a dismissive flip of the hand. "But now I got a problem. Miz Boudreau—I don't know what the woman's saying! She teaches the class . . . in *French*! I'm a new person now, and I'm proud a that. But I don't know what the fuh—what the hell she's *saying*! You know what I mean? I can read the poetry. I don't mean I can *read* it exactly—I'm in the dictionary about eight fuh—about eight times more than I'm in the book . . . but I can read it, I can get through it. Right now we're reading Victor Hugo. That old dude—the world must have been way different back in the day . . ."

"Victor Hugo? I didn't even know he wrote poetry."

"See? Now I know something *you* don't!" He stared straight into Charlotte's eyes. "But you gotta help me! If you don't, I'm fuh—I'm screwed."

"Help you how, Jojo?"

"I passed the Age of Socrates, and nobody thought I could do it," said Jojo. "Now, if I can do okay in real French and this other philosophy course I'm taking this semester—I didn't tell you about that—Religion and the Decline of Magic in the Seventeenth Century—yeah!—if I do okay in that too, the bastards'll have to have microprocessors instead a hearts not to give me a break on this other thing. You know?"

Monotonously: "Help you how, Jojo?"

Jojo said, "Well, the way I figure it is, you know French. The way you were reading that book in Mr. Lewin's class that time—I can't remember the name of the book—I mean, people were looking around at each other—"

"*Madame Bovary*," said Charlotte.

"Yeah! That's the one. If you hadn't said what you said that time, I'd still be—what did you call it?—'playing the fool.' That's what you said, playing the fool. You *know* that stuff. So I figured the only way I can save my—save myself is if I take a tape recorder to class, and then I come back and you tell me what she said. Maybe you could help me with some of the poetry? I mean, I can *do* it . . . but you know metaphors and all that stuff? Sometimes it's . . . you know . . . hard."

Charlotte said, "You know what they *call* people who will do that for you?"

Jojo, tonelessly distrustful: "No. What."

"Tutors."

"No!" said Jojo. "I told you! I'm finished with all that stuff! I'm going—" And Jojo was off on an explanation of why if Charlotte helped him, it would be different . . .

Out of the corner of her eye she spotted Lucy Page Tucker and Gloria coming into Mr. Rayon. They were bound to come close to the table if they headed for the cafeteria rails, and the positioning was perfect. First they would see Jojo, who was more or less facing them. Then their curiosity would get the better of them. They'd be dying to know who the girl was. Charlotte wasn't really following what Jojo was saying, but she figured she knew the gist of it. As soon as his lips stopped moving, she lifted her chin and put on a smile of abnormal animation and coquettishness and said, "Oh, Jojo, Jojo, what makes you think *I*"—she lowered her head, brought the fingers of one hand up to the middle of her chest, opened her eyes wide, and looked up at Jojo—"know enough French to be a tutor?"

"That's what I just got through telling you!" said Jojo, also with great animation. "You're a lot more than a tutor . . . to *me* . . . You're the girl who turned me around! You were the only person who had the guts to stand up to me and tell me the truth! I thought I was cool . . . and all the time I was playing the fool. You're the one who . . . *inspired* me." Now he was leaning way toward her . . . giving her a look of . . . significance. Before she knew it, he had taken her hand in both of his. Charlotte instinctively cut a glance to the left and to the right. Lucy Page Tucker and Gloria—they had both taken trays at the Italian section and were looking back at her. Charlotte, fixing her gaze upon Jojo, manufactured the merriest of laughs and withdrew her hand from his. And the two witches—they couldn't have helped but get an eyeful of it.

"What's so funny?" Jojo wanted to know.

"Nothing," said Charlotte. "I was just thinking of the look on a lot of people's faces when they find out you've really become a student."

Jojo smiled for a moment, then became very serious and once more gave her the look that said he wanted to pour his whole soul into her through her optic chiasma. "Charlotte, I think you know—I hope you know—there's no way you could just be a tutor to me."

Charlotte. Interesting. It was the first time he had said her name in the entire conversation. And that look . . . soulful was the word . . .

In reply, Charlotte gave him a smile of sympathetic understanding, which was quite different—and she meant it to be—from a smile of excitement, joy, or tenderness, much less love. In that same moment she cut another glance toward the Italian section rails to see if perhaps . . . they . . . Still there! They had only moved a few feet along the cafeteria rails. She didn't have time to study their faces to see if they were still looking at her, because Jojo was off on another speech and pouring more soul into her eyes.

"It ain't—id'n just the academic stuff, Charlotte." *Charlotte*; check,

check. "I don't know if you know it or not, but you've showed me like a . . . I don't wanna get all—*you* know . . . but you've showed me a new way to like . . ." He threw his enormous body into it, the struggle to deliver this speech fluently, twisting this way and that, as if to give his brain momentum, and shaping a large lump of invisible clay with his hands. ". . . like . . . you know . . . think about things . . . being at Dupont and everything . . . and it's not enough to just do things with a round orange ball . . . and what a . . . relationship is, or oughta be . . . I'm not very good at saying all this—but *you* know what I'm saying . . ."

Charlotte maintained her benign smile. She sure hoped Lucy Page and Gloria got a load of Jojo's anxious body language.

Greg and Adam were the only ones left in the office at the *Wave*.

"I'm telling you," said Adam, "you'll be the biggest fucking editor in the country, Greg! You'll be publishing the dynamite of all dynamite! This thing is fireproof! It's locked down! We've got two lawyers from Dunning Sponget and Leach, Greg—*Dunning Sponget and Leach!*—who've vetted it and given the thumbs-up!—it's *fireproof!*—it's *libel-proof!*—you'll be the hottest editor who ever worked on a college newspaper and went straight to *The New York Times!* Now that's Millennial Mutant stuff, Greg! We're always talking about public intellectuals and shit—public intellectual is fucking looking at you in the mirror! Carpe diem, dude!"

Pause . . . Pause . . . "Now, who was the last guy we talked to at Dunning Sponget—the old guy, Button, or—"

I think the Fearless Editor's getting over the shakes, Adam said to himself. At least *something's* going right.

31. TO BE A MAN

"Come on in, Mr. Gellin," said Mr. Quat, a ball of fat in a sweater and T-shirt, tilting himself way back in a glorious sprawl in the swivel chair behind his desk. He swept one fat arm up in the air in a beckoning gesture grand enough for a . . . a . . . Adam didn't know what it reminded him of—a pasha?—but he didn't have the capacity to pursue the comparison, not the way his heart was pounding pounding pounding pounding him on on on on into doing . . . whatever he was doing here in Mr. Quat's office.

Was he kidding himself? He knew what he was doing. Otherwise, this was the last place he would be likely to show up. It was just that he wanted to leave himself room . . . to change his mind and bail out at the last minute.

Like most professors' offices at Dupont, this one was small, old-fashioned—dark wooden furniture, dark wooden cornices, a pair of tall double-hung windows side by side—but Mr. Quat's walls were lurid with posters . . . from the 1960s, if Adam knew anything about it . . . a poster of Bob Dylan, rendered so that his hair looked like a conglomeration of hair extensions dyed different hot pastels . . . a poster full of swirly lines and swirly lettering advertising the Grateful Dead . . . a poster with a cobra, proclaiming the martial might of something called the Symbionese Liberation Army—

"So?" said Mr. Quat. "You like my posters?"

"Yes, sir," said Adam. Nerves popped the words out an octave too high. He cleared his throat.

"You know what they are?"

"No, sir. From the 1960s?"

"Ah! So you *do* know your ancient history, Mr. Gellin," Mr. Quat said. He smiled the smile of a man who has known the score for a long time.

The pasha. Maybe the word was pasha because pasha made Adam think of a smug fat man. The same old ratty gray V-neck sweater with a T-shirt visible in the V—or it looked like the same one he wore to Stand Up Straight for Gay Day—hugged Mr. Quat's rolls of fat, which sagged and otherwise changed shape every time he moved. They were bobbing like gelatin at this moment, in fact, as he made another grand, sweeping gesture toward a chair on the other side of the desk, a library chair, the wooden kind with stout arms and a low, curved back. "Go ahead, Mr. Gellin, have a seat."

Adam sat down, and Mr. Quat said, "How do you know about the 1960s? Most students—you might as well be talking about the 1760s."

"I took Mr. Wallerstein's course," said Adam. "Social Crosscuts in Twentieth-Century America."

"*Crosscuts*," said Mr. Quat with a chortle, as if the word was a source of rich good humor. "That's what he calls it? I haven't heard that word since . . . I can't remember. Goes back to Talcott Parsons . . . Everybody underestimates Parsons. Being that tedious to read is a problem." Mr. Quat looked away, out a window, smiling, as if recalling some funny times.

Adam didn't venture a comment. Who the fuck was Talcott Parsons? In any case, Mr. Quat seemed to be in a good mood and kindly disposed . . . Adam knew his beloved 1960s!

"The sixties . . ." said Mr. Quat with an inexplicable chortle. "Seems like an incredible anomaly now, going on half a century or so later." He looked out the window toward the Great Yard. Another chortle without any indication of what was funny. His gaze returned to Adam. "You saw"— *sawr*—"what we've got to work with now . . . Stand Up Straight for Gay Day . . . or subcontractors for the university caterers are paying slave wages to their help . . . most of whom are undocumented Latinos . . ." Another chortle. He looked away. "You can cut the hypocrisy with a knife." He looked back at Adam. "Fifty years . . . and nothing has changed. And you know why nothing has changed?"

He kept staring at Adam while the question floated in the air.

"Yes, sir," said Adam, not knowing what else to do with it.

"It's because you know what all the progressive forces are doing now? They're all busy fighting smoke. Everybody seems to think if the smoke is gone, there's no more fire."

Now *this* comment hung in the air. Adam had no idea what Mr. Quat was talking about. So he said, "Yes, sir."

"And you wanna know why nobody dares try to extinguish the fire again? That's what nobody understands. Nobody's supposed to *see* the fire anymore. That's been demonized—pointing straight at it and saying, 'That . . . is fire . . . you're looking at. Right there.'" He pointed toward the floor with an accusing finger. "That's not allowed, not even in so-called PC circles in academia. Whichever one of them thought up 'PC' was a genius in his own slimy way. It's because of that clever little smear that it's now considered . . . vulgar . . . to call the fire the holocaust—that's the word for it, except that *holocaust* has taken a specific meaning—in Greek it means something completely burned up—anyway, it's 'vulgar' to mention it. You wanna know what PC *should* mean? 'Progressive causes' is what it should mean. You wanna know what it actually means today?"

Mr. Quat's lips stopped moving, and he stared at Adam . . . waiting . . . Adam was baffled. What fire? So he croaked out, "Yes, sir."

"What it actually means is prison-bound citizens . . . prison-bound citizens . . . PC . . . think about it . . . We're being pinned down by snipers and hooligans. You saw the hooligans the other day. They were so brazen, they even put on a paramilitary uniform, the short khaki pants. They're ready to go after something as mild as Stand Up Straight for Gay Day. How many times does history have to repeat itself? This goes back to 1917 in Russia, where the hooligans lost—that was a miracle!—and 1933 in Germany, where the hooligans won—meaning, of course, those who sent them forth, the forces . . . the fire . . ."

Mr. Quat let that one loose in the air like a blimp. Reflexively, Adam said, "Yes, sir," even though Mr. Quat had not asked him a question. Mr. Quat now stared at Adam intently and cocked his head in a way people do when they are just about to excavate your soul. "Now . . . you're probably wondering why I'm telling you all this."

To put it mildly. All that Adam could make out of it so far was that a wind was rising, and in some vague way it was blowing in his favor. Mr. Quat would have never gone on that way about "progressive" this and "progressive" that if he didn't think he was talking to a sympathizer. But Adam didn't dare utter anything more adventurous than his all-purpose standby, "Yes, sir."

"Okay," said Mr. Quat, "I'm going to tell you. In the grand sweep of things"—he made a grand sweep with his hand and forearm—"Stand Up Straight for Gay Day is about as soft-core as protests get. You know what I mean? I've been involved in *protests*."

"Yes, sir."

"Nevertheless, you were right there in the front line holding a placard. That shows courage in two ways. One is the very fact that you were willing to stand up for an unpopular cause. *And* . . . Camille tells me—Camille . . ." The very thought made Mr. Quat break into a huge grin and close his eyes and lower his head and shake it. He looked at Adam again, still grinning. "That woman is . . . a *pistol*! She was born too late, though. If she'd been around in 1968, she would have blown the top off this place!" Grinning grinning grinning he closed his eyes, lowered his head, and shook it some more, apparently having visions of Camille Deng as an acetylene-mouthed Chinese Mother Bloor—Mr. Wallerstein talked about Mother Bloor—battling atop the burning barricades in the streets of Chicago during the war in Vietnam.

Mr. Quat pulled himself together. "Anyway, Camille tells me you're not gay, but you were one of the students willing to stand right there in front of the platform holding a placard reading I forget what, something something 'Queer.' That shows me what we used to call intestinal fortitude. 'Guts,' I believe, is the term that has survived." He who knew the score gave Adam a smile of approval.

"Yes, sir," said Adam, who had lost all track of what the question, if any, might be. His heart pounded pounded pounded pounded.

Mr. Quat cocked his head in that certain way again. "Now, I take it, you can . . . uh . . . shed some light on the Johanssen case. You were his tutor, you said?"

"Yes, sir."

"Okay . . . So what can you tell me about it? Where did that paper come from?"

"Yes, sir," said Adam. "But may I give you some background?"

Mr. Quat granted him another pasha sweep of the arm, as if to say, "Go right ahead."

"Camille and I," said Adam, "and Randy Grossman, the student who spoke right before you?—we're all members of a group . . . well, actually a cénacle is what we call it—like the cénacle in Balzac's *Lost Illusions*?" He lowered his eyes and smiled in an embarrassed fashion, to show that he was aware of the immodesty of the comparison. Now was the time to enter his evidence for the defense. He had worked on it until four o'clock this morning, and he could say it by heart. He told of how hard he and the other Millennial Mutants had worked to take control of the *Wave* and how, now that they had it, they were determined to print *real* stories about Dupont, such as the series on the board of trustees. In explaining what "Millennial Mutants" meant, he was careful not to mention their fundamental assumption, which was that to be a mere college teacher was too humble and self-effacing for words. He quickly moved on to the Mutants' role as the ideological core of progressive causes on the campus, whether it was standing up for gay rights or simply mobilizing students to be active and vote against the Republican Party. He enumerated the many ways they had devoted the *Wave* to that end. Then he moved to the more personal terrain. He came from a family—and he had already rehearsed how to let it be known that his family was Jewish, by packing his great-grandparents, pogroms in eastern Europe, fear of being forcibly dragooned into military service in Poland, Ellis Island, the Lower East Side, and sweatshops into a single sentence, without losing track of the syntax—he came from a family that had fought for progressive causes for generations. That flicked on, in the very moment he spoke the words, a flashback to his father, Nat Gellin, Mr. Congeniality, maestro of Egan's, the Jew who could butter up Irishmen better that any other Jew in Boston, but it was only that, a flash, and did not break up the flow of his words. He had also rehearsed how to let it be known that the Gellins, formerly Gellininskys, were Jews without money, as witness the fact that he was the first Gellin in all those generations who ever went to college. Big Nat, the tender of the sons of Erin, he reasoned to himself, had dropped out of B.U. and didn't count. Furthermore, not even he, Adam, could have come to Dupont had he not been awarded a scholarship and held down two jobs, one delivering pizza at night in a Bitsosushi and the other, as Mr. Quat was aware, tutoring athletes for the Athletic Department. Then he moved to the climax. He had a dream—and now this dream was close to becoming real: a Rhodes scholarship. He omitted the part about the "Bad-Ass Rhodie." He included the part about "opening doors"—and added a part about how, once inside those doors, he would be in a position to devote his life to advancing progressive causes in a substantial way. He figured now was not the moment to mention his intention of becoming a matrix who originates the great theories and concepts that are then spread by "the intellectuals," the people with the dealerships, such as college history teachers . . . if one need edit.

Throughout this recitation, Mr. Quat kept his lips compressed in a thoughtful manner but allowed a friendly smile to play about the corners. He also kept nodding toward Adam with obvious approval and encouragement to continue. During Adam's peroration concerning his dream of reaching the high ground where he could devote his life to progressive causes, Mr. Quat nodded more enthusiastically and continually than ever, even closing his eyes from time to time in the midst of a full bobbing nod, as if to concentrate to the utmost upon what he was hearing.

When Adam's lips stopped moving, Mr. Quat nodded some more and said, "Well—I hope you get your Rhodes. It sounds likc you've worked hard and done well, and I commend you." A pause. "So I guess that brings us up to Mr. Johanssen and his paper." Once more he cocked his head and waited.

Adam took a deep breath. This was it. He was at the border. He either crossed over into unknown territory or stayed here. Which was riskier? If he stayed here, Buster Roth was his strategist. But Buster Roth was not his friend. What was to keep Buster Roth from making him a sacrificial lamb to save Jojo? Nothing. He didn't even *know* Roth, and technically he had been working for him for two years. They were two totally different types of people. Whereas Quat—he had been with the man now for maybe thirty minutes, and he already felt as if he was with a *landsman*, a compatriot. He felt it . . . he *knew* it . . . there was no way Mr. Quat would now turn on him . . . Where would this leave Jojo? That, he hadn't thought through . . . but it stood to reason that if Mr. Quat dropped the case against one of them, he'd have to drop the case against both . . . This limbo . . . this not knowing . . . this having a sword over his neck *constantly* . . . it was unbearable . . . and the window of opportunity was now open . . . while the demonstration was still live in Mr. Quat's memory . . . Now!—and suddenly he was across the border.

"Mr. Quat," he said . . . pause . . . "what I have to tell you . . . well, let me put it this way. In order to tell you, I'm going to have to throw myself upon your mercy. Otherwise, I don't see how—I don't know how it can be done." He gave Mr. Quat a look that asked for immunity ahead of time. Mr. Quat nodded yes, as before, but without the little smile playing about the corners of the lips. "When the Athletic Department hired me," Adam continued, "they gave me a . . . not really a pamphlet, more of a leaflet, I guess you'd call it, with these guidelines for being a tutor and the limits of what a tutor could do for an athlete and so forth. I'm sure it was all very correct. It was like . . . there it was, in print. But gradually you got the message that you should forget that and do whatever the athletes wanted you to do, because the whole program depended on their getting by academically. They were always talking about the 'program.'"

Mr. Quat continued to nod yes, and Adam gradually descended from the overview . . . down to Crowninshield House and the unofficial basketball wing on the fifth floor . . . and being summoned by Jojo at 11:55 p.m. that particular night . . .

"Mr. Quat—I'm not going to hold anything back," said Adam. "I'm going to tell you exactly what happened. I'm—I'm entrusting my own fate to your hands." He could feel his heart banging away even harder. He didn't know whether what he had just said sounded dramatic and morally compelling or dramatic and pompous. However it sounded, Mr. Quat gave him the broad, reassuring smile of a father and nodded yes some more.

Reassured, Adam plunged in.

He told it all, leaving out only the fact that Jojo and his roommate sat in their suite playing Stunt Biker on PlayStation 3 while he worked all night in the library writing about a complex subject against a terrible deadline. He told himself he was making it better for Jojo that way.

He told of the all-night race in the library of Time . . . versus Intellect . . . He told of how even in the very midst of the struggle he couldn't help but admire the subtlety, the complexity, the implicit insight of the assignment itself and regret that he didn't have time to savor the reading that should have gone into the preparation of such a paper. He told of the great ironic satisfaction of coming up with a psychological concept—oh, he knew he hadn't worked it out well—to account for the resonance that the unique psychological makeup of George III—fascinating figure—would have on world affairs—all this, even while knowing full well that this was a—well, an essentially . . . proscribed life preserver he was throwing to a sinking "student"-athlete. Mr. Quat was still nodding yes in a pasha-paternal fashion when Adam reached the coda, the account of how he slipped the paper under Jojo's door at 8:30 a.m. and returned to his apartment in the City of God and crashed for twelve hours.

He stopped and gave Mr. Quat a look of supplication that all but bled for mercy.

Mr. Quat, still reared back in his swivel chair, continued to nod yes in his thoughtful manner. He wrapped a forefinger around his chin and over his goatee and put his thumb beneath his chin, as if he were holding a pipe. He studied Adam's countenance for what seemed like an eternity. The silence turned into a sound inside Adam's skull, a sound like steam escaping from one of those glass vessels for boiling water before it starts whistling. Without a word, Mr. Quat stood up from his desk and slowly walked his pendulous bulk to the other side of the little office, head down. He was still holding his chin like a pipe. Then he walked back the same way, not once looking at Adam. Adam's eyes, on the other hand, never left Mr. Quat's face or, for that moment when he reached the other side of the room, the ruff of hair on the back of his bald head.

Mr. Quat stopped by the side of the desk. He looked down at Adam. Adam was no longer aware of his heart or any of the rest of his torso and limbs—only of the steam. He looked up into the face of judge and jury. The very words, "judge and jury," bubbled up his brain stem.

Mr. Quat spoke. "Mr. Gellin, I take plagiarism very seriously. Offhand, I can't think of a worse crime against scholarship and learning and the entire mission of a university. There may be those weary cynics on the faculty here who think the university can no longer claim to have a mission, but I'm not one of them. At the same time, I resonate completely with what you have achieved here and what you've tried to achieve and your long-range goals, which are also mine. I also think I comprehend the pressures the Athletic Department must have put upon you. In light of that, I can't very well do what I would honestly prefer to do." He gave Adam a trace of a smile, albeit weary. "I think what we have to do—both of us—is make an example of this case—"

An *example?*—

"—because it encompasses so many crucial issues that must be settled *now* . . . the power of an athletic program that has gone out of control, the corruption of the scholarly ideal, the corruption of a mind as bright and promising . . . as yours . . ."

What?—

". . . and it's true that in the short run both of us, me as well as you, will have every cause to regret what will probably happen. But in the long run you will be a better, stronger person, and this institution will learn a lesson that has been a long time in coming."

"*Sir! No! You don't mean*—"

"I'm afraid I do. I'm afraid I must. There's something here bigger than your short-term outlook and my short-term outlook. And when this is all over, you will have every reason to be grateful, along with many others, for the role you've played, however fortuitously."

"Sir! You can't! I came to you in good faith! I placed myself in your hands! You're destroying me!"

"Hardly," said Mr. Quat, with his biggest paternal smile yet. "You're young. That's a tremendous asset none of us comprehends until much, much later. You'll be fine. You've got what it takes."

"No! I'm begging you! I'm begging you! You can't! I'm begging you!"

"I'm sorry. I truly am. But it will be over quickly, now that you've been forthright and told me everything. You won't have to go through an investigation or any judicial process. I know how you must feel at this moment. But trust me. This will be a catharsis, for you as well as for the undergraduate program and the hopelessly, needlessly corrupted young men we refer to euphemistically—without any regard for their true situation—as student-athletes. Without your confession we might not have gotten anywhere. Under the university code, we can't prove plagiarism without finding the specific source."

"Please! I'm begging you, Mr. Quat! I'm *begging* you! Please don't do this to me! You *mustn't* do this to me! I trusted you completely! I put my whole . . . I put my *life* in your hands! I'm begging you! I'm begging you!"

"Mr. Gellin!" Mr. Quat said sharply. "All this begging is not becoming! The ultraright already enjoys portraying us as whiners, handwringers, cry-babies. They portray our concern for the oppressed as something unrealistic, irrational, maternal, softheaded, feminine. Furthermore, they honestly believe that. So for the sake of yourself and all of us—be a man."

32. THE HAIR FROM LENIN'S GOATEE

What's wrong?" said Beverly, seeing Charlotte sitting at her desk in front of her "new" computer and staring into space. "You look like a statue. You haven't moved for the past fifteen minutes. You haven't even blinked. Are you all right?"

So that's the way it works, thought Charlotte. It was precisely *because* she had stood up to Beverly this morning for the first time, and been abrupt and sarcastic, dismissed her as a prurient schadenfreude-driven gossip, that Beverly was now asking an idle question, one roommate to another, about nothing special. Which is to say, open contempt had jarred the Groton snob who shared her room into treating her as an equal. Charlotte took a rueful satisfaction in this discovery about human nature, but it was no more than that, rueful and beside the point.

And brief. Nothing was likely to dislodge Charlotte from the foreboding that, as of half an hour ago, had metamorphosed from the larval stage into a catastrophe, official, documented, beyond fixing.

"I'm fine," said Charlotte without turning her head so much as an inch toward Beverly, who was at her computer in the depths of her jungle of wires, knuckle sockets, and techie toys. "I'm just thinking."

Beverly returned to her instant-message e-mail conversation with Hillary, who was all of three feet away, on the other side of the wall, in Room

514, amid a happy music of electronic-alert *pings* on the screen and Beverly's giggles. The silliness of yakking away with your next-door neighbor via the World Wide Web seemed to be what made it fun.

Charlotte scarcely noticed, so deeply imprinted in her brain was the very image of what she had seen on her screen:

    B
    B-
    C-
    D

Plain B, not B+, in French; B- in medieval history; C- in modern drama; D in neuroscience ... D in neuroscience ... D in neuroscience ... Like many another student before her, Charlotte had thought that if she was pessimistic enough ahead of time, if she steeped herself deeply enough in foreboding, the result couldn't possibly be as bad as she had feared. Somehow the very act of thinking about it with such despair beforehand would be a form of magic that would ward off any truly ill fate. But there her grades had been on the screen, barely half an hour ago, flat out and explanation-proof. She hadn't printed them out. She hadn't clicked on KEEP AS NEW. She had immediately deleted it—which helped what? Nothing. It was just another exercise in magic—not that she had the remotest hope it might work.

B, B-, C-, D ... So many things had been killed in her academic collapse, Charlotte had been sitting there paralyzed for at least thirty minutes, not just the fifteen Beverly had detected. D and C-minus—in fact any grade less than B-minus was tantamount to an F at Dupont these days, except that you wouldn't be kicked out for having failed two courses and barely scraping by in the others. As it was, she would be on academic probation for the second semester, and her parents would be apprised of that fact. Fortunately, Momma and Daddy had no computer, and it would probably take two days for the news to reach them by mail. What was she to do? Why hadn't she mustered up the courage to tell them over Christmas? They would have been ready for what they were about to learn. So now she had to call them—within the next twenty-four hours—to be sure the notification didn't reach them by mail first. She should make that call right now! But she would have to recite those grades to them herself, in all their stony definitiveness. Right now ... but right now she was still in a state of shock, and so she would make that call ... but later. And Miss Pennington ... Once Momma had the bad news, maybe she could revive her plan to ask Momma not to mention them to Miss Pennington. But what if Miss Pennington happened to call Momma? The thought of asking Momma to come up with a little white lie on the subject . . . it was beyond even imagining. *D in neuroscience*—and to think it wasn't many more than ninety days ago that she had been in Mr. Starling's office and he had offered her the keys to the kingdom, to the very laboratory wherein the human animals' new conception of themselves was being created a full generation before they would realize it had happened. She could hear—she seemed to actually be hearing—the change in Mr. Starling's tone of voice that day as he began to speak to her as something more than a student, as a young colleague in this, the greatest adventure in the life of the mind since the rise of rationalism in the seventeenth century—

The telephone rang, and out of sheer reflex she answered.

"Charlotte . . . this is Adam"—spoken with a note of breathless agony. "Something horrible has happened. You've got to help me. *Please* come over here . . . *please!* I need you! I need you right now—"

"Adam! Hold—"

"I'm having a—Charlotte! *Please!* It's all so horrible!"

"What's happened?"

"*Please, Charlotte!* I haven't got the strength—I'll tell you everything—just come—as soon as you can! *Please!* Do this one thing for me, before I—" He broke off the sentence.

"You want a doctor?"

"*Hah.*" A sharp, dry, bitter laugh, it was. "Skip to step three—get a coroner. Step four—organize a celebration-of-his-life committee."

"I'm calling a doctor."

"No! There's nothing—the only person who can help is you! How soon can you be here?"

"You're in your apartment?"

"Yeah." Bitterly: "My little slot, my little hole."

"Well—I'll leave right now. I'll be there—however long it takes to walk over there."

"Please hurry. I love you. I love you more than life itself."

They hung up. Charlotte sat still in her rickety wooden straight-back chair and gave the world another vacant stare. *It's all so horrible?* She had her own catastrophe to worry about. The last thing in the world she wanted to have to deal with was Adam in an "I love you more than life itself" state of mind. But how could she say no? . . . after everything.

She put on her puffed-up hand-grenade jacket and left without a word to Beverly, who was still busy pinging and giggling and bouncing and blinging her instant messages to a relay station two thousand miles away in Austin, Texas.

Charlotte had barely reached the landing when Adam's door swung open. He had obviously been waiting at the very peephole. He stood in the doorway with one of his synthetic green blankets wrapped around him like a cape. His cheeks were gaunt and ashen, and his eyes were a perfect picture of fear. Before she knew what was happening, his arms shot out from beneath the blanket. He was wearing jeans and a plaid shirt in unfortunate shades of hallway green, Rust-Oleum brown, and book-mailer-stuffing gray. He embraced her, causing the blanket to fall to the floor. It wasn't the embrace a boy gives a girl. It was the one Studs Lonigan gave his mother in the doorway when he came home to die, as best Charlotte could remember the book.

"Charlotte . . . oh Charlotte! . . . You came . . ."

She was afraid he'd want to kiss her. But he put his head on her shoulder and made a moaning sound. He hung on for dear life. It was all awkward. Charlotte didn't know where to put her hands. Embrace him likewise? Cradle his head? Everything she could think of, he might take the wrong way. So she said, "Adam . . . come on, let's go inside. Let's get out of the doorway."

So they went inside, which at least got her free of the embrace. She took off her puffy jacket and sat down on the edge of the bed, which was a tortured mess. Adam immediately sat down beside her and began to put his arm around her. Charlotte jumped up and fetched Adam's folding deck chair, the one with the aluminum frame and the wide bands of Streptolon webbing in a plaid pattern that looked even cheaper than his shirt's. She unfolded it and sat down as fast as she could. Adam, still on the edge of the bed, stared at her as if she had abandoned and rejected him.

"Adam," Charlotte said with just a touch of sternness, "you have to pull yourself together."

"I know!" said Adam, close to tears. Then he hung his head. "I know, I know . . . I'm having a—I don't know anymore!" He left his head hanging that way, his chin touching his collarbone.

Charlotte switched to talking as calmly, softly, tenderly, maternally as she could. "I can't do anything, Adam, until you tell me what's happened."

Adam slowly raised his head and looked at her. His eyes were bleary with tears, but at least he wasn't crying. In a morosely low voice he said, "I've been destroyed, is what's happened."

Charlotte stuck to tender and maternal: "How?"

Adam went into a long but reasonably calm and straightforward account of his blighted strategy and his disastrous appointment with Mr. Quat. He looked straight at Charlotte and fought back his despair with deep breaths and sighs. "He wants to make"—deep breath, sigh—"an example. That means he wants to"—deep breath, sigh—"have me thrown out of school. But even if I'm merely—" He looked away and said, "Hah. Merely . . ." He looked back at Charlotte. "Even if I'm suspended is all . . . 'all' . . . that happens, the result is the same. I'll have a suspension—for cheating—on my transcript. There goes the Rhodes. There goes graduate school even, which was my last resort. There goes *any* decent job, even teaching high school. What's left of me?" Deep breath, hopeless sigh. "There goes my big story in tomorrow's *Wave*. It'll be discredited, nullified, ignored. 'Written by a plagiarist' . . . 'a despicable smear job' . . . They'll *hate* me. That's all I'll get out of that story." Utterly forlorn, he hung his head again.

Charlotte said, "What story, Adam? *Who's* going to hate you."

Adam looked at her again, this time with his brow contorted and his eyebrows lopsided. "It's about Hoyt Thorpe."

Charlotte felt her tender, maternal face jerk alert. She was so startled, it must have registered upon Adam, even in his current state.

"It's about how the governor of California bribed him to keep his mouth shut about the Night of the Skull Fuck. I tell the whole story. One of the most powerful Republicans in the country will want my head. He can have it . . . That wouldn't be as bad as having all of Dupont University despising me, students, alumni, faculty, administration, employees . . ."

"Why employees?" said Charlotte.

"Why?" Deep breath. With a profound collapsing sigh: "I don't know . . . I don't remember . . . so you agree about the rest of them, though. That's what you really mean."

"That's not what I said," said Charlotte.

"But that's what you mean, obviously."

In fact, she wasn't even thinking about "all of Dupont," only about Hoyt. She was frantically crunching this information to figure out what it would mean for him. Why? She couldn't have come up with a rational explanation if she had tried. Who stood to get hurt was Hoyt . . . and Jojo. That gave her a start, too.

"What was Jojo's reaction to all this?" she said.

Adam lowered his head again and put his fingers over his eyes and face. In a muffled voice: "I haven't told him."

"He doesn't even *know*? You have to call him, Adam! You told Mr. Quat everything. Isn't that true? You've—you've got to let Jojo know that."

His head still in his hands, Adam began moaning. "Oh, shit . . . shit, shit, shit . . . Jojo . . . I was so sure Mr. Quat would drop the whole case. I thought I was doing Jojo a favor."

"But you didn't tell him about it ahead of time."

Adam shook his head no with his hands still covering his face. "Oh, shit . . . shit . . . shit . . . How can I tell him? He'll kill me. He's done for, the big bastard. Even if they don't kick him out, he's . . . finished . . ." More moans. "He'll miss this whole season, and if he doesn't play this season—if he's suspended for cheating—it won't matter what he does in his senior year. He'll kill me, he'll kill me." Moans . . . pathetic moans.

He was close to whimpering. Charlotte had the terrible premonition he was about to break down in some uncontrollable way. She got up from the deck chair and went to the bed and stood over him. She put her hand on his shoulder and bent down until her face was barely six inches from his, which remained slumped over to a morbid degree. In the softest, tenderest tone she could, she said, "Jojo's not going to *kill* you. He'll understand. He'll know you meant only the best. He'll know you were trying to help *him*, too. You took what you thought was a good chance, but it didn't work. He'll understand what you were doing."

Adam began shaking his bowed head so rapidly and with such a pathetic chorus of moans, Charlotte couldn't help but wonder if he had ever taken Jojo into consideration at all.

Adam took his hands away from his face, but if anything, he hung his head still lower, until his back was humped over like an arch. His eyes were shut tight. He began trembling. The trembling turned into the shakes. His teeth began chattering. You could hear them.

"Put your arm around me, Charlotte," he said in a pitiful way. "I'm so cold."

So she sat down on the bed and put her arm around him and wondered what was coming next. He didn't look at her or at anything else. He began shaking terribly.

"Please . . . bring me a blanket. I'm freezing."

Charlotte stood up, walked toward the doorway, and fetched the blanket from the floor. It was a sickly green. The material was so stiff, so unnaturally dry, so cheaply synthetic, so synthetically horripilate, she could scarcely bear to touch it. Nevertheless, she brought it back to Adam. Slumped over this way, he looked like the sculpture of that Indian, the sculpture called *The End of the Trail*. The Indian is on his horse at the edge of a cliff with nowhere else to go. Indian civilization has come to an end. The white man has exterminated it. That picture, which she had seen in an American history textbook, had always fascinated her . . . and made her so sad. She draped the blanket over Adam's narrow shoulders. When he reached up to pull it closed over his chest, his hand touched hers. His was as cold as ice.

"Hold me—please hold me, Charlotte." His eyes remained squeezed shut.

Charlotte put her arm around him again and pulled him close. He was shaking and chattering so violently, she thought he must have the flu. She put her other hand on his forehead . . . Whatever else he had, he didn't have a fever.

"I'm—I've got to lie down." With that, he let the upper half of his body flop onto the bed. His legs were twisted, but his feet still touched the floor. His eyes remained shut tight. Charlotte lifted his legs and swung them onto the bed. They were so light, his legs . . . She slipped his leather moccasins off. Now he was stretched out on a turmoil of wrenched and twisted bedclothes and blankets, a crumpled clear polyurethane bag from the cleaners with the bill stapled on it, abandoned underwear, socks, a T-shirt, the innards of a two-day-old copy of the *Philadelphia Inquirer*. Part of the blanket Charlotte had fetched for him was under his head and shoulders, but the rest was flopped down over the side of the bed and onto the floor. Charlotte retrieved it once more and made up the bed on top of him as best she could. Adam's eyes were closed, and she hoped he was falling asleep; but with the next breath he said, "Charlotte, I'm so cold."

"I've put your sheets and blanket on top of you. You'll start feeling warmer."

"No, hold me," he pleaded. "You've got to hold me. I'm so cold. I'm afraid, Charlotte!"

Charlotte stared down at him for a moment. Adam was shaking and chattering to beat the band. That left only one thing. She took her Keds off and got under the covers with him, still in her jeans, socks, and sweatshirt.

She embraced him from behind and pressed her body up against his back, just the way he had held her. He shook and rattled, but gradually his torment subsided.

When she got up to turn off the lights, he began pleading in a groggy voice, "No . . . no . . . Charlotte . . . don't go away. I'm begging you! Don't leave me alone. Hold me. You're all I've got left."

So she turned off the lights and got back into bed with him. As long as she held him, his breathing was regular. There they were in the dark. Both of her arms were around him. The circulation in the arm under him seemed to be cut off. She whispered, "Are you asleep?"

"No." The voice of doom.

She knew he was staring wide-eyed and terrified into a black hole. She knew all about that.

She held him that way all night. She sank into naps now and again. Somehow he could tell. She would wake up to him saying, "Hold me. Please don't leave me."

After a while it became pretty tiresome being mother to someone like this. But she was repaying a steep debt. Adam had kept encouraging her, and he had brought her back from the depths. But Adam—she couldn't think of anything to encourage him with.

She was holding a truly doomed boy—and then she thought of Jojo—and then she thought of Hoyt. This poor weak boy she held—he was like some kind of insipid Samson. He had brought the temple crashing down on everybody.

Hoyt came out of Phillips onto the Great Yard so angry, he was muttering to himself loudly enough for people to hear. At this particular moment, heading up the sidewalk that bordered the Yard, he had just become the prissy, fluty, faggoty, "sophisticated" voice of that little fucker Mr. Quat. " 'I'm not trying to cast doubt on your sincerity, Mr. Thorpe. I'm sure you're all *too* sincere. I'm merely suggesting that unconsciously or otherwise you've cobbled together several rather weary nostrums of the religious right and presented them as an argument. And that would be tiresome coming from *anyone*.' "

On a walkway that crossed the Yard diagonally past the Saint Christopher's Fountain and in the direction of Mr. Rayon, he switched to his own voice: "Yeah? And I'm merely suggesting that you're Jesus with his head cut off, flapping around squawking, 'Tolerance! Tolerance! Tolerance for the meek so they can inherit the earth!' and you don't even know it. You think you're some brave little intellectual Jew who's above all this God shit." That's what he *should* have told him. But the fucker would hardly let him say *any-thing* . . . Mr. Jerome Quat and his "intellectual" "wit": "'We value freedom of speech and the play of differing viewpoints here at Dupont, Mr. Thorpe, but may I suggest that in the interest of time, we postpone this particular rant of yours? You can deliver it immediately after class, and I'm sure all who want to hear it will gather round.' Fat, scarce-haired motherfucker . . ."

Students were staring at him as they passed by, but how would they know if he was talking to himself or not? Everybody on the whole campus sounded like he was talking to himself. Everybody had his head keeled over into the palm of his hand talking on his cell phone. The what?—four or five percent?—who didn't walk around the campus with the usual cell phone had the kind with a microphone below the chin and an earpiece so small you had to look for it if you wanted to see it. They'd think that's what he had, and if they didn't—fuck'm.

Well, he had gone and shot himself in the ass again, hadn't he . . . That obese, bald-headed little pisser Mr. Jerome Quat would have the last laugh. He'd give him a lousy grade. But how could the rest of them sit there and just listen to this PC shit and not say anything? Fucking sheep . . . they just swallow the sheep shit he gives them and regurgitate it every time he asks a question. If that's all you do, it doesn't matter whether you believe it yourself or not. It ends up being the only "proper" shit to say, and so you keep on say-ing it because why not be proper and not the kind of person you can't invite anywhere because he might introduce a fart into a proper conversation.

As he passed the Saint Christopher's Fountain—that magnificent piece of sculpture—what was the name of the Frenchman who did it?—a fucking genius that guy—was there another campus in the country with a piece of sculpture that great?—no, there was nothing even close—"*I'm a Dupont man*—I'm imbued with all the strength and all the beauty and all the tradi-tions of that great figure—what's it made of?—bronze, I guess—copper?—nahhhh—has to be bronze"—Hoyt cooled down. There was no way Quat could hurt him now. He wasn't going to have to take a hopeless elevator up to every goddamn investment banking firm in the country trying to explain away his college transcript, which barked like a dog, so he could get a job. Miracles happen, his dad had once told him. "They happen to those who are already ready to roll. No lucky man is simply lucky. He's the man who recognizes Fortune the moment he looks her in the face." Hoyt Thorpe, a

Dupont man, Hoyt Thorpe, a Saint Ray, had been ready, locked and loaded, and the miracle had come. Hoyt Thorpe *had* a job waiting for him, Mr. Jerome Quat or not, and not some flickering-fluorescent-lit cold-call boiler room in Chicago or Cleveland, either, but with the mightiest of the mighty, Pierce & Pierce, in New York. Ninety-five thousand a year to start—to *start*—with no limit in sight. It was hard for him to believe it himself . . . but he had it made.

It was cold out in the Yard whenever a gust of wind blew across the icy crust of the snow that remained. He buttoned up his overcoat. Given a choice, he preferred leaving it open. In the wintertime this was the Saint Ray look, the coolest look on campus: ankle-high boots, khaki pants with no crease, a bulky-knit crewneck sweater, a flannel shirt open at the throat—and on top of all that, a navy melton-cloth overcoat like this one, single-breasted, long, reaching down well below the knees, lined in navy silk, the kind of coat that would be perfectly correct with a tuxedo, too. It was the contrast between the casual stuff and the dressy look of the topcoat that made it so cool. You possessed the full give-a-shit freedom of youth, the MasterCard license, and at the same time you knew about the ultimate sway of the other world, an older world of money and power, two things that had excitements all their own. A coat like this one cost a thousand dollars at Ralph Lauren. Hoyt got his for forty-five dollars in a secondhand clothing store in South Philadelphia called Play It Again, Sam's. Now, that was cool. The long, single-breasted coat gave you a tall, lean, glamorous silhouette. You were fairly bursting with the sexual power of the first ten years following puberty—and at the same time you already knew where the rice bowl was. Hoyt had once heard a friend of his dad's, an old guy with a florid face, say that. Hoyt couldn't have been much more than eight or nine at the time, but he always remembered the old guy saying, "I'm too old, too fat, and I drink too much—but I always know where the rice bowl is."

This train of happy thoughts had just about brought Hoyt back to his old self. By the time he got close to Mr. Rayon, he was humming a disco song called "Press Zero." He could remember only one line: "For additional me, press zero," but he couldn't get it out of his mind . . . "For additional me, press zero . . . For additional me, press zero . . ." By the time he reached Halsey Hall, he was moving his lips and singing the words under his breath. "For additional me, press—"

—he didn't complete the line. What he saw in front of the entrance to Mr. Rayon was too strange. It was cold as hell out here, but there was a regular hive of students, twenty of them at least. Their heads were lowered, and they were silent . . . save for the random chortle by some guy or screamlet of laughter by some girl. What the fuck were they doing? Then he saw the newspapers. They had newspapers in their hands, poring over them . . . outside in the cold. A few others were rooting like maggots to get to one of those metal newspaper boxes with windows that were out front of Mr. Rayon. It was a taxicab-yellow box . . . That would be the *Wave* . . . A bunch of students standing out here riveted by the school newspaper? That was megaweird.

Hoyt joined the throng. A girl piped up with one of those high-pitched shrieks you usually hear at parties. Guys were beginning to make comments. They were so excited, they were taking the Fuck Patois over the top.

"This fucking stuff is . . . too—fucking—much!"

"—fucking *student*! The fuck you talking about?"

"Where's Jeff? Where'd he fucking go? I think he fucking *knows* this guy—"

"—didn't know they could print 'fuck' in the fucking paper!"

"—opera house. Same fucking family!"

"—fucking name? I don't know—Horatio Fucking Fellatio."

"—same fucking one! I was fucking *here*!"

"—blow job! I don't fucking *believe* this!"

Blow job? Hoyt felt like his brain was flushing. He began doing some accidentally-on-purpose body checks in a bid to get to the yellow box before the newspapers were all gone. "Sorry! Coming through! Gotta restock!" he said as he swung his left leg in front of the right leg of a guy slightly ahead of him, a guy in some kind of old military jacket with ghost shapes where chevrons and other insignia had been removed. Hoyt figured the cool authority of his seriously awesome topcoat would intimidate half of them. But the guy with the ghost jacket was stubborn. He gave Hoyt an accidentally-on-purpose shove with his hip. Hoyt battled back by accidentally extending the range of his left calf across the stubborn guy's right shin on purpose. That made Hoyt turn slightly—and he saw a girl, a pretty girl, with that Norwegian look—straight, shiny blond hair a mile long and parted right down the middle—staring at him with big eyes. She nudged another girl, a dog, and they both stared at him. Then the mouth of the hot one— gorgeous!—he loved that Norwegian look, the blond hair, the bright blue eyes, the fine bones of the face, the rolls in the snow, naked, and then into the sauna, naked—her mouth fell open, her eyes widened. She gave him a stare that all but ate him up for two seconds, three seconds—and then she said, "Ohmygod . . . Ohmygod . . . aren't you—*you're him! You're Hoyt Thorpe!*"

Unable right off the bat to think of any other cool response, Hoyt gave her his most charming get-something-going smile and said, "That is true. Had lunch yet?"

All at once, innumerable eyes were pinned on him. A general buzz swept the crowd. *Bango!* The students were in a circle around him, as if beamed there by intergalactic voyagers. A guy standing right in front of Hoyt, near the concupiscent Scandinavian blonde, a tall Chem-geeky-looking guy, with a long neck and an Adam's apple the size of a gourd, said, "Awesome, dude! Did you really say to the guy, 'You're an ape-faced dick—'" He broke it off and turned to a guy with a newspaper standing right beside him. "Wait a minute, How's it go? It's better than that."

Hoyt closed one eye and opened his mouth on that side, as if to say, "I don't know what he's talking about."

The blonde, the fjewel of the fjords, had a newspaper folded over once, twice, in her hand. "Come on. You haven't *seen* this?"

Hoyt shook his head no—but slowly, which is to say, coolly.

The girl unfurled the newspaper and held the front page up right in front of him. There was the biggest headline he had ever seen on a newspaper. Eleven fat white letters on a black band four inches deep stretched across the entire width of the page beneath the logo: WHAT ORAL SEX? Underneath that on the right-hand side:

POL BRIBE$ CHARLIE WHO
$AW HIS GROVE $EX CAPER

Underneath that, a smaller headline:

FRAT BOY WILL GET
$95K WALL $T. JOB
FOR "MEMORY LO$$"

Underneath that: "By Adam Gellin."

Underneath that, a swath of paragraphs printed two columns wide ran to the bottom of the page, where a notation said, "See BRIBE, pages 4, 5, 6, 7."

"Governor of California" . . . "Republican nomination" . . . "paid off

Dupont senior" . . . "coed" . . . "of oral sex" . . . Hoyt's eyes were in too much of a rush to do anything more than scan the first paragraph of the story. The left side of the page was pulling them like an imaging magnet. Other than the headlines, the byline, and the few inches of type, the entire front page consisted of a photograph of a guy. He was in the foreground, coming out of the I.M. with, slightly behind him, a little blond cutie-pie who, even though it was fiercely cold and she was wearing a bomber jacket and jeans, still managed to show a swath of bare belly. The guy, the guy front and center— he was one . . . awesome . . . dude . . . the boots, the Abercrombie & Fitch creaseless khakis, what you could see of them . . . the shirt open at the throat . . . and the coolest, longest single-breasted navy melton-cloth topcoat that ever turned up in a photograph . . . It made the guy look eight feet tall, slender, cool, and Serious Business. Out of the rakishly turned-up collar of the awesome overcoat rose a white, thick, dense neck—well, wide enough, thick enough, and dense enough, in any event—and a face—Hoyt couldn't keep his eyes off that face—a face with wide square jaws, a chin cleft perfectly—guy looked like a combination of Cary Grant and Hugh Grant with a lighter, thatchier, thicker, cooler head of hair than either one of them— cooler because it had no part. There was a slight sneer on the lips, the sneer that says, "I'm money, baby, and you're all fucked up"—a sneer, and maybe people don't like to see a guy sneering, but this was one . . . cool . . . awesome . . . sneer, cool as sneers will ever get. Before the heavy-duty machinery of his brain could even gear up to figure out what this whole goddamn thing might mean, Hoyt thought of three people: himself, Rachel, the Pierce & Pierce succuba of the dream i-bank job; himself; that little nerdy, devious, cowardly, backstabbing, rat-faced weasel, Adam Whateverthefuckhisnameis; himself, himself, and himself. Even the subrational himself sensed trouble on the right-hand side of the page somewhere in all that big type. But that picture—that *picture*! Could any college boy ever look better than that?

It was now one o'clock in the afternoon, and Charlotte was going to some lengths to keep from admitting to herself that after fourteen hours, next to no sleep, one slice of stale whole wheat bread with jelly, a couple of sips of orange juice turning bad, and a patient with insatiable psychological demands, she was good and tired of being Millennial Mutant Adam Gellin's nurse. She was also growing resentful, which she didn't try to keep herself from knowing. For *him*, out of a sense of obligation, she had blown off two classes this morning, one of them being her history course for the new semester, The Renaissance and the Rise of Nationalism. That was sure a great start, wasn't it—after the debacle of her academic collapse last semester. What was worse, in a way, was the fact that blowing it off no longer created in her the same sense of guilt and despair she had felt back in October when she first overslept a class after playing shepherd for a blitzed Beverly half the night. *That* she was aware of very clearly. Then there was the horrible Monday morning following the formal, when she as good as overslept—"as good as," *hah*!—"worse than overslept" was more like it—and wound up sitting through the last half of her modern drama class a clumsy, sweating, panting, disheveled little fool, an object of ridicule for her classmates and an object of scorn for the T.A., who all but buried her final grade.

Final grade . . . a surge of dread . . . All over again she was smack up against it. There was no more avoiding it. She had to call Momma today—it would be infinitely more dreadful if Momma got it in the mail first—and break the news . . . her prodigy's grades for the first semester: B, B-minus, C-minus, and D. Couldn't she just neglect to get into the fine shading, the minuses? Bad idea; the minuses would be coming in the mail, too.

She checked out Adam. He was the same as he had been all day, lying on his side in bed, eyes wide open, staring fixedly at the wall opposite like a crazy person, seemingly out of touch with reality—but if she so much as moved a muscle, he came to life with fearful, anxious questions, beseechings, and guilt triggers, which he pulled expertly. She had to go through a negotiation, make a hundred promises, and provide an itinerary just to go out the door and to the bathroom in the hall. When he himself went, he shuffled out into the hall with that filthy, insane, flesh-crawling green blanket around him, head bent over like an old man's—and insisted she stand in the hall until he was through. If any of the students who lived in the other three slots on this floor had shown up, she would have been mortified.

So how was she going to get time off from her patient to go back to Little Yard and call Momma on the telephone? But she *had* to.

Tenderly: "Adam?" No answer. "Adam?" Again no answer. "Please look at me, Adam." No answer, big eyes still glued to the wall. Sternly: "Adam." No answer. So this time she snapped it out, sharp with aggravation: "*Adam!*"

"Unhh, unhhh"—moan, moan—"Yeah . . . yeah . . . what?"

"Look at me, Adam."

The wild eyes rotated slowly in their sockets. The mouth hung open.

"Adam . . . I have to go back to my room—"

"No! No! Not yet! You can't! I'm begging you!"

". . . back to my room for *just a minute*, and then I'll be right back, *right back*, I promise you."

A piteous moan: "Not yet . . . Oh, Charlotte . . . please, you can't . . . Don't leave me *now* . . . not *now* . . ." And so forth and so on.

He wore her down until she promised not to go. She would just have to make the call on Adam's cell phone, that being the only phone he had . . . right in front of him . . . Well, he knew the whole story anyway . . . and in his current state he had become incapable of thinking about anyone but himself . . .

Adam had resumed shaking, moaning, staring at nothing . . .

"Adam, I'm going to make a call on your cell phone." She picked it up off his little desk—

"No!" He fairly screamed it. "You can't! No! I forbid you!"

For*bid*? That truly did aggravate her. The nerve of him trading on his misery like that. So she opened the cell phone—

"No, Charlotte! I implore you!"

Im*plore*? That was ridiculous. So she pressed the PWR for Power button. She knew that much from watching Beverly—

"DON'T! CHARLOTTE—"

Beep-beep—beep-beep—beep-beep—beep-beeps came popping out of the little device.

"CLOSE IT UP! CLOSE IT UP! YOU'RE KILLING ME!"

Killing you? Charlotte lost count after ten beep-beeps—

Groan groan groaning: "They'll get me! They'll get me!"

The beep-beeps—there was no end to them! Charlotte looked at the little screen, which said, "YOU HAVE 32 NEW MESSAGES."

Charlotte had to talk right over Adam's moans and protests. "Adam! You have *thirty-two* new messages! What's going on? What do I push to get the messages?"

"NO!" howled Adam. His wild eyes were now staring at her from out of a head hung over the side of the bed until it was virtually upside down. "I'm not gonna tell you! They're after me! I don't want to hear them! I'll die!" And so forth and so on.

"You can't just *ignore* them, Adam. Somebody's trying awfully hard to reach you."

"Kill me, kill me," said Adam with a lot of moans. "Don't make me lis-

T
O
M

W
O
L
F
E

ten!" And so forth and so on. He wouldn't give in, wouldn't tell her the first thing about retrieving the messages. Then she saw his laptop.

"Adam," said Charlotte, "I'm going to turn on your computer." Protests, protests, protests. "I'm *going to* turn on your computer, Adam, and see if you have any e-mail." Moans, moans, whines, whines, death, death. "Adam, if you want me to stay here, I have to find out what's going on. I'm just not going to sit here in total ignorance. You won't have to *hear* the e-mails, you won't have to *read* the e-mails. They'll be for my eyes only. Now, please give me your password." Won't won't can't can't end of everything end of everything. "Well, then it's the end of my staying here, too, Adam. You can't treat me this way. I won't have it. You'll never even *know* what's in them, unless you want to. Now, please . . . give — me — the — password."

That went on for many rounds until Charlotte finally wore *him* down and he divulged it. She had to smile in spite of herself. She might have known. It was MATRICA, the first seven letters of "matrical."

Charlotte hunched over the laptop while Adam kept busy moaning and groaning and announcing his impending extinction. New messages — there were so many from yesterday and today, the list ran to the bottom of the screen and beyond. She had to scroll down, down, down to reach the end. There were a lot from Greg, a few from Randy, others from Edgar and Roger, four from Camille, several from what looked like Dupont administrators, many from addresses she didn't recognize and couldn't decode — but one she very much recognized. She clicked on it.

Wails of lamentations from Adam as the printer began its own groaning and lurching and protesting as it came to life and then started stuttering out the message. Charlotte read it again in hard copy, broke into a big now-didn't-I-tell-you smile, and held the sheet of paper in front of her patient.

"This one you'll like," she said. "I absolutely guarantee it. This one is *not* coming to get you. This one's doing exactly the opposite."

Adam still looked crazy, but he had shut up; not a moan, not a peep. Charlotte went over to him and took his hand, which hung off the side of the bed in a posture of abject surrender, palm up, knuckles resting on the floor. She lifted the arm. Adam didn't resist. She folded the piece of paper in two, placed it on his palm, and clamped it with his fingers, manipulating them one by one.

He didn't seem to be aware of it . . . but neither did he let go of it . . .

"I promise, Adam, you'll like it. You'll love it."

It seemed to Charlotte as if minutes went by. Finally Adam turned his head toward his palm and looked at the piece of paper as if it were a small, harmless animal that had unaccountably hopped aboard. Slowly, still lying flat, he drew it toward his face, adjusted his glasses—a sign of interest in life at least—and began to read. Charlotte tried to imagine being inside Adam's head as the news dawned:

> Mr. Gellin,
>
> I have not changed my principles or opinions concerning the matter we discussed. But given the way you have fixed the clock of that insidious ultraright demagogue and enemy of civil justice—I have been watching the CNN coverage for the last hour—I am not going to take any action that might compromise your excellent work. Thus you may consider the entire matter dropped, deleted, forgotten. Plaudits for what you have achieved. Strength for the fight ahead. Never stop battling the fire, which has not died out. Remember the prison-bound citizens. Be scrupulous in your academic work.
>
> Jerome P. Quat

Adam propped himself up on one elbow. He gazed at Charlotte with wondering eyes. Then he swung his legs over the side of the bed and sat up. Still looking at Charlotte, he allowed himself a wary, slightly befuddled smile, but a smile nonetheless.

Charlotte couldn't remember how Lazarus looked when he rose from the dead or if the Bible even got into that, but it stood to reason he must have looked like Adam Gellin did at this moment.

It so happened that Jojo was in the main reading room of the library at about eight-thirty, after team study hall, reading about Plato as a "fitting and yet ill-fitting successor" to Socrates—and puzzling over why these people, these philosophy scholars, kept writing sentences in which the ending contradicted what they said at the beginning or else reduced it to mush—when his cell phone rang.

Oh shit! That wasn't supposed to happen here in the library—you were supposed to put it on vibrator or else turn it off—and the fact that his ring was a digitized rendition of "The Theme from *Rocky*"—*dah dahh daaahhh . . . daaahhhh duhh duh*—made it worse. He hurriedly, furtively opened up the cell phone, hid it between his knees, swung his head about as if somebody behind him were the offender, then got down under the study table, as if he were looking for something, and said sotto voce into the phone, "Hello?"

"How's my Greek friend who grew up Swedish in New Jersey?"

Coach never said "This is Coach Roth" or "This is Coach" or anything else to let you know who was calling. He didn't have to, certainly not if he was calling anybody on the team or close to it. Jojo flinched instinctively—but Coach didn't really sound like he was on his case this evening.

Jojo didn't take any chances, nevertheless. "I'm fine, Coach." He probably didn't sound particularly fine, whispering from under a library table.

"Socrates," said Coach's voice, "you Greeks are one lucky fucking buncha people, that's all I can tell you."

"Whattaya mean, Coach?"

"Our friend Mr. Quat has dropped the whole thing. It's over, Jojo. It never happened."

Silence. Then: "How do you know, Coach?"

"The President just called me," said Coach. "He said, 'You can forget about it. Erase it from your memory,' or words to that effect."

"Wow," said Jojo in a dull fashion, he was speaking so softly. "What happened?"

"I couldn't tell you, Jojo. Mr. Quat is a mysterious fucking dude."

"Wow," said Jojo in the same flat way. "Thanks, Coach. I don't know what to say. I appreciate the hell out of this. You've taken a load off—off my back, is what it feels like."

"I'm glad to be the bearer of good tidings, Socrates. Now you don't have to drink that hemlock cocktail."

"Hemlock cocktail?"

"Jesus Christ, Jojo, you're supposed to be the big Socrates scholar around here! I already *told* you about your boy and the hemlock. You don't remember?"

"Oh yeah, sure." Jojo attempted a sotto voce laugh. "Mr. Margolies mentioned the hemlock, too, Coach. I guess I just got confused about the cocktail part." He attempted a prolonged muffled laugh to show Coach he appreciated him as a wit, too.

They said good-bye, and Jojo climbed up off the floor and back into his library chair and returned to Plato, the fitting successor to Socrates except that it turns out he was ill-fitted. Then Jojo lifted his head and leaned back in the chair and looked up at the room's massive wooden chandeliers and re-flected a bit. A smile stole across his face. Coach . . . The guy was too much. He could be rough. Nobody had ever treated him, Jojo, any rougher without having to roll in the dirt to pay for it. But Coach looked out for you. If any-body else started any rough stuff, Coach was right there by your side, and it was Shoot-out at the O.K. Corral for them that dared fuck with you.

Jojo shook his head and smiled at the same time. Old Quat had been around here for a while. You'd think he would have known. Nobody gave Coach any shit and remained standing afterward. Coach had talked about how both of them, coach and player, too, were examples, whether they wanted to be or not, for everybody on the campus. He hadn't really under-stood what Coach meant at the time. Now he did. Coach was loyal . . . and he was a man.

33. THE SOUL WITHOUT QUOTATION MARKS

I t was nine-thirty p.m. by the time Charlotte left Adam's and walked alone in the dark through the City of God and across the campus and reached Little Yard. What a relief it was to escape at last from Adam's stifling, psychologically polluted sick bay of a slot . . . and what a sour taste remained. She felt used. Adam had made an awfully miraculous recovery from terminal neurasthenia and the imminence and immanence of death. Once he got out of bed and began reading his thirty-four e-mails and started making phone calls and trying to figure out with Greg which TV and newspaper interviews to do and which ones not to bother with, his ego began refilling so fast Charlotte could *see* it and *hear* it . . . Color and clear eyes returned to his face. Irony and intellectual showboating returned to his speech. "Tomorrow" returned to his vocabulary. He was so busy online and on the cell phone, he . . . carved out . . . the time it took him to thank her and say good-bye.

Her sense of relief had lasted barely one block into the City of God, however, and that had nothing to do with the slum's much-feared bad boys, who were not to be seen, in any event. Charlotte's night had just begun, not even counting all the homework she had yet to do for tomorrow. This was "it," and "it" possessed her as she departed the elevator on the fifth floor of Edgerton and walked down the hall. How should she word "it" when she called Momma? Nine-thirty was awfully late to be making the call, given the diurnal cycle of country people, but she no longer had a choice. What would work best? Contrition, confession—a strictly academic confession, that is—humility, a plea for forgiveness, and a promise to make up for "it"? Or what about a by-the-way approach? "Momma, it's me! . . . Oh, I just wanted to hear your voice and find out how everybody is . . . Good, and how is Aunt Betty's angina? . . . That's a relief. By the way, I've run into sort of a glitch in the academic side of things. It's not the end of the world, and it'll be easy to turn it around, but do you remember at Christmas when I was telling you all about . . ." Oh, sure . . . the way she must have looked and sounded to everybody . . . Momma was no fool. She would never swallow the notion that her prodigy's hog wallow in misery had been induced by a glitch. Well, what about a completely true confession, an abject, hold-nothing-*nothing!*-back confession, committing herself to Momma's mercy the way she did when she was a little girl? . . . The blessed catharsis that always followed . . . the blissful balm of Momma's mercy . . . It had always brought peace to Charlotte's heart precisely *because* Momma refused to be "realistic" about "the way things are today" . . . Oh Momma, Rock of Ages, cleft for me, let me hide myself in thee! . . . *Pop.* The very thought chilled Charlotte to the core. It would be as risky as trying to beat a burning fuse to the dynamite.

Round and round such calculations went until Charlotte actually took a couple of steps past the door to her room. She backtracked and opened it—

Bango!—both Erica and Beverly stood there. Ohmygod, how could she even make the call?

Beverly cocked her snoot and said, "Well! I've been wondering where you were. Your phone"—she gestured toward the white room telephone—"what's going on? It's driving me crazy." She didn't say it nicely.

Charlotte was surprised by her own calm and insouciance, insouciance in the literal sense: just not caring.

"You know, it's your telephone, too, Beverly. In fact, you own it. You can pick it up and answer it or leave it off the hook or unplug it. If I'm not here, why would I care?"

Beverly bristled. To her, no doubt, those words were the equivalent of an impudent reprimand. Gesturing toward Charlotte, she turned to Erica and said in a bored manner, "My roomie."

Silence. The moment stretched out . . . stretched out . . . and in that moment it occurred to Charlotte that she still envied the Beverlys and the

Ericas and the Douches and the Psi Phi Trekkies. She envied them for being wellborn, for having money and all the clothes they wanted, for their natural assumption of social superiority and their actual attainment and enjoyment of it. She admitted this to herself, and it seemed like little more than an observation. For reasons she couldn't have explained, if asked, she no longer felt cowed or intimidated by these people. They were what they were, and she was Charlotte Simmons. *I am Charlotte Simmons.* And in that moment it also occurred to her how rarely she had said that to herself over the past couple of months, and how even more rarely did it come burning into her mind with the old fire of defiance.

Perhaps to end the tension and fill the fast-expanding conversational vacuum, Erica spoke up. "Well, Charlotte, I suppose you've been keeping up with the adventures of our Mr. Thorpe today."

Interesting. It was the first time Erica had called her by name. "I heard something about it," said Charlotte.

"You haven't read the *Wave?*"

"No."

"You really *haven't?*"

"I really haven't."

"Ohmygod, I don't *believe* it! You've got to read it! I don't think I've ever intentionally picked up the *Wave*, but today I did. Our Mr. Thorpe has been totally out of control. He's always been totally out of control, but now he's over the top."

Erica paused, as if to see how this might strike the girl who was divested of her virginity by Mr. Hoyt Thorpe in what had been practically an *exhibición* in a hotel. Charlotte was absorbed in something else: the excitement in Erica's voice as she addressed her, the absolutely flashing excitement in her eyes as she questioned this infamous little freshman and studied her face for any little change of expression that might reveal the emotions she assumed to be boiling inside.

In fact, Charlotte was intrigued by how little Charlotte Simmons cared. She replied in a countrified voice, "Goodness me. I had no—iiii—dee-a." She gave Erica a supercilious smile.

That plus the sarcasm left Erica offended and speechless. Erica and Beverly exchanged glances and smiled at one another in a certain smart, galling mock-discreet way they had.

Without another word, Charlotte took off her puffy jacket, hung it on the back of her wooden chair, turned on her gooseneck lamp, sat down, and began reading a monograph titled *Print and Nationalism*. The first paragraph had to do with the extent, demographics, and technology of reading throughout Ancient Greece and Rome—Greece—which made her think of Jojo and his complete lack of guile or irony, which in turn made her think of Erica and Beverly and their excess of both, which in turn made her regret being so sarcastic and arch to Erica, which in turn led her to conclude, with nihilistic aplomb, that it made no difference anyway.

Erica said to Beverly, "You know the word 'chippy'?"

"Chippy?"

"The Brits are always talking about people being chippy. They always have a chip on their shoulder, and they're so insecure, they think everybody's looking down on them."

"I think I know what you mean," said Beverly.

Charlotte's back was to them, and so she had to imagine their little smiles and suppressed sniggers.

Soon they went out, which shouldn't have made her feel unusually fortunate, since she couldn't imagine either of them staying in . . . a dorm room at night . . . before two or three in the morning. They didn't say good-bye.

Damn! Now it was nine-fifty, which would make everything just slightly worse when she called. Charlotte stared at the white telephone for a good two minutes before she screwed her courage up enough to dial . . .

One ring . . . another ring . . . another . . . another . . . four rings!—and such a tiny house!—could they be *out*?—so unlike them . . . another ring!—five—no, God!—if she had to wait until tomorrow to tell Momma, and the letter arrived tomorrow, it would be the same as not calling at all—another ring!—six—

"Hello?" Momma, thank God.

"Momma! Hi. It's me!"

"Why, Charlotte! Did the phone ring a long time?"

"It did sort of, Momma." She pulled *did* out into *dee-ud* in an instinctive and all but unconscious claim to Down Home closeness.

"Your Daddy and me been watching television with Buddy and Sam, and your brothers had on a movie—you know the ones where the whole thing is just one big fireball after the other?" *Farball*.

Charlotte laughed, as if their mutual awareness of silly farball movies was one of the funniest things they had ever shared.

Momma laughed, too. "I just barely heard it ring at all! You sound in a good mood. How *is* everything?"

"Oh, I feel *good*, Momma! And I just feel better hearing your voice! Well, there *is* one thing, Momma, I thought I ought to tell you before you just got it in the mail? You know?" Charlotte sped up her delivery to make sure Momma couldn't slip in a question. "It's sort of disappointing, actually—well, not *sort of*—it *is* disappointing, Momma. Remember how I got four A-pluses at midterm?"

Pause. "I do." A bit wary.

"Well, I think I got too sure of myself, Momma. In fact, I *know* I did. And I started letting a few things slide? You know? And I don't know, Momma, before I could do anything to stop it, it was like a whole landslide, you might say?"

Pause. "Whyn't you tell me what you mean, a landslide."

"Some of my grades fell off real badly, Momma." Charlotte closed her eyes and turned her head so that her deflated sigh wouldn't be transmitted. Then she blurted it all out, all four of the grades, the minuses and everything.

Momma said, "You got four A-pluses at midterm, and these are the grades you got for the whole semester?"

"I'm afraid so, Momma."

"How can that be, Charlotte?" Momma's voice was preternaturally restrained. Or was the word "numb"? "Midterm was early November, best I recollect."

"That's true, Momma. Like I said, I guess things just started piling up too fast, and I wasn't paying attention, and then it was too late."

"*What* was piling up, Charlotte? *What* was too late?" Momma's voice was getting a bit testy—from her being double-talked.

Charlotte quickly discarded all the little cards she had been ready to play. She didn't have any choice. She had to move straight to the radical explanation, which was at least in the orbit of the truth, however remotely.

"Momma—the thing is . . . I got a boyfriend right after midterm. I mean . . . I just . . . *did*. You know?"

No comment.

"He's a real nice boy, Momma, and he's real smart. He writes for the *Wave*, the daily newspaper. As a matter of fact, he might be on television tomorrow, on the news. I'll call and tell you if I find out ahead of time." Ohmygod, that was a blunder. If she turns on the TV and there's Adam talking about oral sex—"Anyway, he's part of a group of real bright students who have a sort of . . . society."

Silence.

"It's exciting just to hear the way they come up with ideas and dissect them. You know?"

"And that's why you ended up with . . . the grades you got?" said Momma. "Because you got a boyfriend and he's smart?"

That hurt like a lash. If it wasn't sarcasm—and she couldn't remember Momma ever being sarcastic before—it was close enough. She felt found out. *Lies!* Momma had always held up the Cross to lies, and they always cringed and died in that merciless, unforgiving light.

"I'm not saying it's because of *him,* Momma! It's because of *me.*" The good daughter generously concedes that the buck stops here. "I guess I got too interested in him. You know? He's very courteous and respectful, and the last thing he would do is try to take advantage—" She stopped, realizing that the fantastic leaps of logic—of illogic—she was making from sentence to sentence were as much of a clue as Momma needed. She charged off in a different direction. "I'm already making a complete turnaround, Momma. I'm setting up a discipline for myself. I'm—"

"Good. So far I haven't understood one thing you've told me, not one thing, except you got terrible grades. When you decide to tell me what's happened—what's going on—then we can talk about it." Momma's voice was terribly controlled, which was somehow worse than testy or sarcastic. "Does Miss Pennington know about any of this?"

"No, Momma, she doesn't. You think I should tell her?" Desperately, Charlotte hoped to receive . . . some low-voltage approval . . . for having come to Momma first.

"What are you going to tell her, Charlotte, the same as you told me?"

Charlotte couldn't think of a thing to say to that.

"Sounds to me like what you need right now is a talk with your own soul, an honest talk."

"I know, Momma."

"Do you? . . . 'Deed I do hope so."

"I'm sorry, Momma."

"Sorry don't change a thing, darling. Never did, never will."

Long pause. "I love you, Momma." The last and lowest resort of the sinner.

"I love you, Charlotte, and so does your daddy and Buddy and Sam.

And Aunt Betty . . . and Miss Pennington. You got a lot of folks you don't want to be letting down."

After they hung up, Charlotte sat stricken in her wooden chair, too empty to cry. She had thought it would be a relief to "get it over with." It wasn't a relief, and she had gotten nothing over with. She was an ungrateful coward and a liar. What she had accomplished was to egest a putrid, obvious lie.

She had even sunk so low as to pass off Adam Gellin, perhaps soon to be on television, as her boyfriend. Such a lie, such a lie, and to what earthly end? Momma wasn't stupid. She hadn't believed a word of it. All she found out for sure was that her little prodigy was, for some no doubt vile reason, a little liar.

"I probably shouldn't be calling you, but I just had to tell you: you're awesom, dude, *awesome.*" As the words came through the receiver of his cell phone, Adam purred. He had been purring a lot this morning. Calls! E-mails!—like a *thousand* e-mails! Letters slipped under the door! Even a couple of FedExes! He was *high,* high in the best way a human being could be high, high with the triumph . . . and high with vengeance satisfied, paid in full. Even this shithole he lived in . . . *glowed* as he looked about it, glowed like some . . . well, holy place . . .

Nevertheless, this particular call was special. He owed this guy . . . a lot.

"Thanks, Ivy," he said into the cell phone. "That means a lot to me, coming from you. I couldn't have—"

"What's better than 'awesome'?" said the exuberant voice. "'Dynamite' maybe? It was fucking dynamite, dude! Mission Ayyyy-complished. I wish you could come over and see the sonofabitch dragging his rotten fucking ass around this place. He hasn't said a word about it, as far as I know, but body language says it all. That fucker's gotten some baaaaaaad news."

"You're the one who's dynamite, Ivy," said Adam. "I gotta run off to this fucking press conference pretty soon, but I gotta ask you again, because I've racked my fucking brain, and I just—cannot—figure—out—how you got those documents from Pierce and Pierce and those tapes from your house there. How did you?"

The voice laughed heartily. "Some things it's better you—especially you—*don't* know. You know what I mean? Let's just say there's certain . . . friends of the family . . . who used to work at Gordon Hanley and have moved along to . . . let us say, *other* investment banks and who've—well, let's just leave it at that. As for the tapes . . . let's just say that most Saint Rays are *above* working with their hands and fooling around with wiring and shit, but every now and then, I guess, somebody comes along who—who—and I think I'll leave *that* . . . at *that*. Do yourself a favor. Forget I even told you that much."

"Look, Ivy," said Adam, "I really do have to run, but we've got to get together sometime and let each other in on the complete war stories."

"Great idea," said Ivy. "Once all this shit blows over. I tell you what. I'll take you to dinner some night at Il Babuino in Philadelphia. Maybe you've heard of it. It's as good as any restaurant in New York, and it's a place where you can hear each other talk. Also, I know there's not a fucking soul in this house who *feels* rich enough to go there. Not even our Mr. Phipps."

"Sounds great!"

"I'll tell you about all the shit that the shitheads, the major shithead and the minor shithead—well, Phipps isn't so bad—what the number-one shithead and his pals have dumped on me. I'll tell you what they fucking did at this formal we had in Washington."

"I know a little bit about that particular formal, Ivy."

"You *do?*"

"Yeah, and I know a little bit about a girl named Gloria."

"You're shitting me! Well, obviously you aren't. You're too fucking much, Adam! You know everything!"

"Not everything, believe me . . . not everything, by a long shot. But hey! We can talk about that, too! Right now I really do have to get to this fucking press conference."

As he lugged his bicycle down the narrow stairway, Adam repeated the words to himself. *Not everything* . . . not everything . . . He hadn't known enough to hold on to Charlotte and make her love him the way he loved her. He could see her from yesterday as if she were still here today. Not even the greatest triumph of his life, not even an accomplishment of this magnitude, was enough to win Charlotte. There was not a more beautiful girl on this earth . . .

But he mustn't let himself be so down right now. There was the press conference, and right after that, a whole segment on the Mike Flowers show on PBS. He just couldn't believe this was all really happening! He couldn't let himself wilt now.

———

Hoyt was drinking alone at the bar of the I.M. with the shell-backed bar stool slump of . . . the loser who comes to a bar and drinks alone.

Not that by the strictest of definitions one could have described Hoyt as alone. His peripheral vision detected yet another student he never saw before in his life approaching him . . . and now leaning over the empty seat beside him and saying, "You're Hoyt Thorpe, right?"

Hoyt turned his head just far enough to get a glimpse of the guy, and he responded, "Yeah," wearily, as if he had been asked the same question a thousand times already, which he had, or at least it seemed like that many. This guy was very tall and very bony and very pale and acne-scarred, and he had an ingratiating smile. He had grown one of those little stubbly patches of beard not on but underneath his chin. He was a tool, obviously.

"Aw-right!" the tool said. "You're awesome, dude! I just wanted to tell you that!" So saying, he made a fist and put it practically in front of Hoyt's nose. So Hoyt made a fist and touched the tool's fist without even looking.

"Keep on truckin'!" the tool said with comradely warmth as he walked away. "Good stuff!"

Keep on truckin' . . . *Good stuff* . . . That was from *Old School* . . . Couldn't you cram in any more cornball Cool into it? . . . you toolshed . . .

It was only nine-thirty, and the evening was just beginning to buzz at the I.M. Fortunately, it was too early for the band and the customary balls-to-the-wall excitement of being "out" at a bar. The sound system was playing CDs . . . Right now lonesome James Matthews and his lonesome guitar were singing and sighing that lonesome . . . ballad? — is that the word? — called "But It's All Right." It was a relief from the usual, in any case.

Anybody looking on probably thought the phlegmatic give-a-shit way he, Hoyt, was responding to all this was intended to show people he was still cool and not being swept away by all the gushing idolatry coming his way. The funny thing — except that it wasn't funny — was that the whole campus took this "exposé" by that little shit Adam Gellin as practically a *King Arthur and the Knights of the Round Table* about him and Vance. The little shit thought he had nailed him with the "bribe" shit. But the Night of the Skull Fuck story was so awesome, people seemed to barely notice the rest. With his own ears Hoyt had heard students quoting that one line — "*Doing?* Looking at a fucking ape-faced dickhead, is what we're *doing!*" — and going into convulsions. What was this so-called bribe compared to that? A nice fat Wall Street job with an incredible starting salary floats his way and he takes it? What's the big deal?

"Hey, dude, sorry to be late." It was Vance, arriving finally.

"Where the fuck've you been?" said Hoyt. "I've been sitting here and having to act like a real asshole to save this fucking seat for you."

Vance slid onto the seat. "I couldn't help it, man. I got hung up at the library with—"

He couldn't even finish the sentence, because a guy came up from behind and said, "Wait a sec—aren't you Vance Phipps?"

Vance acted just like Hoyt, which is to say, bored and uncommunicative.

Once the guy had finished prostrating himself in awe of the Phipps presence and left, Vance said to Hoyt, "Well, monster, you wanted to be a legend in your own time, didn't you? Congratulations. You've done it. You've made it. As a matter of fact, I have a feeling it won't be just in your own time, either. Years from now they'll still be talking about Hoyt Thorpe and the Night of the Skull Fuck."

"And what about you?" said Hoyt.

"Me, too, I'm afraid. But you got to admit, I come off as the Herb of the dynamic duo, the straight man. I didn't get off any great lines like 'Doing? Looking at a fucking ape-faced dickhead is what we're *doing*.' Wow. That state trooper must have one hell of a fucking power of total recall to give the little shit that line, verbatim near as I can recall. Right, Hoyt?" He gave Hoyt a lip-twisted *gotcha* smile.

Hoyt finessed it. "How many months we got left before graduation, Vance?"

"I don't know . . . March, April, May . . . three."

"So I've got three more months to be a legend in my own time and for all time, right?"

"That is true," said Vance. "But you know, you can always come back here every year for reunions, and the Alumni Band will always provide the music."

"Fun-nee. Could I bust my gut any worse laughing? What happens starting in June? You've got it made. You can go to any i-bank you want and get a job. You've been 'hung up' at the fucking library more than once over the past four years, if I know anything about it. Your transcript will be a passport good at any door on Wall Street—*and* your last name is Phipps."

"What the fuck are *you* complaining about?" said Vance. "You've already *got* a job, at Pierce and Pierce, *only* the hottest fucking i-bank there is—*and* you're getting a starting salary *only* fifty percent higher than what me or anybody else is going to get. How ungrateful is *that*?"

Hoyt said, "I got something to show you. It's why I wanted you to come over here."

With that, he descended the bar stool, went over to the rack inside the door where everybody's winter gear was hanging, reached into an inside pocket of his navy topcoat, withdrew a piece of paper, and returned to the bar. "Read this," he said to Vance.

Vance read it. It was an e-mail printout. At the top it said, "Subj: Re: Application." It came from rachel.freeman@piercepierce.org.

Dear Mr. Thorpe,

We are grateful for your interest in Pierce & Pierce and for the opportunity to meet with you when our team was at Dupont. Your qualifications are excellent in many respects, but after a thorough review by our Human Resources executive committee, we must conclude regretfully that your strengths are not a true "fit" with our requirements.

We as a team, and I personally, enjoyed our interview, and we wish you well in finding a place elsewhere in the industry, should that continue to be your interest.

> Very truly yours,
> Rachel E. Freeman
> College Liaison
> Human Resources
> Pierce & Pierce

Vance looked at Hoyt as if waiting for him to comment. A long pause . . . as if Hoyt was waiting for *Vance* to comment. Finally Hoyt said, "What do you make of that?"

"What do I *make* of it? . . . I don't know . . . except that it sounds to me like they're reneging on their offer."

"That's exactly it!" said Hoyt. "They're fucking *reneging*! How the fuck do they think they can get away with that?"

"Uh, I don't know," said Vance. "You get a signed contract or anything?"

"No! I don't have any fucking contract, but on Wall Street it's different, right? Your word is your fucking contract, right? How the fuck else can investors and i-bankers trade fucking *billions* over the telephone every day?"

"I don't know. I hadn't thought of that," said Vance. "Did anyone else happen to hear her promise you the job?"

"That's the fucking point I'm making!" said Hoyt. "Witnesses and shit are not fucking necessary! On Wall Street your fucking word is your fucking bond!"

Puzzled pause. "Well, I don't know. I don't know what to tell you, Hoyt. I don't know what applies to job offers and what doesn't."

"Look," said Hoyt. "There's one very specific reason I had to see you. Your father must know somebody in this fucking area, some lawyer, somebody who knows how to sue their fucking asses off if they try to pull shit like this. How about talking to your father?"

"I don't know," said Vance. "Maybe there's such a person. But one thing I do know. My father doesn't even want to *think* about this whole thing. If he could, he'd get a fucking injunction barring the press from using my name in the fucking story. You know his reaction when he first heard about it? His reaction was (A) why hadn't I told him about it last spring and (B) what kind of a moron had he raised who didn't know enough to go straight to the police when it happened and file charges for assault against the state trooper, Whatsisname. Hoyt—I can't even fucking *go there* where my father's concerned."

Hoyt looked off toward the scruffy black raw-edged "paneling" of the I.M.'s walls and expelled a great sigh of resignation. Then he turned back to Vance.

"What am I going to do, Vance? What am I going to do on June the fucking first? I don't have a job, and you know how much I got to fall back on? Zero! My mother's blown whatever she had, which was like next to nothing, just keeping me going at this fucking place. What am I fucking going to *do*! *Your* transcript's a passport. *Mine*—you have no *idea* how bad my grades are. My transcript's going to look like a police crime site with fucking yellow tape all over the place to keep people away. You think maybe the Charles' Society might give me a lifelong pension for being the coolest guy who ever bestrode the soil of the forty-eight contiguous United States and a legend for all time and forever after? Vance—I am fucking *fucked*!"

He hung his head. Then he looked up at Vance. "One thing I still can't figure out. How the fuck did the little shit get all that shit about Pierce and Pierce? They'd be the last people in the fucking world to give it to him. And those conversations between you and me in the house. I mean, he didn't have direct quotes, but he didn't have direct quotes, but he might as fucking well . . ." He hung his head again and shook it slowly. "Fucked, fucked, fucked, and fucked."

T
O
M

W
O
L
F
E

34. THE GHOST IN THE MACHINE

A month had passed, and by now Coach Buster Roth's basketball team had won twenty-one games and lost none here on the verge of the NCAA national basketball tournament, nicknamed March Madness, which Dupont was highly favored to win again. All home games at the Buster Bowl had been sellouts for several years now, but the jockeying, conniving, favor-promising, favor-cashing in, the flattering, the pandering, the name-dropping, string-pulling, and sheer spending—scalpers were said to be getting a thousand dollars per ticket—to get into tonight's game with the University of Connecticut had reached up-roar proportions. Fights—not physical but via telephone, e-mail, fax, FedEx, and U.S. mail—had broken out among musical alumni for the privilege of playing in the Charlies' Children's Alumni Band, which performed court-side in a block of four rows of a section near one end of the court—Children, as in sons and daughters of the alma mater, Mother Dupont.

At this moment, a full hour before game time, these devoted sons and daughters, attired in mauve blazers with yellow piping—they happily paid for this raiment themselves—were playing "The Charlies' Swing" with un-equaled kinetic energy and brio, not to mention volume. The "Swing," writ-ten by famous Dupont alumnus/composer Slim Adkins, had become a staple of jazz bands all over the world.

The two teams were yet to emerge from the dressing rooms for the warm-ups. At the moment the court was congested with entertainers—the cheerleaders shaking their fannies, the Chazzies dance troupe shaking their fannies, the gymnasts hurling their twirling girls into the air and catching them, and the Zulj Brothers—twin sophomores from Slovenia majoring in clonotic biology (the study of undifferentiated stem cells) who also happened to be jugglers—juggling alarming things such as serially lit cherry-bomb firecrackers. Even after almost a month of it, Charlotte was agog at this zany show that seemed to pop up from out of the floor to the über-exuberant accompaniment of the Charlies' Children's Alumni Band whenever the players were not on the floor. It was the closest thing to an authentic circus she had ever seen in her life.

To tell the truth—had she dared tell the truth—which she hadn't and wouldn't, not even to Jojo—Charlotte felt like part of the pregame show herself. Here she was, a freshman, eighteen years old, sitting directly behind the Dupont bench at mid-court. The only better seats in the arena were those reserved for the Cottontops (namely, the university's most important donors, most of whom were old men with white hair), who sat in the courtside section immediately below. Their wives were called the Pineapples, because most of them had white hair dyed a pale pineapple blond. Many students grumbled about the Cottontops and the Pineapples and their seats, on the grounds that these prize vantage points should go to themselves, the real fans, as opposed to these golden-agers with money who merely wanted to be seen breathing the most precious air there was wherever their sense of privilege told them they ought to be.

Charlotte had no money at all, but she, like them, enjoyed the knowledge that her position was just about the best there was. That much any of her fellow students would realize, and they would wonder who this pretty girl was, if not already aware that she was Jojo Johanssen's girlfriend, Charlotte Simmons. Once that had become known, the world had begun to turn rapidly for Charlotte. She now knew Buster Roth as "Coach," and he knew her as "Char," pronounced *Shar*, short for Charlotte, and just last week he had said to her, "You know, Char, you're the best thing that ever happened to Jojo." "Coach" seemed to credit her—seemed to . . . he had never said that in so many words—with Jojo's sudden turnabout on the court. Over the past month he had become a new player, or perhaps come back as the Jojo of old. He was suddenly so hot at scoring, as well as rebounding, setting picks, and "altering the behavior" of other big men on defense, that he had

T
O
M

W
O
L
F
E

won back his starting position—as opposed to starting home games as the to-ken white boy replaced before the end of the first quarter by Vernon Congers. Charlotte still hadn't the vaguest idea of what "setting picks" was. "Altering behavior," one of Coach's favorite phrases, seemed to refer to physical punishment. Charlotte never noticed Jojo pushing, elbowing, or whacking opponents with his forearms, but he was said to be devastatingly good at these things and at "sumo-tizing" them, which seemed to mean shoving and battering them around with the muscular bulk of his body. One thing she *was* able to see for herself was how high he was now jumping. Seeing somebody 250 pounds and almost seven feet tall launch himself to that altitude was amazing.

Not only Coach but also Jojo's roommate, Mike, and his friend Charles seemed to realize that she was no ordinary girlfriend. This little slip of a girl from the mountains—Charlotte enjoyed imagining how they perceived her—was for Jojo, in addition to whatever else she might be, a mentor, a teacher, and a nanny. It was something—once more she put herself inside their heads—to see the extent to which the little girl had the giant whipped. As far as she herself saw it, Jojo regarded her as the catalyst of the new him—he seemed to enjoy using (and overusing) this word "catalyst"—the student-athlete who was actually a student and who had resolved to lead a life cleaner than that of the playa-athlete he used to be. Charlotte had laid down a few laws on that score herself, and Jojo, like many another convert in the early stages of devotion, clearly found a blissful blessedness in his new asceticism and the bliss of the born-again in obeying her law number one that said they could be boyfriend and girlfriend and go everywhere together but that he would have to *win* her affections in the fullness of time.

Seated on the aisle, as she was, Charlotte was aware of people descending and climbing up the stairs of this particular cliff of the Buster Bowl, but she had long since ceased focusing on them as individuals. They were simply there . . . until she became aware of a figure rather more smartly dressed than the general run of basketball fans—a blue-green tweed suit, a white shirt with a fine blue windowpane check, a black silk knit tie—

An inexplicable sinking feeling came over her—it was Mr. Starling, climbing up the stairs in her direction. It seemed so improbable. She couldn't think of a less likely person to see at a basketball game. On the other hand, this was one of the few college basketball games she had ever been to, and she really had no idea what sort of people were or were not basketball fans. In the next instant Mr. Starling saw her, too. She knew he did, because their eyes locked and he compressed his lips in a grim manner and averted his eyes. Her heart sank—he couldn't, he wouldn't, do that to her—but then, still climbing the stairs, he looked at her again. As he drew close, he smiled. And she smiled, feeling that a . . . catastrophe . . . had just been averted. As Mr. Starling drew abreast of her in his climb, he looked at her imploring face in a tender way, as Charlotte saw it, and said, "Hello, Miss Simmons."

"Mr. Starling! Hi!"

He slowed to almost a halt, still looking at her—

Oh, speak to me, I implore you!

—and then smiled again—*in that way?—in that way?—Don't worry, I hold nothing against you for squandering your gifts?*—and resumed his climb up the cliff of the Buster Bowl.

Charlotte twisted about in her seat—*No! I need to tell you everything that happened!*—but she didn't leap up from her seat, and she didn't call out after him . . . for what was there left to tell him that he couldn't have already easily surmised?

In that instant the band members rose to their feet and launched into a delirious, almost violent reprise of "The Swing." The Chazzies, the cheerleaders, the acrobats, the Brothers Zulj seemed to sink into the floor as quickly as they had popped up. The Dupont team was coming onto the court in their mauve-and-yellow warm-up suits, dribbling what appeared to be a multitude of orange balls. In the warm-up suits—it was astonishing—all the players looked a foot taller than they already were. It was the long pants, mauve with broad yellow stripes down the sides. They brought out the tremendous length of their legs in a way that was lost when they peeled down to their uniforms with the sloppy, droopy shorts that were the current fashion for combat. At this moment they looked like an entirely other order of human beings, like the giants of the species they truly were.

There was no problem picking out Jojo, of course. With the mighty LumeNex lights making his warm-up suit, his mesa of blond hair, and his big white face fairly gleam, Jojo appeared nine feet tall at the very least, and a dense, powerful nine feet, too. When he reached mid-court, he looked up toward Charlotte, as he had taken to doing lately, and spun off a quick comical salute in which he twirled the first two fingers of his right hand up off his brow. The first time he did it had embarrassed her, but by now she felt as if there were a spotlight picking her out of the crowd like a star. Of all the female freshman at Dupont, how many were truly better known than Charlotte Simmons? In a way, the notoriety of her getting her dust knocked off at a Saint Ray formal—which everyone but her had seemed to know was a euphemism for bacchanal—had only made her rise, from social death to the eminence she now enjoyed as girlfriend of the superstar Jojo Johanssen, yet more dramatic, yet more of a feat.

There had come a day a couple of weeks before when two girls in a very sleek white, new European convertible had seen Jojo driving his SUV, the Annihilator, across campus and had pulled up beside him and blown the horn to attract his attention. They waved. Charlotte, in the passenger seat, had craned her neck to see who it was—and she could scarcely believe her eyes. It was Nicole, the magnificent Douche, and another girl who proved to be a Douche herself. Both were yelling and waving flirtatiously to Jojo. When they saw Charlotte's head pop up, they did a double take—and Nicole cried out, in the merriest way, "Hi, Charlotte!"—as if they were great chums! The next day, Nicole came up to her at Mr. Rayon and said Charlotte really should come by the Douche house during the impending spring rush. In fact, she should consider herself formally invited. Charlotte thanked her but said she didn't dare think about sororities, because she couldn't begin to afford to. Nicole said, "Oh, come on, anyway. You never know how things might work out in the end."

So the little country girl from the Lost Province had become quite a campus presence, of sorts, in a remarkably short time, a mere six months . . .

Just then a cheer rose up from the crowd as Jojo, in a warm-up drill, made such an incredible leap that when he dunked the ball, *slammed* it, *stuffed* it, it was as if he had flown up and attacked the net from three feet above. A regular chorus of *Go go Jojos* followed.

Charlotte felt a hand on her forearm and turned. It was Treyshawn Diggs's mom, Eugenia, who was sitting next to her. In that big, hearty voice of hers, she said, "Honey, what kind a diet you got that boy on? He is some kind a *loa-ded—for—bear!*"

Ripples of laughter and chuckles ran all through the immediate vicinity. Eugenia's voice was too much for even the racket and the *Go go Jojos* of the fans.

Treyshawn's twenty-seven-year-old sister, Clare, sitting on her mother's other side, leaned forward laughing and said, "Yeah, Charlotte, don't put so much go-go in the Jojo! That boy's getting out of control!" More laughs and chuckles.

Charlotte smiled and blushed and blushed some more in an appropriate Little Me manner. She noticed heads turning about in her direction. She made a modest point of averting her eyes from them, but she couldn't help but notice a head almost directly in front of her two rows below, a head with a thick stand of silver-gray hair combed straight back and trimmed to just above a crisp white collar, as it turned her way. It was the Dean of Dupont College, Mr. Lowdermilk, and his head was now twisted about, and his ruddy face was smiling at her rosy one, even though she had never even met him. Then, still smiling, he turned back and said something into the ear of a woman next to him, probably his wife, something no doubt along the lines of, "Don't turn around, but two rows directly behind us is Jojo Johanssen's girlfriend. They say she's the reason he's become the hottest athlete at Dupont" . . . or words to that effect, Charlotte felt sure.

Honey, what kind a diet you got that boy on? Charlotte loved that, because it said not one but three things. It said, "You're Jojo Johanssen's girlfriend, you've got him so spellbound he'll do whatever you say—and everybody knows that! Everybody knows who you are!"

And sure enough, barely a minute went by before Mrs. Lowdermilk, if that's who she was, turned all the way around, pretending she was actually looking at something way up the cliff.

Charlotte allowed herself a quick panoramic survey of the stands . . . She wished they were here, although it was supremely unlikely—Bettina and Mimi. Next home game, she'd like for Jojo or Coach himself to get some tickets to them without their knowing where they came from. Charlotte no longer spoke to either one of them. If she happened to run into them in Edgerton, she—cut—them—dead. She would never forgive them, never, not even if the three of them should happen to live together in Edgerton for the next hundred years—for the way they betrayed her, the ghoulish glee she overheard in their conversation when they were sure her life had been destroyed. You snide, insidious—please, my two little snakes, kindly come take a look at me now . . .

Hoyt—he wouldn't be here, either. He and his beloved "brothers" were forever watching that stupid SportsCenter . . . but it was funny, Hoyt never showed any true interest in any sport in particular. All those popped-vein, concussion-batty headbangers scampering across the plasma screen and striving for glory seemed to amuse him as much as anything else. She never heard him express any emotion whatsoever over a Dupont team winning or losing. Yeah, Hoyt was cool. They didn't come any cooler . . . She didn't hate him . . . He hadn't betrayed her at all. Hoyt was what he was, the same

T
O
M

W
O
L
F
E

way a cougar was a fast animal that stalked slower animals, and that was what a cougar was.

Ah, Hoyt. If only you would come take one last look at what you so cavalierly discarded, at what you once loved—and love her you *did*—I know it!—if only for an evening or a single hour or one brief instant.

She didn't *want* Adam to see her as she was now. It would break his heart a little more, knowing that she could never love him *in that way*. A wave of fondness for him spread through her so suddenly, she experienced a sharp intake of breath.

"Are you okay, honey?"

It was Eugenia Diggs, who once again put her hand on Charlotte's forearm.

"Oh, Eugenia"—looking at Treyshawn's mother with a tender smile—"I'm fine. I just suddenly thought of something. Thank you, though."

Well, if she had to disappoint Adam—and she did—she couldn't have done it at a better moment. The moment his big story broke, he became what he had always wanted to be, a voice that made thousands—hundreds of thousands?—stand stock-still with wonder. It was no matrix, his great "scoop" about the Governor of California and Syrie Stieffbein and Hoyt and Vance and the big Wall Street firm, but it would do, for a twenty-two-year-old college senior. It had all turned out for the best.

Why, then, the uneasy feeling, the sometimes desperate feeling, that came over her now . . . and almost every day? If only she had someone to talk to about it . . . to assure her that she was a very lucky girl, after all . . . But there was—when she thought it through—only Jojo. Aside from him, she was as alone as on the day she arrived at Dupont. Jojo was sweet. It was touching, the way he constantly turned to her for help. But Jojo was not made for talks with anyone's soul, not even his own.

She was Charlotte Simmons. Could she ever have that conversation with herself, the way Momma told her to? Mr. Starling put "soul" in quotes, which as much as said it was only a superstitious belief in the first place, an earlier, yet more primitive name for the ghost in the machine.

So why do you keep waiting deep in the back of my head, Momma, during my every conscious moment—waiting for me to have that conversation? Even if I were to pretend it were real, my "soul," the way you think it is, what could I possibly say? All right, I'll say, "I am Charlotte Simmons." That should satisfy the "soul," since it's not there in the first place. So why do I keep hearing the ghost asking the same tired questions over and over, "Yes, but what does that mean? Who *is* she?" You can't *define* a person who is unique, said Charlotte Simmons. It, the little ghost who wasn't there, said, "Well, then, why don't you mention some of the attributes that set her apart from every other girl at Dupont, some of the dreams, the ambitions? Wasn't it Charlotte Simmons who wanted a life of the mind? Or was what she wanted all along was to be considered special and to be admired for that in itself, no matter how she achieved it?"

That was ridiculous—but she was spared responding to that dreary, tiresome query by the Charlies' Children's Alumni Band. The mauve blazers with yellow piping rose from their seats and struck up with an old, old song by the Beatles called "I Want to Hold Your Hand." They played it as if John Philip Sousa had composed it as marching music for a military band with trumpets, tubas, a glockenspiel, and a big bass drum. The two teams had completed their warm-ups, and—*bango!*—the cheerleaders, the Chazzies, the acrobats, and the Zulj twins sprouted up from out of the floor, and all was loud music, merry madness, and *oooooo'n'ahhhhh*s. The Zulj boys were now juggling old-fashioned straightedge razors, blades unsheathed. If they didn't catch every razor by its mother-of-pearl handle—*ooooo . . . ahhhhhh*—upwards of fourteen thousand basketball fans felt as if they themselves were about to lose their fingers. This was the circus's last cavort before the game began.

The ghost in the machine kept prattling away, but there was no possibility of paying attention to it now. In no time the circus disappeared into the floor, the musicians sat down, and there beneath the LumeNex lights, on a gleaming rectangle of honey-colored hardwood, the game was on.

A towering white boy with a skiff of blond hair on an otherwise shaved head seemed to take over that entire court of superb black athletes all by himself, commandeering both backboards—he *owned* them, driving into the hole for slam dunks—don't get in his way, and altering the behavior of UConn's big men—he demolished them like Samson or the Incredible Hulk.

Dupont had sprung to a 16–3 lead before UConn called time-out. The circus sprouted out of the floor, Charlies' Children rose up from their seats, fannies shook, acrobatic girls did gainers in midair, the band's mighty brass wailed with greater fervor—and sheer loudness—than ever before. But the roar of the crowd drowned it out. From cliff to cliff and dome to floor, the cry rang out: *Go go Jojo! . . . Go go Jojo! . . . Go go Jojo! . . . Go go Jojo!*

A bit too late, Charlotte realized that heads were turning toward her in

T
O
M

W
O
L
F
E

hopes of enjoying, sharing in, her ecstasy over the exploits of her boyfriend. *Ohmygod* . . . She sure hoped not too many had gotten a real eyeful of the glum, distracted, thoroughly uninterested look on her face. She clicked on the appropriate face *just like that*. Since the crowd had now launched into rhythmic clapping to the one-beat cadence of *Go go Jojo*, Charlotte figured she had better join in, too. So she worked on keeping the joyous smile spread across her face and clapping with some semblance of enthusiasm.

Ohmygod . . . the band had now thrown itself into "The Charlies' Swing"—and in no time, so potent was the moment, the partisan crowd was bawling away with the words. It obviously behooved Jojo Johanssen's girl-friend to join in.